CITIZENS OF ANOTHER COUNTRY

Citizens of Another Country

Annika Goodwin

For Mom and Dad, who showed me the beauty of the natural world and introduced me to its Creator. The older you get, the more clearly you reflect His image.

Acknowledgments

With sincere thanks to:

My Saviour, Jesus Christ. Thank You for never giving up on me.

Matthew, for your invaluable encouragement

Jesse Christoffersen of 3dCubed for going above and beyond

All who helped with editing and revision: Matthew Smith, John and Jan Goodwin, Lee Gaar, Barbara Goodwin, and Steve Passiourias of bookow.com

Awake, O sleeper, and arise from the dead, and Christ shall give you light.

Ephesians 5:14 RSV

1

Jayka stared at the soothing colors as they swirled across the ceiling, gradually brightening from their slumbrous shades to a rousing, sunny glow. She had awakened at the prescribed time, her chip's biocomponents flawlessly integrated with the intricate workings of her hypothalamus. It didn't bother her that the space above her bed was actually gray, its colors a mentally projected combination of her programmer's recommendations and her chip's algorithms. Jayka rested easy because everything was arranged for her by people and computer systems with an intelligence far superior to hers. She had not had to worry about anything in a long time—not since she was a little girl, fighting for survival in the alleyways of the outer docks.

Occasionally she had flashbacks of that life—scrabbling for food, hiding from the rape gangs in a dumpster, and of course the times when she had failed to remain hidden. She had learned to compartmentalize the daytime flashbacks. Memories that overtook her in the daytime were easier to deal with. She could rationalize that the events were in her past and could no longer hurt her unless she allowed them. Nightmares were more difficult, but eventually the chip helped her determine she was only dreaming. With the help of a counselor, she learned how to address the situation through lucid dreaming. During the dream, Jayka would initially attempt to reason with her assailants. If that failed, she would overpower them, sometimes brutally beating them, sometimes simply killing them to be done with it. However, she found this technique did not usually result in a good night's sleep. Her preferred solution became locking the attacker into club cuffs and taking him to the clinic to be chipped. Letting the State take care of her problems, even in her dreams, gave her a sense of relief. Handling the emotional baggage of bits and pieces of a tragic childhood became just another exercise in trusting the State at the deepest level. Jayka had decided to trust the State all those years ago, the day she walked into the Euthanasia Clinic.

That day itself was beautiful. There was an absence of the acid fog that morning. A cloudless sky seemed determined to redefine the intensity of the color blue. A starling glided to the sidewalk where she lay in a crumpled heap, its iridescent feathers shimmering a pink and teal overlay to its white speckles. The flawlessness of the perfect morning was the last straw for the twelve-year-old girl. How could a morning dare to be so beautiful when her night had been so horrific? She raised her bloodied head and shielded her eyes from the insanely happy sunlight with her broken fingers—the skin of her attacker still embedded under her fingernails.

It was time. And because her parents had never bothered to secure a D.I.N.— a Declaration of Intent to Nurture—it was her right. She remembered laughing at the thought. Even Unspokens had at least one right: the right to die. The thought came to her so suddenly, she felt nearly giddy. No more hunger pangs. No more loneliness. No more beatings. No more pain of any sort. Just the sweet, sweet nothingness that came with the negligible pain of a needle's prick. Maybe her organs could be salvaged and used to help someone else who wanted to live and had the right to do so.

She managed to stand, leaning against a building for support. As luck would have it, she wasn't that far from the clinic—just two blocks away. She inched her way down the sidewalk, stopping to rest frequently. A woman with a thick accent from the outskirts of the outer docks offered her a piece of moldy bread, but she shook her head. It was a kind gesture, but she wouldn't need food where she was going. Besides, she could see the bundle of netting slung over the woman's shoulder, identifying her as a pigeon trapper. She could use the bread for bait. "Ya be needin' sump'n ta eat, ya hare?" the woman called after her, but she shook her head and kept moving. When she arrived at the clinic, she discovered to her surprise that she hadn't the strength to open the door. Maybe she *should* have accepted the bread from the old trapper woman. She stood at the entrance, leaning into the door with all her weight, but it barely budged. Finally, she collapsed, sliding to the sidewalk. A few seconds later the door opened, and she fell across the threshold. She found herself staring into the spotless tile floor of the clinic lobby. "This is not the medical clinic," announced the stocky-framed nurse who had come to the door.

"I know," she croaked. "I come here to die."

The nurse's tone changed as she helped her to her feet. "We get that all the time, honey. But I'm sorry. You're too young to donate yourself. Come back when you're eighteen. Until then, you'd better go to the medical clinic. It looks like whoever worked you over almost did our job for us—"

"I don't got no D.I.N.," she said hopefully. The nurse didn't seem to grasp the seriousness of her situation.

"We get that all the time, too," the nurse responded sympathetically. "I can see if your DNA is on file to verify that. But surely life can't be that bad. Don't you have something to live for? Some*one* to live for?"

She stared at the woman through eyes that were swollen to mere slits. "How do it look like ma life ain't that bad?" she asked in disbelief. "Just do ya job an' stick me."

"Now see here, young lady," the nurse said sternly. "I will do my job as I have been trained by State law, and I can't do anything about your situation until I make certain everything is legal. If you want to transition to the Source and donate your remains, there are plenty of people in line waiting for them. But first I need a sample of your DNA so I can verify your status. All it takes is a swab of your mouth, and then I can run it through the database to see if you're on file. If you're not, well, you're in luck."

She sighed as the nurse helped her to a chair. It was a slow day at the Euthanasia Clinic. She was the only one in the lobby. The girl bleakly surveyed the shiny floor as she waited, too depressed and weak to raise her head. As if anticipating the emotional and physical state of some of their clients, the clinic had enlisted the talents of a State-sanctioned artist to create a design made of bits of colored tile. It was a multicolored starburst pattern that was both intricate and soothing. She was still staring at it when the nurse returned. "It's beautiful, isn't it?" the nurse commented, nodding at the mosaic as she opened a package of swabs with a gloved hand. "It's supposed to be the artist's rendering of the

Source, but from what I've read, the Source is more beautiful than anyone can ever describe."

The nurse swabbed the inside of the girl's cheek, dropping the sample into a tube and capping it off. Then she procured another swab and repeated the process. "They want us to take a second sample for another study they're conducting," she explained. "There. That's done. Now there's just a few more minutes waiting—uh…you never did tell me your name."

The girl sighed again. "Scrap Dog," she said simply. It was the only name she had ever known. The rag-tag group of street children she ran with had christened her the day they met, when they took pity on the starving girl and threw her a chew bone they had found in a dumpster. Her parents, whom she didn't even remember, had never called her anything but "girl," or "hey you," and referred to her as "it." They dropped her off in the Shaw one morning, hurrying away when she was busy looking at pigeons. She began to cry when she realized she was alone, and that's when she met her first friends. The oldest girl in a gang of street urchins walked right up to her and told her to shush. "Be quiet, girl! Ya cain't be drawin' no 'ttention to yaself," she said. But Jayka would not be consoled. "Dang, girl. Shut you *up*. Here. This'll keep ya mouth busy," the older girl said as she pulled the bone out of her pocket. The toddler then chewed on the factory-made bone until she managed to get to the marrow and suck it dry.

"Ain't she a little scrap dog!" laughed one of the boys. Even though none of them had ever even seen a dog, they had all heard stories of a time food was so plentiful that not only did people keep dogs for pets instead of eating them, but they actually fed them their leftovers! The name stuck. The group adopted her, caring for her as best they could, even though it was an inconvenience. They had all known the pain of separation, whether by death or dumping, and they abided by an unspoken code to help and protect others like them.

If they had still been around, she may have never been in the situation she was in now. One by one, they had disappeared. None of them had D.I.N.s, and the State was looking for new subjects for a study. She reflected with reticence that this may have been the same study to which the nurse referred.

"Well, I have a bit of good news for you!" said the nurse brightly as she returned ten minutes later with an orderly and a cot. "You don't have a D.I.N., and—"

"Good. Then let's get on with it," the girl mumbled.

"I wasn't finished! The second test we ran makes you an excellent candidate for a new program. It's that study I was telling you about," The nurse began.

"I think I just want to die instead," she said dismally. The thought of being a medical experiment was almost more unbearable than the pain of living.

"Actually, being an Unspoken, you don't have a voice in the matter," the nurse said, as she quickly administered a sedative. In seconds, the girl was unconscious, her frail body transported to the gurney and wheeled into the back of a waiting van.

A few days later, she was allowed to regain consciousness. The medical team at the State research facility had found it was easier on subjects if they remained sedated while blood was drawn and tissue samples were taken, all the while addressing their nutritional and vitamin deficiencies intravenously. Many of them were so malnourished that the shock of being put through a battery of tests could cause major setbacks and delay their implementation into the study.

The spearhead of the pilot program promised it was a chance for the State to see the future of humanity—its potential for harmony and collective strength. It was a chance for a life and a destiny much better than that afforded by simple totalitarian rule—a chance for humanity to evolve into a unified whole, giving it the power of limitless possibility. "We have been held back by a belief we no longer acknowledge," explained the director of the study when he was securing funding for his program. "In the ancient text of Genesis, the Judeo-Christian God thwarted the unity of mankind by confusing their language, creating many languages. Now, we all know this is simply a myth used to explain why there are many different people groups. But in all myths, there is an element of truth. Imagine what we could accomplish if we were able to understand each other at the deepest personal level. Imagine if there were no cultural or political boundaries, and we could communicate on a level playing field. That is what I am proposing by implanting my subjects with a chip and linking them together from an early age. I want to show the world what I believe is possible when people collaborate."

"Is forced collaboration a true measure of humanity's potential, or is it merely an extension of totalitarianism at the neural level?" asked a member of the think tank.

"On the contrary, Ira, as we have seen throughout the development of humanity, we, as a species, seem bent on collaborating. We form family groups and people groups, and when those fail, we form gangs such as exist in the outer docks. People want to collaborate. They *want* to belong. We are simply giving them the opportunity to take ownership of that desire to belong and see its fulfillment."

"Are you certain we aren't presenting them with the opportunity for the State to take ownership of their freedom of thought?" Ira countered.

"If anyone should understand the danger of separation and the desire to belong to something greater, *I* do," came the reply.

Ira Owens studied the man, who was just a few years younger than he. He seemed so sure of himself, though he had risen in scientific circles from literally nowhere—a man who had walked into the outer docks from somewhere deep in the Preserve, with no memory of the route he had taken to escape the isolationist outpost of his origin. He had willingly turned himself into the State, claiming he had been held at the outpost against his will. Attempts to retrieve his memory of the whereabouts of the hidden community through hypnosis had failed, despite the cooperative nature of the subject. In the end, the most promising prospect for memory retrieval was eventually invented by the young man himself, who showed a remarkable aptitude for technology—especially considering his background. In theory, the chip would be no different than the implants already in use. It was simply a tool that aided brain function, much as implants aided the body's ability to counteract disease. But Ira didn't trust it.

"With the chip will come the ability to excel…to become the person you have the potential to be," the man was saying. "And the obvious next step is to give people the ability to connect with each other at a deeper level. Think of it. We already connect with our visors using social media platforms. Linking will just remove the clunky bit of yesterday's technology—a kind of obsolete middle man, if you will—and replace it with its new incarnation. It's really no different in theory than visiting a social media site, except that it's more efficient and more intimate. And with the safeguards I've invented to keep out would-be 'mind-stalkers,' this advance in technology will be the end of loneliness and isolation —maybe even of prejudice. It may well be the beginning of racial and political harmony and could be the next evolutionary step of humankind."

At this last boast, a ripple of soft laughter was heard from the older members of the group. But there was a nervous edge to it, as if they could almost believe its veracity. Ira swallowed. If the man didn't have such a passion for his idea, it could possibly be swept under the rug and forgotten. But its purpose was so close to State ideals. And the fact that it originated from the State's "poster child" and was glorifying all the State could do for humanity on an individual basis, as well as a whole…no, this idea wasn't going away. But surely the others could see the danger in it? Ira didn't trust this man, no matter how charming he was or how convincing his arguments. "I'm sorry, Joseph," Ira said firmly. "I don't feel this study is morally or ethically sound. There are too many gray areas where individual freedom is concerned. What's to keep the State from taking over someone's thought processes?"

"Are you suggesting the State would do such a thing?" the man asked cleverly.

Ira clenched his fingers around the arms of his chair, safely hidden under the table from the camera recording the session. "Of course not. But if some corrupt individual was placed in a position of power, it could be a possibility."

"Ahhh. I understand your concern," the man replied. "But this only validates the moral rectitude of my proposal. Government officials could be implanted with a chip that has checks and balances to ensure they only operate with the good of the people and the State in mind."

Checkmate. Ira nodded slightly and kept his mouth clamped shut. He seemed only to have aided the man's argument, considering the change in the expressions of the scientists surrounding the table. Dr. Joseph Moses later presented the sessions of the think tank to government officials, who—after they understood it—seemed very keen on his idea. Which is how the chip came to be approved by the FDTA, or Federal Drug and Technology Administration. And how Dr. Moses eventually gained approval for his study on a group of linked individuals. Which is how a girl named Scrap Dog came to be lying in a bed at the State research facility, regaining consciousness with Dr. Moses at her bedside.

"Good morning, Jayka," he said pleasantly, as her eyes fluttered open and she tried to focus on objects in the room.

"Where am I?" the girl asked, her head still foggy from the sedative. "And *what* did ya call me?"

"Jayka. It's a Qatari name meaning *conqueror,* only spelled differently. It seemed a better moniker than the one you gave at the Euthanasia Clinic."

"Scrap Dog. That's what I go by," she said stubbornly. "And I didn't sign up fuh no medical study. I may be an Unspoken, but I still got one right—the right to die. And I claim that right."

"Ahh, but that is where you are wrong, my friend. You are not an Unspoken. Someone has come forward with a Declaration of Intent to Nurture. You no longer have the right to die until you are of age to make a decision of such finality," Dr. Moses said with a calculative smile. "Although I think perhaps you may change your mind by that time."

At this, the girl swore vehemently. "There ain't no one who come forward with a D.I.N. fuh the likes o' me. I would jus' like ta see ya prove it, whoevah ya are. An' then we'll get on with my rights, cuz—"

She stopped jabbering as the man lifted up his electronic tablet for her to see. "That don't do me no good." she said bitterly. "Ya think I can read?"

"Very well, I'll read it for you," Dr. Moses said patiently. "But I'll have you note that this is the State's official website, and if you'll look at this square on the tablet, a scan of your retina will confirm that this document is, indeed, intended for you." He held the tablet close to her face, and immediately the word "Jayka" emanated from its speaker. "Would you like me to read it to you?" Dr. Moses asked.

The girl squinted. She was still having a hard time understanding why anyone would come forward with a D.I.N. The fact that she had been an Unspoken up until now would have given them the right to do anything they wanted to her. A Declaration of Intent to Nurture would seem to complicate things for them. Who had done it? And why?

Dr. Moses took her silence as consent and began to read. "As guardian of this individual, I hereby declare my intent to nurture them by providing them with all proper nutritional, medical, and educational care at my disposal. I declare that this individual, Jayka, is solely my responsibility, and that I am bound by the law of the State to protect, care for, and nurture them until they are of an age and mentality to care for themselves. Signed, the State."

The girl sat dumbfounded. "Do you know what this means, Jayka?" Dr. Moses asked.

"I am property of the State," she sighed.

"Not property," Dr. Moses corrected her. "You are a daughter. You're not an Unspoken anymore. You have a voice now. They didn't give you a last name because they thought you might like to choose one for yourself when you turn eighteen. In the meantime, the State will feed you and clothe you and educate you. And when you're eighteen, if you still want to die, your wish will be considered after you have undergone counseling. But we hope you'll change your mind. You have a lot to live for now."

The girl's attention was diverted by the smell of something delicious. A cart was being wheeled into her room, and on it was a plate of food that smelled incredible. Her eyes widened. "Is that *new* food?" she asked incredulously. "Food that ain't been eaten on?"

"Yes, of course!" Dr. Moses said. "You are a daughter of the State—the most benevolent political entity humankind has ever known. Why wouldn't you receive the very best?"

She sat up eagerly, the plan to end her life strangely forgotten. "This is more food than I've seen in three weeks put together!" she exclaimed.

"It's actually quite a small portion. We didn't want you to overeat and get sick," Dr. Moses apologized, but the girl was stuffing forkfuls of mashed potatoes and chicken into her mouth and didn't seem to hear him. Halfway through the plate, she forced herself to slow down. It didn't seem possible that the food was unlimited, and she had learned to pace herself to conserve supplies.

"Are you getting full already?" Dr. Moses asked.

"Nah, I just wanna make sure I got some leftover," she said.

"You should know that whatever you don't eat will be thrown away. We don't want you to get sick by eating food that has been left out."

She looked at him in consternation. "But that's what I been doin' ma whole life!" she exclaimed.

"Well, not anymore. And just so you know there's more where that came from, you can keep this with you," Dr. Moses said, handing her a granola bar.

She stared at it wonderingly. "I seen the wrappers fuh these things, but I nevah had one what still had somethin' in it."

"Well, enjoy. Or just hold onto it. It's up to you," Dr. Moses told her, and paused as he studied her thin form. "You'll find that all the things they told you about the State back in the outer docks—it's all lies."

The girl stopped chewing and looked at him guardedly. "Oh, yeah?"

"I can see that you don't believe me. But I came from the Preserve. And the State adopted *me* as one of its own, too. I have never regretted my decision to come here. And even though it wasn't your decision, I don't think you'll ever regret being adopted by the State."

The girl looked at her bedside companion with new respect. "You came from the *Preserve?*" she asked. "What was it like?"

Dr. Moses smiled and settled back into his chair. "Prison," he said bluntly. "Trust me. You're going to love it here."

The girl chewed thoughtfully and seemed to stare into space. "Jayka," she repeated softly. "It ain't a bad name."

That had been eight long years ago. With proper care and nutrition, Jayka had matured into a striking young woman. Education and integration into society helped erase the accent that had identified her as a pariah. And while not all of the things the State asked her to do were easy, with the help of implants and the chip, she had developed coping mechanisms and was able to rationalize and even champion what was required of her. She had become part of an elite group of operatives that fought for the State's ideals. In fact, a few members of her old gang had been recruited earlier, and now they fought alongside each other. But they now shared a bond much greater than the gang they had formed as children —a bond at the neural level. The scared, beaten little girl was a memory Jayka could almost forget. While the outer docks crew had cared enough to try to save her, only the State had the means to help her rise above her poverty and give her a real sense of purpose. And that was a debt of gratitude Jayka would never forget.

2

Shadows stretched across the crumbling road, gradually softening into murky twilight. Macy kept her post near the edge of the woods. Surely the Kind Man would bring Craig back and lead them to camp, and they would eat a meal with the younger humans. But the longer Macy waited, the more restless she became. The humming noise had never stopped since she had detected it that morning, its pervasive drone setting her canine senses on edge. She whimpered and set her head on her paws. An hour passed. Her stomach growled. A dog could get terribly hungry while she was waiting for her Master to return; but the Kind Man had told her to stay, so she would.

What if something had happened to Him? She knew her Master would never abandon her, and she had never seen anything that could overpower Him. But what if He couldn't get out of the flying machine that had taken Craig away? Maybe she should try to follow them—but no, He had told her to stay. She was so confused. She raised to a sitting position and whimpered again. And then— she couldn't help it—she lifted her head and let out a long, lonely howl.

"Macy, My dear little friend! Don't be distressed," said a familiar voice.

Macy stopped in mid-howl and jumped up and down in a ragged circle around her Master.

"I was with you the whole time. You were just having trouble seeing Me because your worry got in the way of your faith in Me,"[1] the Kind Man explained as He rubbed her ears. "Our friends back at camp are worried as well, and *their* fear is also overshadowing their faith. If I had allowed you to go back sooner

---

[1] Can a dog have faith? Maybe not in a spiritual sense, but anyone who has owned a good dog has surely wished themselves to be the type of person the dog thought they were. But Macy knows the Master, and her faith, though only that of a dog, is not misplaced.

—before dark—they would have tried to rush to the rescue. Now they have to wait and think and pray a while before their next move. Let's go see them, shall we?"

Macy fell in step with Him but whined and looked behind them as they left, wondering why Craig wasn't there yet. "No, he's not coming," the Kind Man said with a hint of sadness, but then His eyes brightened. "He loves Me…so much that he chose to listen to Me and follow My will. It won't be easy for Him. But I am with Him always. And his obedience is a key part of My plan."

Macy's tongue lolled out the side of her mouth as she looked up at her Master. She trusted Him—with her own life *and* everyone else's. She dropped her head and sniffed eagerly at the leaves of the forest floor as the Kind Man retraced their steps of that afternoon. Eventually, she heard the sound of voices, and she let out an excited snort. The Kind Man chuckled as Macy's tail began wagging so hard that it threw her off balance. Suddenly the voices at the campsite fell quiet as the group wondered at the source of the crashing sound in the brush. Macy could stand it no longer. She gave a bark of greeting and bounded into camp.

"Macy, you scared us to death! We thought you were a bear or something!" Dania laughed nervously.

"Yeah! Craig said he wasn't going to be gone long. I look forward to hearing what happened," Thom said as they all peered into the darkness of the surrounding forest, waiting for their youth pastor to arrive at any moment.

Macy watched the young humans as they waited and listened for the sound of approaching footsteps. She looked to the Kind Man for guidance, but He, in turn, was watching the teens to see their reaction when their leader didn't appear.

"Macy, where's Craig?" Garrison asked, pointing into the woods.

"I bet he's just taking longer to get here," Lydia suggested. "Macy can go under green briars when we have to find a way around."

When it became obvious that Craig wasn't coming, they all looked at Macy. "Where's Craig, Mace?" Garrison said.

Macy stood up eagerly, but when she looked at the Kind Man, He shook his head and gave her the command to stay. She whined and lay down, settling her head on her paws.

"Something's wrong," Garrison said. "We need to go find him!"

"In the dark?" Dania asked worriedly. "We can't see anything."

"But if Macy would lead us…" Garrison said, looking at the dog expectantly. "Take us to Craig, Mace! Com'on, Macy, go find Craig!"

The "Go Find" game was one of Macy's favorites, and she almost always found the person she was looking for. But as her eyes shifted to the Kind Man, she could see His gentle command still held firm. She was to stay at the camp, at least for now.

"I've never known her to refuse a game of 'Go Find,'" Garrison said, the tension mounting in his voice.

"Well, maybe she knows Craig is alright. Maybe he's just taking his time," Thom suggested.

"Or maybe she's afraid and too stubborn to go back that direction," Garrison muttered crossly.

"Craig said if for some reason he didn't come back before dark, we shouldn't go looking for him," Dania said.

"Macy isn't the only one who's afraid," Garrison said pointedly. Dania bit her tongue and looked down, walking to the other side of the clearing. For one thing, she knew Garrison was right. She *was* afraid. But for another thing, he was a new Christian. She needed to be patient with him.

"Don't you think that if something was wrong, Macy would be acting funny, trying to get us to follow her?" Lydia asked.

"You guys sure put a lot of stock in this mutt's decision-making abilities," Garrison said. But then he remembered all the times Macy had led him places —even before they had left Adullam—and every time, something significant had happened. Since they had been on this journey, she had helped them find sources of food and water and safe places to camp. At first, he had thought it was serendipitous, but it had happened too often to be coincidence. Was she really that smart, or did God have a hand in it?

Chandra, who had kept uncharacteristically silent until now, could hold her tongue no longer. "Why don't we vote on it?" she asked. "If the majority thinks we should leave and go looking for Pastor Craig, we'll go. If not, we'll wait 'til morning."

"Why don't we *pray* on it?" suggested Lelah. Normally timid, Lelah's voice was surprisingly loud and had the confidence that comes with wisdom.

"Now, there's the voice of reason," Thom said.

Garrison watched as his companions gathered in a circle and put their hands on each other's shoulders. He reluctantly did the same, but secretly wondered how long this prayer meeting would last. Craig could be in trouble, and every second might count!

After a few minutes of praying to themselves, Lelah's voice gained in strength. "Father, we know that the angel of the Lord encamps around those who fear Him, and delivers them.[2] We ask in the name of Jesus that the promise of your Word be fulfilled, and that You will send Your angels to be with Pastor Craig—wherever he is—and that You will deliver him from any harm."

"Yes, Father," added Thom, "and we know that Your Word also says You will never leave us or forsake us. So we can say with confidence, 'The Lord is my helper, I will not be afraid; what can man do to me?'[3] We know that You haven't left Pastor Craig, and You haven't left us. We know You are our helper, and You will be with us, no matter what we go through or who comes against us. We thank You right now for Your hand of protection over Pastor Craig. Give us wisdom, Lord, so that we can know what to do."

As Thom finished praying, he began to pray in the Spirit, and the others began to do the same. Garrison was at a loss for how to pray, when suddenly one of Miss Genevieve's verses came to mind: *"Likewise the Spirit helps us in our weakness; for we do not know how to pray as we ought, but the Spirit himself intercedes for us with sighs too deep for words. And he who searches the hearts of men knows what is the mind of the Spirit, because the Spirit intercedes for the saints according to the will of God—Romans 8:26-27,"* [4] he quoted quietly to himself. "Well, God, I could certainly use some help praying now, because I don't know what to do," he said under his breath. And as he looked to Jesus for help, the Holy Spirit supplied the words. Praying in the Spirit, Garrison knew he was asking God's perfect will for the situation at hand.

---

[2] See Psalm 34:7
[3] See Hebrews 13:5-6 RSV
[4] Romans 8:26-27 RSV

The group continued praying for their pastor, breaking off individually after a while. Lelah could be heard claiming the promises found in God's Word. Lydia was singing choruses about the Lord's goodness and His protection and provision. Chandra was chattering as usual, talking to Jesus just as she would talk to any close friend about a problem. Dania and Thom and Garrison were praying in other tongues, their requests and the cries of their heart known only to God.

And Macy? Macy was hungrily crunching on an unsuspecting mouse that had wandered into camp and skittered right past her nose. She licked her lips and surveyed the scene, watching as the Kind Man listened to each prayer. When one of the youths would fall silent, He would minister to them. Macy couldn't understand what He was saying, but it reminded her of the times when Craig would get out the precious object and talk while looking at its leaves.[5] Whatever the Kind Man was saying to the teens right now, Macy could see it was giving strength to the humans. Her stomach growled, and she looked hopefully around the camp for any signs of dinner. In the edge of the girls' tent, she spied another mouse sniffing around the pockets of Chandra's backpack. Macy crept slowly to the tent and with another swift *chomp* had procured another snack. "Macy, what are you doing? Stop biting my backpack!" Chandra exclaimed, running over to investigate. "Ewwww! Nasty! What's that in your mouth?" she asked. "Is that a mouse tail? Hey, everybody! Macy caught a mouse!" Laughter erupted in the campsite. Their concentration was broken, but a deep peace had settled over them after the time spent in prayer.

"I'm not sure how everyone else feels, but I think we should wait until morning to go look for Craig," Thom said. "I have peace about it in my spirit that everything's going to be alright."

"I agree. It's dangerous to go wandering around when we can't see. Maybe tomorrow Macy will lead us in the right direction," Dania said.

Garrison sighed. At the beginning of this journey, he had been confidently in the lead with Craig, knowing that none of the others had ever ventured beyond the borders of their community and knew very little about surviving in

---

[5] In *The Image Bearers,* Macy watched as Craig would hold a Bible study for the teens each morning, get out the precious object (a Bible) and read from its "leaves."

the wilderness. But now that a crisis had occurred, he found himself deferring to those who were spiritually older and wiser, even though they might be physically younger and had less survival skills than he did. "I can't explain it, but the feeling I had earlier to rush off and help Pastor Craig just isn't there anymore. It's like God is asking me to trust that He'll take care of him. Besides, with Macy not being very cooperative, there's not much of a point in trying to find him in the dark. I know how to track a deer or a rabbit I shoot with an arrow in broad daylight, but going after Craig now would be like tracking in the dark with no blood trail—at least, I *hope* there's not a blood trail."

"Oh, my goodness! I really think he's ok, Garrison," Lydia said quickly.

"Maybe he just went farther than he realized, and it got dark before he could get back. I bet he just bedded down for the night. He'll probably walk into camp in the morning," added Thom.

"Yeah, and he'll probably be wondering why we aren't up already, making breakfast," Chandra laughed.

The group departed to their tents—except for Lelah, who sat on a rock for a while, praying softly. Macy ambled over to her and put her head in the girl's lap. "You know where he is, don't you?" Lelah asked. Macy's tail beat a steady rhythm on the ground, and she licked the girl's hand. Lelah stared over the top of the cedar brake surrounding the clearing. They must be very close to their destination. The humming sound, although not terribly loud, could not be ignored; and the sky had a strange glow off to the north that must certainly be city lights. "Because he hath set his love upon Me, therefore will I deliver him: I will set him on high, because he hath known My name. He shall call upon Me, and I will answer him: I will be with him in trouble; I will deliver him, and honor him. With long life will I satisfy him, and show him My salvation," [6] Lelah quoted. "These are promises You made to us, Lord. But sometimes I wonder…is the deliverance You talk about always a physical deliverance? It says right there in that passage that You will be with us in trouble. So that implies we're going to have trouble sometimes. And of course, Jesus said 'In the world you will have tribulation: but be of good cheer; I have overcome the world.'[7]

---

[6] Psalm 91:14-16, KJV
[7] See John 16:33

Father, I just wonder if maybe Craig is in some sort of trouble we can't get him out of. Like, maybe he ran into those people Wisteria was talking about, and they locked him up somewhere. Your Word *does* say You will be with us in trouble. And I *know* You can deliver us from anything. But sometimes maybe You allow us to walk through the fire so that we and everyone else can know You will be walking through it with us, right by our side.[8] So wherever Craig is, I know You're with him. I just ask that You give him Your strength and peace for whatever he has to face and that he'll know You're right there."

A mist had begun to seep through the trees, draping a gauzy veil over the tents and the unused firepit. Lelah scratched Macy's ears, hugged her jacket closer against the chill of the night air, and quietly made her way to bed.

---

[8] See Daniel 3:19-25

3

Sunlight crept over the hills of the Preserve, making its way steadily westward to the little campsite in the clearing. Garrison was already up as the light topped the nearest hill. It set the mist afire with a golden glow before burning it out, leaving nothing but a slight dampness that clung to everything. Garrison wondered if he should risk making a fire. He decided against it and instead walked around the edge of the cedar brake to keep warm, making a point to step on every twig in his path. He was ready for action now that dawn had arrived, and the others couldn't wake up soon enough for him. Macy followed closely behind him, her red nose bumping against his calves when he slowed his pace. When the noise of clomping boots and snapping twigs didn't work, Garrison began to whistle.

Thom was the first to make an appearance, stumbling out of the boys' tent. "Dude. Not cool," he grumbled, rubbing the sleep from his eyes.

Garrison gave him a wicked grin. "Come on, man. It's daylight. Besides, Craig may need our help."

"What about devotions?" Chandra asked, peeking around the flap of the girls' tent. "Craig would want us to start the day with God."

"Craig may be in serious trouble, and God can go with us. Haven't you read that Enoch walked with God?" Garrison quipped.

"Yeah, and God took him," Lydia joked. "I'm not quite ready to leave."

"Ready to leave camp, or ready to meet Jesus?" Chandra grinned. "If you're not sure, I can pray with you about that."

"Yes, yes, thank you Chandra," Lydia smiled sarcastically back at her. "If Garrison keeps waking us up early, I may need your help praying because I might break one of the Ten Commandments."

"Which one?" Chandra asked.

"Thou shalt not kill," Lydia said, glaring at Garrison.

Dania emerged from the tent, with Lelah close behind. "Hey, I'm not saying we should have an extended Bible study, but I do think it's important we start our day with prayer and the Word," Dania said.

"Definitely," Lelah agreed.

"Well then, let's get to it, so we can get going!" Garrison said impatiently.

"You know, it's probably a good thing to wait around camp just a little bit, in case Craig was just waiting until morning to come back," Lydia suggested.

Garrison said nothing, but he knew she was right. If Craig had gone too far to come back before dark, it might take him a while to get back to camp the next morning.

"Does anyone have a scripture they want to share?" Dania asked.

"There's this one I'm thinking of, but I can't remember where it's found," Chandra began. "Something about the eyes of the Lord and roaming around on the earth?"

"I think I know the one you mean," Lelah said, grabbing her Bible and flipping to the Old Testament. "It's in 2 Chronicles. Here it is. 2 Chronicles 16:9—'For the eyes of the Lord run to and fro throughout the whole earth, to show Himself strong in the behalf of them whose heart is perfect toward Him.'[9] There's more after that, but that's the part you're talking about, isn't it?"

"That's it!" Chandra exclaimed. "Because I was thinking…Craig's heart is perfect toward God. I mean, obviously, nobody is perfect, but if you're a child of God, you are perfect to Him, because your sins are all forgiven and you are washed clean by the blood of His Son. So we don't need to worry about Craig, no matter where he is, because God is going to show Himself strong for him. And you know, we don't need to worry about ourselves, either. Because even though we're not perfect, we are perfect to God, because He has forgiven us, too. When He looks at us, He sees us through the blood of His Son. So no matter where we go or what happens, He will show Himself strong on our behalf," Chandra bubbled over, her eyes shining.

---

[9] 2 Chronicles 16:9 KJV

"Chandra, sometimes you take forever to say anything, but I'm glad you said that," Garrison said genuinely. He looked around at the others. "I'm sorry I've been so hard to live with. Sitting still doesn't come naturally to me, especially if I'm worried about something."

"Well, instead of worrying, let's pray,"[10] Thom suggested. "Then we can go ahead and pack everything up and be on our way."

The group huddled together, and Thom began to pray as the others joined in agreement. "Father, we ask that You go with us today. Watch over us and watch over Craig. Please help us to find him, or for him to find us before we leave camp. We know that You *do* show Yourself strong on behalf of Your children, and we are trusting in You for this promise to be fulfilled. In Jesus' name we pray—"

"Amen," the group all said together.

"Does anyone have anything to eat?" asked Chandra.

"There's still some of those peanuts from Dania's grandpa," Lydia suggested. Dania's grandfather was one of the main farmers in Adullam, keeping the community supplied with fruits, vegetables, and legumes. As a going-away gift, he had given the group thirty pounds of roasted peanuts. At the beginning of their journey, Dania carried little but the peanuts and her water canteen, as the team attempted to distribute weight evenly among individuals. But her pack had grown steadily lighter as they traveled, and they began to ration the peanuts more carefully. Now each teen grabbed a handful to eat while they broke camp. It wasn't much of a breakfast, but they knew they would need to eat something for the journey.

"Ok, are we ready?" Garrison asked as he surveyed the campsite.

"I really thought he would come back," Chandra said.

"I think we've given him enough time to come if he was able. Agreed?" Garrison said. The others nodded. Garrison shouldered Craig's backpack and turned to Macy, who was watching the group from the edge of the clearing in the area where she and Craig had left the day before. "Okay, Macy. Go find Craig!"

Macy stood up and looked up at the Kind Man, Who was also standing at the forest edge. He smiled gently at her and walked into the woods, beckoning her

---

[10] See Philippians 4:6

to follow. Macy's tail wagged furiously and she bounded behind Him. Garrison smiled at the others, now confident that Macy would show the way.

For a short while, the group retraced Craig's steps. Macy was keeping track of the scent trail as she followed her Master. But soon after leaving the clearing, the Kind Man left the scent and veered to the east. Macy stopped for a second, snorted, and waited until her Guide turned around to look at her. She pricked up her ears and wagged her tail hesitantly, looking at Him with a question in her eyes. "Yes, I know," He told her. "We are taking a different route." Macy snorted and once again bounded after Him, her tail wagging confidently again.

The group followed her for an hour, picking their way among the oaks and maples. At one point, the scenery changed dramatically. Trees vanished and the earth looked as if it had been turned over by a giant shovel. Each footstep created a swirl of dust that was wafted away by the slightest breeze drifting over the barren landscape. "What happened here?" Lydia wondered aloud.

"Do you think it was some sort of explosion? Maybe a bomb!" Chandra said excitedly.

"It looks more organized than a bomb going off. Look at those big piles of dirt," Thom commented, gesturing to the huge mounds of soil and chunked-up limestone scattered around the area.

"Maybe they were mining for something," Lelah suggested. The group walked gingerly through the site, wondering what kind of toxic dust they might be breathing as they passed through the former location of Steelville. They had no way of knowing they were traversing a former settlement. Nothing remained of the town, which had long been demolished in the State's search for specific minerals to supply the construction of the causeways.

After a mile or so, the wasteland ended abruptly and they found themselves surrounded by trees again. Flowering dogwoods had recently shed their blossoms, which littered the forest floor as if an enthusiastic flower girl had flung them wildly at some woodland wedding. Sandstone boulders dotted the surrounding slopes, peeking out from under their thick blanket of last year's fallen leaves. A few miles later, the slopes steepened and converged, and a stream could be seen trickling at the bottom of the draw. The teenagers followed Macy to the bottom and refilled their canteens, taking care to strain the water through the water purifier bottle Dawson had given to Craig before they left Adullam. "I guess it's a good thing he left his backpack at camp," Lydia remarked as she poured the filtered water into her canteen.

"Yeah, but what if he runs out of water before we get to him?" Chandra asked worriedly.

"I'm sure we'll find him before then," Dania reassured her.

"Wait a minute," Garrison said suddenly, holding up his hand for the group to be quiet. "Listen."

After a few moments' silence, Chandra spoke up. "I don't hear anything except the creek."

"I don't either," Thom said.

"That's what I mean," Garrison said. "Do you guys hear the humming noise anymore?"

They became quiet once again. "No," Dania broke the silence. "But maybe we can't hear it down in this creek bottom. Maybe the hills are blocking it."

"Maybe," Garrison said doubtfully. He turned to Macy, who was waiting on top of a smooth, gray boulder nearby. "Macy, go find Craig!" he said, but before he could finish the command, she was already plodding dutifully behind her invisible Guide.

"It's nice of her to go slow for us," Chandra said, as they puffed their way up the slope.

"Yeah. I remember when we first left Adullam, she was following *us*," Thom mused. "But then at some point, it seemed like we started following *her*."

When they got to the top of the slope, Garrison held up his hand again to signal them to stop. "Do you hear it?" he asked them.

The group strained to hear, but the only sound was Macy's footsteps crunching through the leaves.

"This can't be right," Garrison said. "Craig wouldn't have gone farther away from the city. The humming should be getting louder. I can't hear it at all anymore."

"Me neither," Lydia said.

"Well, maybe Craig went this way for a reason," Lelah said tentatively.

"Why would he do that? It just doesn't make sense that he would head away from the sound of civilization," Garrison replied.

"Maybe he's taking a different way there," Lelah suggested.

"How could he know a different way? He's never even been there before!" Garrison exclaimed in frustration. Once again, his worry was getting the best of him.

"I mean that maybe he was trying to find a safer way. Or maybe he was being led by the Holy Spirit," she replied calmly.

Garrison was quiet as he thought about her remark. "I guess it's possible. Macy seems pretty sure of where she's going."

The youths put their doubts aside and continued following the dog. Instead of any signs of civilization, they seemed to be walking through denser stands of old-growth timber. By mid-morning, the peanuts they had eaten for breakfast had worn off, and they stopped to inspect their backpacks for any available food items.

"If you're tired of peanuts, I've still got about a pound or two of jerky," Thom offered.

"Why didn't you say anything about that this morning?" Chandra huffed.

"I usually save that for our dinner, remember?" he explained. "But let's eat some now. We just have to try to conserve some for dinner tonight." He doled out a piece of goat jerky to each member of the group, and they continued their trek as they ate.

"I really thought I would be better at using a slingshot," Thom said, chawing his way through a piece of the stringy meat.

Dania smirked. Several of the group had made slingshots for the journey, hopeful that they might be able to dispatch small game. She and Thom had been holding shooting matches since before they left Adullam. "I still think I'll get something before *you* do."

"And what'll you do with a squirrel or a rabbit if you actually get one?" Thom countered.

"Garrison already showed me how to clean one before we left home," she said smugly.

"We'll see what happens when the time comes. *If* the time comes," Thom replied.

For the last half hour, the group had been making their way slowly to the crest of a high ridge. The trees thinned out as they reached the top, allowing them to look back over the way they had come. From this vantage point, the travelers could see for miles. "Can you tell how far we've gone?" Thom asked Garrison as they surveyed the scene.

Garrison was quiet for a moment. "I really don't think we've come as far as you might expect," he said, shielding his eyes from the sun. "Do you remember the old mine tailings we ran across? I think that's them right there." He pointed to a bare, gray spot in the otherwise verdant landscape.

"I think our camp was just a little farther that way," he began and then drew in a breath, his eyebrows raised in surprise. "Look north of where we were camped." He pointed to a silver ribbon that lay across the land in a smooth, polished curve.

"That sure is a big river," Lydia remarked. "You can see it for miles."

"Yeah, most rivers are hidden by trees here and there. This one must be a whomper," Thom added.

Garrison sighed and scratched his head thoughtfully. "I don't think that's a river," he said, "for exactly the reason you mentioned. Look at it. It's never hidden by the trees. Whatever that is, it's *above* the trees. Once in a while, it looks like a hill might hide it from us, but for the most part you can see the whole thing until it gets too far away to see. I think that might be one of those big transport systems Viv told me about one time. It's the main way they travel between cities these days."

"That's a causeway. She told me about that too," Chandra said. "She said she always avoided it when she came to visit because it was heavily monitored. That and the older roads."

"And I think that's one of those older roads there," Garrison said, pointing to a gray line south of the causeway. "That's even closer to our camp."

As the group silently surveyed the scene, they saw a white object rise up out of the trees from the old road. "What is that?" Chandra asked nervously.

"A helicopter?" Thom ventured.

The helicopter made a methodical sweep of the area surrounding the campsite. As they watched, a smaller object appeared on the horizon, rushing to join the helicopter in its search. It, too, began a methodical sweep of the area around the old road. "That must be one of the surveillance drones," Thom said.

Garrison tried to swallow a lump in his throat. "I think I know why Craig never came back to camp," he said quietly.

$$4$$

CRAIG stood at the window of the small apartment where he had been personally escorted by Dr. Moses, the childhood friend he had known as Yosi Manaba. A thousand questions rushed through his mind, some of which he had asked his old acquaintance. Dr. Moses had merely smiled patiently and reassured him that all would soon be made clear. He had offered no explanation as to what had transpired since he left Adullam, nor had he explained the nature of his current endeavors in the place he now obviously called home. Before departing, he told Craig that he would return in the morning after his guest had gotten some much needed rest. "You are welcome here, Craig! You have no idea how happy I am that you've come," he reassured him. But Craig had a sickening feeling akin to what a fly must feel when it first finds its wings are stuck in a spider's web.

Sleep had eluded him, although his accommodations included a soft bed and a mechanically interesting chair that allowed its occupant to lean back and elevate their feet. He had tried the chair out of curiosity, but his nerves, coupled with a slightly upset stomach, rendered the prospect of sleep out of the question. Instead, he explored the apartment.

In a spacious refrigerator he had discovered a plastic tray divided into separately packaged portions of mashed potatoes, a mysterious meat with a curious texture, and green beans devoid of seasoning. The meal came with instructions for using the microwave, which was embedded in the apartment wall. While he was heating the tray, he ravenously devoured several little cups of chocolate pudding that lined the shelves of the fridge. Chocolate was scarce in Adullam; few occupants had ever tried it, but he remembered it from his boyhood when the community still carried a small supply. The pudding had a faint chemical taste, but hunger spreads a magnificent table.

Having left the city at a very young age, there were many aspects of modern life of which he was ignorant. A full bathroom gave him an option of personal hygiene he had never before experienced: a device above his head which sprayed water out of the wall into the bathtub. It was *hot* water too, he discovered, as he nearly scalded himself trying to understand its operation. His own bathtub in Adullam had offered only lukewarm water which had been heated by solar power. If it had not been for the monotonous gray walls, the apartment would have seemed luxurious by Adullam's standards. And then, of course, there was the door which was locked from the outside, reminding him that he was not a guest, but a prisoner.

He had been standing at the window for some time, watching a thick, dingy fog that slithered its way through the city in a serpentine path, illuminated by traffic and streetlights. As the sun rose, the source of the fog was revealed: a strangely colored river that swallowed sunlight instead of reflecting it. He sighed and rubbed his eyes. Daylight. He could not stop thinking about the group of teens he had left behind. They would be stirring in camp now, waiting for him to show up. But no—surely, they had been discovered by now. He fought the urge to panic and once again turned to his Heavenly Father in prayer. "Lord, I know I was doing what You asked me to do. But I don't see how we can fulfill our mission if we all get captured and no one ever hears our message." He prayed silently, for he remembered the stories his parents had told him about how society was closely monitored. Even a private conversation in one's own home wasn't really private. Suddenly a scripture came to his mind. "Thou wilt keep him in perfect peace, whose mind is stayed on Thee: because he trusteth in Thee,"[11] he said softly. As he spoke the verses out loud and meditated on what he had said, fear still attempted to rise up in him. "I'm not listening to you, Fear. I choose to listen to the Word," Craig said firmly, and repeated the verse. His thoughts then drifted to another verse, and he smiled as he recited it. "Peace I leave with you, My peace I give unto you: not as the world giveth, give I unto you. Let not your heart be troubled, neither let it be afraid."[12] As he

---

[11] Isaiah 26:3-4, KJV
[12] John 14:27, KJV

said it, he could almost imagine Jesus saying it to His disciples shortly before he was betrayed and taken into custody. Jesus had known the doubts and fears that would plague His followers after He was crucified. He had tried to prepare them by offering them the kind of peace that passes human understanding. Many of them would face persecution. Some of them would be martyred. And yet here was a promise they could hold onto, no matter what they faced. It was something the world couldn't take away from them…something that defied explanation: peace in the midst of suffering, hardship—even beating and torture. All they had to do was believe what Jesus said and receive it.

Craig thought about Peter when he had been imprisoned by Herod. While Peter slept in jail, the church prayed for his release. While they were praying, an angel visited Peter, loosed him from his chains, and then led him out of the jail.[13] Craig was certain the teens were praying for him. He also knew that their whole community was praying, as well. It wouldn't have been impossible for an angel to appear at any moment to help him escape. But Craig also remembered that eventually, Peter gave his life for the gospel. The group from Adullam had known this would be a possibility for them before they left home. "Whatever You have planned, Lord, count me in. As long as You're with me, I can do what You ask me to do," Craig whispered. Inexplicably, a wave of peace flooded his soul. Craig raised his hands in praise and wept, knowing that he was experiencing firsthand the type of inexplicable peace Jesus had promised. The presence of the Lord was with him as he had never felt it before. The words of Jesus seemed to surround him as he worshipped: *"Lo, I am with you always, even unto the end of the world."*[14]

Suddenly, he heard a knocking at the door. He walked to it, and then remembered he couldn't let anyone in, even if he had tried. "Uh, hello?" he ventured.

"Good morning, Craig Goforth," said a voice from behind the door. "It is required of me that I ask your permission to open the door."

"Um, ok…" Craig replied, confused.

The door slid open to reveal the soldier Yosi had called Jayka. "I would not have asked. But for reasons unknown to me, Dr. Moses ordered that I proceed in this manner."

---

[13] See Acts 12:1-11
[14] Matthew 28:20, KJV

"Well, that's considerate of him, I suppose," Craig said cautiously.

"Indeed. It is a very unusual way to deal with a—" Jayka stopped herself suddenly, and then continued, "…*guest.* Dr. Moses has informed me that you are his *guest.*"

"I have never encountered the inability to leave guest quarters," Craig mused.

Jayka regarded him coldly. "Your quarters are another unusual matter," she said, her eyes surveying the bed, recliner, spacious kitchen and the open door to the full bath.

"I'm not complaining. It's much more comfortable than I'm accustomed to," Craig said quickly. "Are all apartments here as lavish as this one?"

Jayka gave him a steely glare. "If you're done offering insincere compliments, I will conduct you to your meeting with Dr. Moses."

"I hope I didn't seem insincere. It really is a very nice apartment." Craig attempted to sound affable, but his effort was wasted on Jayka, who simply stepped aside and motioned for him to walk with her down the hall.

"May I ask you a question?" Craig asked as they walked from the gray-walled building into a gray brick courtyard.

"You just did," said Jayka in her cold, emotionless tone. "But as I mentioned, I have been instructed to indulge you in tedious social protocols. Proceed."

"Why is everything the same color of gray? Is there some law against color?"

"Hardly. The gray you see is the natural color of the brick we use for building. Paint is not only unnecessary, but harmful to the microbes embedded in the material."

"Microbes?"

"Yes. For self-repairing bricks. And the general populous either wears visors or are implanted with a chip, both of which allow them to choose whatever color they want to see projected on the walls. Paint is expensive and oppressive."

"Oppressive? How is paint oppressive?" Craig asked, mystified.

"Because if something is painted a certain color, there is no way *not* to see it. What if those who pass by don't like the color? Or what if some have color vision deficiency, and are made to feel excluded when they realize they are not viewing the color as the majority sees it. Some colors have even been shown to induce violence in certain individuals. By allowing people to choose their own color for their surroundings, they are made to feel at ease. No one person's preference is forced upon another. In the State, equality is taken very seriously. Every voice matters. But oppressors are not tolerated," Jayka explained.

"I would think painting your own home a certain color would be viewed as self-expression," Craig said. "Are people here unable to express themselves?"

"It would obviously depend on the circumstance. If their form of self-expression offends others, the State may find it necessary to take action."

"Well, what if, for example, I find your hair color to be offensive?" Craig asked. "Not that I think that, of course," Craig added hastily as Jayka shot him a glance.

"Obviously, something as personal as a hair style would unlikely cause offense in others. Citizens of the State are trained from an early age to respect the rights of others and not infringe upon their personal freedom of expression," Jayka said with an air of impatience.

"How is that different than the color someone might choose for their house?" Craig persisted.

"You have made several references to housing as if personal ownership is somehow involved. The state provides all housing for its citizens. But even if the occupant had a choice in the matter of color, a house is a stationary object—a permanent part of a neighborhood. A neighborhood is collectively shared by all of its residents. To project a permanent color onto a house would be viewed as an act of defiant self-expression—much like graffiti."

"Oh, I see. So it's okay to express oneself in deeply personal ways such as hair color or clothing—"

"As long as that self-expression does not harm others," Jayka interjected. "Obviously, if the State did not draw the line somewhere, anyone who lost their temper could insist that beating their fellow citizen was their right to express themselves."

"So who determines what is actually harmful? What defines someone as an oppressor? It's easy to see the harm one might cause by beating up their next-door neighbor. But what if I wanted to share some information with my neighbor that might cause them temporary mental or emotional discomfort but would completely change their lives for the better? What if I knew something bad was coming? Something they could only avoid by deciding to trust Someone I could introduce them to? Someone who provided a way of escape?"

Jayka stopped suddenly and turned to face him. "Craig Goforth, if you know of a dangerous plot against citizens of the State, you are required by law to divulge that information."

Craig's pulse quickened. "I will gladly share this information."

"Then I must take you to the proper authorities," Jayka announced.

Craig winced. This wasn't going exactly as planned. "But this is something so important that everyone must hear it," he explained. "It can't be limited to just a few people in authority."

"The administrators will determine if the information you provide reveals a credible threat to the State. Then they will prepare in an orderly fashion and either conducts citizens to safety or effectively eliminate the threat altogether. There is no need to cause panic and disrupt society if the threat you speak of isn't imminent or even plausible. In fact, most matters of national security are handled quietly, and citizens have no knowledge they were ever in danger."

"Who are these administrators?" Craig asked. "How do you know they are acting in the citizens' best interests?"

"All administrators are implanted with a chip which guides them in their decisions. They cannot deviate from their protocol to protect citizens—and the State, as a whole," Jayka explained.

"I've heard about this chip," Craig said. "But I didn't know citizens were required to have it." His mind flew to Viv. He wondered if this could be the reason no one had seen her in so long.

"Not all citizens," Jayka clarified. "Just those in positions of governmental authority—although most citizens are eager to be implanted. The chip gives the individual the ability to unleash their full potential."

"But someone had to program the chip. How do you know if the programmer is operating with the good of citizens in mind? Who programs the chip? I would like to meet this person."

Jayka paused, giving him a sidelong glance. "Not just anyone can have access to the programmer," she said. "His identity is protected from the general population. This knowledge requires a certain level of security clearance."

"It seems like a lot of power to give to one person," Craig said incredulously. "Someone who can control a person's mind seems like someone who could wield almost absolute power. And you know what they say about power. Power tends to corrupt, and absolute power corrupts absolutely."[15]

Jayka looked at him skeptically. "I have never heard this aphorism. But it would seem to contradict everything I have learned about the State. The State is part of the most powerful political entity on earth, but it is not corrupt. Corruption in government has been eliminated. The State acts in the best interests of its citizens. It takes care of them, protecting them from external forces and even protecting them from themselves. If it were not for the State, I would have been dead long ago, a victim of outer docks' violence, disease, or perhaps starvation. In order to provide this level of security and care, absolute power is not only helpful, it is necessary. The longer you stay here, the more you will come to appreciate this power."

Craig was silent for a moment. "There is only one entity Who has absolute power. And it isn't the State," he said softly, but firmly.

"We will see who this threat is. You will reveal it to the administrators, willingly, or by force," she said. "I recommend you do so willingly, as the alternative is not…pleasant."

"As I said earlier, I will gladly share this information. I would prefer to have the audience of the State, as a whole, so its individual citizens can make up their minds for themselves, but if the only audience I am granted is a roomful of administrators, so be it."

"A wise decision," Jayka commended him as they exited the government housing facility and climbed into the military transport that awaited them.

---

[15] A quote by 19th century English historian Lord Acton

5

MACY watched patiently while the teenagers set up camp in the wooded flat just above the river bottom where the Kind Man and led her. Their confidence in her ability to guide them had initially waned when they realized she hadn't been taking them to where she had last seen Craig. "I knew we were placing too much confidence in that mutt," Garrison said exasperatedly.

"She may not have found Craig, but just think what would have happened if she *had* led us in that direction," Lelah insisted.

Garrison shook his head. "But isn't this a missionary trip? Didn't we come on this journey to meet people and tell them about Jesus? At some point, we're going to have to take the risk and just knock on the front door. All Macy has done is lead us in the opposite direction."

Macy could sense the irritation in Garrison's voice as he looked at her, and she hung her head, her tail tucked between her legs. There would be no ear scratches tonight. Her gaze shifted to the Kind Man. "They don't understand that you were doing exactly as I asked," He told her. "You're a good dog, Macy. I am very pleased with you!" His hand rested on her head, and she leaned into Him. Having her friends be mad at her was hard, but pleasing her Master was the most important thing to Macy in the whole world. She wasn't certain why the young humans spoke roughly to her when she was just following in her Master's footsteps. Wasn't He *their* Master, as well?

There were many times throughout the journey when they seemed to be ignoring Him. In the morning after they looked at the sacred object, they always took time to listen to Him. But as soon as they got ready to leave, they stopped paying attention. Could it be that they didn't know He was always there with them, ready to help and guide them? There were many times when Macy could see the Kind Man was talking to them, but they didn't seem to hear. Humans were certainly a strange lot. Macy had seen the Kind Man walking the path ahead of them, telling certain snakes to leave the area, and they obeyed. Even the breeze listened to her Master. Macy had felt it change directions to cool them down in the heat of the day after a few words from Him. Early in their journey, there was a time when the sky grew black and the wind was bending the trees nearly horizontal, threatening to blow the travelers off their feet. The humans were talking excitedly about something in the sky that was headed their direction as they frantically headed for low ground. The Kind Man had simply held up His hand and told the strange thing in the sky to be still…*and it was.* If the sky and the animals listened to Him, why didn't her bipedal companions? It was difficult for a dog to understand.

While her traveling partners finished setting up camp, Macy dutifully dug up the wild onion the Kind Man showed her and brought it back to Thom. Thom praised her and petted her, showing the onion to Garrison. "Look what Macy found," he said, brushing the dirt crumbles off the little bulbs. "We could make an onion soup if we had enough of these."

Garrison held up the onion and looked over at the mongrel, who lowered her head, expecting to be scolded again. He sighed. Garrison was still annoyed with his four-legged friend, but he showed her the onion and asked her to "go find." Macy's ears perked up and her tail wagged madly as she made eye contact with him. This was her chance to please him, to prove to him that she was still a *good* dog. She happily bounded away through the woods, and a few minutes later they reached the spot the Kind Man had shown her: the edge of an open meadow where wild onions grew in stringy clumps in a carpet of clover. Garrison smiled in spite of himself. "Good girl, Macy," he told her. When he realized he hadn't thought to bring the foldable camp shovel, he began looking for a sharp rock to use for digging at the base of the plants. "Maybe you could 'go find' a rock shaped like a shovel," he joked.

But Macy wasn't listening. Her ears pricked forward and her nose quivering, her attention was focused on the brown, furry animal she could see a few yards away. It also was digging, slinging dirt in brown arcs behind it, completely oblivious to them as it worked to increase the size of its den. Macy raised one of her front paws and pointed her nose in the direction of the plump little digger. Garrison, who was busy at his own digging, didn't notice. Finally, Macy could stand it no longer; and the softest of barks slipped out as she kept on point. Looking up, Garrison froze as he spotted the groundhog. "Oh, Lord," he prayed under his breath, "Please help me get 'em!" Garrison pulled his slingshot out of his back pocket. He was pretty certain he could dispatch a squirrel or a rabbit, but he hadn't thought about the possibility of anything bigger. The shot would have to be a perfect one. Presently, the creature's head was mostly underground. He looked around to see if any sticks large enough to use as a club lay nearby, but the edge of the meadow was free of larger fallen branches. A trip into the woods would likely result in crunching leaves and snapping twigs, which would alert the animal to his presence. The slingshot would have to do. While he had been harvesting the onion, he had dug up a rock that would work well for a projectile. He looked at his canine companion, giving the hand signal for *"stay"* and barely uttering the word above a whisper. Carefully watching where he placed his feet, Garrison crept forward, timing his movements with the groundhog's digging. When he was only ten yards away, he stopped, scarcely believing how close he had been able to get. The animal was so absorbed in its home improvement project that it barely lifted its head from the hole. Garrison waited, the slingshot pulled back and his heart pounding. A few seconds later, the 'hog paused in its digging, raised up to look around the meadow, and Garrison released the rock.

To his amazement, it clonked the animal right in the head, knocking it over and stunning it. For a second, Garrison was frozen in shock at the successful shot, and his prey began to revive and threatened to escape down its hole. But Macy was already there, the command to *"stay"* forgotten in the excitement. In an instant, she grabbed the animal around the neck with her strong jaws and began shaking it furiously, snapping its neck. Garrison rushed forward, the adrenaline pumping through his body. "Good job, Macy!" he exclaimed, as the dog gave the groundhog one more vigorous shake before she dropped it at his feet. "Oh, Macy, what a *good* girl you are!" he exclaimed, vigorously rubbing the ruff of her neck. Macy was ecstatic, her whole body wiggling with delight.

Every groundhog Garrison had ever eaten was tougher than shoe leather, but he wasn't going to complain. Empty stomachs made everything taste better.

"Thank You, Jesus! I couldn't have done it without You—*and* Macy," he said gratefully. He cleaned the animal, taking care to remove the scent glands that would spoil the flavor of the meat. He gave Macy the head to chew on, and they headed back to camp.

The other teens nearly cheered when Garrison came into camp holding up their supper. "What *is* that?" Chandra asked.

"It's a groundhog! Macy found it for me—I had no idea it was there."

Chandra's eyes widened in surprise. "Isn't that kind of small, for a hog? Was it a piglet?"

Lydia laughed. "Not a hog—a groundhog. You know… a woodchuck."

"Oh," Chandra laughed.

"Did Macy lead you to the onions?" Thom asked.

Garrison paused and dropped his head with a sheepish grin. "Yes. But I totally forgot to bring any. Macy showed me the groundhog before I managed to dig up any of them. They're in a field not far from here in that direction," he said, pointing the way they had come. "I'm sure Macy'll take you, won't you, Mace?" Macy watched Garrison point. She then took a few steps in that direction, stopping to look over her shoulder at Thom.

"Ok, girl, I'm coming," Thom said.

"Hey, wait for me!" Dania said, grabbing her slingshot. "Maybe we'll find something else to eat!"

"I wanna come, too!" Chandra and Lydia said in unison.

"Well, take the shovel. It'll make digging easier," Garrison advised.

Lelah procured the shovel from Craig's backpack, and the group was on their way, trailing behind Macy through the whippy saplings of river maples, buckeyes, and sycamores.

Garrison set to work making a fire. The group was convinced that if they kept it small and used the driest wood they could find, it wouldn't be detected. But Garrison wasn't going to leave it to chance. "God, I know You gave us that groundhog. And since You gave it to us, You knew we would need to make a fire. So please, just don't let the State find us until we're supposed to be found. If that time isn't now, then please hide the smoke."

The groundhog was barely enough to make a meal for the group, but if they made a stew with it using the wild onions, they could stretch it. He divided the carcass into smaller portions and put it in the pot, bones and all. Last of all he included the heart, which he had carefully saved, lamenting the fact that he couldn't dredge it in flour and fry it in butter.

When the others returned an hour and a half later, the groundhog was bubbling nicely in the pot. Thom was beaming from ear to ear, his hands holding up the ends of his shirt to create a makeshift pouch. "You're not gonna believe this," he gushed.

"Man, you must've found a lot of onions!" Garrison said, eyeing the shirt, which was stretched out with the weight of the harvest.

"Not onions. Mushrooms! Morels! Tons of them—the most I've ever found!" He lowered the hem of his shirt and a couple of large, creamy yellow mushrooms tumbled out onto the ground. "That's why we took so long. They were everywhere! I can't believe you didn't see them."

"Well, they *are* pretty hard to spot," Dania said.

"Not when there are practically groves of them!" Thom exclaimed.

"You nabbed that cluster before the rest of us could even begin looking!" Dania complained.

"Only fifteen of them were in the cluster. All the rest I found were scattered here and there. You could have found them if you had really been looking," Thom protested.

Chandra was nearly bubbling over in excitement. "I found twenty! Once you see one, it's easy to see the rest of them. They're all over the place."

"Well, you definitely have the eye for them," Lydia remarked. "I only found seven."

"Oh, yeah, and here's the onions," Dania said, holding out several bunches. "At least I didn't come back empty-handed!"

After carefully cleaning the dirt and insects from the wild edibles, they deposited them into the pot. That evening, before darkness fell, they shared the best meal since they had left Adullam. They extinguished the fire at dusk, but talked long into the night about what they should do next. "If we would make a *big* fire, the State would come to *us,*" Chandra suggested.

"I don't know. Maybe we should sneak in," Lydia offered. "Then we could make contact on our terms."

Various scenarios were discussed, but no clear plan emerged. "Maybe we should just start heading back toward the causeway and follow it from a distance far enough they won't be looking," Garrison said.

"I'm not sure there *is* a place they won't be looking, with all those drones," Dania reminded him.

Garrison looked thoughtful for a moment. "Yeah… but if the Lord stood between the Egyptians and the Israelites as a pillar of cloud by day and a pillar of fire by night,[16] I bet He can somehow hide us from the State. When Viv found me, she said she couldn't believe I hadn't been seen since I was following the road so closely," he explained. "I think that if God doesn't want them to find us, they won't find us. Not that I think we should go announce ourselves by walking right down a road, but if it's God's time for us to be discovered, there's no forest or cave that could hide us."

"You have a point," Dania said.

They all agreed they would head back to the causeway in the morning and finally went to bed, their sleep uninterrupted by hunger pangs or the growl of an empty stomach.

---

[16] See Exodus 13:21 and 14:19-20

6

Macy was awake long before daylight. This morning, it wasn't hunger gnawing at her insides that had awakened her. Grateful for her help in procuring their meal, the missionaries had made certain Macy got her belly full of the woodchuck stew. She had consumed every drop they had given her and was full even before she had crunched up the last bone. She was in the middle of a dream about chasing a giant groundhog down the streets of Adullam when she heard the sound of her name. Macy's eyes opened, and the Kind Man was crouching before her, the light that emanated from Him softly illuminating the thick grass where she had curled up for the night. "Macy," He said again, "I have a job for you today." Macy raised her head eagerly and slowly stood up, wagging her tail and stretching out each back leg as she always did after a good sleep. She tipped her head to her Master and snorted a "good morning" to Him, following Him dutifully across the campsite to the girls' tent.

The Kind Man paused at the tent flap, beckoning Macy to follow, and then passed through the canvas as if it wasn't there. Macy pushed her way under the flap, delicately stepping around the girls, who were snuggled together for warmth. Her Master was waiting for her near one of their backpacks, tapping it with His finger. Macy approached and sniffed the pack, recognizing it as Dania's. It smelled a little like the girl, but most of her scent was overpowered by the small remaining stash of peanuts contained in the pack. A bit of the peanut pouch protruded from the lip of the pack. The Kind Man was tapping the pouch, waiting for her to retrieve it. Macy looked up at Him with a question in her eyes. She had been scolded severely at one point for stealing a piece of jerky from Thom's pack. But her Master persisted. "Go ahead. Take it," He said in a voice that was gentle, but firm. Macy carefully tugged at the pouch until it landed on the floor of the tent with a soft *plop* and a rattle of peanut shells. Lelah moaned slightly, turning over in her sleeping bag. Macy froze. In an instant, the Kind Man was beside the sleeping girls, and a deep peace flowed from Him like a warm spring breeze. Soon, Lelah was snoring softly. Macy picked up the pouch and followed the Kind Man back outside the tent. "Come on, My little friend. *Let's go!*" He said in the tone He used when He was taking her on a great adventure. Macy wiggled with excitement, the threat of being caught stealing forgotten. She bounded after Him into the woods.

The Kind Man led her around briar patches and tangled sprawls of multi-flora rose, over logs and through giant sandstone formations. As light kissed the hilltops, they arrived at a spring, the stony lips of its mouth hidden by a veil of green moss. Her Master waited as she drank the cool, clean water until her thirst was slaked. Then Macy once again grabbed up the peanuts in their drawstring bag, and they followed the spring as it flowed to the south. This part of the landscape hadn't yet felt the warmth of morning sunlight. The spring branch was hugged on both sides by steep, rocky slopes covered with tall white oaks, eastern red cedars, and a smattering of short leaf pines. Mayapples stood guard over the occasional morel peeking through the leaves of the forest floor. The Kind Man slowed His pace and came to a stop, giving Macy a chance to survey the area. About twenty yards downstream of them, the hollow began to open up, offering a small patch of level ground mounded up with years of fallen leaves. There, nestled in the leaves, was a large lump which moved ever so slightly. A loud, buzzing sound coincided with the movement. The noise was unsettling, yet slightly familiar. Macy's ears cupped forward to catch the sound, her hackles raised. Her study of the creature was interrupted by the sound of the Kind Man chuckling. She looked up at Him questioningly. "No need to be afraid, My friend," He said in a reassuring voice and slowly approached the lump. Macy followed Him with caution until they reached it, and then her fears were completely alleviated, for she *knew* this lump. With a whine of greeting, she gingerly stepped forward and licked the creature on its nose.

A series of snorts erupted from the lump, and it raised a fuzzy gray head, bleary-eyed from sleep. "Akkk! Gi' back!" it yelped, grabbing for the spear at its side. Macy whined again and set back on her haunches, her tail thumping a leaf-rustling rhythm. "Ehhh, what's dis?" Macy whimpered and wiggled in reply. The creature slowly put down the spear and unfolded its bony legs, joints popping. "Well, I'll be," it said in wonder. "It's *you!* Ya didn' happen ta bring anytin ta eat wit' ya, didja?" As if she understood every word, Macy picked up the bag of peanuts and dropped it beside the old woman. Suddenly, Zelda's day was off to a great start.

Back at the campsite, Garrison was just beginning to wake up. A low mist had gathered over the area just before dawn, and a staccato of light rain began falling on the tent. He scrunched down deeper into his sleeping bag. Rain made great sleeping weather. "Oh, no!" he said, coming fully awake with a start. "Lord, we don't need rain today!" He put his hand on Thom's shoulder and shook it roughly. "Get up, Thom! It's starting to rain! Maybe we have time to pack up the tents before they get too wet." As if on cue, the light sprinkle suddenly gained momentum and transformed into a torrential downpour. The group had learned to make certain their tents were on higher ground to avoid water that might pool underneath them, but the two boys rolled up their sleeping bags just in case water seeped in through the floor. They looked helplessly across the campsite to the girls' tent, where the flap opened as Dania peeked out to assess the situation. Seeing the boys, she shook her head and shrugged, closing the tent flap again. There was nothing to do but wait.

And wait. The rain lasted into noon, long enough for the girls to get hungry and discover the peanut bag was missing. "Surely it didn't drop out of my backpack," Dania said worriedly.

"There wasn't very much left, anyway," Lelah reassured her.

"Well, there was probably enough for us all to have a good handful. Every little bit helps! I was kind of counting on those for breakfast."

"Me too," Chandra said, and then added hopefully, "but I'm sure maybe it's just somewhere in the tent. Maybe it got pushed around under the sleeping bags somehow." They all rolled up their sleeping bags and emptied each backpack, just in case it had been put into the wrong one by mistake.

"I hope it's not out there getting soggy by the fire ring," Dania lamented.

"If you left it outside, it's probably coon poop by now," Lydia muttered crossly.

"I'm almost positive I put it in my backpack yesterday morning. In fact, I'm sure of it. I just don't know what could have happened to it." Dania's voice quavered, and she bit her lip as tears began to form in her eyes. The stress of the trip and the unexpected loss of their leader was finally catching up to all of them.

Instantly, Lydia regretted her remark and put an arm around her friend. "Oh, don't worry about it. It's just peanuts. Yesterday, God gave us mushrooms, onions, and a groundhog. Don't you think He can take care of us today?"

"Yeah," Chandra added, "and if a coon *did* eat them and we can catch him, he'll taste even better fattened up by peanuts!" The girls' tent filled with laughter.

Sometime early in the afternoon, the rain stopped. The teens emerged from their shelters and surveyed the scene. The tents were soaking wet, and the slight depression of the fire ring was a mud puddle. Although the girls' sleeping bags were still dry, some water had managed to seep through the tent floors and into some of the backpacks, dampening a few items of clothing. Lelah strung up a paracord clothesline between two trees to dry out their clothes.

"So much for getting a morning start," Garrison commented. "I vote we let the tents dry out completely before we pack them up."

"By that time, it could be nightfall, but I agree with you." Thom said.

"This isn't a bad place to camp. Except for the firepit being a mud pit now," Lydia said.

"Should be interesting trying to find dry wood for a fire," Dania remarked.

Chandra brightened. "Well, if we're going to stay here another night, let's go find some more mushrooms," she said enthusiastically.

"Yeah, rain really makes them pop up," Lelah added.

"Did anyone happen to save one back from the stew?" Garrison asked. "I was thinking maybe we could show one to Macy and tell her to 'go find'."

"I think we threw them all in the pot," Lydia said, looking around the site. "Where *is* Macy, anyway?"

"I haven't seen her," Garrison suddenly realized. "I bet she found some place out of the rain—maybe a hollow log somewhere, or a cedar thicket. She'll turn up." But he was slightly worried. Macy was usually the first one to greet him in the morning, and there had been no sign of her.

The group spent the rest of the day foraging and managed to collect enough mushrooms to make soup. The hope for a bumper crop of morels due to the recent rainfall was quickly dashed when they discovered the rain had been localized to a forty-yard radius around their campsite. However, this time Garrison managed to find a cluster of eight under a sycamore tree. "I thought they were supposed to grow under ash trees," Dania said. She still hadn't found one.

"One thing I've learned about mushrooms is that they don't play by the rules," Garrison said with a grin as he broke the stems off at ground level.

"Well, I wish I could just at least find *one,*" she said regretfully.

"You have to have an eye for them," Thom said. "Some people really have a hard time seeing them."

"Yeah, they are so well camouflaged that—Thom, look *out!*" Dania exclaimed, pointing to a place near his feet.

Thom jumped backward. "What?"

"Don't you see it?" Dania asked.

"Is it a mushroom?" he asked excitedly. "No, I really don't see it. Where is it?"

"Not a mushroom! The huge snapping turtle you almost stepped on," she said, frantically pointing to a mud-colored shell that resembled a large rock.

"Whoah! Where did that come from?" Thom exclaimed.

"Well, we *are* pretty close to a river," Garrison said. He found a thick, sturdy stick and proceeded to wave it in front of the turtle's face. After a decent amount of hissing, the animal finally had enough of being teased and lunged forward to grab it. Garrison pulled on the stick until the turtle's neck was stretched out, and with the other hand, grabbed the ax he was carrying to use for firewood. With a swift, hard *chop,* the turtle was dead.

"Oh, why did you have to *kill* it?" Dania asked.

"Because turtle soup is delicious," Garrison explained, picking up the animal by its tail to let the blood drain out.

"You can eat them?" she asked.

"Of course! There are several different flavors of meat on a turtle. They're really tasty. Haven't you ever tried one?" he asked.

"We don't eat much fish from the river back home because of mercury levels," Thom explained. "I'm not sure if the same holds true for turtles, but we have goats and chickens to eat anyway."

"Well, you're in for a treat," Garrison beamed. "They're kind of hard to clean, but they're worth it."

That night, when the group sat around the fire with servings of turtle and morel soup, Dania had to agree. "I had my doubts, but you were right. This is great!" she said between slurps.

"Now, if Macy would just show up from wherever she's run off to, we have plenty left over for her," Garrison said. He had a sinking feeling that something may have happened to the mutt. The teens had been calling for her intermittently as they foraged, but with no results. They had even left their small fire going after dark, despite the risk, in case the smell of smoke would help her find her way back to camp. *Macy, where are you?* he asked under his breath. He had been praying for her all day, and he didn't doubt the others had, as well.

As if in answer to his silent question, the group suddenly heard a couple of short *yips* from the darkness of the surrounding trees. "Macy! *Macy*, you get over here!" Garrison yelled, flooded with relief as the dog pounced her way into camp. "We were so worried about you! Where have you been all day?" he scolded her while she licked his face.

Suddenly, the group could hear a noise in the brush from the direction Macy had come. "Rarf!" Macy barked happily, and broke away from Garrison to plunge into the darkness again. She emerged back into the circle of firelight, tugging a bedraggled figure by her tattered pantleg.

"Leggo ma leg!" Zelda bellowed, trying to keep her balance and swat at the dog with her spear at the same time.

"Wisteria!" Chandra exclaimed, and ran forward to give her a hug. Zelda stiffened and yowled in protest at first, but Chandra would not be deterred.

"Hummph," she finally managed. "Imagine runnin' into you'ns again. I figgered you's all in jail somewhere's, done been chipped, spillin' da beans 'bout me an' ya kinfolk. But I sees ya still out here, wanderin' aroun'."

"Yup," Garrison said. "What are you doing here? I thought you were headed in the opposite direction."

Zelda squinted. "I should ask you'ns the same ting. But den, mebbe I's a lot more turned aroun' den I realized. Somehow, I got turned aroun' funny, an' I couldn' rightly tell which way I was goin'. I wandered aroun' fer a long time, but I coudn' make heads 'r tails of which way ta go. Den, I runs outta food, an' I got real weak-like. An' I couldn' tink straight. An I lays down by dis stream. An' da next ting I know, I get woked up by *dis* slobberin' animal," Zelda said, pointing a knobby finger at the dog. "An' ya know what? She brung me dis!" Zelda held up the peanut pouch, now empty. She patted Macy happily. "If it hadn'a been fah dis pooch, I tink I mighta starved."

"That's where it went!" Chandra exclaimed. "We couldn't find it." Everyone looked at Macy, but this time, there was no scolding.

"Well, come over by the fire. We have a delicacy tonight—turtle and mush-room soup!" Dania said, quickly scooping some into a tin cup.

Zelda shuffled forward eagerly and took the cup, slurping noisily. Her eyes opened wide in surprise. "Dis is da best ting I ever et!" she exclaimed, squatting down by the fire. "Even better 'n da fish sammich I had back in da docks." She looked around at the faces as she smacked and gulped, and then she suddenly stopped, looking around again. "Say… where's dat udder fella—da older one what was in charge?"

The group looked at each other silently for a moment. Finally Dania said, "We think he may have been captured. He was scouting ahead one night and never came back. And we saw a helicopter and drones flying around the direction he went."

Zelda stopped chewing, her eyes wide. "Den dey got 'em. He be tellin' 'em everyting dey wanna know," she said slowly. "Whar was ya when it happened? Did it happen close ta here?" she asked worriedly.

"No, we're several miles away from there now. We think we were close to a causeway. We could hear a humming noise," Garrison offered.

Zelda glared at him and shook her head in disapproval. "I told all of you'ns what'd happen if'n ya kept head'n dat way. An' jus' look. Now yer leader'll be da one dat'll lead 'em straight *to* ya. How come ya didn' listen? Ya didn' believe me, didja?"

"Well, from everything Viv told us, what you said sounded about right," Garrison replied. "But like we told you earlier, we have to reach the people in the State. They need to hear about Jesus."

"Oh, dat *stupid trade!*" Zelda spat. "Pipah and Selah, dat's all dey could tink about. Get'n people ta cozy up ta Jesus so dey could trade 'im deir sins fuh his rightways-nus. Why's dis Jesus-God so bent on collectin' sins? What's 'e do wit' em all?"

"He doesn't collect them," Lelah said. "He completely removes them from us, so all our guilt is gone. In the Psalms, it says 'as far as the east is from the west, so far does He remove our transgressions from us.'"[17]

Zelda watched her through slitted eyes. "But I still can't feature what 'e gets outta it. How come a great big god what created da whole world an' everyting in it keers 'bout us folks? Keers 'nuf ta send de only son 'e ever had on a suicide mission? Dat don' make no sense. An' if dis god is smart 'nuf an' powerful 'nuf ta create da whole world, he sho ain't crazy 'nuf ta do sump'n dat don' make no sense."

"Actually, He *does* do things that make no sense—as far as this world is concerned," Lelah said. "The apostle Paul said 'For the preaching of the cross is to them that perish foolishness; but unto us which are saved it is the power of God.'[18] Many people of the day thought a savior should be a victorious king, so they couldn't accept one who was crucified. That was a sign of weakness and defeat. But Jesus didn't stay dead. He rose again. He defeated death, so that we could have eternal life!"

Zelda regarded her quietly for a minute. So many things, unlikely things —impossible, even—had happened to her in the last twenty-four hours. She had been lost and wandering for several days, out of food and nearly out of her mind. She had drunk the last drop from her canteen, unable to find water. Being dehydrated was beginning to cloud her ability to think. The last thing she remembered was lying down in the leaves, wondering if she would ever get up again. She had begun to think of Piper, wishing she could hear the girl's voice. And then, through cracked, dry lips, she had formed her first prayer. "Jesus, if'n

---

[17] Psalm 103:12, RSV
[18] 1 Corinthians 1:18, KJV

ya really is real, could ya help me? I needs food, and I needs water. But even if'n ya don' give me dat, more dan anyting, Ida just wish ya'd take keer a Pipah. I sho wish I could see 'er again." She had fallen asleep, and when she awoke, it was to the sound of trickling water. She raised up on her elbow and saw that she was lying beside a spring branch. Zelda barely had the strength to squeeze the water through the old filter Selah had given her, but she knew if she got sick from tainted water, it would be the end of her. She filtered a cup and rested, and then another. After a while, she gained enough strength to fill her canteen, but the effort it took wore her out. She lay down again in the leaves, wondering how she could have been so confused that she hadn't noticed she had laid down right beside a spring. "Well, God, I guess you's off da hook for da water, but I still needs food, ya know," she said weakly, and drifted to sleep. The next thing she knew, she was waking up to Macy licking her on the nose. Her first thought was of roast dog with mashed potatoes, even if she knew she didn't have the strength to kill the animal, much less clean it and cook it. But then the dog had dropped a bag in her lap. When she opened it and discovered the peanuts, she was too stunned to move for a minute. As she munched away, she wondered if the kids were nearby. If they were, maybe she could camp with them for a while—just until she felt well enough to go on her own. "Well, Jesus, I don' know fo sho if'n ya done it, but I gots food now. So just in case, I'ma gonna say thank ya. But ya know, I could really use some help. I needs ta find dose kids. But no tellin' where dey is. So's if'n you could just get me to 'em somehows, I'd be terrible grateful." Zelda wasn't sure what she could do to say thank you to an all-powerful God. What could she possibly have that He could want in trade for His services? As she was mulling it over in her mind, crunching up the last of the peanuts, the dog was pushing her with its nose. She slowly hobbled to her feet, barely able to stand, much less shoulder her pack. But as she stood there, washing down the peanuts with the freshly filtered water in her canteen, she felt her strength revive. She filtered another canteen of water and looked down at the mutt, who was staring expectantly at her. "Ok, poochie. Where's ya people?" At this, Macy barked softly and moved a few paces away, looking over her shoulder to see if Zelda would follow.

Thus began their trek that day. Zelda would pause to rest, and eventually, Macy would tug on her pantleg or bark until she got back up and followed her. It wasn't a terribly long distance, but it was slow going. "I may never catch up to dem kids if'n ya don' keep 'em in one place for a while," Zelda muttered to God under her breath. "Ain't no way I can keep up wit' 'em, if dey's on da move." But she kept following the dog, even after nightfall, because Macy wouldn't let her stop. "Akk!" she had complained, when wet branches began to slap her in the face as she moved through a stand of timber near a river bottom. One minute, she had been crunching through dry leaves, and the next, she was slogging through wet piles of them, her boots slipping in the mud. "Musta been a heavy rain come through here," she marveled. And the next thing she knew, the dog was dragging her into the circle of firelight, and she was getting the first hug she had gotten since Piper disappeared.

A deep longing pierced Zelda's heart as she continued her scrutiny of the young folk around the fire. "Is you folks somehow kin ta Selah?" I can't figger it out, but you an' Selah an' Pipah—ya'll favor eachudder somehow. I knows ya cain't be related ta Pipah, cuz she was borned in da outer docks. But still, ya looks alike somehow. Or ya acts alike."

Lelah looked confused for a moment, but then smiled in comprehension. "That's Jesus you're seeing, shining out from inside of us. You see, when someone accepts His free gift of salvation, He puts His Spirit inside of them. Any similarity you see between us is because of Him."

Zelda studied her for a moment, chewing thoughtfully on a piece of turtle meat. "Hmmm." She held out the cup hopefully, and Dania gave her another serving of the soup. "So you kids is bent on goin' on dis suicide mission, jus' like Jesus? Cuz dat's what it is, ya know. Suicide. Ya ain't gett'n out alive."

Lelah swallowed and stared into the fire. "Nothing is impossible for our God. He can deliver us from the State. But even if He chooses not to, we're still going." The other teens nodded as they all regarded Zelda solemnly.

"We would have been long gone earlier, but it started raining this morning and we didn't want to pack away the tents and the other gear before they dried out," Garrison added. "If it hadn't been for Macy leading us all the way out here on a wild goose chase and then disappearing—and then if it hadn't rained, we probably wouldn't have crossed paths again."

Zelda regarded him through hooded eyes, remembering the requests she had made to a God she wasn't sure she believed in. Well, He had certainly delivered, and she still had nothing to trade for it. To take something without offering anything in return was what she considered stealing, and there was no room for that in Zelda's particular set of morals.

She looked at the young people and sighed. They were going to get themselves killed—she was sure of it. But then a memory flashed through her mind. When she had taken Selah back from the Preserve to the outer docks, they had seen a Pod-Op. He was so close, and he never saw them. She had thought of the incident many times and couldn't make sense of it. There was no way he couldn't have seen them, and yet he hadn't. And then Selah had told her that story of how when she was by the causeway, she had run into a man and a female soldier. The man could see her and had helped her, but the woman couldn't see her at all. Selah had said it was because God had hidden her from the woman and had allowed the man to see her. Could she be right? Could God do something like that? Suddenly a funny feeling came over her. "Ok, I'll do it," she heard herself say.

"Do what?" Lelah asked.

"I'll take ya. If ya can get me ta where ya hear da causeway, I tink I can get us back and help ya sneak in like I done helped Selah. Udderwise, ya'll is just walkin' to ya deaths."

The teens were in shock for a moment, unable to think of anything to say.

"Well, the less of ya gets chipped, da less likely I is ta get found out," Zelda offered in explanation. But she was thinking instead how she wouldn't owe God anything anymore. She was going be square with Him again—to pay up what she owed. Actually, more than she owed, she smiled. Bringing the kids back to the wall was a huge risk, a much larger prize than some drinking water, a bag of peanuts, and a localized rainstorm. Of course, those things would have been impossible for her to procure for herself; but after all, they were from the hand of what was supposed to be an all-powerful God. Surely since she was risking her life to help His servants, that would be considered an overflow payment for what amounted to Him as a food delivery and a drenching from a giant watering can. But then in her mind she saw a picture of a man on a cross, bloodied and beaten and rejected by the very ones He had come to save. How could she ever be square for that? Zelda scowled and spat over her shoulder. *"Dat* ain't da trade I's makin'," she growled under her breath. "I do dis ting—get 'em tru da wall, and we's square."

After a few notably weak protests from the girls when she refused to share their tent, Zelda shuffled to the dry area outside camp and bedded down in the leaves.

7

CRAIG settled into the seat of the official-looking vehicle, coughing nearly uncontrollably after walking through the river fog that had not yet dissipated. As Jayka informed the driver of their new destination, Craig noticed that the car was black, while the bus that passed by and the few cars that were on the street maintained the same monotonous gray theme. "Why is this car black?" he managed to choke out the words before having another coughing spasm. "I thought color was oppressive."

Jayka opened a compartment in the ceiling of the vehicle, and a mask attached to a tube tumbled out and hung six inches from his face. "Here. Put this over your nose and mouth and breathe deeply," she instructed.

Craig did as he was told, and soon the burning in his nose and lungs subsided. "My apologies are in order," Jayka said, in a tone that did not hint at actual regret or contrition. "I forgot you would have no knowledge of the fog and wouldn't realize it's best not to inhale while moving from the building to the safety of the vehicle."

"That's some fog," Craig said after he had regained the ability to speak. It was then that he noticed pedestrians were equipped with some form of goggles or glasses combined with a mask. "What's in it that makes it so hard to breath?"

"It's a form of pollution called acid fog. It is an unfortunate consequence of what happens when businesses grow too big and think their profit margin is more important than the health of citizens and the environment. Certain implants help citizens breathe a normal amount of pollution, but the fog requires additional protection. You may have noticed the breathing apparatuses attached to people's visors?"

Craig nodded.

Jayka reached into a different compartment of the vehicle and procured a mask similar to the ones worn by pedestrians. "You can use this mask when we arrive at our destination. If you are released back into my custody, I will make certain you are fitted with a proper breathing apparatus."

"*If* I am released?" Craig said apprehensively.

"Yes. The administrators may want to keep you for a longer period of time for intensive questioning."

"But what about Yosi—I mean, Dr. Moses?" Craig corrected himself. "Isn't he expecting me?"

"Any immediate threat to society must be routed through the proper authorities first. If you do not cooperate, you will be redirected to a facility where your cooperation will be obtained without your consent."

"But I *am* cooperating," Craig said hurriedly.

"Which is very wise, as I pointed out earlier," Jayka said. "Continuing to cooperate will procure a more favorable outcome."

The vehicle rolled to a stop. "We have arrived at our destination. Remember to put on the mask," Jayka said.

"What about you? Where's your mask?" Craig asked.

"I have been trained to abstain from breathing for long periods of time. Much longer than is necessary to move from this vehicle to the building," Jayka explained. With that, she opened the door and waited for Craig to follow.

As he stepped out onto the pavement, he noticed that the building in front of him, just as the car, featured some colors other than gray: notably an imposing, official-looking pattern of red, black, and cream-colored stone forming the State's insignia. He was going to ask Jayka about the apparent double standard in the law about color when he glanced at her and remembered she was holding her breath until they reached the door. Once inside, however, there was no time for casual chatting, as he was immediately whisked away by two very intimidating men in black suits. "Uh, Jayka? Aren't you coming with me?" he asked over his shoulder, wondering why he should find her continued presence comforting when she had shown him only the bare minimum of courtesy. "Do they realize I offer no threat?"

"That will be determined shortly," Jayka said levelly.

Craig glanced at the men on either side of him. "Hi, my name is Craig Go-forth, and I was just telling Jayka there that—"

"Save it," was the tight-lipped response he received from one of his steely-eyed escorts.

Craig clamped his mouth shut and studied the polished tile floor of exquisite green and black marble. It suddenly struck him why the government wasn't following its own rules about color. In a society where the individual could tailor-make their environment to suit their preferences, the State was the only constant. No one could bend it to suit their whims. The State was calling all the shots—the one reality upon which citizens could not project their own preferences. It was a brilliantly simple statement of the nature of totalitarian rule. Craig swallowed nervously. In a world where citizens' feelings were coddled and superficial indulgences were granted to placate the masses, he was bringing the news that reality and truth were not subjective. In a society where everyone's needs were provided by the State—an entity that adopted an image of immutability—he was bringing the message that there was one need the State couldn't meet. His message that the world would eventually be judged because it was unwilling to receive God's free gift of love and salvation from sin would surely be viewed as offensive, if not fantastical. Indeed, the very idea of sin would probably be offensive to them. *"God, what am I supposed to say?"* Craig prayed.

"And when they bring you unto the synagogues, and unto magistrates, and powers, take ye no thought how or what thing ye shall answer, or what ye shall say: For the Holy Ghost shall teach you in the same hour what ye ought to say,"[19] came the answer. He knew the scripture. It had always sounded so heroic to him when he was a little boy—to be able to stand up for Jesus before authorities, wholly depending upon the Holy Spirit to supply his words. But now that the time had come, his mind grappled for control. Surely, he should have some sort of plan ...a well-presented argument. He had studied apologetics. He could argue his case, beginning with examples of Jesus' life, ministry of teaching and healing, and His death and resurrection—all of which were historically documented by several sources. His mind was racing, constructing his opening statement, as

---

[19] Luke 12:11-12, KJV

the men opened a door to a room that housed a small table with a single chair on one side and two on the other. They pushed him into the seat that was by itself, and before he knew what was happening, his wrists were snapped into handcuffs that were then snapped to a ring on the table. The men left abruptly, leaving Craig sitting alone, staring at a one-way mirror. He looked around in confusion. According to his parents' recollections of the society they had left, this was nothing but a police interrogation room. He wasn't appearing before a room full of government officials, as he had assumed. Didn't the fact that he came from outside of the State label him as an elevated threat? Didn't it warrant him a bigger audience?

Suddenly the door opened, and a man wearing a casually tailored brown suit entered the room, took off his suit coat and placed it on the back of his chair. "Hello, Mr. Goforth. I'm Detective Conlin Riedert. I understand you were discovered trespassing in the Preserve, and are a…guest of Dr. Moses," the man said conversationally. Craig noticed there was a slight hesitation before the word *"guest,"* as if to acknowledge it was a euphemism.

"Yes, that's correct," Craig said, his heart pounding.

"However, you have been brought here because our source indicates you may have information concerning a threat to the citizens of the State," the man continued, looking at Craig with a question in his eyes.

Craig swallowed. "Yes. I was hoping I might be able to share news of this threat with a larger audience, so preparations could be made to avoid it."

Detective Riedert tilted his head back ever so slightly. "Well, *I* am your audience now. If you'll just share with me the nature of the threat and any details you might have concerning it, I'll make a full report to my superiors. From there, they can decide how best to proceed." Riedert pulled out his chair and sat down opposite him.

Craig searched the man's eyes and then looked down at the table. He could try holding out for a larger audience, but from the way Jayka made it sound, any information they wanted could be extracted from him if he refused to cooperate—including the whereabouts of Adullam. It appeared Detective Riedert might be the only witness to his message. He had better make it good. All the arguments he had rehearsed on the way struggled to form a cohesive, convincing theme. *"Lord,"* he prayed silently, *"Help me to say the right thing."* And once again, the scripture came to his mind, *"Take ye no thought how or what thing ye shall answer, or what ye shall say: For the Holy Ghost shall teach you in the same hour what ye ought to say."* He looked across the table at the man.

"I couldn't help but notice how the State takes great pains to keep citizens from being offended—even to the point of using a special kind of gray brick for everything so people can choose their own color with their visors or with the help of an implanted chip," Craig began.

"Yes," said Riedert slowly, with one eyebrow cocked.

"And it also places a high value on the rights of the individual, since it provides a means for citizens to keep from offending others and even has laws against offensive behavior."

"Yes."

"I also notice that the State offers a constant in the lives of citizens. No one, for instance, can change the color of its insignia. And it continues this comforting role as a constant, benevolent benefactor by attending to citizens' needs beyond their delicate social sensibilities of color preference by providing each one with housing and the means with which to improve oneself."

"Mr. Goforth, you're not telling me anything I don't already know. And while your observations of our way of life are accurate and from an outside perspective must seem very interesting, I'm not certain where this discourse is going or what it has to do with any threat," said Riedert with a hint of impatience.

"If you'll give me a chance, I'll explain."

"Well, get to the point, or we'll skip the cordialities and I'll send you up the line to the extractors," said Riedert darkly.

"Understood," said Craig quickly. "You see, the entity I represent shares a few things in common with the State. No matter what kind of image a citizen or government may try to project upon Him, He remains the same. He also puts a high price on the individual and desires to protect and provide for those who serve Him. But while the State has taken great pains to keep its own *citizens* from being offended, it has done *nothing* to keep from offending the entity I serve. In fact, the State may not realize it, but it has done many things that seem *designed* to offend Him. And this type of behavior didn't start with the

State. It started before your State even existed, although its nature was already in operation."

"Are you saying that you are from a government that existed before the State?" asked Riedert skeptically.

"I am saying I represent a kingdom that existed before the State, or any other government, existed," Craig said.

"A *kingdom?* Well, that sounds rather impressive," Riedert said with the slightest hint of sarcasm. He leaned back in his chair and steepled his fingers together. "But it also brings to mind the many authoritarian governments of the past which sought to control their subjects like mindless cattle."

Craig wondered if the man even realized the irony of his last statement. "Oh, no. It's not like that at all. 'Of the increase of His government and peace there shall be no end…upon His kingdom, to order it, and to establish it with judgment and with justice from this time forth and for evermore,'"[20] Craig quoted. "He cares so much for people that He sent His Son as His representative, as a demonstration of His love."

"Mr. Goforth, I'm confused. Are you talking about an individual, or a political entity? First you say you're serving an entity, then you say a kingdom—which, by the way, no longer exist in our present day—and then you seem to be talking about a person. So which is it?"

"I serve both an individual *and* His kingdom."

Riedert scratched his nose, rested his elbow on the table and sat his chin in his hand. "I'm still waiting to hear of the threat you were so convinced we need to know about."

"The One I serve is more powerful than you could ever imagine. He finds certain mindsets and behaviors to be offensive. He has promised that someday, citizens and their governments will be judged for these offenses. But He sent His Son to provide a way of escape from the coming judgment."

"Oh, he did, did he?" Again, derision laced the detective's tone.

"Yes. You see, these offenses can't simply be erased from a record by the hand of any man. Someone had to pay for them. And instead of having *us* pay for them, the Son I spoke of earlier took it upon *Himself* to make the payment."

---

[20] See Isaiah 9:7

"Ok, Goforth. I'll play along, for the time being. So how was restitution made for these offenses?" Riedert asked with a sarcastic smile.

"The Son gave His life and paid for the offenses with His blood."

The detective leaned back in his chair and rolled his eyes. "Mr. Goforth, you understand how preposterous this all sounds? That kind of barbarism hasn't taken place for thousands of years."

"True. And indeed, it did happen thousands of years ago. The event is well-documented. And not only His death, but His appearance as a living, breathing person after His death. Indeed, He is still alive."

Riedert raised his eyebrows and scratched his forehead. "Well, bringing people back from the dead isn't all that uncommon today, but thousands of years ago they didn't have the technology or medical know-how to accomplish such a thing."

"But the One I serve has always had the ability to do it," Craig insisted.

"What's more, eternal life seems to be an ongoing quest for humanity, but no one has ever found a fountain of youth. Your commander in chief seems to have found the secret, if he's been around for thousands of years and can bring his son back from the dead." Riedert added.

"The Father says that to those who are thirsty, He will give freely from the fountain of the water of life,"[21] Craig said.

"Well then, why haven't I heard of him? Because this is all news to me," Riedert said, drumming his hand on the table impatiently.

"You haven't heard of Him because your government has attempted to erase Him from the History books and to dismiss Him as a myth. But He can't be erased or dismissed. Someday He will come back, and the only way to avoid the coming judgment is to admit we have been wrong and to believe in His Son and the sacrifice He made. If we do this, we will be forgiven and escape judgment."

Riedert's eyes smoldered as he regarded Craig. "Well, you've wasted enough of my time," he said. "But just out of curiosity, what is the name of this father and son duo?"

---

[21] See Revelation 21:6

"God the Father and His Son, Jesus," Craig said, trying to make his voice sound strong and firm, but the room made it sound tinny and small and swallowed it up.

Riedert turned to the one-way mirror. "Get this nut-job out of here," he said brusquely.

"Where am I going now? Where are they taking me?" Craig asked, as his escorts reappeared and unlocked his handcuffs.

"If it were up to me, you would be sent straight to clean-up. But since you're from the Preserve, you're going back to Dr. Moses—with a recommendation for referral to a river clean-up penal colony. Without you knowing it, Mr. Goforth, you've been living off the good graces of the State this whole time you've been trespassing in the Preserve. And now that you've been apprehended, you've taken it upon yourself to present your belief in a mythological kingdom and its ruler as an absolute truth, rather than just a privately held notion. A waste of the State's time and resources, since the threat you spoke of was completely unfounded."

"I'm telling the truth," Craig said. "And someday you'll know it. I truly believe we are in the last days before His return."

Detective Riedert chuckled. "You know, I *have* heard of this kingdom of yours before. You aren't the first person who has come here talking about the last days. But you know what? The members of that religion have been talking about the last days for centuries, and nothing ever happens."

Craig looked at Riedert meaningfully. "Everyone has a last day," he said evenly.

Riedert shook his head. "I'm truly sorry for you, Mr. Goforth. You're obviously delusional. But if anyone can straighten you out, it's Dr. Moses." He dismissed the group with a wave of his hand, but his eyes followed them as they clopped down the marble hallway. He had interviewed many religious fanatics in his day, and most of them were successfully reconditioned. But there was a low success rate among the members of the Jesus sect. The ones who had really bought into it just couldn't seem to let it go. What was the difference, he wondered? No matter. He would file his report, Dr. Moses would do his thing, and if the patient lived through the treatment, he might provide intelligence as to the whereabouts of any other people living out in the Preserve. Afterward, there was even a chance he could be integrated into society. Riedert's part in the matter would be finished as soon as he turned in the report. He shook his head as he thought of the sincere look on Goforth's face when he was describing the blood sacrifice that was made to pay for humankind's offenses. The very idea that someone could actually believe something like that—it showed how far humanity had come with the State to guide it.

Detective Riedert made his way to his desk and began filling out the report. He was about to check the box that indicated referral to a clean-up colony if Goforth proved to be incapable of being integrated into society. He paused. Christians who were this serious about their belief almost always refused to admit that their faith was just one of many ways to reach the Source. It was as if they really believed it, as if they had some sort of proof. Even the ones who didn't seem unhinged acted as if they truly believed what they were saying. When he would press them for their reasons for believing something so implausible, almost all of them claimed to have a personal, life-changing experience they couldn't deny when they became a follower of Jesus. The ones who had been found with a Christian Bible or parts of a Bible claimed that their god himself promised them things through his book, and that they were simply believing the things they had read in it. He sighed. Poor dupes. He left the box untouched. There was little hope Goforth would survive the treatment, so strong were his convictions. He sent the report to his superiors via his visor.

Riedert had held out as long as possible to avoid having the chip implanted. He had seen too many early experiments on Discards to be comfortable with this particular implant. But he knew his time was coming. People with jobs like his were required to be implanted. Everyone in his department had been reassured the success rate was 99.9%. Only those with a stubborn holdout that didn't match up with the State's ideals were at risk of an unsuccessful procedure. Almost unconsciously, he opened his desk drawer and rifled through the examples of confiscated books he had taken from interviewees. There was a Koran, a copy of the Lotus Sutra, and the Bhagavad Gita. He pawed to the back of the drawer and found it: a book simply titled *Holy Bible*. *What made the followers of this religion so much more stubborn than the others?* he wondered. Why did they choose death when all they had to do was say their god was one of many ways to reach the Source? Were they afraid of the judgment Goforth had mentioned? What was the cause for offense that was bringing judgment? Riedert was fascinated by neuroses and sought to understand them and their cause. He flipped down his visor and searched through the list of curators at the Museum of Religious Convergence to find one whose emphasis of study was Christianity. Maybe they would have some insight into how to help these people, or at least how to get them to cooperate.

8

Conlin Riedert <conlin.riedert@dd.s.gov>

To: rhys.bradley@mrc.s.gov

Subject: Inquiry into Christian fanaticism

Dear Curator Bradley

I have recently interrogated a member of the Christian religion and was reminded of their tendency to be fanatics. In many cases, they insist that their belief is the only one that leads to the Source. Unfortunately, when they are sent to reconditioning, they don't usually have a successful implant procedure. Returning them to society to be productive citizens is one of my main objectives, so I was hoping you could help me understand the reason behind their intolerance of other beliefs. I don't think they could be victims of brainwashing, considering there is no known school of traditional Christian teaching in existence in the State today, and copies of their Bible are rarely found in circulation. Any insight you might provide into this matter may assist in further investigations and the health and well-being of citizens recovering from this mental incapacity.

Best Regards

Detective Conlin Riedert

Department of Defense

St. Louis Branch

Rʜʏs sighed as he read the email. Detective Riedert may have meant well by sending the subjects of his interviews to reconditioning, but the result would be a negative outcome. Some Christians were left brain-damaged since they would not recant their beliefs. The internal mental conflict was too great to survive. The State usually "recycled" those patients, harvesting their organs or, in the case of those who were brain-dead, using their body as a vehicle for experiments with chip technology and its ability to utilize the brain in control of motor functions. As horrific as it sounded, it was no government secret. It was touted as ground-breaking research for coma patients or for those who suffered from stroke or some form of paralysis.

He wondered how he should answer. If there was any possibility that the reconditioning could be delayed, maybe he could speak to the authorities in question and convince them to let him have a word with the patient. He could at least reaffirm this person's hope in Christ before they went under the knife. Of course, that could be personally incriminating since installation of the chip might reveal any recent memories, and the subject could expose him unintentionally. He shook his head. It was too risky. He began composing his reply, deciding to play it safe.

Rhys Bradley <rhys.bradley@mrc.s.gov>

To: conlin.riedert@dd.s.gov

Dear Detective Riedert,

I have noticed in my studies of Christianity that proponents of the faith are actually very tolerant of people with differing beliefs. In the past, much humanitarian aid has been funded by Christians for members of other religions who are experiencing persecution. Their insistence that their way is the only way to the Source seems to stem from their claim that they have a personal relationship with it, and does not strike me as intolerance for others, but rather a result of their desire to share the way to the Source with humanity. One might argue that they are acting in love and concern, rather than intolerance. Perhaps the subject in question could be given another chance to rethink their position on proselytizing before they are sent to reconditioning.

Respectfully

Rhys Bradley, Curator

Museum of Religious Convergence, Christian Studies

Rhys sent the email, praying for a delay in the patient's processing. Most of the time, a Christian could fly under the State's radar if they were careful about how they witnessed. If Riedert was still holding the subject for interrogation, there was still a glimmer of hope.

He glanced through the queue of electronic notices he had received from the state. Most of them were regarding updates to the State's Bible Collaborative Project and requests for editorial assistance on the *My Truth* devotional blog. But several of them were reminders to make an appointment for chip implantation. As an employee of the Museum of Religious Convergence and an editor of the *My Truth* blog, he was expected to take the chip. His superiors explained it would ensure proper treatment of subject matter in his editorial duties. Rhys had been searching for other employment options since he had received the first notice, but it was difficult not to raise suspicion. His position was a very respected one, and leaving the museum for a different job was almost unheard of. Besides, it was obvious that Rhys enjoyed his occupation. That would leave little reason for his decision to leave except to avoid implantation, which was suspicious in and of itself. After all, why would someone want to abstain from taking the chip unless they didn't trust the government or had something to hide? And Rhys had much to hide. Not only was he a Christian, but he was a member of an underground church. Being chipped could result in the exposure of all its members and their subsequent arrest.

Suddenly, Rhys's visor indicated he had an incoming call. It was Riedert.

"Hello, Detective Riedert. Did you see my email?" he asked, trying to sound casual.

"Yes, I did. And that's why I'm calling. I'm afraid the offender has already been sent to reconditioning, but I'm interested in what you have to say on convincing Christians not to proselytize. They just don't seem to understand that everyone has the freedom to believe whatever they want. If there's any way I could convince future interviewees that they can follow their own beliefs without having to insist they have an exclusive pass to the Source, I'd love to hear about it. It has to be a better option for them than taking the chip. I've seen some of the results of failed implantation, and it isn't pretty."

"No, it isn't," Rhys said grimly. "If you'd like to talk, I'm always open to helping fellow citizens like the person you just interviewed."

"Well, he wasn't a citizen, but most of the people I interview are."

"Well, I don't mind helping Discards either."

"Actually, he wasn't a Discard. I can't really say much beyond that."

Rhys paused. Perhaps the man had been an Unspoken. "Well, whatever the case, I'd be glad to help, if I can."

"Are you free for lunch?" Riedert asked.

"I think I can work it in."

"Great. There's a nice little sandwich shop almost midway between our offices. It has a good view of the river, and since the windows are tinted, you can almost forget how nasty it is."

Rhys chuckled. "Send me the address and I'll meet you there." There was something about Riedert that was likeable. Of course, the man's job was determining when people should be sent to reconditioning. Possibly hundreds of people had suffered at his hand. But quite feasibly, Riedert had thought he was actually helping them. If he didn't care about people, why would he bother to find out what made Christians less likely to succeed in being reconditioned? There was a chance that Rhys could actually make a difference if he could direct Riedert in how to proceed when he questioned Christians.

When he walked into the eatery, he surveyed the tables and booths lining the windows and saw a man in a brown suit raise a sandwich in salutation. He made his way to the booth and slid into the seat opposite the man. "Detective Riedert," Rhys nodded as he sat down.

"That's me. Thank you for meeting me. And may I recommend the Reuben. Hands down, it's the best in town."

"I never could get a taste for sauerkraut," Rhys said apologetically.

"Your loss. But their Philly Cheesesteak is a close second."

Rhys smiled and ordered the cheese steak sandwich.

"So, Curator Bradley—"

"Oh, you can call me Rhys," Rhys said. The title *curator* had always sounded so stilted to him.

"Is that how you pronounce it? I thought maybe it was 'rice', like the grain. But it rhymes with geese and fleece."

"Indeed," Rhys smiled.

"I always wondered why they never made a universal phonetic alphabet that was more user friendly than the one we have so that everyone could know how to say everything."

"Maybe that's in the works," Rhys said affably.

"Naw. Now that we've got the chip, everyone will be able to understand everybody," Riedert replied. Rhys thought he detected a hint of disdain in the man's voice.

"I keep getting notices about making an appointment for implantation," Rhys ventured.

Riedert looked up from his sandwich. "Yeah," he said with a full mouth. "Me too."

"So, you don't have it."

"Not yet." Riedert glanced furtively around the room. "And to be honest, I'm not in any hurry."

"Me neither," Rhys confided.

"I've seen too many failed attempts. Which brings me to the reason I asked you here today. I just don't seem to be able to get these Christians to understand that their god is the same god as everybody else's. It's just that everyone uses different names for it."

Rhys exhaled slowly, praying silently for wisdom. "The problem you're having actually relates to a key concept of their belief. Jesus said that He is the way, the truth, and the life, and that no one comes to the Father, except through Him."[22]

"Yes, I've heard this little litany before. But if religions could just realize that they are all serving the same thing—"

"But they aren't," Rhys interrupted.

"How do you think?"

---

[22] See John 14:6

"Well, if the gods of all the different religions of the world are just different representations of the Source, how does that explain religions that have multiple gods? Or a 'good god' and a 'bad god,' if you will?"

"Well, I think these are just humanity's attempts to explain the archetypal conflicts within us. They're just assigning human traits to the Source. We all know that the Source is just the energy of life—the impetus behind the big bang. And while some people believe it is a rational supreme being, of sorts, the truth is that no one really understands it. But if some people want to attach personality traits and names to it, that's fine. So long as they maintain a grip on reality and realize that these are just ways to help them understand it, and they can't go around preaching these beliefs to people unless they ask for it. With these Christians, it's like they believe they've had a personal encounter with the Source that changes their life."

"Who's to say that they didn't?" Rhys asked.

Riedert started to open his mouth, and then regarded Rhys thoughtfully, a smile creeping across his face. "Well, no one, of course. Because that would be religious discrimination."

"Exactly," Rhys smiled back at him. "It may not be your truth, but it's their truth," he said, quoting the catch phrase of the *My Truth* blog to make his point. He didn't agree with it, but it highlighted the internal conflict of the State's position on the matter.

Riedert grinned. "Which shows the inherent dilemma in the State's treatment of religion. But this doesn't solve my problem—or theirs. No matter whose truth is what, the law says that believers of any sort of religion cannot actively seek new converts unless they are approached by an interested party."

"How can someone decide whether or not they are interested in something unless they have been exposed to it?" Rhys asked.

"I assume they're still teaching about the basic religions and philosophies of the world in high school."

"They do. Just a barebones introduction to each. And then what is considered the best part of each faith is used to explain the Source."

"Which means we can all be one big happy family," Riedert said as he leaned back in his seat. "Except for the Christians. And some of the Muslims. The hardcore Muslims still want to kill everyone who believes differently."

"But not the Christians," Rhys said quickly.

"They did, during the Crusades."

"That was a dark time in the history of their religion, when they were following the teachings of man rather than those of Jesus," Rhys explained.

"I think we're straying off topic here," Riedert said. "What I want to know, is why do these Christians think they have had a personal encounter with the Source?"

Rhys thought for a moment, carefully weighing his answer. "From what I understand, Christians believe that they have a spirit, soul, and body. Before they ask Jesus to forgive them and ask Him to be Lord of their life, they believe that the spirit part of themselves is dead. But when they ask Jesus to be the Lord of their lives, He brings their dead spirit alive with His Spirit and lives within them. They become a sort of walking, breathing temple of their God."

"Like demon possession in the Satanic faith?"

"No, not at all," Rhys said emphatically. "They do not claim to be controlled or manipulated in any way. But they can ask their God for help and they believe He is with them always. Many of them say they feel as if something heavy was lifted from them when they became a Christian. And many say they suddenly feel clean inside."

Riedert's eyes lit up. "I've heard more than one of them say that. Do you suppose they are using a psychedelic drug?"

"No. Their religion teaches that they shouldn't even be drunk with wine,[23] much less use the more dangerous, mind-altering drugs. Whatever happens to them, it is apparently a result of what their God does to them on the inside."

"Or what they *think* he does," Riedert quipped. "But they must really believe it, or they wouldn't insist to the point of being sent to reconditioning."

"Detective Riedert, what would be the harm in simply explaining to them that they need to be careful of how they share their faith, and then just sending them home instead of to reconditioning? You, yourself said it rarely has good results."

---

[23] See Ephesians 5:18

"Well, I've actually considered doing that unless it was a repeat offender. But my superiors keep pushing the chip. They say Dr. Moses is close to a breakthrough in the hard cases where a citizen's ability to think rationally has been compromised."

"Their ability to think rationally?" Rhys repeated. "Some of the best thinkers—the innovators, inventors, artists, and philosophers in history would not have been described as rational thinkers. Some of humanity's best work was produced when conventional or rational thinking was pushed aside. If Edison had been thinking rationally, he would have given up on trying to find the perfect material for the filament of a light bulb after the first 2,000 attempts. But he stubbornly persisted, and it changed our way of life."

"But the Christians I've met aren't inventing new philosophies or things that improve society. They're fixating on ideas that are offensive and even oppressive."

"It seems to me that they are exploring a way of thinking and believing that turned dictatorial regimes into democratic forms of government. The tenants of Christianity shaped our judicial system and helped create one of the longest running success stories of free society in our time."

"If you're referring to our State's previous form of government, aren't you overlooking all the oppression of racial and religious minorities?"

"Of course, it wasn't perfect. It was a work in progress. But members of racial minorities rose to positions of judges and lawmakers and even the office of President. This was possible because of the freedoms put in action by the Declaration of Independence and the Constitution of the United States of America."

"Don't you mean the Declaration of Dependence?" Riedert asked.

"No. That wasn't its original title. As you know, I have access to unaltered historical documents."

"You sound like a true believer," Riedert smiled, eyeing Rhys speculatively.

"I'm merely stating historical facts."

"Isn't your job at the Museum of Religious Convergence supposed to be to show how the different religions actually complement each other and are really parts of the same whole?" Riedert asked skeptically.

Rhys's pulse quickened. He decided to redirect the conversation. "You asked me why Christians think their version of God is the only one and why they think they've had a personal encounter with the Source. What I have found in my studies is that Christians who display the strongest adherence to their faith have had an experience they describe as being 'born again.' It is a life-changing moment they say transcends any other positive encounter they have had, whether in the arts, athletics, intellectualism, philosophy, or exposure to another religion. There is a long list of people who were committed Christians who, historically, have changed the world for the better."

"For example?"

"Isaac Newton. Johannes Kepler. Blaise Pascal. William Wilberforce. Martin Luther. Florence Nightingale. Martin Luther King, Jr.—just to name a few. Nearly every leading university in the world was founded by Christians."

"I'm sure you could pull up just as many examples of people from other religions who positively impacted society."

"Perhaps. I don't know. You contacted me because my emphasis was on Christianity. I'm just telling you what I've found in my area of study."

"It sounds like you think maybe letting the Christians make more Christians would make the world a better place," Riedert said, his eyes narrowed.

"I never said that. But history would suggest that to be true. I am merely a protector of information and an editor of spiritual musings of the citizens of the State. You asked for my opinion based upon my knowledge of the faith, and I've provided it to the best of my ability." Rhys paused. He felt like God was nudging him to do something more. "Most of my information is limited to documents. It would be very interesting to meet this person you interviewed. I have never met any Christians who were dangerous enough to be interrogated by the Department of State Defense. I feel it would do much to add to my understanding of the pitfalls of this faith and would help me in my editorial duties."

"Well, I'm afraid that is out of my hands now. As I said, he's been sent to reconditioning."

"Any chance you could put in a good word for me? Let them know it could go a long way in helping me understand the subject?" Rhys pressed further. "If my questioning him produced any new insights, I could share my findings with you."

Riedert chewed thoughtfully as he considered the proposal. "Well, I guess it couldn't hurt."

Rhys smiled and nodded. "I appreciate that." He took a bite of the sandwich he had ordered. "You were right about this place, Detective Riedert. I don't know when I've had a better sandwich. I think it's the bread."

"Isn't it great? They make it fresh here. So much better than the government standard," Riedert said enthusiastically.

They finished their lunch, Riedert promising to pursue Rhys's permission to interview the offender. Rhys walked out the door with a feeling of relief. He had felt like he had been under unofficial scrutiny during the entire conversation. Probably State interrogators had that effect on everyone, he reasoned.

As they parted ways, Riedert watched Rhys make his way back to the museum. He wondered if all the curators had such a burning desire to learn all they could about their area of expertise. He shook his head. Of course, they did. That's probably why they were chosen in the first place. But something seemed a little off about this guy. He seemed unusually quick to defend historical proponents of a dangerously monotheistic dogma. Then again, anyone who was unchipped and still willing to venture into the lair of the main programmer after ignoring requests to comply with the procedure was gutsy, to say the least. He sighed. The guy was probably just a nerd of academia, jonesing to delve deeper into his studies. Riedert had to admire his drive. He flipped down his visor and put in a call to Dr. Moses' office. "Yes, hello. This is Detective Riedert with the Department of State Defense. I just sent a person I interviewed over for reconditioning, but I was wondering if it might be possible to hold another interview. A curator from the Museum of Religious Convergence has shown a particular interest. Says he thinks it could help further his insight into Christianity." Riedert paused. "Well, as soon as you find out, could you let me know? The offender in question doesn't seem like someone who would interview too well after being implanted, if you know what I mean. Yes, thank you. I'd appreciate it." Riedert ended the call and gazed out over the sluggish Mississippi as it oozed its way through the city. The fog had been especially acrid that morning, but it had all burned off, and it was turning out to be a nice day—for everyone except Craig Goforth. With any luck, they would hold off on the procedure, but it was surely inevitable. At least, since Goforth had already been in Moses' custody and was destined to go back to him, Riedert didn't have to harbor any guilt about the affair. One thing was certain, though. Once someone was sent to Dr. Moses, they never came back the same.

9

Viv looked at her reflection in the mirror. She had carefully parted her hair, leaving the silvery white half completely on the right side and the crimson red half on the left. A strand of royal blue outlined the front edge of the right side, curving around the bottom of her chin. "I can do all things through Christ, Who strengthens me,"[24] she said to the girl in the mirror. Her voice sounded shaky, and the eyes staring back at her betrayed her fear. She turned away from the mirror and knelt at her bedside. "Jesus, I know You are with me. I know I'm in this position for a reason. Help me to follow Ya lead. Ya Word says You would give us the peace that passes all understandin',[25] an' I really need that peace right now. Please, Lord Jesus, give me the words ta say, an' keep me safe today. Help me ta hear Ya voice an' obey," she prayed under her breath.

Since she had become an employee of the State, she suspected their surveillance of her may have become more intense. She had been attending classes for the past several weeks that covered how to recruit Discards and guide them through the transition process. Ainsley Abbot, who had recruited Viv for the position as liaison for the Outer Docks Transition Program, explained that even though they had hired her for her personally successful transition and her unique perspective in the matter—facts that would lend to her believability with her audience—she still needed training so that she could see the situation from the State's perspective.

Viv had initially wondered if they would force her to take the chip to speed up the learning process, but Ainsley quickly put her worries to rest when she showed up for the first training session. "In this case, the fact that you haven't yet been

---

[24] See Philippians 4:13
[25] See Philippians 4:6-7

implanted with the chip only increases your chances of success," Ainsley had reassured her. "As I'm sure you're aware, many Discards find the idea of being implanted with even the most basic health implants as threatening, much less having one installed in their brain. If you had the chip—well," Ainsley paused and smiled as she studied Viv, "your credibility would be shot. Let's just cross that bridge when we come to it, shall we?"

Viv nodded enthusiastically, and Ainsley gave one of her musical laughs. "I can see you're not completely sold on the idea of implantation."

"I have Audio-boost," Viv said in self-defense. "And, of course, I have all the health implants."

"A good start," Ainsley said. "Of course, the chip makes most of the old standard implants obsolete. It really is nothing to worry about. It's just an improvement on what we've been doing for years, with the bonus of enhanced brain function, storage capacity and retrieval, and the social connectivity Dr. Moses is so fond of preaching about."

"I've heard 'im call it the next evolutionary step of humankind," Viv said in what she hoped was a reticent tone.

"Oh, yes. Quite right. No more crutch of those primitive notions of religion. No more separation by race or social status. Prejudice and disunity among people groups will be a thing of the past. There will be no more people groups, per se—just people, working together as a whole. There's no limit to what we can do! I foresee a day when we even do away with the bonds of mortality," Ainsley boasted.

Viv's eyes widened. "Are they workin' on a way to reverse the agin' process?"

Ainsley's musical laughter floated through the room. "Oh, nothing as tedious as that." Her eyes narrowed as she watched Viv. "I like you, Viviana. You show a certain spark and freshness that is invigorating. Maybe someday, I'll be able to discuss this with you. For now, you'll just have to dream and wonder. But I wouldn't wait too long to arrange for implantation when you get the go-ahead," she added, giving Viv a playful smile. "Besides, I think it would be enriching to link with you. Such a difference in thinking. I'm sure I would find it stimulating."

Viv looked away, uncomfortable under Ainsley's study. Every time she was around the woman, she had a feeling of unease, as if she had just entered a predator's lair. She had dutifully come to all the training sessions, but felt they offered her no advantage. When she had signed on, she hadn't realized she wouldn't only be helping Discards to transition, but she would also be recruiting people. It would take more than just a familiar face to convince them to want to *defect*, as Discards called it, to the State. On her last trip back to the docks to find her father, she had been called "Deserter," an insult hurled at her from the window of an upper story apartment as she wove in and out of the dismal alleyways. No, if you left the outer docks, it was either because you were so desperate you really *wanted* to leave, or were taken into custody. Any success in getting Discards to leave would only occur if they had already made up their mind.

Which was one reason she was so nervous this morning. It was her first time going back to the outer docks as an employee of the State—what many Discards would consider a true traitor. It was the first time she had been concerned for her own safety upon entering her old neighborhood. She was to arrive on her bike, as if nothing had changed, and mingle with residents in meeting places like the Shaw. But this time, a garbage truck would be shadowing her from a distance. All of the trucks were equipped with defensive weapons and crowd control features such as tear gas and tasers. They even had spring-loaded nets to assist with the capture of troublemakers. At the least sign of trouble, Viv could be targeted as the cause of trouble and netted so as not to blow her cover. Eventually, of course, word would get around that "the Deserter" now worked for the State; but hopefully by that time, her honorable intentions of helping out her former dockmates would be made clear. Ainsley had made it all sound so easy, as if it would run without a hitch, but Viv knew better. The outer docks was a volatile area where the least bit of tension could erupt into rioting. If the situation escalated, the garbage truck driver would probably have to use deadly force to protect her, completely undermining their purpose. Viv was afraid the driver might overreact, stepping in too quickly by misreading the danger level, putting both her and the people she was trying to help at risk. Even then, her only real source of safety would come from God. As soon as she had the thought, the peace she had longed for descended upon her. "Thank Ya for keeping me safe, Lord. Please, keep ma dockmates safe, too. They need to know Ya. They won't get the chance if someone is shootin' at 'em," she prayed.

She made her way to the first floor of her apartment building where her bike waited in one of the charging docks. The truck was scheduled to meet her at a stop just outside the gateway. From there it would follow her, keeping her within sight and making a "food" delivery along the way so as not to arouse suspicion. Viv motored her bike out of the garage and zipped out onto the road toward old Hwy 44. She glanced toward the route she normally took when she left for Adullam. It was one of the few approved roads for non-causeway travel that ventured into the Preserve, and its travelers freely passed through the outer docks in a protective tunnel that ended once the motorist had reached the boundary wall. It was rarely utilized, but citizens who had medical conditions that made it difficult to use the causeway could use it by obtaining a permit. Viv had been given a permit right after she had been implanted with Audio-boost. They were usually only valid for one year, but Viv's had never been revoked, even after six. Every time she remembered this, she breathed a prayer of thanks. She knew Who was keeping her permit valid and her GPS system undetectably disabled.

The gate to the Dead Zone loomed ahead, and a garbage truck waited on the side of the road. She slowed to idle speed and came up alongside the truck. The driver's side window rolled down and the truck operator turned to her with an expressionless face. Viv's breath caught in her throat. She knew the driver. His eyes had a look of caution as he spoke. "Hello. You must be Citizen Viviana Delacruz," he said. It was Luciana's husband, Chess. Knowing their interchange would be monitored, she worked quickly to conceal her expressions of recognition and relief.

"That'd be me. And you are?"

"Chester Clarkson. And this is Ed Eleck," Chess replied, nodding toward his companion in the passenger seat. "We'll be your escorts today—and for all future trips into the outer docks."

"I really don't think this is necessary. Discards know when somethin's up, an' if I got a food truck followin' me aroun', they's gonna know somethin' ain't right," she said, forcing herself to sound resentful.

"Well, believe me, we have better things to do with our time than to babysit one of the State's poster children, but we have our orders. Don't try to lose us, or we'll report you. We'll follow at a discreet distance, and we'll be monitoring your every move." He paused and took something out of his pocket had handed it to her. "Slap this on your bike. It will allow us to hear you and any interchanges you have with the Discards. If at any time you feel your safety is compromised, just say the words 'meal ticket', and we'll be right there."

Viv took the device, which appeared to be a simple decorative magnet, and attached it to her fuel tank. "Thanks. Just try ta stay outta sight, ya hare?" she said irritably, and could barely conceal her smile when Chess gave her a slight grin. She turned away and sped into the Dead Zone with the closest thing to a burnout that you could do on a hoverbike. *"Oh, Jesus!"* she prayed silently. *"Ya done outdid Yaself again, givin' me someone I can trust as an escort!"*

The Dead Zone flashed by, startling as always in its stark, lifeless expanse. She throttled down as she passed through the gateway to the outer docks, giving Chess a chance to catch up. A dreary, aching feeling pressed down upon her as the gray ghettos rose up ahead. She was almost home.

Behind, in the garbage truck, Ed reached into his snack box and pulled out a bag of peanuts. *"Genetically engineered to be allergen-free!"* boasted the package. "Well, you think she's gonna have any luck?" Ed asked. "I mean, do you think she's just going to stir up trouble?"

Chess shifted in his seat, turning left down an alleyway. He noticed Viv was taking him past dumpster drop points, making it appear as if he was just following a normal truck route. "I guess we'll find out," he said nonchalantly. "I don't think she wants trouble any more than we do."

"Are you sure about that? What if she's trying to start a rebellion, like that religious kid we gave our lunches to several months ago?" Ed said warily.

Chess grimaced. He had found out only recently that his codriver was responsible for the young girl's incarceration. And then he had learned she was responsible for Viv's conversion. The little underground church continued to pray for the girl, although they didn't even know her name. "You know, Ed, I don't think that girl was trying to start a rebellion. She had just found something to believe in and wanted to share it with others."

"Well, that's a problem. I find it offensive," Ed retorted, as if that justified his assessment of her. "Anyway, I'm going to be watching this one."

"Well, I would hope so," Chess said matter-of-factly. "It's our job."

They followed the bike for half an hour, pausing to empty half of their garbage at a drop site when Viviana conveniently slowed to a walking pace. When they were finished, she almost imperceptibly increased her speed. None of the Discards noticed due to the frenzy of activity at the dumpster as food scraps were snatched up and fought over. The bike slowly put distance between them, but Viv's destination was clear. She was headed for the Shaw. The two watched as Viv entered the social hub of that part of the outer docks. They parked the truck in an alleyway to observe and listen from a distance.

Viv was aware that the area wasn't on any of the garbage trucks' normal routes, but it seemed like the most promising location for recruitment—unless, of course, the presence of the truck flagged the situation as a trap. She sighed and shook her head. The truck could just as easily attract people who were hoping for a food delivery. She decided to stop second guessing herself. When she had left her apartment that morning, she had a strong impression that she was supposed to come to the Shaw.

Viv floated her bike to the eastern red cedar that guarded the "park," marveling that it had survived all these years. One might have expected it to be broken apart for firewood. Although open fires were prohibited in the outer docks, people still managed to attempt them when electricity went out and temperatures dipped below freezing. Some Discards revered the tree as a religious icon or a sacred meeting place and might have tried to protect it. But in the end, the desire for survival always won. Sacred objects and precious memories would be handily destroyed if it meant you could burn them to stay warm in the winter or could trade them for food. The cedar was the only tree still living for several miles, and how it had managed to survive surrounded by asphalt, plagued by acid fog every morning, and a target of cold, desperate Discards was anybody's guess. She swung her leg over her bike and slid off to approach it, her hand resting on its scraggly bark. "Hello, old friend," she said softly.

"What's she saying?" Ed asked.

"I think she's talking to the tree," Chess responded.

"Oh, great. They didn't tell us we'd be following a loony."

"I think that tree is special to the people that live here," Chess explained. "Haven't you seen the surveillance footage of how they congregate around it in the middle of the day? It's a special meeting place."

"What are they, tree worshippers?" Ed asked, intrigued. "Kind of a bad place to be, if you're a tree worshipper. Aren't many trees around here."

"No, I don't think they worship it. I just think that's why it's special to them. It's the only one for miles. It's the only thing that isn't made out of gray brick or pavement. In case you hadn't noticed, most of the Discards don't have Vista Visors. Most of them use the old phones. So what might be blue or red or even rainbow to us would be just plain gray to them. That would have to be depressing," Chess explained.

"Well, in case *you* hadn't noticed, they're here by choice. If they want to have a better life, they can leave this dump and come to the State. All they have to do is get the health implants. From what I understand, if they take the chip, they can skip the immigration classes they usually have to take and have any job they want. I wish I could have had it so easy," Ed said resentfully.

"I don't think there's anything easy about it for them," Chess countered. "They would have to leave the only place they know as home and allow people they don't trust to put something in their body that they've heard could make them sick, or worse yet, transform them into a mindless slave. That's why the State is sending this girl. They're hoping she'll be someone they might trust more than someone from the mobile clinic."

"I've also heard that part of the reason they're giving them such a good incentive to leave is because they're looking for test subjects," Ed went on, as though he hadn't heard anything Chess said. "They want to see if they can be controlled. If they did that, we'd have the perfect river clean-up crew, or whatever other dangerous job there is. They could send 'em on those long flights to Mars where a lot of them don't end up surviving the trip—or if they do survive, they go crazy from trying to live on that little colony in what amounts to a space station on the ground." Ed's voice grew more animated as he warmed to his subject. "And from what I hear, they're working on doing genetic experiments combined with chip technology to make humans able to live in the Martian atmosphere without a spacesuit. *That's* probably what this whole thing is about!"

"Ed, get a grip on reality. These are Discards, not Unspokens. They can only do experimental work on Unspokens. You've been spending too much time on social media. Don't you think maybe the State just wants to help people?" Chess said, knowing their conversations were always monitored.

Ed looked at Chess, his eyebrows raised in a skeptical expression. "That is, without a doubt, the worst case of brown nosing I've ever heard," he said. "Help Discards? Come on."

Chess glanced at the cab camera and then back at Ed meaningfully.

"Yes, I know, we're being recorded. But the State also knows they're not fooling anybody—except maybe the Discards, if they pull this off," he puffed his lips out in disgust. "Hard to believe that girl would betray her own people like this."

Chess shook his head. "She doesn't seem like the type to do that," he remarked.

Ed leaned forward in his seat. "Oh, yeah? What type is she? Is she your type? If it doesn't work out with you two, I get dibs."

Chess slammed on the breaks, ramming his passenger into the dashboard. "Hey!" Ed yelled.

"That's enough, Ed. This girl is a citizen of the State, and she's trying to do something nice for the people she grew up with. She deserves to be treated with some respect," Chess said with a scowl in his partner's direction.

"Ok, ok," Ed said with a sneaky smile. "I can see you have a thing for her. I'll back off 'til she dumps you."

"I only have a 'thing' for my wife. So, drop it," Chess said quietly.

"Oh, for the Source's sake! Can't you even joke around? You're so square you're cubed," Ed complained, but suddenly fell silent as they both noticed someone else approaching the tree. It was a man in a ragged flannel shirt and jeans so dirty and old they had morphed from blue into a faded yellowish green.

"Vivvy?" a voice came in over the monitoring system. "Vivvy, is that you?" said the man, his arms outstretched as he came toward her.

"It looks like we may have a situation!" Ed said excitedly.

"Easy, Ed. She knows the code word. She hasn't said 'meal ticket' yet."

The man continued his approach, limping slightly. Viv just stood there, a strange expression on her face that Chess couldn't quite read. Suddenly she reached toward the bike, and the sound of an indie rock band blasted through the cab of the trash truck.

"What's she doing?" Ed yelled, covering his ears. "Turn it down!" he exclaimed, reaching for the volume control on the monitoring system. The two watched as Viv stepped away from the bike a few paces, moving with the rhythm of the music. The shabbily dressed man seemed to take her cue, and shuffled a few sideways dance steps. "I think she's trying to make him feel at ease," Chess said with a confident tone. "Look! It seems to be working." The man seemed to be smiling at Viv, nodding his head as he grooved to the music.

As soon as she turned on the radio, Viv turned her back to the truck and mouthed the words, *They're listening.* She smiled, the corners of her lips trembling as tears began to form in her eyes. She had no idea how she would have reacted when this moment came, but now that it was here, she was surprised at her own emotions. When she spoke, it was with the assurance that her dance partner alone could hear her. "Dad! It's so good ta see ya!"

10

Viv's mother, Ariana Delacruz, had finally given up any hopes of her boyfriend escaping addiction. She left the outer docks while pregnant and went through the implant procedures of becoming a member of the State. Once Viv was born, she had declared intent to nurture her child, ensuring Viv's citizenship since she had been born in the state *and* had a D.I.N.

Two months later, however, Ariana returned to *her* old addiction: Viv's father. So Viv grew up in the outer docks, hearing stories of a different life from her mother—a life that was rightfully hers as a citizen. When she was eight years old, her mother's despair of life finally became too great for her to overcome. She took Viv with her to the Euthanasia Clinic. Viv remembered watching from the waiting room as her mother spoke to a nurse behind a clear glass window. The nurse had looked through the window at Viv and nodded to Ariana, and then turned away to open a medical cabinet. When she turned back around, Viv could see a hypodermic needle. Ariana smiled at her as the shot was administered, and then the nurse came to the door and beckoned for Viv to come in. "Vivvy, I need ya ta go with Nurse Cara. I'm gonna be goin' away now, an' I need ta know ya gonna go back ta the place where I use ta live —back in the State. It's not safe for ya here." Ariana's voice sounded strangely peaceful.

"I don' hafta stay with Dad?" Viv asked excitedly. "I can go see the place where they gots food all in rows on shelves?"

"That's right, Vivvy."

"How long do I get ta stay there?"

"Forever, if'n ya like," Ariana said sleepily.

Viv stayed with her mother, wondering about the trip provided by the State and why her mother had to be asleep in order to take it. Maybe it was such a long journey that it was easier to pass the time that way. When her mother woke up, she would be in another place, on an amazing adventure, she thought.

"Nurse Cara, can I go with Mama on her trip?" she asked suddenly.

The nurse looked as if she didn't know what to say at first. "This trip is just for grownups," she finally explained. "And besides, you are going on a wonderful trip of your own! You're going to the State, and you'll get to see all the food in the stores. And they even have toys! And new clothes," she added, glancing at Viv's threadbare tee shirt and her shoes riddled with holes.

"New clothes? My size? That ain't been owned before?" Viv asked incredulously. "They must have some jackpot dumpsters in that city! So when can I leave? And when will Mama be back?"

The nurse smiled sadly and opened her mouth to say something, but was interrupted by a commotion in the lobby. Someone was yelling and causing a scene. Viv's heart sank. She knew that voice. It was her father.

"My name is Dan'l Salgrove, an' I wanna see my wife! Don' you stick her! Don' you dare stick her!" he was yelling.

"Calm down or we'll give you something to *make* you calm down," said a doctor who was attempting to pull him away from the window. "And Citizen Delacruz doesn't have anyone on file as her legal partner."

"Hey! That's my little girl! That's my Vivvy! What're ya doin'? Are ya gonna to kill her, too?" he yelled, throwing the doctor to the side and lunging toward the door.

Viv was accustomed to her father's temper tantrums. She was usually good at calming him down. She opened the door and glared at him. "I don' know what ya been smokin' this time, but these people ain't hurtin' no one. They's just helpin' Mama go on a trip," she said.

But her father wasn't listening. His eyes were on the prone figure on the cot. "Ariana…Ariana," he mumbled softly, and stumbled forward to kneel by her side and rest his head on her lap.

"Don't worry Dad. She'll be back after her trip," Viv declared and thought a moment. "I'm sure ya could go with her if'n ya wanted."

He raised his head, looking at her with an expression of helplessness Viv had never seen in him before, and then he scowled fiercely at the nurse and the doctor. "Is that what ya told 'er? That she's goin' on a trip? Ya lyin' devils!" he got up slowly and put a protective hand on Viv's shoulder.

Nurse Cara took a tentative step toward Viv, her hand held out in her direction. "Sir, Viv is a citizen of the State. It was her mother's wish that she go there and claim full citizenship," she said.

A stream of expletives spewed out of Dan'l's mouth as he glared at the clinic staff. "Viv is stayin' with *me,*" he said in a firm voice.

Viv tugged on her father's shirt to get his attention. "But Dad, I wanna go where they gots food in stores just for the takin', an' new clothes, an' toys, an' …" her voice trailed off as her father's eyes bored a hole right through her.

"Viv, ya jus' don' understan' what these people jus' did to ya mama. She ain't goin' on no trip. They done killt her."

The words plunged through Viv's heart like a knife. Her father must be mistaken. She turned to look at the doctor, who was speaking in a sedate voice and behaving as if nothing out of the ordinary had happened. He was accustomed to deescalating situations with outraged family members who showed up seeking their loved ones. Ultimately, the decision to die was up to the patient; and as long as they went through the required counseling session, neither Discards nor unchipped citizens were discouraged from pursuing that end. The planet could only support so many people, and assisted suicide was viewed as an important part of population control. Properly functioning organs were harvested and sold to any Discard who needed a life-saving surgery and somehow had the means to pay for it. The fact that Discards were offered the option of suicide or the ability to purchase organs made available from previous suicides was considered an act of benevolence by the State. "It's what she wanted," he said soothingly. "She had been through the counseling several weeks ago and had gone through the proper protocols before the treatment was administered."

"Treatment? Is that what the State is callin' murder these days?" Dan'l gripped his daughter by the arm and yanked her into the lobby. "Come on, Viv. Let's get outta here before they kill us, too."

"Sir, since your alleged daughter has citizenship, she has the right to make the choice for herself where she wants to live," Nurse Cara insisted.

Viv's eyes were round with terror as she looked back at her mother's still form. "Mama? *Mama!*" she cried. She whirled around to face the nurse. *"I hate you!"* she screamed. Then she turned to her father. "And I hate *you, too!*" She broke free and ran out the clinic door. After wandering the streets for several hours, she realized she had nowhere to go but home, where her father was waiting. He was already stoned out of his mind when she got there. She didn't want to stay with him, but she didn't trust the people at the clinic now, either. It would be another six years before she finally went to one of the free mobile health clinics and announced that she was a citizen and had come to claim her rights.

"Oh, is that so?" said an exhausted nurse who was at the end of his shift. "You know, I hear that story at least once every time we do a tour."

"Yeah, it *is* so. I'm ready to receive the rights of full citizenship." Viv would not be deterred.

The nurse sighed and held up his palm. "Ok. Flash me your palm and if it reads, I'll give you a free trip to the State."

Viv's heart began to thud. What if her mother had made up all the stories about going to the State to have her baby? She knew that citizens were given certain health implants at birth, plus an identification device called Palmscan, but the only proof she had was her mother's word and the tiny lump she could feel in her palm. Ariana had taken care not to flash palms with Viv to make the beep that indicated one citizen had made contact with another, because it would throw her father into a rage. Viv was warned that she could never tell her friends the truth about her birthplace, since she would most certainly become the target of bullying. Her father wouldn't talk about it. He had even told her it was all a lie.

Viv locked eyes with the nurse, summoning all her courage to raise up her palm and bring it close to his. Suddenly, she felt a small vibration in her hand and heard a soft *beep*. The nurse gasped slightly, and his eyes opened wide. "By Jovies!" he exclaimed. "How did you get that? What are you doing here?"

Viv breathed out a sigh of relief. It was all true. There would be no more fighting. No more scrambling. No more being stuck with her father and his drug addiction. She looked at the nurse. "My ma tol' me I was born in the State. I don' wanna be here no more. I wanna go home." And with that simple exchange, Viv was whisked off to a different life.

She wouldn't see her father again until three years later, when she needed his help. In her quest for a decent job, she had found she could gain a distinct advantage in the hiring process if she could prove she was the child of a Discard. She had needed a DNA sample. Although Discards didn't believe in getting implants, they were required to be registered with the State as a resident of the outer docks when their parent or guardian declared intent to nurture—the official D.I.N. that insured they weren't considered an Unspoken. Viv's father was in the registry as a Discard. She just had to prove it.

It had been difficult enough to locate him. But once she did, he refused her request. His brows wrinkled into a scowl, he glowered at her and said, "Before ya left, ya tol' me ya wished I wadn't ya dad. Now, ya wanna prove it. Well, *you* can go ta—"

"Okay, okay, Dad. I get it. Ya mad at me, an' I don' blame ya. But I was just tired o' takin' care of ya all the time, workin' hard for food an' then seein' ya trade it off for dope. I wanted a better life. I didn' wanna be trapped no more. Mama gave me a chance at a better life. That was her dyin' wish. Surely ya don' begrudge 'er that?"

"Yer ma shouldna nevah left the docks in the first place."

"Come on, Dad. Ya always tol' me ya gotta look out for numba one. An' that's just what she was doin'. Plus, she was lookin' out for me, too."

"But she left *me* to do it!"

"And she came back, because she couldn' stand life without ya."

"An' *you* can't stand life *with* me!"

"Aw, come on, Dad. All I need is one hair. It's the only thing I've asked from ya since I was old enough ta know ya couldn' give me anything anyway." Viv hadn't meant the words as an insult, but she could tell by the look on her dad's face that they sank in like a barb.

"Git on back to Mother State, ya deserter," he said, spat on her bike, and walked away. Stunned at first, Viv watched her father disappear around a corner, and then glanced back at the glob of sputum as it rolled down the surface of the seat. She quickly reached in her pocket and pulled out the collection tube provided to her by the State lab, collecting a large portion of the saliva before it hit the ground. How ironic that, by giving her the insult he reserved for the most detestable characters he knew, her father had provided her with the sample she needed.

When she came back as an Outer Docks Transition Liaison, she hadn't counted on seeing her dad. And yet here he was, two years older and showing his age. Life without health implants in the polluted environment of the outer docks had taken its toll. He smiled at her as they danced to the music under the old cedar tree, his nearly toothless grin telling the story of non-existent dental care coupled with drug use. His skin showed signs of acid-fog burn, but his dancing surprised her. He wasn't jittery or jerky in his movements, and the shuffling gait he had exhibited earlier seemed to be the result of an injury rather than being drunk or high. She looked into his eyes as they drew near to each other. They were clear. "Dad? By Jovies, are ya sober?" she asked, her eyes wide.

Dan'l Salgrove grinned and threw his head back in a joyous laugh. "Vivvy, things is changin'. I'm not the same man ya used ta know."

Her heart sank. She had heard those words before. But as Viv looked her father up and down, she could sense that something was definitely different about him.

"I ain't even the same man I was *yesterday!*" he continued.

Viv studied him again. "I can tell somethin's different, but I can't figger out what."

"Well, ya see, there's this gang from the outskirts that come to the Shaw sometimes. They's just reg'lar kids, but a few weeks ago, they came, an' one of 'em gets up by the tree and starts singin'. He can sing like a bird, too! An' he starts singin' about some meetin' they's havin' in the outskirts. Says they's providin' a meal fa anyone what wants ta come to the meetin', an' 'e says for us ta bring a bowl with us."

"Sounds fishy," Viv said.

"That's what I thought, too. So I didn' go," Dan'l explained. "No one else did, neither, 'cept this little girl what was so hungry her gut got the best of 'er.

An' when she came back, she was tellin' everyone about a big mess o' some o' the best stew she ever had, plus some story they had tol' her about a better way o' life. Well, that got folks's hopes up. They could tell she'd had vittles cuz her gut wasn't sunk in no more. She tol' ever'one they's gonna have another meetin' next week, an' we all better come with a bowl or a cup if we wanted ta get some good grub an' give 'em a listen. But most people still thought it was prob'ly a trap. Even so, the next week, five more people up an' went. An' when they come back, they tell the same story: free stew—all they keered ta eat. An' when they was full, they listened to some sorta tale about Someone who could give 'em a better way o' life." Dan'l paused, and Viv was surprised to see tears forming in his eyes. He shook his head, as if he, himself, couldn't believe what he was saying.

"Say on, Dad!" Viv urged him.

Dan'l grinned and continued. "Well, by this time, people is startin' ta get excited. Where was these outskirts folks gettin' the food ta feed anyone what shows up? Maybe they really *did* have the answer to a better life. So next time, I goes with 'em. Me an about a hundred other people. An' ya know what? There's this apartment as far out o' the docks as you can get. An' there's a line o' people goin' by the door o' this little apartment in Zelda's old neighborhood."

"*Zelda!* That *is* as far out as you can get," Viv interrupted. Everyone knew Zelda, the pigeon trapper. She was the oldest Discard from the farthest neighborhood nearest the Preserve.

"I know," Dan'l agreed. "An' when we walk up to the door, there's this young lady handin' out the stew. She says to be sure and come back for seconds, cuz they had plenty."

"A young *lady?*" Viv asked. No one referred to anyone as a *lady* in the outer docks, unless it was to say someone was "your old lady."

"I know that sounds funny. But there's somethin' differ'nt about 'er. It's like she lit up the whole street. An' the kids from the gang that tol' us about the meetin' in the first place—there's somethin' differ'nt about them now, too. It's like they's all happy about somethin'. An' then, when we gave 'er a listen, we found out what they was happy about." Dan'l craned his neck around Viv to glance at the van. "Are ya sure they can't hear us?" he asked.

"Not as long as I got this music blastin'," she replied.

Dan'l stopped dancing and looked at Viv with a serious expression. "Now Vivvy, I want ya ta hear me out on this. This thing that happened ta me, it's the most important thing that ever happened to me in my life."

"Say on," Viv nodded encouragingly.

"Viv, they tol' us about a man named Jesus who came ta save the people on this planet. He came thousands of years ago. The only thing is—this Jesus, He wasn't just a man. He could heal people. An' He gave His life ta save us. He died on a cross an' came back ta life. He was God, Vivvy. But 'e cared enough ta come down an' *die* for us!"

Viv couldn't believe what she was hearing. "Dad, do ya *know* Him now? Did ya meet 'im an ask 'im ta come into ya heart?"

Dan'l's eyes opened wide. "Viv—do *you* know 'im *too?*" he asked in amazement, and suddenly he jumped forward and embraced her in a bear hug.

As her father clung to her, sobbing like a child, Viv thought she could hear a noise above the sound of the music. She turned to look at the trash truck and could see its lights had been activated as its engine roared to life, and the warning siren used in crowd control was beginning to blare. She shook her head as she stared at the cab of the truck.

"Dad, let go!" she yelled in his ear. "There's gonna be trouble!" She hated breaking off the embrace, but there was no other safe option.

Inside the truck, Ed was on point. "See there! That man is attacking her!" he said excitedly. "Move in! Move in!"

Chess was certain he had seen Viv signal for them to stand down. "She hasn't said the code word," he said.

"She may have said it five times by now. We can't hear anything with the music going!" Ed insisted.

"Let's just wait and see what happens," Chess said hopefully.

"If that girl gets a knife in the gut, it'll be on you," Ed warned.

Chess hesitated, his foot lifting off the brake. Suddenly, the bedraggled man released Viv and stepped away, maintaining a respectable distance. Viv was nodding and smiling. Chess let out a sigh of relief and turned to Ed. "I understand your concern, Ed. I was worried, too. But this girl is from around here. She knows how to handle herself. If we had moved in, we would have blown her cover."

Ed settled back in his seat, obviously disappointed the situation had been defused. "I don't like it," he growled. "After all, this girl is trusting us with her life."

"And if she's trusting us, we need to trust her, too," Chess countered.

"Well, when we get to talk to her again, we need to tell her to keep the music down. How can we hear her call for help if we can't hear a blasted word she's saying?" Ed grumbled.

And in an instant, Chess realized that was Viv's plan, exactly. He hoped it wasn't as obvious to his coworker. He focused his attention on the scene by the cedar tree. A few more Discards had filtered into the Shaw, attracted by the loud music. From their vantage point, Chess and Ed could see Viv was making conversation with a few of them, but they didn't seem very receptive. As they watched, the old man who had approached Viv in the first place seemed to be trying to bridge a gap between her and the onlookers, albeit unsuccessfully. He patted her on the shoulder and nodded his head vigorously. Ed sat up and took notice when Viv pulled the man close to her in a sideways hug, but Chess looked at him and shook his head. "It's fine. She initiated that," he said firmly. Ed puffed out his lips and drummed the armrest of his chair nervously, sinking back in his seat again.

Viv could tell the Discards weren't interested in anything she had to offer, so she kept quiet about the transition program. If anything, they seemed suspicious of her, on high alert for some reason. *Well, of course,* she reasoned. Her visit was suspicious, since she had only come back in the past to obtain the only thing her father could have given her. After all, she was a deserter. There were only two reasons she might have come back this time—to settle a score or to spy on them for the State. She turned to her dad and smiled sadly. She wasn't certain what to do now. Dan'l was certain to take some flak for receiving her so warmly. "Dad, I think maybe I'd better go," she said.

"But ya just got here," he protested. "I can take the heat. I used ta take it for ya mama when she first came back."

"I'll be back, Dad. I gotta rethink how to connect with ma old dockmates. There may be a few who wanna do what I did—who wanna leave for a better life, an' I can help 'em with that. But they won't let me help 'em if they don't trust me."

Dan'l's eyes shone. "Vivvy, there's plenty of us who *have* got a better life now. We got somethin' that the State can't offer. We gots hope. We gots forgiveness. We gots the love of God, an' Jesus in our hearts. Plus, we gots a free hot meal every day, since they've started havin' the meetin's every night. Shoot, even them what don't want nuthin' ta do with God can come ta get the free meal. That's more than the State has evah done for anyone aroun' here."

Looking at her father, Viv felt as if her heart would burst. She had thought someday she might get the chance to witness to him, but someone had beat her to it. She wished she could thank whoever had told him and wanted desperately to ask more questions about the meetings in the outskirts; but the less said about it, the better. If the State ever found out, they would certainly investigate, and that could be the end of it. "I'll be back, Dad. I promise," Viv said, and squeezed his shoulder before climbing back on her bike and heading leisurely back in the general direction she had come, taking care to avoid the alleyway where the trash truck was parked. She turned off the radio and spoke above the humming of her hoverbike. "I'm headin' to the Euthanasia Clinic on Beat Street," she announced to the listening device, and kept at a slower pace until she could see the truck behind her.

The bike floated casually over crumbling streets that were sprinkled with crab-grass and dandelion shoots which had taken hold in the cracks. Viv didn't know how the State would feel about her trying to discourage people from seeking the clinic's services, but she figured she could argue it would be good publicity for the State to offer people an alternative to suicide. Depressed people were probably her most promising candidates anyway, she reasoned, since Discards considered the choice between suicide and defecting to be a toss-up. If she could make just one person think twice before listening to the clinic's drivel about transition-ing to the Source, perhaps she could convince them to make a *different* type of transition. She unconsciously slowed the bike to a walking pace as she turned onto Beat Street, her right foot repeatedly pushing off the curb as she went. The buildings leading up to the clinic inched slowly by. She was surprised that nothing had changed. Buildings and billboards in the State changed almost monthly, but here it was the same drab gray tenement houses, the same dilapidated streets. A sickening feeling settled over her as the clinic came into view. Viv hadn't seen it since that fateful day her mother had enlisted its services. She had taken pains as a child to avoid it. But maybe she could prevent another child from losing a parent if she could convince one of their clients that there was something worth living for. However, that wasn't the only reason she had planned her visit. She had unfinished business here. She parked her bike, squared her shoulders and pushed open the door.

"Hello? May I help you?" asked a receptionist who was obviously confused as to why a well-dressed, well-put-together citizen of the State would be visiting a Euthanasia Clinic in the outer docks.

"Hello. My name is Viviana Delacruz. I just wondered if Nurse Cara still works here? She would have been here about eight years ago," Viv said.

The receptionist looked confused. "No. No one works at a Euthanasia Clinic for more than three years at a time," the receptionist explained.

"Why is that?" Viv asked.

"It takes a toll on the healthcare worker. It's difficult work, helping people make their transition to the Source."

"You mean it's depressing," Viv said bitterly. "As if that's on ma news feed." She shook her head. "Is there any way I could get a message to 'er?"

"Healthcare workers' contact information is confidential," the receptionist said in a no-nonsense voice.

Viv sighed and looked around, her eyes resting on the room behind the windows. It was empty now. Apparently, it was a slow day at the clinic. "I don't need to know her contact information. I just wondered if I could leave a message for her."

"Well, as she doesn't work here anymore, and I don't have high enough clearance to have access to past personnel files, I don't have any way of getting her a message," the receptionist stated, squinting her eyes as she studied Viv speculatively.

"I just wanna tell 'er I forgive 'er," Viv said, looking away from the windows and back to the woman at the desk.

"Forgive her…" the woman repeated slowly.

"Yeah. She administered the shot to my ma when I was eight years old. I didn't understand what was going on, and when I found out, I took it out on 'er. I just wanted to say I was sorry, and that I forgive her."

The woman looked at Viv, nonplussed. "Forgive her for what? For helping your mother transition to the Source? Why on earth would she need forgiveness for that? You should be *thanking* her, instead."

Viv opened her mouth and quickly closed it before something she would regret could come out of it. She had come here to grant forgiveness and make peace with her past, but as she stood in front of the naïve receptionist, she realized she had already forgiven Nurse Cara, even if she never saw her again. "Just tell 'er if ya see 'er, ok?" Viv said and quietly turned around and exited the clinic. She could see the trash truck parked down the street. She hopped on her bike and turned it on. "Guess that's it for today," Viv said so that Chess and Ed could hear her. "I'm headin' back to the State."

Inside the cab of the trash truck, Ed looked quizzically at Chess. "She must've been desperate to try to drum up business from the suicide clinic. Guess she found out it was a *dead end*," Ed laughed and slapped the armrest of his chair to celebrate his own joke.

"Very funny, Ed," Chess mumbled sarcastically.

"Awww, you old stick in the mud. You have to admit, that was a good one."

Chess rolled his eyes and pulled up to the dumpster two blocks past the clinic to make one more "food delivery." He was eager to hear about the day from Viv's point of view. There would be much to discuss at the next meeting of the underground church.

11

THE wiry-haired man scratched his bristly chin thoughtfully. His clothes, which were worn and slightly dirty, had been strategically selected; and the day's old growth of whiskers wasn't a result of sloppy hygiene. Since poverty was a thing of the past in the State, everyone knew this musician was playing a part in an elaborate scenario, hoping someone else would decide to play a supporting role. Romantic hook-ups with no thought of commitment were a normal way of life. Marriage was actually discouraged by the penalties one incurred when paying taxes, and many people regarded monogamous relationships to be confining and emotionally dangerous, since those who practiced it were placing their proverbial interrelational eggs all in one basket. Marriage wasn't illegal, but citizens were encouraged to have any sort of romantic relationship they wanted. The more partners you had and the more interesting scenarios you played, the more followers you had on social media. Hopeful individuals could seek a basic relationship where they were simply themselves, or they could post what kind of role playing they enjoyed on dating sites which vetted their subscribers. The more daring ones would venture out on the street, dress as their character, and wait to see what happened.

The middle-aged man ran his fingers through his greasy hair as he leaned against the subway wall. His hand rested on his guitar case as he listened to the *whoosh* of the trains when they passed through the tunnels and the whine of their breaks as they came to a stop. Doors opened, and he seemed to be staring off into the distance. But a careful observer would note he was actually watching people as they exited the cars. He kept a record of every passenger, using his chip implant to play back footage in his mind. He was paying careful attention to those who used the stop on a set schedule and those whom he had never seen before who might be visiting the area to shop or meet with friends. And then there were those who arrived infrequently but at least made a weekly, albeit sporadic appearance, like the girl who was exiting the car now.

He watched her stride across the platform toward the stairs, her boots clopping out a steady, purposeful rhythm that echoed through the station. It was a slow time in the subway, when most people had already made their evening commute. Time and date recorded, he eyed her up and down until she vanished from sight. Then he picked up his guitar case and followed the path she had taken, up the stairs into the chilled night air. He could see her colorful, red and white hair bobbing up ahead as she meandered down the sidewalk, stopping occasionally to peek in a window of one of the many curiosity shops lining the street. The wiry-haired man kept his distance, content to watch, recording her every move. She had been on his watch list for a long time, but some things were worth the wait.

Viv made a careful study of the street ahead as she walked to the secret meeting place of The Closet, the underground church hosted by the proprietor of Talk-o-Lot Chocolate Café. Everyone seemed to be going about their business. No one stopped at the café tonight since it was closed at 2100 hours on weekdays. The myriad of eateries, bars, shops, and galleries on 9th Street offered a variety of ways to occupy their time. There was enough foot traffic from the nearby college—even on a weekday night—that it was unlikely she would be noticed passing into the alleyway. Even so, she made a point to stop and look into shop windows to appear as if her only agenda was shopping. Every member of the church had separate arrival and departure times so as to diffuse suspicion, but one couldn't be too careful. Luciana had mentioned they might need to consider alternative meeting places and had asked for suggestions.

Viv wondered if her days attending the church were numbered. The group had known about her new position as Outer Docks Liaison from the time she was hired, but when she had suggested she might need to stop attending, they wouldn't hear of it. "Hebrews 10:24 and 25 says 'let us consider how to stir up one another to love and good works, not neglecting to meet together, as is the habit of some, but encouraging one another, and all the more as you see the

Day drawing near.'"[26] Luciana said, putting a reassuring hand on Viv's shoulder. "You need us, and we need you."

"I just don't want to take any chances that I might lead the State straight to ya," Viv had said anxiously.

"We'll let God take care of that. We can try meeting in other places. But until then, I want you to know we expect you to be here. If you don't show up, we'll be worried!" Luciana had replied. So Viv continued to attend. She continued pausing at displays in the various windows as she strolled down the street, trying to appear as unsuspicious as possible, and then disappeared into the alleyway beside her destination when it appeared on her right. It was empty except for the café's trashcan, along with a few stray bags of trash that apparently wouldn't fit. She made her way quickly to the side door of the shop, rapping out a specific number of knocks in a prescribed cadence. The door opened, and she slipped inside.

"Viviana!" Stasi exclaimed, and grabbed her in a bear hug.

"It's about time you got here," Celidor grinned. "After all that talk last time about it not being safe since you got that government job, I was wondering if you would be here."

"Viv knows better than to ignore her pastor," Luciana said as she gave Viv a warm embrace.

"Ya got that straight. I was afraid Luciana would call down the wrath o' God on me if I wasn't here," Viv joked.

"I thought I was going to have to call down the wrath of God on that man that was hanging on you in the outer docks," said Chess, as he stepped forward to squeeze her shoulder.

"Oh, Chess! Ya don't know how glad I was to see ya that day! That was an answer ta prayer! But ya don't have to worry none about that dude. That was ma dad! An' ya never gonna believe this. He got saved!" Viv bubbled over.

"Oh, praise God!" Luciana exclaimed.

"That was your *dad?* No wonder you turned up the music so you could have a private conversation. And it's a good thing, too. If Ed had heard what he said about being saved, he would've jumped on it and reported it."

---

[26] Hebrews 10:24-25, RSV

"Was it that obvious what I was doin'?" Viv asked worriedly.

"No, not really. We just thought you were trying to attract people with the music. But after a while, I figured it out. I don't think Ed did, though," Chess reassured her. "I'm thrilled to hear your dad met Jesus! You've been praying for him for a long time—well, we've *all* been praying for him."

"Yeah, an' that's not all he told me," Viv said, her eyes wide with excitement. "There's a revival going on in the outer docks! That's where he got saved."

Melford stepped forward with his guitar. "A revival! I wish I could play at it," he said wistfully.

"I wish we could all go," said Ranger enthusiastically.

"Even though I know it's impossible, I would love to be a fly on the wall," Rhys chimed in.

"Chess, what's wrong?" Luciana said, as she noticed his thoughtful frown.

"It's just that…we've not seen any suspicious activity on our routes—no big gatherings or anything," he explained.

"It's in the outskirts—as far out as ya can get. The trash trucks don't go out that far. Someone out there is holdin' meetin's an' feedin' folks. An' then they're tellin' 'em about Jesus an' singin' songs about 'im. Dad says people out there have got hope now. Isn't it amazin' what God can do?"

Chess looked at Luciana with a concerned expression. "If large groups of people are gathering somewhere out there, the State is bound to find out sooner or later. We need to pray for them."

"Well, amen to *that*, but I'm sure God is going to help keep them hidden," Viv said. "I know He's kept some of my other friends hidden for years now. And besides, since the Discards are gettin' food outta the deal, they're gonna do all they can to keep it quiet. They wouldn't wanna rat out the revival to the authorities. They'll do whatever it takes to keep gettin' a free meal ticket, even if they aren't interested in hearin' 'bout Jesus."

Chess's brow wrinkled in confusion. "Where in the world are they getting enough food to feed that many people?" he wondered aloud.

"I'll bet God has something to do with that!" Contessa said with a sparkle in her eyes.

"I'm certain of it," Luciana said confidently.

"When we pray for the revival, I'd like us also to remember a certain detective I met and a fellow believer who has been taken into custody," Rhys said.

"What's his name?" asked Luciana.

"The detective's name is Conlin Riedert, but I don't know the name of the Christian in custody. I just know it's someone who has already been sent to Dr. Moses, so he may not have much time before they chip him. Riedert asked if he could meet with me because after interviewing the man, he wanted to get some insight into why Christians are so different from the followers of other religions. I asked Riedert if I could meet the fellow. I just felt like God was asking me to do more, although I'm not certain what I'm supposed to do. Maybe just to encourage him somehow if I get to see him. I'm not sure."

"I'll keep my ears opened when I'm at work," Viv interjected. "I work in the same building as Dr. Moses. I hardly ever see 'im, but with my Audio-boost implant, I can hear things most people can't."

"We certainly have some things to pray about," Luciana said. "Let's go ahead and open in prayer and get started, because some of you have to get up very early in the morning."

The group bowed their heads, and with Luciana leading them in prayer, they all called upon the Lord to help their brothers and sisters in captivity and those attending the revival in the outer docks. Then Melford led them into worship with a song he had written himself. As Viv sang, tears streamed down her face. She felt more strongly than ever that her presence was putting the group at risk. After the service, as the members were saying their goodbyes, Viv once again voiced her concerns to Luciana.

"Before anyone leaves," Luciana announced, "Let's go ahead and agree on a different meeting place. Who said they had a defective Geeves unit?"

"I do," Stasi said. "It's always been a little glitchy. They usually send someone out to fix it in a few days, but it hasn't been working for two weeks now. Still, you never know when a repairman will show up." She grinned mischievously at Contessa. "Contessa, I've always wanted to throw you a baby shower!"

Contessa stared at her friend, mortified. "Stasi, I'm not even pregnant! What kind of rumors are you trying to spread?"

"But don't you want to have children?" Stasi asked with an innocent expression.

"Well, of course, *someday*, but I want to save that for after I get married!" Contessa protested.

"Well, there you have it. Contessa is going to have a baby…*someday*. Let's all meet at my place and throw her a baby shower. If anyone asks what we're doing there, that's what we'll tell them. And even if they reboot the Geeves unit, we can still read scriptures. The monitors don't know if we're reading from just one source. In fact, Luciana can preach and even use notes if she wants to. They don't know what the Bible says. They'll probably think it's just something out of *My Truth* anyway. Just one time isn't going to arouse suspicion. We can figure out our next meeting place while we're there, and pass it around on scraps of paper as if we're playing one of those games like they play at baby showers."

"Stasi, that's a great idea!" Celidor exclaimed.

"I love it," Luciana said.

"My place on Thursday at 1900 hours, if that works for everyone," Stasi said. "We don't even have to stagger our times, since it's for a party. Let me send you all an 'invitation' with my address, and that'll be the icing on the cake." She turned to Contessa. "Speaking of cake, what kind do you want? White? Marble?"

"You don't need to—" Contessa protested.

"We have to make it look real," Stasi interrupted. "Besides, I like cake."

As the group laughed at Stasi's antics, Viv was reminded of Chandra. She wondered how the youth group back in Adullam was doing. She missed Julie and Dawson and Garrison.

"You ok?" Chess asked.

Viv realized with a start that she had been staring off into space with a worried look. She turned to him with a wistful smile. "I'm just wondering how some friends of mine are doing. I guess I finally realized I may never see them again." Viv's voice broke, and she turned away to hide her tears.

"Your dad and your friends in the outer docks?" Chess asked.

Viv wiped away her tears and attempted to compose herself. "Well, I may see *them* again. Especially since it's my job to recruit them. I'm talking about the people who gave me the Bible. It's just not safe for me to visit them anymore. Too much risk of me being followed."

"What if one of *them* threw a party like Stasi is doing, or had a game night? Even if you were being monitored and couldn't have a regular church service, at least you would be able to see them again," suggested Rhys, who had overheard them. It was difficult not to hear everything that was said within the confines of a janitorial closet.

Viv sighed. She had never told her friends at The Closet where her other church family lived. Everyone had agreed that the less they knew, the less dangerous it would be for all concerned. "It just isn't possible for me to go see them."

"Well, maybe they could come see you?" Rhys persisted.

Viv shook her head and laughed. "Naww. I wish I could explain it to you. They couldn't come here, even if they tried. They would stick out like a sore thumb."

"Well, as far as your friends in the outer docks are concerned, I think you'd better steer clear of the revival in the outskirts so they aren't exposed. I know you want to see your dad, but it's probably safer to go to a different area next time," Chess cautioned her.

Viv nodded in agreement. It was her time to leave, so she said her farewells and started out the door. A thought struck her before she stepped outside. "Luciana, is there any other way to leave this alleyway besides the street?" she asked.

Luciana's brow furrowed in confusion. "Well, no…I don't suppose so," she began, and then grabbed Viv by the wrist. "There's the fire escape ladder next door. From the roof, you could go to the opposite side of that building and climb down the ladder on the other side. The alleyway between those two buildings is open on the far end, not a dead end like this one." Luciana fixed Viv with her gaze. "I guess I didn't realize you were that certain you were being followed."

Viv couldn't ignore the uneasiness she had felt since she left the subway. "I can't explain it. I just don't think it's safe for me to go back the way I came."

"Well, take the ladder, then. But if for any reason you don't feel safe going down the other side, just come back. We'll take the risk of being discovered over the risk of you falling from a rickety ladder."

Viv smiled and hugged Luciana tightly. "I love ya." She then looked at the other members of the church who hadn't yet left. "I love *all* of ya. I don't know what I'd do without ya." Then she stepped outside. A glance to the darkness on her right revealed nothing but the trash she had noticed earlier. To her left, the street was open and empty. There was no telling who might be back at the subway entrance, perhaps watching to see where she would emerge. Hopefully, there would be more foot traffic when the others left. She walked quickly to the opposite side of the alley where the ladder hung. It looked slightly rusty, but didn't shift when she put her weight on it. She climbed quickly to the roof, strode across to the other side, and located the other escape ladder. Viv had never been afraid of heights, but coming down was decidedly sketchier than going up. She white-knuckled the siderails of the ladder as she found her footing on the rungs below and descended as quickly as she dared. There was less light in this alley, and one look down made her feel as though she were descending into a black abyss. Six feet from the bottom, she missed a step and gasped, realizing that the bottom section was missing. She craned her neck in the darkness, attempting to see where she would land. A dumpster had been stationed just beneath the ladder. Having grown up in the outer docks, Viv had a great deal of experience with dumpsters, including finding the best footing around the rims when you couldn't trust the lids to hold your weight. She stepped onto the edge and walked on the rim to the lowest point, neatly kneeling and simultaneously spinning around as she made a quick bound away onto the brickwork below. "Ah-hah!" Viv congratulated herself on her safe landing, and then breathed a prayer of thanks. "I know Ya had way more to do with that than I did," she told the Lord softly. A series of flashbacks of dumpster-diving rushed through her mind as she picked her way out of the alley and made a quick study of the street. Her father was still in that life, she realized with a twinge of sadness. She wondered briefly if she could convince him to join her in the State, and then laughed at herself for even considering it. Dan'l Salgrove was one of the loudest protesters of State control. There was no way he would give up one ounce of his freedom, no matter how much hardship he had to endure to maintain it. She shook her head, bringing herself back to the present. She was going to have to walk several blocks to reach the next subway station, and the night wasn't getting any younger.

Back at the church's meeting place, Luciana and Chess were the only ones left. "I wish I could make sure Viv gets home safely," Chess remarked.

"I have a feeling Viv can take care of herself better than most of the men in this city," Luciana reassured him.

Chess grimaced. "I don't like it. I'd walk all of the women home if I could."

"Well, Stasi and Contessa have started leaving together," Luciana said. "That's safer, and there's nothing suspicious about that."

"And there's absolutely nothing suspicious about a husband and wife walking home together," he added. "So let's get to it, shall we? You're one of those early morning people you mentioned earlier, remember?"

Luciana kissed her husband warmly. "My protector," she smiled. "You and the Lord watch out for me." The two stepped into the alley, Luciana making sure the door locked behind them. When they reached the street, it was empty except for a few tipsy customers exiting the micro-brewery a few doors down.

"No acid fog tonight," Chess commented as they walked.

"Yes, it's a *lovely* night," Luciana murmured, burying her face in his arm as she stifled a yawn.

"You need to get more sleep, young lady," Chess said, hugging her more tightly in the cool night air.

Back in the alleyway, one of the bags of trash moved slightly. A figure in tattered clothes rose to his feet, making a note of his location and the time. He rubbed his bristly chin thoughtfully, and then recoiled at the smell of the trash on his hands. Guitar case in hand, he exited the alley, his wiry hair swinging with each step as he made his way to the subway station.

12

SELAH rubbed her eyes and squinted at the sunlight coming through the tattered, lime green towel Zelda had hung for a curtain in her bedroom. At least, it must have been lime green at one time, she reflected sleepily. Selah still wasn't used to having the sun in her eyes while she was in bed since she was accustomed to getting up before dawn. However, meetings were held in the evenings after all the trash trucks had finished their deliveries so that groups of people enroute wouldn't attract attention from authorities. Amazingly enough, whenever a meeting was held, the acid fog that habitually crept over the banks of the Mississippi and rolled through the outer docks failed to make an appearance. At first it seemed a coincidence. But as the meetings had grown from one night a week to two, then three, and finally a nightly event—with no acid fog in sight—Selah knew God was holding it back.

After feeding the crowd, Selah would teach them about the love of God and the redeeming power of the blood of Jesus Christ, and would end with an invitation to receive Jesus as their Savior. When the meetings first began, it was obvious that everyone was just there for the food. Selah was concerned that if she fed the crowd first, they would leave before they heard about Jesus. She considered preaching first and making them wait until the end to be fed, but was counseled against it by Bally, who had become an invaluable help to her.

Much like an armor-bearer in the Old Testament was a help to his commanding officer, Bally helped Selah prepare for the meetings. She tried to make certain she was getting enough rest and remembered to eat in the midst of feeding the crowds. She watched out for her safety and educated her on outer docks etiquette. "Miss Selah, if'n ya wait 'til da end ta fill deir bellies, dey's gonna take it as a insult. Like you's holdin' sump'n over deir heads like a queen. An' dey wouldn' be *wrong*. 'Cain't have none o' my stew 'til ya done listen ta what I say,' uh-huh. Dat's what dey'd be tinkin'. You'd have a powerful ruckus on ya hands if ya made 'em wait, an' dey'd likely run off wit' da stew pot. After all, dey don' know God keeps addin' to da pot. When dey look in dere, dey may tink dat's all dere is an' dey's gonna make sure dey get it afore someone else does. But if'n ya feed 'em from da start, dey knows ya keer about 'em, no matter what dey showed up for. An' I kin tell ya right now, dey's *all* just showin' up for da food. But when dey see ya keer 'nuf ta feed 'em wit' no strings attached, some of 'em's gonna stick aroun' ta listen—most likely, da ones dat is ready to make a change. An' den when da others see da change in deir dockmates, dey's gonna come an' listen, too."

Selah realized she was right. But to everyone's surprise, from the very first meeting, almost all who came to be fed stayed to hear what she had to say. "You has got a bangity way o' talkin', Miss Selah," Drey said in her nasally voice. "It's like, ya got dis accent we could listen to all day. An' what you is sayin', well, *no* one talks about *dat*. Not in front o' no crowd. Dey's too skeered ta get locked up by da loon dockers. An' here ya is, astin' folks ta come listen."

"Ain't nobody gonna report ya, though," Tunes piped up. "Cuz dat'd be da end o' da meal ticket."

"He not wrong," Bester added. "Only ting is, some o' da gangs may wanna keep it on da low down."

"Why?" Selah asked. "There's enough for everyone."

"Yeah, but dey don' know dat. Plus, if everyone in da outer docks starts makin' a migration to da outskirts ta get some grub, da State is gonna know sump'n's goin' on. Da State would start investigatin'—maybe even send in a spy or da chipmates or sump'n. An' den dat'd be da end of it," Bester explained.

"What's are chipmates?" Selah asked.

Bally rolled her eyes. "Bester, dey's called *Pod-Ops*. Were ya borned under a rock or sump'n?"

"Well, everyone aroun' here calls 'em chipmates, cuz deir minds is somehow connected by da chips dey got in deir brains. An' dey is nuttin' ta mess wit. Dey can snap ya neck jus' like *dat*," Bester said, smacking his hand down on the counter. "Da gangs gonna do everytin' dey can ta make sure dis news about da meetin's don' travel too far."

"But that's terrible," Selah said, her voice filled with frustration. "I want to spread the good news to everyone I can, not just whoever the gangs say can come."

Andrew sat up straight in his seat on an old crate. "Miss Selah, dis news 'bout Jesus is so good, not even da gangs can stop it, even if dey tried. Cuz dem what gets saved is gonna go tell da people dey know, an' *dey'll* tell da people *dey* know. Ya can't stop it. It's like da story Jesus tol' about da starter someone puts in bread dough. It don' take much. Jus' a little makes da whole lump o' dough rise up,"[27] he said confidently.

"That's good preaching, Andrew," Selah said with a smile. Andrew blushed and looked away. "But I still don't like the idea of people who want to come being held back."

"Da way I see it, we just do what God wants us to do. We do our part—da part we know how ta take keer of—an' God, *He* gonna do da rest," Tunes said with resolve.

Selah looked around at the small group of teenagers, marveling at how their faith had grown in the few short weeks since they had been saved. They still had much to learn and a lot of maturing to do, but God was doing a quick work in their lives.

Since that conversation, meeting attendance had more than doubled. It was thrilling to see people being saved and healed and delivered from spiritual darkness. Selah was humbled that God was using her in ways she had never imagined. But the late nights were beginning to take their toll. Every night after the salvation invitation was given, people would linger, asking Selah to pray for them. Many of them had physical ailments and didn't trust the State to treat them. Some suffered from anxiety or depression. Still others had an addiction of some sort. Selah never turned anyone away, but it meant that sometimes she didn't get to bed until the early hours of the morning. Last night had been one of those nights. She rolled to a sitting position on the couch cushions and buried her face in her hands. "Lord, I am *so tired,*" she mumbled.

---

[27] See Matthew 13:33

As if on cue, a knock was heard at the door. Selah sighed deeply and pulled on a jacket over her pajamas. As she stood up, the soles of her feet tingled from standing for hours on the platform of pallets the teens had made so that she could be seen and heard over the crowd. The knocking continued.

"I'm coming," Selah croaked, her voice hoarse from trying to project loud enough for everyone to hear. As she opened the door, she was relieved to see Bally.

"Man, Miss Selah. Ya look like leftover death," Bally commented.

"Well, that's good news. At least I look better than I feel," Selah said.

Bally surveyed her with a solemn expression. "I knows ya ain't getting' enough rest. An' ya ain't gettin' enough time alone wit' Jesus. Ya can't just keep pourin' stuff out if'n ya don' keep takin' it in."

"I need to prepare a message for tonight," Selah said firmly. "Since I get up in the middle of the day now, there's not really much time left to do all the things I need to do."

"Such as?" Bally asked with raised eyebrows.

"You know. Spending time in the Word and prayer. Finding the scriptures I need for tonight's message, and being sensitive to the Holy Spirit about what I am supposed to say. And just basic things like laundry."

"Well, I can do ya laundry! Why didn' ya say sump'n afore now?" Bally sputtered.

"Bally, you are not going to do my laundry," Selah said, embarrassed she had mentioned it.

"Why? Ya tink I won' do a good job?" Bally sniffed.

"No, of course not! I mean, yes, of course I know you would do a good job. But I'm not going to ask someone to handle my dirty clothes."

"Why not? Didn' someone do it for all o' us when we was just ankle-biters?" Bally persisted.

"Yeah, but I'm not an ankle-biter anymore," Selah said.

"Maybe not, but ya gettin' to da point where ya can't take keer of yaself. Ya gots to have someone watchin' out for ya. An' dat someone is *me*. I know it, in my spirit," Bally said, with the voice of authority. "Now, if you is too proud to let me get a blessin' from God by bein' obedient to da task what He's ast me ta do, I suppose I can sit back an' miss whatever blessin' He had stored up for me. Or ya could let me help an' let Jesus have dat extra time alone wit' ya ta pour some strength back into ya."

Selah was too tired to argue. Besides, through the fog of her mind, something of what Bally was saying made sense. "Ok, Bally," Selah relented. She trudged wearily to the bathroom.

"I got a surprise for ya when ya git done in dere," Bally said as she poured a cup of water from a bottle in the refrigerator.

"Ok," Selah called from behind the door. As she washed her face with water from their limited supply, she wondered what the surprise could be. Most likely a barely used item of clothing in her size that Bally had retrieved from a dumpster. Just last week, she had been the recipient of an almost new pair of sneakers that were much more comfortable than her old boots. But she found herself wishing it could be an apple, or her mother's blackberry cobbler, or a chunk of one of her father's smoked hams. Anything besides stew. As soon as she thought it, she scolded herself. "Lord, I am thankful for the stew. Please keep multiplying it," she whispered. She emerged from the bathroom to see Bally waiting by her seat at the table, a smile spread wide across her face.

"Sit down, Selah," she ordered, gesturing to the old five-gallon bucket that doubled for a stool. Selah noticed she kept one hand behind her back.

Selah obediently sat down and reached for the cup of water Bally had poured for her. "Thank you for bringing more drinking water. I was almost out," she remarked.

"Dat ain't da surprise," Bally said and with a flourish pulled her hand from behind her back and produced an apple. It was bruised and had a dent in it, but it was otherwise a complete apple, not the normal cores that were found in the dumpsters.

Selah was shocked speechless. Finally she stuttered, "Wh-where'd you get that?"

"When I come to ya door dis mornin', dere was dis little lady from da Shaw neighborhood waitin' here. Name's Idy. She was afraid to knock on da door cuz she figgered you was asleep. When she saw me, she almost didn' give it over, but Idy an' Mama, dey go way back. So she knew she could trust me. She says ta tell ya dat ya prayed for 'er last week. Dat poor woman been dealin' wit' back pain fa ten years. An' she says after you prayed, she went home an' didn' feel no differ'nt. But when she woke up in da mornin', da pain was gone. Now, she says she knows Jesus is da One what healed her, an' she been praisin' Him ever since. But when she found dis *whole* apple, she jus' felt like God wanted 'er ta give it ta *you*."

Selah looked wonderingly at the apple and cradled it in her hands. And then, much to her own surprise, she began to sob.

"Selah, what's wrong?" Bally asked, confused.

Selah's mind was flooded with images of the apple orchard back home—the branches bowed low with a bounty of fresh, perfect fruit, their delicate fragrance filling the breeze. And yet this one battered apple seemed like it was handed to her directly from God. It was the most beautiful apple she had ever seen. "It's so wonderful, Bally!" Selah exclaimed between sobs.

Bally didn't understand what was going through her friend's mind, but she recognized physical and emotional exhaustion when she saw it. "Now, you eat dis up, Miss Selah," she ordered. "Do ya want any stew dis mornin'?"

Selah giggled. "I think I'll skip it for now," she said as she wandered into her bedroom to retrieve her pocket knife. She cut the apple neatly in half and handed one half to Bally.

"No ma'am. Idy gave it to *me* ta give ta *you*," she protested.

"And since it's mine now, I'm giving half of it to *you,*" Selah insisted.

Bally reluctantly took the half and studied it. "Seems a shame to cut it up like dat, since it was whole." Suddenly her eyes grew round with wonder. "Selah! What if God is gonna use dis apple like 'e used da stew? I can't eat dis." She set the half down on the table. "I'm gonna wait an' see if He turns it into a whole apple again."

"Well, I'm eating *my* half," Selah said, and bit into the apple with a noisy crunch. She tried to remember the woman who had back pain, but she had prayed for so many. She didn't remember feeling anything different connected with many of those who were healed when she prayed, but then she was reminded that Jesus had said to the woman with the issue of blood, "Your faith has made you whole,"[28] and that Paul had looked into a crowd while he was preaching and had perceived that a man there had the faith to be healed.[29] God was the One who gave to each person the measure of faith.[30] *She* wasn't the one who could heal—she was merely a vessel being used to heal other broken vessels who reached forth in faith and received. "Thank you, Jesus," she whispered.

Bally regarded her from her post by the kitchen counter. "You go on back an' study, Sis. I'll let ya know when it's time to get ready for the meetin'."

Selah nodded and smiled. "Thank you, Bally. Not just for keeping me on schedule, but for being my friend and having my back."

"We all have ya back, Miss Selah. We's honored to be called ya friends," Bally said pragmatically.

Selah took one last look at Bally's half of the apple before she retreated into her room to study. She wouldn't be surprised if it was whole again when she emerged.

The book of Romans had been on her mind all that week. The study Bible she used and notes she had taken were spread out on the floor in front of the window. Selah paced back and forth in the room for a while as she prayed for the Lord's help with the message, but her exhaustion and her sore feet eventually convinced her to sit down. She opened the battered old folder Miss Genevieve had given her which contained the many sermons written by the wise old woman of God. Sitting cross-legged on a couch cushion under the window with her back against the wall and the folder propped up on her knees, she began to study. After about an hour, her back began to hurt. She stretched out on her stomach on the cushion in an effort to find a more comfortable position and continued to read. The meal was served at 6 p.m., with the service immediately following. There was still time between now and then to fine-tune her message. She knew the points she wanted to make and the scriptures she wanted to use, but she felt like it was lacking something. It was difficult to come up with stories to illustrate

---

[28] See Mark 5:25-34

[29] See Acts 14:8-10

[30] See Romans 12:3 Even our faith is given to us by God. We have no room to boast in any spiritual area of our lives because every gift we have is from Him! Although Selah reflects that those who were healed in the meetings had the faith to be healed, healings can also result from the faith of those praying for the sick, as in Mark 2:3-12

her points when she had such a different background than her audience, and as of now, she still felt like she needed to keep her origin a secret. But surely she could find some common ground if she put her mind to it. She closed her eyes, searching her memory for stories Miss Genevieve had used. The pencil she held made a droopy scrawl across the page of notes as her grip relaxed, and Selah was sound asleep.

Selah's boots made crunchy noises in the gravel as she made her way down the alley by Zelda's place. "That's odd," she thought to herself. "I thought this alley was paved in asphalt." She looked down at her feet and realized she was walking on a carefully manicured pathway. Lush vegetation lined the path and brushed against her arms like soft, leafy curtains as she walked. She could almost forget she was in a slum, until she looked above the leaves of elderberries, blackberries, and wild grape vines to see the dismal gray walls rising to the heavens. The wild plants that walled the path were vibrant. She wondered at their ability to cope with what little light the buildings allowed to reach the ground. Her gaze returned to the path, and she could see a gate ahead of her. Of course! It was the gate to the garden she was tending. It was remarkably similar to the gate surrounding Miss Genevieve's old place. She raised the weathered wooden latch and swung it open. As soon as she stepped inside, she spotted an empty watering can by a tomato vine which was slouching against its support stake, limp with thirst. Unlike the plants along the pathway behind her, many of the garden's specimens were wilted and in dire need of water. But the only water available was what was left in the bottle in Zelda's refrigerator. She would have to make a trip to the nearest hydrant, which was almost two miles away. The rows of beans and hills of squash and cucumbers stretched out before her, the length of the building. How would she be able to carry enough water to care for all the plants? She looked down at a cucumber the size of a gherkin, stunted and shriveled from water deprivation. With a sigh, she turned around and headed back to the fence. It was going to take all day to carry enough water to furnish the whole garden. But she had to. She was taking care of it for her employer. She didn't want to displease Him. As she grabbed the watering can and walked out the gate, she marveled at the vibrance of the plants outside of the garden. How was it that they thrived, when it was so dry? "They depend on Me," said a voice in explanation. Selah looked up into the kindly eyes of a man who looked strangely familiar.

"How do you manage to carry enough water for all of them? They're thriving! You must be giving them buckets and buckets of it!" Selah exclaimed.

The man smiled patiently. "The water I give them is different than the water from the hydrant. They are never thirsty because this water springs up from within them now—into everlasting life. They know that depending on other sources will leave them thirsty, so they continue to drink from My water that I constantly supply for them."

Selah's heart jumped. Maybe this man could help her. "Do you think you could water this garden for my employer? I feel terrible that it's in such poor condition. I just don't have the time because I have to go back and forth, carrying the water. If what you say is true, then all it would take for this garden to be healthy would be for you to give these plants a drink. Then the water would somehow be inside of them, and they would never run out."

Sadness passed across the man's face as He looked at Selah and then at the garden, and then shook His head. "I'm afraid I'm not allowed to do that," He said simply.

"Why not?" Selah asked. "I know my employer would be grateful. He won't stop you. I don't even care if He pays you instead of me. I want this garden to look good for Him, but I just can't do it all by myself."

"He is not the one keeping Me from helping," said the man, as He fixed her with His gaze. "You are."

Selah frowned, and anger and frustration came boiling to the surface. "But I just asked you for help! I'm not stopping you. I'm begging you, please help me!"

"Selah, don't you recognize Me?" the man asked sadly.

And suddenly, Selah understood why the man standing before her had looked so familiar. He was her employer, the Master Gardener. But before He had become her employer, He had been her friend and her closest confidant. They used to spend hours together, planting seeds and listening to each other talk. She loved the sound of His voice, and often told Him so. When she grew tired, just the touch of His hand revived her. And the water He gave her was sweet and cold. When she drank from His cup, it was like she was somehow drinking from an icy cold spring. The amazing thing was that the cup never ran out. Any time she reached for it, it was full to the brim, ready to slake her thirst. "Oh, Master!" she cried. "How could I forget all the wonderful times we spent together?"

The Master smiled and placed a comforting hand on her shoulder. "You became so involved in working for Me that you stopped spending time with Me. You started missing our morning meetings. Do you remember? I would arrive, and you would already be at work instead of waiting for Me at the gate. When I called out to you, you would say you were too busy to visit, but maybe the next day you would have time. Eventually, you stopped looking up when I called. You stopped drinking from My fountain and started trying to do everything by yourself. Don't you remember, Selah, that without Me, you can do nothing? I am the vine, you are the branch. Whoever abides in Me, and I in him, he will bear much fruit, for apart from Me you can do nothing. If you don't stay connected to the vine, you will wither up and die."[31]

"But I was working for You the whole time," Selah protested weakly.

"Yes. But you forgot all about our friendship. When you stopped waiting on Me so I could help you, My hands were tied. I could no longer renew your strength because I wasn't allowed over the threshold."

Selah looked down in shame, tears running down her cheeks and hitting the parched ground in dusty little poofs. "How can You ever forgive me?" she asked.

"I took care of that a long time ago. But maybe we could just spend some time together. I would really enjoy that," the Master said.

Selah nodded. "Would you like to take a walk?"

The Master held out His hand. "Why don't we go back to the garden?" He suggested.

Selah smiled gratefully and clasped His hand. Strength instantly flooded her soul. They entered the garden together, and the latch shut behind them.

Selah awoke with a start. The room was dark. There must be a storm, she thought, and raised up on her elbows. She stood to her feet and looked out the window, but there was no rain. The sky was dark, though. Light from the streetlamp was splashing against the apartment. She rubbed her neck, which had a crick in it. And then she realized she had been asleep for much, much longer than a few minutes. She fumbled for the light switch and found her sneakers, pulling them on and barely pausing to tie them. How long had she

---

[31] See John 15:5-6

overslept? And why hadn't Bally awakened her? The people would be restless. They might leave before she could feed them or say anything to them about Jesus! She grabbed her Bible and a few notes and rushed out the door, looking around wildly for the food line. What she saw took her completely by surprise.

Around the pallet platform was a large crowd of people, perhaps the largest they had ever had since the meetings had begun. Tunes was still on the platform below the streetlamp, leading worship. Or was he? He seemed to be lost in worship, not even singing, yet the sound of voices rose up all around the alley, amplified by the buildings. It was a sound of worship such as she had never heard before: pure, honest, adoring, and it was swelling up from the crowd in sweet abandon. She looked around and saw Bally, her hands raised and eyes closed. "Bally," she whispered as she sidled up to her. "What's going on? What about the meal? Where's the stewpot?" Bally opened her eyes and looked at her friend with a confused expression. "Why didn't you wake me up? How long have the people been waiting?" Selah continued.

Bally smiled and shook her head. "Miss Selah, I tried ta wake ya up, but you was so tired, ya didn' even budge when I shook ya. Da people have done been fed. Da stewpot is back in da fridge. Everyting' has been taken keer of." She stopped talking and clasped Selah's shoulder. "Don'tcha feel dat?" she asked. "It's like Jesus Hisself is here, walkin' aroun' in dis alley, stoppin' to hug ever'one."

Suddenly, a loud "Whoop!" was heard from somewhere in the crowd.

"Dere's anudder one!" Bally exclaimed.

"Another what?" Selah asked.

"People has been bein' healed while we's praisin' God, wit'out no one prayin' for 'em!" Bally said, her eyes shining as tears streamed down her face. "Every time it happens, dey lets out a holler to let everyone know. Oh, Miss Selah, dis is so much easier, lettin' God do all da work."

As soon as she heard the words, the dream came flooding back to her and the convicting power of the Holy Spirit settled upon her. Selah dropped to her knees. "Oh, Jesus, I've been so wrong," she repented. "I'm so sorry I let my service to You take first place before our relationship!"

Bally put a hand on her shoulder. "Selah, is ya ok?"

Selah lifted her hands as the warmth of God's presence poured over her. "I am *now*," she said, and laughed with joy as another shout of praise was heard from someone who had just received their healing.

13

WHEN Ira arrived at work at 0700 hours, he was surprised to see Dr. Moses waiting for him at the door with a welcoming smile and a steaming cup of coffee. "Good morning, Ira. I certainly hope you're feeling better." He sounded genuinely concerned as he offered him the cup.

"Much better, thank you," Ira said, taking a sip. The coffee was deliciously richer than the government standard. "This is great coffee," he remarked.

"The beans are from a small farm in Panama. I ground them fresh this morning and made it in my personal coffee bar," he explained. "I had a feeling you might need some fortification for the task ahead. I know you had a rough day yesterday, but I'm afraid I'm going to have to ask you to power through with this project. We've had an incident with the rogue program. It has been detected in another system within this building after one of my employees was ejected from the interface she was attempting to reprogram."

Ira instantly recoiled. The man was lying to him, as he had the day before. Much to Ira's dismay, he had discovered the "rogue program" was actually the protective neural wall of a young girl named Piper who had been chipped against her will. No doubt, this other system Dr. Moses referred to was another human being.

"Disturbing, isn't it?" Dr. Moses said, noticing Ira's revulsion but completely misinterpreting its cause.

Ira opened his mouth, tempted to tell the man exactly what he thought of him, even if it meant he might end up in a penal colony, but Dr. Moses continued before he could say anything.

"I'm concerned if we don't find a solution, we may have to abandon these systems altogether, and much useful data will be lost."

"Abandon these systems?" Ira didn't like the sound of that.

"Yes. If the program can't be stopped, the systems will need to be terminated. It will be too dangerous to allow them to exist if the virus can't be contained and reversed."

"No!" Ira said fervently. "I mean, there's no need to lose all that data," he added quickly, as Dr. Moses raised his eyebrows at the emotional outburst.

"I knew I could count on you to keep plugging away at this," Dr. Moses said, with some relief. "It's a lot to ask of someone under such stressful circumstances, but you really do appear to be our best chance at stopping this, since you aren't in any danger of being infected. All the other top programmers in the State have already taken the chip. I wish I could help you, but I just can't risk it. You're going to have to fly solo."

"I'll do my best," Ira said.

"I know you will. Your work ethic won't allow you to do otherwise," Dr. Moses said in a tone that suggested he expected no less. "I'm going to give you a look at the other system. Perhaps seeing the program in a different setting will reveal its commonalities between its infection of the two systems and any weaknesses it might have."

"It couldn't hurt," Ira nodded, wondering whose mind he was being asked to violate today.

Dr. Moses led him again to the office with the special interface suit specifically designed to allow him to form an artificial virtual link using a Vista Visor. As they entered the darkened room, Ira was startled by the movement of a figure that had been leaning against the wall opposite the door. "Allow me to introduce you to Ainsley Abbot. She spearheads Employee Interrelations in the State and private sector, and was involved in the incident I referred to earlier. Needless to say, she has taken a special interest in this project."

Ira nodded a hello at the woman as she slipped out of the shadows into the halo of light surrounding his work station. She was dangerously attractive. He was reminded of the beautiful pattern on the timber rattlesnake he had seen at the zoo. As a child, he had thought how marvelous it would be to stroke the rusty stripe on the viper's back, even though he knew it would be a foolish mistake.

Ainsley seemed to assess him with a sweep of her dark eyes. "I've heard a lot about you, Ira," she said with a voice as smooth as honey. "I look forward to watching you work."

"Watching me?" Ira asked.

"After yesterday, I thought it might be helpful if we kept a closer watch," Dr. Moses explained. "If things appear to be getting too stressful, or if the visor is turned off again, we'll be able to communicate with you through the earpieces in the suit and talk you through it. And we'll be able to monitor your heart rate and blood pressure through the suit's sensors, as well. If I had thought of that earlier, we might have avoided yesterday's unpleasantness."

Ira sighed. He could feel his blood pressure rising already. "Actually, I think I'll be alright without that. Just knowing someone is watching me makes me feel nervous."

"Don't be silly," Ainsley said, fixing him with her penetrating gaze as she placed her hand on his shoulder and let it slide down to caress his elbow. "Think of us as your backup team, cheering you on from the sidelines. We'll be monitoring you from Dr. Moses' office. When we see that you need help, we'll be right there to offer encouragement."

Ira could have sworn he heard the sound of slithering. Knowing he could do nothing but agree with them, he nodded. "Very well."

"Excellent," Dr. Moses smiled, and he and Specialist Abbot exited the room.

After one last nervous swig of his coffee, Ira donned the suit. He was faced with a terrible moral dilemma. If he cracked the code, he would be breaching an individual's neural wall without their consent. If he failed to crack the code, in all likelihood, Piper and this new test subject would be euthanized. He sat motionless in the chair as he pondered his situation. Of course, he had to preserve life if he could, even if it meant the most private aspects of a person's life were wrongfully invaded and exposed.

"Ira, is everything ok?" said Dr. Moses' voice in his ear. "Your blood pressure is elevated."

"Yes, I'm not surprised." Ira laughed. "Stage fright."

"You can do this, Ira," Ainsley said. "Just pretend we aren't even here."

It was an impossible request. Ira exhaled slowly. As he reached up to turn on the visor, he heard yet another word of encouragement in his earpiece. "I know the plans I have for you. Plans for good—not evil—to give you a future and a hope."[32]

Ira froze. That was the scripture he had seen on the table at the café he had visited last night—the one the man called Jesus had spoken in his dream, or whatever it was. Had the woman in the café been a government plant? Did Dr. Moses have him followed? Piper had yelled out that scripture reference to him in the hall. Did Dr. Moses know about the incident? Did he know that Ira knew she wasn't just a "computer system?"

"*What* did you say?" Ira ventured. If Moses was toying with him, he was going to find out now—bring it out into the open. If he was going to die in a penal colony anyway, they might as well all be on the same page.

Ainsley's voice came through the earpiece. "I was just telling you to pretend we aren't here."

"No, I mean after that. One of you said something right after that," Ira insisted.

There was silence on the other end of the connection, and Ira feared his suspicions were confirmed. But then Dr. Moses said, "We didn't say anything, Ira. You're good to go."

Ira frowned. He had not just imagined what he heard. He slowly peeled off the headpiece of the suit and looked around the room. No one was there to have spoken the words where he could hear them. He needed time to think about this, and he couldn't do it with Moses and Abbot watching every vital sign.

"Ira, is there a reason you've taken off the headpiece?" Moses said over the intercom, a slight edge to his voice.

"Uh, yes. I realize this is inconvenient, but I really must use the restroom," Ira said quickly.

"Of course," Dr. Moses replied.

In the office on the top floor, Ainsley Abbot muted her microphone and stared hard at Dr. Moses. "He's stalling, for some reason. And his blood pressure is still elevated."

---

[32] See Jeremiah 29:11

"He's nervous, Ainsley. It's perfectly normal. I would be more surprised if he *weren't* nervous. Think about how you would react if you were in this situation," Moses replied diplomatically. "The man knows that the only reason he's here and not in prison is because we think he can help us. And if he can't, well…he may find himself in prison again."

"*I* wouldn't *be* in this situation," Ainsley retorted.

"No, of course not. You don't have the programming skills necessary," Moses said pointedly.

Ainsley glared and stood up to pace the room. "Every minute he delays is time the virus spends building and spreading and mutating."

"And every added stress will only hinder his progress. Give the man a little space. He only asked to go to the restroom, for goodness' sake. When he gets settled and gets in 'the zone,' he won't disappoint. I've seen him at work before. Even if the other top programmers I mentioned earlier hadn't taken the chip, Ira would still be my first choice."

"Well, he'd better get settled soon, or we'll have to instate plan B."

"I'd rather not go with that option. I feel that we're so close to a breakthrough on the mental block created by this dogmatic religion. If we can break the girl, we'll have the key to opening the minds of all those who have been imprisoned by this particular belief system."

Ainsley sat down again and leaned back in her chair, a slight smile curving her lips. "This isn't just about the success of the neural link composite, is it? This is *personal* for you."

Dr. Moses gave her a sidelong glance, as a rhinoceros might acknowledge the harassment of a mosquito. "I'm curious to see if there's a common thread between Piper and this woman you brought in," he said, completely ignoring her question.

Ainsley's smile broadened as she swiveled in her chair, her eyes fastened on Moses. "Ok, Joseph. I won't pry. But as far as Janice Druthers and the girl sharing anything in common, I don't see it. Druthers is an inherently weak person with a simple mind, prone to seeking validation from others. As far as I know, the only religious conviction she might have is the drivel being spoon-fed to her from the State devotional blog. From what you've told me about Piper, she is incredibly strong, having survived things that would send most people to a Euthanasia Clinic. And her faith in the Christian deity goes beyond conviction. It's who she is, now. As much as you hate Christianity, you can't deny that her faith, however misplaced, is probably the only thing that has kept her alive. One might even argue that since that is the case, her faith might not be misplaced at all."

"Spare me the justification of morals to which you claim no adherence," Moses said coldly. Ainsley's musical laugh rippled through the room. "I can see I've struck a nerve. I do hope you'll take me into your confidence someday. What happened out there in the Preserve, Joseph? Did you really grow up in a cult, like the rumors say?"

Moses remained silent, continuing his vigil of the empty interface suit in the office on the live cam. When it was obvious that he wasn't going to respond, Ainsley continued. "Okay, Joseph. I'll leave it alone. But as far as the virus is concerned, the only commonality between the two affected subjects is their desire not to have their privacy violated. If something else is at play here, we can't see it yet. I know you that think this coding is something the girl created to prevent you from forcing her to recant her faith. But Janice really has no faith, to speak of. We need to look at other probable causes."

"And we are," Moses finally spoke. "It's possible Citizen Druthers succumbed to the virus because she was in a weakened state brought on by your questionable 'counseling' techniques. Piper could have simply wandered across her neural boundary and introduced it before we knew what was happening. Perhaps she was the second figure you saw with Janice before your link with her was severed."

"It's possible, I suppose," Ainsley said thoughtfully, remembering the incident during the link when the unseen force had whisked her off her feet and blown her back outside of Janice's mind as easily as a breeze would pick up a leaf and send it tumbling down the road. The figure she had seen with Janice didn't look like that of a small girl. Of course, people could project themselves any way they wanted to within a link. It all depended upon the strength of the person's self-image. But one with a trained eye could see beyond the façade to determine if any of the projection contained qualities intrinsic to the individual. And the glimpse she had of the figure beside Janice had seemed to reveal something more permanent than a projection. It looked as genuine in appearance as Janice, who had neither the self-image nor the skill to project anything but the truth when it came to neural linking. No, the individual she had seen appeared to be exactly as it presented itself. Ainsley shuddered involuntarily. Whoever or whatever it was, she had never sensed such power before. If it were the source of the virus, they were dealing with more than just a master programmer.

Ainsley had some knowledge of unexplained power. Her father and mother had dabbled in the occult. They were eventually taken into custody by one of the State's hubs in Jacksonville, Florida for proselytizing. Ainsley, who had been temporarily taken into foster care, was reassured by her mother during a virtual meeting over Vista Visor that they would soon be together again. "Don't worry, Ainsel. We're telling the State everything they want to know in order for us to be released."

"But they'll know you're lying," Ainsley had said matter-of-factly. "They can always tell."

Her mother had glanced at her father, who had smiled broadly. "We're not lying, Ainsel-cakes," he lied. "We're just telling them we agree that all religions are serving the same god—the Source."

"But we worship—" Ainsley faltered. She didn't even like speaking the name of the dark force her parents served. Other children whose parents came to the secret meetings treated it as if it were a game. But she had seen things she couldn't explain. Things that made it hard for her to sleep at night.

Her mother smiled and laughed. "I know you've been having nightmares, honey. But you'll get used to them. I did. I learned to walk around in them and embrace the darkness."

Her father shifted his hulking weight, and Ainsley could almost hear the bench creak and groan over the visor connection. "You see, Ainsel, it's all part of the plan. If we agree that every road leads to the Source, we're distracting people from the only road that leads to our enemy. If no one can find their way to Him, it hurts His kingdom. The more things we can do to hurt His kingdom, the more power we'll be given."

"Are you sure that's how it works?" Ainsley asked in a trembling voice, and immediately regretted it. Even though she was in a completely different part of the city and her parents were locked up in a State mental ward, she could feel her father's anger.

"Are you questioning me?" he asked in a voice that was eerily soft.

"No, Papa," Ainsley answered quickly.

"Because if you were, I can send someone to check on you."

"No! No, I wasn't questioning you," Ainsley said fervently. The visitors who came to her in her dreams were the reason she was afraid to go to sleep in the first place.

"That's our Ainsel of darkness," her mother crooned proudly. Her parents used fear to control her. And even though the nightmares hadn't stopped, she felt safer with her foster parents than she did at home.

But the reprieve didn't last. Her parents were eventually released after they agreed to stop seeking new converts, and Ainsley was returned to them. She found some semblance of a normalcy during school hours. When she learned of a scholarship to a high school for accelerated learning in St. Louis, she made academics her top priority, earning excellent grades in junior high that eventually won her a seat in the program and a ticket out of her nightmarish homelife. Away from her parents, Ainsley vowed to herself to never be controlled by anyone or anything else again. *She* was in control now. After all, there were different, less obvious means of controlling others than using fear. That was just one method of manipulation. Ainsley honed her craft by nurturing the sympathy, lust, pride, and insecurities of others to bend their wills to her whims, all without them realizing it. When the chip was introduced, she knew there were very few people who could stop her, and very few who would know what she was doing.

Last year, she had a surprise visit from her parents after a press release about her work with people who were transitioning to life with the chip. "We're in town for a convention," her mother explained, "and we wondered if we might get to see you."

Ainsley felt a rush of fear that she hadn't experienced in years. She could make the pretense that she was too busy at work, but then they would probably just stop by the lab and disrupt her professional life by casting spells at her workplace. No, she would choose their meeting place. "Let's meet at the Museum of Religious Convergence," she suggested. "They have a nice café there, and we can browse through the religious artifacts. They have some excellent statues of Baal."

"Sounds like an enlightening place," her father approved.

As they meandered through the galleries of the world's religions, Ainsley shared some of her insights into the human psyche and her work with people who were having difficulty adjusting to life with the chip. "Oh, honey! We are so proud of you. I knew that amazing brain of yours would open doors for you. You'll be able to do so much more than we ever could."

Ainsley's breath caught in her throat. "What do you mean?"

"The Church of Satan is lucky to have someone like you on the inside, working for the kingdom of darkness. That's one reason we came to see you. We wanted to make sure you haven't lost your way. And I can see that you haven't," her mother said with a sly smile.

Her father seemed to size her up. "You've come a long way from the little girl who was afraid to go to sleep. Now, you can be the reason someone *else* is afraid."

Ainsley's eyes flashed in anger. "There are more ways to deal with people than by using fear," she hissed.

"Of course," her father smiled. "That's just *our* way. You've opened up a whole new world of possibilities—with your interpersonal skills and the power of the chip. Congratulations, Ainsel-baby. We couldn't be more proud."

When they had said their goodbyes, Ainsley realized the darkness had followed her from Jacksonville to St. Louis. She thought she had escaped it, but instead, she had just stopped running and embraced it, as her mother had advised her all those years ago.

There had been very little resistance to her methods—socially, professionally, and electronically—until her experience with Janice. Ainsley stood up and walked to the windows that overlooked the city, the mappings of each block of gray buildings reminding her of the initial layout of a person's neural net before it branched into the amazing intricacies of the human mind. She had gone uncontested until now in her control of people who resisted chip protocol. But this figure she had seen beside Janice was a new element. And as long as the code present in Piper and Janice kept her from accessing their minds, there was no way to tell who it was or what it wanted, nor was there any way to keep its influence from spreading. "I think this is too dangerous, Joseph," Ainsley said suddenly. "I think we need to end it."

Moses turned to her and said firmly, "If it comes to the point where I feel that is our only option, we will do what is necessary to protect ourselves and all the others. For now, we are going to let Ira take a stab at this."

Ainsley looked away, rolling her eyes in frustration. The problem with Moses was that she hadn't found a way to control him. Or had she? She smiled as she remembered his reaction to her insinuations earlier. If she couldn't manipulate him, she could certainly find other ways to undermine him, professionally. "Okay, Joseph. We'll try it your way, for now. After all, you're the boss. But I hope that Ira gets his mind in the game soon, or we may be out of other options."

In the privacy of the bathroom, Ira pressed his forehead against the cool metal wall of the stall in an effort to focus. The voice in his head had repeated the words of Jeremiah 29:11. It claimed it had made plans for him. It claimed it wanted good for him, not evil. What was it Piper had told him was the reason he had been allowed inside the meadow that comprised her inner world? *"Jesus tol' me He was bringin' someone here who looked at things differently—someone who could help us."* Ira straightened up in the stall. Was the Jesus program trying to communicate with him, outside of the artificial link? He didn't see how it was possible that such a program could exert its influence without the use of a chip or a visor. And both of the times he had heard these words, the visor had been turned off. Was he losing his mind, or had the program somehow evolved and developed the ability to make an organic link, with no physical contact?

"There are some things you can't explain," Grandfather had told him once. Ira had been busy explaining how science had removed the need for faith and had created a world that could be based on logic, rather than fear or suspicion or the projections of human emotions on the workings of the universe. Grandfather had shaken his head. "You keep at it and you'll explain away all the wonder in the world. There's more to life than what you can explain with science or see with your eyes." Ira often wondered if Grandfather secretly believed in a higher power. If he had, he had never mentioned it. It was dangerous for parents and grandparents to teach their children about religion, since that was viewed as the

State's responsibility. Only the State could be trusted to present religion in a way that was unbiased toward any particular faith, and parents who ignored this fact were relieved of the burden of childrearing so they could concentrate on their own mental health while the State provided a stable environment for their children. "Ira, have you ever seen a program that matched the complexity of the human brain?" Grandfather had asked. Ira had to admit that he hadn't. "If you took the components necessary to make a computer and put them on a table somewhere, if you gave them enough time, could those components come together and write a code that would enable them to function independently?"

"I know what you're trying to say," Ira said flatly.

"I'm not sure you do. Just answer the question," Grandfather had insisted.

Ira sighed. "Inanimate objects can't simply jump up and start doing things. Someone has to be there to assemble them and write a program for them. The human brain is a different matter, altogether. It's organic. It evolved over centuries, responding to stimuli that the body was exposed to. Comparing the brain to the disassembled parts of a computer is like comparing a mechanic to a wrench."

Grandfather looked up at the ceiling as if in deep thought. "Let me rephrase the question. The human body is made up of cells which are made up of proteins and amino acids. If we put some amino acids together, could they build a human body?"

"No. With some help in a lab, maybe. But not by themselves."

"Well, that's what evolution is asking us to believe."

"But they have the code necessary to do it," Ira said. "DNA tells each cell what to do in order to make an organism that can live and reproduce."

"Who made the DNA? Who thought *that* up?" Grandfather asked determinedly.

"Over millions of years, carbon, hydrogen and water molecules mixed together in the ocean and eventually formed—where are you going?" Ira asked as Grandfather walked out of the room.

"You've got a heck of a lot of faith," he called over his shoulder. "It takes way more faith to believe in that than it takes to believe that Someone was there to create the components and write the program."

Sometimes talking to Grandfather was like talking to a brick wall. But he wished the old man was still alive so he could talk to him now. If the program—or person—called Jesus had found a way to jump from a brain implanted with a chip to the conscious awareness of someone like himself who was unchipped, no one was safe. There was no privacy left in the world. And yet, the minute he had felt uncomfortable in his encounter with Jesus, the whole scene had vanished and the lines of coding had reappeared. "Oh Grandfather," Ira whispered. "I wish I could ask you about this. What kind of an answer would you have for me?" Or what kind of question, Ira mused. Grandfather often answered Ira with a question. It was an irritating habit, but it had made him think for himself. What kind of question would Grandfather have asked him now?

Ira rubbed his chin thoughtfully. *"Do you have any reason to believe you are in danger?"* he could imagine Grandfather asking. He had to admit that he didn't. Jesus had only spoken to him. He had never forced him to do anything or made him feel out of control. He had only asked him to trust Him and to accept His "gift of life," as He had put it. And when he had hesitated and begun to feel uncomfortable, Jesus hadn't pushed the idea any further. He had simply disappeared. That would have been the end of it, had it not been for the girl appearing in the hallway, yelling out *"Jeremiah 29:11!"* and the incredible coincidence of that same scripture verse being carved into the table where he had been seated by the woman at the café who just happened to know so much about Jesus. Suddenly, Ira's eyes widened, and his heartbeat quickened. It was a setup. But not in the original way he had thought. It wasn't some State plot hatched up to examine his loyalty. It was just as Grandfather had said. Someone was behind it all. Someone had orchestrated the whole thing—written the program—and not just the one inside Piper's brain, if that was even a program at all. There were too many coincidences for it to have been by chance. Maybe this Jesus was some sort of genius programmer, such as the world had never seen, who had created the world's first blending of an organic and computer virus—one that could jump from biotech interface to an unchipped brain. Or maybe there was, as Grandfather had told him, more to life than could be seen. In any case, Ira was going to find out. He eagerly strode out of the bathroom and back into the office, and without a word slipped into the interface suit.

The soft, blue lighting that illuminated the work station dimmed slightly as he flipped down the visor. Dr. Moses and Ainsley would be expecting him to turn it on to access the program. He wondered if the Jesus persona would activate if the visor was in operation, since there was the possibility that the interchange would be monitored. Perhaps he needn't worry about whether or not the visor was running, since he had somehow heard the voice speaking to him out of thin air (or inside his head, as the case may have been). *"Ok, I'm going to turn it on now, because that's what they expect,"* Ira said silently to himself or whomever else might be listening. There was no answer—only the gentle hum of electronic devices. He leaned forward in his seat and flipped on the visor.

14

"WELL, *that's* progress," Ainsley said to Dr. Moses as Ira's visor flickered to life.

Moses kept his eyes on the monitor, choosing to ignore her sarcasm. Ira was the man for the job. He felt it "in his spirit," as his father would have said. Moses narrowed his eyes at the religious terminology as his childhood memories resurfaced. No one could understand why he felt so strongly about this.

When Craig had appeared on the road near the causeway, Moses had thought he might finally have opportunity to talk to someone who could identify with him; but after hearing Craig's interview with Detective Riedert, he realized that the man had been brainwashed. There was a whole community of people out there who were living under a belief system that Moses had found to be restrictive and isolating. He knew that Christians were comforted by being united with others who believed in the same God and the same ancient religious text. But Joseph Manaba felt that religion had been crammed down his throat since he was born. His parents had told him Bible stories and taken him on vacations where they attempted to show him the "wonders of God's creation," as they liked to call it. For them, every bird song, every mountain peak, every sunset, was a work of art by the Master Artist. They tried to convey this sense of wonder to their son, but since vacations meant less time for electronics, Joseph had grown to resent them. He was fascinated by computer gaming and absorbed by the idea of programming. So when his parents took him from the city to live somewhere in the middle of nowhere, Joseph (or Yosi, as he was nicknamed) was devastated. A brilliant child, he had few friends who could relate to him. Those who had similar interests were located across the State, or in some cases, across the globe.

His only communication with them was over the internet. Suddenly, that avenue of socializing was cut off, and Yosi felt he had no one. His parents certainly couldn't understand the intricacies of computer coding, and even if they had, they would have placed low priority on it. Their lives were consumed by their love for God. Moses smiled grimly as he remembered a scripture his father had quoted frequently: "Set your affection on things above, not on things on the earth. For ye are dead, and your life is hid with Christ in God."[33] Of course, he knew now what the scripture meant. It was some grandiose idea about dying to your old nature and allowing the Spirit of God to live in you and work in you. But at the time, Yosi thought it was the most depressing thing he had ever heard, and quite an accurate description of his situation. He felt he might as *well* have been dead; and he certainly felt hidden, because no one could find them.

No one, that is, except those people who were like-minded. After a while, families inexplicably began to arrive, appearing at the little homestead after leaving the city and wandering around for several days in the wilderness. At least after that, he had some people his own age, even if none of them understood his passion for technology.

Over the next few years, it wasn't unusual for several new families to arrive every few weeks. The homestead grew to a town. And then the stream of new arrivals slowed to a trickle. Families that had come most recently mentioned they had been concerned they would make it out of the city at all, as the government had begun to make crackdowns on enforcement of the Free Land Initiative, which had abolished private property. Walls were being constructed to keep people from encroaching from the cities into what was just then being labeled "the Preserve." Administration at the time ruled that the planet knew best how to take care of itself, and rather than man interfering with ideas of conservation, or "wise use," they adopted a policy of noninterference. The land, it was believed, knew how to heal itself. The stronger species would survive. Never mind that many of those species were non-native and invasive. Unchecked, they began to crowd out native plants and animals, disrupting natural ecosystems and destroying years of careful land and species management. The State wasn't con-

---

[33] Colossians 3:2-3 KJV

cerned. Everyone was expected to adhere to the rules of consolidation in order to create the largest land mass of undisturbed wilderness possible.

Need for swift travel over the long distance between major cities evolved into a tech race that required mining for the necessary materials. The government easily changed its tune, making exceptions and provisions for companies to be able to mine within the Preserve. It was for the overall good—"the future preservation of the planet," they said. But when the development of the new causeway alloy in factories yielded a new kind of pollution, it was clear that the environment wasn't top priority on the State's list. Legislators pointed fingers at the private mega corporations whose unethical practices and blatant noncompliance with EPA laws had been conveniently overlooked until the infrastructure desired by the State was complete. The public, which had always been easily influenced by the media, called for the abolishment of big business to prevent any future environmental disasters. The government swiftly complied with what the people had been surreptitiously guided to ask for. Everything was falling into place for the State. The people were now physically contained, and the power of free enterprise was slowly slipping from their grasp. Health implants created as a result of pandemics cultivated in the new densely populated areas improved the life of citizens, but also terminated pregnancies when the baby was genetically predisposed to vulnerability to specific viruses or diseases or had what were termed "unresolvable defects." When populations recovered and eventually spiked, medical technicians made certain that implants would automatically and indiscriminately terminate pregnancies without the consent or knowledge of parents until the desired population level was reached. In the same way, demographics were also effectively controlled, the outcomes depending on the desires of administrators of the world government, which was itself only in the stages of infancy.

Moses was aware of the government's questionable methods of gaining control. But only with its power and resources would he be able to reach his goal of global consciousness. He reasoned that with this goal achieved, all administrators would become transparent. Checks and balances would be put in place. Corruption would be a thing of the past, no one could hide their motives, and no one would ever have to be lonely again. There would be no need for the belief system that had left him feeling trapped and intellectually isolated. Intellectual freedom would be paramount, and that included freedom of worship. But no one could force their personal philosophical or religious concept on another. The Christian God had no place in the new world order, as far as he was concerned. There would be no need for it, since the human race would be neurally connected and harmony of consciousness would be achieved.

When he had left Adullam, he had some inkling of the vision he had for society. He just didn't know if it could be accomplished with existing technology. By the time he reached the city and was picked up by authorities, he knew his purpose in life. When they asked him who he was, he answered easily. "My name is Joseph Moses," he told them. His given name was Joseph, and like the biblical Joseph, he was a dreamer—a visionary. And similar to Moses in the book of Exodus, he was going to lead his people out of bondage—not from literal slavery, but from the physical and intellectual confinement of spiritual darkness into intellectual enlightenment and what he believed would be the next evolutionary step of humankind.

15

Janice Druthers sighed contentedly as she surveyed the beautifully patterned brickwork before her. Her protective wall was complete, filled with the promises of God. She had spent hours meditating on the verses that compiled her boundary, made available to her—ironically—by the very chip that was intended to abolish dependance upon their truth. Since it gave her the ability to access files and memories easily, she could call up any one of them at any time she needed. Piper had helped her with the initial foundation of the wall, and when it was clear they needed divine help to finish before Ainsley and Dr. Moses attempted to force their way in, Piper asked for it. She simply asked and believed, and they received.

Now that Janice's wall was complete, Piper had told her she needed to start making new pathways of thought in her mind. These pathways couldn't be like the old ones, which were founded upon what Janice had wanted out of life before she met Jesus. And Janice found she didn't mind it, because she didn't have the same desires as before. In fact, she had decided to run everything through "the Filter," as Piper called it. Whenever Janice would begin to think about something, she would use Philippians 4:8 to determine if it was worth thinking about, or if it was something that might make a path that led to destruction. "If it's not true, honorable, just, pure, lovely, admirable, virtuous, and praiseworthy, it's not worth havin' ya mind camp out on it," Piper had told her.

Piper then gave her a verse to start her first new path—Psalm 37:4. "Delight thyself also in the Lord; and He shall give thee the desires of thine heart." Janice sat still for a while and thought about what the verse meant to her. When she had called out to Jesus, He had lifted her up out of the turbulent ocean of madness she had landed in when Ainsley had pushed her out of her own mind. He had placed her upon a solid rock that was impervious to the storm raging around her, had whisked Ainsley away, and had set Himself down as the new foundation of her life. She no longer hated herself because she knew that Jesus loved her. Janice knew she wasn't perfect, but if Jesus loved her, He must see her as someone who was worthwhile. "You thought I was worth saving," Janice said wonderingly, as she stood at the beginning of her new path.

"Indeed, I did," Jesus whispered to her.

Janice turned around to see Jesus standing behind her, His eyes full of unconditional love. "Oh, Jesus, I don't know what You saw in me, but I'm glad You saw it!" she exclaimed.

Jesus beamed. "I made everyone with a specific purpose in mind. What I saw in you was the original plan I had for you before the curse of sin took hold. But one thing that every person shares in common is My love for all of you.[34] I am not willing that any should perish, but that all would come to know Me and want a relationship with Me."[35]

Janice bit her lip. "Piper said I need to start making paths. But what if I do it wrong? I don't want to disappoint You!"

"Daughter, I know your heart. And it is perfect to Me. Did you know that I am constantly searching the earth for those whose hearts are perfected in Me?"[36]

Janice blushed. "Oh Lord, You of all people should know I'm not perfect."

"To Me, you are perfect. Perfect doesn't just mean without fault—although since your sins have been forgiven and forgotten, you are blameless in My eyes. But perfect also means completed and made whole. You used to search here and there for happiness and depended on the approval of others. But now, as My Word says, you are complete in Me.[37] And I have seen the results of that in your life, because you are continually seeking ways to draw closer to Me," Jesus explained. "You never have to question My love for you. As you learn more about Me and walk with Me down these paths you are creating, you may make mistakes. But I will be with you to help you overcome them; and in this process, you will become stronger."

---

[34] See John 3:16
[35] See 2 Peter 3:9
[36] See 2 Chronicles 16:9
[37] See Colossians 2:10

Janice smiled gratefully. "Thank You, Jesus!" She looked again at the prospective pathway, which was still nothing but a barren wasteland from her former life. But across the desert expanse, a golden glow emanated from the center of her mind. This, she had learned from Piper, was the peace of God. "I love the feeling of peace You've given me," Janice said. "I just wish I could make this desert wasteland into a beautiful garden. Is there any way we could do that?"

Jesus looked across the desert. "Some of the most beautiful gardens have a desert theme and contain plants that are quite breathtaking. Take this cactus, for instance," he said, indicating one of the saguaros that stood like giant sentinels across the expanse.

Janice looked up at the cactus, which was festooned with arm-like branches. One of the arms was stretched down toward them, as if warning them away with its spines. She realized it was connected to a painful memory. "I don't like thinking about that one," she said.

"I know," Jesus said. "That's why you grew spines all over it. You wanted to keep yourself away from the memory by putting up a barrier. But I came to heal you of your past hurts. Are you willing to face them and forgive those who hurt you so that I can do My work of healing in your life?"

Janice looked closely at the cactus. Piper had told her something about forgiveness. She said Jesus had shown her parts of her life where she needed to forgive someone. Piper even had to learn to forgive *herself*. She had also said it wasn't easy.

"I really don't like thorns. They hurt," Janice said timidly.

"I know," Jesus said.

It was then that Janice noticed the ragged scars around his brow. Suddenly, she felt ashamed she had mentioned the spines on her cactus. She looked into Jesus' eyes and declared, "If You can wear thorns for me, I can deal with the thorns I made for myself."

Jesus smiled gently and put His hand on her shoulder. "We'll do this together," He said, as they faced the painful memory. It was an old one, where her classmates had made fun of her. She could still hear them calling her names like "fat" and "stupid." Tears began running down Janice's cheeks. She hadn't thought about the incident in a long time. Suddenly, she felt Jesus' reassuring arm around her. "You know, a lot of people made fun of Me, too. They called Me names and said things about Me that weren't true. I know just how you feel."

Janice looked up at Him, surprised. "They said bad things about *You?* But You are the Son of God! Why did You let them do that?"

"They didn't know what they were doing, so I asked My Father to forgive them. The people who hurt you didn't really understand the damage they were causing you—and themselves, spiritually. You can hang onto the hurt they caused you, or you can forgive them and pray for them, like I did for those who were cruel to Me," Jesus explained.

Janice thought about each person involved, and one by one, she began to name them and tell them she forgave them. She looked up at the cactus. The spines seemed to have lost some of their sharpness, and suddenly, a feeling of compassion came over her for her old classmates. She wondered if they had ever even heard of Jesus. "Oh, Jesus! I want them *all* to meet You. Is there any way I could introduce them to You?" she asked.

Jesus smiled. "I would love that," He said. "Why don't we ask My Father to prepare their hearts for such a meeting? And you can also ask that others would be placed in their pathways to be effective witnesses for Me. They can introduce Me to the classmates you won't see again. You can pray for those witnesses to be sensitive to the way I'm leading them. Ask all of these things in My name, and they will be done."[38]

Janice bowed her head and began to pray. When she was done, she raised her head and looked at the cactus in amazement. A bright bunch of yellow and white blooms had opened at the end of the branch that was stretched toward them, as if it were offering them a bouquet. "Oh, my goodness!" she exclaimed.

"It's a good beginning to a wonderful garden," Jesus commended her. "You delighted yourself in Me, and because of it, you have begun to have the same desires I do. Forgiving those who hurt you and telling them how much I love them is something very dear to My heart."

"It's making my old, scary cactus look beautiful!" Janice mused.

---

[38] See John 14:13

"It certainly is," Jesus agreed. "And that brings us to the next step on your path: 2 Corinthians 5:17—*Therefore if any man be in Christ, he is a new creature: old things are passed away, behold, all things are become new.*"

As Janice spoke the words with Jesus, clusters of Mexican Gold Poppies and Coulter's Lupine sprang up on either side of the pathway ahead. "That's incredible!" Janice marveled as she took in the flaming orange blossoms and spikes of vibrant blue that were spreading outward from the path, spattering the hillsides with their colorful hues.

"Isn't it?" Jesus laughed. "Your past is over, Daughter. You are a new creation in Me. And as you apply My promises to your life, every part of you is becoming beautiful, for all of the promises of God in Me are yes and Amen.[39] You will still encounter a cactus here and there. But I will help you to soften their spines and to turn them into something lovely."

Suddenly, a gentle thumping sound could be heard, as if someone was tentatively knocking on a door. Janice looked apprehensively toward her wall. "What's that?" she asked nervously. "Is Ainsley trying to get in? Is she trying to trick me into opening the door?"

"No, that isn't Ainsley," Jesus said, looking toward the wall with a pleased expression. "It's the grandson of a friend of Mine. Over many years, My friend asked Me to prepare his grandson's heart to receive Me, much as you just asked Me to prepare the hearts of your old classmates. He also asked Me to place people in his grandson's path who would be effective witnesses of My love."

"Did anyone ever do it?" Janice asked. "Did anyone become an effective witness?"

Jesus smiled at her. "Yes. Two of My followers have already been in contact with him and have told him of My love. And I have met him before, but he isn't sure I'm real."

"How could anyone meet You and not know You're real?" Janice asked, dumbfounded.

"If the gospel is hidden, it is hidden to those who are lost. The enemy has blinded the minds of those who don't believe so that they can't see Who I really

---

[39] See 2 Corinthians 1:20

am."[40] Jesus explained. "That's why I need people like you and Piper and your friend Luciana."

"Luciana?" Janice blinked. It seemed like an eternity since she had thought of the outside world. "Does Luciana know Who You are?" And then Janice remembered the night Viv had met her at Talk-o-Lot Chocolate. "Luciana was trying to tell me about You, wasn't she?"

"Yes, she was."

"Oh, and so was Viv!" Janice said sadly. "I didn't understand. I hadn't met You yet, and I didn't think You were real," Janice said sadly.

"But then, because Viv had told you about Me, you called to Me when you needed My help."

"I wish I had listened to her earlier," Janice said regretfully.

"Don't worry about the things in your past that you can't change. You have had to go through some very difficult things because of the choice you made that night to take the chip. But because you did, you can be an effective witness for Me now."

Janice's eyes opened wide. "You want *me* to be a witness?" she asked worriedly. "But what if I say the wrong thing? What if he won't listen? What if I make him decide not to accept You because I mess it all up?"

Jesus looked at her patiently. "Janice, all I'm asking you to do is to tell him the truth. What he decides to do with that information is up to him. Will you do this for Me?"

Janice swallowed nervously. "I'll try. But can You help me?"

"Of course, I will," Jesus said.

"Then I'm all in," Janice said bravely.

Jesus grinned. "That's My girl."

Once again, a knocking was heard. "I'm coming!" Janice said as she made her way back down the path to her wall.

---

[40] See 2 Corinthians 4:3-4

16

Iʀᴀ glanced back and forth at the scene before him, a bit surprised at his surroundings. Dr. Moses and Ainsley had described this particular "system" as being protected by the lines of code that had appeared after Ainsley had been ejected from the program interface. "Or kicked out of someone's mind, rather," Ira seethed. The fact that the two would attempt to strong-arm themselves past a person's neural boundary to form a forced link was reprehensible. The fact that they thought they were tricking him into doing the same thing so that he would proceed unhindered by the restrictions of his conscience was almost as bad as the crime, itself.

But what appeared before him was not the code he had seen when he first encountered Piper's neural boundary. It was very much a physical representation of a wall—different than Piper's impenetrable fortress of natural red rock, but just as formidably impassable in its own way. As far as he could see from left to right was a wall made of perfectly cut stone bricks, their color ranging from burnt sienna to a sunbaked, creamy yellow. The bricks were arranged in such a way as to form a meticulous pattern of damask roses and intertwining, bristly vines that reached from the ground skyward to a towering, indeterminable height. The immense roses were so artfully created within the pattern that they seemed three-dimensional, as if one could come close enough to lean into a blossom and be enveloped in its scent. And then there were the thorns that stood watch over the vines, as if to warn those who intended harm that their power to protect the resident behind them was nothing with which to trifle. Ira stared in fascination for a few moments, his eyes taking in the impossibly intricate pattern created by the mere stacking of multicolored bricks. He had never seen another wall like it, in the world of neural boundaries *or* the physical world. "There's no way I would intrude upon someone with so grand a presence as the person behind this wall," he mused to himself.

No sooner did the thought occur to him than a door appeared in the brickwork. Ira's heart jumped, his body tingling with adrenaline. Just as it had with Piper's wall, a door had appeared out of nowhere when he had thought about the act of approaching it. Seemingly made of pure gold and gothic arch in shape, it was adorned from top to bottom in a delicate arabesque pattern. Ira gasped at its beauty. "Oh my goodness!" he whispered. *Who lives here?* he wondered. And he realized that even had he not been assigned the task of decoding this neural boundary, he was captivated by its beauty and longed to see the person who lived within. Without even thinking about what he was doing, he approached the door and knocked tentatively, as a subject might approach a queen. He waited with anticipation. There was no answer at first. Dare he knock again, or would he offend the occupant? He waited for what seemed like a polite interval, and then knocked.

From somewhere behind the extravagant wall came the reply. *"I'm coming!"*

Ira drew back from the door. Would this person be at risk if she opened it? What should he do? Would Dr. Moses and Ainsley be able to see what was happening? Suddenly a thought occurred to him. Maybe the Jesus persona within the program could erect some sort of a neural firewall to keep them out. Actually, maybe that's what had happened in the first place. Well, it couldn't hurt to ask. It seemed to be reading his thoughts anyway, so why not put forth the proposal? "Uh, Jesus—or whoever you are—I would really like to meet the person behind this door. But surely you must know they're in danger if Dr. Moses and Ainsley can see that it's being opened. Can you please keep them from finding out? I don't want any part of harming this individual. I'm backing away from the wall now. I don't know how to warn this person without alerting Dr. Moses to my intentions." As he was attempting to think of something he could say out loud to warn the person behind the wall, the door opened.

Ira gasped, in spite of himself. Standing in the doorway was a woman wearing a simple, yet elegant dress with a lovely floral print. He couldn't put his finger on it, yet something about her struck him as stunningly beautiful. "Hello," she said warmly. Her eyes were the color of an inviting pool of water under a sun-bleached summer sky. "Won't you come in?"

"Uh, uh, why I'd be delighted," Ira stammered shyly, and gulped as he passed through the threshold. He waited as the woman carefully shut and bolted the door behind her, and then ventured to say, "I'm actually surprised you let me in. I fear you are in serious danger."

"I suppose you're referring to Dr. Moses and Ainsley," the woman remarked. "You don't need to worry about them. I'm not going to let them in."

"I'm just afraid they'll realize I made it past your door. I wanted to warn you, but I wasn't sure how to do so without them knowing about it," Ira said worriedly.

"It's okay. Even if you had warned me, I still would have let you in," the woman said with a genuine smile.

That was it, Ira realized. That was part of it, anyway. Her beauty was based on her genuineness, as well as something else he hadn't quite figured out. "Why? Why would you have let me in?"

"A friend of your grandfather's asked if I would talk to you," she said simply.

Ira closed his eyes, trying to remember his grandfather's friends. Being rather eccentric, Grandfather hadn't had many. Having no success, he opened his eyes again to the scene of the woman in what appeared to be a flowering garden in the desert. "What is this friend's name?" he queried.

The woman paused, as if she was gathering courage to tell him something extraordinary. "His name is Jesus. He's been trying to reach you, but He told me you weren't certain He was real."

Ira felt as if the ground had dropped from beneath him. "What do you mean, real? Like a real person? Or like a real part of a computer program?"

The woman giggled, and it was such an infectious sound that Ira found himself laughing with her—and delighted to do so. "Jesus isn't a computer program," she said.

"A computer programmer, then?" Ira ventured.

"No, well—maybe," the woman seemed to ponder for a moment. "He certainly could be if He wanted to, but that seems like a boring pastime for someone like Him." The woman gestured to her wall. "He made that for me in about two seconds," she said, staring at the patterned brickwork as if it were a love letter. And then Ira knew the rest of the secret to her beauty. She knew she was loved.

"He made this wall to protect you because He loves you so much," Ira said, astounded.

"Yes," she said in amazement. "I don't understand what He sees in me, although He did try to explain it. But that's the thing. It's not just me that He loves. He loves us *all*, and He's trying to let us know. He wants to help us be what He created us to be."

"You mean, when He programmed—uh, *made* your wall?"

"No. When he created *us*. Not our neural wall, but all of us, as individuals."

"All of whom? Who do you mean?"

"Well, Piper and your grandfather and you—even Dr. Moses and Ainsley. By all, I mean *all* of us—the human race."

Ira paused to consider what she had just said. It was obvious that, just like Piper, she believed that Jesus was not just one of many mythological names for the Source. To her, Jesus was *the* Source. The God of the universe. And then something else she had just said registered with him. "Now, wait a minute," he said, flabbergasted. "Are you saying that you know Piper?"

"Yes. Piper came to teach me how to protect myself by learning God's Word. Jesus told me He had also asked her to talk to you about Him. And He asked Luciana, too," the woman explained.

"Luciana? Do you mean the woman at the café?" Ira's head was reeling.

"Yes. How is she doing? I haven't been able to see her in a while," the woman asked with concern.

"She seems well," he replied and wrinkled his brows in amazement as he considered the careful planning involved in all of the coincidences he had experienced in the last twenty-four hours. Her explanation fit in with his theory that the whole thing was a set-up. "So you're saying Jesus asked you and Piper and Luciana to talk to me because he was a friend of my grandfather?"

"Yes. Because your grandfather asked Him to send people to talk to you about Him."

"Why didn't Grandfather just tell me himself?"

"Would you have listened?" the woman asked. "I know that when one of my best friends told me about Jesus, I didn't understand. I didn't believe. It wasn't until I was at my last resort that I called out to Him for help, and He answered. When I called out to the Source, nothing happened. But when I called on Jesus, He rescued me! And you know what? If it hadn't been for my friend telling me about Jesus in the first place, I might not have known to call out to Him. So in a way, I guess she's responsible for me being saved."

Ira stood watching the woman and suddenly realized he hadn't even asked her name. "I'm sorry, but I've been terribly rude. I didn't introduce myself when I knocked on your door. My name is Ira Owens."

The woman smiled shyly. "My name is Janice Druthers. I'm so pleased you came."

Ira blushed and cleared his throat. "It's unfortunate that we've met under these circumstances. I'm afraid I've been asked to attempt to break the very code that is protecting your mind. I would have refused, but I don't have much of a choice. They think that this protection that you and Piper have is some sort of malware that is spreading. You may be in serious danger if they don't think I can solve this problem."

A shadow of worry passed across Janice's face, but then she smiled as if reassured. "Have no anxiety about anything, but in everything by prayer and supplication with thanksgiving let your requests be made known to God. And the peace of God, which passes all understanding, will keep your hearts and your minds in Christ Jesus."[41] As Janice spoke the words, a golden glow seemed to emanate from the center of her mind, warming them both with a feeling that was foreign to Ira.

"Wha-what is that?" Ira asked, basking in the light as it fell on his skin.

"That is the peace of God," Janice said, with a faraway look in her eyes. "It's still new to me, but I don't know how I got along without it for so long!"

"I've never felt anything like it." Ira stood perfectly still, afraid that if he moved, the moment would be spoiled.

"Would you like to keep it?" Janice asked suddenly.

---

[41] Philippians 4:6-7, RSV

"Uh, I, well, what do you mean? You mean you can give it to me somehow?"

Janice laughed, but not in a way to make him feel small. He could see she was delighted that he was interested. Everything about her was so genuine, like Piper had been.

"*I* can't give you peace. But I know Someone Who can. And you've already met Him once."

"I assume you're talking about Jesus," Ira said. Unwilling to throw away what he felt were logical explanations for the order of the universe, he asked her again, "Who is he? If he's not a programmer, then who—or what—is he? Is he a physical representation of the code that makes up your wall?"

Janice smiled patiently. "Jesus is the Son of God. He left Heaven to come down here and live like one of us. He wanted us to know that He understands what we're going through because He's been through life down here. He understands what it's like to be hurt and depressed and rejected. He understands, and He *cares*. So when I talk to Him, I don't have to wonder if He has any idea how I feel. He knows *exactly* how I feel, and He wants to help me be an overcomer. That's why He is helping me build new pathways of thought in my mind—pathways that lead to a stronger relationship with Him. I just started this one," she said, gesturing to an inviting trail that meandered through the glorious desert vista.

Ira found himself wishing he had time to go on a hike. "That is quite lovely," he said. "But can you tell me, has Jesus found a way to make this program jump from someone with a chip to someone who doesn't have one?"

Janice looked at him quizzically. "I'm pretty new to this technology stuff since I just got the chip, but I can tell you that Jesus doesn't speak to me the way the chip communicates by interfacing with my brain. He doesn't use a program. He just talks to me—like you're talking to me. And He shows me what He's like through His Word. When I learn a new verse and think about it, it helps me to understand Who He is and what He's like. It makes me feel closer to Him."

Ira shook his head. "But I heard his voice in my head. It was like someone was trying to tell me something."

"Well, what did He say?" Janice asked.

"He said he had plans for me that were good and not evil, to give me a future and a hope," Ira said. "It's a scripture reference—Jeremiah 29:11."

"Wow, that's a good one! And you see, He *was* trying to tell you something," Janice said. "He was telling me something similar just today. When I was wondering what He saw in me, He told me that He had made everyone with a specific purpose in mind, and what He saw in me was the original plan He had for me before the curse of sin took over my life."

"But why is he telling me all of this now? Why was he silent my whole life and all of the sudden he starts talking to me?" Ira said, surprised at his own perturbation.

"Maybe He was waiting for you to listen," Janice suggested. "Were you listening before? Maybe He's been trying in a lot of different ways for a long time, but you weren't ready to listen."

"Well, I'm listening now," Ira said, trying to keep his voice down. "So what exactly is he trying to tell me?"

Janice put her finger on her chin as she considered the question. "It sounds to me like He is trying to encourage you," she finally said. "Maybe He wants you to know your life isn't an accident. There was always a plan. You're going to do important things that only you can do, because you have a unique way of looking at things."

Ira frowned thoughtfully. That sounded remarkably similar to what Piper had told him—that Jesus was bringing someone to help them who "looked at things differently." He sighed and wondered—if Jesus really was the Son of God, why would he need help from anyone? And what did he mean, that Ira looked at things differently?

His thoughts were interrupted as Janice began speaking again. "You know, God is all powerful. If He wanted to, He could get things done without help from anyone. But that would mean that He would be forcing His will on us. God doesn't work like that. He doesn't want a bunch of mindless slaves. He wants sons and daughters who are willing to work *with* him. If He just made things happen like He wanted to, He would be taking away our free will—our ability to make choices, or even the knowledge that we weren't the ones making the choices for ourselves. Plus, we wouldn't be able to get in on the fun of helping

Him out with His plans. They really *are* good plans," Janice insisted. "The One Who planned out the universe certainly knows what He's doing in the world."

Ira stared at her. "How did you know what I was thinking?" he asked her. "Oh of course—the neural link. You can read my thoughts."

Janice looked at him quizzically. "No, I can't. I can see you and hear you talking, but for some reason it doesn't seem like a regular link. Is your chip working correctly?"

"I don't have a chip. This is a virtual link with a Vista Vi—" Ira stopped suddenly. Of course, she couldn't read his thoughts. He was speaking out loud, just quietly enough to keep Ainsley and Dr. Moses from hearing. But the visor was picking it up and transferring it to the scene.

"Do you know why people think you're different?" Janice asked him suddenly.

Ira thought a moment. "Well, I suppose because I don't want the chip, even though I'm a bio-interface programmer. I'm not keen on humanity's headlong plunge into technology. I think people should still be able to think for them-selves, the old-fashioned way."

"I'm sure that's part of it," Janice said. "But I don't think that's what Jayka was talking about when she said that she had heard you were different."

"You've met Jayka? Did she tell you that?"

"No. Actually, Jesus told me about that incident."

Ira stared at her again. How could Jesus have known about that incident? It had happened during Ira's jaunt out into the Preserve. No one else was around. The only way the Jesus persona could know is if he had been in contact with Jayka. But Jayka was a top-secret Pod-Operative. Did this mean that the mal-ware had bypassed even that high level of security firewall?

Or alternatively, if Janice was lying about Jesus telling her, perhaps she had become privy to the incident if Jayka had formed a link with her to extract information. Still then, Jayka's thoughts weren't open to the chipped general public. Even if she had formed the link with Janice, it would have been a one-way street. Pod-Ops had fail-safes that ensured the link went only one way when dealing with people under a certain level of security clearance. Ira shook his head. The whole scenario was based on Janice being untrustworthy, and for whatever reason, he could not imagine her as anything other than honest. "I guess I don't know what you mean," he finally said. "How did Jesus find out about that?"

Janice smiled, and the desert scene behind her seemed to change. The blue of the lupines took on a more intense hue. A Vermillion Flycatcher flitted skyward from a thorny patch of Wait-a-minute bushes, hovering over the landscape in a blazing red display before fluttering back to its perch. Ira had to marvel, because every time Janice thought about Jesus, it seemed as if the whole of her neural world increased in brightness. "I didn't realize it until I met Him, but Jesus knows everything that happens," she was saying. "He knew about me even before I would give Him the time of day. And He knew about you when you were trying to help that young girl out in the Preserve—Selah, isn't it?" Without waiting for an answer, Janice nodded, as if satisfied with the information she had somehow obtained.

Ira's blood ran cold as he realized his secret was no longer safe. "Wait a minute. Did Jesus tell you about that, too?" he asked. If Janice knew of his act of treason, then Ira had even more incentive to keep her neural wall intact. But how could he do that without endangering her life—without Dr. Moses "shutting down the system," as he had phrased it? It was a no-win situation.

"Nothing is impossible, with God," Janice said suddenly. "I found that out when I was sinking in a sea of madness after Ainsley kicked me out of my mind. Remember—I told you that Jesus rescued me. And you may feel like you're in a no-win situation, but He can rescue you, too."

"How are you doing that?" Ira said, flabbergasted.

"Doing what?"

"It's like you're reading my thoughts, but we're not really linked, and I didn't say anything out loud this time. So how did you know what I was thinking?" Ira sputtered.

"I didn't. But Jesus did. Like I said, He knows everything. And He just asked me if I would tell you those things to encourage you and to let you know that He can help *you*, too," Janice explained.

"He just asked you?"

Janice nodded.

"But I don't see him anywhere," Ira said, confused and frustrated.

"There's more to life than what you can explain with science or see with your eyes," Janice said suddenly.

Ira swallowed. Those were his grandfather's words. "Ok. You have my attention. You and Jesus, both. If Jesus is somehow here, right now, may I please speak to him again? When I first met him, I remember that just being near him was overwhelming. I couldn't even stand up without him helping me. At first, I thought he might really be who he said he was. But then I thought someone was trying to trick me. I thought he was part of the rogue program I was trying to decode. But after my experience yesterday, meeting Piper and Luciana, I have so many questions. And now, talking with you, I don't see how Jesus could just be malware, or a programmer with ill intent. If what you say is true, he saved your mind and your life. I just wish I could speak to him again, face to face. It seems like everything is leading me to the implausible explanation that there really is a God, and his name is Jesus."

Janice tilted her head forward slightly and began to speak. "Jesus, I'm not sure why Ira is having trouble seeing You. Will You give him the ability to see You again?"

Suddenly, within the virtual world of the visor, Ira's vision momentarily fogged over, as if he had been wearing sunglasses in a cold building and suddenly stepped out into a blistering summer day. He blinked and tried to rub his eyes, and as he did so, a strange substance detached itself from their surface and dropped to the desert floor, wrinkling up like a shed snakeskin. Ira watched in fascination as the slight stirring of a breeze picked it up and blew it end over end to become snagged on a branch of treacherous Teddy-bear cholla cactus. The elements of the desert scene sharpened in focus. He could see every scale on the translucent skin as it fluttered in the arid breeze. And then, much to his horror, it seemed to change color, regaining substance as it revitalized into a semblance of a snake and dropped to the ground. A segment of the cholla dropped with it, as if attempting to hitch a ride. But somehow, the serpent managed to avoid the clutches of the cactus spines. To Ira's dismay, it seemed to grow, raising its scaly head in his direction, and with a quick flick of its tongue, darted toward him at mind-bending speed, determined to reattach itself to its host. Ira cried in terror, jumping backward, but there was no way he could escape something that moved so swiftly.

What happened next took place in a half second. From out of nowhere, a sandaled foot came crushing down on the head of the viper, turning it into a smoking mass of ash. Ira looked up into the face of his rescuer and instantly fell, prostrate, amid the poppies and lupines. He wondered what kind of tarantulas or scorpions might be lurking there with him on the desert floor, but he felt as if he belonged there, far, far beneath the Man who had come to restore his sight. "Jesus," he found himself sobbing.

Jesus knelt down to lay a gentle hand on Ira's shoulder. After a few seconds, Ira managed to say, "Janice said You knew my grandfather. If he really knew You, why didn't he tell me about You?"

"He tried, in his own way," Jesus said softly. "You just weren't listening. You were wearing blinders over your eyes—put there by the enemy. He's been handing them out left and right via the State's media, religious, and educational systems. People readily accept them from the entertainment industry as well. But My daughter, Janice, prayed for you to be able to see."

"Janice is Your…*daughter?*" Ira asked incredulously.

"Yes."

"Because she believes in You?"

"Because she believes, *and* received Me as her Lord and Savior. The enemy believes also, but he has no part in Me," Jesus said firmly, as He helped Ira stand up on shaky legs.

"I don't understand why You've taken all the trouble to convince me of Who You are, but I believe in You now. You really are Who You say You are. I can't explain it, but I know it. You're not a piece of malware. You're not a computer programmer or a hacker. Y-you are actually God, aren't…aren't You?" Ira stammered.

"Yes, I Am," Jesus answered, and steadied Ira as he was nearly swept off his feet by the power of those words. "Will you follow Me, Ira? I have loved you from the day I created you, and I long to call you My son."

Ira leaned forward into Jesus' breast and began to sob again. "Yes, Lord. Yes, I *want* to follow You! I want to be able to trust the one I'm following. It seems like no one understands the difference between right and wrong anymore. Even if I never get out of this mess, I want to know that I'm on the right side—*Your* side: the way of goodness and truth."

As Jesus embraced him, Ira could feel His tremendous, unexplainable love. "Oh, I am so glad you came to this decision!" Jesus cried. "I am so happy to call you My son. Your desire to be on the right side of things has always been a delight to Me. That is one of the things that everyone who knows you can see."

Ira stumbled backward as the improbability of the situation hit him. "Is that what Jayka and Piper were talking about?" he asked. "They said I was different, or that I saw things differently. Is that what they meant?"

"Indeed," Jesus said. "Morality is almost unheard of today, especially in someone who doesn't know Me. In the past, your government taught Biblical principles through its public schools. When that kind of teaching was removed, the general moral condition of the nation began to decline. It spread like a sickness, until My Word was treated as powerless, or only a historical record—sometimes, not even a reliable record. Even the ministers of My gospel began to doubt the infallibility of My written Word, leaving themselves and their congregations vulnerable to the enemy's lies. But there is a remnant of people who still believe. And it is in the teaching of their children," at this point, Jesus paused and smiled as he looked at Ira meaningfully, "*and grandchildren*, that some semblance of My truth has been preserved."

"But I can't understand why Grandfather never said anything about You, specifically. I knew he was peculiar about some things, and extremely old fashioned when it came to our government, but he never mentioned Your name," Ira said.

"Instead of words, he tried to live his life before you as a testimony. It was the most effective way he knew how, since the government began monitoring what people were teaching children at home. Even Christians who somehow manage to escape the detection of Geeves units worry about their children being questioned at school. If you had been taken away to be raised by the State, he would have lost all of his influence with you. You would have grown up a very different person."

Ira swallowed hard as he thought about his grandfather. "I wish he could have known that I would eventually meet You," he said suddenly.

Jesus grinned. "Don't worry. He knows."

Ira's brow wrinkled in confusion. "What do You mean? Of course, You must know he passed away."

Jesus chuckled. "Your grandfather didn't cease to exist. He just made it home before you. And he was very excited I was going to come meet you today. In fact, they're all making quite a celebration in Heaven right now about your decision."[42] Jesus placed His hand on Ira's shoulder. "You have a lot to learn. But right now, we need your help with some things in which you are already well-versed."

"How can I help?" Ira asked.

"Well, you know how you've always loved programming?" Jesus asked.

Ira looked at his feet. His love of bio-interface technology seemed to be at complete odds with God's plan for humanity. "I'm really sorry about that. I'll give it up. It's so unimportant, compared with the plans You must have."

"Actually, Ira, I created you that way. I gave you the intelligence and the desire to learn how to do these things. And now, that talent and skill are essential to My plan," Jesus said.

Ira's eyes opened wide. "That's why I've always loved it and been good at it?"

Jesus grinned at him. "You always had the choice of what to pursue. But, yes. That's why."

A feeling of purpose settled over Ira as he considered the words of Jeremiah 29:11 in a new light. "Ok. What do you need?"

---

[42] See Luke 15:7

17

The pain in Zelda's back made her wake up earlier than her traveling companions. She rolled to her side, eyes still closed, and the bed of leaves she had made the night before protested with a rustle and crunch. She slowly became aware of the humming sound of the causeway, so constant it had become background noise. Today, if they made good time, they would probably reach the wall.

Suddenly she felt a warm, wet sensation smearing across her nose. Her eyes shot open as she sputtered and wiped her gnarled hands across her face. Macy was staring at her, head cocked as she studied the prone figure. Zelda raised to a sitting position. "G'back, mutt!" she growled.

Macy wagged her tail and gave Zelda one of her characteristic lopsided smiles, but she backed away to a respectful distance. Even though it was still dark, the birds were beginning to stir, making attempts to welcome the coming daylight with the first few tentative notes of territorial song. Macy had been listening to them with the Kind Man, who always made a point of being still enough to listen in the mornings. She had observed Him for long enough to realize He wasn't just waiting for the day to begin and the birds to start singing. He was waiting for the humans to wake up, ready to visit with them and available to give them strength if they chose to seek His company.

Zelda, however, was listening to her own stomach growl. She raised herself to a sitting position. After fishing a piece of roasted squirrel from last night's dinner out of her pocket, she chewed on it appreciatively. She had eaten well since she had decided to stay with the young folk and lead them back to the wall. They had dined on turtle and mushroom soup, groundhogs, rabbits and squirrels—what would have been considered sumptuous fare in the outer docks.

Every time it seemed like they would certainly go hungry, her companions would pray, and the food was provided. Sometimes, it was a patch of lambsquarters and mushrooms. More often than not, one of the group would be successful at apprehending game with a slingshot. Zelda began to wonder if God was giving them special treatment. One day she asked Lelah about it. "It just seems like ever' time ya needs sump'n, ya ast 'im, an' 'e gives ya whatcha need," she said, the brown wrinkles in her face twisted into a questioning look.

"Well, He promises in His Word that He will supply all our needs according to His riches in glory by Christ Jesus,"[43] Lelah explained.

"So all ya hafta do is ta ast 'im."

"That's what He promised," Lelah had said as she pointed to Philippians 4:19 in her Bible.

"Dat don' do me no good," Zelda said. "I can't cipher out all dem symbols. But dat's what it says, eh?"

"Yup."

"Do ya believe ever'ting ya read?" Zelda had asked, her head tilted back as she assessed the girl.

"No, but I believe everything I read in this book," Lelah explained. "It's God's letter to us."

Zelda was quiet for a moment as she considered that bit of information. "You tol' me once dat God keers about all of us. How come 'e just talks to da ones what can read? How come 'e doesn' show up 'imself and say stuff ta udder folks? Cuz if'n it wadn't fah Pipah an' Selah an' you'ns, I wouldn'a had no *idee* about dat Jesus dude."

Lelah brightened. "God talks to us in other ways besides His Word. Some people have had dreams and visions, and sometimes you can hear what He wants to tell you on the inside. Some people say they have even heard His voice. But His Word is the most reliable source. Even if you can't read, someone who *can* could read it to you. That's why it's so important that the ones who know about Jesus tell the ones that don't. That's why we're willing to risk going to the State. Jesus gave us a mandate to go into all the world and preach the gospel—that

---

[43] See Philippians 4:19

means the good news—that God loves us and wants to forgive us. We just need to accept His free gift of salvation and let Him be the Lord of our lives."

Zelda rocked back on her haunches, her arms wrapped around her knees as she considered the prospect. "If people knew dat ever' time dey ast for grub dey'd git it, dere wouldn' be no hesitatin'. But Pipah tol' me 'bout da time Jesus fed a whole passel o' people, an' den when dey wanted to make 'im king, 'e went somewheres else. So mebbe 'e don' wanna be a king. Mebbe 'e don' want people followin' 'im aroun' all da time, astin' 'im fah stuff."[44]

"Those people wanted Him to be their king for the wrong reasons," Lelah explained.

"Dey tought 'e was gonna be dat 'victorious king' like you was tellin' me 'bout earlier?"

"That's right. They realized that He must be the One all the prophets had written about. But they didn't understand that His kingdom is much bigger than any of the kingdoms on earth. They were focused on what He could do for them immediately—like giving them food and giving them victory over the people that ruled over them. But God's kingdom isn't just about what is happening here and now in the world around us. His Word says 'the kingdom of God is not meat and drink; but righteousness, and peace, and joy in the Holy Ghost.'[45] Jesus told the people who asked Him about it that it wasn't something you could see. He said, 'the kingdom of God is within you.'[46] It is a different kind of kingdom—one that lasts forever."

Zelda scowled. "Well, ya can't blame dem folks fah wantin' food. But I wanna know sump'n about dat forever kingdom stuff. Selah said dat someday, dem folks what makes da trade wit' Jesus will get ta live togedder in Heaven forever."

"Makes the trade?" Lelah asked, confused.

"Yeah. Dey trade deir sins fa his rightways-nus."

"That's true," Lelah said. "Jesus never sinned, but He took all of our sins upon Himself. They died there on the cross with Him. And He gave us all of

---

44 See John 6:1-15
45 Romans 14:17, KJV
46 Luke 17:21, KJV

His righteousness as a free gift. We just have to believe Him and trust Him to receive it."[47]

"Now, don't dat seem like a stupid trade to *you?*" Zelda exclaimed.

"That depends. It sounds like a great deal for us. But for God, it does seem pretty foolish, since it's definitely not an equal trade," Lelah admitted. "But that's how much He loves us. He was willing to die for us and take on our sins so that He could separate us from them. Because He did that, we don't have to be separated from *Him.*"

Zelda studied Lelah for a moment. "All o' you'ns talks like ya knows 'im. But how can ya know someone ya cain't even see or hear, rightly?"

"Well, when you make the trade, God's Spirit comes to live inside of you."

Zelda looked at Lelah askance. "Huh. Well, *dat's* differ'nt."

Lelah giggled. "It's *very* different. God's letter to us says 'Therefore, if any one is in Christ, he is a new creation; the old has passed away, behold, the new has come.'"[48]

"Dat almost sounds like what da State says about da chip. I reckon if people knew da trade would change 'em to a new person, dey might be skeered ta go tru wit' it. Dey prob'ly jus' want what goodies dey can git outta da deal, an' not hafta live any differ'nt."

"You're probably right," Lelah reflected. "But getting the chip is completely different than having God's Spirit live inside of you. From what we've heard about the chip, it can be used to manipulate people and force them to do what the government wants. God's Spirit will never force you to do anything. He won't control you like a puppet. But when you become one of His children, you *want* to live differently. And if people only knew the peace that comes from making Jesus Lord of your life, they wouldn't let that stop them. Just think, you wouldn't have to worry about what happens after you die."

"I didn' used-a worry 'bout dat none. Not 'til Selah said I could see Pipah again if'n I went ta Heaven. I used-a jus' figger dat when ya die, ya jus' stop livin'," Zelda confided.

---

[47]See 2 Corinthians 5:21
[48] 2 Corinthians 5:17, RSV

"Our physical bodies stop living, but our spirits live forever. It's up to us to decide where we want to live for eternity," Lelah said carefully.

"Well, what all kinda choices do we got?" Zelda asked, her interest piqued.

"It's simple. You can live with Jesus in Heaven and with all the other people who have given their lives to Him, or you can live in the lake of fire with Satan and his angels."[49] Lelah said in a serious tone.

"Well, what kind of a choice is *dat?*" Zelda spat. "Who would be stupid enough ta choose da lake o' fire?"

"Seems like a pretty obvious choice to me," Lelah agreed.

"Yeah—*If'n* ya believes in all dat," Zelda had said quickly and turned away, determining that their little chat was over.

The conversation played over again in Zelda's mind as she peered into the dark forest, trying to distinguish one tree trunk from another. She stood slowly to her feet and winced as she straightened out her back. Ever since she had reasoned she owed God something for saving her from starving to death, she felt like she couldn't rest until she had paid Him back. But as she listened to the incessant droning of the causeway and thought about the possibility of being captured, her heart began to race. The shadowy trees seemed to stretch their arms toward her, inviting her to remember that she was now a free woman, out from under the watchful eye of the State. Why should she risk losing *her* life to pay back a God who cared so little for life that He sent His only *Son* to die? What difference could it possibly make to *Him?* If He was all powerful, surely He could keep the kids safe if He wanted to. She could leave now, before they all woke up. They were close enough that they would find the wall by themselves. Even if their God decided not to protect them and they got caught and chipped and ratted on her, she had heard of a place where she could hide—an old cave her grandpa had told her about that was near a place called Lee's Bird, or maybe it was Lee's Burger. She couldn't remember exactly. But if she could find that cave, she was sure she could wait it out until the excitement died down. Later, when people stopped combing the woods, she would make her escape.

Her eyes darted to her homemade spear she had left leaning against a tree, along with Selah's bow and the pack that held her meager belongings. If she

---

[49] See Revelation 20:15 and 21:8

was careful, she could gather her things without waking anyone and be on her way. She gently slung the pack and the bow over her shoulder so as not to make any rattling noises. Grabbing the spear which doubled as a walking stick, she gingerly picked her way out of camp. Macy followed closely behind. Zelda had no worries that the mongrel would return to her friends. After all, they were the ones who fed her. She just needed to put as much distance between herself and the teens as she could before dawn.

But there was a feeling that kept rising up inside of her as she walked. It was similar to the feeling she got the few times she had cheated someone—a feeling that she owed somebody and needed to settle an account. Zelda stopped. She had made a deal with Someone. And not just any someone. She swore softly under her breath and lifted her eyes to the sky that was beginning to turn from black to a grayish blue. "How's I supposed to get 'em dere wit' out gettin' caught?" she whispered hoarsely. "It's an impossumble sitch-iation. If'n ya loves 'em so much, why don' ya take 'em yaself?"

There was no answer from the heavens. Zelda scowled. "Okay, Mister. If'n ya really wants ta hold me ta dis here deal I made wit' ya, stop me from leavin'. Jus' try an' stop me," Zelda growled under her breath, and resumed her stealthy escape.

"*Rarf! Rar-rar-rar-rar-rarf!*" Macy exploded in a volley of barking.

Zelda froze. "Shut up, ya stupid, traitorous mutt!" she commanded with as much authority as a whisper could afford.

Macy would not be silenced. She not only barked, but she began running from tent to tent, waking up all the occupants and returning at last to Zelda, where her barking continued. Garrison was first to emerge, followed by the others, looking bleary-eyed into the darkness. "Macy, what is it?" Garrison asked, as he stumbled sleepily onto the scene. Gradually, he was able to make out the figure of Zelda at the edge of camp. "Wow! You're up early," he commented. "Do you know what Macy is barking at?"

Zelda shook her head. "I got no *idee*." She looked down at the dog, who was happily wagging her tail as she stared at the old woman.

"You look like you're all ready to go," Garrison noted.

"Yep. I tink we kin reach da wall today, if'n we make good time. Dat's why I gots up so early," Zelda lied.

"Well, in that case, we'd better get moving!" Garrison said. "Do you think we have time for breakfast?"

Zelda's stomach growled. "Dere's always time fah breakfast," she said reproachfully. As she followed Garrison back to the campfire ring, she glared at Macy and mumbled under her breath, "Okay, Big Guy. Ya proved ya point. I'll keep ta my end o' da bargain. But after dat, we's square."

Macy fixed Zelda with a watchful eye and settled down beside her when the old woman hunkered down by the firepit. "You kin call off yer dog," Zelda said bitterly.

"What did you say?" Garrison asked as he lowered the food bag that had been hanging from the limb of a sturdy Burr Oak.

"Nuttin'," Zelda muttered. "I wadn't talkin' to *you*." She was halfway ashamed for attempting to break her deal and halfway irritated that God had accepted her challenge.

With their energy fueled by the prospect of reaching their destination, the group did make good time. The closer they got, the less conversation was made. The awareness of how easily they could be discovered was sharpened by Zelda's painstaking precautions to avoid detection. She made certain they never left the canopy of trees, and if anyone made a noise above the level of a footstep crunching the unavoidable leaves, she would whirl around and glare at them.

Finally, around midday, Zelda raised her hand for the group to stop. "There's a crick up ahead," she announced.

"A crick?" Thom repeated.

"Yeah, a crick. You know, wit' water an' crawdaddies an' such."

"Oh, she means a creek," Garrison said.

"Yep. A crick. Except I said it da right way," Zelda said, her eyes narrowed. "Anyways, we ain't too far now. I kin take ya to da wall an' show ya how ta get in. But I tink ya oughta wait 'til nightfall. If ya hafta walk tru da fog, it won't be no picnic, but it's safer'n waltzin' in at broad daylight."

"We're not scared of being able to see in the fog. We'll just take it slow," Chandra said.

Zelda raised her eyebrows. "Not dis fog," she said. "It'll make ya choke an' make ya eyes burn. If'n it's bad enough, it'll burn ya skin. But alls ya kin do is pull ya shirt up over ya nose an' squint ya eyes real tight, like da rest of us. You's gonna be walkin' straight north til ya come to a road right near da first docks ya see. Take a right at da first passel o' docks. An' once'd ya be walkin' down dat road, ya need ta look for sump'n on da side o' one o' da doors. Once ya make sure it's da right place, you'ns kin knock on it an' git outta da open."

"How do you know they'll let us in?" Lydia asked.

"Cuz it's Selah I'm a-sendin' ya to," Zelda replied. "Leastways, I tinks she still be dere. She said she wanted to tell da Discards 'bout Jesus. So if'n she ain't been caught yet, she still be dere."

"How do we know which place is hers? What do we look for?" Garrison asked.

"I'm a-tryin' ta tell ya," Zelda said in exasperation. "I left a cipher on da side o' da door. Here, I'll show ya." With that, Zelda found a stout twig, squatted down in the leaves and brushed them aside to give herself a clean writing slate. First, she drew two squares in the dirt with a two-way arrow between them. On the square to the left, she drew four lines growing out of the top and a line coming from the bottom right corner, angling upward. On the square to the right, she drew four lines coming out of the bottom of the square and a line coming out of the top left corner, angled down. "Dere. When ya see dat by da door, ya know dat's da place."

"Is that a turkey?" asked Dania, pointing to the box to the left.

Zelda frowned. "A turkey!" she spat out the word in disgust. "Now why would I put a turkey on da side o' da door?" She held out her left hand and placed it beside the box. "Dat is a *hand.*" She traced the arrow lightly with the stick she had used for a pencil until she was pointing to the box on the right. "Dat is anudder hand, 'cept on da opposite side. Dis cipher means 'good trader'. Means you'll git a fair trade—mebbe even better'n fair, cuz da hand on da udder side is upside down, emptyin' out its goodies." Zelda leaned back on her haunches and squinted at the group. "Now—speakin' o' tradin', I need sump'n from you'ns."

"Well, maybe we better wait 'til we reach the wall first," Garrison said, and winked at the old woman when she looked insulted.

Zelda shook her frizzy head. "I made a cipher fah you'ns, and now I need ya ta make a cipher fah me." The teens looked at each other, nonplussed, and Zelda hurried to explain. "Can you'ns cipher out what da name 'Lee Bird' looks like? Or it might be Lee's Burger. It was a long time ago my grandaddy tol' me 'bout dat town, an' I can't remember da name exactly."

"Wait a minute," Thom said. "I think I know where you're talking about. My dad went there as a kid. There's a famous cave near the town. He got to tour it before it was closed to the public."

"On-a-doggy Cave?" Zelda asked.

"Something like that," Thom smiled.

"Well, my grandaddy tol' me dat Lee Bird is a dangerous place," Zelda lied. "All sorts o' caves an' sink holes a body kin fall into. If you kin cipher it out fah me, I'd sorely appreciate it. Dat way, if'n I see a sign fer it, I'll know to head da opposite direction. I wanna stay as far away from dat place as possumble."

"I'd be glad to," Thom said. "I just need something to write on—and something to write *with.*"

Zelda fumbled in one of her pockets and pulled out a rag of questionable cleanliness. "Here," she said eagerly, holding out the scrap of soiled cloth.

Thom took the rag without batting an eye. After locating a rock with a flat surface, he smoothed out the cloth and looked around at the group. "Does anyone have a pencil?" he asked.

"Craig probably brought something," Garrison said, and opened up the youth leader's pack. After rifling around for a minute, he produced an ink pen that had been provided by Viv, who had often brought things with her on her visits to Adullam that she thought the community might need.

Thom wrote the words *Leasburg* and *Onondaga* as best he could on Zelda's handkerchief and handed it back to her. She squinted at it and gave him a snaggle-toothed grin. "Dat'll do," she said happily. As she looked around at the teenagers, her expression darkened. "You'ns understand dat de rest o' dis here journey is very dangerous, huh? Ya knows dat ya can't make no gabbin' and no big noises. After da sun goes down, I'm a-goin' ta show ya da place where I got tru da wall. Den I is gonna leave, an' you'ns is gonna go inside. Right now, we is gonna stay put an' outta sight til I say so." When she was satisfied that they understood the brevity of the situation, Zelda cocked her head to one side and eyed them speculatively. "Dis might be a good time ta ask dat god o' yourn ta watch out fer ya."

The youths exchanged glances and nodded. "That's an excellent idea, Wisteria," Dania said. They all huddled together in a circle, putting their hands on each other's shoulders. Dania and Lelah made certain to include Zelda, who shuffled uncomfortably at first, but then stood, mesmerized, as she watched the group petition their God. They thanked Him for His protection and provision they had already received and prayed for their own safety and that of Zelda as she traveled into the Preserve. At the end of the prayer, they made certain to thank Him for the answers to their requests. When the prayer was over, Zelda held up her hand to ask a question.

"You'ns call dis god ya pray to 'Fodder.' Like 'e's ya daddy or sump'n."

"That's right," Lydia said. When Jesus taught His followers how to pray, He started the prayer by calling God 'Father'."

"But he was really *Jesus'* fodder. You'ns ain't even kin, an' ya callin' 'im Fodder."

"Well, when we trade our sins for His righteousness, God adopts us as his children," Lydia explained.

"After da trade, we becomes God's chillens?"

"That's right," Garrison said. "The Bible says that 'For as many as are led by the Spirit of God, they are the sons of God.' Then it says that we 'have received the Spirit of adoption, whereby we cry, Abba, Father.'[50] Abba is an intimate Hebrew term for Father, by the way. It is similar to Daddy, but it also shows respect and a willingness to obey."[51]

"So you all has made da trade, an' dat makes you 'is chillens!" Zelda said and looked at the group as if she were trying to imagine such a thing could be true. "What happens if ya do sump'n bad—like *really* bad? Does 'e un-adopt ya?"

---

[50] See Romans 8:14-15
[51] For more information on this subject, visit https://himpublications.com/blog/meaning-abba/ and https://www.logos.com/grow/what-does-abba-really-mean/

Thom spoke up. "His Word to us says that if we confess our sins, He is faithful and just to forgive us our sins, and to cleanse us from all unrighteousness."[52]

Zelda's eyes opened wide for an instant. "Ya mean 'e'll forgive ya an' clean ya up all over again? Even dough ya went back on yer end o' da deal?" she asked incredulously.

"That's what His Word says," Lydia affirmed.

"Hmmph. I knows a lotsa natural-made fodders what won't do dat," Zelda remarked.

"God's love is greater than our ability to love," Lydia explained. "In fact, Paul said that we can't even begin to understand it."

"Who's Paul?" Zelda asked.

"He wrote part of the Bible," Lydia said.

"But I thought you'ns said it was *God's* letter to us," Zelda said, confused.

Lydia took a deep breath, praying as she did so that the Lord would help her to explain it to their guide. "Well, many times, God uses people to get things done. It's how He likes to do things. He asks His children to do something, and they get to be a part of doing His work. That's how the Bible came into existence. God inspired men to write down what He wanted us to learn. Paul wrote several letters to people, but what he wrote was inspired by God."

"Oh, yeah? Can ya read me one o' dem letters, afore we goes any furder? We can't be makin' a lotta noise da closer we git."

"I can read you part of one," Lydia said. She pulled her Bible out of her pack and found the scripture she was looking for. "This is from Paul's letter to the Ephesians," she began.

> 'For this reason I bow my knees before the Father, from whom every family in heaven and on earth is named, that according to the riches of His glory He may grant you to be strengthened with might through His Spirit in the inner man, and that Christ may dwell in your hearts through faith; that you, being rooted and grounded in love, may have power to comprehend with all the saints what is the breadth and length and height and depth, and to know the love of

---

[52] See 1 John 1:9

Christ which surpasses knowledge, that you may be filled with all the fullness of God. Now to Him who by the power at work within us is able to do far more abundantly than all the we ask or think, to Him be glory in the church and in Christ Jesus to all generations, for ever and ever. Amen.'"[53]

"Dats a lotta words," Zelda commented.

"Do you understand what it means?" Lydia asked.

"Not really. Just a lotta gabbin'."

"Paul was praying for the people he had led to Christ. He was praying for them to have strength and to grow in their relationship with God. Then he prayed that they would be able to understand how much God loved them—except the love of Christ is greater than we can understand!" Lydia said.

"The last part of it is one of my favorite parts of the Bible," said Thom. "He was saying that by God's own Spirit and His power that works within us, He is able to do much more than we ask for—or even can think of to ask."

Zelda squinted her eyes. "I reckon I'll hafta tink on dat fer a while. It's hard to understan' how a great big god would wanna come an' live inside one o' us."

"It's still hard for me to understand," Garrison said, "but all I know is that He did it for me, and He'll do it for you, too, if you'll ask Him."

Zelda seemed to snap out of her study. "We don't got time fah stuff like dat. I'll tink about dat when I'm free an' clear o' da State, off in ma new home in da woods."

"But what if something happens? What if you get caught, or worse?" Garrison insisted.

"If'n I git caught, I reckon I kin still ast 'im if I wanna make da trade. If'n I git kilt, I'm a-gonna come back ta haunt all o' you'ns!" Zelda growled, and the conversation was over.

The rest of the afternoon was spent resting. As much as the teens wanted to visit the creek to replenish their water bottles and look for crawdads, Zelda advised otherwise. "Dey'll be watchin' da waters," she warned.

---

[53] Ephesians 3:14-21, RSV

After awaking from a nap, Zelda passed the time by turning over rocks to look for grubs which she collected in the old yogurt cup she had brought in her pack. Intrigued, Dania finally asked what she was doing. "I'm a gatherin' up some vittles," she explained.

Dania paled. "You're going to *eat* all of those?"

"I'd be glad ta share," Zelda said generously, tipping the cup in Dania's direction to offer her one of the plump, white larvae.

Dania couldn't keep from gagging. "No, thank you!" she managed to whisper.

"Suit yaself," Zelda said. "You'd be glad to eat dese little worm nuggets if'n you'd growed up where I did. We find 'em dere sometimes, but dere ain't a lotta bugs in da outer docks. Dere ain't a lotta dirt ta find 'em in, neider, less'n ya goes to da outskirts, where I come from."

"How do people survive?" Dania asked.

"Dumpster divin' an' pigeon trappin'." Zelda said. "Dat, an' makin' dope ta sell. I hear some folks'll agree ta suicide demselves if da State promises ta give deir fambly some foods."

"The State will give food to the families of people who commit suicide?" Dania asked in amazement.

"Dey don't really kill demselves. Da State does it for 'em. It's just one way ta guard against overcrowdin'. Ever'one's gotta stay in da city, so dey can't let da number o' peoples get too outta hand. Dey're always lookin' fah ways ta keep da number o' peoples down," Zelda explained.

Zelda warmed to her subject. "Peoples 'll do nearly anyting fah food. Some Discards is crazy enough ta risk sneakin' into da city ta git stuff we just can't git in da docks."

"How do they get away with stealing stuff? Aren't there cameras everywhere?" Dania asked.

"Oh, dey don't steal it. Dey trades dope fer it. Dere's people on da inside dat meets 'em. I don' know how dey gits past da Dead Zone, but dey do it somehow. Mebbe dey go underground in da storm drain tunnels. But I don' know how dey survive it. Too many fumes from da river ta be safe. But dat's de only way I can figger." She stopped suddenly and looked Dania in the eyes. "Mebbe dat's how you'ns 'll get into da city."

Dania's pulse rate quickened as she pondered the prospect of sneaking into the city via an underground tunnel filled with toxic fumes. "I never thought about having to sneak in after I'd already snuck in," she said.

Zelda, seeing the expression on her face, put a knobby hand on her shoulder and patted her. "Don' ya worry none. If dat god o' your'n is anyting like ya say 'e is, 'e can bring ya tru it. 'E brought ya dis far, didn' 'e?"

Dania swallowed and nodded. "Thanks, Wisteria," she said.

Zelda smiled. She felt a little guilty about keeping up her alias, but she couldn't chance the kids knowing her real name. She didn't have much family left, but she didn't want the distant relatives she still had in the outer docks being tracked down by authorities.

When night fell, the group filled up their bottles with water they filtered from the creek. A crescent moon offered minimal light as they began the slow trek through the woods. Branches whipped them in the face, stinging their cheeks and occasionally hitting them in the eyes. Garrison nearly plowed into Zelda as she grunted to a halt when she was caught across the neck by a green briar vine. After a few choice cuss words and a small amount of sawing with her knife, she was on her way again. After two hours of achingly slow progress, Zelda stopped and turned around and leaned over to whisper in Garrison's ear. "Dat's da wall up ahead," she said.

Garrison's heart leapt into his throat. He looked, but he couldn't see anything —just trees and darkness beyond. But the knowledge that he might see Selah in a few hours filled him with anticipation. She was going to be so surprised at how he had changed! As he followed the waddling figure in front of him, he wondered what it would be like to see his old friend again.

Suddenly, he tripped over something in the path. He scrambled to his feet and gasped as the object he had tripped over grabbed him by the arm. "You idjut!" Zelda whispered. "Dis is da place. Now sit tight while I gits da brick out."

The rest of the group arrived in single file, huddling around Zelda as she gently tugged the brick from side to side. "Once ya gits tru, I'll put it back inta place," she said after moving it out of the way. Her original plan had been to show them the secret opening and then hightail it into the woods. But on the off chance that they were never caught, they would need a way to get out again. What if they didn't do a good job of replacing the brick and the passageway was discovered? She decided to stick around to ensure everything was put back properly.

"Thank you for all your help," Garrison said, squeezing her shoulder before he dropped to the ground and began scrunching through the opening.

The rest of the group began to express their thanks, but Zelda shushed them and held her finger to her lips. As soon as Garrison was through the wall, she motioned for the others to hurry through. Lelah was the last in line. Before she crawled through the hole, she stepped near Zelda and gave her a kiss on the cheek. The old woman put her hand to her face in wonder. It was the first kiss she had been given since she was a little girl. She had forgotten what it felt like. She watched as the soles of Lelah's shoes disappeared through the opening. Then she pushed the brick back into place. After stepping away from the wall, she looked into the sky, putting her hands on her hips. "We's square now," she whispered, and then she picked up her belongings and faded into the darkened forest.

18

"Excuse me, Curator Bradley?"

"Hmm?" Rhys pulled himself out of his study of the ancient Hebrew manuscript he had been translating. It had actually already been translated, but he wanted to see what State "adjustments" had been made. If an accurate translation didn't match the State's agenda, it was altered until it came in line with current ideals. The State version had been heavily edited, and Rhys had just discovered some of its inaccuracies as he reviewed one of the historical books in a copy of the *Codex Leningradensis, the* oldest Hebrew manuscript of the entire Old Testament. When his new secretary called him by his title, it barely registered that someone was trying to get his attention.

"Everyone just calls me Rhys," he said warmly. "What can I do for you, Alicia?"

"Dr. Moses' office just sent you an invitation to visit their facility today between ten and eleven hundred hours. Something about interviewing one of their *guests*." Alicia stressed the last word as if she were dubious about its correct application, considering the circumstances. People didn't usually visit Dr. Moses' facility unless they were employed there or being held in custody.

"Ah, yes. Please let them know I accept their invitation." Rhys leaned away from the climate controlled, protective case that contained the ancient text. Every time he accessed one of these manuscripts, he feared it might be his last. He had been hand-copying passages of them and secreting away the copies, translating them from Greek and Hebrew and distributing them to the other members of The Closet. Now that Viv had become a member, some of the urgency to copy and translate had been removed. She owned a King James Version of the New Testament, which was one of the translations Rhys considered reliable.

Some of the meanings of the old English words had changed a little, but it was definitely a translation they could trust. His fingers rested lightly on the case. If only he could take pictures of the pages and translate them later. But photos by curators were strictly forbidden. The information was deemed too sensitive to risk being put into the hands of the public, even if it was written in Greek. If citizens became aware of how both history and the basic tenets of religion were altered by the State to accomplish its agenda, it could have an adverse effect on the semblance of peace and unity that was touted by those in control of the government. So Rhys copied the information when he could.

Today, however, he would have to leave his project to visit the Christian in custody. He wasn't certain why the Lord had impressed upon his heart to pursue an interview with the man. He only knew he was supposed to try. "Father, help me to say or do whatever it is I am supposed to say or do," Rhys prayed quietly. Then he folded up the piece of notebook paper on which he had been translating and tucked it into a pocket before he headed out the door.

Rhys had never visited Dr. Moses' facility before. It was home to the elite special forces team, the Pod-Operatives, who had been recruited, chipped, and altered by Dr. Moses, himself, and who were constantly being monitored by and updated with the latest technology. It was also home to Dr. Moses' pet project, the Liberation of Individuals from Oppressive Religion and Ideology Through Biotechnology. It was an unwieldy title, so most people referred to it as Operation Liberation, and called the facility "Liberation Station." Dr. Moses was pleased with the nicknames, but he knew the only reason his project was approved was because his mission to completely erase humanity's dependence upon faith in a supernatural being fit right in with the State's agenda. The only religion that was accepted by the State was a belief that the government was the ultimate power and authority, leading humanity into the next phase of cultural and physical evolution through its purported reliance upon science and statistics. Citizens didn't question the science, which was founded upon studies skewed to support the State's desired outcomes. They had been gradually conditioned to accept State authority as truth. So long as their physical needs were met, citizens led blissfully ignorant lives. Everyone knew that dissenters were sent to reconditioning therapy. Successful patients were reintegrated. Unsuccessful patients were chipped, and those who reacted well to the implantation were free to resume life in society. The change in such individuals upon their return was a subject of concern for their friends and family, but since any questions might result in a similar outcome for those who might ask the questions, the questions were never asked.

Freedom had slipped through their fingers. It had happened not through an obvious takeover by a hostile international force, but slowly—like a blight spreading across the globe in the post pandemic world, as dangerous political ideologies shed their spores and were carried by politicians seduced by the power they could wield in a believable lie. Differences were accentuated between people groups who had previously been making strides in better treatment of each other. Sins of the past which had been forgiven and laid to rest by the victimized were resurrected by the media and treated as though they had never been addressed. State schools taught that this was a symptom of the corruption of those in power. Well-meaning individuals rallied to the cry that the earth belonged to everyone, and wealth should be distributed equally, regardless of the work ethic of recipients. The only answer, they were told, was a complete reorganization of society—the surrender of land and possessions so that everyone could begin again on an even playing field. People who had worked their whole lives to pay for their homes were vilified as selfish capitalists. The failure of past socialist regimes and the suffering of their countries' populations were conveniently left out of world history classes. Socialist utopias were made popular by futuristic movies and weekly series on streaming services. The push toward a unified world government was increasing and the goal was nearly achieved.

Rhys rubbed his arms briskly as he made his way to the subway station, chilled by more than just the low temperature that morning in late spring. Sometimes it was overwhelming. He knew he was exactly where God wanted him to be, but he couldn't always see that he was making much of a difference. How could one man fight against an ideological sickness that was taking over the world? The words of the apostle Paul came to him suddenly. "For we wrestle not against flesh and blood, but against principalities, against powers, against the rulers of the darkness of this world, against spiritual wickedness in high places. Wherefore take unto you the whole armor of God, that ye may be able to withstand in the evil day, and having done all, to stand."[54] Paul had explained it. Christians weren't expected to fight with their wits or their fists. God had given them spiritual armor with supernatural power. "Stand therefore, having your loins girt about with truth, and having on the breastplate of righteousness; and your feet shod with the preparation of the gospel of peace; above all, taking the shield of faith, wherewith ye shall be able to quench all the fiery darts of the wicked. And take the helmet of salvation, and the sword of the Spirit, which is the word of God."[55] Rhys stopped in midstride as he realized this passage in Ephesians was heavily influenced by one of the passages he had just been studying in Isaiah.

> "Yea, truth faileth; and he that departeth from evil maketh himself a prey: and the Lord saw it, and it displeased Him, that there was no judgment. And He saw that there was no man, and wondered that there was no intercessor: therefore His arm brought salvation unto Him; and His righteousness, it sustained Him. For He put on righteousness as a breastplate, and a helmet of salvation upon His head; and He put on the garments of vengeance for clothing, and was clad with zeal as a cloak."[56]

When no one was able to stand up for truth, when those who refused to do evil became victims of it, and when there was no judgment passed on this injustice and no one to step in and fight for what was right, the Lord Himself stepped in. He put on His armor of righteousness and salvation. The apostle Paul was not calling upon us to put on just *any* armor. He was asking us to put on the same armor God used when He was going into battle. Every adopted child of God had access to their Father's armor. They weren't expected to do it on their own strength or in their own power, but to rely upon the strength and power of God, Himself! Rhys felt goosebumps as the realization hit him. It wasn't a matter of one person submitted to God making a difference. It was a matter of that one person and the Commander of the angel armies going into battle together.

---

[54] Ephesians 6:12-13, KJV
[55] Ephesians 6:14-17, KJV
[56] Isaiah 59:15-17, KJV

The passage in Ephesians ended with "Praying always with all prayer and supplication in the Spirit, and watching thereunto with all perseverance and supplication for all saints."[57] Rhys was about to visit a fellow 'saint,' a brother in the family of God, and the man could certainly use his prayers. He passed the rest of the commute in silent prayer for this brother he was about to meet, wondering if this might be his sole purpose in coming.

When he entered the building, he was met by a young man whom he suspected was a Pod-Op. The operatives didn't always wear uniforms, but they had a distinct presence about them that transcended a uniform—an uncanny alertness and quickness of movement when it was required. "Welcome, Curator Bradley," the man said, giving Rhys a quick visual assessment. It took less than a second, but Rhys knew he had somehow just been scanned for weapons. "Dr. Moses is waiting for you."

Rhys was a little surprised. "Dr. Moses? Well, I hadn't thought to disturb him or take up any of his time with this interview."

"It's no bother, truly," the Pod-Op said pleasantly. Rhys was always taken off guard when the operatives appeared so personable. They were trained to adjust to any situation, after all. But Rhys was well aware that if he had posed any threat, he could have been dispatched with one well aimed, concentrated blow to the skull. He smiled stiffly and followed the operative without another word.

Dr. Moses was, indeed, waiting for him by a door numbered 304. "Rhys Bradley," he said warmly, extending his hand in the State's gesture of greeting. Rhys returned the gesture so that their hands were an inch apart; and without actually making contact, their Palmscan implants synchronously vibrated and beeped.

"I'd like to thank you for this opportunity," Rhys said. "It isn't often one has the chance to interview a Christian with such a strict adherence to the faith. They seem to be a dying breed."

"Well, hopefully, we can help the affected individuals and just call it a dying *creed*," Dr. Moses quipped with a smile. Rhys noticed that the smile didn't reach the man's eyes. "But before you go in, I'm going to need you to sign a

---

[57] Ephesians 6:18, KJV

non-disclosure form. The contents of this interview will be confidential. I know you understand the importance of classified information, since you deal with it on a daily basis." Dr. Moses waited while Rhys made his signature on a hand-held tablet. "I'll be outside, observing and recording this interview." At that, Dr. Moses gave a simple voice command and the opaqueness of the wall separating room 304 from the hallway faded, giving them a view of a modestly but comfortably furnished sitting room. "The wall will still appear opaque from the other side. I feel it's important that we give the appearance of you being alone with Craig. He may be less likely to open up with me around. Perhaps you will find the answers to any questions you may have if I just watch from a distance," Dr. Moses explained, and then flashed his hand over the palm scanner on the outside of the door to open it. He looked at Rhys and nodded toward the door, indicating he was expected to make an entrance by himself.

Rhys gave him a thin smile and stepped through the threshold. The door shut behind him, and he could hear the mechanical click that indicated a locking mechanism had been operated. He looked around the empty room. "Hello?" he ventured.

"Hello?" a voice called tentatively back to him, and a man appeared in the doorway of an adjacent room.

"Uh, hello, Citizen..." and suddenly, Rhys remembered the man wasn't a citizen, and Dr. Moses hadn't given him any name except Craig. "Umm, Craig, isn't it?"

"Yes, my name is Craig. Craig Goforth," the man said quickly. Rhys could tell he was nervous but was making a tremendous effort to be congenial. "Are you the scholar from the museum?"

"Rhys Bradley," Rhys said, and smiled and nodded. The man stepped forward and offered his hand as if he would like to have his palm flashed. Rhys automatically extended his hand even though he knew the man wouldn't have Palmscan, and he was surprised when Craig clasped it and simultaneously made eye contact. The effect was startling, as the old custom of the handshake greeting had fallen out of favor with the onslaught of the first pandemic. He smiled and squeezed back, attempting to recover from his initial shock.

"I'm glad to meet you," Craig said. "Yosi said you'd be coming."

"Yosi?"

"Uh, Dr. Moses," Craig corrected himself. "That was his name back home."

"Back home?"

"Uhh, yeah. He and I grew up in the same community," Craig explained. "When I left, I didn't plan on telling anyone about my home town—in order to keep them safe. I only planned on telling them about Jesus. But it turns out everyone already knows there's a community out there somewhere, since Dr. Moses is here." Craig paused and shook his head. "I still can't believe it's him! His dad would be so happy to know he's alive."

Rhys was dumbfounded. "You're from somewhere in the Preserve?" he asked in wonderment. "I know very little of Dr. Moses' past—only that he escaped from an isolationist outpost. Are you telling me you're from a whole community of Christians?"

"Yes. We've been waiting for the right time to send someone back to the State. And now is the time! I wasn't certain how I would be received. But I can't complain of my treatment so far. I'd just like a chance to share the gospel. The detective who interrogated me didn't seem very receptive."

"Well, you apparently made an impression on him, because that's why I'm here. Detective Riedert contacted me because he wanted some insight into why certain Christians refuse to agree that their God is the same as everyone else's. I'm certain you're aware that if you have trouble understanding that concept, the State will be obliged to help you," Rhys said cautiously.

"You mean with the chip?" Craig said. "Yeah, I've heard about that."

"So, they told you?"

"Well, I asked one of their security escorts. She was kind enough to explain that if I didn't divulge certain information, I could be *made* to divulge it. She said most people *want* to get the chip. I still can't believe people want something put inside of them that could control their thoughts and actions. It's the antithesis of freedom. But even if they did put that thing in me and could make me sing and dance and tell them whatever they wanted, my heart would still belong to Jesus. Nothing can separate us from God's love, because His Word says so. 'Neither death, nor life, nor angels, nor principalities, nor powers, nor things present, nor things to come, nor height, nor depth, nor any other creature, shall be able to separate us from the love of God, which is in Christ Jesus our Lord.'[58]

Rhys's breath caught in his throat. That was the verse he had heard Viv quote when she came to her first meeting at The Closet. "That's a beautiful passage from the book of Romans, isn't it?" Rhys asked.

"Romans 8:38-39." Craig was quiet for a moment. "You know, I was concerned at first that they would put that chip in me and make me tell them where I came from. But the whole community was aware of the risk. If God wants the State to find them, they'll be found. But if not, they'll remain hidden."

"Have they asked you yet? How to get there, I mean?" Rhys couldn't help but ask.

"Not yet, but I'm sure it's coming. To be honest, I'm not certain I could find my way back. It felt like wandering around, really. I wasn't sure where I was going. I just had a general direction. And then I found the road. Actually, I believe God led me to it. He gave me the choice of whether or not to reveal myself. I chose to say yes—to let myself be found. I'm not sure what's going to happen next, but if He asked me to do it again, I'd do it."

Rhys swallowed uncomfortably. He felt like such a phony. He was a member of an underground church. Shouldn't he be proclaiming the love of Jesus to the world, as this man so desperately wanted to do, instead of living a double life? But he wasn't the only person involved. If the government found out he was a true believer, there would be questions. If he didn't answer their questions satisfactorily, he would be chipped, and the others might be exposed.

Or would they? "So you believe that even if you are implanted with the chip, they can't make you reveal the whereabouts of your community?"

Craig shook his head. "Not if God doesn't want it revealed."

"Are you aware that resisting the chip can have serious physical consequences?" Rhys asked, wondering if Dr. Moses was going to step in and extract him at any moment.

Craig seemed to stare off into space for a moment. When he began to speak, Rhys wondered if the man had somehow figured out that Rhys was also a true

---

[58] Romans 8:38-39, KJV

believer. "Fear not: for they that be with us are more than they that be with them."[59]

"I'm sorry, what was that?" Rhys asked.

"It's a passage from the book of 2 Kings, the sixth chapter. The prophet Elisha is speaking. He is describing what he sees in the spiritual realm when his servant brings him news that their city is surrounded by an enemy's army. When he prays that the servant's eyes be opened to the truth, the young man can suddenly see horses and chariots of fire surrounding him and Elisha. You should look it up some time, if you have a good translation," Craig said, looking at Rhys intently.

"I-I'll try to remember that," Rhys stammered, keenly aware that the protected manuscript in his office contained the complete Old Testament. He would certainly look it up when he returned to his office. "But back to the reason for this interview. There aren't very many people in the world today who feel the way you do about your religion. They believe that there are many roads to God. The State's view is that all religions are worshipping the same deity, just by different names."

"What is your view on that?" Craig asked.

Rhys framed his answer carefully. "Naturally, being a student of Christian literature, I am intrigued by Christianity's view of God. But I was wondering if you realized that you might be able to avoid chip implantation if you could simply believe what you believe, and keep it to yourself unless someone asked you about it."

"Is that what Christians in the State are doing these days?" Craig asked. "Keep the good news a secret unless someone asks them about it?"

Rhys didn't answer, so Craig continued. "Are you familiar with the Great Commission?"

"Are you referring to Jesus' charge to His followers to go into all the world and preach the gospel to everyone?" Rhys asked, his discomfort growing by the minute.

"Yes, that's it."

"Mr. Goforth, anyone who does that in the State may end up not even being able to verbalize at all, let alone preach."

---

59 2 Kings 6:16, KJV

"So are there any true Christians left in the State?" Craig asked.

"I don't know how to answer that," Rhys said truthfully. If he said yes, he would be questioned later. If he said no, he would be lying.

"Let's just say that there are," Craig continued. "Let's just say that there are little pockets of believers throughout the State, meeting in underground churches, much as Christians had to do in places like communist China and India and Islamic countries throughout history."

"Ok," Rhys said, hoping the cameras couldn't capture the fact he was beginning to perspire.

"You know the thing about those little underground churches? They wouldn't be doing it unless they felt they knew something important enough to risk their lives for. They would have to be careful who they trusted. But somehow, God would lead them to the people who were going to be receptive to the gospel. Maybe all they are able to do is to plant a seed. Then maybe a member of another church waters that seed. Eventually, that seed will grow, if it has fallen on the heart of someone who is ready to receive it. The person who planted the original seed may never know that it ended up growing and producing a crop. But if the seed is never sown, what chance does it have of growing?"

"So you're saying that a true Christian is going to somehow tell others about Jesus. There may be different methods, but a follower of Christ will naturally want to spread the news."

"That's right. But I also understand that there may be believers left in the State who have different ways of reaching others. God has called them into a different way of ministering. My way is pretty straight forward. It's what God asked me to do, so I'm doing it. But it's not any more or less important than the people who have to meet in secret." Craig shook his head and laughed. "I really don't know why I'm telling you all this. I'm not sure I'm answering your question. But for some reason I think I should tell you that what you're doing at the museum is really important. Maybe you don't even believe what you're studying, but it's important that people are still studying it. God's Word will not return unto Him void, but it will accomplish what He sends it forth to do."[60]

---

[60] See Isaiah 55:10-11

Rhys gulped. Craig was quoting one of the passages he had been translating before he left the office. He suddenly realized that he had not been sent to comfort Craig. Craig was comforting *him*. He cleared his throat as he tried to maintain his composure. "Well, I want you to know I'm glad you came here."

"You are?"

"Certainly. It's a pleasure to have met a Christ follower."

As Rhys stood up, on a sudden impulse, he stealthily slipped his hand into his pocket, his fingers closing over the piece of paper on which he had written a scripture earlier. He extended his hand for Craig to shake again, nodding his farewell. As he began to relax his grip to withdraw his hand, hoping Craig would be able to smoothly receive the note, Craig held on. "Psalm 11," he whispered. "Believe it." Then he relaxed his grip. Rhys smiled as he tried to maintain his composure, withdrew his hand, and turned to go. The door opened for him, and he stepped out into the hall, where Dr. Moses was waiting for him.

"Well, Curator Bradley? Did you find the answer you were looking for?"

Rhys gave Dr. Moses a bemused smile. "Fascinating," he said simply. "Once again, thank you for the opportunity."

"You're quite welcome. And may I remind you of the non-disclosure form you signed."

"Of course," Rhys said. He cocked his head sideways as he appeared to consider something. "I'm curious—is the man telling the truth, or is he completely unhinged? Is he really from the community you escaped from?" Rhys had believed everything Craig told him, but he was curious as to what Dr. Moses would say.

"Craig is more deluded than unhinged. But yes, he's from my 'home town,' if you will." Dr. Moses said.

Rhys wished he could say something that would convince Dr. Moses that chipping the man would prove fruitless, but there was nothing to say. "I believe he would certainly give me insight into how to go about changing the original texts to make them devoid of their original intent," Rhys ventured, hoping to delay the inevitable. "If it's possible to meet with him again and discuss the most meaningful passages, I would be able to make some valuable progress in further editing the State Bible."

Dr. Moses seemed to consider his request for a moment. "Perhaps. I'll let you know." He smiled at Rhys and turned to the same Pod-Operative who had been there earlier. "Conall will show you out."

Rhys nodded and began to follow the Pod-Op.

"Oh, Curator Bradley," Dr. Moses called after him. "Thank you for the valuable service you are doing to dispel the lies that have held humanity captive for so long."

Rhys nodded his head and turned again to follow the Pod-Operative to the door, amazed at the hatred this man had for the Christian faith.

Back in room 304, Craig went into the bathroom and opened his hand to reveal the folded piece of paper. A loose translation of the words of Isaiah 59:21 were written there: "My Spirit which is upon you, and my words I have put in your mouth will not leave you. They will be on your lips and on the lips of your children and grandchildren from now forward and forever."[61] His heart jumped as he realized Rhys was a fellow believer. He quickly folded up the paper, knowing that if it were discovered, Rhys would be in danger. Uncertain as to what he should do with it, he finally hid it in the water tank of the toilet.

On the way back to his office, Rhys's mind was racing. There had to be something he could do to save this man. But how? How could one fight against the political ideology of the world when the majority of the population was deceived and deluded into believing the status quo was convenient, if not right? The image of Craig's face as he spoke his parting words came back to him. He wondered at the significance of Psalm 11 and couldn't wait to look it up. When he entered his office building, he hurried to his study and found the passage in the ancient text.

As he read it, he realized it was about trusting God. While David's friends were advising him to flee to the mountains to escape his enemies, David was proclaiming his trust in God for protection. "If the foundations be destroyed, what can the righteous do?"[62] the doom-and-gloom-crowd cried worriedly. But David's faith would not be shaken as he affirmed in the next verses that God is still on the throne, and he sees it all—the wicked *and* the righteous. David went

---

[61] See Isaiah 59:21
[62] Psalm 11:3, KJV

on to say that God tests and approves the righteous and fights for them, but the evil deeds of the wicked and those who love violence do not go unnoticed. They will eventually be punished.

Rhys sat back in his chair. He was a relatively new Christian who had come to believe in Jesus by the convicting power of the Word of God. His spirit had been in turmoil on his way to Liberation Station as he thought about the state of the world. But the power of God's Word had stepped in as he meditated on the passages in Isaiah 59 and Ephesians 6. He reflected on the truths he had discovered that day. He was expected to go to battle, but he would not be alone. He would be wearing the same armor worn by the Lord of Hosts, Who would be fighting beside him. Now this passage in the Psalms was telling him there was no need to worry or to run and hide. God saw the efforts of His people, and He knew all about the current spiritual and political state of the world. He would fight against their enemies. Even though the foundations of American society and the world's common sense had been destroyed, the followers of Christ would not be shaken, for Jesus, Himself, was *their* foundation. A sense of calm descended on Rhys, chasing away his agitation as he thought about God's promises. "Lord, I will do whatever I can to help Craig or any other believer who needs help in the fight for what is right," he prayed. He looked again at the last verse of Psalm 11. "For the Lord is righteous, He loves righteous deeds; the upright shall behold His face."[63] Rhys knew it wouldn't always be easy or safe, but it would be worth it.

---

[63] Psalm 11:7, RSV

19

Sᴜɴsʜɪɴᴇ struggled to penetrate the stagnant, oily cloud atop the gray tenement buildings. For the last few weeks when the acid fog had crawled out of the river, it had deviated from its normal behavior. Instead of lying low to the ground in the mornings and evenings, spreading through neighborhoods and choking residents with its acrid fumes, it would almost immediately climb to the tops of the buildings where it waited to be burned away with the rising sun or blown away with the breath of a welcome breeze. Most areas of the State were still plagued by this particular form of air pollution, and the citizens coped with masks and visors. But the outer docks seemed to have an invisible shield the fog couldn't penetrate. It skated around neighborhoods to hang menacingly above the Discard dwellings, but it posed no threat to breathing. "Like some great big *Somethin'* is hidin' us under its wing," mused Dan'l Salgrove. He stopped in midstride and peered whimsically into the dirty gray mass of pollution that licked at the rooftops. "Is that You up there holdin' back the fog?" Dan'l asked and giggled like a boy. Somehow, he knew it *had* to be God keeping the fog at bay so that residents could attend revival meetings and not have to worry about battling for every breath. "We sure do appreciate it, Lord," Dan'l said gratefully. Tears welled up in his eyes. He still found it hard to believe he could converse with the Creator of the universe.

Most people would think you were crazy if you told them you could talk to God and hear back from Him. But the girl at the revival meetings—Selah, she was called—said anyone could hear God by reading or listening to His Word. She said it wasn't just written to people thousands of years ago, but it was for all people in every age. Even if some of the stories applied to the way things were done in ancient times, the truth behind the accounts stayed the same: some people do bad things; some people do mainly good things. But they all need a Savior, and His name is Jesus Christ. No matter how good or how bad you are, He can save you from sin—or even from the notion you are good enough to save yourself. Dan'l never had to worry about being fooled by the latter. He *knew* he was bad news, and had known it for a long time.

But there were others…Dan'l shook his head. There were others who didn't think there was such a thing as sin. "They don't play by the same rules," he thought, and then corrected himself: "They don't *believe* in rules." Dan'l was thinking of a gang that was gaining prominence on the south side of the outer docks. All the Gateways cared about was power, and they did whatever was necessary to keep it and grow it. Taking their name from the St. Louis Arch, they claimed they were gatekeepers. They had found a way to bribe certain unchipped citizens of the State who craved excitement and claimed their lives were empty and meaningless. Although citizens were allowed by State law to visit the outer docks, they were required to report back inside the city walls by nightfall, at the peril of their own lives. It was rumored the gang had found a way to peddle people back and forth through the Dead Zone undetected and would offer passage to those willing to pay the price. "Can you believe that?" Dan'l said in disbelief to the starlings that were fighting over a scrap of bread they had managed to snatch during a garbage delivery. "We's out here fightin' ovah trash, an' they's gettin' bored with easy livin'." The starlings were playing tug o' war with the bread crust, which suddenly tore apart and was gone in seconds. "That's jus' how it is with us out here. There ain't enough ta go aroun'," Dan'l mused. Food, not drugs, was the ultimate medium of exchange in the outer docks. With the help of the Gateways, State citizens snuck back and forth for the adrenaline rush of a night with the outcasts. In return, they brought food. The Gateways used it to get whatever they wanted from their dockmates—drugs, sex, hauling water, and gang allegiance, to name a few things.

Up to a few weeks ago, they had the monopoly on food. But since the revival had started, business was down. Dan'l had seen some of the members hanging on the fringes of the crowd, even going through the line for stew. He had been waiting for them to make their move, for surely they must view the revival as competition. He had even managed to press through the crowd and tell Tunes, the worship leader. But Tunes didn't seem worried. Said something about how the book of Proverbs said when a man's ways please the Lord, He would make even his enemies to be at peace with him.[64]

But when Cosmo, the leader of the Gateways, showed up at a meeting, Dan'l feared the worst. The crowd parted to let him and his gang members through to the first of the food line. But to Dan'l's surprise, Cosmo went through the line and ate with the rest of the crowd, staying through praise and worship and some of the message. He left before the invitation to receive Christ was given. And that seemed to be the end of it.

Except that Dan'l knew it couldn't be the end. Cosmo wouldn't tolerate a competitor—unless he had somehow found a way to capitalize on it. The next time Dan'l tried to attend a meeting, there were gang members stationed at the main routes to the outskirts, demanding either allegiance or drugs or services in return for passage. People in Zelda's old neighborhood didn't have to worry since they already lived near the meeting place, but the days of anyone else freely attending the meetings seemed to be over. Cosmo had found an easy way to capitalize on what should have been a free meal. Some of the guards were even claiming that Selah had joined the Gateways and that she expected part of the cut. Long standing attendees knew better, but those who had never been before didn't know what to think. Dan'l wanted to tell Bally so she could tell Selah, but he couldn't get past Drey and Bester. He had given them the message, but he wasn't certain it was getting through. And then he wondered—Viv had connections now. Maybe *she* could take care of it somehow. He kept his ears opened, but hadn't heard any news of her being in the area lately. She could be working the docks on the other side of the city, for all he knew. The situation seemed hopeless until he remembered the Euthanasia Clinic. It stood to reason that the people there would know how to get in touch with her. Dan'l's face fell. Those people at the clinic had killed his wife. He wanted no dealings with them. He gritted his teeth and decided to push the idea out of his mind. Surely God could take care of His own business.

He made his way to a working hydrant and proceeded to fill up an old water bottle. Reesa Shockley, a lady who lived in his neighborhood, was so old she

---

[64] See Proverbs 16:7

couldn't go out to get water anymore. Dan'l had been bringing her a bottle every day for the past couple of weeks. He even managed to save some stew for her from the meeting one night. So far as he knew, she didn't have anyone looking out for her. "Hey, Miss Reesa!" he said cheerfully when she opened her door. "I done brought ya some water."

Reesa Shockley flattened down her frizzy gray hair with shaking fingers. "My, my, little Dan'l Salgrove," she said with a toothless smile. She looked him up and down. "Well, not so little anymore. But I remembers when ya was knee-high to a grasshopper." She always gave him the same greeting, taking the water with a trembling hand. "Come in, come in," she motioned, stepping aside out of the doorway to allow him passage. Her polyester print dress hung down over the sagging flesh of her bosom. Dan'l had never seen her wearing anything else. Its Hawaiian colors were still vibrant, and except for a few snags in the material, it seemed to defy the ravages of time. "Don't ya'll have nuttin' better ta do than bring water to an old lady?" she asked.

"No, ma'am," Dan'l answered. "Unless'n ya wanted me ta find a way to take ya to the revival in the outskirts."

Reesa looked at him, nonplussed. "The what?"

"The revival. They's havin' meetin's in the outskirts, an' they serve up stew like what I brung ya the other day."

"Oh, the *meetin's*," Reesa reminded herself. "Yeah, I heard tell o' them meetin's. My nephew, Reggie, been a time or two. Don't reckon I'll ever be able to make it out there."

"Well, we might be able to pack ya out there on a bike," Dan'l suggested.

Reesa stared at him. "Ya gots a bike?"

Dan'l looked sheepishly at the floor. "Nah."

"Well, no matter. I'd fit on one o' them like a whale on a skateboard." She shuffled backwards to an ancient recliner draped with crocheted blankets used to cover its ragged holes. With a few grunts, she lowered herself into the chair and grimaced with a pain in her bones that was familiar to the aged. Next to Zelda, Reesa was the oldest person the outer docks had produced in quite a while. "Take a seat, wherevah ya can find one," she said, gesturing to a stack of flattened out cardboard boxes and a stepstool made out of pallet wood.

"Thank ya, Miss Reesa," Dan'l said, and eased himself onto the stack of boxes. "Say, I haven't heard ya talk much about ya nephew. I guess I didn' know ya had family in these parts."

Reesa squinted at him, her eyes dulled by cataracts and the effects of years of acid fog. He wondered if she had heard him and began to repeat himself, but she interrupted. "Ya haven't heard me talk about 'im cuz I don' see much of 'im. 'Cept lately. He been comin' round now an' then. Thought 'e wanted somethin' at first, but 'e started bringin' me stuff. Water. Food." She stopped in mid-story, fixing him with her gaze. "I don' tell no one else 'bout this. Cain't trust no one. But ya been good to me, Dan'l. Ya been bringin' me water, so I think I kin trust ya." She reached in between the armrest and the chair cushion and pulled out a box of flavored crackers. "Can ya believe it?" she said wonderingly. "Crackers in a box. I never seen the like."

"Lawdy, Lawdy," Dan'l said, puffing his lips out to show he was impressed. "Only crackers I ever seen are the broken ones, an' they ain't nevah in a box."

"Get this," Reesa said, leaning forward conspiratorially, "They's nevah been opened, afore I opened 'em." She leaned back, her eyes wide and her eyebrows raised.

Dan'l felt an uneasiness begin to nibble at the edges of his mind. "Miss Reesa, howdja nephew *git* that? They ain't no way someone jus' threw *that* away."

"Well, if ya was rich enough, back in the day, ya could throw 'em away, jus' ta show off. But now, no one's rich. They's all the same in the State, they say. All got the same opportunities now, so long as they put in a full shift."

"So how's he come acrosst that?" Dan'l asked warily.

Reesa leaned even farther forward. "Says some State person give it to 'im. Outta the goodness of their heart."

Dan'l cleared his throat. "Miss Reesa, do you really believe that?"

Reesa slapped the arm of her chair, and the crackers rattled in the box on her lap. "Lawd, no! But who is I ta look a gift horse in the mouth?" She looked at him a moment and smiled sweetly, gingerly opening the box. "Here," she said, proffering it as if it were a tray of canapés. "Try one. They's crispy."

"Oh, no, I couldn't," Dan'l said, shaking his head, but his stomach growled.

"Now, if'n ya don' take one o' these, I'm gonna be powerful offended," Reesa said sternly. "It's not often I can pay someone back for all the kindnesses they do. You wanna rob me o' this opportunity?"

Dan'l hesitantly reached in the box and retrieved a cracker. It was, indeed, crispy, just as she had described. It snapped when he bit into it and crunched pleasantly between his teeth. The flavor was cheesy, with a hint of spicy hot sauce. He chewed it slowly, luxuriously, savoring the first fresh cracker he had ever eaten. "Now, that *is* somethin'," he remarked after he had swallowed. He looked uneasily around the apartment. If Reggie was a member of the Gateways—as Dan'l strongly suspected—he might view anyone who visited his aunt as someone who trespassed on his turf. "Your nephew been comin' aroun' a lot lately?" Dan'l wanted no run-ins with the Gateways. If Reesa was being cared for now, there wasn't much reason for him to keep coming by. In fact, it might be viewed as an insult—as if the man couldn't take care of his aunt.

"He come by every week lately," she said. She reached over the side of her chair and lifted up the flap of a cardboard box she used as a table, revealing a row of brand-new bottles of water beside some of the dirty ones he had brought her earlier.

Dan'l's heart jumped. Her nephew *must* know someone else had been coming to visit her. Hopefully he would appreciate the effort and wouldn't take offense. He shifted his weight and carefully disembarked from the unsteady tower of boxes. "Well, I'd better get goin'" he said with a grin.

"Sho do appreciate-cha," Reesa said. "Can ya see yaself to the door?"

"Certainly, ma'am," Dan'l said and turned to go.

"Oh, an' I almost forgot to remember," Reesa said suddenly. "Ya remember how you's askin' me if I had seen that girl o' yourn lately?"

Dan'l nodded.

"Well, I ain't seen 'er. But Reggie, 'e was askin' about 'er."

Dan'l's heart jumped into his throat. "He was? What'd he wanna know 'bout *her* for?"

"How the blazes should I know? But he said he saw you with her at the Shaw a while back. He wanted to know what you two had ta talk about, since he knew you'ns had been on the outs," Reesa divulged. "I tol' him y'all had made up an' was just prob'ly catchin' up on things. He said that the Deserter had better be careful. An' he also said that if anyone tells anyone from the State about the meetin's in the outskirts, there'll be hell ta pay."

Dan'l swallowed. "No reason ta tell anyone from the State. They'd shut it down fa sure."

"That's what I tol' 'im. I tol' 'im ya wouldn' be that stupid," Reesa said with a meaningful tilt of her head.

"No, ma'am," Dan'l said, feeling slightly sick. "Well ma'am, I needs ta go. Thank ya for the cracker."

"Oh, you is sho 'nuff welcome," Reesa said sweetly, slipping one of the crackers into her mouth and giving it a good workover with her gums.

Dan'l ducked out the door and looked up and down the hall. If a member of the Gateways had seen him with Viv, they might both be in danger. He had to get a message to her somehow. A sinking feeling came over him. He took a deep breath, squared his shoulders, and headed out of the apartment building in the direction of the Euthanasia Clinic.

Half an hour's stroll later, he pushed open the door and stepped inside. A worried receptionist was standing up behind the counter. "Mr. Salgrove, I'm going to have to ask you to leave, unless, of course, you would like to transition to the Source," the girl said anxiously.

Dan'l frowned. "I'm sorry, I don't understand."

"Facial recognition listed you as a potential threat to this facility. You made verbal threats to staff members here eleven years ago, and for that reason, I am going to have to ask you to leave, or you will be removed."

Dan'l looked at her helplessly. "But that was *years* ago. I'm a different person now. And I needs to get a message to my daughter."

"I'm sorry, sir, but I have to ask you to leave *immediately*," the woman looked over her shoulder down a hall—*probably*, Dan'l reasoned, *checking to see if anyone was responding to the silent alarm she had undoubtedly pushed.*

Dan'l backed toward the door. "My daughter works for the State. Her name is Viviana Delacruz. I need to talk to her. It's very important. If you'll just send her the security footage of what's happening right now, she'll know how important it is that I see her," he said hurriedly, and swiftly exited the building as a couple of medics appeared from the hallway. He stood outside in the sunlight, blinking in the heat that radiated from the asphalt and silently praying they would get her the message. He only hoped it wouldn't cause her any problems with her employers. But if the Gateways were concerned that Viv knew about the meetings, she would have far worse problems than a reprimand at work.

Dan'l walked down to the corner of Beat Street and Blues Avenue and turned south in the direction of the outskirts. He had started arriving at the meetings several hours before the Gateway members stood guard to take payment for passage. To play it safe, he turned into one of the nicer sections of the docks where the buildings were less etched by the fog, exiting it after several blocks when he could enter the outskirts by a less traveled, albeit less convenient, route. The walk had taken longer than he liked, but he smiled when he saw the first of the crumbling apartment buildings. It was just as he had suspected. There were no guards stationed here.

"Dan'l Salgrove," said a voice behind him.

Dan'l's blood ran cold. He pasted a smile on his face and turned around slowly. Standing in the alleyway behind him was a member of the Gateways, his association made obvious by the arch-shaped tattoo where his left eyebrow should have been. Gang initiation included removal of the left eyebrow by painting it with either water from the river or the condensed droplets of acid fog collected by leaving a glass container underneath a downspout. A few members had lost the sight in their left eye in the process. It was considered a badge of honor.

"Afternoon!" Dan'l said affably.

"You sure do have a roundabout way a goin' to the outskirts," said the young man, a half-smile playing on his lips.

"Walkin' is good for ma bum leg. Keeps it from gettin' stiff," Dan'l said while patting his right knee.

"You think I's some kinda chip-whipe?" the man asked, rubbing the fuzzy stubble of his goatee. "I followed ya all the way from my Aunt Reesa's to the suicide clinic. Then you was wandering around the Upscales, an' now you is out here. Kinda makes it look like you's tryin' to avoid somethin'."

"Miss Reesa yo aunt?" Dan'l said, trying to sound pleasantly surprised as his heart began pommeling his ribs. "Why, you must be Reggie."

"Whose nephew I is ain't none o' your concern. But who I run with, now, that *is* a concern for *you*."

"You're one o' them Gateway fellas, ain't ya?" Dan'l stated the obvious, but he didn't know what else to say.

"That's right, genius. And we wanna know why you is talkin' to people from the State. First, it's the Deserter at the Shaw; now, it's Suicide goons. Why you hafta go an' blab ya mouth for, Dan'l?" Reggie said, his eyes cold.

"First off, the Deserter is my daughter. An' I wasn't blabbin'. I was lookin' for 'er. Dat's why I went to the Euthanasia Clinic. I's tryin' ta find 'er. I thought maybe I could send 'er a message. Been two years since I seen 'er last, an' we wadn't on the best o' terms then. So when she turn up at the Shaw the other day, I was powerful glad ta see 'er. Ya never know when the last time ya see someone really *is* the last time." Dan'l said.

"Yeah, you know, that is the first thing you said that sounds like ya got a brain in that head," Reggie said, closing the gap between himself and Dan'l in a few strides. "Mebbe ya oughta listen to yaself on that one. Better yet, mebbe ya oughta tell ya daughter them words o' wisdom."

"Well, I'm sure I can let 'er know, next time I see 'er," Dan'l said, nodding as he turned to be on his way.

"You said you wanted to send 'er a message. I think I'd rather make *sure* she gets my message," Reggie said, yanking Dan'l around by the shoulder so he could look him in the eye. "See, what you don't *get* is, you start blabbin' about the meetin's in the outskirts, the State's gonna shut 'em down. An' they gonna start takin' a real close look at the docks on the south side. Now, we don't know how that girl gits the food ta keep runnin' the show. We's lookin' into that. But for right now, as long as them meetin's don't get too big, they's good fa business. We don't mind a few local folks knowin' 'bout 'em. We can collect without havin' ta put out any capital. But when idiots like you keep blabbin' to State folk, it waves a red flag. State gonna wanna know what all the commotion is, an' how they's gettin' all that food."

"Ain't ya worried they gonna wonder the same thing about *y'all's* operation?" Dan'l dared to ask.

"We don't raise no commotion. We fly under the radar. Somethin' you need ta learn how ta do. An' somethin' you gonna tell the Deserter, real clear," said Reggie, and suddenly his fist crashed into Dan'l's jaw. Dan'l staggered to the ground, his world spinning sideways. But Reggie wasn't finished. After several kicks to Dan'l's gut, Reggie rolled him over on his left side and grabbed his right leg, twisting it at the knee until a crunching sound could be heard. Dan'l screamed in pain, and suddenly Reggie was right in his face. "You don' hafta worry about rememberin' to tell the Deserter ta keep 'er mouth shut about them meetin's. Cuz I just sent the message for ya." Reggie stood up and surveyed his work with a smirk as he stepped back and then swaggered down the alleyway in the direction Dan'l had been walking.

For a few minutes, the only sound was Dan'l's ragged gasps and moans and the hum of the causeway in the distance. Dan'l hovered on the brink of consciousness, knowing there was very little chance of help arriving. He had purposefully chosen a less traveled route to the outskirts, hoping he would be undetected. But after only a few minutes, he could hear footsteps approaching. "Hey, bro? Are ya okay, man?" said a nasally voice. Dan'l opened his eyes and was amazed to see Drey and Bester squatting on the pavement in front of him.

"Gateway Gang," Dan'l mumbled.

Drey looked up and down the alleyway. "Well, dey's gone now."

"I gotta get to the meetin'. I gotta talk ta Selah," Dan'l managed to say, spitting out blood between breaths.

"Ya'll ain't in any shape ta go to da meetin'," Bester said. "Ya'll need ta go to da health clinic."

"I ain't goin' ta no clinic. The Gateways see me with any State folk, they gonna *kill* me, nex' time. You take me ta Selah. *Please!*" Dan'l begged.

Bester looked at Drey doubtfully, but stood up. "If'n you can stay wit' 'im, I got an *idee*. I tink Bally's mama might have a rolly chair dey kyped from da clinic years ago." He reached into his jacket and pulled out a partially full bottle of water. "Dis only have a few swallers left in it, but ya try an' git 'im ta drink it," he said, handing the crinkly old plastic to Drey.

"Hang in dere, Mister," Drey said as Bester's footsteps pounded down the alley. "Whatcha name, anyhow?"

"Dan'l," Dan'l breathed out his name and gasped for his next breath.

"You's dat dude what told us da Gateways was collectin' on da meetin's," Drey said. She held the bottle to his lips and Dan'l took a swallow, choking and coughing as he did. Drey felt helpless, and then she laid a hand on Dan'l's shoulder and did the only thing she knew that could help. "Lord, dis man is in terrible need of Ya help. I know You is on a healin' rampage lately. So rampage 'im up, real good, wouldja please? Fodder, I ast it in da name of Ya Son, Jesus."

Dan'l listened, captivated and soothed somehow by the simple plea for help. Just the thought that someone else cared enough to pray for him was surprising. And then, Drey began to say something else. Dan'l couldn't understand any of it. It sounded like a different language, but as she prayed, a power seemed to emanate from her voice and the hand that rested on his shoulder. The pain began to subside a little. By the time Bester arrived with the wheelchair, Dan'l no longer felt as if he were going to lose consciousness at any moment.

"Now, we is gonna try ta git ya in dis here rolly chair," Bester said. "We gonna try not ta hurt-cha, but I 'pologize in advance if'n we do." With that, the two teenagers hooked their arms under the crook of his shoulders and dragged him into an upright position. Dan'l cried out in pain, in spite of himself. He had felt better after the prayer, but as a searing sensation shot through his knee, he feared it would never work again.

"I's sorry," Drey said. "We's tryin' ta be gentle."

"Jus' git me to the meetin'. What's you two doin' out here, anyway? Ain't ya sposed ta be down by Zelda's place already?"

Drey looked at Bester. Neither one of them had understood why Selah told them to go to the Upscales. She just said she had what she called a "burden" for someone in that direction. She had a feeling that they should go there and invite people to the meeting that night. "I don' know, rightly," Drey confessed. "But I tink it was God's *idee*."

20

"I can't believe we're here!" Dania whispered to Thom, her eyes shining.

"I know," he replied, his eyes fixed on the streetlights in the distance. "I hope we can find the place Wisteria told us about before someone sees us." The small band of teens had quietly trekked toward the lights in the distance after emerging on the other side of the massive, gray brick wall. Although their guide had warned them of treacherous fog, it was nowhere to be seen.

"We should be coming to a road soon," Dania remarked.

Almost as if on cue, Garrison, at the front of the line, stopped and turned to face the others, pointing to the ground. *It's the road,* he whispered when they had all come within earshot.

"We're just supposed to follow it until we reach the apartments and then turn right, *right?*" Lydia asked.

"That's what she said," Chandra nodded.

"Jesus, go with us!" Lelah prayed, her teeth chattering slightly.

"Are you cold?" Thom asked.

"No, just really scared!" Lelah admitted. "I know God is with us, but I'm still nervous."

Garrison took a deep breath, hoping he could sound brave for the others. "Me too. But as you said, God is with us, and He asked us to do this. He wouldn't bring us this far and then abandon us."

"Wisteria said the same thing—in other words," Dania said.

"Well, I guess we'd better keep moving. We need to get there and find that apartment before daylight," Thom said.

The group moved forward, their feet scarcely making a sound on the old asphalt. As the minutes dragged by, the lights in the distance grew brighter, and they began to make out the shapes of buildings. A few moments later, they could hear something no one had expected. Garrison stopped and looked back at the others. "Do you hear singing?" he asked. They strained to listen to the sound that was carried to them on the whisp of a breeze.

"I hear it," Dania said, and pushed to the front of the group. "Come on!" she said excitedly.

"Wait a minute," Lydia protested. "If there's some sort of rally or gathering, it might not be safe. Everyone will see us."

"Yeah, I was hoping we could find where Selah is staying first, without anyone knowing," Chandra said reluctantly.

"But if they're all concentrating on something else, maybe they won't notice us." suggested Dania.

"I think we should wait 'til they leave," Lelah said. "Then we should move in."

"But what if they stay out all night? What if they're there 'til morning? Then we're out here in the open, and they'll see us," Chandra said worriedly.

"How about if we hang back in the alley, and if it looks like it's getting close to dawn, we can sneak behind that first group of buildings; but one of us can work our way around to the front of them and check for that symbol beside the doors. If they find the symbol, they can come back through one of the alleys and get us," Garrison proposed.

"Sounds like as good a plan as any," Thom said, and the others nodded. They continued forward. As they drew closer to the scene, the sounds of the voices grew more distinct. Someone was playing a guitar. The group crept as close as possible without being noticed, keeping to the cover of shadows cast by stacks of pallets and cardboard boxes worn soft and ragged with use. The crowd had completely filled the street between the row of apartment buildings. Many of the people had their hands raised in the air. Most of them were singing.

"Do you hear what they're saying?" Dania asked in amazement. "It sounds like a worship song!" They strained to hear, drawing as close as they dared. "I just want to peek around that building," she said eagerly.

"I'm not sure it's safe," Lydia cautioned.

Suddenly, Thom felt a tug on his shirt sleeve and jumped. When he looked down, a little boy was smiling up at him. "Hey, brah! Are you'ns from da udder side o' da docks—uppa da city?" he asked.

"Uhhh, I uhh," Thom fumbled.

"We're not from around here," said Dania quickly, as the whole group turned and realized they had been discovered.

"Well, dat's ok. Lotsa folks from all ovah da docks been comin' ta dese here meetin's. You'ns is all welcome. Dey done put da food pot away already, an' da singin' is almost ovah, but dey's still gonna have da talkin' part. So ya ain't missed da whole ting," the boy said, his dirty face spread wide with a smile.

"You're sure we're welcome?" Garrison asked doubtfully.

"Well, as long as da Gateway Gang don't come by an' want ya ta pay up," the boy said, his brown eyes wandering around the perimeter of the gathering.

"The Gateway Gang? Is that the group who's putting on these meetings?" Dania asked.

"No, ma'am. Miss Selah's da one what started 'em" he explained, as the teens looked at each other in wonderment. "Hey, ya knows what? Ya'll kinda sound like 'er, a li'l bit. Do ya'll come from da same part of da docks as what she does?" the boy continued.

"I come from her old neighborhood," Garrison answered truthfully.

"Well, I don' know how ya got aroun' da Gateway Gang, but jus' don' let 'em find out ya here. Dey been chargin' people ta get in."

"And Selah knows about it?" Garrison asked, confused.

"I tink she knows, but she can't do nuttin' about it," the boy explained. "Listen, if'n ya'll will just follow me, I can lead ya aroun' close to da front. As long as ya don' try ta go back home, ya shouldn' run into da Gateways. Dey don' keer nuttin' about da meetin's. Dey just like to recruit new members from da folks what's comin' or ta ast 'im ta do stuff."

"Ok," Garrison agreed, raising his eyebrows as he looked back at the others. They nodded, and the group followed the boy back behind the row of buildings. The music had stopped, and after a few moments, someone began to speak. As they neared the end of the first building, the boy turned left into an alleyway, and the sound of the person speaking funneled its way to them through the brick-walled darkness. Garrison's heart jumped. It was Selah's voice. His pace quickened until he reached the edge of the streetlights. She was standing on some sort of rickety looking platform, a Bible in hand, looking out over the crowd. Gone was the timid girl who had been afraid to leave their home. In her place stood a young woman who was speaking of God's love in a voice strong and sincere. It was a simple salvation message, but the anointing was so heavy that people were coming under conviction, kneeling right where they were as the Holy Spirit moved through the crowd like a powerful wave. Garrison and the others stood, transfixed, as the message was preached.

"You didn't tell me she was a preacher," Thom whispered to Garrison.

"She wasn't," Garrison replied, his eyes never leaving the platform.

In a short time, an altar call was given, and from their limited view of the crowd, the teens could see several hands raised to receive Christ. Selah began to lead them in a simple prayer of salvation. "Jesus, I know I'm not perfect. I've sinned, just like everybody else. But I believe You are the Son of God, and You came to save me. You died on the cross to be the perfect sacrifice for my sins. Then You rose from the dead, and You are alive forever! Please forgive me for my sins and come into my heart. Be my Lord and Savior! And please, help me to live for You," she said, pausing between phrases so the people could repeat the words after her.[65] When the prayer was finished, spontaneous clapping and cheering broke out from the crowd. Then several young people who appeared to be in charge came to the front of the platform with Selah and began to pray for anyone who came forward.

Garrison was itching to push his way to the front, but he felt a hand on his shoulder. "We shouldn't get in the way of God moving here," Lelah said softly.

Garrison bit his lip. "I know," he said and forced himself to continue watching from the shadows.

"If'n ya'll wanna go up fah prayer, dat's ok," their little guide said encouragingly. "I got healed o' da croup."

Garrison smiled. "We'll just wait until everyone else has had a chance."

---

[65] If you haven't asked the Lord Jesus to forgive you and to be the Lord of your life, why not do it right now? He created you, He loves you, and if you'll allow it, He'll help you to become everything He created you to be.

The boy shook his head in exasperation. "Den ya'll is gonna be waitin' a long, *long* time. You'ns can at least get a little closer," he suggested.

The group inched forward, but stuck to the alley. Suddenly, a loud, nasally voice was heard above the crowd. "'Scuse me, I need ta get tru here," said a stout teenage girl sporting orange dread locks and freckles. She was pushing a man in a wheelchair. "Dis dude needs prayer—*real* bad," she said. The crowd parted quickly as they saw the physical state of the man and realized the situation.

"I needs ta see Selah," the man said weakly as he reached one of the teens up front. Selah made her way through the crowd and laid her hand on his shoulder.

"Drey done prayed for me," he said, "but I needs ya ta pray for ma daughter."

The crowd fell silent. Garrison thought he could detect a few mutterings, and the word "Deserter," was spoken a few times.

Selah stood up tall and surveyed the crowd. "This man is asking for help for his daughter. No matter what she has done, Jesus can forgive her," she said firmly.

"She ain't done nothin' wrong, 'cept ta leave the docks an' work for the State," the man was saying.

"It ain't right," said a voice in the crowd.

"None of us were right until Jesus found us," Selah said above the murmuring. The voices grew silent.

"She's in danger," the man was saying. "The Gateway Gang done this to me, an' they's gonna do it ta her if she come back here. They think she been reportin' back to the State 'bout these meetin's, but she didn't know nothin' about 'em 'til I told 'er. An' I know she won't tell no one 'bout 'em, neither."

"How ya know she won't?" piped up a woman standing nearby.

"Cuz she loves the Lord Jesus, jus' like we do," he said.

There were some audible gasps from the crowd. A few people nodded and grinned. "Da Deserter done found Jesus!" someone said excitedly.

"How ya know she ain't fakin'?" asked a skeptic, but he was immediately shushed by those around him.

"Hallelujah!" said another. "Dat jus' proves dat God can save *anybody!*"

Selah waited for the crowd to quiet down and knelt beside the man again. "What's your daughter's name?" she asked.

"Viviana Delacruz," the man said.

Garrison turned back to the others. "Did you–?" he asked, but they all nodded before he could finish. They listened as Selah and the whole crowd began to pray for Viv's safety and for healing in the man's body.

"Do you have a place to stay tonight?" Selah asked the man when they were finished praying.

"Mama says 'e can stay at our place," said a tall, striking girl who had been helping conduct the crowd during the altar call. "We can figger out how ta get 'im home in da mornin'."

"Tell your mama 'thank you' for us, Bally," Selah said.

"Come on, Dan'l. I'll take ya," said Drey as she and an older boy wheeled the chair back through the crowd.

A few more people came forward for prayer after that. The crowd began to disperse, and Selah finally dismissed those who lingered, bidding them goodnight and telling them there would be another meeting the following night.

"Come on!" The little boy said, grabbing Garrison by the arm. "She gonna go home if'n we don't hurry!"

The group reluctantly came out onto the street, the boy nearly dragging Garrison in Selah's direction. Suddenly, Bally was standing directly in their path, her eyes fixed on the group with a fierce expression. *"Can I help you?"* she asked in a voice that suggested they would have to get past her to get to Selah.

"It's okay, Bally. Dese here folks is Selah's homeys. Dey come ta see 'er," the boy said.

Bally stooped to look him in the eye. "Hazen, ya cain't believe everting' ya hear."

"Aww, come on! Lookit how dey's dressed! Dey even sound like 'er," the boy insisted.

Bally stood up and regarded Garrison with a skeptical eye. "Where ya'll from?"

"We're not from around here. Like Hazen said, I'm from Selah's neighborhood," Garrison offered.

"Well, ya *do* sound like 'er," Bally remarked.

"My name is Garrison, and—"

Bally's eyes grew round, and she spun around. "Selah!" she called. "Selah, git ovah here!" she hollered.

Selah, who had been heading back to the apartment for a good night's sleep, turned slowly around. She stared for a minute in streetlights, blinking in weariness and confusion, until a look of shock and recognition registered on her face.

Garrison's smile broadened. "Hey, Selah," he said.

Selah's mouth dropped open, and then she ran to embrace her old friend. "You're alive!" she exclaimed, and then backed away to look him in the eye. "Have you been in the city this whole time?"

Garrison shook his head. "We just got here," he said.

"But you left home last year! What happened?" Selah was bubbling over with questions.

"Miss Selah, I hates ta interrupt, but we need ta get dese folks offa da street," Bally said sternly. "Come on!" She turned to go, then whirled back around to look at Hazen. "Now, you git on home. It is way past yo' bedtime."

Hazen stuck his tongue out at her and ran down the street, his bare feet making a soft pattering sound on the pavement.

"So much has happened since I saw you last," Selah gushed, hanging on Garrison's arm as they walked to the apartment.

"We have a lot to catch up on," Garrison agreed. "Hey, I haven't even introduced you to my friends—" he began, but Bally interrupted again.

"I don' wanna be rude, but shut up an' git inside," she said urgently, and ushered them through the door.

Laughter filled the apartment as the teens, their bellies filled with stew, visited long into the night. Finally, when the conversation became punctuated with yawns, Bally stood up and cleared her throat. "Alright. I know y'all has prob'ly got miles more o' gabbin' ta do, but we all gotta git some sleep. No tellin' who saw ya when ya came in, an' not ever'body is gonna believe da story about bein' from anudder part o' da docks."

"But we didn't actually say we were from the docks. I said I was from Selah's old neighborhood. And technically, that was true," Garrison said. "I wouldn't have lied about it."

"Well, we can jus' keep on lettin' 'em believe you'ns is from da nort side if'n dey wants ta believe it. Da Gateways is gettin' way too uppity. Dey find out ya know how ta live on da outside, dey might just force ya ta take 'em back out dere wit' ya. Or mebbe dey jus' turn ya in ta da State ta show dey can be counted on ta keep order. Anyway, no one *in* dis room needs ta tell no one *outta* dis room nuttin' 'bout where y'all come from."

Selah watched Bally for a moment, and then said, "I think we should come clean to the others about where I'm really from."

Bally raised her eyebrows and opened her dark eyes wide with caution. "Absolutely not! I's da only one what knows about it, an' dat's da way we gonna keep it. At least fa now."

"I think we should pray about it," Selah said firmly.

"I tink we should go ta bed. We kin pray in da mornin'," Bally said irritably. She looked around the room at the others. "I'm sorry we don' have cushions fer all of ya. Ya just gonna hafta sleep on da floor."

"Are you kidding?" Chandra laughed. "We've been sleeping on the ground. This is the best place to sleep I've had in weeks. No ticks, no spiders, no snakes, no mosquitoes! It's heaven!"

"Well, until I learned about the outer docks from Wisteria, I was dreaming of having a nice soft bed," Garrison said. "But I agree with Chandra. This is great."

"*Wisteria!*" Bally snorted.

"I mean Zelda," Garrison laughed. When the group had told the story of how the old woman had guided them back to the hole in the wall, Bally and Selah knew immediately that it had to be Zelda.

"I just can't believe she came back after having gotten away," Selah marveled. "I hope she makes it to a place where she'll be safe."

"If anyone can get her to safety, Macy can. That dog has a sixth sense about things," Garrison said. "I miss her already."

"Well, ya jus' better be glad she stayed wit' Zelda, cuz if she came dis side o' da wall, she'd get et up," Bally remarked. "Now come on. Fo' da last time, we gotta git some shut-eye."

The girls stayed in Selah's room while the boys unrolled their sleeping bags in the living room, where Bally usually spent the night. Overcome with exhaustion and the excitement of the day, they were all asleep in a matter of minutes.

21

JAYKA sighed. It wasn't often she allowed her feelings to interfere with her sense of duty, but sometimes it took tremendous effort to complete a task she felt was a poor use of her skill set. While the rest of her team had been sent to scour the sector of the Preserve where Craig Goforth had been apprehended, looking for other members of an isolationist outpost, she had been sent to babysit the man, himself—instructed to continue this farce of playing host to a long-lost friend. The man was a criminal, and should be treated as such, as far as Jayka was concerned. She wasn't certain why Dr. Moses was showing him such consideration.

And now this. Jayka permitted herself a slight scowl as she scanned the rolling hills. A breach had been discovered in the wall, and she had been sent to retrieve the Discards. It was a task normally performed by monitors flying drones. It made no sense that she, the leader of her team, had been singled out for such a routine assignment unless she was being punished or tested. She had searched her memory files for any failings on her part—any infractions—and had found nothing that would deem it necessary to saddle her with such a denigrating function…unless it had been the incident where she advocated for clemency in the case of Ira Owens.

Although Ira was already proving himself useful in Dr. Moses' research, could her handlers have viewed her part in Ira's release as a sign of weakness—a dangerous deviance from State protocol? She had felt, at the time, that Ira's show of remorse for his negligence of losing a subject he had been monitoring and his valiant attempt to correct the error at the risk of his own freedom had earned him a little leniency. Perhaps the administrators didn't see it that way. Perhaps this was her chance to prove she still believed in and followed the directives of the State, and would do her duty to the fullest, even in the most menial of tasks.

Jayka reviewed the information she had gathered. The breach appeared to be a natural one caused by the growth of a vining plant at the junction of the wall and a drainage port in a section that dipped down below the view of the wall cameras. There had been little rain near the city in the last few weeks, so she was unable to locate any footprints—only broken twigs and trampled grass supporting her theory that she was dealing with more than one Discard.

For the first few miles, they were easy to follow. Deer and mountain lions and humans, alike, all chose the path of least resistance. Jayka had followed the trail to a creek and lost it. She walked through the shallow water, attempting simultaneously to think like her quarry—who might be using the waterway to hide their trail—and to avoid disrupting whatever sign of their passage that might remain on the shoreline. Continuing this way for a half mile, she scrutinized the banks until she found the tiniest of clues—a scrap of thread snagged by a multiflora rose bush on the opposite side of the creek.

Jayka waded ashore, scanning the forest floor. She found at least three distinct sets of prints in the sandy portion of the bank, although there could have been more. The footprints of those who crossed first could have been disrupted by those who came after them. They all led deeper into the woods, where the trail faded from footprints in the soft shores of the creek to the slightest disturbance of saplings and brambles. Some signs were obvious, as when a member of the party had broken a greenbrier vine in half to allow easier passage for the rest of the group. An overturned stone dislodged by a foot, a bent sapling with bruised leaves—these hints let her know she was still on the right track. But her greatest find was a place just off the east side of the trail where the entire party had appeared to gather in a huddle. Jayka squatted down in the leaves to study the scene. In the middle of the circular disturbance of forest undergrowth was a space where the earth had been swept clear of leaves. Someone had scratched something in the dirt—a crude drawing of squares and lines. Both squares had four lines radiating from one of their sides. One square's lines were on top, the other's lines were on the bottom. Each square had another line protruding from the side nearest the other square. The square with four lines on top had a single line coming from the bottom corner and pointing at a forty-five-degree angle to the right. The other square's single line came from the top and pointed at a forty-five-degree angle to the left. Had they been drawn more precisely, one would have been an upside-down mirror image of the other. Between the two symbols was a two-way arrow. Jayka catalogued the image in her memory and studied the surroundings carefully. Someone had clearly felt it was important to show this pictograph to the rest of the group. She didn't need to search the internet to know its meaning, for she knew it from her childhood. The squares and lines depicted hands. It was the Discard symbol for "good trader" given as a token of respect from one person to another by leaving the drawing somewhere near their house or place of trade. It brought more business to the trader because it meant you could depend on them for a good, honest transaction—perhaps even one in which you felt you had the upper end of the deal. This differed from the pictograph in which the hands were exact mirror images of each other, which merely meant you could make a decent, fair trade. But why had they left the symbol here, in the middle of nowhere? She stood up and surveyed the area, located the trail and once again was on her way.

Twenty minutes later, Jayka froze as her enhanced hearing detected the cracking of a twig up ahead. She crept silently in the direction of the sound and was rewarded by the additional noises of stumbling and an occasional curse word. She moved through the trees as silently as she could, drawing ever closer to her quarry. The noises had stopped, and up ahead the trees began to open slightly into a small clearing. And then she had visual contact. This would be easier than expected.

"Stop, in the name of the State!" she demanded in a commanding voice.

The woods erupted in an explosion of activity. Three Discards began scrambling in three different directions from the clearing, until one of them looked back and suddenly ordered the others to stay. "Okay. We's stopped. Now, whatcha gonna do 'bout it?" asked the apparent leader of the three. "I know you's alone, chipmate."

Jayka did a quick mental assessment of her opponents. All of them were sporting Gateway tattoos, which elevated the danger level slightly, but she still wasn't terribly concerned. And if things got out of hand, she had a little 9mm she kept tucked behind her back, out of sight. It was a matter of pride among Pod-Ops that weapons were rarely necessary, as the operatives, themselves, were considered a sufficient weapon in a world where both the right to bear arms and the accessibility of them to anyone other than those who enforced State law had been eliminated.

"How ya know dat, Dune?" one of the men was saying. He looked as if he were ready to bolt into the woods at any moment. "How ya know dere ain't any more of 'em close by?"

"Cuz if there was, there wouldn'a been no announcement. We woulda been surrounded first, an' then told ta surrender." Dune grinned, exposing a tooth that sported a gold filling. "She's just bettin' we's gonna be scared enough ta stay put so she can get out the club cuffs. Square up, homies. If it had been just two of us, I woulda had us skip clean outta here. But three crewmates against one girl chipmate? That's pretty good odds."

The others seemed to relax a little, sizing up the lone Pod-Op as they slowly began to flank her. One of them picked up a sizeable rock. The other slipped a shank from a side pocket of his pants. Jayka smiled in spite of herself. She enjoyed a challenge. It wasn't *much* of a challenge, but it was better than the usual options. "I'll give you one more chance to come along peacefully. Otherwise, I cannot guarantee that you will come out of this situation without physical damage," she warned.

"Get 'er, boys!" Dune ordered, and the three descended upon her at once. What happened next was a whir of motion that was nearly impossible to follow. With a few combined techniques from her arsenal of Krav Maga and Brazilian Jiujitsu, Jayka had all three opponents on the ground, two completely still and the one who remained conscious, moaning in pain. She strapped restraints on their wrists and ankles and sent a simple message via her chip to the main dispatcher. "Request transport for apprehended subjects at my coordinates." She checked the pulses of the two unconscious men. She knew she had broken some bones, but it was her sincere desire to capture them alive for questioning. Satisfied they were merely unconscious, she searched them for weapons and then continued her study of the clearing.

A charred area ringed by stones told the story of a small campfire. Jayka frowned thoughtfully. None of her prisoners had possessed a lighter or even any of the more primitive tools used to start a fire. She glanced at the conscious prisoner, who had stopped moaning and was looking bleakly around the clearing with an eye that hadn't yet swollen shut. "How long have you been here?" she asked. "How did you start that fire?"

There was no answer from the man, who appeared to be struggling to maintain consciousness. "Answer me, or I'll ruin your remaining good eye," Jayka threatened.

"We jus' got here," the man mumbled weakly.

"Wrong answer," Jayka said menacingly, and drew her fist back in front of the man's eye.

"Please!" he flinched, "I don't mind ya messin' up the other one. It was wrecked anyway by the river-brandin'. This is the only good seein' eye I got left!"

"Why your pathetic band of miscreants persists in such a primitive act of self-mutilation is a laughable mystery," Jayka said, in a tone that did not suggest she found anything remotely funny. "So tell me—the truth, this time. How long were you here? Long enough to make a fire with coals that have grown cold, so I'm assuming you were here overnight."

"No," the man persisted. "I swear—we left the docks this mornin'. Dune found a place in the wall where we could get through. Me an' Ox didn' wanna go, but he said this was our chance to rise in the ranks." There was a pause as the man contorted in pain.

"Continue," Jayka demanded. She could hear the sound of the transport approaching.

"We saw this place where someone had a fire an' we were just lookin' aroun' when you busted in on us."

Jayka had been monitoring the man's body language for telltale signs of lying, but she was convinced his pain was overriding any attempt he could make at deception. "I believe you are telling the truth," she said simply and let her fist drop to her side. "How did the one you call Dune manage to afford a gold filling?" Jayka asked, but the roar of the transport engine hovering over the clearing drowned out any further attempts to communicate. It didn't matter. Dr. Moses would get it out of him, one way or the other. A cot was lowered, and Jayka secured the conscious man onto it. One by one, the prisoners were extracted from the sight. "Go on without me," Jayka said via the chip to the pilot of the chopper. "I'm going to take a look around."

She waited for the sound of the rotors to fade into the distance. Slowly, the birds begin to sing their varied melodies, adding interest to the monotonous chorus of humming mosquitos in the background. She carefully walked the perimeter of the clearing and finally found what she was looking for—a stalk of wild dwarf larkspur, its stem broken and the deep purple flowers on its lower half slightly crushed. Once she had found that, it was easier to see the next clue —an old fallen log with scuff marks on the bark. And then it was as if the forest opened up to her and she could see the path clearly. It was a game trail, she was fairly certain, but it had been used by humans recently. If the men she had apprehended weren't the culprits, then how many Discards had escaped through the hole in the wall? Jayka's heart quickened. This was no menial assignment, after all. They had needed someone they could depend on to perform a thorough investigation. A wave of relief surprised her. Was she so insecure in her position that she had surmised she was being punished for some reason? If the State had adopted her, why did she feel she had to constantly prove herself worthy? Why did she feel she owed a debt she could never repay?

"Focus!" she commanded herself, dropping her introspection to once again study the game trail before her internal protocol could issue a warning to stay on task. It made sense to her that someone would take this route. It was easier. The path of least resistance, after all. She continued following the trail, which meandered southward and just slightly to the west. Gradually the sound of the causeway became nothing but a faint hum, and eventually it disappeared alto-gether. The game trail was growing fainter, and she was becoming concerned she had lost it altogether when she stumbled upon another campsite. She discovered the remains of a second campfire. Two large squares of earth had been cleared of rocks and sticks. Someone had put up a couple of tents, she realized. She found slight damage to the bark of two trees near each site where a rope must have been tied to support a tarp or canvas. There must have been a heavy rain at the time the camp had been used, because she was able to distinguish seven sets of prints in the hardened mud, as well as those of something in the canine family. "A dog?" Jayka muttered. She had never known of a Discard owning a dog. There were stories of people owning them in the past, but they had all been eaten long ago. Dogs as pets were a luxury of the citizens of the State. A dog wouldn't have lasted five minutes in the outer docks. She walked around the campsite in a slowly widening circle. The game trail seemed to have disappeared completely. But then she saw a stand of mayapples, their umbrella-like leaves spreading like a miniature fairy village among the tree trunks. Leading through the mayapple grove was the fresh sign of broken stems and leafy umbrellas turned topsy turvy. Jayka smiled with satisfaction and once again continued her pursuit. The terrain was hilly, predominately oak forests, with a river she knew to be the Meramec curving gently through the hills. At one point, she thought she detected the barely audible hum of the causeway; but once again, that faded into silence.

It was slow going. The trail was difficult to follow, even for a person with her tracking skills. Occasionally, she would run across one of the old roads and their accompanying signage. Each time, she was able to pick up the trail again on the other side of the road, so it seemed these Discards were playing it safe and avoiding the heavily monitored areas. But eventually at one of these intersections with the roads, the trail did not reappear on the other side. Jayka looked up and down the stretch of dilapidated highway. She could see a sign in the distance, and by using her enhanced sight she could make out the word "Leasburg" with an arrow and a number two indicating mileage. She frowned. Her internal GPS unit had indicated she was actually still within a few miles of the wall, but until she saw the sign, she had thought it might be malfunctioning. The tracking was taking much longer than anticipated. She turned the opposite direction. Leasburg was closer to the causeway, and any Discard who truly wished to evade capture would choose to put as much distance between himself and the causeway as possible. After walking a mile or so down the road, alert for any evidence of the Discard leaving the trail, she encountered a sign, warped and cracked from neglect, that read, "Onondaga Cave State Park."

Jayka had information in her databanks about all the caves in the area. Historically, caves had always been good hideouts. Meramec Caverns, which had been absorbed by the expanding city decades ago, had been sealed off to keep Discards from trying to escape, though it would have been a futile endeavor since the underground portion of the cave existed entirely within the outer wall. But Onondaga, located a few miles outside of the city, would have been a tempting place for a Discard to hide. The old visitor center had been torn down years ago as the State attempted to return all the tourist caves back to a natural state, but the airlock system was still intact. Unless they knew the entrance code, anyone seeking refuge would quickly find they were at a dead end. Despite all her implants and the chip algorithms that performed the function of predicting outcomes in any situation, Jayka still relied heavily on her gut instinct; and she had a good feeling about the cave. An abundance of cave lore had been spread around the outer docks. Those who were daring enough to dream of escape always silenced those skeptical of their survival in the Preserve by pointing to the possibility of hiding in a cave for protection against the weather and wild animals and as a way to evade detection by the drones. It was implausible, of course, but it was a dream to hold onto in an otherwise dreary, hopeless existence. Again, Jayka's mind wandered back to the days when she, too, had dreamed of escape. She quickly shoved the memories of her past aside as they tried to resurface. She had to be alert now, not incapacitated by scenes of her horrific childhood.

The crumbling highway offered an easier path than the woods, which was choked with thick undergrowth from a lack of controlled burning management. State philosophy was that the earth knew best how to care for itself. If it needed to be burned off, a lightning bolt would eventually set off a fire. The cities, surrounded by their motes of outer docks and a Dead Zone, would be protected, with a calculated loss of lives that included no citizens of the State, thus a purge of the superfluous for both nature and metropolis.

It was now late afternoon. Jayka had left the wall in the early hours of morning when she had just enough light to discern signs of a trail. She had encountered the men just before midday. Her focus in tracking and the terrain she had covered–with no food to refuel her energy—were beginning to take their toll. When old H Highway crossed the Meramec River, she stopped to filter a drink of water and noticed some tracks in the mud. It was just one set of human tracks, and again, the prints of a canine. What had happened to the other Discards?

Could that account for the difficulty she had tracking? The disturbance in the mayapples near the campsite had seemed large enough to be caused by a group of people. But if a dog were there, crashing playfully through the brush in circles around the human, that could explain all the broken plants. She wondered how close she was getting. The damage of the mayapples had looked fresh enough, but it could have been a day or two old, as their tender stems didn't bounce back like the stronger saplings. The tracks on the riverbank supported the theory that she wasn't far behind. As tempting as it was to rest, she felt she had to press on, at least until she reached the cave.

Light was fading as she approached the site of the old visitor center. She sat down with her back against a low retaining wall that had once bordered a pollinator garden. A few of the native species remained, although much of them had been displaced by Canada thistle. She ate one of the two energy bars she carried in her jacket pocket and washed it down with the water she had filtered into her flask. If she needed more food, she could always send for it. Things were so different from when she was a little girl, fighting for survival with the other orphans. She had someone to take care of her now.

"But at what cost?" The question seemed to rise out of nowhere, surprising her with its insinuation. The safety and provision she was given was worth any cost of personal freedom, she reasoned. Jayka ran a quick diagnostic of her mental processing and physical condition, which was a default exercise when a Pod-Op experienced any feelings of disloyalty to the State. The results revealed she was exhausted from the constant state of vigilance she had maintained throughout the day, and she needed to rest. The darkening woods spread their shadows across the old parking lot. There was no protection here from predators. She needed to either build a fire or find a safer place to sleep. She looked over her shoulder at the only visible remains of the visitor center—a cinderblock wall set into a mound of earth, its airlock door nearly hidden by the limbs of a fallen oak. The cave was the obvious choice. It offered protection from predators and any unforeseen weather changes. There was no sign of the Discard. Hopefully, he was still nearby, even though he had undoubtedly failed in his attempt to enter the cave.

Jayka climbed to her feet and made her way across the cracked sidewalk. When she gained a clear view of the door, she wondered if she would be able to gain entrance after all. She knew the code, but the keypad was partially obscured by the blunt stob of a limb that had bludgeoned it as the tree fell, lodging itself against the buttons. She placed her shoulder under the limb and attempted to move it, but it had the effect of a mouse trying to move a boulder. Frustrated, she pushed with all her might, and her left foot slipped backward with the effort, making contact with the airlock door. Jayka whirled around as the door pushed in with a slight creak. The airlock had been compromised. She pushed the door all the way open, shining a flashlight into the gloomy interior, which was lit only by the dim, solar-powered exit signs. She half expected the Discard to be huddled inside, but there was no evidence to suggest anything had been disturbed since the last group of scientists had traveled to the park to take water samples in the cave's famed Lily Pad Room. She shone her light at the second door on the other side of the air lock. It would be cold and damp inside the cave, itself. The airlock would be warmer and offered adequate protection through the night. She chose a spot on the floor near the door and removed the pistol from her waistband, laying it beside her within reach. After taking off her jacket and rolling it up to place beneath her head, she lay down on the concrete floor and closed her eyes. A few minutes later, her eyes popped open, and with a hint of irritation, she sat up and removed the remaining energy bar and flask of water from the jacket pockets to make a more comfortable pillow. Finally satisfied with her accommodations, Jayka relaxed. The full force of weariness from the day's exertion descended on her, and she drifted into a deep sleep.

When she awoke, she was confused at first, alarmed at the soft, red color emanating from the exit lights. She was accustomed to waking gradually. Her chip had always utilized the gray walls and ceiling of her room as a blank slate for projecting colors used to stimulate her brain to a state of wakefulness. She felt groggy. Then she remembered where she was. How long had she been asleep? Three hours. Her chip confirmed it. She automatically reached for the pistol she knew to be on the floor beside her, but could only feel the hard, cool concrete. Immediately, she was in a crouching position, searching for the gun and ready for combat, if necessary. Her heart was pounding. What good were the martial arts against one well-aimed shot from a 9 mm? She half-expected to hear the sound of the gun at any moment, but she appeared to be alone in the room. She shone her flashlight around to confirm it. Jayka was, indeed, alone. Although there was no sign of her pistol or the energy bar, the flask of water was where she had left it. She stood motionless for a few seconds, calculating probabilities. She had slept with her back against the outer door all night, so that meant someone had already been inside the cave when she took shelter in the airlock. Jayka silently cursed herself for being such a fool. If she had discovered the airlock door was opened, why hadn't she suspected someone else could have made it there before her arrival? By flashlight, it had appeared the room was undisturbed. But she had been tired and could have missed any subtle signs that had been left. Why hadn't her chip calculated *that* probability?

Jayka calmed her pounding heart and gathered her thoughts. She knew she should alert her Podmates and call for backup, but she would rather handle the situation herself—especially since she had lost her weapon. Her mistake would eventually be revealed since she was chipped together with her team, but at least they would see she had corrected her error.

She turned her thoughts back to the situation at present. How had this Discard managed to sneak from the cave back into the airlock and take the items without waking her? And, more importantly, why hadn't they killed her when they had the chance? Perhaps this person was not violent by nature. Perhaps they only took the gun to be used as a tool for procuring food. If that were the case, she might be able to reason with them. She cautiously walked to the cave door and slowly opened it.

The darkness surprised her, smothering her with its thickness. How could anyone find their way in this blackness? Then her eyes adjusted and she saw the handrail and a barely discernible footpath. Somewhere up ahead, a dim light source was lending some definition to the surrounding formations. Jayka searched her databanks. There was an old lighting system still in use by visiting scientists. Light switch stations were found along the handrails at intervals. Whoever was in here had gone deep into the cave—deep enough they thought their section of lighting wouldn't be noticed. Jayka crept stealthily forward, her hand on the railing to guide her. She would refrain from using her flashlight so as not to alert the Discard to her presence until she was closer. Once she was near enough to be heard distinctly, perhaps she would be able to convince them to surrender. Looking back on her experience as an orphan, she couldn't imagine any circumstance in which she would have been willing to give up freedom from both the outer docks *and* the State. Even when she had been adopted, it had not been her choice. She was just fortunate it had worked out in her favor. Jayka shook her head. Why did she keep experiencing these treasonous thoughts? She made a note that when she got back to the State, she needed to ask Dr. Moses to run a full diagnostic. Once again, she forced herself to focus. It should have been easy in the cave, with the only noise being the soft sound of trickling water. It was strange that the less distractions she had, the more bombarded she was by questions she had never considered. She gripped the handrail, allowing the cold, damp metal to ground her thoughts in the present.

Somewhere up ahead was a person who was alone and most likely afraid. Although they might not be violent by nature, they were undoubtedly desperate, as they had taken the chance to brave the Preserve in a quest for freedom and had the nerve to steal her firearm at great risk of waking her. Fear and desperation might override their nonviolent tendencies and cause them to overreact. Should she announce her presence and try to talk them out of their escape, or should she wait for the opportunity to take them by surprise and secure the weapon? Her chip ran the algorithms for favorable outcomes as she advanced stealthily forward, taking care not to let her boots scrape against the textured concrete footpath.

It wasn't as if she were unhappy. She had a place to sleep, food to eat, clothes to wear, and a purpose in life. She even had some notoriety, as Pod-Ops were viewed with honor—selfless individuals whose lives were completely dedicated to upholding the laws of the State and protecting its citizens. A Pod-Op had no relationships, outside that of other Podmates and their personal handlers. Relationships and families were considered too much of a distraction and a liability. If you loved someone, you could be controlled by them or by someone who threatened to harm them. So Pod-Ops lived a life free of compromising emotions that could endanger them, their Podmates, or other citizens. Whatever semblance of love and friendship they experienced was fulfilled in their loyalty to their team. And if they encountered emotional hardship because of it, there were drugs to counteract the effects of that. In Jayka's experience, the only people who had ever cared for her had been other orphans like her, and many of them were now on her team or other teams. She wondered what would have happened to them all if they hadn't been discovered by Dr. Moses and given a chance to have a good life. Would they all have been dead by now?

Or would they have survived and had families of their own? *"If I had a family,"* Jayka said silently to herself, *"I would* never *abandon my child as I was abandoned. I would love her and teach her how to survive. I would—"* suddenly, Jayka slipped on the steep downward grade of the path as her foot came in contact with something slippery. She almost went to her knees, but caught herself with the handrail. A disgusting odor filled her nostrils. She put her flashlight on the lowest setting and shone it on the path. There, smeared in a brown streak, was the reason she had nearly fallen: a fresh pile of feces. Jayka wrinkled her nose in disgust. It looked similar to human waste except smaller, and it somehow smelled worse. Of course. It was the dog. The Discard must still have the animal with him. This could prove problematic if it decided to attack her. Jayka was trained in self-defense against other humans, but dogs had never entered the equation. She flicked off her light, noticing just before she did so that there was a steep drop-off on the other side of the railing. She would have to be more careful, or another misstep could be her last.

"What would it be like to have a dog?" she wondered as she continued down the trail. A handful of scenarios began to play in her head in which she was the owner of a Bull Mastiff or a Great Dane or a German Shepherd. The dog would accompany her on missions. It could track people by scent. It could attack criminals. It could—*"Stop it!"* Jayka screamed silently in her head. She was having tremendous difficulty concentrating. She wondered if the fact that she was underground was interfering with her chip's ability to connect with the nearest communication tower, and if that was somehow diminishing her ability to think clearly. She needed to find this Discard and get out of this cave.

She moved forward, this time with more caution as she thought again of the black abyss that had been revealed when she had used her flashlight. She wasn't certain how well the old handrails were maintained. Putting all of her weight on them, as she had when she had nearly fallen, could prove to be a fatal mistake.

The source of light was growing stronger. It was just ahead, hidden by a turn in the path and a rather large formation. She crept as close as she dared and peeked around the large flowstone that had been a showcase display in the time of tours. There was a place just off the path where someone had spread a blanket. Something shiny lay on the ground beside it—the wrapper from her stolen energy bar, she realized. There was no sign of the 9 mm or the Discard and the dog. She squashed the sudden impulse she had to go investigate the scene. They must be close by, she reasoned. In fact, this was probably all a trap. And then, in the eerie stillness of the cave, she heard something growl right behind her.

Squashing her impulse to whirl around and attack, she kept her voice low and soothing. "You do not need to fear me. I am unarmed. I have come to rescue you from the dangers of the Preserve. Please keep your dog at a reasonable distance."

There was no answer, but there was another low growl, this time further away. "I mean you no harm. I was an Unspoken once, but I was adopted by the State. If you come back with me and declare that you experience mental health problems that led you to trespass in the Preserve, I can speak in your favor. I may be able to help you to become a citizen. There is an outreach program for Discards in which they can receive help for their mental instabilities. Just think —you will no longer experience want. You will get all the food you could ever need and will have a safe place to sleep."

Another low growl, this time from even farther away. She began to slowly retrace her steps as she spoke. "I was without hope when the State rescued me. I went to the Euthanasia Clinic to end my existence, but instead, I was entered into a program where I became what I am today. I have purpose now," she said. But for the first time, the words felt hollow. She tried a different tack. "Listen. I know you're hungry. I can get you anything you want to eat. *Anything.* And it won't be someone else's leftovers. It will be hot, fresh food made just for you." She peered into the darkness, but even with her enhanced vision, it was hard to distinguish shapes. Then she heard something to her left, on the side of the walkway where she had seen the drop-off. There was a shuffling sound, and then a scrabbling, and a shriek, followed by a thud. Suddenly, the cave was alive with the sounds of excited barking and yipping. Jayka turned on her flashlight, and she could see the dog running back and forth near the edge of the drop-off. The animal stopped and looked down the path directly at her. And suddenly, it was running toward her at top speed. Jayka froze and put up her arms defensively in front of her face, expecting the animal to attack when it reached her. But instead, it barreled by her, nearly knocking her off her feet. Jayka could hear its claws scratching against the concrete. She cast the beam of her light in the direction of the sound and could see the dog as it left the trail and picked its way around the otherworldly mounds of earth and strangely shaped calcite formations. It had made its way to the bottom and was whimpering and barking at a prone figure at the base of a canopy of flowstone. Jayka made her way down, following the route the dog had taken. When she neared the site, the dog was shoving its nose under the hand of its master. It stopped and looked at her, but to her surprise, it did not growl. It almost looked as if it were trying to tell her something, and then it barked. The dog would take a few steps toward her and bark, and then run back to the body, nuzzle it again, and then run back to her and bark again. Jayka tried to swallow the lump that was forming in her throat. Even though she had never spent any time with dogs, she knew that this animal was asking her for help. She approached the figure. It was a woman—extremely old for a Discard. She looked vaguely familiar. Jayka felt for a pulse, and there was none. She could see where the woman had hit her head on the rock formation as she fell. "You almost made it, sister," Jayka said. Suddenly, she felt a stinging sensation in her eyes and realized she was beginning to cry—something she hadn't done in several years. Her emotions were kept in check by the chip and emotion-leveling drugs. But here, in this cave, with an old dockmate and the dog she had somehow protected, Jayka's emotions began to usurp all her programming. "I am so sorry," she said in a voice choked by tears. She searched the woman's pockets and found a fixed blade knife and the pistol. "Why didn't you use it? You could have gotten away with it. You could have buried my body here and left it." If only she hadn't pressured her. If only she had given up her quest. She didn't know how the woman would have survived in the wild, but at least she would have had the chance to try. "You died free, ancient one," Jayka said respectfully. She removed a small headlamp from a band around her arm and put it on so she would have her hands free to negotiate her steps back to the path with the weight of the body. The medical examiners would want to look it over, and in any case, she couldn't leave it in the cave. The dog looked up at her and wagged its tail hopefully as she shouldered the body. "She's dead," Jayka said, even though she knew the animal couldn't understand her. She began to carefully pick her way through the obstacle course of stalagmites.

When she finally made it back to the path, she gently set the body down near where the woman had made camp. The light sources strategically placed around formations near the site cast a soft glow on the old Discard, and Jayka couldn't shake the feeling that she had met her at some time or another. She ducked under the railing of the path to inspect the campsite, while the dog, who had followed her closely the whole time, licked the woman's face and whimpered.

The blanket was ragged, but serviceable, and she decided to wrap the body in it. She pocketed the energy bar wrapper to keep the cave free of litter. The State was very serious about keeping environments as natural as possible. The only reason the lighting system still existed was because to remove it would have caused more disturbance than leaving it intact, and it *did* prove useful for the speleologists. She stood up and looked around. Somewhere nearby, there had to be a stash of supplies. No Discard would have chosen to enter the Preserve without at least a cooking pot for heating water to render it drinkable. She shone her flashlight in the surrounding area, sending the shadows cast by giant stalagmites and stalactites dancing crazily against the cave walls. As her light fell across an immense portion of creamy colored flowstone, Jayka spotted something tucked within a crevice of the calcite deposit and went closer to investigate. Inside was the stash of supplies she had been looking for—a ragged old bag and something she couldn't readily identify. It was a polished piece of wood with a string attached to both ends, and she realized she was looking at a recurve bow. Further investigation yielded a quiver of arrows. Inside the worn canvas knapsack, Jayka discovered live traps, small foothold traps, a lighter, a device for filtering water; and at the bottom of the bag, she discovered a wad of netting that made her heart jump, for she finally remembered where she had seen this person before. Just prior to being "recruited" by Dr. Moses, when she barely had the strength to make it to the Euthanasia Clinic, this woman had seen her struggling and had offered her a piece of bread. It was the old pigeon trapper from all those years ago.

Jayka could no longer hold back her sobs as thoughts of that day pushed through any mental defenses she had built. She sat on her haunches, her hands clasped to her face as she attempted to gain some form of control. She was startled by a nudge against her elbow and was surprised to see the dog looking up at her with soft brown eyes, its tail wagging tentatively. As years of pent-up emotion were released, the animal curled up around her ankles and rested its head on one of her boots, its presence strangely comforting. When Jayka finally stopped sobbing, her tears spent, the dog raised its head and studied her with a gentle expression, its tail making a soft thump on the cave floor. It was then that Jayka knew the dog was coming with her. There was no scenario in which she would leave it behind. She cautiously extended her hand for the animal to investigate and was rewarded with a lick. Jayka sniffed in amusement, and suddenly realized she had forgotten how to laugh. Even when she was in the outer docks with her posse of friends in the most dismal of circumstances, they had always had something to joke and laugh about. Jayka stroked the dog's mottled fur. "Well, Scrapdog," she said, resurrecting her old nickname, "it looks like you're coming with me."

She knew she would have to make two trips to bring the body as well as all of the woman's belongings. With the dog following her closely, she picked up the lifeless bundle and began the hike back to the entrance. Each time she encountered one of the light switch stations, she flipped it on. It was difficult enough negotiating a path that was steep and damp in places without the added danger of not being able to see. It was then that she discovered the reason the woman had fallen. One of the rails was bent out over the drop-off. It must have given way when she had leaned on it. Just at the edge she spotted what looked like a walking stick with some colored cords at one end. She would have to investigate on her way back.

When she finally reached the airlock, she set the body down and turned to go back inside. The dog seemed to hesitate to leave its old master, but then followed her back into the cave. When they reached the broken railing, Jayka knelt down to pick up the stick and realized it was a makeshift spear. One end had been whittled out to fit the handle of a sharpened screw driver, which had been bound there with a rainbow mishmash of shoelaces. Jayka smiled. The old woman had been extremely resourceful. As she stood up, she was surprised to see something scratched on a large column formation right next to the path. It was another pictograph. Jayka shone her light on it to get a better view. Once again, it was a trade symbol. But she had never seen one made in this particular fashion. One hand was in the stalactite portion of the column, with the lines indicating fingers pointing downward and the thumb pointing to the right. It was much larger than the other hand, which was located on the stalagmite portion, with little fingers pointing upward and the thumb pointing to the left. In the middle of the smaller hand was the letter, "Z," and the traditional, two-way arrow was drawn at the point where the two formations had met. Jayka stood staring for a while, perplexed, and catalogued it in her memory. The speleologists would have a fit, of course. If there were a way to remove it, they would do so, and Jayka was glad to have captured the image for further study.

The dog watched her dolefully as she gathered the old woman's things. "I wish I knew your master's name," Jayka remarked. "But I am certain I can find someone who does." With that, she headed in the direction of the exit. The dog trotted ahead of her on the way back, eager to leave the underground lodging.

Zelda blinked. One minute, she had been in the cave, falling through blackness —the next, she found herself lying in soft, green grass in the bright sunshine. She thought she remembered a chipmate coming to the cave. She had stolen some food and had taken the girl's gun so she couldn't force her to go back to the docks. Had it all been a dream? She could hear the sound of water and was reminded of the time she had been lost in the Preserve and had fallen asleep in the leaves by a spring branch. Maybe she was just asleep. Maybe she was still safe inside the cave, snoring away while Macy kept a restless watch. She sat up. If this was a dream, it was the most realistic one she had ever had. She was near the banks of a crystal-clear river, surrounded by the gentle swells of verdant hills and a spattering of colossal pine trees. She rose to her feet and realized something was missing. The familiar pain in her old bones was completely gone. She looked around, taking in the pristine wilderness. High overhead, a hawk circled, its bronze-barred wings glowing in the sunlight. In the river beside her, she spied a flash of movement just beneath the surface, and a trout jumped. Zelda cackled gleefully. This was the best dream she had ever had. The only thing that would make it better were if Piper could share it with her. She knelt down at the riverbank. If this really was a dream, it wouldn't hurt to drink the water. She scooped up some of it in her hands and drank deeply. It was icy cold and invigorating. Somehow, it seemed to give her energy. She peered into the water and was startled to see someone staring back at her—a young woman with milk chocolate skin, extremely curly, ginger brown hair and a surprised expression. She spun around, but there was no one behind her. She looked back into the water and realized she was looking at her own reflection, minus twenty or thirty years. This dream just got better and better.

"It's hard to believe, isn't it?" said a friendly voice to her right. She jumped. She hadn't seen anyone earlier when she had gazed at the vast expanse of meadows and pine groves, but now there was a woman standing beside her on the riverbank. She was wearing a white outfit of some sort.

"It shore is," Zelda giggled. "Dis here is da best dream I ever had!"

The woman grinned. "This isn't a dream, Zelda."

Zelda's brow furrowed in consternation. "Course it is. I ain't looked like dis in prob'ly thirty years. An' dere ain't no sich places left on dis earth dat is dis beautiful, wit' clean runnin' rivers like dis, an' no drones flyin' aroun' chasin' ya. Dis here is perfect. I don' wanna wake up."

The woman smiled patiently. "You're not asleep. You're actually more awake than you've ever been. And I've been sent here to make sure you make it the rest of the way home."

"Home?" Zelda said blankly, and then she frowned fiercely. "I ain't goin' back to dat rat hole. Dis is my dream. Now, don't you go spoilin' it."

At this, the woman burst into laughter, clapping her hands in delight. "I know this is all very hard to understand, but maybe I can explain it to you, if you'll allow me."

Zelda tilted her head back. "I'm listenin'."

The woman turned and pointed off in the distance to what appeared to be the sun resting on the horizon. "Do you see that?" she asked.

"Yeah," Zelda said. "Looks like da sun is startin' ta set," she remarked, but as she studied it, she realized that it wasn't getting any darker. "It ain't settin'. It looks like it's jus' sittin' dere, shinin'."

The woman smiled. "That's where we're going. The light you see isn't the sun. It's coming from inside the city. There's no need for the sun there."

Zelda squinted in confusion. "I don' get it. If dat is your answer for da sun, how come it don' hurt ma eyes none?"

The woman held out her hand. "If you'll just come with me, I'll show you."

Zelda stared at the woman. Well, if it was a dream, it wouldn't hurt to go investigate. She cautiously extended her hand, and the woman clasped it tightly. Suddenly, they were standing before a gate and the high walls of the shining city, which appeared to be clear as it radiated from within. The base of the wall was embedded with jewels of every color, and the intricately carved gate was made of something that reminded her of the buttons on her grandad's old western shirt. "What is *dis* place?" she asked, completely fascinated.

"This is your new home! It's the one Piper told you about."

"Pipah! Is she in dere?" Zelda asked eagerly.

"No," the woman replied. "It isn't time for her to come home yet."

"Well, I tink I'll jus' wait for her outside da gate. It's really purty out here. Mebbe I'll try ta catch me a fish. Or mebbe I'll take a nap under one o' dem pine trees. Dey gots soft needles underneath 'em to lay down on."

"This is nothing compared to what's on the inside of the walls," the woman reassured her.

Zelda thought for a moment. "It's jus' dat—I been waitin' all my life ta get outta da city walls where I come from. All dis beautiful nature—da trees an' da streams an' such—I been dreamin' 'bout it ma whole life. I don' know if I wanna spend much time in a city."

The woman grinned. "These walls are just the border of Heaven's back country. There are plenty of beautiful creeks to swim in and forests to explore beyond these walls, and the trees by the river of life have twelve different kinds of fruit!"[66]

---

[66] Revelation 22:1-2

Zelda was mesmerized. She had never before eaten fresh fruit, much less picked it off of a tree. She looked around her. She thought she would have woken up by now, but she was still here.

"Like I said, you're not dreaming," the woman remarked, as if she were reading her mind. "Do you remember when you were hiding in the cave?"

"Yeah," Zelda said slowly. The memory was fuzzy, but she could still piece it together. "I was just gonna step offa da trail in da shadows where dat chipmate couldn' see me, an da railin' gave way. But I thought dat was part o' dis here dream."

The woman shook her head. "No. That actually happened. You died, Zelda. You hit your head."

Zelda's eyes opened wide, and she gaped at the city gate. "If dis here is Heaven, dere ain't no way dey're lettin' me in dat *place. I don' mind waitin' out here. Mebbe dat way, I'll see Pipah when she makes it home, even if it's only fer a minute."*

The woman smiled again. "Do you remember Selah?"

"Yep. Nice girl. Not sure how smart she was, wantin' ta teach all us Discards 'bout Jesus, but she had a good heart."

"Do you remember the trade she told you about between God and man?"

"Course I do! I called it da stupid *trade, cuz God didn' get nuttin' good outta da deal. He jus' give us everyting an'—" suddenly Zelda stopped as she remembered. There, back in that cave, she had kept thinking about Piper and Selah and what they had said. She knew she wasn't good enough to get into Heaven, and she knew that's where Piper would end up. If anyone would go to Heaven, she was sure it would be the girl. And she desperately wanted to see Piper again. The girl was the only friend she had ever had. She decided then and there that if God would have her, she would make the trade—her sins for His righteousness.*

"Wait a minute. I made dat trade! I left a marker of it on dis place where da roof stooped down ta meet da floor—cuz dat's what it was like! God stooped down an' met me right where I was when I was reachin' up fer Him."

"That's it, exactly," the woman said, and then seemed to remember something. "Oh, my goodness. I've been so rude! I just realized I never introduced myself. My name is Genevieve. I'm waiting for a friend of mine, too. Would you like to come inside and wait for your friend with me?"

Zelda smiled, her youthful freckles sprinkled across her nose and cheeks. "Dat sounds mighty fine."

The two turned toward the gate, which swung wide for them. As they stepped inside, Zelda somehow knew her adventures were just beginning.

22

D R. Moses opened his eyes, a look of pleasant surprise registering on his face. The corners of his mouth curved into a smile as he looked up at Ira and Ainsley, who were standing beside the chair at Ira's workstation. "Excellent work, Ira. I don't know how you did it, but you've managed to do the impossible. I was able not only to approach and pass through the interface of this system, but I even did a little light programming of my own that should help mitigate the neurologically disruptive effects created by the malware and will allow a citizen to be more emotionally receptive to treatment."

Ainsley rolled her eyes. "I see little value in your concern for a patient's feelings about our methods. A doctor doesn't apologize for having to rebreak a fracture that has healed incorrectly. Once a subject's life changes for the better, they'll come around to our way of thinking."

"I believe it is *completely* necessary that the citizen understand we are helping them before they embark on the journey," Dr. Moses insisted. "A doctor explains to the patient what needs to be done before he rebreaks the bone."

"Some patients wouldn't understand the explanation if you gave it to them," Ainsley fired back at him. "Take this particular… *system* that Ira has been working on," she said, gesturing in Ira's direction. "Some systems are clunkier than others."

Dr. Moses gave Ainsley a look of warning, which Ira pretended not to see. "Nevertheless, the effort must be made," Moses said firmly.

"Were you able to extract any information about the anomaly I detected at the border of the…*system interface* when the link was severed?" Ainsley asked, purposefully pausing before the euphemism as she referred to the incident in which she had been forcibly removed from Janice's neural network. It had left her unsettled. Being an extremely strong personality and a decent programmer, Ainsely wasn't accustomed to being denied access to any area within a subject's neural boundary. But this force she had encountered was like no other, having given her the sensation of being picked up and physically tossed out of Janice's mind, much as a whirlwind would pick up a leaf. When she had looked back, she had seen someone or some*thing* with Janice. She couldn't shake the image from her mind, nor the feeling of powerlessness she had at the time.

"I saw no such anomaly," Moses said.

"Then how do you know it won't happen again?" Ainsley asked. "It needs to be dealt with—completely eliminated. Just because you didn't see it doesn't mean it isn't in there somewhere, infiltrating and degrading other parts of the system."

Ira, who had been quietly listening to the interchange, felt an inner nudge to say something. "If I may, I can possibly assuage Specialist Abbot's concerns," he began.

"Doubtful," Ainsely snapped.

"Continue," Dr. Moses urged him.

Ira cleared his throat. What he was about to say could put him in danger, because it would reveal that he had known all along that he hadn't just been working on an interface system, but on the neural boundary of an individual. "As I was working on this project, I met an interesting personality connected with the interface," Ira began carefully. He looked Dr. Moses square in the face, deciding it was now or never. "She told me her name was Janice Druthers. She was very reluctant to allow you access because no basis of trust had ever been established. But when I explained that I was trying to help her, she allowed me to write the program I've just shown you."

Dr. Moses studied Ira for a moment. "You are full of surprises today, Ira. I would have thought that once you discovered the true nature of the system interface, you would have politely declined, on moral grounds."

Ira was careful to maintain eye contact. "Knowing I don't have much of a choice and knowing I might be able to help a fellow citizen was all the convincing I needed."

Dr. Moses seemed to consider something as he looked at Ira. "You know, I didn't even see Janice's mental projection when I accessed her neural network. She seems to have been tucked out of my way, allowing me access with little or no distress to her while I made the preliminary adjustments that will give her the ability to view our methods objectively."

"That was the plan. Don't you agree that the less stress a citizen encounters, the better?" Ira asked.

"Absolutely," Dr. Moses agreed. "I highly suspect that Citizen Druthers hadn't the mental capacity to fully comprehend what chip implantation entailed and how it would affect her life."

"That was my point, exactly," Ainsley interrupted.

Dr. Moses shot her a glance and continued. "Apparently, the lab technicians failed to recognize this during the preliminary screening. If they had, more efforts could have been made to ensure she understood exactly what she was getting into. But since we've passed that point, we have to regain her trust, not violate it," Dr. Moses said with a meaningful look at Ainsley. He turned again to Ira. "What you have done for Citizen Druthers today shows tremendous empathy and is a service to both her and the State."

"Empathy—is that what you're showing the subject in 201?" Ainsley asked cattily, her eyes boring into Dr. Moses. "You know as well as I that the girl is underage. She has a D.I.N. She's hardly an Unspoken to be used as experimental fodder. Ahh, but you're doing her a service—that's how you justify it"

He stared evenly back at her. Ainsley was as guilty of human experimentation as he was, and her treatment of Janice had proven it. "I've explained that situation to you before. That girl has harmed herself and others with her words and has repeatedly declined to stop her illegal behavior, although having been given several months to do so. People who reject the rules of the State have forfeited their rights to freedom of thought and can be programmed accordingly. But those upstanding citizens such as Janice, who are simply attempting to become better people and have come to us for help should not be coerced into anything!" Dr. Moses said it with such conviction that even Ainsley believed he meant what he said.

Ira looked down as he realized they must have been discussing Piper. And then his eyes darted back to Dr. Moses. "If you'd like, I could help you with this particular individual using the same method I've used with Citizen Druthers," he said.

Ainsley and Moses snapped out of their verbal sparring match to stare at him. Ainsley's lips sprawled into a generous smirk as she looked from Ira back to Dr. Moses. "Yes, Joseph. Why don't you allow Ira to have a crack at that one? Oh, wait, you already did, didn't you? And it didn't exactly work out."

Dr. Moses' eyes had a distant look as he managed to conceal his anger at Ainsley's revelation. His only show of emotion was a stiff, forced smile. "Ira, I'm afraid I haven't told you the complete story about this particular situation. The individual in question is actually the original host of the rogue program." As he watched Ira, comprehension suddenly dawned that the man had known all along. "But I can see you already knew that."

"Yes. But I think I understand your intentions. And I am certainly willing to do whatever I can to help individuals cope with the stress of implantation so that they can learn to use the chip as a tool to better their lives rather than it becoming the source of a nervous breakdown or a complete neurological disconnect," Ira answered truthfully.

"Well, well, Ira!" Ainsley said sarcastically. "You're certainly becoming adept at the balancing act of morality versus self-preservation."

Ira smiled and straightened his glasses, which really didn't need straightening at all. "So it would seem."

Within Janice's neural boundary, Piper and Janice safely observed the program Ira had written. "So he called it a firewall?" Piper asked.

"Yes, that's what he said."

"What does it do, exactly?"

"It's a kind of barrier that keeps programmers out and lets us go about our regular lives. They can even create programs that interact with it so that they think they're making progress. But all it really does is keep them out while making them think they're in. And it can also interpret the coding they wrote so that we can see what they were *trying* to do. Wasn't that clever?" Janice grinned.

"It sure was!" Piper exclaimed. "Jesus tol' me Ira was gonna help us. He said Ira could see things differently. I didn't know he could also make *other* people see things differently!"

Janice laughed at Piper's double meaning. "Oh, and Jesus had him do something else, too. It has something to do with someone who's going to be chipped really soon."

"Someone dangerous?" Piper asked.

"No. It's someone who's going to help us. But He asked us to pray for him because getting the chip is going to be really scary for him at first. It's going to make him feel really sick, like it did you."

Piper's face fell. "That was the scariest time of my life, and the pain made me just wanna die. Isn't there any other way?"

"I think if there was, Jesus wouldn't allow this to happen. Jesus already gave him the choice of whether or not to be captured, and he made his decision. He decided to say yes to serving Jesus—even if it meant dying for Him," Janice explained.

"But it makes Jesus hurt," Piper said. "I can tell how He hurts when we're hurting, can't you?"

"Yes, I can. I know our lives are precious in His sight.[67] He knows how it feels, and He hurts for us.[68] But His Word says He'll never leave us.[69] Psalm 91 says He'll be with us right in the middle of whatever we're going through.[70]"

Piper brightened at Janice's words. "Wow, Janice! You're really learnin' how ta make good pathways in ya mind with all them Bible verses ya been learnin'!"

"And just think, it was you that got me started doing it!" Janice beamed. "You know, I think that pretty soon, you may be helping a lot more people learn about building up their walls and making new pathways of thinking."

"I hope so! But for now, maybe we should jus' do what Jesus asked us to do right now, an' pray for this fella who's in trouble."

---

[67] See Psalm 116:15
[68] See Hebrews 4:15
[69] See Hebrews 13:5
[70] See Psalm 91:15

Janice and Piper joined hands and began to pray. In the small apartment just one floor above their rooms, Craig's anxiety began to lessen. He could tell something was coming, but he knew that whatever it was, He could face it with the help of the Lord.

23

SELAH stood on the porch step, looking up at the slot of clear sky above her between the apartment buildings. Throughout the revival, the acid fog had maintained its deviance from the norm by keeping close to the rooftops, leaving the streets open for travelers. Occasionally, when the streets were once again deserted, it would swirl languidly down to stalk the vacant sidewalks, caressing the dingy gray bricks of the buildings and stroking the crumbling asphalt. But before the sun was up, it would lift once again to the height of the roofs, where it dissipated in the early morning sun. But last night was different. The fog had never risen from the river, but stayed within its banks, as if it had been issued a warning that it could go no further.[71] Selah knew this because she had been up all night, thinking about what would transpire that day. Looking up at the phenomenon of the crystal-clear morning gave her assurance that they were doing what God had ordained. Soon, three different families who had given their lives to Christ and were eager to find ways to serve would be arriving to escort ministry teams to their homes in various parts of the docks. The people were hungry for God's Word and for weeks had been asking if Selah could teach classes in the daytime, but she was already weary from ministering at night. She had thought about asking Bester, Drey, and Bally to hold Bible studies in the alley or nearby homes, but Bester and Drey were faithful altar workers and were just as exhausted as she was. Bally had her hands full being Selah's armor bearer and managing people who came to the door in the daytime. Even if Bally's little brother Andrew (or Mouse, as he was known in the neighborhood) hadn't been so painfully shy and had agreed to teach, the threat of the Gateway Gang extorting food or services only further complicated the situation. Add to all those

---

[71] See Job 38:11

difficulties the fact that none of her fellow ministers could read, and it seemed they were faced with an impossible situation. Selah had been praying about it for weeks. Every time she thought she had come up with a solution, she felt like she was facing a closed door. When she would pray in the Spirit, she had no clear direction, except to wait.

Then the missionaries from Adullam had arrived, and she had known immediately why the Lord had impressed upon her to wait. Now the day had come when the teams would be leaving. Thom and Dania would be going with a family that lived in the Upscales. Lydia and Chandra would go with a couple in the southwest sector of the docks and would be accompanied by Andrew. Being timid, Andrew was very adept at avoiding confrontation and would likely keep them out of trouble when they were out and about. Garrison and Lelah would go with a family to the East Side. Each team would hold daily Bible studies in the host family's homes and would minister in the local neighborhood. The hope was that eventually, the growing number of believers in the outer docks would mature in the faith and gradually extend their ministry until the West and North Sides were reached and city of St. Louis was encircled by the good news of Jesus Christ.

Selah struggled to swallow the lump in her throat. She was thrilled that God had heard her all along—indeed, He had been answering her prayers from the minute she began praying about the situation. Garrison had told her about the dream he had in which he and the other teens had been sent out as missionaries from Adullam. It had occurred the night she had prayed about it and recorded it in her journal, which she had faithfully kept since arriving in the city. After allowing the teens to acclimate to outer docks life, Selah had explained the situation. It was obvious to all of them that this was God's doing, and much prayer was then directed toward finding host families. To everyone's surprise, the families approached them almost as soon as the teens began seeking the Lord about it, and preparations were quickly made. Ever since she had come to the city, Selah had felt the weight of the ministry on her shoulders. Having other mature Christians around to pray with her had been a comfort she had missed since leaving her valley. Now they were leaving her, and although it was an answer to many prayers, she felt a tinge of sadness.

"What do you see up there?" said a familiar voice coming from the window to the side of the porch.

Selah turned to see Garrison grinning at her. "The sky. It's clear. Good traveling weather," she replied.

Garrison held her gaze with his penetrating hazel eyes until Selah couldn't help but blush and look away. It had been almost a year since she had last seen him, and a great deal had happened. She had grown by leaps and bounds in her faith, having learned from Miss Genevieve about fasting and prayer. She had been filled with the Holy Spirit, set off on a journey to reach people in the State with the gospel, witnessed God's miraculous protection and provision, and served in the revival that was taking place. And yet this one individual could make her feel vulnerable and weak at the knees. Her heart jumped as the door behind her opened and she realized he was coming outside. *This is ridiculous,* Selah thought to herself. *I am a woman of God. I should be more mature than this.*

Garrison stepped out onto the porch and looked up at the sky. "It is *incredibly* clear, for here," he said. "That acid fog is no joke." He had stayed awake long enough one night to see the fog hanging low in the streets. Being ever adventurous, he had decided to add the acid fog experience to his resumé and had slipped out the door, only to immediately regret it. A half hour later he had managed to stop coughing, but only after waking up everyone else in the apartment.

"Selah, that boy don' got no sense," Bally had told her afterward. "I don' see what you see in 'im, although 'e *is* easy on the eyes."

Selah's face had reddened. "What I *see* in him? I grew up with him. He's just an old friend."

Bally looked at her with a knowing expression. "Uh-huh. We'll go wit' dat fa now. But someday, you gotta come clean wit' yaself about da way ya feel about dis dude," she said sagely and dropped the matter.

Selah wasn't really sure how she felt. When the group of teens had shown up at the revival, she had a hard time grasping the idea that Garrison had stayed in another isolated community for most of the time since he had left their valley. It seemed like the last thing he would have done. And to discover he had given his life to the Lord, received the baptism of the Holy Spirit, and felt called to be a missionary—it was such a different scenario than the one that had played in her head. A year ago, she had even considered what it would be like to be married to him, but so much had transpired. The girl who had those fantasies was naïve, a child compared to who she was now. Yet here she was, blushing and speechless standing next to him.

"I came all this way to find you, and now you're sending me away," Garrison said with a mock expression of remorse.

Selah smirked back at him. Garrison hadn't even known Selah had left their hidden community until the group from Adullam had run into Zelda. "Do you know how many times I wondered what was happening to you?" Selah asked. "When you left, I couldn't decide if you were living a life of luxury like you imagined it would be, or if you were rotting in some prison cell."

"Looks like we were both wrong," Garrison mused, surveying the empty street and the fog-scarred faces of the apartments. The outer docks was a juxtaposition of modernity and squalor. Free housing and electricity, but potable water only came from hydrants in specific locations. Food was free, but came in the form of scraps in the dumpster deliveries. Ambitious Discards could earn credits as plumbers, electricians, and street cleaners, but the incentive to get ahead was very low. Discards could only use credits to buy advanced medical care. The only way they could raise their standard of living—aside from rising in the ranks of a gang—was to move to the State. This would require them to trust the government enough to allow it to alter their bodies with health implants and dictate what they taught their children. The system kept Discards dependent on State support for food and housing, although it was meager, even when they had refused to trust the government enough to live by most of its rules. In the eyes of outer docks residents, they were punished either way. Only those with the most intense mistrust of government lived here. Nearly half had been the last to be rounded up from the most rural areas—people who had been termed *hillbillies* and *rednecks*, many with a history of vigilantism in their distant past. Interestingly enough, most of the rest had come from inner city ghettos, where gangs similarly had their own sense of justice and there was intense mistrust of police and any type of authority. The unlikely conglomeration of people with a few core similarities had somehow learned to get along since they had a common enemy. When you added to the mix a dependence on that enemy for survival, the hatred and mistrust ran deep.

"You don't know how many times I wanted to show you around Adullam. It's like our little valley, except without the fear of the outside world. The people there are like family to me. I know you would love Mark and Julie and Dawson and Sophia and Craig," Garrison's voice trailed off as he thought about what kind of situation Craig could be in now.

As if reading his mind, Selah said reassuringly, "We won't stop praying for Craig. He's in God's hands. There must be a reason God allowed him to be captured. It must be part of His plan. We just need to remember not only to pray for Craig's protection, but that God's plan for him will be fulfilled."

Garrison nodded. "I know. But it's hard not to worry. Do you think it's true what some of the Discards have said about Viv working for the State now? I just can't believe she'd do that unless she was forced."

"Well, maybe she *was*," Selah suggested. After hearing tales of Viv's heart for Jesus, it didn't make sense she would choose to work for a government that was so anti-Christian in its policies.

"So, you think she could have been chipped?"

"Your guess is as good as mine. But if she *had* been chipped and they were forcing her to spy on us, I think we would've seen her at the revival. And we know she knows about it because Dan'l told her. From what he described, it sounded like she was still trying to hide her faith from the authorities. My guess is the reason we haven't seen her is that she's avoiding this area to keep us safe."

Garrison nodded. Craig and Viv weren't criminals. They were people who believed in Jesus and wanted to tell others about Him. He hated the thought of what the State could do to a human being within the bounds of the law. One of the original intents of the First Amendment had been to ensure that citizens were allowed to worship as they pleased and were not limited to the confines of a State-established religion. But the Amendment had been turned backwards on itself, with the combined religious texts of the world's faith comprising a State-sponsored Bible that was the only religious text allowed in circulation. The State's official stance was that anyone could believe anything they wanted, as long as they accepted the fact that all religions led to the Source. If the members of a religious sect believed that their way was the only way, they were considered intolerant, even if they didn't try to force their beliefs on others. Even just presenting such a controversial notion was offensive to many and resulted in reconditioning therapy for those who held that belief.

Garrison smiled as he realized that the slum-like prison of the outer docks was now the freest place in the State. The gospel was spreading, unhindered in an environment where monitoring wasn't as intense. While Geeves units seemed a "convenience" for citizens—a virtual butler that followed commands for thermostat settings, lighting, and entertainment options—the huge selling point for Geeves was that it could watch over you, monitoring your movements and vital signs, alerting emergency responders if need be. The home was also monitored for would-be intruders, so citizens could feel completely safe. Many were happy to swap the lack of personal privacy for the peace of mind it afforded them. Outer docks residents did not have this luxury; and even if they had, they would have declined it. Their distrust of technology meant the only monitoring taking place was through cell phones, the occasional Vista Visor, street cameras and interactions with people such as waste truck operators and health clinic employees. Ironically, the lack of the most current technology was a boon to the revival, the news of which was spreading by testimonies of healing, salvation, and a free meal. It was the best and worst kept secret of the day, depending on what side of the city wall you called home.

"There's Akayla and Jefferson," Selah said suddenly. Garrison looked up to see a couple coming down the street toward them. "Thom! Dania!" Selah called as she brushed past Garrison to open the door.

Garrison watched wistfully as Selah went into the house to make sure everyone was ready to go. He knew that soon he would be leaving, as well. After all the waiting at Adullam, things were moving so quickly now. He wished he could spend more time catching up with Selah, but God had other plans. Maybe someday he could pursue the idea of a relationship with her, but now didn't seem like the right time. "But if not now, when?" he asked out loud. Their mini-journeys within the city weren't without danger. They could be reported by people who were more interested in getting rewarded for cooperating with the State than in hearing about the gospel. Or they could be threatened by the

Gateway Gang to keep quiet so the revival could maintain a low enough profile to avoid State detection while still allowing room for them to profit from it. There was a chance they might be apprehended and he would never see Selah again. He should at least tell her how he felt about her. But she was so focused —would she be irritated at him for even bringing up the subject?

"Good mornin', Garrison!" said Jefferson as the couple approached the porch.

"Morning!" Garrison said affably. "Thom and Dania should be out any minute."

"Can ya believe this weather today?" Jefferson exclaimed. "I tol' Akayla that the Lord sure is givin' y'all a good send-off!"

The door opened and Selah returned, followed by Thom and Dania, who were toting their backpacks. "Are ya ready, then?" Akayla asked. "Can we help carry anything?"

"Oh, no. We lugged these things up and down all kinds of hills to get here," Dania said.

"Well, then, isn't it nice ya don' hafta do that no more?" Jefferson said as he deftly slipped the pack off of Dania's back and slung it over his shoulder. "Lawd, chile. Watcha carryin' in here? Which is it, a fridge or a stove?"

The group laughed and then Dania turned to hug Selah. "Thank you so much for your hospitality, and for teaching us so much already about how to handle ourselves here."

Selah smiled as tears threatened to come to the surface. "Thank *you* for answering the Lord's call," Selah replied. "If you need anything, don't hesitate to ask. We don't have much, but we'll figure out something."

"Now, don' ya worry 'bout a thing, Miss Selah. We gonna take real good care of ya friends," Jefferson said, making a point to look her directly in the eye.

"Thank you, both," Selah replied.

Suddenly, Dania turned to Garrison and put her hands on his shoulders, fixing him with her snappy brown eyes. Garrison thought he detected a flash of something on Selah's face as Dania inclined her head to him to whisper. "And *you*, you watch over Lelah. Sometimes she gets so preoccupied with the conversation she's having with the Lord that she's not paying enough attention to what's going on around her."

"I'll do my best," Garrison replied, grinning and throwing a quick glance in Selah's direction. Was it his imagination, or did she look perturbed? As soon as the group left, he decided he would chance saying something to her about the way he felt. What did he have to lose? He was convinced they had been friends long enough that if she didn't share his sentiment, their friendship would survive. And as time went on, maybe she would change her mind. To his surprise, he began to sweat as the two of them watched the first team departing. He'd better do it now, before he lost his nerve. "You know, Selah—" he began, but her focus was on the street in the distance.

"Look! Can you believe it?" Selah said. "They're early."

Garrison sighed, clenching the porch rail as he looked beyond the first group to another group of people who were coming. His heart sank. It was his host family. It had taken more courage for him to work up the nerve to tell Selah how he felt than it had for him to leave their valley. And now he had lost his chance. He looked at her hopelessly. He wanted to kiss her—to tell her she was his best friend and he had missed her so much. He wanted to tell her he would rather stay here with her than to be anywhere else in the world.

Selah was watching him, confused. "Aren't you going to go get ready?" she asked.

Suddenly Garrison didn't care if he didn't have the perfect circumstances for his announcement. "Selah, I—"

"I'll go tell Lelah," Selah interrupted. "I'm not even sure she's awake yet!"

Garrison stared helplessly after her and turned to welcome the family that was almost there. "Good morning!" he called, hoping his cheerful greeting would hide the disappointment in his voice. Overhead, the sky was beginning to change from the sunny glow of morning to a deep, flawless blue.

24

A_{INSLEY} leaned back in her chair, rubbing her perfectly manicured fingernails along the sculpted edge of her jawline. She paused to study the glossy, smoky green of the nail polish, and then her eyes darted back to the man sitting across the desk from her. "If you suspect something, I fail to understand why you decided to come here to inform me. This information could easily have been shared through a link."

"We had an agreement. How I fulfill my end of the agreement was left up to my discretion."

Ainsley's eyes flashed in anger. "Your business is discretion, Wayne—which is why I trusted you to make good decisions. But this method could hardly be considered discreet."

Wayne thrust out his chin and leaned back in his chair, matching Ainsley's body language. "I wanted the opportunity to see your species in its natural habitat," Wayne countered, a humorless smile deepening the wrinkles in his face. He would not be intimidated. Or at least, he would not *admit* to her that he was intimidated. There was a reason he had chosen not to link with her. There was no chance he would make the same mistake twice. He had barely managed to disengage with any of his private life intact, and the feeling of violation he had felt was unnerving. She had enjoyed all of it. He could still see the look on her face when she saw that he understood what she was doing.

Ainsley glared, but a leer was playing at her lips. "How very brave of you to venture into the dragon's lair."

Wayne huffed dismissively. "As I said, something's going on there. It's worth closer monitoring. It's not on any set day, but it's always after 2100 hours."

"A simple perusal of the alley cam video footage will probably suffice," Ainsley said.

"No. That's the thing—the reason they've gotten away with it this long. There aren't any alley cams in this neighborhood. I'm not sure why, but I checked."

"Easily rectified," Ainsley sniffed.

"But not if it's obvious. It needs to be done covertly. Possibly rigged up in a lamp pole by a State worker with some story about working on the lighting. Maybe even something across the street, so they won't suspect anything." Wayne stopped for a moment as a medical alert on the floor directly below them chimed, directing nurses to a patient's room. He tilted his head back, eyeing Ainsley up and down. He trusted her like the very devil, but she was stunningly attractive. "What's this have to do with biotech, anyway? Isn't this more in the realm of the Department of Defense?"

"You let me handle the nuances of my job, and if you find it difficult to handle yours, I can manage those, as well," Ainsley said, giving Wayne's suit the same, careful perusal he had given her figure seconds earlier. "I must admit, you clean up rather well. I barely recognized you, if it weren't for the hair."

Wayne self-consciously smoothed back a greasy strand that had escaped his pony tail. "I haven't been an informant for this long by being careless."

"Could have fooled me," Ainsley quipped. "Next time, send me a location, and I'll meet you there—if you find the process of linking overwhelming," she added with a vicious grin.

Wayne cleared his throat and stood up. "That's all I have, for now."

"Thank you, Wayne. The deposit will be made into your account. I want you to set up somewhere else now. Say, the Hill district?"

Wayne nodded and turned to exit the office, heading to the elevator with his long, swaying stride. The elevator was empty. He was relieved, although he couldn't imagine anyone recognizing him. Ainsley had made him nervous, with all her talk of discretion. What did *she* know about it? He had been doing this for years. It was out of her realm of expertise, and her anxiety was just bleeding off onto him. He glanced at the lighted numbers of the building's levels as the elevator descended. How many poor citizens were housed here, their brains being altered and probed? How many of those people were here because he had informed on them? He looked at the ceiling of the elevator, focusing on the lighted tiles above in an attempt to distract himself from the unpleasant thought. Wayne had never had to see the results of his investigations. Ainsley had never revealed her actual position in the State government. He had assumed she was with the Department of Defense because they were the only ones who had his contact information and were authorized to share it. Having worked with them for years, he trusted them to pass along the information he divulged. But he had only recently become acquainted with Ainsley Abbot. If she was based at Liberation Station, she was bypassing protocol, which was perhaps why she was so annoyed with him for coming there in person. Not that she had given out the address. He had followed her.

The elevator reached ground level, and Wayne stood ready at the door, so absorbed in thought that he nearly plowed into the girl who was waiting to enter. His breath caught in his throat in spite of himself, and he quickly concealed any look of recognition he might have shown. "Excuse me," he said stiffly, allowing the woman entrance as he stepped aside. It was the same girl he had followed to the café. She was unmistakable, with her red and white hair and her striking features.

"Sorry," she smiled as they passed. As he glanced back at her, he noticed she was studying him carefully. Here was another reason Ainsley had disapproved of his appearance at her workplace. Not only was she avoiding the proper channels, she was spying on one of her own. He cursed himself as he strode down the hallway to the exit. He would have to lay low for a while and do some research on his next area of surveillance. He may have done more damage to his career today by avoiding the personal discomfort of a link than he would have if he had just let Ainsely have her way with him. But he was accustomed to sharing other people's secrets, not his own. Maybe the girl wouldn't recognize him, but he wouldn't give anyone the opportunity again. He was going to report this to his contacts in Defense as soon as he had the chance.

Back in the elevator, Viv couldn't shake the feeling that she had seen the man she bumped into somewhere before. She stopped on the fourth floor and made her way to Ainsley's office. The door was opened, and she stopped at the threshold, smiling as Ainsley swiveled in her chair with a welcoming wave. "Do come in, Viv. I've been wanting to talk to you about your visit to the outer docks, but I've been swamped. How is recruiting going?"

Viv came into the office and stood in front of the desk. "Not too many prospects yet. It'll take time ta win their trust," she said.

"Please, sit down," Ainsley gestured to the chair. "Tell me all about it."

Viv perched on the edge of the chair and proceeded to relay the events of that day, carefully telling the story of her dance session in the Shaw as being a way of attracting Discards and making them feel at ease. Her visit to the Euthanasia Clinic was easy to explain, since people were more likely to give themselves up to the State if they felt they had nothing to live for.

Ainsley listened attentively and came around to the front of the desk, leaning against it as she faced Viv. "I know you may feel your visit was fruitless, but you're laying a foundation. Don't be discouraged. You have a certain spirit about you, Viv. People are drawn to you. They can't help it!" Ainsley said, looking deeply into Viv's dark eyes.

Once again, Viv felt a wave of discomfort sweep over her during Ainsley's scrutiny. She decided to change the subject. "I was just wondering—when I got on the elevator, I ran into this guy who looked familiar, but I've never seen 'im here before."

"Oh?" said Ainsley, her eyebrows raised slightly. "Describe him to me."

"Well, he was wearing a nice suit, and his hair was slicked back in a pony tail. He had kinda long legs," Viv said, straining to remember details. "His eyes were light colored, and his hair was kinda grayish blond."

Ainsley's eyebrows crinkled. "I can't place him. Must have been someone to see Dr. Moses."

Viv nodded. "Back to the recruitin' business, I've been thinkin' o' just goin' on ma own, without the escort. You know, just ta try to make some connections without the food truck breathin' down ma neck. Discards have a sixth sense about these things. They're gonna catch on, if the only time they see me is when a food truck is around."

Ainsley tilted her head, seeming to consider the suggestion. "You're right, of course," she finally said. "But it's a little dangerous."

"I can handle myself. I know how ta watch fa trouble. I just need to get them ta trust me, an' they won't do that if they think I don't trust *them*."

Ainsley tapped her nails on the desk and stared out the window for a few moments, then suddenly turned to Viv and fixed her with her gaze. "Ok, Viviana. Take some time to make connections. We'll give it a trial run. But I want you to inform me when you leave, and I want to know when I can expect you to return. If you fail to report back at the right time, we'll send in someone to extract you. Depending on their discretion, that could prove a hindrance to your success in future recruiting endeavors."

"Thank ya, Ainsley," Viv said, standing up to leave. "I appreciate the opportunity. I think it'll make a huge difference." She made her way to the door.

"Oh, Viv," Ainsley said nonchalantly as Viv stepped into the hallway.

Viv turned to face her.

"How is your father doing?"

Viv's face paled, but she managed a tight smile. "He seems to be doin' real good. Thanks fa askin'." She realized all at once that Ainsley must have reviewed the footage of the food truck cameras. She had found out who her dance partner had been, and had known all along that Viv had chosen not to divulge that information.

Ainsley sauntered over to the door and leaned on the frame, her eyes on an even level with Viv's. "I understand your desire for privacy, but you really should know you can trust me." She reached over and caught the blue strand of Viv's hair, running it through her index finger and thumb. "I was thinking we could take some time together and build on that trust. What do you say you meet me for dinner?"

Viv swallowed nervously and backed into the hallway. "I-I actually have plans tonight. Maybe another time?"

Ainsley gave her a wicked smile. "Ok, Viviana. But don't keep me waiting too long. I think it's important that supervisors and their employees trust each other. And since you aren't chipped, the only way I can think of to get you to trust me is to spend time with you. Unless you're ready for the procedure, of course?"

Viv's blood ran cold. "I'm sure we can work out a time ta meet," she said quickly. "It's just that I can't do it tonight."

"Very well. Until next time, Vivvy."

Viv turned quickly and strode down the hallway to the elevator, her heart beating a frantic prelude to a fight or flight response. Her father was the only one who called her Vivvy. Was it a coincidence, or had Ainsley somehow managed to extract the audio from the footage of their conversation? If she had, then she would know about the revival and that she and Dan'l had both accepted Christ. She sucked in her breath as another possibility hit her. Where was her father now? Was he still in the outer docks? Or was he here, in custody? She had to find out. She didn't doubt that they had planted a tracking device on her bike, so going into the docks without first informing Ainsley was out of the question. And after her recent exchange, Viv wasn't ready to talk to Ainsley anytime soon. The meeting of the underground church was tonight at Stasi's house. Maybe Chess would know something. She walked out of the building, her heart still pounding.

High above in Liberation Station, Ainsley watched the bike speed away and closed her eyes, putting in an order for a camera installation across the street from the Talk-o-Lot Chocolate Café. She was well aware that the best strategy for finding the purpose of the secret meeting may have been to keep her mouth shut and let Viv unknowingly reveal it. But she genuinely liked Viv. She was young, beautiful, and charismatic. The fact that she wasn't chipped made her exponentially more interesting. It practically guaranteed that Viv was in no actual danger of being chipped at Ainsley's order. But Viv didn't need to know that. Of course, it would be ever so much more exciting to legitimately gain her trust and to entice her into a relationship willingly, but Ainsley wasn't opposed to using whatever leverage she had to get what she wanted.

She once again reviewed the footage Wayne had carefully downloaded from his chip and hand-delivered to her, her lips curving into a slight smile as she realized what great lengths he had gone to in order to avoid linking with her again. He had served his purpose. And he had made it clear that he suspected she was overstepping her bounds. She sat down behind her desk and closed her eyes.

Two blocks away, Wayne staggered and leaned against a parking meter. "Wha —No! *No, I won't let you! Keep out!*" he yelled. Passersby on the street made a wide berth around him, assuming they were witnessing one end of a private conversation. People had arguments all the time while linked. It wasn't unusual for their discussion to become so heated that they actually verbalized instead of just keeping the thoughts within their heads. Wayne clenched the meter, his face screwed into an expression of desperation as he slid to the sidewalk. "Someone, help me!" he cried weakly.

A five-year-old boy stopped and tugged on his mother's hand. "Mommy! He needs help!" he implored.

His mother jerked him away, busy looking at the schedule she was scrolling down in her visor. "No, he doesn't, Alphie. The State takes care of everyone. He's just pretending."

Wayne's eyes were fixed on Alphie, but all he could see was his broken neural wall. He had never seen it from the outside. It had seemed impregnable, but she had blasted through it as if it were made of cardboard. He could just make out her svelte figure, clad in an exquisitely tailored aubergine suit with long, flowing coattails. She was heading to the core of his neural network. He struggled to stand, floundering in the foundationless mire outside of his mind. "You can't do this!" he called to her. And then, to himself more piteously, *"How is she doing this?"* Then he suddenly remembered. Whatever she was doing, she couldn't get away with it. All was well. His chip would report anything out of the ordinary. Soon the EMTs would arrive, and everything would be alright. He slowly paddled his way back to his neural boundary. If she was trying to intimidate him, it had worked. But she wouldn't get away with it. He pulled himself back over the broken border. Being a fan of old southwest lore, he had fashioned it to look like the wall of the Alamo. He panted with the exertion. The ground outside of one's own network was bottomless, like quicksand. It was good to be on solid footing again. He stood up and looked toward his core. There she was, casually picking her way toward him through the beautiful gardens he had created in his mind.

"It's been fun, Wayne, but I have to go now," she said playfully.

He cursed and lunged at her, but she nimbly stepped aside and he landed on a neatly trimmed topiary. She smirked as she stepped back over the boundary. "Interesting choice of wall designs," she said cattily. "The Alamo, isn't it? How appropriate!" And then she blinked out of sight.

Wayne stood to his feet. For someone who seemed so intelligent and confident, she was certainly making some vital errors. His chip would have recorded everything. He scratched his head and was surveying his broken wall, when suddenly he felt an unusual feeling in his chest. It was as if a heavy weight was sitting on it. He ran to the center of his neural core and accessed the pull-down menu for his vital signs.

Pulmonary function: not responding. Heart rate: 32.

She must have made it all the way to his neural core and had done something. But how? Those functions were accessible only to the chip's host, and then only for monitoring purposes. Wayne looked around wildly to see when the call to the paramedics had been made. It should have been put in as soon as he had been pushed out of his mind, but there was no record of it. He rushed to do it manually, but it seemed like everything was slowing down. It was becoming difficult to think. The lights in his neural network were growing dimmer, and he could no longer see the menus.

Outside on the sidewalk, people stepped around the prone figure. It was none of their concern. The State would take care of everything.

25

MIST wrapped the district of East Saint Louis in a gauzy coverlet, softening the sharp lines of the state's architectural design. The East Side was historically a dangerous area, but it had been completely revamped after its former residents refused to comply with State imperatives and migrated to the outer docks. Walls once splashed with graffiti had been torn down and replaced with the standard, self-repairing, gray brick used as the building block of modern society. Scrupulously clean parks, with their sculpture gardens and carefully placed benches, utilized the State's version of Feng shui. Revered for their purported connections with the Source, leaders of various religious traditions were invited to provide input for the best flow of energy to yield a harmonious experience for park visitors

Viv pulled the respirator part of her helmet more snugly around her chin as she crossed the Mississippi, where the fog would be at its most caustic. She had never entered the Dead Zone from this area. She glanced at the aluminum gates of the city's famed Karl Marx Park as she passed. They had been fashioned to look like the more traditional wrought iron, which rusted profusely in the fog and was no longer utilized for construction. Hardy yew bushes just inside the park's entrances struggled to thrive, despite meticulous care from city gardeners. Their leprous topiarian forms peeked through barred gates in the shroud of vaporized acid like zombies held back in the gloom. Viv shivered involuntarily and hugged the sides of her bike with her legs. She had never felt safe in this part of town. Perhaps it was a lingering feeling of past events, when the social class riots of 2037 had resulted in atrocities regarded too violent for textbook material. History clung to the area like the ticks that clung to her pant legs in the Preserve. No matter how hard the State tried, there were some elements of the past that couldn't be erased.

Viv turned her thoughts toward the trip ahead of her. Rather than talk to Ainsley about it, she had opted to leave a message for her at the office, informing her of the time of departure and when she could be expected to return. After last night's meeting at Stasi's apartment had yielded no information as to her father's whereabouts, Viv knew she had to try to locate him herself. She had decided to enter by the East Side so as to appear to be expanding her recruiting area, and then make her way slowly to the southwest, stopping at all the working hydrants and any areas of public trade. Once she got to the South Side, she would leave her bike at the Euthanasia Clinic and go on foot. She doubted Ainsley would send someone to follow her in the outer docks, since they would stick out like a sore thumb. Simply leaving the bike in a public area would give her a chance to find her father without being tracked. Her bike's bio-recognition theft system would keep it from being stolen or vandalized, as it was programmed to autopilot its way to her key fob signal should an individual not matching her Palmscan attempt to steal it. Most Discards knew better than to tamper with a vehicle, which not only gave a verbal warning that its security system was in place, but was also capable of delivering an electric shock before relocating itself.

Viv swept quietly through the entrance to the Dead Zone. The fog was thickest here. She could barely see the edge of the road to her right, and the lack of any buildings made it seem as if she were floating along a bridge with no sides. She didn't even realize she had strayed from the road until she became vaguely aware her bike was making hardly any noise. Traveling in the State, the bike gave a characteristic hum as the wind it generated pushed against the pavement, which was textured for the safety of vehicles with wheels. But now it was strangely quiet. She came to a dead stop and studied the ground beneath her. It was the smooth concrete block finish of the Dead Zone. She hadn't realized the roads through the zone were anything but straight. Either she had veered to one side, or the road had curved. She began again, moving at a slow crawl as she moved slowly to the left for a few yards and then to the right in an attempt to rediscover the road. A working GPS system would come in handy now, she mused. Her dysfunctional unit had been a godsend when she was visiting her friends in

Adullam, since she couldn't be tracked. But now that she worked for the State, her days of freedom and wandering out in the Preserve, undetected, appeared to be over. Anxiety gripped her chest like an invisible iron glove. Would she ever be free again? *"Jesus, I don' know how much longer I can do this. But I don't see any way I can get outta this job without lookin' suspicious,"* she prayed silently. If she had known that the last time she had been to Adullam would possibly be *the* last time, would she have left?

She had been a fool not to stay, she thought angrily. But then Dawson's words came back to her. *"You may be the only source of the gospel to the people back in the State. You may be their only hope of meeting Jesus!"* he had told her.

She felt like she had failed miserably. After all, Janice had taken the chip after Viv had tried to witness to her, and Viv's reaction to her friend's decision had nearly landed her in reconditioning therapy. Viv had accepted Ainsley's job offer because she felt she had no choice.

But did she? She had soothed her conscience by telling herself she could be a witness to the Discards she was trying to recruit. However, her efforts to save her own skin had brought her in contact with her father, who was later recorded at the Euthanasia Clinic saying he had to get a message to her. She knew he would never have visited that clinic unless he felt someone's life was at stake. Now all she wanted to do was to make sure he was safe. That, and leave the State forever and go back to Adullam, where she would never have to worry about being open about her faith. *If only the citizens could see Jesus for Who He really is*, she thought. Then they wouldn't report her. They would understand—and possibly believe. And if enough of them believed, and if the gospel was preached and lives started being changed, how could the State squash that kind of hope?

It was already happening in the outer docks. She had thought she should steer clear of the revival so the State wouldn't find out, and maybe she should. But what would stop her from letting Discards in other areas know about it? She could hand out little packages of Sytha-meat jerky here and there and tell people about the meeting in the outskirts of the South Side. No Discard would rat her out, simply because she was giving them food when she told them. As the plan began to take shape in her mind, hope rose up within her. Maybe it wasn't a mistake for her to leave Adullam, after all. Maybe she *could* make a difference.

"Oh!" Viv exclaimed, as a figure suddenly appeared directly in front of her. She swerved to the left but couldn't avoid collision. The bike made contact with a sickening thump, knocking the person to the ground. Viv stopped the bike and leapt off to check on the unexpected pedestrian. What kind of a State employee would be walking in the Dead Zone in this kind of fog? She could see the huddled form a few feet away, struggling to get up. "Jovies, I didn't see ya in this fog! Are ya okay, then? Let me take ya to get some help!" Viv said as she approached. But the silent figure only gave her a quick glance through the full-face respirator mask he wore, jumped to his feet and disappeared into the fog. Viv's heart skipped a beat as she realized she had just hit a Discard who was sneaking into the city. She had heard stories about people making it to the inside, but had always assumed they traveled underground through the toxic fumes of the sewage tunnels. How they could survive it was anybody's guess. Without a respirator and a full body suit, it would be impossible. But this Discard had somehow acquired a very sophisticated mask. As long as he had a liaison waiting for him at the gate, he could make it undetected above ground when the fog was this thick.

Viv climbed back aboard her bike. To continue to search for him would be pointless. The fog was impenetrable, and the man obviously didn't want to be found. She studied the smooth bricks beneath her as the bike hovered slowly above them. Once again, she began her slow, weaving pattern, looking for the road. Her search was interrupted a few minutes later by the wall to the outer docks. All she need to do now was travel along the base of it until she found the gate. She wasn't certain whether to go left or right, but for some reason, left seemed the better choice. After only a few yards, a sudden opening in the wall to her right confirmed she had made the right decision. She passed through the gate and inched along the roadway, taking care to be more observant this time. Her ride was more dangerous now, since she would be encountering obstacles such as buildings, dumpsters, and any debris or pallets stacked near the road. The fog probably wouldn't thin out very quickly, since her route would eventually curve back toward the river as she angled to the southwest. She could feel a stinging sensation on her neck and quickly zipped the bodysuit up more closely to her helmet. The sooner she could get out of this area, the better.

But the farther she went, the slower she had to go. She glanced at the tenement buildings on either side of her. She could faintly make out light in some of the windows. If she had still been living here, she would have knocked on a door and asked if she could stay until the fog lifted. Although she wasn't known in this part of the outer docks as "the Deserter," she had known very few Discards who would simply open their home to a strange visitor from the State. Viv crept along the road, coughing despite the respirator in her helmet. This was the worst fog she had ever seen. "Jesus, I think I made a mistake comin' this way. Please help me outta this mess! Take away the fog, or help me ta get outta the fog," she prayed desperately and pushed down on the accelerator. A few moments later, her bike reared up and threatened to roll over backwards with her as she ran up on an overturned trash can. Viv was thrown to the ground, landing awkwardly on one foot before her helmet crashed into a nearby porch step with a loud *thwack!* She lay still for a moment, dazed, as the bike righted itself. Light spilled into the fog as the door to the apartment opened, and Viv could hear quick, light footsteps coming her direction.

"Phoenix, you get back here!" called a man's voice from the doorway. "You can't go out when it's like this!"

"But Daddy, someone's out here an' they needs help!" Suddenly, Viv felt a little hand on her shoulder. "You gotta come inside," Phoenix said, and then burst into an uncontrollable fit of coughing from the fog. Viv snapped out of her daze and struggled to her feet, but her ankle had other ideas.

"Pheonix, you is in so much *trouble,*" said another young voice from the doorway, drawing out the last word to emphasize just how much trouble Pheonix was in.

"Hush, Sparta. Get inside. Phoenix, git in this house an' let me take care o' this," said Phoenix's father, tying a scarf around his face as he came down the steps.

Another adult wearing a cloth mask appeared in the doorway behind him. "Wallace, let me give you a hand," said the figure, who was following closely behind. Viv strained to see the man who had just spoken. His accent seemed off, somehow, and there was something familiar about his voice.

"I think I'm okay, I just can't see three feet in this fog," Viv said as she struggled to stand. "Wouldja mind if I came in 'til it clears?"

As she spoke, the man who had come to help stopped in midstride. Then he was down the steps in one leap and at her side, helping Wallace assist her into the house. Once inside with the door safely shut, Viv took off her helmet and stared at amazement at Wallace's helper, who was ripping off his mask. "Garrison! How —what—I can't believe it!" she cried.

Garrison was grinning from ear to ear as he grabbed her in a bear hug. "Lelah, get in here! You're not going to believe this!" he called in the direction of another room.

Suddenly, Lelah appeared and squealed with delight, and Viv almost thought she had died in the bike wreck and gone to Heaven. "What are y'all doin' here? How did y'all get here?" Viv asked.

"Will ya let the girl sit down?" said a salty voice from the kitchen doorway. "Cain't ya see she's hurt? Whadja do to ya leg, honey?"

"I think I landed funny on ma foot and twisted ma ankle," Viv said as they helped her to a wooden bench made of pallet boards. "But where's the little guy what came out ta help me? If it hadn't been fa him, I might still be out there, chokin' in the fog." She looked around the room, and a six-year-old boy rushed forward to introduce himself.

"I'm Phoenix, and you're pretty," he said with a gallant smile, as his parents grinned and shook their heads in amusement.

Viv smiled back at him. "Thank ya so much for comin' to ma rescue."

Phoenix blushed and went to stand beside his big sister. "I can't believe ya flirted like that!" she said to him in a loud whisper hidden behind her hand.

"I wasn't flirtin'! It's da truth!" Phoenix said fiercely, and started coughing again.

"Now, you stop talkin'," Pheonix's mother ordered. "I'll fix ya up some hot water fa steamin'."

The feisty woman, whom Viv later learned was called Annabel, retreated to the kitchen to make a soothing treatment for Pheonix's burned throat. Memories of sore throats caused by acid fog came back to her, along with the practice of leaning over a pot of hot, steaming water with a cloth draped over your head so you could breathe its soothing steam. Discards had varying degrees of hoarseness to their voices from vocal cords that had been persistently irritated by exposure to the fog, and Viv was no exception. Her voice had a slight raspy edge to it which some people in the State found endearing or even alluring. To her, it was just another factor that branded her as different. "Listen, I wanna know how y'all got here. Say *all!*" Viv looked from Garrison to Lelah imploringly.

"We came as a missionary team," Lelah explained.

"A team of just you and Garrison?"

"We started out with Thom, Dania, Lydia, Chandra, Garrison and me—and Craig," Lelah said, glancing at Garrison as she mentioned their youth pastor. "We ran into an old woman out in the woods on our way up here—"

"Yeah, and you're not going to believe this, but she said she helped Selah sneak in," Garrison interrupted.

"Are ya yankin' ma chain, Way Man? Is Selah really here?" Viv asked incredulously.

"Yup. Anyway, that's how *we* got in, too. The old lady decided to help us. She thought we were crazy for coming here. Said we were giving up everything she had always dreamed of having."

Lelah smiled warmly as she remembered their old friend. "She told us her name was Wisteria, but we found out later it was Zelda."

Viv's eyes opened wide. "I remember Zelda from *way* back. An' Selah must have started the revival, am I right?" Viv asked.

Garrison and Lelah exchanged glances. "Yes, she did. Have they heard about it in the State?" Garrison asked.

"No. Not that I know of. I found out cuz ma dad went, and he got saved!" Viv exclaimed happily.

"Oh, Viv, that's wonderful!" Lelah cried, sidling up to her on the bench and hugging her tightly. "We actually met him when we first got here. He wanted Selah to pray for you." She looked at Viv searchingly. "We were so worried about you. You stopped coming and we thought maybe something had happened."

"Yeah, I figgered y'all would wonder what was up, like maybe they finally caught me an' chipped me, or somethin'. Turns out I got a job with the government." She paused as she saw her hosts stiffen slightly. "Let's just say it was an offer I couldn't refuse," she explained in a dark tone. "I'm s'posed ta convince Discards to come to the State an' start a new life, like *I* did. So I went to the Shaw, an' who should I run into but ma dad? An' he tells me about the revival. But ma new boss saw the video footage, an' now I'm wonderin' if she mighta had him arrested so she can keep me under her thumb."

Lelah brightened. "Well, you don't need to worry about that anymore, because he's staying with a friend of ours until he gets better."

Viv looked at her, nonplussed. "Gets better? Is he sick?"

Garrison cleared his throat. "Have you heard of the Gateway Gang?"

Viv's face darkened. "What happened?"

"Dan'l said they wanted to send you a message. They don't want you coming around on their turf. They've been capitalizing on this revival, keeping people away unless they have something to give in exchange for passage, and you being around as the eyes and the ears of the State puts their business endeavors at risk. They like the revival, so long as the State doesn't find out about it," Garrison explained.

"Is Dad okay?" Viv asked worriedly.

"His knee is really messed up, but he's better since we prayed for him," Lelah said.

"I'd like ta see 'im, but the Gateways'd prob'ly finish 'im off if I tried." Viv scowled. "Keepin' people from goin' to the revival unless they pay somethin'!" she huffed.

"It ain't ideal, but we don' know what ta do about it," said Wallace. "They's gettin' too big fo' their britches, the Gateways are."

"I won't *nevah* join *them*," Pheonix proclaimed.

"I'm glad ta hear it, Pheonix," Viv smiled, and then looked wonderingly at her friends. "Can ya believe that of all the places I could flip ma bike, it jus' *happens* to be in front of the house where y'all 're stayin'? It's like Dawson says—divine coincidence. Ya can't plan stuff like that, but God can." Her head was overflowing with so many questions she couldn't decide what to ask first. "So where are the others?" she finally asked.

"Thom and Dania went to the Upscales," Garrison said.

"Chandra and Lydia went to the southwest," Lelah added.

"Where's Craig? Did he stay with Selah in the outskirts?" Viv asked, her face brightening. "How is he? I've really missed hearing him preach."

Lelah bit her lip and looked down. Viv looked back and forth at them, alarmed. "What happened?"

"They caught him when we were still out in the Preserve," Garrison said.

Viv's blood ran cold. "They would want to find out everything he knew," she said.

"Does that mean–?" Lelah asked tentatively.

"They done chipped 'im," Sparta said, her bright eyes wide with fear.

"Now, we don' know that for sure, honey," Annabel reprimanded her daughter gently.

"If he isn't chipped yet, they'll prob'ly get around to it," Viv said dismally. A look of determination came across her face. "But I bet I know where he is."

26

CRAIG arose as he heard the door to his quarters open with a *whoosh.* It was time for breakfast, and every mealtime someone would bring him a tray of food. Sometimes it was a woman with blond hair woven into a series of complicated braids captured behind her head. Sometimes it was a middle-aged man with a beard contained behind a mesh covering. Both of them were clothed in the same serene shade of green, and neither of them ever spoke to him, although he had attempted to converse with them on several occasions. This time it was the woman. "Good morning!" he said amiably. "Thank you for bringing me breakfast. Do you have a big day planned today?"

The woman's eyelids fluttered slightly as she made a conscious effort not to look him in the eye. Craig took the tray and thanked her again. The woman stepped away from the door, and it slid closed. Several times he had wondered what would happen if he would bust out the door when his tray was delivered. But what would be the point? Where would he go from there? He would only get himself labeled as dangerous and untrustworthy if he pulled such a stunt, and perhaps be taken to a more restrictive environment. He had been here ever since being released by Detective Riedert, and had seen no one except the museum curator and the people who delivered his food. He wondered what had happened to Yosi. The man was obviously important, or Craig was convinced he would have found himself rotting in a prison cell or already implanted with a chip instead of waiting in a comfortable apartment, albeit in isolation. Perhaps Yosi was protecting him out of a sense of nostalgia for his old community. Or was he simply preserving him to deliver to his superiors in order to advance himself? Perhaps he was just busy. Or maybe the lack of communication was some sort of tactic to make him nervous.

He sat down in the comfortable chair in the sitting room where he had met with Rhys. The plate of food in his lap was a feast compared to what he and the others had been eating out in the woods. Suddenly he found he wasn't hungry. He picked up the tray and sat it down on the floor by the door, where he had been instructed to leave it when he was finished. He couldn't just stay here, calmly eating his meals while his real mission was being neglected. He walked back to the chair and knelt down beside it. "God, I need You!" he cried softly. "You asked me to come here to spread Your Word. But how can I do that if I'm trapped in this room?" He closed his eyes and buried his face in the chair cushion. Scriptures he had committed to memory floated to the surface of his mind, and he spoke them out loud to remind himself of the promises they contained. *"May the God of peace Himself sanctify you wholly; and may your spirit and soul and body be kept sound and blameless at the coming of our Lord Jesus Christ. He who calls you is faithful, and He will do it.*[72] Lord, You called me. You are faithful. I know You asked me to step out in faith when I left Adullam, and I know You asked me to step out onto the road so I would be caught. And here I am. There has to be a reason that You asked me to do those things. I'm not here by accident. Your Word says 'The steps of a good man are ordered by the Lord: and He delighteth in his way. Though he fall, he shall not be utterly cast down: for the Lord upholdeth him with His hand.'[73] Father, I'm trusting You, that You're ordering my steps. I know I'm not here by accident. Now, please show me what I can do to further Your kingdom from where I am." Craig knelt with his face against the chair until the marks of the fabric were imprinted in his forehead. He forced himself to be still and listen. When fear and worry rose up, he fought it with God's Word. "God hasn't given me a spirit of fear; but one of power and love and a sound mind,"[74] he said aloud, and focused on what it would be like to stand face to face with his Creator. He had made the choices he made because he loved Jesus and wanted to serve Him. Suddenly, a passage of scripture began to unfold in his mind, as though he were reading it.

A disciple is not above his teacher, nor a servant above his master; it is enough for the disciple to be like his teacher, and the servant like his

---

[72] 1 Thessalonians 5:23-24, RSV
[73] Psalm 37:23-24, KJV
[74] See 2 Timothy 1:7

master. If they have called the master of the house Beelzebul, how much more will they malign those of his household.

So have no fear of them; for nothing is covered that will not be revealed, or hidden that will not be known. What I tell you in the dark, utter in the light; and what you hear whispered, proclaim upon the house-tops. And do not fear those who kill the body but cannot kill the soul; rather fear Him who can destroy both soul and body in hell. Are not two sparrows sold for a penny? And not one of them will fall to the ground without your Father's will. But even the hairs of your head are all numbered. Fear not, therefore; you are of more value than many sparrows. So every one who acknowledges Me before men, I also will acknowledge before My Father Who is in heaven; but whoever denies Me before men, I also will deny before My Father Who is in heaven.[75]

Craig's breath caught in his throat. He had the distinct feeling that he was on the brink of something—something that would not be easy and would not make sense. He raised his head, his fingers gripping the chair cushion. "I trust You," he said. He heard the door open, and there was a pause as the woman hesitated to pick up the untouched tray of food. Then he heard a slight rattling of a juice box and the plate when it slid on the tray as it was retrieved. The door *whooshed* shut again. Craig remained in an attitude of prayer and fasting throughout the day.

And the next day.

And the next.

The trays remained untouched by the door until they were taken away once an hour had passed. On the morning of the fourth day, Craig was sitting in the chair, feeling rather weak, when he heard the door open behind him at the normal time. He waited for the tray to be placed on the floor, but instead, he heard the footsteps of someone crossing the threshold. It wasn't the woman. She used a slightly perfumed soap with a distinctive scent. His sense of smell had been heightened by the days of fasting, and he couldn't detect that particular smell. It wasn't the man, either, he reflected absently, because the man had a

---

[75] Matthew 10:24-33 RSV

slight limp. Whoever it was, they were approaching the back of the chair with the tray of food—hashbrowns and bacon and eggs, by the smell of it. And then Dr. Moses was standing in front of him, holding the tray with a rather bemused expression on his face.

"I suppose this is your way of getting my attention?" the man said as he sat the tray of food down on the coffee table directly in front of Craig.

Craig didn't change positions. He was too weak for social graces. He smiled wanly, noticing he had been right about what was on the menu. "No."

Dr. Moses sat down in the chair opposite him. "No?" he said and then allowed himself a mirthless chuckle. "Of course not. You're trying to get God's attention. Asking him to get you out of this mess. But he won't, you know. All your fasting is pointless. He doesn't exist. He's not going to save you."

"No," Craig said.

"You agree that he's not going to save you?" Dr. Moses asked, intrigued.

"He already saved me. I'm just saying that's not the reason I'm fasting. I'm trying to line up my thinking with His—and trying to lay aside all my plans and preconceived ideas about what this was supposed to be like."

"What *was* this supposed to be like, Craig? Did you think the State was going to allow you to stand on a street corner and preach? To hold a revival in a tent? You're so blinded by your misplaced faith that you can't even see that this little hunger strike isn't doing any good. If you would just let me help you, I can show you a place where you can anchor your faith—one with solid facts that can be proven."

"We walk by faith, not by sight,"[76] Craig said softly.

Dr. Moses' eyes narrowed. He doubted that the man would listen to him, but he had to try. "Let go, my friend. Let go of your dusty dogma. God *is* real. He just isn't who you thought he was. Humanity has discovered that when we are connected, we are unstoppable! Our combined intellect, aided by technology, has solved the problems of disease and world hunger and emotional instability. No one has to be sick anymore, or hungry or lonely or depressed or insane. We've cracked it, Craig—the puzzle of humanity! We used to rely on superstition and mythology and religion to fill in the missing puzzle pieces, but now the

---

[76] See 2 Corinthians 5:7

puzzle is complete! You don't have to wonder if God is real, because in a sense, he is, because *we are it!* We are the ones our ancestors told stories about. Science explains how we evolved over centuries, making miniscule advancements over the eons. We came to the point of sentience and reason and adopted stories to explain our beginnings, but now we can see that in a sense, *we were* that beginning! The source of all life is now looking back upon its origins and realizing that everything is connected. And now we're taking the next step in that process of realization: a massive mental collaborative. A global consciousness, if you will. We've evolved from a being who seeks merely to survive, into one who seeks to understand why they exist and what kind of miracles they can achieve if they work together as one."

Craig swallowed. "Like a super species of bees or ants," he mused. "So who gets to be the queen?"

Moses pushed the tray of food toward Craig and leaned back in the chair. "Ahh. So you *were* listening."

"Someone has to be the queen. Otherwise, there would be chaos. Who gets to play god in your world, Yosi? Is it you?" Craig asked evenly.

"This isn't a sci-fi movie, Craig. I'm not an evil genius bent on ruling the world. I am merely an architect assisting in the next evolutionary step of humanity. When the whole world is connected via a mental link, we will understand each other—not only on an emotional level, but linguists theorize that we will develop a new language based on the essence of thought. It will be quicker than our clunky vocabularies and will convey ideas and emotions in an instant. And much like your Christian view of the church as the body of Christ, all of the parts will work together for the good of the whole."

"But someone has to be the head of that body," Craig insisted.

"Those with leadership skills will naturally become the collective decision makers, although with the advanced mental capabilities made available by the chip, those suitable for leadership will be more numerous than one might suppose. And I know you're thinking that we might be paralyzed by an internal war for dominance, but think about it: when you make a decision, do you fight with yourself?"

"All the time," Craig confessed. "Sometimes I know the right thing to do, but I don't want to do it. I have to convince myself the inconvenience or my own personal preference shouldn't overcome my ability to make the right decision."

"Ahh, but now we have the chip and its ability to perform algorithms weighing the probable results of decisions to do that tedious work for us. Except the chip will be free from bias, making decisions purely based on our good. The combined brain and computing power of billions of chipped individuals will determine where we go from here."

Craig was silent for a moment as he studied the man across the coffee table. He had a brilliant mind, but all Craig could see was a lonely, angry little boy. And suddenly he understood. "You act as though you're doing this for the good of humanity. It sounds noble and some would even call it 'godlike.' But that's not why you're doing it."

"I know better than to ask this question, but I am curious. Why do *you* think I'm doing it?" Moses leaned forward, propping his chin on his clasped hands as he rested his elbows on his knees.

"You're angry. You've never forgiven your father for taking you away and isolating you from the rest of the world. He never understood or appreciated your gift. This is your chance to show him—and the world—that you matter."

Moses' eyes grew cold, and his smile disappeared. But Craig continued.

"What you aren't willing to accept is that you *already* matter, and always have. Even if you never came up with the chip and its potential to connect the whole world, you mattered enough for the God you don't acknowledge to send His Son to pay for your sins so that *He* could connect with *you*. That's what your father really wanted for you. Even if he didn't understand your passion for technology, he loved you. He wanted to connect with you. But even more than that, he wanted you to connect with your heavenly Father."

"Well, now he'll get a chance to connect with me. Because like it or not, I *will* find Adullam. And you're going to help me."

"By shoving a chip into my brain without my consent? Is that the way things are handled in your utopian world of collaborative consciousness?"

Dr. Moses' lips formed into a thin line that might have passed for a smile. "It would be so much easier for you and for everyone concerned if you would consent willingly. If you don't fight it, you'll understand how much better things will be for everyone. Once the whole world is united, there will be no need for people starving in the borders of our cities. They will finally understand what it is we're trying to accomplish! We can reverse the effect of pollution on our planet, preserve endangered species, selectively guide the genetics of our progeny to produce greater minds and healthier vehicles to contain them. There will be no limit to what we can achieve if we work together!"

Craig was silent for a moment, seeming to study his hands. Then his eyes rose to meet Dr. Moses' gaze. "There was another time when humanity felt this way. It didn't work out so well. Do you remember the story of the Tower of Babel?" he asked quietly.

"Ahh, yes. The confusing of the languages," Dr. Moses smiled reminiscently. "I actually used that myth to expound upon my reasoning to secure the pilot program for the chip and my study of linked individuals. It's how the Pod-Op program came into being. Our antiquated belief system had its evolutionary purpose. It kept us under control. It created a moral standard that kept us from completely annihilating each other. But now that belief is holding us back. We don't need a mythological subscript to guide modern society. We can take care of ourselves now. We are in command of our own destiny, and it's a good destiny, if we will all work together."

"You can't really believe that everyone will have the same opinion about how things should be run," Craig stated.

"No, of course not! But the chip will weigh out the best option for the planet and its species as a whole—as I explained earlier—and the correct decisions will be made."

"What about those who don't want to be chipped? I've heard that it doesn't work out very well for people who are not compliant."

"If they make the right choice—the choice to allow the technology to blend with their mental processes and aid them in their thinking and learning—then they will have taken a brave first step into a new world of unlimited possibilities."

"And if they don't? If they don't choose to comply?"

"It's unlikely they'll survive. But it's their choice. Isn't that what you say about where we spend eternity? 'God doesn't send us to hell. We choose to go there.'"

"It *is* a choice. But the choice of whether or not to comply with the chip isn't a choice about where to spend eternity. Eventually, we'll all have to face the ultimate consequences of the choice we made of whether or not to accept Christ's free gift of forgiveness. *That* is the ultimate choice. And no matter how noble you think you're being and no matter how far you go in this utopian dream of yours, until you forgive your father, you won't ever progress beyond the decision you made as a child to punish him for isolating you."

Dr. Moses' eyes glittered in the dim light of the sitting room, and he rose to his feet and paced back and forth along the length of the wall. Finally, he turned on his heel and fixed his gaze on Craig. "How much do you trust your god, Craig? What lengths would you be willing to go to in order to prove that he's real and that he's worth believing in?"

A strange feeling came over Craig, because he knew exactly what Dr. Moses was going to ask him next. He knew that Moses wasn't really giving him a choice. But he knew that it didn't matter. All that mattered was that God was with him, right there, at that moment. The peace was overwhelming. "Give it to me. I'll take it. 'The Lord is on my side; I will not fear: what can man do unto me?'[77]"

Dr. Moses' eyes widened in momentary astonishment, and then he left the room, taking the tray with him. The procedure required that the patient abstain from food or drink, and Craig had been on a three-day fast of food and water. The chip was already made, its biocomponents having been grown in the lab using the DNA sample they had taken from the man upon his arrival at the facility. They could begin preparations immediately. Craig had unexpectedly taken away the unpleasantness of forcing someone to take the chip against their will by his act of volunteering—Dr. Moses assumed—in an effort to prove the Christian God would protect him. Moses shook his head. If the man would just receive it with an open mind, he would survive it and would understand. It would all become clear. And if he could get someone like Craig to understand, perhaps Craig could reach other Christians and free them from their prison of religious mind-control. Eventually, they could even help his father and the people of Adullam to see the truth—if they could ever find them.

---

[77] Psalm 118:6, KJV

Back in the apartment, Craig sank to his knees and stretched out flat on the floor. Once again, he knew God had asked him to make a decision which seemed to make no sense. It was possible Moses had even thought he had risen to the bait to prove that God was real and would be his protector. But as he lay there, basking in waves of inexplicable peace, he knew he had made the right decision. What Moses or anyone else thought didn't matter—only what God had asked of him mattered. And although he couldn't understand it, he had decided once again to obey. A voice echoed in his mind: *"Fear thou not; for I am with thee: be not dismayed; for I am thy God: I will strengthen thee; yea, I will help thee; yea, I will uphold thee with the right hand of my righteousness."*[78]

---

[78] Isaiah 41:10 KJV

27

Iʀᴀ blinked within the helmet of the interface suit. It had taken some work to convince them he needed to wait until the chip was implanted to install the new program in the most recent subject. Moses was very keen on him installing it onto the chip directly, but Ira knew he couldn't risk creating such a version. Moses would undoubtedly study it to discover how Ira had achieved the impossible, and its true purpose would immediately become apparent. For that reason, Ira had insisted it was housed in the juncture of technology and organic matter—the initial melding point of neural-tech interface—requiring him to tailor-make the program specifically to each individual. Because of this, it would need to be programmed on site via link or virtual link after implantation. "Very well, Ira. I'm certain that, as the program engineer, you understand all the nuances of its design. But in the future, I'd like you to work toward developing a version that can be integral to the chip and will then spread through the neural interface from there. If the malware we encountered earlier can't be destroyed, every person on the planet who is susceptible to the virus will need to have the benefit of your antiviral program. Surely you concede that it would be laborious for you to be the sole programmer and installer?" Dr. Moses said with a smile.

"Indeed," Ira affirmed. "And as soon as I figure out how to create a universal version that can diverge into the varied personalities of its hosts, I'll be glad to implement it. But now, that type of homogeneity could create a whole new subset of problems. I still need to work on the ability of the individual to generate an appropriate defense response to those with whom they do not wish to link. Can you imagine a standardization of minimal resistance to link initiation? I may have given *you* a way in, but not everyone should be allowed access to a person's mind without their consent. And who's to say a standardized version wouldn't have the effect of manufacturing identical responses to other stimuli? I'm not willing to risk the subsuming of personality traits that could result in such a venture."

Dr. Moses sighed and shook his head. "You're quite right, of course. The moral clime you insist on espousing can be extremely limiting and irritating at times, but I agree with you on this point. We need to work toward a version that allows access of doctors, programmers, and therapists to their patients, yet allows the individual to raise up a wall against neural predators. I truly believe this program will eventually become part of the chip's mandated security software. But this must be done correctly in order for us to win the confidence of those who are still hesitant to be implanted. Of course, they never need know about the malware, since we already have the antidote, so to speak. But if they see their fellow citizens becoming copies of each other on some neurological level, they'll want to know why; and then we would have to make a cover story for both the malware and your program and possibly begin all over again to gain their trust."

So Ira was allowed to continue his rescue mission uninterrupted, and Moses and Ainsley were none the wiser. He looked around the quiet mindscape. The man had been implanted only two days ago and had been kept heavily sedated to aid in his healing process during the initial growth of connections between the biocomponents of the chip and his brain. Every precaution had been taken to ensure success and guard against rejection by the host, but this was a critical stage. Ira was concerned that any interaction he might have with the neural net could prove permanently damaging. *"Jesus, please keep him safe,"* he prayed silently. *"Keep his mind intact. Guide my steps so that I will cause no harm."*

Every chip was programmed to recognize an individual's natural neural boundary. People normally created their own protective wall, even without implantation, to shield themselves from hurt that came from interactions with others or trauma from accidents or incidents that couldn't be processed all at once. With the possibility of a neural link came the necessity to build a neural wall that was even stronger than the psychological one that was already there. The chip worked with the host to strengthen their wall, even giving them the option to tear down what had been built and begin again with what was considered a stronger foundation provided by the chip. Most people were reluctant to tear down a wall that had taken them years to build. Which was why he was slightly confused about what he saw.

So far as he could tell, there *was* no wall. Ira knew he was standing just outside the normal location of a boundary. He could see a beautiful light that glowed from the neural core, and he could vaguely make out the shapes of pathways that marked the man's memories, but the wall was nowhere to be seen.

It was disturbing, to say the least. Ira wasn't certain what good his firewall program would do if there was no wall to hide in the first place. He dare not attempt to speak to the host, for he was convinced, simply by the veiled manner in which Moses had discussed him, that the man was in a psychologically fragile state. From what Ira could gather, he had volunteered to be chipped, but had a limited understanding of what that meant and was a product of years of brainwashing. What sort of brainwashing was left up to Ira's imagination.

Perhaps installing the program would give the man some time to build his own wall. Ira began to take a step forward, but then stopped. It didn't make sense. If he had been brainwashed, wouldn't there be *some* sort of wall? That form of mind control depended on barriers that kept out the truth of what was actually taking place in the outside world. Something wasn't right. He might be forced to speak to the man, after all.

"Craig Goforth? Can you hear me?" Ira whispered softly.

There was no reply, only a gentle breeze that began to blow from the neural core, traveling outward to where a border should have been.

"I'm going to come in now. I'm here to help you." Ira took a step forward.

Suddenly, light exploded all around him as a bolt of lightning seemed to leap from the ground. Ira was propelled backward, landing flat on his back and knocked momentarily unconscious. When he came to, his whole body tingled, and his heart was pounding madly in his chest. He cautiously raised his head. Standing between him and the man's mindscape was the most fearsome creature he had ever seen. It appeared to be a human in form, but it was like no other human Ira had encountered. He estimated its height to be fifteen feet. It was clothed like a warrior, with a sword strapped to its belt. Its right hand rested on the hilt of the sword, and its eyes rested dispassionately on Ira. They were the eyes of a soldier, ready to follow orders from its commanding officer. As if the creature's height and sword weren't intimidating enough, wings stretched from behind its back, forming a forty-foot barrier to protect the man's neural network.

Ira's breath caught in his throat. He exhaled slowly, and while keeping as low a profile as possible, began inching his way backward. When he had gained a respectable distance, he cautiously crept to his knees. The creature was still watching him, its eyes fierce and vigilant, like a bird of prey. Ira trembled. There was no way he could get past this being. He was about to turn off the interface suit and give it up as a lost cause when he remembered why he was here. This was about protecting the man. The winged creature was obviously trying to do the same thing. Perhaps Ira could reason with it. Or alternatively, if this was the product of brainwashing, perhaps he could poke a hole in its argument. He slowly stood to his feet. "Whose side are you on? Are you for Craig, or against him?" Ira said, trying to sound brave. His voice seemed muffled, as if Craig was protected even from the intrusion of sound.

"Neither. I am an officer in the army of the Almighty One. I am commanded to hold this boundary," said the creature in a voice that could level the trees on a hillside.

Ira attempted to stand to his feet, visibly shaking. "I'm here to help the man you're protecting," he said meekly.

"Your species is known for its lying tongue," the being answered, and drew its sword. "Proceed at your own peril."

Suddenly a voice sounded across the mindscape. "Stand down, Benaiah. This is the man I told you would be coming."

The being immediately folded its wings and stepped aside, revealing Jesus standing within the neural network. Ira was awash in relief. "Jesus! Thank God —I mean, thank *You*, You're here!"

Jesus held out his hand, beckoning for him to come forward. "It's alright, Ira. You may pass the boundary now."

Ira hesitated, his eyes still on the mighty warrior. "I can't even *see* the boundary. I mean, the only reason I knew it was there is because I know where it's *supposed* to be and—and that…*thing* was standing guard over it," Ira said, as he hurried to Jesus' side, his eyes still on Benaiah.

"Benaiah is an angel," Jesus explained, leading Ira deeper into Craig's neural network.

"An angel?" Ira said, peeking around Jesus' shoulder. "In all the pictures I've seen, angels either look like fat little babies with tiny wings or women with long, flowing hair and harps or trumpets."

Jesus raised his eyebrows and smiled. "There's a reason why, whenever you read many of the accounts of angelic beings speaking to humans, the angel usually reassures them and tells them not to be afraid. Of course, not all encounters are like this. Some people interact with angels without ever knowing it. Some angels are messengers, while some minister to people's needs. Benaiah is a warrior angel."

"I can see that," Ira said, glancing back at the boundary, which was once again shielded by Benaiah's wings.

"He is guarding Craig from the north. There are three other angels stationed around the boundary, guarding the south, east and west sides."

"Why is there no boundary?" Ira asked. "Does it have something to do with the man being brainwashed?"

Jesus sighed. "Craig isn't brainwashed."

"So Moses lied again," Ira said coldly. "I suspected as much."

"Joseph doesn't think he's lying. He thinks that people like Craig have been brainwashed into believing in Me. It suits his agenda very nicely, allowing him to fancy himself some sort of champion of humanity and freedom of thought. But deep in his heart, he knows the truth. The seed was planted there long ago by his parents. True freedom only comes from total surrender, which is why Craig has dropped his neural boundary. He has surrendered everything to Me—even the very essence of who he is. Which is why we are defending him so fiercely."

Ira swallowed. "I would very much like to meet this man," he said softly. "But I was afraid any interaction with him might prove damaging to his mind."

"Not as long as I am here," Jesus said. "I have come to heal him and to reveal to him the purpose of his being implanted with the chip. I'm going to go visit with him now. The fact that his wall is down gives you the ability to install the connections and accompanying safeguards needed for him to complete his mission. I want you to begin installing the firewall. Benaiah and the others will be there to aid and protect you should you need it." Jesus stopped for a moment to make eye contact. "Ira, Craig is the man I'm going to use to reach nations. He is going to speak to every implanted individual. He needs to be able to talk to them, undetected by any 'guard-dog' protocols that may report him as a possible threat. If he's marked as suspicious, no one will want to initiate a link with him."

"Wait a minute—you mean he's going to talk to every chipped person on the planet? There are already over a million in the State, alone. I'm not certain what the number is overseas, but the World Health Alliance has promoted it aggressively. In China, they've already been implanting babies for several years now, and you know how staggering their population is—even after years of population control measures. It would take him years—even a lifetime—to talk to everyone. In fact, I don't think it's humanly possible!" Ira exclaimed.

"That's correct. It isn't," Jesus said simply.

"So how is he supposed to do this?" Ira asked.

"You know how Joseph keeps preaching about a massive collaborative link?" Jesus said with a slight grin.

"Yes, but we're a few years from figuring out the logistics of that. The human brain isn't capable of handling multiple links. We'll need safeguards to keep people from being overwhelmed by all the information. Security programs will need to be created to protect the individual's rights during such a link. A governing body of administrators will need to be in place to direct all the information. If any participants suffer psychological malfunction, it could act as malware that could infect the whole system. And not to mention that any power-crazed programmer who has the skill necessary could sway the course of human history by usurping individual freedom and instating themselves as the sole administrator. The checks and balances haven't been put in place. The infrastructure just isn't there yet." Ira stopped talking as he noticed Jesus was watching him patiently.

"Are you finished explaining to Me how it can't be done?"

"Yes," Ira said meekly.

"Joseph wants a link in which all of humanity can understand each other by being able to feel what everyone feels and communicate through thought. He thinks this will bring unity to the world. But it won't. Just because people understand each other doesn't mean they'll immediately work together. The world governments know this."

"Then why did the World Health Alliance mandate that Dr. Moses should receive funding?"

"There is a spirit which works against Me and everyone who represents Me. This spirit of antichrist does what it can to deceive nations and people groups around the world. It manipulates people and stalks individuals who look promising to sway the masses. Adolph Hitler was one of these people, although I know your history books have been rewritten to paint him in a positive light. I could name others over the centuries, but my point is that even now, prospective programmers with intelligence, ambition, and skill are waiting in the wings. They're waiting for the chance to hijack such a link, once it is created. Some of them will do it with their charisma, which will create confusion and dysfunction similar to the world's political crisis in the first half of this century. People will gravitate toward any unifying force to bring stability and safety within their own minds. It is the perfect opportunity for the antichrist, himself, to step in."

"And You're asking me to create such a link?" Ira asked, dumbfounded.

"No. I'm giving you the wisdom you need to provide protection against it. The type of link I want you to create doesn't involve intruding upon anyone's mind. You are going to create a free space where people can congregate, undetected by the government, and hear the message of salvation as Craig delivers it. They will be aware of each other, but will not be linked to each other. It will be a safe place for them to come and accept Me and learn to worship Me, since the world system has made it so difficult for My children to meet together. As they come and the invitation is given and accepted, I will meet them there. When they receive Me, I will provide them with the protection they need against the type of link the world system wants to use. They can stay in the safe space where Craig is teaching for as long as they need until such time as they can retreat within their own minds and create their own secret, holy place. As they grow in

Me, they will venture out and invite others. People within geographical proximity will form lasting friendships with others they know they can trust, and eventually, underground churches in the outside world will form. My church will grow, and the gates of hell will not be able to stand against it!"

Ira was silent for a time, nearly overwhelmed by all that was expected of him. "How will Craig be able to process a multiple link? Everyone else will experience it as singular input, but Craig will have to link with every one of them."

"Not exactly," Jesus said. "Craig merely needs to be able to speak to every one of them, in the same way a speaker interacts with a crowd. Everyone can hear the speaker, and everyone is aware of noises made by people in the crowd. But while someone on the back row can't converse with someone on the front row, they can both hear what's being said from the platform. Craig needs to be able to send a message. Whether or not people engage with him to listen to that message is up to the individual. If they're not interested, they can close their minds to it. But if they change their mind later, the door is always open. People in the crowd will have the option to speak with each other afterward, but it still won't be an actual neural link. More like just talking to a neighbor over the proverbial backyard fence, rather than hopping the fence and invading someone's property. It's important that My children be able to form relationships so they can learn from each other and receive encouragement from this fellowship. In the future, Craig will be discipling those who have already accepted Me, and he will always give an invitation to receive My gift of salvation at the end of his messages."

"But what about those who are diametrically opposed to the idea of receiving You?" Ira asked. "Won't they notify the authorities?"

"That's where the firewall program you designed will come into play. When the authorities attempt to track the link history, it will be undetectable. As I said, it isn't a regular link. Craig is much like a voice crying out in the wilderness, preparing the way for Me to come to each individual. Those who hear the voice and wish to listen will come closer and receive. Those who aren't interested will dismiss it and shut it out. Those who are opposed may attempt to report it, but no traceable link will have been formed," Jesus explained.

"I'm not sure how to do this," Ira confessed. "I mean, I have a few vague ideas, but I can't guarantee success."

"I can," Jesus said quickly and looked at Ira meaningfully. "You do your part, and I'll do Mine."

Ira stared at Jesus blankly for a moment, his mind still racing with a myriad of probabilities of failure. Finally, he shook his head, attempting to focus. "Okay. I'll do everything I can."

Jesus smiled and placed a reassuring hand on Ira's shoulder. "Okay then. Let's begin."

28

CRAIG pushed his way through the bristly branches of a Douglas-fir and stared in wonder across a wide opening in the trees. As he gazed over the scene of reddish-orange Indian Paintbrush and lavender aspen daisies, he knew he must be somewhere in the mountains. He had seen pictures, and this was exactly how he had imagined it would be. Just a few moments ago, he had awakened on a bed of soft pine needles to the sound of a river as it tumbled joyously through a forest of enormous ponderosa pines. Craig had never thought of a river as being joyous, but the word definitely fit this one. He had followed it until he came to a vast clearing.

"This must be a dream," he thought to himself. The meadow was incredibly picturesque, dotted with the vibrant orange, blue, yellow, white and purple of a multitude of wildflowers. Overhead, the sky was a deep, clear blue he had only experienced on crisp October days, when the humidity was low enough there was no haze. He drank in the fresh air, which was heavily scented with pine. Looking down at his feet, he noticed he was standing on a well-worn trail. How had he not seen it before? It was inviting as it wound its way through the flowers, its surface worn smooth by much use. Craig had always wanted to visit the mountains, and the path seemed to beckon him. He decided to follow it. The grass, drenched in morning dew, reached out into the trail and brushed his pantlegs as he walked, soaking them through to the ankles and chilling his skin. To his left, the river chuckled merrily, as if it were daring him to a race. It careened along its banks and around large boulders, pushing against their granite surface as if it were giving them a playful slap of *"Tag, you're it!"* He stopped when he reached what seemed to be the center of the clearing and turned in a complete circle. If this were a mountain meadow, where were the mountains?

"You removed them," said a familiar, reassuring voice somewhere to his right. Craig turned and was temporarily blinded by what he assumed was the morning sun coming over the tree tops, but then the light seemed to envelope him, bathing him in its brightness. It was not painful to look at, and it seemed to have a life of its own. The light suddenly reached levels that allowed him to discern shapes, and he was able to make out the form of a man.

"Hello," Craig said tentatively. "What do you mean, I removed them? How could I remove mountains?"

"You created them in your mind. Many of them are beautiful, made of promises I gave you. Some of them were made of fear you refused to release. But when I asked you to surrender everything, you did. And that's when the mountains came down."

Craig stood very still for a moment, trying to process everything that had just been said. Suddenly he realized why the voice had sounded so familiar.

"My sheep know My voice," the man said gently, as if reading his thoughts.

Instantly, Craig knelt and pressed his face to the ground. "Jesus!" he said in awe, his voice muffled in the mountain grasses.

Jesus reached down and laid a hand on his shoulder. "I am so pleased with you. You have been so much more than a faithful servant. You have been My friend."

Tears cascaded down Craig's cheeks as the magnitude of the situation overcame him. "I've failed you so many times," he protested, as memories of past mistakes flooded his mind.

"To Me, you are perfect," Jesus said.

"Perfect! How can that be?" Craig sputtered.

"When My Father and I look at you, We don't see any past mistakes. Every time you fell, you confessed your sins to Me and determined to get back up. My blood covers it all. We only see the blood, and it is more than enough to cleanse you from all of your sin."[79]

Craig didn't know what to say. He could only weep. After a while, Jesus took him by the hand and helped him to his feet. It was such a familiar feeling

---

[79] See 1 John 1:9

that Craig suddenly realized this wasn't the first time it had happened. It was a different setting, perhaps, but it was just another time among many. Craig found himself looking in wonder into the face of his Savior. "Am I in Heaven?" he asked. "I thought there would be more people here."

Jesus chuckled. "You're not in Heaven yet, son. But soon, there will be more people here than you can imagine. I've come to prepare you for your mission—the mission I called you to when you left Adullam."

Craig looked around the empty meadow. "Where is this place? Am I dreaming? Is this a vision? All I remember about the State is a bunch of gray buildings, and air that made me choke, and being held prisoner. Oh—and they were going to surgically implant a computer chip in my brain!"

"And they did," Jesus said. "The place you see is the world you created in your mind. It is a beautiful place, although not without its dangers. But you have made a practice of following the right path—the path that always leads you to Me. You've taken side roads, but they always led back home, because deep in your heart, you were determined to follow Me. My Word that you hid in your heart has helped you throughout the years to stay on the right paths. And you guarded your mind with My promises, protecting yourself with a wall of tremendous mountains like you always dreamed of visiting. A few portions of that wall were a result of your fear of being hurt by others, but when you determined in your mind and heart that you would serve Me, no matter the cost, you gave Me the access to your mind and heart that I needed to make you a vessel of My message to the nations."

Craig could barely believe what he was hearing, but he knew it must be true because of its source. "I don't understand. Why would I need to take down the protection of Your promises? If they are Your promises, I know You will keep them, so shouldn't I hold onto them?"

"I always keep My promises. But sometimes I fulfill them in ways you don't expect. What you did was to remove any preconceived notions of how things should happen."

"But how will I be safe if there are no walls to protect me?"

Jesus smiled again. "I'd like to introduce you to a few people. They are your fellow servants, and they have been charged with keeping you safe." At this, Jesus turned toward a gentle rise in the meadow that culminated in an outcropping of stones. The two wound their way among the various rocks, which grew in size the closer they came to the center of the formation. Eventually, the two were climbing from boulder to boulder.

"This reminds me of the goat pasture back home where I would take the youth on rock climbing expeditions," Craig remarked. "I guess it wasn't a very spiritual thing to do, but we had a lot of fun."

Jesus stopped climbing for a moment and gave Craig a quizzical look. "Why would you think it wasn't spiritual?" He asked.

Craig paused in the middle of finding a foothold on a boulder. "Well, I guess because we weren't talking about You the whole time. I wasn't teaching them any scripture, or anything. We were just enjoying each other's company."

Jesus looked back at the rock that He had been scaling and grinned as He continued His climb. "You were *showing* them scripture. That is sometimes more effective. You were teaching them about fellowship—about forming relationships with other believers. That's a practical application of Hebrews 10:25," Jesus explained.

"Not forsaking the assembling of ourselves together, as the manner of some is; but exhorting one another: and so much the more, as ye see the day approaching,"[80] Craig muttered the verse to himself, and then looked at Jesus questioningly. "I always thought it was just talking about going to church services. You know, warning people that if they stopped getting together to worship You and learning about Your Word, it would be easy to fall away from the Truth."

"Yes. That's part of it. But who you spend time with and what you do when you're not in a place that has been set apart for worship—that also shapes who you become. Being with My original disciples wasn't just one sermon and miraculously multiplied meal after the other. It was little moments and long, grueling hours of regular, everyday labor. Following Me isn't about a program or a religious meeting or reading scripture and applying it to just certain aspects of life. It *is* life. It is living and breathing—the act of being My child and part of My

---

family. It is keeping the awareness of My presence with you as you form friend-ships and memories. If you allow Me into *every* aspect of life, it will be a life more abundant than you could ever experience on your own."

"The awareness of Your presence…You mean not necessarily Your presence, but the awareness of it?"

"I am with you *always*. But you are not always *aware* of Me. I see everything —when you're at your best *and* your worst. You just tend to choose not to think of Me when you're at your worst, as if that means I won't notice what you're doing."

Craig cringed inwardly. He knew it was true, but a part of him always liked to think that Christ only saw the good in him.

Jesus smiled gently. "I know it's hard for you to understand, but My love for you doesn't change, even when I see you at your worst. I simply love you, and you can't do anything that will change that. So since I am always with you, why not include Me, even when you're not feeling super-spiritual, so to speak? Don't you see that I'm not just a moral axiom? I'm your friend."[81]

Craig was speechless. He knew that Abraham had been called a friend of God, but he had never felt he was in the same category. He wanted to ask Jesus why he had been chosen for this special mission, but they had reached the top of the rock formation and were looking down into a small depression. A slim, bespectacled man was busily typing on a keyboard that seemed to be formed directly in the smooth surface of a chunk of granite. The man flinched and looked up as he noticed movement, but then relaxed as he saw Jesus.

"Ira!" Jesus called in greeting. "I know you're busy, but I wanted you to meet Craig and explain to him, in simple terms, what you are doing."

The man's eyes widened for a moment, and then he stepped forward, tenta-tively looking from Jesus to Craig.

"It's okay, Ira. No harm will come from you speaking to him. I want him to know some of the people who are helping to make this possible," Jesus explained.

Ira cleared his throat. "It's an honor to meet you, Mr. Goforth. I'm Ira Owens, and I'm a biotech programmer. I just finished installing a firewall that will keep

---

[81] Proverbs 18:24 (RSV) says, "There are friends who pretend to be friends, but there is a friend who sticks closer than a brother."

you safe from unwanted links or questionable upgrades. Dr. Moses or his associates may try to link with you, but they will simply be interacting with a pseudo-neural network where they can enter coding—or at least attempt to enter it—while you appear to be in a nonreactive state."

"Okay…" Craig said slowly, trying to understand.

Ira glanced at Jesus, Who nodded for him to continue. "All that means is that you're safe from anything that Dr. Moses or his staff might attempt to do. Now I'm writing code that will allow you to speak to millions of people from a virtual platform. Anyone who has a chip will able to hear your message, and they can either listen or block it out."

"But doesn't Yosi—er, I mean Dr. Moses—have the chip?" Craig asked.

"Yes, and so does Ainsley, one of his programmers. But each chip has an IP address. Biotech programmers have a different type of IP address identifying them as such. It's meant to give them easier access so they can more readily link with and program their patients. And I've identified these versions of the chip as trojan horses—uh, do you know what that means?" Ira paused as he realized Craig may have no knowledge of any type of computer terminology.

"I actually do understand. The families where I'm from have a limited use of computers and phones on our own private network that was created by Dr. Moses, himself, when he was just a teenager. All our kids get an education, and that includes the history of technology—at least up to the point where our parents left the State." Craig said. "So you're saying that their IP addresses will be labeled as a threat, no matter how innocuous they may seem, and the firewall won't allow them access, and my, uh, *system* won't extend an invitation to them to hear my message?"

"That's right. For everyone except them, when you begin to speak, it will be like someone tapping on the window of their mind, if you will. They can open the window and hear what you have to say, and if they're really interested, they can visit your IP address."

Craig looked around the meadow. "They're going to come here? Are there very many of them?"

Ira glanced at Jesus, Who grinned and said, "There are quite a few. Several hundred thousand who are old enough to understand and respond. The actual number is in the millions, since so many toddlers and infants have been implanted overseas."

"How will I be able to accommodate them all? How will they be able to hear me?"

"A link isn't like the outside, waking-world where hearing depends on sound waves," Ira began. "In here, we are dealing with the connection of thought. The first mind links involved only two people. And eventually it was discovered how to link a group of seven for the Pod-Op program, but only after many unsuccessful attempts that resulted in the mental and emotional acuity of the subjects being compromised. Finally, they achieved success by engineering the chips from the beginning to be parts of a single unit from the moment of implantation, where each subject shared hazy neural boundaries with the others. But that sort of link isn't possible on the scale we're talking about. Successful links of the traditional sort have been made between three people, where two individuals cross the threshold of one person's neural boundary. However, even that one extra person increases the blood pressure of the host. When an attempt was made to involve just four people, the cortisol level in the host's brain was too great to continue without risking injury to their prefrontal cortex—"

"Wait, wait, wait," Craig interrupted. "You're saying that a link with just four people can cause brain damage, and yet I'm going to host a link with thousands?"

"Not exactly," Jesus said and placed a reassuring hand on Craig's shoulder. "This beautiful place that you've created in your mind is currently accessible only to the three of us. What Ira is doing is making it possible for people to hear you without having a traditional link."

"I only recently figured out how to make it accessible for those who aren't chipped, as well. I'm creating an amplifier—a projector, of sorts—that originates from your mind. It will be a hub in the internet, almost like a website people can visit, much as they visit media sites via their Vista Visors or links, and it will appear as such. While you will be able to see everyone who is listening via chip, there may be many more who are tuning in through Vista Visor."

"But what's to keep the government from shutting it down?" Craig asked.

"It isn't an actual website. And they don't know that. So although they may attempt to shut it down, the only way that could actually happen is if you stopped talking, or…" Ira paused.

"Or if they removed me from the picture," Craig finished the thought. "Even if the people who are against it can't get through the firewall, millions of other people may be watching online. Dr. Moses is going to find out. And even if he can't shut it down, he could shut *me* down, couldn't he?" Craig asked, looking from Ira to Jesus.

"It's a huge risk," Ira admitted. "If you want, we can take the safer route and only allow access by the chipped—"

Jesus held up His hand to stop Ira. "That's not what he's worried about," He said, and looked at Craig with a tender expression. "He wants to make certain to have time to complete the message and to reach as many people as possible."

Craig smiled as he looked into Jesus' eyes, because He knew what he'd been thinking. "And not only that, but I want to make certain they can be discipled. I don't want people to just get saved and then just sink or swim. I want to be able to stick around and teach them. And how can I do that if I don't survive the sermon?"

"Well, I've been working on a solution to that, as well. Something that will keep the main message and any teaching points alive and undisturbed for the future reference of all who come," Ira said with the intensity of someone who is passionate about their work. "I was thinking you could prerecord some lessons that teach the basics of living a life for Christ. Nothing fancy or esoteric, just easy to understand lessons that people can use in personal application."

"You mean something like a youth pastor might teach?" Jesus said, grinning at Craig.

"Exactly. I mean, I *guess*. I'm not sure what a youth pastor is, but I'm guessing it means someone who teaches young people about Jesus. Anyway, that's what we need. Quick, straightforward access to the Truth. I know there are a lot of deep thinkers out there who may feel it's too simple to be anything worth listening to, but—"

"You just let My Holy Spirit tend to that," Jesus said firmly.

"How am I going to find the time to do all of this before they start getting suspicious? How much time do I have?" Craig asked.

"Time doesn't pass exactly the same in here as it does in the waking world," Jesus explained. "You know how a dream can seem like it took years, and yet it was only a few minutes of your sleep? You'll have more time than you think. And I'll be here to help you. And now," He said with a gesture in the direction of the tree line, "I'd like you to see your neural boundary, or at least, where it used to be. We need to leave Ira alone so he can work." Craig nodded to Ira, who smiled briefly and then once again turned all his attention to entering code.

Jesus and Craig made their way carefully down the stack of boulders to the floor of the meadow and headed toward the forest once again, leaving on a different path. A stand of aspens stood starkly against the dark background of spruce and fir trees. As they drew closer, they could see clusters of blue and white columbines nodding in the breeze at the forest edge. "I can't believe how beautiful this is," Craig said. The slim, white-barked trees on either side of them stretched skyward, their smooth trunks dotted and etched by black markings. "I love the contrast of black and white on the bark of these trees."

Jesus glanced back at Craig. "A stand of aspen trees is actually a single organism. The individual trees share a root system. Each black mark on their trunk is an indication of either a place where a branch was broken off by a natural, self-pruning process or where the tree was somehow injured. But even if a tree sustains a serious injury, the grove, itself, won't die. The black marks on these trees in your neural network are old injuries you allowed Me to heal." Jesus paused by a tree that had an intricate pattern of black markings and rested His hand on the old wound that had healed over. "Sometimes My children experience heavy emotional damage, but if they are rooted in Me, they can survive and grow again. The scars can become something beautiful."

Craig ran his hand along the cool, white bark surrounding the scar. Suddenly he looked at Jesus, tears forming in his eyes. "I'm not afraid to die—especially not now. But…I know it isn't right to worry, but I'm concerned about the others. I don't know what's happened to them. Are they finding enough food? Are they going to be taken into custody? Will they survive?"

"They are all safe. They made it to the State, and they have already seen many souls added to My Kingdom," Jesus said.

Craig's mouth dropped open. "How? How did they get there without being seen? Is someone helping them?"

"My plans don't usually involve just one person or even one group of people. One of My children—you know her as Wisteria—helped the missionary team you led to sneak into the outer docks."

"Wisteria got saved?" Craig exclaimed. "That's wonderful!"

"You should have heard the cheering in Heaven," Jesus laughed. "Her given name is Zelda, by the way. Once there, the youth made connections with Selah—"

"Selah? They found her? That's incredible!" Craig interrupted.

"My son, Hazen, helped out with that part," Jesus said with a chuckle. "Adults often lose patience with Hazen because he's so precocious. But children his age have such great faith! I so much enjoy spending time with them. Hazen and Peter share a lot of the same attributes."

"Peter? Is that someone else in the outer docks?" Craig asked.

"No," Jesus laughed. "I mean Simon Peter, one of My first disciples."

"Oh!" Craig exclaimed.

"Hazen has invited many people to the revival, and because of him, his entire family received Me as their Savior."

"A revival?"

"Yes. Selah and My servant Genevieve laid the groundwork for the revival that is just beginning. Thom and Dania, Lydia and Chandra, and Garrison and Lelah have formed into three different teaching teams being hosted by different families that are part of My church in the outer docks. In fact, I just helped Viv to find Garrison and Lelah. So you are correct. You don't need to worry. I have always had a plan, and I have everything under control."

Craig followed Jesus silently down the path for a while, a lump forming in his throat. Why did he ever worry about things? His guide, his Redeemer, was the omniscient Creator of all the earth, and nothing was too hard for Him.[82] He had

____

[82] See Jeremiah 32:27

orchestrated all of these events from the beginning and formed the personalities of each individual involved, making certain they would be prepared and would be in the right place at the right time to fulfill His plan. "You are amazing, Lord," he whispered.

To Craig's surprise, Jesus suddenly turned around and grabbed him in a bear hug. "I'm so proud to call you My son!" He said. When He let go and turned back toward the trail, Craig could see tears in His eyes. "Many people think I don't care about what happens to them, or that I'm angry with them. They have believed the enemy's lies. So when My children return My love, I just want to spend more time with them, showing them Who I really am and what I'm really like. Zephaniah tried to tell them how I feel. 'The Lord, your God, is in your midst, a warrior who gives victory; He will rejoice over you with gladness, He will renew you in His love; He will exult over you with loud singing.'[83] He turned once more to Craig, His eyes shining. "I love you so much!" He exclaimed, and momentarily clasped Craig around the shoulder in a side hug as they walked as Father and son.

"There are so many things I'd like to ask You," Craig said. "Like, the Trinity —can you describe what it's like? I get so many questions about that from my students, and it's hard to describe."

"I tried to explain to My disciple, Philip, how I am in the Father, and the Father is in Me.[84] And then I tried to explain to them about My Holy Spirit. That really blew their minds—that the same Spirit that is part of My Father and Me would be able to abide in them! It's hard for you to grasp these things now because you depend so much upon what you can see with your eyes and what you can explain with human reasoning. But someday, you will know, just as I know and understand you better than you know yourself!"[85]

Craig sighed. "I can't wait to get to know You as You know me!"

"Well, you're going to have to wait, because you still have work to do!" Jesus replied with a smile and then continued their trek. A few minutes later, He slowed the pace and the trees parted to reveal something Craig couldn't identify.

---

[83] Zephaniah 3:17, RSV
[84] See John 14:8-11
[85] See 1 Corinthians 13:12

At first, it appeared to be a thick fog that covered the area in front of them. As they drew nearer, Craig began to see outlines taking definition in the fog. And then he realized it wasn't fog at all, but a being that was so large he had thought it was part of the landscape. What had been vague shapes became the distinct outlines of feathers, and then a voice that seemed to come from somewhere on the other side of the wall of feathers was heard, saying, "Hail, Master! I keep watch, else I would show the reverence of which You are worthy."

"Greetings, Hallel. Your vigilance is noted," Jesus replied. He turned to Craig. "Meet my servant, Hallel. He is the angel guarding the east side of your neural boundary."

In response, Hallel turned slightly and Craig could see the angel's head above the immense wings. Hallel nodded, glancing at Craig out of the corner of his eye while retaining his watchfulness at the area outside of the boundary.

"Another angel, Benaiah, is guarding the north. His name means 'God builds.' I am building a wall of protection around you with My strength. Xander guards the west. His name means 'Defender of the people.' He is defending you as you bring the message of deliverance to a people who have forgotten that I am their Defender. Asaf guards the south. His name means 'gatherer of people,' and he will guard you as you gather My people to hear of My love for them."

Craig felt strangely weak as he stood in the presence of Jesus and the angel, and suddenly Jesus reached out to steady him with a strong hand. "Be strengthened," Jesus said simply, and all of the weakness disappeared. "I understand that this is overwhelming to you, but I want you to know that I am with you. Just one of these angels can subdue an army of men, and each of them can call in reinforcements from the armies of Heaven if need be. I have given them the honor of guarding your boundary because they embody their names. They are My faithful servants, and they will defend you as you do what I have called you to do.

Craig stared in wonder, thinking about the meaning of each of the names, and then realized Jesus had explained the meaning of each of them except for the one standing before them: *Hallel.* He was fairly certain Hallel meant praise.

But what did that have to do with the theme of guarding, protecting, gathering and building?

Knowing his thoughts, Jesus said, "When My people praise Me, I draw near to them quickly. It makes Me want to spend time with you. You've read that I inhabit the praises of My people.[86] Your praise brings My presence. You don't need to worry about fighting your enemies. I will go before you. When you praise Me, it confuses the enemy. They will fall into their own traps and fight against each other."

Suddenly, Craig felt a familiar feeling coming over him. It was the same feeling he would get sometimes when he was about to teach the youth on Sunday nights back in Adullam—an excitement for his topic coupled with a desire to connect to his listeners. "Thank you for showing me all of this. I'm ready to get started!"

Jesus laughed joyously. "I knew you would soon begin to feel the anointing of My Holy Spirit. Just go ahead and start teaching as if you have an audience. Your messages will be recorded as memory files and available for future believers to access. Once Ira is finished with his part of this mission, I want you to livestream and tell everyone about Me. Tell them that even if they lose their life for My sake, they will find it."[87]

"That won't be an easy thing to sell," Craig stated.

"None of it is for sale," Jesus said matter-of-factly. "It's free. At least to humankind. But it cost Me everything."[88]

Craig nodded and swallowed. Jesus had already done the work. All he had to do was tell everyone about it. He turned away from Hallel's expansive, outstretched wings and looked toward the path they had just taken and imagined all the faces of the people who would need to learn about Jesus. "Thy word is a lamp unto my feet, and a light unto my path," he began. "If you're watching this, you may have a lot of questions about how to live this new life you've been given. One of the most important things you can do is to read God's Word."

---

[86] See Psalm 22:3

[87] See Matthew 16:25

[88] Jesus gave up His glory and omnipotence to come to earth as an infant, and then He gave His life as a sacrifice for the sins of all humanity.

Suddenly, Craig looked to Jesus with a question in his eyes. "How will they find access to *that?*" he asked.

Jesus smiled. "Just before we go online, one of My daughters is going to drop by and provide us with a copy we can offer as a free download."

Craig grinned. "You thought of everything, of course."

Jesus chuckled. "You just teach. I'll do the rest."

29

Jayka awoke, but it was *not* at the prescribed time. The ceiling was dark, and when she checked the time via her chip, she discovered it was 0400 hours. What had awakened her? A soft, pitiful whimpering came from a corner of the room. Jayka raised up slightly and a rhythmic thumping could be heard against the floor. "Good morning, Scrapdog," she mumbled sleepily. And that was all the invitation Macy needed. Soon, Jayka's face was being covered in slobbery kisses. Jayka knew she should protest and demand some sort of obedience and respect from the animal, but all she could do was giggle. She couldn't decide which was the stranger sensation—being licked in the face by an animal, or being able to giggle again. She couldn't remember the last time she had laughed.

And then she sat bolt upright as the realization of what she had done jolted her completely awake. She had brought in an animal from the Preserve—sneaked it in, actually. The Preserve was to be left untouched, unchanged…exactly how one found it. She had violated State protocol. Even if she had obtained an animal legally from within the State, she would probably have had to go through the lengthy animal adoption application process just like any other citizen, which included background checks, health screenings, and home assessments. Although she knew she could pass through the process with flying colors, the fact remained that she had bypassed it entirely. The State was stringent on its ethical treatment of animals, and would-be animal caretakers had to be vetted before being approved for guardianship. Even if she had gotten the proper licensing, there was no precedent for a Pod-Op having a pet. She had possibly violated her *own* protocol.

Macy gave a soft *woof* to remind the human that she was there, and why weren't her ears being scratched? A delicious feeling of excitement rushed to the surface of Jayka's emotions and pushed aside any concern for proper procedure as she scratched Macy vigorously behind the ears. The dog was staying. She didn't care how many protocols she had to violate.

But caring for an animal brought new responsibilities. It had to be fed. It needed exercise. Jayka's eyes opened wide as she realized it also probably needed to go outside to relieve itself, and perhaps that was why it had awakened her in the first place. Right on cue, Macy trotted to the door and looked at it and then back at her. Well, it was still early, after all. Maybe no one would see them. She was certain none of the other Pod-Ops were awake. The waking phase programmed into all of their chips didn't begin until one hour from now. She slipped on her street clothes and retrieved the survival pack she kept in her closet, procuring a roll of paracord. Macy waited patiently while Jayka fashioned a makeshift leash and collar. The dog lowered her head and emitted a barely audible, high-pitched whine as Jayka slipped the collar over her head. "I'm sorry, but this is necessary by State law. It's for your own safety," Jayka apologized. "I will attempt to find you a more suitable collar or harness as soon as possible; but for now, this will have to do." And then, just before she opened the door, Jayka's heart began to pound. What if one of the other Pod-Ops in their housing unit *did* happen to be awake? What if they were discovered? She accessed her chip and did an assessment of the waking status of the other six with whom she was linked. She couldn't detect any Beta or Alpha brain waves, which meant her Pod-mates were most likely still asleep, just as she had known they would be. She turned to Macy and looked into her eyes. "You have to be quiet," she said in a whisper. Macy cocked her head and pricked her ears forward. Inwardly scolding herself for thinking the animal could understand her, Jayka took a tight grip on the leash and opened the door.

The hallway was deserted. Jayka let out a breath of relief, and the two made their way down the hall and to the door that led to a dimly lit inner courtyard where residents could play basketball or even practice climbing the walls of their barracks if they so desired. There was no grass in the commons area, but there were also no cameras since it was inaccessible to the general public, and Pod-Ops provided all the surveillance footage that would be needed from their own memories. Jayka assessed the courtyard and found it empty. She then scanned every window that faced the area for heat signatures of any operatives from a different Pod that might be awake and watching from another floor. Finally satisfied that no one was watching from above, Jayka led Macy into the commons area and let her off of her leash.

The animal began an immediate inspection of the potted yew bushes that sat in the four corners of the courtyard, sniffing in the normal places other animals would mark their territory. Finding no evidence of the canine version of a message board, she trotted to a corner from which she could view the entire area and be flanked with the protection of two walls. Facing the yard, Macy did her business. Jayka had encountered dogs in the State before, but many of them were the yappy, unpleasant sort with little trace of intelligence. This dog showed a level of alertness and self-preservation that was admirable, she decided. Once Macy was finished, Jayka used the sandwich bag she had brought to dispose of the evidence and sprayed water on the area with the hose used to water the yews. She then proceeded to water the bushes to allay any suspicion associated with the hose being used in only one spot and not for its designated purpose. As she was doing so, Macy carefully sniffed all of the chairs in the courtyard and sat down beside the one Jayka always chose, in one of the corners beside the healthiest looking shrub. Jayka was filled with a sense of pride as she realized the animal had not only displayed intelligence and a keen sense of smell by choosing the very chair she always sat in, but had also chosen that area as her place to rest. The dog had chosen to trust her. Jayka coiled the hose back in its reel and went over to her new friend, giving her the ear scratches she loved so much. Her eyes rested on her hands as she caressed the dog's fur. Those hands were capable of so much damage. It had been a long time since they had been used to show affection. She was momentarily transfixed as memories of past encounters with criminals of the State flashed through her mind. Bones had been broken. Bodies had been bruised and beaten. Several had not escaped with their lives. Some suspects she had apprehended were not in the act of any wrongdoing, but she had merely been told they were enemies of the State. She was simply carrying out the orders of her superiors. How many of those people had been just like the old Discard in the Preserve? How many of those people had lived lives similar to the one she had lived in the outer docks? Jayka shook her head and attempted to change her focus. The self-doubt she had experienced while in the cave, the questions she had about the State's motives—it was happening again for no reason. She couldn't blame this on being in an underground environment that was interfering with her chip's ability to connect to communication hubs. What was going on? She needed to order the diagnostic she had promised herself she would ask Dr. Moses to run. Suddenly Macy placed her paw on Jayka's lap and looked at her with soulful brown eyes. The diagnostic would reveal all. The dog would be confiscated and put up for adoption. Her questionable thoughts might be viewed as treasonous, or at least a case for mental instability, possibly resulting in a selective memory wipe. Jayka had always opted to keep her memories, when possible. She learned from them. But perhaps in this case, she considered in a moment of introspection, she was being selfish.

Pod-Ops worked together as a unit when in close proximity. When on separate assignments, they were able to practice distancing—the act of operating completely independent of each other. Once the members were all back at base, they would meet at a scheduled time for datashare. The memories of each Pod member were transferred to the other members of the team, after which they all operated as a synchronous unit again. Since the scheduled datashare from her pod was delayed due to Tyrell still being on assignment, now would be an ideal time for a selective memory wipe. She could rid herself of the whole affair: the accidental death of the Discard, her confusing feelings of guilt, her attachment to the dog and all the responsibility it brought. The dog would be well-cared for, since animal adoption was taken very seriously by the government. None of her Pod members need be confused or distracted by the questionable doubts she had experienced regarding the State. She could arrange to report to Dr. Moses this morning, before anyone else was awake. This was the logical choice.

She stood up, convinced she had made her decision. Suddenly, an image of the old pigeon trapper came to mind—not from her recent time in the Preserve, but from her childhood in the outer docks, when the woman had tried to give her a precious commodity: a piece of bread. Jayka felt a slight pressure on her foot as the dog stepped on her shoe and leaned into her leg. Tears formed in Jayka's eyes. No. She would not do it. She would—

"Jayka, what are you doing?" asked a voice from the window to her right. It was her Podmate, Sloane.

Jayka turned casually toward the window, her hand resting protectively on the ruff of Macy's neck. "This animal needed to relieve itself. I hope I did not awaken you," she said simply.

"You didn't. I've been called in to check on some disturbances in the southwest quadrant. Why do you have a dog?"

It wasn't an accusation. It was a simple question, and Sloane had a right to know. "This matter is classified. I will inform you later if I am able unless they selectively wipe my memory once the mission is complete. In the meantime, I suggest you wipe this memory. If it becomes declassified, you will obviously all have privy to the information once we datashare. If not, the memory will only cause problems for all of us later, as I will have no knowledge of it."

"Understood," Sloane said.

"Successful mission to you."

"And to you as well."

Sloane closed the window and returned to her preparations. Jayka looked down at Macy, her heart pounding. The lie had come so easily, but she couldn't keep this secret forever. The spark of a plan began to kindle in Jayka's mind. There was a perfectly reasonable explanation for her behavior, one that would make sense to her superiors and would exonerate her of all guilt. She just needed a little more time. She slipped the leash back over Macy's neck. "Come on, Scrapdog. Let's go for a walk," she said. Macy's ears pricked up, and she trotted obediently beside Jayka.

Once the two made it outside of the Pod-Op barracks, Jayka strode boldly out the main entrance of the Liberation Station compound and began the familiar route she took when relaxing off-duty. There was no point in trying to be secretive once she had left the station. Pod-Ops were closely monitored. Their chips were constantly tracked. She wondered if Sloane would perform the memory wipe, as she had suggested. If not, she might have to incorporate the lie into her plan.

She began to jog, an activity that always helped her think. Beside her, Macy kept pace, glancing at her for cues and maintaining a watchful eye on their surroundings. Jayka felt a sense of pride well up within her again. Not everyone could say they had been chosen by such an intelligent animal.

An hour later, the pair was still jogging through various neighborhoods. Jayka's Podmates would be awake by now. She wondered if they would question her absence at breakfast, although since they were off-duty, it wouldn't be unusual for one of them to be spending time off-base. The morning wore on as Jayka continued playing out different possibilities in her mind. She avoided using the chip's algorithm function. Although it would have been easier, it would also have made a record of the probability exercise. She would have to do it the old-fashioned way and think for herself.

Not all of the Pod-Ops' memories were sent straight to a memory file on the chip, where they could be accessed during datashare or a diagnostic. Routine attendance to personal hygiene, for instance, was stored organically in the hippocampus. Memories were routed according to their importance, and anything relating to a mission was stored directly on the chip. It might be possible for her to designate the storage area of the memories she was making now, although she had never attempted such an exercise. If all else failed, she could make a detailed plan, write herself a note of it, and perform a memory wipe on herself before the next datashare to avoid any record.

Macy lagged momentarily behind as the two passed a food truck selling bagels and breakfast sandwiches, and Jayka suddenly realized the dog must be hungry. She bought a couple of Syntha-sausage sandwiches while Macy watched every move. "Hey, those aren't approved for animal consumption," protested the man as she immediately gave one to the dog.

Jayka turned to him, momentarily confused. "They're good enough for humans, but not for animals?" she asked.

The man gave her a sideways smirk and explained, "Hey, you know how it is. They have rules about that kind of thing. Ever since the State determined animals can't be owned like property, but they're all citizens of the State, the rules are tougher. Now, *I* don't care if you feed your dog Syntha-meat, but the State prefers you use the State's label, when possible. Something about it being more natural."

"How is it more natural? Syntha-meat is still synthetic protein, whether or not it comes from a food truck like yours or a State-approved dog food factory," Jayka quipped, perturbed at the man's explanation.

"Syntha-meat! No way, hume. That's not what *I've* heard. Now they're using Unspokens. That, and Discards who donate themselves for organ use at the Euthanasia clinics. As long as their meat isn't contaminated with drugs, of course. Nothing but the finest for our four-legged friends—"

"Quiet! I should have you arrested. Such lack of concern for human life is revolting," Jayka retorted coldly.

"Well, haven't you heard? The latest bill that's up for approval says that Unspokens aren't actually human. Actually, they're saying they aren't even *alive*. And get this—they're looking to expand the ruling to include Discards who won't agree to become citizens." The man paused as he saw the look on Jayka's face. "Hey, don't shoot the messenger," he said, raising his hands for comedic effect before going back to his grill to flip over a slice of Syntha-bacon.

Jayka stood still, accessing her chip for the latest in State Capitol news. The man should be detained for spreading misinformation, in the least. But as she read her newsfeed, she discovered it was all true. Suddenly bereft of an appetite, she gave her own sandwich to Macy, who wolfed it down in two bites.

The two continued at a walk, Jayka deep in thought. She had known for years that Unspokens had no rights, but to rule that they weren't human and weren't even alive was not scientifically sound. And as far as the ruling on Discards, how were they getting around the Declaration of Intent to Nurture? Discards who had D.I.N.s had always at least had the right to live. She knew enough of State politics to realize that Discards were a valuable object lesson. If you didn't play by the State's rules, you could end up like one of *them*. It had always been a key talking point that encouraged unity among citizens. Why would they want to completely annihilate the whole subculture when they served such a valuable purpose?

Jayka slowed to a standstill as she realized it must have something to do with their research on creating a collaborative link. They must be getting close to a breakthrough. She had heard Dr. Moses say that eventually, the world would share thoughts much as she did with her Podmates. He was convinced that it would be a terrifically unifying transformation of society—even of humanity, itself. She wondered if he understood how difficult it could be to share one's mind with several others. When she was first chipped together with the other members of her Pod, she had enough trouble with her own problems without dealing with the ones banging around inside the heads of six other teenagers. But then they had given her the emotionally deadening drugs, the hormone inhibitors, everything they had provided for her and continued to administer to make certain she maintained the emotional stability necessary for a soldier who had been neurologically augmented. Was this on the horizon for citizens of the State?

As a soldier, she had made a vow. She had given up her rights in order to protect her fellow citizens; and it seemed that *potential* citizens, such as she had been before being recruited, were in danger. But she had also made a vow to abide by the State's rulings and uphold its laws. She felt an obligation since the State had adopted her. After gaining her freedom from the outer docks, she had been manipulated to give it up out of that sense of obligation; and as a Pod-Op, she was considered government property.

There it was again, those feelings that painted a less than desirable picture of the State, even if she felt she owed the government a debt she could never repay. If she had the diagnostic run and the problem addressed, things would be better, she reasoned. But could she trust a government which had ruled that people such as she, who were born unloved and unwanted by their parents, were not actually *alive*? She was definitely considered a living human being *now*. What was the difference between now and *before* the State had adopted her?

Her thoughts were interrupted as she found herself approaching the Soulard district. Up ahead, there was a street lined with various shops and businesses. Most were State-affiliated, but a few were privately owned. Jayka slowed to a walk as she surveyed the various shops. She thought she had remembered a pet supply store in the area, but a search of the internet revealed nothing but a few bars, cafés, an odd assortment of clothing boutiques, and a hair salon. A little bit of everything, but nothing that she needed. Suddenly, something in the window of one of the shops caught her eye. She made her way quickly to the storefront of *The Consummate Costumery*. A sign in the window claimed to provide the perfect outfit for everyone and for any situation: parties, creative romantic relationships, or even those who identified as a super hero. She stopped and looked in the window at the mannequin that was dressed in tight leather straps and knee length boots. A steel-studded leather collar with a chain lead was fastened about its neck and held in the delicate hand of another mannequin who was dressed as Little Bo Peep. Jayka smiled. They had exactly what she needed. However, the shop didn't open until 0900 hours, and it was only just now 0756. She stood there for a while, considering if she should simply wait there, when suddenly Macy emitted a low *woof*. Jayka followed the dog's gaze to a man working on a light pole adjacent to them. It must have gone out, she decided, but then realized the man was not replacing an L.E.D. at all, but installing something additional beneath the light source. She zoomed in using her 2nd Sight implant and could see it was a surveillance camera aimed at the shop across the street. A few minutes later, the man climbed down his ladder. As he turned to her and smiled, she did an immediate background check identifying him as an employee of the Surveillance Division with Level 2 Clearance. "Good morning!" he said affably. "They say those L.E.D.s last forever, but this is the third one I've replaced in the last month."

"Is that so?" Jayka said in her best friendly voice.

"Yep. Now, you have a day!" he said cheerily as he grabbed his ladder and tools and loaded them into the utility vehicle parked by the curb. Jayka frowned in disgust. Even after all these years, she couldn't get used to the way the State encouraged citizens to refrain from telling anyone what kind of a day to have. That, coupled with the man's deception, left a sour taste in her mouth. She looked across the street at the shop that had been deemed an area of concern. It looked to be nothing more than a café. As she stood looking at it, she couldn't help feeling drawn there. There was something about it—a warmth, almost— that seemed inviting. She felt a tug on the leash and looked down to see Macy wagging her tail as she looked toward the door of the café, where a woman with long, silvery grey hair was setting out a clapboard sign advertising the daily special. "Well, we have about an hour's wait before the costume shop opens. Why don't we give it a try, whaddaya say, Scrapdog?" Jayka said, lapsing into the accent of the Discards.

The silver-haired woman looked up and smiled warmly as the two crossed the street and headed her direction. "Good morning," she said. "That's a fine-looking dog you have there. Is she any particular breed?"

Jayka stared at Macy as she began to access her chip to run an assessment of the dog's heritage, and then stopped suddenly. She looked at the woman, who was waiting with an expression of genuine interest. "I have no idea, actually," Jayka confessed.

"Well, those are usually the best kind anyway, and rare these days," the woman said. "My name is Luciana."

"I'm Jayka. And this is Scrapdog," Jayka said, nodding to Macy, who barked a greeting.

"Would you like to come in?"

"Yes, we would," Jayka said. As the two stepped into the cozy café, an unfamiliar but welcome feeling seemed to lap at the edges of Jayka's being, like the waves of a tranquil lake. "What *is* that?" Jayka asked warily. "Are you using an ambiance-enhancing drug in the ventilation system?"

"What? No, we don't do that sort of thing here," Luciana said firmly, but kindly. "But many of our customers seem to think we have a warm, peaceful vibe."

"Peace," Jayka said slowly. "So that's what it feels like."

Luciana looked at her intently. "Welcome to Talk-o-Lot Chocolate. Follow me. I have a table just perfect for you."

Jayka followed the woman to a booth in a corner from which she could safely view all the customers and anyone who might come into the front door. It was almost as if the woman knew where Jayka would feel most comfortable. She slid onto the bench, and Macy curled underneath the table at her feet. "Would you like some time to look over the menu?" she asked as she handed Jayka an old-fashioned laminated piece of paper with a copy of the café's offerings.

Jayka stared at the menu and took it, perplexed. She glanced at the area above the counter where a digital menu readout would normally be posted. In its place was an old-fashioned chalk board, its items displayed in whimsical, yet legible script. "This is highly unusual. I've never been to an establishment that had a non-digital menu board and hard-copy handouts."

"We strive to be an area where people can engage with each other, rather than with a screen. Most digital menus are so distracting, with their constant flipping between the regular selections and the daily specials. In fact, we ask that our customers check in their Vista Visors at the door, but I had a feeling you don't have one," Luciana said knowingly.

Jayka wondered if it was that obvious that she had been implanted, or was the woman simply working on that assumption since she wasn't using a visor or wearing one on top of her head? "Interesting," she said, wondering if the café's unusual practices were the reason for the State's surveillance. She glanced around the room. At the side nearest the window, a couple was seated and seemed to be engaged in a very stimulating conversation. She accessed her Audio-boost implant and discovered they were planning a State-sponsored excursion to view the Grand Canyon. A few booths away, a group of college students were discussing an upcoming exam. A woman sitting at the front counter was wearing an anxious look, and a barista stopped in the middle of making a latte to place a comforting hand on the woman's arm and offer words of encouragement. It was such a different environment from most eateries, which were normally dead silent as customers plugged into the internet via whatever means they possessed, completely ignoring their human companions. She looked back at the woman. "What do most people order?" she asked. Jayka rarely opted to eat out, even though the mess hall at her barracks had a limited variety of food. It had always seemed such an abundance compared to the meager offerings of a back alley dumpster. She was accustomed to receiving gratefully anything she was given and had never considered looking for something else.

"Do you like caramel? Our *Buttery Bon Voyage* features caramel and sea-salt."

Jayka remembered the first time she had eaten caramel. It was drizzled over a piece of apple-crumb cake she had been given in the hospital while she was still recovering from the implantation procedure, and the richness of it had made her slightly sick. She glanced down at the menu. "Do you have anything with chocolate?"

Luciana smiled. "We would probably be charged with false advertising if we didn't, considering our name. I'll bring you a mocha latte. That's fairly safe."

"Are some of your drinks considered dangerous?" Jayka asked.

Luciana laughed and then realized Jayka was being serious. "No, of course not. I just meant that if you like chocolate, the mocha is a safe bet."

Jayka nodded, and as the woman left the table, she continued her survey of the room. Did the State consider this café to be dangerous, or was it suspected of being a meeting place of dissidents or a drop point for contraband merchandize? Perhaps the owners of the establishment had no involvement in whatever crimes were being committed and the spot was just a location of suspected criminal activity. She ran a scan using 2nd Sight and could find no obvious deviations from the normal equipment or supplies used in the restaurant business. There was an unusual concentration of electronic devices stored in a cabinet near the front door, but further inspection revealed that it was Vista Visors collected from the customers upon entering the café. Other than the front register's computer, the only other electronic signatures were very faint—so simplistic they were almost indetectable. But they were definitely there, and that was rather unusual for a café that leaned toward anachronism. She scanned under the counter, where the highest concentration of those particular signals was found. It appeared to be a stack of shirts. The barista behind the counter was wearing one, and so, she realized, was the woman who had waited on her.

"That's a very interesting shirt," Jayka said cordially as Luciana came back to the table with her drink.

"Why, thank you," Luciana said. "A friend of mine designed them. I thought he did a nice job."

Jayka studied the printed fabric, with its steaming cup of coffee and the name of the café emblazoned on the front. "Do you have any for sale?" she asked.

Luciana seemed to study her carefully for a moment. "No. But I'll give you one, free of charge."

Jayka stared at her suspiciously. "Give it to me? How can you afford to give away merchandise?"

"Our customers have helped us build a successful business. I simply want to give them something back in return," Luciana said.

Jayka's augmented senses recorded a slight elevation in the woman's blood pressure. "Are you the owner?"

"I am," Luciana said. "And I would be happy for you to have a shirt, even though you're a first-time customer."

"Then, I will gladly take one," Jayka said as she studied the woman for further signs of nervousness, but Luciana simply smiled and walked away to the counter to retrieve one of the shirts. As she sorted through the stack for the correct size, Jayka could hear her whispering. She once again accessed Audio-boost.

"Father, I place this in Your hands. Watch over us. And help us to show her Your love," the woman was saying.

Jayka frowned. To whom was she speaking? Her father? Whom was she talking *about*? When the woman came back to the table, all signs of elevated blood pressure had disappeared. "If you need anything else, just let me know," she said as she handed Jayka the shirt. "You mentioned that you could feel something different when you walked in. Peace is sometimes hard to come by these days. But you can still find it if you look in the right place." She nodded a farewell and left Jayka to sip on her mocha.

Jayka glanced at the shirt but decided not to study it too carefully until she had left. If the shop had somehow implanted a tracking device in the material to study the habits of its customers, it was just a workaround of the old data-gathering methods used by the private sector when cell phones and virtual assistants tracked peoples' buying habits, locations, and even listened in on their private conversations. Such practices by privately owned businesses were now forbidden, being a violation of privacy and punishable by law. Now only the government was allowed to freely do such a thing, and since the groundwork had been laid for the technological means to accomplish it and the public had been desensitized to being spied upon, the transition from private to strictly federal use had been easy and painless. Only the State could be trusted with such sensitive material.

Jayka needed to keep her suspicions as inconspicuous as possible. In an attempt to appear as if she were merely another customer enjoying herself, she smiled and looked around the room, pretending to study the decorations and the antique furniture. And it was then that she noticed the table where she was seated. She had been so preoccupied, as she always was, with assessing the risks of her environment and being placed in the best location to monitor her surroundings that she had overlooked its design. Certainly, she had seen the intricate carving under its protective glass cover, but it wasn't until now that she studied it closely: "Peace I leave with you, My peace I give unto you: not as the world giveth give I unto you. Let not your heart be troubled, neither let it be afraid."[89]

It wasn't unusual for small businesses to use inspirational quotes from various works of literature as decorations in their establishment. She had seen passages from *My Truth* that had originated from Confucious or the Koran or the Christian Bible. All had been edited heavily during their homogenization into the State's religious text and shortened even further to make a tasty, bite-size spiritual tidbit for citizens to easily digest. Jayka was certain the quote on this table did not match its parallel in the State bible, for the Source rarely, if ever, referred to itself in the singular form, preferring to use the pronoun "we" to promote a sense of inclusion. Another odd thing about the passage was that it referred to "the world" as if it were something separate from the speaker and his or her audience. She wondered about the significance of the distinction. It was a very unconventional mode of thought, especially in the modern State. She suspected it could be a direct quote from the original text, although how the person who carved it would have been able to acquire such a subversive piece of literature, she was unsure.

The woman who called herself Luciana had told her she had a table perfect just for her. The quote carved on the table's surface was about peace, which was apparently the unfamiliar feeling she had experienced when she walked in the door. There was something about the people who worked here—something about this place that was different from other establishments. Luciana had claimed they didn't use drugs to enhance the mood, but she could have been lying. Of course, as long as the drugs were registered with the State and purchased from a State-sponsored facility, their use was completely legal. She wondered if the chemical might interfere with any higher thought processes or inhibit physical performance in any way. If not, she should probably recommend it to her superiors as a replacement for some of the ones administered to her Pod. On the other hand, if the drug were suitable, wouldn't it already be used in the Pod-Op program?

---

[89] John 14:27, KJV

This could be the explanation for the installation of the camera across the street. A powerful new designer drug, indetectable to her heightened senses, was possibly being used in this shop prior to State approval. The owners might also be dealers, and the only advertisement they needed was the feeling their patrons experienced when they walked in the door, coupled by word of mouth. Jayka glanced down at the shirt. Perhaps this was the way the dealers connected with the buyers. This was obviously someone else's investigation, and she should hand over the shirt to her superiors so they could place this evidence in the proper hands.

Across the street, the costume shop was opening for business. Jayka knew she should get up and leave, but she hesitated. If there really was a drug in the ventilation system, perhaps she should run a self-diagnostic to see if any of her processes were adversely affected. Jayka stared off into space, pretending to be lost in thought while she checked her systems. That was strange. Everything was normal. Actually, her blood pressure was better than normal, and the level of stress hormones in her blood were lower than usual. She took her time finishing the mocha. This could be the perfect opportunity to connect with the dealer and arrange for a meeting. Of course, she would inform her superiors when she had gathered more information. She looked across the room toward the register and found that Luciana was watching her. Jayka smiled, and Luciana made her way to the table. "Can I get you anything else?" she asked.

"Actually, I was wondering if I could just move in!" she said with a laugh. "This place makes me feel like I never want to leave! I don't suppose there's a chance I could take this feeling with me?" she ventured. It was a statement that could be interpreted as either innocent small talk or a discreet invitation to sell.

Luciana gave her a sidelong glance and then placed her hand on the carved table. "Peace. It's free, made available to us if we'll just reach out and take it. But it was very costly to the author of this quote."

Jayka stared. Was this the offer? If it was free, what was the catch? And what did she mean about the author of the quote? "How do I get it?" she finally asked.

"Well, I suggest that you meditate on this quote. If you're still interested a week from now, come by and see me, and we'll talk," Luciana said.

"Meditate?"

"Yes. Think about it for a while."

"I know what meditate means," Jayka said shortly.

"Well then, give it some thought, and if you're still interested, come by. Of course, you're welcome anytime, even if you decide against it," Luciana said, and glanced down at the shirt on the seat beside her. "Don't forget your shirt."

That clenched it. Somehow, the shirt was involved.

"I won't," Jayka said. She paid her bill and visited the costume shop across the street, purchasing the collar and leash for Macy. As she had sat there in the café, she had also formulated the plan for keeping the dog. She made her way back to Liberation Station. "Good morning, Conall," Jayka said to the Pod-Op who was acting as front door security that day. "I need to see Dr. Moses if he's available."

Conall nodded and was silent for a moment as he accessed his chip. "It looks like he's rather busy today," he said, his eyes on Macy.

"It's a matter that needs immediate attention and is related to the mission I just returned from late yesterday evening. It involves this animal," she added, noting his attention was fully focused on the dog.

Suddenly Macy stepped forward, her tail wagging slowly, and looked up at the man with a lopsided grin. Conall grinned back, in spite of himself. "Hello," he said. Macy sat on her haunches and lifted up one paw as if in greeting. In a moment, Conall had stooped to her level and was holding the paw, staring into Macy's brown eyes. "You're quite an animal, aren't you?" he said, and glanced back up at Jayka. "This dog isn't like the ones you normally see around," he commented. "She doesn't look like a purebred."

"Of that, I am certain," Jayka replied. "But she seems to show a remarkable amount of intelligence."

Conall stood back up, and nodded toward the elevator. "He says he'll see you. I guess he already knew about the dog."

"Of course," Jayka said. She had known there was no point in hiding it. That's why she had come up with the plan. She went up the elevator and made her way down the hallway to Dr. Moses' office. The elegantly carved wooden door swung open upon her approach.

"Hello, Jayka. I've been very interested to hear about your mission. The three Discards you apprehended are being questioned, and an autopsy is being performed on the woman you found in the cave," said Dr. Moses as he came around to the front of his desk. "Conall informed me that this is an animal somehow related to your mission."

"Yes," Jayka said. "I found her in the cave. She seemed very disturbed by the Discard's death. I believe she had formed an attachment with the woman."

"Is that why you brought it back with you?"

"Yes. I realize the Preserve is to be left exactly as it was found, but I do not think this animal originated from within the Preserve. I do not think the woman had been out there long enough to befriend and tame a wild dog."

"Very well. I will contact the Ministry of Animal Care and arrange for someone to come pick it up. I'm certain they'll find a good home for it."

Jayka swallowed and felt her heart rate increasing. It was fear, she realized. She was afraid her plan wasn't going to work. She adopted an attitude of calm as she continued, surprised that she was more nervous now than during any combat she had experienced.

Maintaining her poise, she related her mission from start to finish, supplying Dr. Moses with recorded footage of her encounter with members of the Gateway Gang and her discovery of the woman's campsite in the cave. He was especially interested in the trading symbols on the cave formation. "If these are trading symbols, I wonder who she was expecting to trade *with*? And what was she trading?" he asked.

Jayka shook her head. "I don't understand it, either. The sign means someone powerful is being very generous to someone weaker. It is definitely a trading symbol, but I've never seen it arranged in that manner."

"Hmmm." Dr. Moses stroked his chin. "Fascinating. Do you suppose the woman was considering setting up a trading post there? Was she expecting other Discards to arrive? The three gang members weren't far behind. Perhaps she had delusions of setting up the cave as a place for escapees to shelter for the night and stock up before heading out farther into the Preserve. Although how they would have known about Onondaga is anyone's guess."

"I had heard of it," Jayka said quickly.

"Yes, but you have access to virtually unlimited knowledge—" Dr. Moses began.

"No, I mean before—" Jayka interrupted, and caught herself. "—Sir. Excuse me, Sir."

Moses looked at her intently for a moment. "Do continue."

"When I was a girl, there were stories. Everyone talked about escape, but there were always those who said it was pointless. Where would one hide, after all? How would one keep safe from the wild animals and hide from the drones? And then the dreamers would insist they could hide in the caves. Onondaga was one of the names circulating back then, and some people even had a vague idea of where it was."

"So do you think this woman could have known more were coming?"

"I don't know," Jayka said truthfully.

"Well, it's worth investigating," Dr. Moses said. "Perhaps we should allow the breach in the wall to remain unrepaired and see who wanders outside?"

"That sort of decision is not within my parameters," Jayka said.

Moses chuckled. "It was a rhetorical question."

"I understand," Jayka said.

"Well then, I suppose this debriefing is over. You may leave the dog with Conall. Someone will be here soon to pick it up and prepare it for adoption," Dr. Moses said.

"I think it might be wise for the animal to stay with me," Jayka said, trying to keep her voice devoid of emotion.

"I'm sure Conall can handle it. You need to go back to your quarters and get some rest after your mission."

"I don't disagree that Conall can handle her. However, the dog seems to have formed an attachment to me in the absence of her owner, and I do not want to cause her any distress," Jayka said matter-of-factly.

Dr. Moses studied Jayka for a moment. "We can have it sedated. When it wakes up, it'll be in the clinic at the Ministry of Animal Care, and once it's adopted, it'll adjust to its new owner."

"With all due respect, I do not think you understand the trauma this animal has just experienced. Her owner fell to her death. The dog was whining and licking the woman's face, trying to get her to wake up. She refused to leave her side, and when the transport came to retrieve the body, she became very agitated and would not have let them approach if I hadn't reassured her. I requested that the transport bring a hover bike because I wanted to retrace my route and see if there might be any more Discards outside the wall. At the time, I had not considered I should bring the animal back with me. When I happened to look back, I could see that she was following me."

"It sounds like you are saying you want to keep it because it followed you home," Dr. Moses said, slightly amused.

"Hardly. But then I reasoned that her presence in the Preserve might cause a disturbance in the ecosystem."

"The disruption wouldn't have lasted very long since it most likely would have been eaten by a mountain lion or a wolf pack, but I appreciate your attention to detail, as always. However, I really don't think you should have to care for the animal any longer than necessary. You have duties to perform, after all."

"Twenty-first century police used to employ canine units. I think this animal could be a valuable asset to our team."

"A distraction, more likely," Dr. Moses said, a hint of irritation in his voice. "Leave it with Conall. That will be all."

"I'm afraid I can't do that," Jayka said calmly, staring straight ahead. "Section 121.8 of the Declaration of Independence of Animals states that animals have the right to life, liberty, and the pursuit of happiness, and whenever it is within our power to provide these rights, we must do so. Section 122.5 states that knowingly causing an animal emotional duress is strictly forbidden and punishable by up to five years in prison. I am sworn to uphold State law. I cannot comply with your request."

Dr. Moses came around to stand in front of Jayka in an attempt to meet her gaze. Since she was a full foot taller than he was, it didn't work. "You will have to go through the application process, just like everyone else," he said stiffly.

"Then it is a good thing someone from the Ministry of Animal Care is on their way. They are bringing an application with them, since it has the requirement of a fingerprint produced in the presence of one of their notaries to verify identity. I already sent my certificate of health and employment history."

Dr. Moses was silent for a full five seconds. "This will be a disruption to your team, Jayka. I cannot allow it."

Jayka finally lowered her gaze to look him in the eye. "By State law, you cannot stop it." With that, she turned on her heel and exited the office, with Macy following close beside her.

30

BEADS of sweat popped up on the forehead of the sleeping man. They pooled in a worried crease in his brow and trickled across the ink-embedded skin above his eye and down his eyelid, finally rolling down his cheek onto the blanket below. He moaned slightly and turned over on the bed fashioned of pallets. Although its comfort looked questionable, a layer of cardboard removed the sharpness of the edges of the boards. On top of the cardboard was a double-layered homemade mattress. The bottom consisted of a mat woven of clothes found in the trash. The top layer was formed of contraband plastic bags of the type used by superstores before they had been consolidated into the State-run corporation, Unimart. Wadded together and packed inside a sheet wrapped around the whole affair, they afforded the sleeper a mattress of comfort that was unparalleled in tenements of the outer docks.

The man moaned again, and the woman beside him roused. She slipped out from under the blanket and quickly dressed in the gray daylight of the alleyway window, glancing briefly at the man as he tossed and turned in his sleep. She wrapped a shawl around her statuesque form and exited the room to the main living area, where several figures lay sprawled sleeping on the floor. Making her way to the front entrance, she placed her hand carefully on the doorknob, turning it silently. "Back home, then?" asked a figure seated beside the door, his back to the wall and his hand resting on a bent knee.

The doorknob made a slight rattle as the woman tensed, almost imperceptibly. She turned and smiled at the man, pulling the hood of his sweatshirt away from his face so she could arrest him with her eyes. "Unless you have a better idea?"

The question could have been taken as a proposition, but if he accepted it, he knew she would tell the man in the next room. It was really an insult, veiled as an invitation. "Nahh. Ya know I don' git paid ta think," he smiled evenly back at her, his eyes conveying that he neither trusted her, nor thought his boss should, either.

She stood looking at him for a moment and ran an ebony finger across his arch tattoo. "Then I guess I'll be going," she said, smiled like a demon, and slipped out the front door.

The man unconsciously swiped his hand across the place where she had touched him, as if trying to rid himself of dirt or a stray cobweb. The woman was trouble. He knew it instinctively, and so did the man who slept so fitfully in the next room. But the leader of the Gateways hadn't risen to the top and brought his gang to preeminence by being afraid to take risks. Cosmo was attracted to the woman for a reason. She was cunning, that much was obvious. But wits without the means to use them strategically were worthless, so she must have that in her favor as well, although Cade knew nothing about it. He had been serious when he said he wasn't paid to think, but he did plenty of figuring to himself.

Ever since those three dimwits, Dune, Ox, and Tank had been captured after they made their little escapade through the wall, tensions in the ranks had been high. For weeks, rumors had been circulating about a breach in the wall. Several people had gone looking for it, but Dune had gotten a tip that it could be out past Zelda's old place. Maybe the people who were going to the meetings out that direction weren't just going for the free meal. Maybe they had just been using them as a distraction while they looked for any possible weak spots without the gang knowing. Maybe they had been able to break through and leave. That was Dune's reasoning, and he and his buddies had decided to check it out. Any idiot with any sense of loyalty would have known they needed to report their discovery to Cosmo, rather than take matters in their own hands and explore on their own. If the Gateways had gained access to the Preserve, it could have been an unprecedented generation of revenue and leverage. They could have expanded their namesake—being not only the gateway for customers from the State to the outer docks, but for both citizens and Discards to the Preserve.

But the three had ruined it. The State knew about the breach because the trio had led them right to it. Cameras had probably recorded them headed toward the wall, and security had been notified when they hadn't returned. If they had come back, nothing would have seemed suspicious. But they hadn't. Cade had seen the female Pod-Op slipping through back alleys in the outskirts and had followed from a distance. He watched as she disappeared into the area that dipped below camera surveillance. It was too risky to follow after that; but he waited, and she didn't return. That afternoon, a helicopter had been seen leaving the city heading south and returning half an hour later with two stretchers attached. *"Idiots!"* Cade mumbled. What had they been thinking? Well, obviously, they *hadn't.* They still hadn't learned the rules. Loyalty. Obedience. Submission to the leader. If you wanted to rise in the ranks, those were the rules. Until you were powerful enough to become his right-hand man—could be trusted with his very life—only then could you either defend him to the death, or take his life and become the next gang lord.

Cosmo was the best leader the Gateways had ever had. But this woman had Cade worried. In the beginning, when Cosmo had first showed up with her, he seemed to be in control, confident that the woman had some skills that could be useful for making contacts in the State. But where had she come from? Cosmo was tight-lipped about it, so for all he knew, she *was* from the State, masquerading as a Discard from the north side. And lately, Cosmo had seemed distracted …maybe even a little stressed. It didn't help that the three had been captured and would undoubtedly be chipped, sharing all the secrets they knew about the gang and its operations. That was why Cosmo had contacted Angel this time, although what she could do about it, Cade had no idea. He rubbed the ring he wore on his middle finger with the thumb of the same hand. A present from Cosmo, it represented the wealth the leader had brought to the gang and his intention to trust Cade as his right-hand man. Cade wondered if that trust was enough for Cosmo to listen to his concerns. He would have to find the right time—a time when they wouldn't be interrupted.

Suddenly a scream erupted from the bedroom. The men on the floor jerked awake, and Cade was at the door in two strides. Cosmo was sitting up in the bed, breathing hard, his eyes wide and staring straight ahead, his body wet with sweat. "Cosmo! Y'okay, bro?"

"'T'snuttin'. Bad dream. Bad, bad dream." He looked around the room. "Angel leave?"

"Yeah, man. About ten minutes ago. You want I shoulda kept 'er here?" Cade asked worriedly.

"Nahhh. Nah, man. She got a job ta do. She say she got da Twit-head Triumvirate handled."

"Triumvirate? What's she mean by that?"

"It's some fancy word fa three people. Ox, Dune, an' Tank."

"How she kin do that? They's locked up, gettin' chipped an' all." Cade asked, before he could stop himself.

"Barricade, I *tol'* ya dat if'n ya need ta know, I'll *tell* ya. I kinda thought ya understood dat by now," Cosmo said testily.

Cade nodded, but decided to risk one more question. "Ya sure we kin trust 'er?" Cosmo's eyes shifted from their focus on the imaginary point on the wall at the foot of the bed to bore into Cade. "If'n I didn' trust 'er, do ya tink I woulda sent 'er ta do a job?"

"No. It's jus', there's somethin' about 'er that don't add up."

"She's already proved 'erself by findin' us a way ta git tru da Dead Zone. Givin' us legit connections ta meet us, Stateside. It ain't like she ain't takin' no risks fo us, 'erself." Cosmo was silent for a moment as he wiped the sweat from his face with the blanket. "Heard anyting 'bout da meetin's in da outskirts lately?"

Cade exhaled in relief. Apparently, Cosmo had decided to put aside the matter of his judgment being questioned. "Not since Reggie taught the Deserter's daddy a lesson. I think she got the message, cuz no one seen 'er since. We know 'e done tol' 'er 'bout the meetin's, cuz 'e tol ever'one 'bout 'em. But she ain't gonna come investigatin' now, that's fa sure. That secret's safe, as long as Angel does her job."

"She will," Cosmo said, glaring at Cade.

"I didn' mean nuthin' by it," Cade said.

"Sounded like ya did."

"No, bruh."

Cosmo glared again at Cade before throwing back the blanket and finding a pair of pants from the various items of clothing scattered on the floor. "Grab Sho-Low and Creep. We gonna pay a visit to da Stewmakah."

"Just them two? That's all?"

"Yeah, dat's it. Outskirts is my ol' stompin' grounds. We ain't gotta make no big show." Cade turned to go and Cosmo was left alone. He put on his pants and, after looking around the room for a clean shirt, decided the occasion called for a brand-new henley that had never been worn by anyone else. It still had the tag on it—one of the new trades he had acquired from their business with the thrill-seeking citizens of the State. He started to remove the tag, and then thought better of it, leaving it dangling from the bottom as a status symbol: no holes, no stains, *and* the tag still attached. He sat on the edge of the bed, his eyes wandering to the window where the light of morning was determinedly forcing its way through the layer of fog just above the rooftops. It made him remember a detail of his nightmare. He had never before experienced a dream that intense. Just when it seemed things were going to turn around and help was within his grasp, someone had stolen the help he needed right out from under him. While the feelings connected to most dreams dissipated with the light of day like acid fog, the emotions connected to this dream held on. He felt like he did when a deal went bad—like there was unfinished business.

"We's ready." Cade was in the doorway with two men who were giants by comparison to most of the outer dock residents.

"Yeah, boss. Whatevah you got goin', we's down for," said the shorter of the two men. "Ah mean, if ya wants ta fix someone up real good so they don't talk no more, we's with ya. If'n you's goin' ta the State, we's with ya. If ya—"

"Sho-Low, shut-*up*. Ya don't get paid ta talk," Cade said exasperatedly. "You could learn a thing 'er two from Creep."

Creep, his face streaked by frightening scars earned in countless brawls, shifted his weight and clasped his hands behind his back, his eyes staring straight ahead.

"Creep *cain't* talk. He gots no choice but ta be quiet," Sho-Low protested.

"Exactly," Cosmo said with finality. "An' y'ain't gonna be roughin' up nobody. Not unless someone gets a dumb *idee*. I wants ya two on ya best behavior. No screw ups. No tinkin' fo yaself. Just be cool. I'll let ya know."

"That's no problem, bruh. We cool. We down with it. We—"

"Sho-Low!" Cade exclaimed as Cosmo glared. Sho-Low clamped his mouth shut and nodded.

"Fall in," Cosmo said and headed out the door. The group headed down the street, Cade walking beside Cosmo and the bodyguards a few steps behind, their eyes darting here and there, seeking out any possible threats. Few were brave enough to challenge the Gateways, but there was always a chance.

Cade glanced at Cosmo as they walked. He was unusually quiet. They hadn't been to the outskirts since the two had gone through the line at one of the meetings to sample the free stew everyone was talking about. Cade was interested in hearing what the Stewmaker had to say, but Cosmo had wanted to leave as soon as the music stopped. Maybe now they were finally going to see what was so important to her that she would give away a fortune in food every night. She had to be getting something in return. Or maybe they were going to ask about her supplier. The Stewmaker had plenty of explaining to do. As far as Cade was concerned, she was a State spy. There were too many unknowns. For one thing, there was no way she could keep up a steady supply of fresh food without knowing someone on the inside. That and the fact that no one had ever heard of her. She said she was from somewhere else, but Cade had checked with some of his contacts up north, and no one had heard of her there, either.

It was one of those mornings where the acid fog never dropped to street level, hovering above the buildings for an hour or two after daylight and then dissipating to reveal a crystal-clear sky. The weather phenomenon was becoming so frequent it was almost commonplace now. People were already lounging around on their porch steps, enjoying the ability to breathe freely this early in the day. Some of them had already made a trek to the nearest dumpster, staking their claim as the first on the scene just in case a food drop arrived. The closer they got to the outskirts, however, the less people were hanging around near dumpsters. They passed a few folks on the street, but they weren't in any particular hurry to beat their dockmates to a food drop. Cade noticed their faces didn't seem hollowed out, like the people in most of the outer docks. *Must be all that good eatin',* he thought to himself.

The gang members were nearing Zelda's old neighborhood now. Cade noticed a young boy watching them from behind a porch stoop. He darted out into the street and rushed off ahead of them. "Hazen!" Cosmo called. The boy turned slowly and watched them warily. "Whatcha hurry, little bro?"

"No hurry, I just gotta get goin', dat's all," said the boy.

"Where ya headed?" Cosmo didn't seem to want to let it go.

"No place special," the boy answered, fidgeting with a dirt smudge on his foot.

"Well, it look like we's headed in da same direction. Why don' ya walk wit' us? I hadn't seen ya since ya was a squallin' ankle-biter," Cosmo said with a smile, but Cade knew what was happening. Hazen was in the Stewmaker's camp, and he was undoubtedly going to warn her they were coming. The boy fidgeted some more, and then fell in beside them as they walked. There was no point in refusing them. There were always consequences for not meeting their demands, even when they seemed like a friendly invitation.

"So how's ya been? How's da fam?" Cosmo asked as they walked.

"Good," said the boy, and offered no further information.

"Jus' good, huh? Dat's it? Ya don' got no news fa ya ol' homey?" Cosmo asked with a grin.

Hazen shot him a glance but kept his mouth shut.

"Man!" Cosmo exclaimed and turned around to include Sho-Low and Creep in the conversation. "Can ya believe dat? I been snubbed by da little man in ma ol' hood!"

"It's almost like 'e *wants* ta get ruffed up, ain't it?" Sho-Low began.

"Shut up, Sho-Low," Cosmo barked. "He's a kid. What *is* you, a milliwatt light bulb?"

"I's jus' sayin'—"

"Well, stop sayin'. Dat's all ya do is *say*. Da problem is, ya nevah *tink*," Cosmo growled. "But you *is* loyal to da cause. An' you's powerful strong. Dat's why you's one o' ma main men. Jus' don' lose ya place by runnin' ya mouth."

The group walked along in silence for a few seconds. "He always like dat?" Hazen asked Cosmo, nodding his head toward Sho-Low.

Cosmo threw his head back and guffawed. "Yay-dat! He sho is, little man. Cain't stop gabbin'. But—" he said, throwing a glance at Sho-Low, who was watching them silently, "he doin' a purty good job right now."

"What dat ting on ya shirt?" Hazen asked, eyeing the price tag dangling from the hem.

"Dat is what dey have on a shirt when it still in da sto. Dis here is a brand-new shirt, ain't nevah been worn by no one," Cosmo said, his eyes narrowed.

"'Cept you," said Hazen.

"Yeah, I da first," Cosmo agreed, and looked at Hazen speculatively. "Hey Hazen. Whatchu tink 'bout bein' first at stuff?"

"It's da best," Hazen said, his eyes shining. "I was first in ma family ta meet Jesus. An' I tol' all o' dem 'bout it. Dey *all* know 'im, now."

"Jesus? Who dat? Oh, now wait a minute. Some o' my boys been to ya meetin's. Dey said da Stewmakah talk 'bout the Jesus ever'one swear by like e's a real god, 'r sump'n. Is dat who ya mean?"

Hazen swallowed nervously and then squared his shoulders and met Cosmo's gaze. "Yeah, dat Who I mean."

Cosmo stared evenly back at him for a few seconds. "Hmmph. Ok. Well, whatchu tink 'bout bein' da first ankle-biter ta join ma gang?"

"I ain't no ankle-biter," Hazen protested.

"Man, I don' know," Cade began.

"Hush, Barricade. Let da man decide," Cosmo said, his eyes sparkling and a smile playing on his lips.

"No, sir, Cosmo. I don't hang wit' no gang," Hazen said, his voice shaking slightly.

Cosmo stuck out his bottom lip thoughtfully. "I guess ya ain't as grow'd up as I thought. Dat's ok. You's got plenty o' time ta change ya mind."

"I ain't changin' it," Hazen said boldly and turned left up an alleyway.

"Where's *you* goin'?" Cosmo said, coming to an abrupt halt.

"Home," Hazen said, without turning around.

"Naw. You's comin' wit' us ta see da Stewmakah. I bet she be glad ta see ya. An' if'n ya don't come wit' us, maybe I can come home wit' ya so we can continue dis conversation. I ain't seen ya mama in a long time. She ain't bad lookin'. Course, she nevah had time fa *me* when I lived out here," Cosmo said with an edge to his voice.

Hazen stopped in his tracks, his little fists clenched, and turned around slowly. "I'll come wit' ya alright," he said between gritted teeth.

"Dat's ma boy," Cosmo said as Hazen fell in beside them again, and he rumpled the boy's curly hair in mock affection.

The dilapidated apartment buildings of the outskirts crouched on either side of them. Cracks crawled across the sidewalks and up the sides of the buildings, which lacked the microbial additive of modern concrete. That self-correcting feature was reserved for places like the Upscales, which were closer to the Dead Zone. In the outskirts, residents counted themselves lucky to even have electricity. "Man, oh man," Cosmo said as he looked around. "Dis place needs a redo. I don' know how it can look any worser dan it did when I was here jus' a month ago, but somehow, it do." He glanced down at the little figure beside him. "Ya know da ting about bein' in a gang, little man, is ya gots powah. Ya gots connections. You an' me, we could be a part o' shapin' up dis neighborhood. I gots a job fa you, if'n ya wants. Bein' you's little an' all, you's harder ta see. An' you's quick, like a little bird, too. I bet you's could zip across da Dead Zone in nuttin' flat."

Hazen kept his lips tightly sealed and his eyes straight ahead. Cosmo chuckled. "Ok, little man. Ok. Look, we's here at Zelda's old place. An' dat's where da Stewmakah's stayin', ain't it?" Cosmo looked at Hazen pointedly, but the boy said nothing. Cosmo smiled and chuckled again. "You do gots some spark, boy," he said, and headed toward the porch. "Don' worry. I already knowed dis was da place—on account of da tradin' picture." He gestured to the symbol of the hands on the side of the door and was about to knock when the door opened and Bally slipped outside.

"What do *you* want?" Bally said tartly.

Cosmo was all smiles. "Well, if it ain't Bally girl! My you is lookin' nice an' fresh dis mornin'!"

"Which is mo' dan I kin say fa *you*. You look like ya hasn't slept in a week. Ya been samplin' ya batches?" Bally snipped.

"Oooo girl, you knows I like a sassy mouth. But I ain't here ta see *you*, princess. I's here ta see da Stewmakah," Cosmo said, leaning against the doorframe in a pose that suggested he wasn't going anywhere until he got what he wanted.

Bally crinkled her eyebrows. "Stewmakah!" she sputtered, opened her mouth to say something else, and then suddenly a strange look crossed her face. She shut her mouth and looked down at Hazen, noticing him for the first time. "What is *you* doin' here? Wit' *him?*"

"I ain't *wit'* him, Bally. Not on purpose," Hazen said. Bally read the worry in his eyes. "I was on my way ta tell ya you was gettin' visitors, but—"

"But I ast 'im ta walk wit' us. So we could get reacquainted, like," Cosmo interrupted, smiling sweetly.

Bally glanced down at the small boy. She could tell he was trying hard to be brave. "Well, dat was mighty neighborly," Bally said and gave Hazen's arm a squeeze. "But now dat you'ns is all reacquainted, I reckon' Hazen kin skedaddle."

"I reckon' not," Cosmo said, placing his hand firmly on Hazen's bony shoulder. "We's got business togeddah, don't we, little man?"

Hazen looked up at Bally desperately. She cleared her throat. "If'n ya wants to meet da Stewmakah, ya bettah let Hazen git home," she said firmly.

Suddenly, a deep voice coming from behind Sho-Low startled them all. "Let him *go!*" The sound reverberated between the buildings. Cosmo, Cade and Sho-Low all turned around and stared. Creep was standing in the road, backing away slowly, his eyes wide. "Let him go, *now!*" Creep repeated.

"Creep, you kin *talk!* You been holdin' out on us all this time!" Sho-Low began jabbering, and then he stopped as Creep turned without a word and hurried down the street from the direction they had come, looking back over his shoulder every once in a while, as he half-walked, half-jogged away. "What got inta *him?*" Sho-Low asked, looking around at the others.

Cade was still staring at the retreating hulk of a man as he disappeared around a corner. Cosmo was strangely quiet, and his hand shook a little as he removed it from the doorframe and let it drop to his side. He turned to Hazen and backed away a few steps. "Mebbe ya better git on home, little man. Say hi to ya mama fo me."

No one had to tell Hazen twice. He spun around and sped off down the street as fast as his little legs could take him. Cosmo watched without a word as the wiry figure ducked into an alley, out of sight. "Cade…Sho-Low, you go make sure Creep is ok," he said, his eyes on the empty street.

"We be back," Cade said, and the two took off at a jog.

Cosmo turned around slowly and faced Bally again. "If'n it ain't too much trouble, I'd like ta see ya friend what holds da meetin's," he said.

Bally's eyebrows raised in surprise at his change in tone. "Stewmakah, huh?" she said. "Wait here. I'll see what I kin do." She slipped back inside, and a few minutes later, the door opened and Selah and Bally both stepped out on the porch.

"I heard you were looking for the Stewmaker," Selah said. Cosmo stared. And then, without really knowing why, he went to his knees and began to sob. Bally looked at Selah, her eyes wide, and Selah stooped down so she could be at eye level with the man. "He's closer than you think," she said. "He knows who you are. He loves you, and He wants you to be part of His family."

For a few moments, the only sound was that of Cosmo sucking in his breath in ragged gasps. When he finally regained control of his emotions, he wiped his nose on the sleeve of his brand-new shirt and fixed Selah with bloodshot eyes. "Who is he? I see him every night in ma dreams. It's da same dream every night. I'm at one o' dese meetin's o' yourn, wit' hundreds o' folks gaddered roun'. You is dishin' out da stew, an' I's at da last o' da line. I's afraid I ain't gonna git none. But den I see it ain't jus' you up dere. Dere's someone standin' right behind ya. I ain't never been aroun' no one like dat afore. It's like, 'e looks at ever' one in da crowd—I mean, *ever'* one, an' 'e sees 'em fa who dey really are—da good *an'* da bad. But it's like 'e don' care how bad dey are. An 'e's sayin' ovah and ovah, 'All you'ns who is thirsty, come to da waters. Even if'n ya don' have no money, come, buy an' eat! Why ya spend ya money fah dat what ain't bread, an' why ya work fah what don't fill ya up? Come to Me, so ya soul can live, an' I will make an everlasting covenant wit' ya.'[90] An' I seen men o' ma own crew what done da worst o' da worst, an' dey go up to 'im an' say dey's sorry. An' 'e jus' takes 'em up an' holds like 'es deir bruddah o' deir daddy o' sump'n. An' when 'e lets go, dey ain't da same person. I mean, dey looks da same, but dey's differ'nt. An' I tink to maself, I gotta git up dere afore 'e leaves. I gotta see what 'es doin' to 'em. Cuz dey all seem like dey's happier dan I ever seen 'em, an' deir eyes is somehow da same as *his* eyes. An' den I knowed it—I knowed it ain't *you* dat been makin'

---

[90] See Isaiah 55:1-3

all dat stew. Somehow, dis guy in da dream is makin' it. Where is 'e? Tell me 'e's real, Miss Selah. Cuz den in da dream, jus' when I's gonna git ta meet 'im, dis woman shove me outta da line, an' she say, 'You ain't nevah gonna be one o' *his* crew. *Dis* is where you belong.' An' den she shove me into dis alley, but it ain't a alley. It's a big black hole, an' dey's screamin' down dere. Dey's doin' stuff ta people down dere dat ain't anyting I evah thought o' doin' ta no one, even ma worst rival. An' I'm fallin', an' all I can see is da dark an' dese hands o' all dese people reachin' out to me, screamin' fah help. An' den I hit da bottom, an' I wakes up."

Selah took Cosmo by the hand. "The Man you saw is real. His name is Jesus. And if you really want to be part of His family, there's nothing that can stop you from coming to Him."

Cosmo sat back on his haunches. "Dat dude is Jesus? Like Jesus-God? Like dey swear by? Nahhh. I always thought God was jus' a story dey use ta tell ta make kids be good. But dis dude was real. He *had* ta be real. Dat dream was realer dan anyting I ever saw when I was awake."

"Well, let me show you something, and then you can tell me what you think," Selah said, and went back inside, with Bally following close behind. As Selah headed toward the pallet table where her Bible lay open, Bally nimbly slipped around in front of her to face her friend.

"Selah! I know what you's tinkin', an' you can't show him dat Bible!" she said in a harsh whisper, her eyes round. "He could be jus' lookin' for an excuse ta sell ya to dah State! Ta make 'imself look good in deir eyes. You show 'im dat Bible, an' he got all da proof 'e needs dat you is an enemy o' da State! I'm not sayin' not ta tell 'im how ta git saved—I mean, we *all* want dat. But dere gotta be a way ta do it wit'out showin' 'im you got a contraband book!"

Selah looked at Bally levelly. "Those words he heard in the dream were from the book of Isaiah. They may not have been word for word, but they were said in a way he could relate to."

"I *know* dat," Bally said, one eyebrow raised. "I may not know what book it was from, but I know I heerd ya say dem words afore, when we's doin' Bible study. Cain't ya jus' *tell* 'im about it? You bring dat book out dere, how ya tink ya gonna be able ta prove to 'im dat it say what you says it say? It ain't like 'e can *read*, or nuttin'. Fah all *he* knows, you is just makin' it up dat it say da same ting."

Selah looked down for a minute as doubt began to creep into her thoughts, but she knew she should show Cosmo the passage of scripture he had inadvertently quoted. She looked back up at Bally. "I have to do this," she said. "His soul may depend on it." She grabbed the Bible off of the pallet table and headed back outside. Before she could say a word, Cosmo saw what she carried, and his eyes opened wide. "Yes, it is what you think it is," Selah said, fixing him with her gaze. "But what I have to show you is worth being reported."

Cosmo looked up and down the street, and satisfied it was empty, he leaned in and looked over Selah's shoulder to see as she flipped through the pages to the book of Isaiah, chapter 55.

> "Ho, every one who thirsts, come to the waters; and he who has no money, come, buy and eat! Come, buy wine and milk without money and without price. Why do you spend your money for that which is not bread, and your labor for that which does not satisfy? Hearken diligently to me, and eat what is good, and delight yourselves in fatness. Incline your ear, and come to me; hear, that your soul may live; and I will make with you an everlasting covenant..."[91]

She looked up at him intently.

"Dat is da same as what he was sayin' in ma dream!" Cosmo exclaimed. "Ain't ya gonna read da rest of it?" Cosmo asked, looking at the verse, and then back at Selah.

"The rest of the chapter?" Selah asked.

"No, you stopped right dere where it say 'covenant'. I don' understan' dat part where it say about how he loves some dude named David."

Bally's mouth dropped open. "Cosmo, you kin read?"

Cosmo glared at her. "Yeah, I kin read. Ma Aunt Marva taught me. An' don' be tellin' no one. It come in real handy sometimes when State folk tink I cain't." He turned back to Selah. "It say right here, 'I will make wit' you an

---

[91] Isaiah 55:1-3, RSV

everlasting covenant, my steadfast, sure love for David.' So what does dat mean about David? Who is he?"

"David was a king of Israel," Selah said. "But he wasn't always king. He grew up taking care of sheep, protecting them from predators like bears and lions. David loved God and wrote songs to Him. He sang and played instruments to worship Him. God saw his heart and chose him to be the next king of Israel. He promised David that someday someone in his family would be king forever."[92]

"How can dat happen? No one can live forevah. Ever'one die *some*day," Cosmo said skeptically.

"It can happen, and it *did* happen. God sent His Son, Jesus, in the form of a baby who came from David's family line. You know—Jesus-God, the one they swear by," Selah added, to make sure he understood. "And Jesus lived the perfect life, teaching people about His heavenly Father. But He was put to death on a cross, even though He didn't do anything wrong. He paid the debt we owed for our sins."

"So he *did* die," Cosmo said.

"But 'e didn' stay dead!" Bally jumped in, too excited to hold her tongue. "He rose from da dead an' now He lives so dat He kin give *us* life! Alls ya hafta do is tell 'im ya sorry fo' ya bad doin's and tell 'im ya want 'im ta be ya Leader. Not jus' *any* jefe, but da Lord o' ya whole life! If'n ya gots His help, you can stop ya bad doin's an' have a new life, livin' fah *Him*."

Cosmo looked from Bally to Selah. "What y'all been addin' to dat stew?"

Selah laughed. "We haven't been doctoring it up with anything. And we haven't doctored up the Word of God, either. What Bally said is true. And the words Jesus spoke to you in the dream are true."

"But what about all da bad tings I done? You tellin' me dis Jesus-God is jus' gonna live an' let live?"

"No," Selah said in a serious tone. "He didn't live and let live. Like I said, He *died*. He gave His life for yours, so you could trade your sins—your *bad doin's*, for His righteousness. But like Bally said, the grave couldn't keep Him down. He really did rise again. I can show you where it says that in the Bible."

---

[92] See 2 Samuel 7

Cosmo put his hand on Selah's arm to stop her as she began to turn to the gospels. "Dat's ok. I believe ya, an' we ain't got much time," he said, looking up and down the street again.

"You believe us?" Bally asked incredulously.

"Yeah, I believe ya. Cuz if'n Jesus-God is still dead, how he able to talk to me in da dream?" Cosmo replied. "Listen, y'all. Y'all prob'ly know I done a lot o' bad doin's. I don' know what ma crew gonna do if'n I tell Jesus I's sorry an' want 'im ta be da Leader o' ma life. But I know dat jus' as real as da Stewmakah was in da dream, dat dark place in da alley was da real ting. Dere is some place like dat, an' it ain't a place folks kin git out of, is it? I mean, once you's dere, you's stayin' dere forevah. Is dat place what dey call Hell?"

"True, dat," Bally said. "But ya don' hafta make it ya home turf."

"Hell *is* real, but you don't have to go there. You have a choice," Selah echoed.

"Dat's easy fa you ta say. But folk like me what's done lotsa bad doin's, we's made fa goin' dere," Cosmo insisted.

"Nope," Selah said firmly. "Hell was made for the devil and his angels.[93] The Bible says that God made us in His own image. In the very beginning, before anyone ever did anything bad, God and humans had a perfect relationship. God walked with them and visited with them in the garden that He had made for them. When the first couple sinned by eating fruit from the only tree God told them not to eat from, that's when the friendship was messed up. But even back then, God already had a plan in place to send His Son to save us.[94] And in the book of Isaiah, just like He was doing in your dream, He was telling everyone—not just the people He had originally made a covenant with, but He is inviting *everyone* who is searching for something they can't seem to find to come find what they need in *Him*. Anyone who is thirsting for something more out of life because nothing seems to satisfy them can find it by coming to Jesus."

"So how do I do dat? Jesus ain't here like 'e was in da dream. It ain't like I kin jus' walk up to 'im an' say I's sorry."

"Actually, He *is* here. The same prophet who wrote the scripture you quoted also wrote these words," Selah said, turning to Isaiah 57:15. "For thus says the

93 See Matthew 25:41
94 See Genesis 1:26-27, 3:1-15

high and lofty One who inhabits eternity, whose name is Holy: 'I dwell in the high and holy place, and also with him who is of a contrite and humble spirit, to revive the spirit of the humble, and to revive the heart of the contrite. For I will not contend for ever, nor will I always be angry; for from Me proceeds the spirit, and I have made the breath of life.'"[95]

"Contrite is a fancy word fa meanin' ya really are sorry fa all ya bad doin's," Bally supplied. "Miss Selah explained dat to me."

"So if you really are sorry for what you've done, His Word says right here that He will meet with you and forgive you and bring your spirit to life. You'll be part of His family. You may not be able to see Him with your eyes, but you'll be able to see Him with your heart—like you did in the dream," Selah explained.

"Do I hafta be dreamin' ta tell 'im?" Cosmo asked.

"I wasn' dreamin' when *I* tol' 'im," Bally said. "An' 'e came an' forgave me an' took *me* in."

Cosmo looked down. "Well, I *is* sorry for all I done," he said, tears suddenly brimming to the surface and slipping down his cheeks. He hid his face in his hands. "Jesus, if me bein' sorry means Ya really is here, den please take me into ya family. Please forgive me. I want You ta be da Leader o' ma life. I don' know how to stop dese bad doin's, but I don' wanna do 'em no mo. Dey say You kin help me. Please help me." Cosmo's sobs were muffled by his hands as he crouched down on the porch steps. Selah and Bally knelt with him, and Selah placed her hand on his shoulder. After a while, he stopped crying and looked at Selah between his fingers.

"He *will* help you, Cosmo. You belong to Him now," Selah reassured him.

"I really one o' His crew now? Dat's all it takes? I don' gotta do nuttin' ta prove maself?"

"You can't do anything to earn a place at His table. You just did the only things you need to do to be accepted into His family. You believed Jesus is the Son of God and that He died to save you, you are sorry for what you did, and you asked Him to be the Lord of your life. And now that you've done that, He's going to help you make the changes you said you want to make."

---

[95]Isaiah 57:15-16, RSV

"Dis is weird, y'all," he said suddenly, wiping his face with his sleeve. "I ain't nevah got sump'n fa nuttin'. An' dis Jesus, He jus' gave me everyting!" Cosmo broke down again, but this time, a smile began to spread across his face as he cried. He stopped suddenly. "I know you say I don' gotta do nuttin', but I *wanna* do sump'n ta show 'im how glad I is ta be part o' da fambly." A look of shock crossed his face. "Oh, man. Dere's sump'n I done—some work I gave ta someone, an' I gotta stop it right *now!*" he said. He jumped down the porch steps and stopped suddenly as he saw Cade and Sho-Low coming back up the street, with no sign of Creep.

"Where's Creep?" Bally wondered out loud.

"I gotta feelin' Creep ain't gonna show his face here," Cosmo said mysteriously. "I gotta go!" And with that, he ran to meet the gang members before they could get any closer to see the book Selah was holding.

"Come on, y'all, we'ns gotta git back to da homegrounds," Cosmo said.

"We found Creep, but when we tol' 'im ya wanted ta see 'im, 'e just shook his head. He back to his ol' creepy self. He ain't sayin' *nuthin'* now." Sho-Low said.

"Dat's ok. I'll talk to 'im later," Cosmo said. "Listen, Cade, I gotta getta message ta Angel, zippy-like. Get me a runner—Trajan, if 'e's available."

"Trajan has got a run tomorrah," Cade reminded him.

"Well, da plans have changed. Now 'e's runnin' tonight."

"What is so king that you gotta push off the drop tomorrah?" Sho-Low asked.

"Dat is nunya. Cade, get Trajan. Dat's da dat." He looked at Cade expectantly.

"Now?" Cade questioned.

"Yay-dat! Now is *king!*" Cosmo said emphatically.

"Ok, I'll run ahead an' bring 'em back to the homegrounds," Cade said nervously. "Is everything up, man?"

"No, everyting is *not* up. Everyting *south* until we git dat message ta Angel," Cosmo said.

Cade whirled around and took off running. Cosmo began to jog, and Sho-Low matched his pace. If he couldn't cancel the order he had given previously, he would have the lives of three men on his hands. "Please, please let us git to 'er in time," Cosmo said.

"What?" Sho-Low asked.

"I wadn' talkin' ta *you*," Cosmo retorted.

"Well, I is de only one here, so who was you talkin' to?"

"Nunya." Cosmo was quiet the rest of the way home. When they got there, Cade was waiting at the door with Trajan.

"I hear tell ya needs a bird," Trajan said. "I'd rather pack the *bundle* tomorrah."

"I'll pay ya da same as for da bundle," Cosmo said—if'n ya gits dis message dere zippy." He wrote on a piece of paper, folded it up and gave it to Trajan, who took it but looked up at Cosmo doubtfully. The gang all knew Cosmo could read and write and were sworn to secrecy, but Angel wasn't part of the gang.

"Ya sure ya don' wanna just *tell* me the song?" Trajan asked.

"No."

"What if I lose it?"

"You *plannin'* on losin' it?" Cosmo asked him pointedly. "Git it to 'er. Don' wait til dark. Use a food wagon. I'll bonus ya." He handed Trajan a small black box. "Take da locater."

Trajan raised his eyebrows and took the box, which was a modified version of a radar detector used to locate State vehicles. He was gone in a flash, the box out of sight but in operation.

"Did the Stewmakah tell ya somethin' so king ya gotta tell Angel?" Sho-Low asked.

Cosmo looked at him and was quiet for a moment. "Yeah." He didn't offer any more information, but changed the subject. "Did you'ns tell Creep I was mad at 'im? Cuz I ain't. I just wants ta talk to 'im."

Cade and Sho-Low exchanged glances. If a gang member refused a direct order, the consequences were clear. "He know the rules," Cade supplied.

"Well, I needs ta talk to 'im. An' tell 'im I extend'n da scepter."

"Extend'n the scepter?" Sho-Low squawked. "Ain't no one done that since my great grandaddy was alive an' the city was walled off. An' then, there was a good excuse, on account of Ol' Sic'em had good intel."

"I know dat. An' I tink dat Creep knows sump'n cuz 'e saw sump'n. An' I wanna know what 'e saw. When you see 'im—"

"We prob'ly won't see 'im. He ain't gonna show 'is face roun' here," Sho-Low interrupted.

"Well, put da word out dat I needs ta see 'im an' I know why 'e left. I know what 'e saw."

"What 'e saw? What'd 'e see? Did you see it, too?"

"Jus' do it," Cosmo said gruffly, his patience wearing thin.

The two headed down the street, and Cosmo was left alone with his thoughts. Angel had seemed pretty sure that she would be able to get rid of Ox, Dune, and Tank. He didn't know her plan or what kind of timeframe he had, but it would be tricky for Trajan to make it there with the message in time, especially since he was doing it in broad daylight. "Jesus," Cosmo prayed softly, "I heerd ma Aunt Marva pray lotsa times. An' I even seen tings happen when she prayed. Now, I don' know nuttin' 'bout prayin', but I know you can make sump'n outta nuttin', on account o' all dat stew ya make ever' night. So mebbe You kin make nuttin' outta sump'n, too. I know what I done is wrong, an' I's tryin' ta stop it. But I don' know if'n it kin be stopped. Please, Jesus—if ya keer anyting about dem dudes, please protect 'em somehow!" Cosmo went inside the apartment and into his room and began pacing back and forth as he prayed. It wasn't long before he heard the front door open and there was a knock at his bedroom door. When he opened it, there was Creep, trying very hard to conceal his discomfort at being there. "Creep! No worries, man. We's ok. Where's Sho-Low an' Cade? Dey found you so quick!" Cosmo looked around Creep's hulking form for any sign of the other men. Suddenly, a little head peeped around from behind Creep's leg. It was Hazen, looking ridiculously tiny next to the giant of a man.

"Hazen! Whatchu doin' roun' here? I tol' you ta go home, man. You don' want none o' what happens roun' here," Cosmo said hurriedly. He looked at Creep. "Did you drag 'im here? Didja tink mebbe ya needed some sort o' bribe ta save ya skin?"

Creep shifted from one foot to the other uncomfortably and shook his head. Hazen spoke up. "Nah, bruh. He didn' make me come here. I heerd you was lookin' fa him an' extendin' da scepter. An' I heerd from Selah what happened on da porch steps. I talked Creep into it. Didn' I, Creep?" Creep nodded vigorously and looked nervously at Hazen and then back at Cosmo.

"Creep, I knowed ya saw sump'n back in da outskirts. Sump'n dat skeered ya *real* good."

Creep nodded again, his eyes wide. For an instant, his eyes darted to a space just behind Hazen and then back to Cosmo.

Cosmo stared at the empty space. "Creep, I know ya don' wanna talk. So I jus' wanna ast ya, an' you can jus' nod if'n what I say is true. You see some big, big dude wit' Hazen, don'tcha? Great big bodyguard dude?"

Hazen's forehead wrinkled. "Huh? Whatchu talkin' 'bout? Dere ain't no one here 'cept you, me, an' Creep!"

Creep looked bewilderedly at Hazen, and then at Cosmo and suddenly found his tongue. "You little liar! That muscle o' yourn is the only reason I come, cuz I's skeered *not* to! An' he's the reason I ran away from the Stewmakah's place when we's tryin' ta git ya to join up. Now don'tchu git me killed, cuz I's doin' what ya tol' me I had ta do."

"Chill, Creep. Ain't nuttin' gonna happen to ya. I don' see it, but I knows what ya see," Cosmo said, looking respectfully in the vicinity right behind Hazen.

"What is y'all smokin'?" Hazen asked. "Dere ain't nuttin' dere."

"But dere *is* sump'n dere, little man, cuz I seen it in da dream I had," Cosmo said. "I seen ya runnin' aroun' in da dream, an' dis big dude—bigger'n any dude I ever seen—was right dere wit' ya. Dat's why I's tryin' ta git ya ta join up, cuz I thought dere must be sump'n special 'bout ya." He turned to Creep. "How long you been able ta talk?"

Creep shuffled uncomfortably. "I always been able to talk. But it's like you bein' able to read. Folks don' know 'bout it, means ya gits ta learn stuff ya might not, otherwise."

"Hmmm. Dat's wit, Creep. Now, I'm gonna tell ya sump'n, even though I know ya can rat me out, cuz it's dat important. I'm gonna tell ya why we went ta see da Stewmakah. An' I tink mebbe you's gonna believe me, on account o' you kin see our little man's guardian angel, here," Cosmo said.

A look of shock crossed Creep's face, then softened as he looked from Hazen to the warrior-like figure right behind him, whom nobody else seemed able to see. He turned back to Cosmo and nodded.

"I'm gonna tell ya 'bout da One what sent dis here angel ta protect Hazen. He's powerful. He's King. An' what's more—an' dis is da part I don't rightly understan'—He loves us like a daddy an' wants us ta join up wit' 'im."

And then, as best he could, Cosmo began to share the gospel with his henchman, with Hazen filling in the gaps. By the time Cade and Sho-Low came back empty-handed, Creep was all smiles.

"Creep! We been lookin' all ovah fa you!" Sho-Low exploded. "Whatchu so happy about?"

"I jus' met mah Maker," Creep said, his scarred face turned angelic.

"What's that s'posed ta mean?" Sho-Low asked Cosmo.

"Listen, boys. Tings 'r gonna be differ'nt aroun' here from now on. We's dealin' in a differ'nt line now. We's negotiatin' da ultimate repo. All we gotta do is git da info to dem crazy folks in da State what can't seem ta find nuttin' ta satisfy. Dey's our prime candidates. Dey's our customer base. Dem, and anyone else in dere dat'll listen. We gonna take 'em ta see da Stewmakah. It ain't gonna be safe. It'll be risky, fah sho. But if we pull it off, y'ain't gonna believe da reward, y'all!" Cosmo said excitedly.

"Big payoff?" Cade asked.

"Bigger'n big," Cosmo said.

"What's they payin' with? MRE's? A shipment o' canned food what cain't be tracked? New socks an' undies, enough fer a whole neighborhood?" Sho-Low asked.

"Nah, man," Cosmo said, his eyes shining. "A clear head. A clean feelin' inside. No mo' fightin' on da inside." He beat his fist against his chest. "What we dealin' now, it make ya into a new man."

"That's crazy, man," Sho-Low said, and quickly added, "I mean, it sound crazy-too-good-to-be-true."

"It *is*, an' it *ain't!*" Cosmo said.

"What're they payin' with? What's the profit?" Cade asked.

"It's already paid for. But dey gotta look at tings differn't, fah sho. Look, I'll explain it all to ya in good time. First, we gotta get some interest goin'. We gotta git a big group what's ready ta sneak in wit'out knowin' da score. Shouldn' be too hard, wit' da way some o' dem thrill-seekers tink."

"What're we doin', bruh?" Sho-Low asked excitedly. "Come on, lemme in on this."

"I will. You'll see. Jus' git a group ready, an' when we gots say, ten of 'em—"

"Ten! We ain't nevah brought in that many at the same time!" Sho-Low sputtered.

"I know, but I tink we kin make it work," Cosmo insisted.

"Ahhh, I git it. You an' Angel got some plan," Sho-Low grinned.

"No! She ain't ta know about dis. Not til later. I gotta wait til I find out if Trajan got'er da message, an' what she did wit' it. Mebbe den, we kin let 'er in on da deal."

"If she has as many connections as ya say she has, she might could help," Sho-Low persisted.

"No way, bruh. Let's keep dis between us four til we git it goin'," Cosmo said with finality.

"You mean, us five," Cade said with raised eyebrows as he spotted Hazen's bare foot sticking out from behind the door.

"What he doin' here?" Sho-Low exclaimed. "Y'all joinin' up afta all, little man?"

"Nahh, man. But 'e's helpin' us, ain't ya, little bruh?" Cosmo said and looked at Hazen with a searching expression. "Only if'n ya want to," he added.

"If he want to? How much he know?" Sho-Low asked.

"Only what we's dealin'," Cosmo said mysteriously.

"Wait—*he* knows what we got, an' ya won't tell *us* yet?" Sho-Low protested.

"I don' like it, man," Cade said. It was rarely that he expressed his opinion, but entrusting the secret of a supply with a non-gang member—and a child, at that—was a terrible idea.

"Oh, I tink he understands dat a lotta lives depend on it," Cosmo said, making eye contact with Hazen and giving him a wink.

Hazen nodded and kept his face expressionless. If he smiled back, no one would believe their ruse.

"Good. Now you head on home an' make da contacts we need," Cosmo instructed. "You know da ones."

Hazen nodded, his curls jiggling with each movement, and then sped out the door, out the building and onto the street.

"Wow, that's cold, man," Sho-Low grinned. "You got that po' kid scared ta death."

Cosmo rubbed his hand thoughtfully over his goatee. "Well, I tink 'e knows dis is serious bih'ness. He won't go spillin' it ta anyone but who we need 'im to." He looked at Creep, who returned his gaze. The other two couldn't be trusted yet. Creep had learned much from keeping silent over the years, and this time was no exception. He shuffled his feet and headed out the door.

"Where he goin'?" Sho-Low asked.

"Gonna make sure our message gits delivered," Cosmo said. "An' now, we's got a lotta work ta do. Start puttin' out ya feelers to da reg'lars. If we kin git mo' dan ten, dat'd be even bettah."

Sho-Low and Cade walked out the door, and Cosmo exhaled slowly. He had gone from dope-dealing to hope-dealing in one day, and while it was an exhilarating feeling, he had his worries. "Jesus, Man, dis may be a one-shot deal. But if'n You kin reach dese people, dey is gonna tell all o' deir junkie bros, an' all o' deir thrill seekin' buds. I jus' don' know what ma boys is gonna do when it all goes down. Dey may turn me in. Dey prob'ly will, I 'xpect. But I don' keer. If'n dey could justa seen what I seen in dat dream, dey'd savvy. An' if dey could jus' meet Ya an' know Ya, da way I jus' met Ya." He walked to the window and looked into the alleyway at the gray brick wall of the neighboring tenement building. A crushing feeling of responsibility for the gang members rested on his shoulders like a two-ton boulder. "I been takin' ever'one in da wrong direction. Help me turn dis aroun', Jesus," Cosmo whispered. "An' please, please, save dose men. Save Ox, Dune, and Tank. Help Trajan ta get da message ta Angel in time. Or make sump'n happen dat keeps 'er from doin' da job." He glanced up at the sky and opened the window to get a better look. It appeared that the fog, which had already cleared earlier that morning, was rolling in again, even though it was well before the time it would normally have done so. He closed the window and walked out the front door. Although the air was still clear below, the murky sky was dark as an executioner's hood. People in the street, their gazes lifted upward, were trying to find places to shelter. But the fog seemed to roll up from the river and head northward, bypassing the outer docks and settling thickly on the city.

31

THE citizens of the State were already busily about their daily routines when the fog descended on the city like a black vulture. Silently alighting on each rooftop, it didn't stop there, but continued its languid, swirling descent until the streets and cars were damp with it, filling the air with caustic fumes. There was no warning. The usual grace period afforded by meteorologists during which individuals could run for cover was nonexistent, because there had been none of the normal indicators that an event of this type would occur. People scrambled for cover, choking and wheezing as they grappled with their ineffective breathing apparatuses and ducked into the nearest shop or business. No enhanced pulmonary implants or standard issue respiratory device could have prepared them for this.

Ira stood in the doorway of the artificial interface room. The second floor was strangely quiet, except for the occasional beeping of monitors and the footsteps of nurses attending to patients. Dr. Moses usually met him at the ground level and accompanied him to his workspace, eager to offer his newest insight into their quest for the global link. However, this morning he had left a note for Ira at the front desk, explaining that he wouldn't be able to meet with him that day and asking him to continue installation of his program, which they had dubbed Welcome 1.0, into three newly implanted subjects. Ira was glad Moses had left detailed instructions, because he was concerned that Specialist Ainsley Abbot might have her own ideas about how he should use his talents during Moses' absence. His brow furrowed in confusion. Where was Ainsley? She usually showed up around 1000 hours, but she was already ten minutes late.

Raised voices at the end of the hallway interrupted his musings. "But until this clears up, no one is going anywhere," one of the nurses was saying in an agitated tone as she looked out the window. It was the nightshift crew. All the people who started their workday at 1000 hours were strangely absent.

"Excuse me," Ira said as he stepped into the hall and approached the pair. "Have you seen Specialist Ainsley Abbot today?"

"No," said one of them. "But my guess is she's stranded somewhere, just like everybody else."

"Stranded?" Ira asked, perplexed.

The nurse gestured to the window. "Haven't you seen it? Oh, I forget—they have you stuffed in that windowless room. The fog rolled in out of nowhere. It's the thickest I've ever seen!" She stepped aside so Ira could see.

Ira pushed his spectacles up his nose and squinted. The fog was heavy and swirling like smoke. "I thought you had the glass dimmed."

"No! It's just that thick out there. Like pea soup."

"But no soup I'd want to eat!" added the other nurse.

They all stood silently looking out the window for a few moments. "I wonder how long it will last?" Ira said. "Dr. Moses is just across the campus in the barracks. I guess he might be able to make it back over here with the right kind of respirator."

"Are you crazy? That kind of fog can burn your skin in a matter of seconds," said the first nurse. She sighed and looked at her colleague. "Looks like we'll be getting some overtime." A monitor a few rooms away began to chime. "It's time to turn the big guy in 205. Can you give me a hand?" The pair walked back up the hall, their fatigue from already working a full shift evident in their stride.

Ira glanced back out the window, his heart rate suddenly increasing to a heavy thump-*thump* against his ribs. He walked quickly back to the artificial interface room and donned the suit. This could be the best possible chance he would ever have to complete the project he had *actually* been working on. He stood at the virtual boundary of Piper's neural network and knocked on the small, recessed door in the stone. It swung open immediately, and he was greeted by Piper's sunny smile. "Ira! I was waitin' for ya. Jesus said ya was comin'," she announced, beckoning him inside.

"He did?" Ira asked. Ira shook his head. "Of course, He did." Ira was still getting used to the fact that Jesus was omniscient. "Did He tell you why I was coming?"

"No, He said He would let ya explain that yaself. But He *did* say it was important."

Ira cleared his throat. "Indeed. It's about Welcome 1.0—I mean, the firewall program I installed. I've figured out a way to give it the characteristics of a virus. Not a cold or flu type virus, but the kind that computers get."

"I know about those. I may have growed up in the outer docks, but some folks still have phones, and a few have visors, and they'd get them viruses sometimes. But why wouldja wanna make it into a virus? I thought it was good the way it was."

"It is. But everyone deserves the right to be protected from people they don't want in their mind—to be protected from mind control. And I can't make a version of it that goes on everyone's chip before being implanted because any programmer could look at the coding and see what I'm really doing. I had to keep it organic to make my intentions undiscoverable. That's what gave me the idea to arm it like a virus. The funny thing is, Dr. Moses has been asking me to make it universal. He thinks it's a key component for his goal of global consciousness."

Piper laughed. "So yer doin' what Dr. Joe asked ya ta do, but it's doin' the opposite o' what 'e thinks?"

"Something like that," Ira smiled, and then his expression sobered. "Unfortunately, I can't allow the virus to infect anyone who has a programmer's chip. If they had the virus themselves, they would see what was really going on. So I engineered it to reject any host with that type of I.P. address."

"Programmers get differ'nt chips than ever'one else?"

"Yes. Their chips have added protections since it was thought they might be targets of cyber-attacks. Of course, I guess Welcome 1.0 really *is* a type of cyber-attack, but it's a benevolent one. Anyway, the built-in protections aren't anything that could keep my virus out. I just programmed the virus to recognize those chips. Programmers can carry the virus, but they can't get it."

"Oh, Ira! That's brilliant!" Piper exclaimed.

Ira blushed. "So now that I've explained what it does, would you mind allowing me to tweak the version I installed on you? You'll be the first person to have it."

Piper beamed. "I'd be honored! An' when ya done, can I give it to Janice?"

"I was hoping you would!" Ira said. "And after that, if you and Janice could visit some of the other patients here, it would help me out. I'm not certain how much time I have, and I want to infect—er—install the virus on as many people as possible before Moses and Ainsley get back. Any help would be appreciated."

"You got it!" Piper affirmed.

"And then I'd like you to go visit Craig. He already has the firewall program, but you'll have the virus version and something else he needs."

"Is he ready for the Bible download?" Piper asked excitedly.

"Yes. And once he has it and gives out the invitation to listen to his message, it'll be available to everyone. Plus, anyone who visits his I.P. address will automatically receive Welcome 1.0, since he has it."

The two began hiking through the green meadow to the large, white-barked sycamore tree at Piper's neural core. "Do ya think Ainsley an' Dr. Joe is gonna be able to figger this thing out before it spreads very far?" Piper asked suddenly.

"All we need is a few programmers to act as carriers. With all the trials they're running on the global consciousness project, it shouldn't be long before it's spread around the globe."

Piper smiled. "You sure are smart. I mean, Dr. Joe is *brain* smart, but you're brain *and* heart smart."

Ira blushed again. "Well, I just think it's important to do the right thing when you have the power to do so. And I believe that even more strongly now that I've met Jesus."

Piper gave him a sidelong glance. "Ya know that what ya doin' ain't safe, don'tcha?"

Ira sighed. "Yes. But I really feel like it's what I was made to do."

"I know how ya feel. Ever since I met Jesus, I know'd I was made ta tell everyone about 'im. So when is Craig gonna give his speech?"

"My guess is, as soon as you get the Bible download to him."

Piper's eyes opened wide with excitement. "Come on, Ira, we gotta git movin'. There's souls ta be saved!" With that, she skipped ahead across the meadow, her long, golden brown hair rippling behind her.

32

Ainsley closed her eyes and let the hot, steaming water of the shower wash away the dirt and filth of the outer docks. It was important to her to have her hand in everything. The illicit relationships she had were just a bonus, and her implants protected her against any diseases or viruses to which she might be exposed. She could understand why the thrill-seekers made their secret treks to the outer docks. There was something about the danger of it all that gave her a rush. Add to that the benefit of the power base she was building, and her motivations for the clandestine visits were obvious. Cosmo had no idea of the dangerous waters he was treading by trusting her.

But Cade did. She buried her face in a plush white towel. She knew he didn't trust her. But she was fairly certain she could control him. And now that she had Ox, Dune, and Tank implanted and ready to divulge information—willingly or unwillingly—she could use it as leverage. Cosmo had ordered their execution to keep his secrets safe, but there was no way he could know she was the very person he should be worried about discovering that information. She had briefly considered that it might be nice to have three personal bodyguards under her complete control, once she had programmed them. But that would blow her cover too early. She would have all the protection she needed once the global consciousness project was initiated and she had muscled her way into command. So once she had stripped the three of all pertinent intel, she would dispose of them, as planned. The deaths would cement her alliance with Cosmo while revealing to him none of the information she had gathered. It would look like an accident to her colleagues, of course. She could say it was a result of them resisting the chip. Or she could blame it on Ira.

Ainsley scowled and threw down her towel. How she hated that man! If he wasn't such an invaluable programmer, she would have used her influence and her skills of manipulation and deception to get him back on track for incarceration or sentencing to a river clean-up crew. His morality was infuriating. And she had nearly run out of patience with his incompetence at finding a way to install Welcome 1.0 onto the chip in a way that would align with his moral scruples. Moses insisted it was important the program be done correctly the first time, with no risk of compromising the host's safety so they could continue to present the appearance of trust—especially since the program was an antidote to the virus discovered in Piper and Citizen Druthers. Ainsley angrily ripped through her hair with a brush. She supposed he was right. They had to at least give the appearance of being trustworthy. Her eyes narrowed as she sighed. Appearing trustworthy had never been her forte. Manipulating people whose minds were bent on advancing themselves, *that* was easy. But those like Ira— and even, to a lesser extent, Joseph Moses—those were hard nuts to crack.

Ainsley stopped yanking at her hair and cradled the brush in her hands as she was hit with a sudden realization. Ira was the most talented programmer she had ever met. It wasn't that he was unable to figure out a way. He *had* to know a way. He was stalling. She dressed quickly and was getting ready to head out the door when she received a weather alert via chip. "Geeves, undim the windows," she said, walking into the area of her apartment that had a view of the street below. "I *said*, Geeves, *undim the windows!*" Ainsley barked.

"Windows are not dimmed, Ainsley," Geeves responded pleasantly. "However, there is an extreme weather anomaly interfering with visibility at this time."

Ainsley stepped within inches of the glass and stared into the gray-green billows of toxic fog. "Perfect. I'm already late."

"Leaving the building would be inadvisable at this time," Geeves announced. "Probability of bodily harm from acid fog: 99.8%"

"Thank you, Geeves," Ainsley said sarcastically.

"Happy to help," was Geeves' mild reply.

Ainsley stood there for a few moments, drumming her fingers on the windowpane. Well, there was absolutely nothing to keep her from carrying out her plan, since the three men had been chipped. Linking with them at this early stage wasn't necessarily advisable, but it wasn't as if she was planning on letting them live, anyway. A sly smile curled the corners of her lips, and she returned to the mirror. It looked like there would be time to dry and style her hair, after all. She turned on the hairdryer and began leisurely pulling the brush through her hair, which had been permanently straightened using gene therapy. There was no need to hurry. She could do the job in a matter of minutes without ever leaving her apartment. In fact, waiting a while could be advantageous, since Ira was set to install Welcome 1.0 on the three patients this morning. It would ensure her access and her success. She nearly giggled. If Ira only knew what he was helping her accomplish!

Across town in the Pod-Op barracks, Dr. Moses continued his surprise inspection. He had hoped to detect any noticeable deviations from normal behavior in Jayka's Pod by showing up unannounced. However, everything appeared normal in all the Pods except for the inclusion of the dog in daily life. If anything, blood pressure was the lowest it had ever been, being normally high in Pod-Ops due to the neural stress of being linked and the physical and emotional stress of their duties. Nearly every Pod had been introduced to Macy, and she was enjoying more attention and pampering than she had ever before experienced. The Pods were lining up in the hall for the short walk to Liberation Station for full diagnostics when the fog began to roll in. "It appears as though our diagnostics will have to wait," Dr. Moses said. "You may all return to your quarters, except Jayka."

Jayka, who had just turned to go, turned back around, holding tightly to Macy's leash. Dr. Moses stood looking at her with an almost sheepish expression. "It appears I may have been wrong."

"About what, Sir? About the dog being a distraction?" Jayka asked, keeping an even tone to her voice.

"No. I was right about that. The dog *is* a distraction, but in the best possible way." He knelt down in front of Macy, who cautiously inched her way forward. "I'm still not certain about the wisdom of taking this animal on missions with you. She could prove more of a hinderance than a help in that capacity. But after seeing the way each unit interacts with her and after taking your vitals— well, of course there are many variables involved. But this is the first time the collective blood pressure of the Pods has approached anywhere close to normal. The only notable difference is the animal's presence."

Jayka attempted to hide a smile as Macy suddenly scooched closer to Dr. Moses and licked him on the nose. "Umph," Moses said, wiping the slobber off his face as he rose to his feet. "Well, I've never been comfortable around animals, but I've read of the use of service animals during the earlier part of this century to help lower anxiety in their owners. Of course, that practice fell into ill favor since the idea of exploiting animals became so offensive. However, I believe the spirit of the law may have been misinterpreted in this aspect. And since you have gone through the proper legal channels for adoption, as long as she remains at the barracks during missions, I think her presence could be an asset not only to you, but to the mental health of the entire program."

"Yes, Sir!" Jayka replied, doing her utmost to remain expressionless.

"Oh, for goodness' sake, Jayka. Go ahead and smile. I can tell you can barely keep from it," Moses said with a sparkle in his eyes.

Jayka met his gaze and grinned broadly. "Yes, Sir! Thank you, Sir."

Moses looked down at Macy, who wagged her tail and pricked her ears forward. "So, does she know any tricks?" he asked. "I suppose that might be viewed as offensive, in some circles."

"I taught her to bark on command," Sloane said, peeking around the corner.

"She knows how to shake hands," Conall offered as he stepped into view.

Moses' eyebrows knitted together. "How many of you stuck around and listened to our conversation?"

A few more Pod-Ops came from around the corner. "You didn't say we had to leave. You just implied we could return to our quarters, if we wanted to," stated Conall.

"So, I did. Ok. Let's see what she can do," Dr. Moses said with a bemused expression, and Macy began an impromptu performance, coached by a hallway full of soldiers who patted and praised her with each accomplishment.

As Jayka stood back and watched, she suddenly felt an unexpected knock at her neural wall. She glanced around the room. Her group hadn't been able to datashare since Tyrell hadn't returned from his assignment, so their thoughts were undisclosed to each other. It could have been any one of them trying to get her attention, but their body language suggested otherwise. They were all very much engaged with the dog. It must be Tyrell, she thought, and ducked into her quarters so she could give the link her full attention. Just inside the door, she closed her eyes and concentrated. She hadn't given much thought to the construction of her inner world, as the State occupied most of her waking and sleeping moments. The mindscape resembled her old neighborhood in the outer docks, with crumbling streets and dingy gray buildings. But at the edge of her neural boundary, a bright, golden spot glowed in the darkness. Jayka jogged to her wall and stood, transfixed, at what she saw. Standing on the other side of the door to her neural boundary, and knocking very politely, was a young girl holding a bouquet of flowers. Jayka stood utterly still. She had never seen this girl before. Although she had sent countless messages with her chip, she had never formed a link with anyone outside her Pod except for Dr. Moses and one of the medical doctors at Liberation Station. "Hello. Who are you?" Jayka asked cautiously.

The little girl's smile lit up the dark world outside the neural network like a miniature sun. "Hi! My name's Piper. An' I was just wonderin'—have ya ever wondered if the people who are s'posed ta be lookin' after ya are really doin' things for the right reasons?" the girl said.

"You're from the outer docks," Jayka said, recognizing her own accent in the girl.

"Yup."

"Are you an Unspoken? A recruit for the Pod-Op program?" Jayka asked.

"Nope. I got a D.I.N. But they chipped me anyway."

Jayka bristled. The girl didn't look more than twelve. "How is that possible? It's against State law."

"They said I offended people by what I said and that I had ta take it back. But I didn't, cuz it was so important. So they chipped me."

Jayka seethed. She could see herself mirrored in the girl at that age, although she never remembered being so happy. How could the State have treated her as an Unspoken when she had a D.I.N.? Unless it had something to do with the possible new rulings about Discards who wouldn't agree to become citizens. "This is outrageous! I'll do all I can to see this injustice is rectified. But I still don't understand how you found me. How did you know to come to me for help?"

The girl laughed, and the sound was like music in the darkness. "I'm not askin' fa help. I come ta *bring* ya some. On account of what I said earlier. Ya know, how sometimes people say they wanna help ya, but really they's really jus' usin' ya?"

Jayka suddenly remembered all the doubts she had been having about the State.

"It's hard ta find people what's trustworthy, but I know Someone ya can trust. An' He tol' me ta come visit ya. He said ta tell ya that if ya ever decided ta trust 'im, He'll give ya His peace. An' then yer heart won't be troubled no more, an' ya won't hafta be afraid."

"The quote on the table!" Jayka exclaimed, her heart pounding. "Does this have something to do with that shirt? Are you running a sting operation for the State? I was doing my own investigation. I think they're selling a designer drug called Peace. I wasn't *actually* buying. I was trying to get to the bottom of things."

Piper shook her head. "Nahhh. Ya got it all wrong. Peace ain't a drug. It's a gift. It's somethin' that happens to ya when ya meet Jesus."

"Jesus?"

"Yeah. He's the best. You can trust Him with ya life. An' also, there's someone else you can trust. Y'already know 'im. His name's Ira."

"Ira Owens? You know Ira?"

"Yup. He looks at things different than most people these days."

"Yes, I remember that about him," Jayka admitted.

"Anyway, Dr. Joe has been tryin' ta break into ma head without askin'. That's when Jesus helped me build a wall ta keep 'im out. Only they was gonna kill me if they couldn't get in. So Ira made this program ta keep me safe, an' let 'em think they're in; but they're not, an' they're none the wiser. An' what's more, they want Ira ta spread the program aroun' ta everyone. That's one o' the reasons I'm here."

"So you're saying that the program Ira designed isn't actually doing what Dr. Moses thinks it's doing? But why are you telling me all this? Don't you know I work for the State? Don't you know they can find all the information they need —including this conversation—by accessing my chip?"

"Not if you accept this gift from Ira," Piper said, holding out the bouquet.

"I am not authorized to link with anyone except my Podmates and Dr. Moses and my doctor," Jayka said, standing her ground.

"I'm not askin' ya ta link with me. I'm just askin' that ya take this gift an' think about what I said. If ya still wanna spill the beans about everything, it won't stop ya. It just gives ya the choice. The choice ta think fa yaself."

Jayka thought for a moment. She trusted Ira. His comments he made while in the Preserve testified to his respect for human life. And ever since her last mission, the motives of the State had been called into question in her own mind. Just opening the door to receive Ira's gift wasn't an actual link. Besides, Dr. Moses had *ordered* Ira to spread it around—if, indeed, the girl was telling the truth. She scanned the bouquet. It was a program, just as the girl had said. "Very well. I will take a closer look at this program." Jayka opened the door and reached for the flowers. As she did, their fragrance wafted through the doorway. "That's strange. I never noticed the sensation of smell so strongly before in my neural net," she said, burying her nose in the flowers and inhaling deeply. A few butterflies fluttered out of the blossoms and drifted on a gentle breeze toward her neural core.

"I sure hope ya give Jesus a chance," Piper said, as she stepped away from the door and blinked out of sight.

Jayka closed the door and turned back to her neural network. It was then that she realized the program had somehow been installed. She recognized it as a firewall, but she could also tell it was undetectable to anyone but her. It was just as the girl had said, only better. For the first time since she had been implanted, she felt as if she was in control of her own mind—as if she had free will. Suddenly, she heard a knock at her door. She looked up, but no one was there. The knocking continued, and it was then that she realized it was the door to her quarters. She exited her inner world and opened the door to the hallway.

It was Sloane, laughing so much she was almost crying. "You just missed it! Scrapdog hacked up part of her breakfast on Dr. Moses' shoe!"

"Lovely," retorted Jayka, but she couldn't keep from smiling.

33

Trajan sprinted down the street. The sound of the food truck rattling up to the intersection behind him gave him an extra burst of speed. There was only one dumpster in this area, but he had to beat the truck there and get in place before it dumped its contents. The alley was just ahead to his left. With any luck, no one would be there to get in his way. He rounded the corner, feet pounding the pavement, and swore under his breath. A small crowd ringed the dumpster in hopes of a delivery. He ran full speed toward them. A few of the taller men stood their ground, their arms folded over their chests. "Ya'll can keep the food," Trajan panted. "Keep it all. I's hitchin'." One of the men eyed Trajan's wiry frame, which lacked bulk and was built for speed. "Or go ahead an' block ma way, an' we'll see how that ends up for ya," Trajan suggested. The man moved out of the way, his eyes on the Arch tattoo. Another man gave him a leg up. "Thanks, bruh," Trajan said, and slipped out of sight just as the truck began backing down the alley. The crowd parted as it drew near, and Trajan readied himself. The whine of the hydraulics on the lift bed announced an on-slaught of garbage that cascaded down over the courier. He squinted, dodging a broken coffee table, but he was unable to avoid several black, leaky plastic bags, smelling profusely of spoiled milk. As the bed began to lower again, Trajan launched himself from the lip of the dumpster into the back of the truck. It rumbled out of the alley again, and Trajan surveyed the situation. The back was almost empty, so that, at least, was in his favor. As the truck bounced over the rough roads, Trajan picked through the trash. He could smell food that was fairly fresh, and located a cardboard box of take-out from a barbecue restaurant. It was Syntha-Ribs, still dripping with a smoky sweet sauce and a side of potato wedges. Trajan wolfed it down, sopping up the last of the sauce with one of the potatoes. Hitching a ride on a food wagon was dangerous, but at least he had the pick of the loot. Suddenly, the truck stopped and began backing up. Trajan clung to a brace beam on the top of the compartment, waiting for the rough ride that was coming. As the truck dumped its contents, the driver turned on a vibrating mechanism that encouraged every last scrap to slide out into the dumpster. Trajan gritted his teeth, working feverishly to maintain his grip on the greasy beam. Finally, it was over. The truck bed lowered again, and the back slammed shut.

This was Trajan's least favorite way of sneaking into the State. He much preferred crossing the Dead Zone at night or early morning when the fog was still thick. Angel had provided them with protective suits and commercial grade respirators and usually sent someone to meet them at the other side. The gang only used the trash trucks anymore as a last resort, when there was no time to plan ahead. He wondered what was so important that it couldn't wait until the scheduled drop.

Once the truck was in the yard with the others, he would push his way through the crack of the dump door and sneak quickly onto the street. After that, there was no need to hide. To the people of the State, he was just another citizen, playing a part in a romantic adventure. *Somewhere out there is some freak whose dream it is to find a poor, lost, dirty Discard who needs a bath and a hot meal and a whole lotta lovin',* he mused. "Lucky fa me," he muttered, smelling the stench on his clothes.

After about a half hour of driving over the smoother streets of the State, the truck finally pulled into the yard and parked. Trajan waited for another ten minutes after the operators left the cab, and then pushed and shimmied his way out the small opening at the back. He darted between the rows of trucks, always keeping one between him and the surveillance cameras on the dispatch building. He was crouching under a truck near the gate, which was opening for the workers leaving in their vehicles, when the sky visibly darkened. It suddenly became much more difficult to breathe. Trajan pulled his shirt up over his nose, but the fumes were making his eyes stream with tears. He was going to have to make a run for it, out the gate and to the nearest subway station over a block away. A few of the workers who were on foot were grappling for their visor masks as they rushed down the sidewalk toward the nearest bus stop just outside the gate. Trajan could see them abandoning the stop and running across the street into a warehouse. In severe fog events, businesses were required to allow fellow citizens to take shelter. The gang had learned that from Angel. That, and to go stand on a subway platform by the security camera and act like you were fishing for romance. Soon, she would send someone to make the exchange. They were always wearing a special pendant fashioned after the Gateway Arch.

But that bit of information wasn't going to help him today if he couldn't make it to the subway. The fog was so thick already that he could barely make out the warehouse across the street. He rushed forward toward the gate and plowed right into a car that wasn't visible until it was a foot away. Suddenly, the car window cracked open and a voice said, "Get in! Hurry!" Trajan didn't argue, but jerked open the back door and jumped inside. Immediately, a specialized filtration system vented the toxic air that had seeped in and pumped in emergency oxygen from a reserve tank that was built into the car.

"Thanks," Trajan said, his eyes and nose running from the acrid fumes.

"Pew*ee!* Caught a spill, did you?" asked the driver, as his nose wrinkled at Trajan's odoriferous clothing.

"Uhh, yeah. Sorry 'bout that." Trajan watched the man warily, trying to decide if he should try to explain himself. Most citizens of the State knew little of the gang tattoos, but a food delivery driver would certainly recognize it. "I'm goin' fishin' for a lady friend now that ma shift's ovah, an' I thought the outfit might be more realistic with a little smell on it."

"Really getting into the part, huh? I think you nailed it. You got the accent down, and you even got a fake tattoo," the driver said. "But you may have gone overboard with the smell."

"Guess I'll find out," Trajan said.

"Where you headed?"

"Just the nearest subway station."

"Once you catch this fish, where are you taking her for dinner?" asked the man conversationally.

"Hadn't thought that far ahead."

"Well, my wife runs a nice little café in Soulard. Here," the man said, handing Trajan a business card over his shoulder.

"Huh. Okay," Trajan said, looking at the card he couldn't read. "Thanks."

"Sure. Well, this is your stop, but if you just want to stay in the car until it clears up, that'd be fine," the man said. "Don't you have a respirator of any kind?"

"Nahh, man, I'm fine," Trajan said, and quickly exited the car to let as little fog inside as possible. He should have brought a respirator, but Cosmo had been in such a hurry that Trajan didn't think there was time. He figured Angel could probably get him another one. He ducked into the subway station, which was crowded with people seeking refuge from the fog, and made his way to the specified area. He often wondered what kind of connections Angel must have, that she knew someone who monitored surveillance footage. He only hoped that whoever it was would notice him amidst the crowd and contact her, because whatever the message was, it must be important.

At home in her apartment, Ainsley was leaning back in her zero-gravity chair with her eyes closed. This was much more relaxing than performing the link in her office, she decided. She was concentrating on Dune when suddenly there was an alert at the control station in her chip. She turned back toward her neural core, wandering barefoot through the white sand she had chosen for her mindscape. It was simple, yet warm and inviting. And the contrast between the sand and the black memory pits made them easy to avoid. She skirted the edges of one of them, a bitter incident from childhood when she had been locked in a closet for a day as punishment for being afraid of the dark. She frowned fiercely, turning away from the scene and concentrating on the sparkling white sand. The control center was just ahead.

She studied the pull-down window for her surveillance cameras. One of her personalized alarms had been activated on a subway cam. She had programmed this particular camera to recognize the Arch tattoo and send an alarm to her exclusively. When she accessed the live feed, she could see one of Cosmo's boys —the fast one called Trajan. "Now, what could be so important that it couldn't wait until tomorrow?" she wondered aloud.

"I'm sorry, Ainsley. I don't understand your request."

"Shut it, Geeves," Ainsley mumbled crossly. "I wasn't talking to you."

If Cosmo thought anyone was going to venture out into the acid bath to take a memo, he was sadly mistaken, Ainsley thought to herself. She couldn't think of anyone to send to retrieve the message, not even the ones over whom she had leverage. She turned back in the direction of her neural boundary and was about to stroll back out into the white sand, but the nagging feeling that something was wrong wouldn't let her alone. She sighed and opened her eyes. Being a government employee, she had commercial grade respirators and protective clothing designed to handle this type of fog. Of course, employees were always advised to stay home in cases such as these unless it was an emergency. "It better be good, Cosmo," she said as she slid out of her chair.

The trains were still running, even though nobody could exit the stations. She left the respirator and suit on during the ride. No one would question her behavior, considering the circumstances. She was dressed in a government issued hazmat suit in the worst fog event the city had ever seen. They would all assume she was dealing with important State business that couldn't be delayed. And the suit would double as a disguise. She didn't want any surveillance cameras identifying her in case the nuances of the exchange were captured on film. When the train pulled up to the stop where Trajan waited, she stepped out onto the platform and casually made her way in his direction, the arch pendant in her hand. Enough attention would be drawn to her by her attire without including the bizarre placement of a bit of decorative jewelry on a hazmat suit. The crowd gave her a wide berth, fully aware that her protective gear might have residual traces of acid fog. When she got to Trajan, she turned around and pretended to be watching the train schedule display, her hands behind her back. She held the pendant in her right hand, rolling it through her gloved fingers like one of the fidget devices commonly used to alleviate tension. After a few moments, she turned to her left and walked down the platform toward the nearest bathroom. A glance behind her told her that he had gotten the message and was following from a distance. Once inside the bathroom, she entered a stall and began unzipping the suit. A few minutes later, Trajan entered the adjacent stall and slipped her the folded piece of paper. "Angel's eyes only," Trajan said.

Ainsley couldn't help but laugh. She didn't know which was funnier, the idea that anyone from the State could decipher the outer docks pictographs Cosmo had taught her to interpret, or the idea that they would trust someone to deliver the message without peeking. She opened the note. To her surprise, there were no symbols, but words that left nothing to the imagination: "Red light on the Twits." Beside the order was both Cosmo's symbol and his written name. So he could read and write. It was a powerful secret, and he had just let her in on it. He either trusted her with it or was that desperate to save his men.

"Should I wait 'til I git an answer?" Trajan whispered. Sometimes it took the better part of a day for Angel to respond.

Ainsley finished removing the suit and shoved it and the respirator under the stall. "That won't be necessary," she said. "You can tell him I'll take care of it."

Trajan's eyes opened wide as he recognized the voice. The accent was gone, but there was no mistaking the underlying tone of superiority that always implied she was one step ahead of everyone. He cracked open the door and watched as Ainsley exited the stall in her bespoke suit and smoothed her hair down at the mirror. "As long as we're sharing secrets," she said flippantly, "You can let Cade know he was right about me. I always knew he thought I was a citizen—not some Discard who flipped to make a profit. But there's no cause for alarm, as long as your people don't cause any trouble. I've enjoyed our little escapades, and our interactions provide useful information. However, I do have one condition. Bring me the one Cosmo calls "the Stewmaker." I'll give you a week's time. If you don't, I can't guarantee that I'll carry out his request, nor can I guarantee your operations will continue to run so smoothly." Ainsley withdrew a tube of lipstick from her pocket and applied it leisurely. When she was done, she made eye contact with Trajan's reflection in the mirror and winked wickedly before leaving the restroom, the picture of poise and power.

34

SELAH scuffed her feet through the weedy vegetation behind Zelda's apartment building. She had made limited treks into the stretch of land between the apartment and the wall to have time to pray, but they usually ended up in her being discovered by someone who needed counseling or prayer or some sort of assistance. While she wanted to help people, she was fully aware that there was a reason that even Jesus spent many hours alone in prayer. But she had never been one who could stay cooped up inside for long. After she and Bally had prayed with Cosmo, the morning seemed much too bright to spend inside. She looked down at the weeds. Dandelions and plantain made up a large portion of the species present, along with cleavers and cockleburs, which she had always hated since their seed pods stuck to her clothes. Often lodged in Maggie's tail, they used to scratch the back of her neck during milking when the Jersey would be swishing at flies. "I wish I could kill every cleaver and every cocklebur on the planet!" Selah used to gripe.

"Now just remember, they both have medicinal uses," Asha had said.

"Well, whatever good they are isn't nearly as big as the *bad* they are," Selah had sputtered. Her mother had always found something positive to say in any situation. Suddenly Selah was overcome by an intense longing to see her parents. She closed her eyes and hugged herself tightly as if she could force her emotions to comply with her wishes, but the tears slipped out between her tightly squeezed eyelids despite her best efforts.

"Will I ever see them again in this life?" she whispered to the only One Who could know.

"Miss Selah? Is y'okay?" said a small voice behind her.

She wiped the tears from her face and turned around to see Hazen watching her worriedly. "I'm fine, Hazen," she said, swallowing the lump in her throat. "How about you?"

Hazen smiled. "I'm fine, but I gotta tell ya sump'n. Cosmo wants ta invite a buncha folks to da meetin's." His face fell and he continued apologetically, "Well, it's really jus' 'bout ten people, but dat's mo' dan dey ever brung at da same time afore. It ain't safe ta sneak mo' dan dat across da Dead Zone at one time."

Selah stared. "Dead Zone? He's going to bring people from the State? How?"

"I don' rightly know how dey do it, but dey do. It's folks what don' got no sense an' cain't seem ta git enough o' danger an' 'citement."

Selah's gaze shifted from Hazen to the tall form that was coming around the side of the building. "Hi, Creep! What's going on?" she asked, trying to sound calm, even though her nerves were as taught as a fiddlestring.

"Oh, you don' hafta worry 'bout him none," Hazen said. "He been followin' me ever since we left Cosmo's. Creep done got saved, din'tcha, Creep?"

Creep smiled, exposing his broken teeth. "I sho 'nuff did," he said. "He's tellin' the truth, Miss Selah. But ain't none o' the rest o' the gang knows nuthin' 'bout it."

"Yay-dat!" Hazen affirmed. "An' dey don' know yet dat dey's totin' folks to da meetin's. Dey tinks dey is gonna deal some new drug or some big adventure dey ain't nevah had afore."

"Well, if you give everything to God, it can be the biggest adventure of your life," Selah laughed. "Isn't Cosmo worried about the government finding out? If he brings all these people from the State—"

"Miss Selah, come *on!*" Hazen said exasperatedly. "Dey ain't gonna tell when dey been breakin' da law all dis time by sneakin' in at night like dey do, an' tradin' stuff like dey shouldn't. Dey'd be cookin' deir own goose."

Selah nodded. "Well, I'm glad he let me know. I'll tell the altar workers. Now we know how to pray." She turned to Creep. "Did he have any idea when they'd be coming?"

Creep shook his head, back to his nonverbal self.

"I'm sure Creep'll let us know, won'tcha?" Hazen asked the giant of a man, who smiled and nodded and turned to go.

"He looks scary, but 'e really ain't," Hazen said sagely.

Selah belly laughed. "Hazen, I used to wonder if you would ever give us a moment's peace, following us around like you do. But I'm glad you stuck around. You're a soul winner! I think you've won more people to the Lord and invited more people to the revival than anyone I know!"

"Mama says I stick like a cocklebur," Hazen said, eyeing the prickly seed pods that were stuck to Selah's bootlaces.

"Well, you know what *my* mama says about cockleburs?"

Hazen shook his head.

"They have good medicine. And so do you, Hazen. You just keep sticking around and spreading the good news."

Hazen grinned shyly and whirled on his heel, running back the way he had come.

Selah wondered how long it would take for Cosmo to arrange things. They needed to start praying for their guests *now*. She wasn't sure how receptive they would be if they realized the only thing they were getting out of their dangerous trip from the State was a revival meeting, and she dreaded Bally's reaction. But when she told her friend, she was in for a surprise.

"But you jus' don' understand, Selah," said Bally when she heard the news. "Dese people get deir thrills outta danger. Dey come ta see how we live out here. Dey come ta be one of us for a night. If'n dey see dat ever'one in dis part o' da docks is goin' ta dese meetin's, dey is gonna be *all in*."

"Yeah, Miss Selah," Drey drawled in her nasally twang. "Dis is gonna be da *ultimate adventure* fa dem type o' folks."

"But we needs ta pray, fa sho," Tunes said. "Dere's a jillion ways dis could go wrong."

"Cuz if'n it's all jus' a game ta dem, dey ain't gonna take it serious-like," Bester added.

"Well, let's pray!" Selah exclaimed. "And if anyone is headed to the neighborhoods where the teams are living, let them know so they can pray, too."

As the teens were praying, Trajan was making his way through the State's transit system, by all appearances, a government worker on business important enough to brave the weather conditions. It wasn't always easy for someone who couldn't read, but he understood the diagrams of the routes and was able to match the letters of the last stop with the letters on the current route readouts. After the farthest subway stop, he began walking. Road traffic had ground to a halt since visibility was zero, and it appeared that all the buses and shuttles had temporarily suspended operations. He had made this trip before, but he usually stayed in a safehouse that Ainsley provided until closer to nightfall, when the fog would rise and give him cover. At that point, one of the gang's contacts usually gave him a ride closer to the Dead Zone, and he would wait for an opportunity to sneak in. This time, although the fog made it easy to leave early, it also meant there was no one available to give him a ride. He walked the three mile stretch to the border, sweating inside of the stuffy suit. Hopefully, the border guards wouldn't be there yet since it was it was only the middle of the day and hours away from the restricted access period. He was just about to waltz through the gate when the barrier arm unexpectedly dropped. His blood froze as he spotted the guard inside the station, barely visible through the fog. "You've gotta be kidding!" The man said through the speaker in the protective glass. "What's so important they made you come in this mess?"

Trajan shook his head and shrugged his shoulders, as if he couldn't believe it, himself. "Didn't they issue you a vehicle? Of course not," the man answered his own question. "They just suspended all vehicular traffic within the city. And yet, here you are, still required to do your job." He shook his head in disgust. "Just hold on a minute." The guard turned around and fumbled at a desk behind him. Trajan kept silent, wondering if the man was just pretending not to be suspicious so he could report him. He fidgeted in the suit, casting a glance to the foggy escape of the Dead Zone. Just as he was about to slip out of sight, the man turned around and passed him a key fob using the isolation drawer built into the side of the station. "Here. You can take the spare they use for the clinic. I know you can't see it from here, but it's just around the side, there," the man explained, gesturing to his right. "I won't have someone's life on my hands because I let them walk into the Dead Zone on a day like this."

Trajan gave the man a thumbs up and nodded enthusiastically, stepping around the corner to retrieve the vehicle. It wasn't much, a boxy affair that had been used to deliver emergency medical supplies to the Euthanasia Clinic, but considering most of the old dilapidated electric cars in the outer docks barely held a charge, it seemed like a luxury sedan. And it was certainly better than walking. The car's navigation system would get him to the gate with no problem, even in the fog. As he approached, the doors opened for him, and he slipped inside. "Destination?" asked a pleasant female voice that was the car's A.I. system.

"Outer docks," said Trajan in his best attempt at a State accent.

"Accessing current road conditions," said the car, and then an alarm chimed. "All road travel within the State has been suspended," the voice notified him. Trajan cursed under his breath and started to get out of the vehicle when he spied the guard waving at him through the window and motioning him to wait.

"Temporary override due to emergency: authorization DZ-143," the car said. Trajan looked back at the guard, who was waving and smiling. He waved back and gave another thumbs up. "Fasten your seat belt," the voice commanded pleasantly. When Trajan did nothing, the car spoke again. "This vehicle will not operate until the seat belt is fastened."

Trajan looked around and located the belt, buckling himself in.

"You may take off your hazmat suit if you like. I have vented the dangerous particles that were present in the atmosphere," the A.I. continued.

"No, thanks," Trajan said simply.

"Very well. Destination arrival time, approximately five minutes."

Trajan sat back in the seat and enjoyed the ride. Ten minutes later, the car was still piloting its way across the short stretch, having underestimated the fog's ability to interfere with the satellite connection. But eventually, they crossed the border to the outer docks and into a bath of sunshine. "What the—?" Trajan sputtered as the car came to a stop in the remarkably clear daylight.

"I don't understand the request. Please repeat the instructions," the A.I. suggested.

Trajan considered his options. He obviously couldn't take the car to the gang headquarters, and it would report him if he got out and took off the suit. He needed to leave it in a place it would normally be left, where it would seem natural for him to end his trip. "Southside Euthanasia Clinic," he said.

"Very good. Estimated arrival time, twenty minutes." The car began the journey, and Trajan leaned back in the seat and felt like he could finally relax. The whole trip had been a rushed job and extremely risky. He still wondered what was so important that it couldn't wait until tomorrow evening. If he had gotten caught, Cosmo probably would've given orders to have *him* killed, just like Dune and his buddies. *"Dune. What a chip-whipe,"* Trajan thought to himself. But then he wondered if he was any better, risking his life to do Cosmo's bidding. Cosmo thought he knew what was best for the gang, but he didn't even know Angel wasn't born in the docks. He had been trusting a natural-born citizen of the State the whole time, counting on her for contacts and inside information. Trajan squirmed in the seat and remembered what she had said about Cade— *"You can let Cade know he was right about me. I always knew he thought I was a citizen—not some Discard who flipped to make a profit."* Trajan looked out the window. Cade had always been cautious. He was loyal, but he wasn't stupid. He usually tried to steer their leader away from doing things that jeopardized gang operations, but sometimes Cosmo wouldn't listen to reason. If Cade had known without a doubt that Angel was a citizen, maybe he would've stood up to Cosmo and they wouldn't be in this situation. Trajan shifted in his seat again, fiddling with the seat belt buckle. "Please do not unbuckle the seat belt. This vehicle will cease operation if the seatbelt is undone," the car warned him. Trajan swore again. He was trapped. The whole gang was trapped, and it was Cosmo's fault.

The car pulled into the parking lot at the Southside Euthanasia Clinic and parked on the side of the building. "You have arrived at your destination. You may unbuckle your seatbelt," the car said amiably. Trajan's lip curled back in a snarl as he unbuckled and exited the vehicle. Freedom was why his great, great grandmother had decided to move her family to the outer docks, wanting nothing to do with the State and its rules. Even their cars told you what to do. And now they were all under Angel's thumb. What was the point of barely surviving in the outer docks so you could be free if you weren't really free, after all? He strode out of the parking lot, careful to keep up the appearance of a State worker on official business. Shucking off the suit in the nearest alley, he wadded it up with the respirator into a tight bundle he could carry under his jacket. He pocketed the key fob, figuring it might come in handy if they needed a way to transport the girl. He was a street away from headquarters when he caught sight of Cade walking ahead of him. "Cade! Wait up, bruh!" he called.

Cade turned around. "Trajan! Hey, man. You's back sooner than I thought. Reggie said the State havin' some fog bog an' no one kin drive."

"You been to the clinic? I jus' came from there."

"Yeah, man. Cosmo got somethin' big cookin' an' Reggie hadda get the word out. Gotta getta ride fo' da circus."

"Reggie ain't wrong. Ever' since 'e got the orderly job, we got good intel outta there." Trajan patted the hazmat suit. "The gatekeeper thought I was a State worker in ma garb, an' 'e lemme borry a spare set a wheels they had sittin' there, stateside! Used some sorta override thing ta fix it so it took me, even with the lockdown!" He laughed and flashed the key fob to Cade. "I kep' it, cuz we may end up needin' it."

Cade's eyes widened. "Dude! That's *king*. But don' ya think the guard'll report it afta ya don' go back ovah?"

"Nahh, man. That's the thing. We got somethin' we gotta do fa Angel real zippy, an' we may need this for a delivery."

"Since when do we make that big of a drop, that we need a sled? Watchu got goin', man?"

Trajan slowed their pace and dropped his voice as they neared Cosmo's apartment. "Angel has a message fo' ya. She said you were right about 'er not bein' a flip. Man, she's a *State* baby. She been playin' us like a fiddle. But she say ever'thing cool an' she'll do what Cosmo ast an have bih'ness as usual, so long as we tote 'er the Stewmakah. We gotta week ta do the job."

Cade came to a halt and his face darkened, but he said nothing.

"Hey, I's jus' the bird. Ya gimme a message, an' I sing it. They gimme a message, I fly it back. What could I do? She got us between a rock an' a hard place," Trajan said apologetically. "I risked ma hide fa Cosmo, an' 'e don' even know 'e been had. How we gonna git outta this, bruh?"

"We cain't. We gonna hafta work with what we got. An' what we got is the devil an' a doofus." Cade glanced up and down the street to make certain they weren't being overheard. "We keep this between us. We gonna see what Cosmo got up 'is sleeve that 'e think is so big. Reggie says 'e can make it happen in a day, if'n this fog clear up. Reggie gonna round up the circus. We kin fetch 'em with the sled, an' tote 'em back out with the Stewmakah, all in the same drop."

"Stewmakah's good fa bih'ness. Bring in a lotta loot from the hood folk. Cosmo ain't gonna stand fo' it," Trajan said worriedly.

"What choice do we have?" Cade whispered.

"What about the circus? What they gonna think when we up an' snatch da Stewmakah an' drag 'er back with 'em across the Dead Zone?"

Cade smiled. "Ahh, man. Them freaks is gonna love that. That is right up they alley."

"But what about the crew?"

Cade placed a hand on Trajan's shoulder. "You let me worry about that. For now, you don' tell no one. You tellin' *me*, that was *king*. I won't forget that, bruh."

Trajan felt a rush of power as he nodded. Things were going to be different now.

35

"I can't believe what you're telling us!" Celidor exclaimed. "The revival in the outer docks was started by some people who sneaked in from the *Preserve?*"

Viv looked at her friends from the underground church. They still called it The Closet, although they had stopped meeting in its namesake in Luciana's café since the Holy Spirit had been leading them to meet in different locations. Currently they were at Stasi's house, since her Geeves unit was still offline. "Remember when ya asked me where I got my Bible? Well, that's where. But I couldn't tell ya, 'cause if any of ya got caught, it'd put 'em in danger."

"You've been in the Preserve? Off of a causeway, I mean?" Contessa asked, her eyes round in disbelief.

Viv nodded.

"How did you manage that? How did you do it without getting caught?" Melford asked incredulously.

"When ya first get the Audio-boost implant, it messes with ya sense of balance. Makes it darn near impossible to use the causeway or take a plane. So they give ya a medical permit ta use a few other roads in case ya still need ta get to another city. It's only s'posed ta be for a year, but fa whatever reason, mine still works. I know, 'cause I never got flagged, even after six years."

"You've been sneaking into the Preserve for six years?" Rhys asked, dumbfounded.

"Nahh. Only about two. I started sneakin' out when I was thinkin' about endin' it all. I didn't wanna just go to a clinic, ya know. I thought if I was gonna take the final exit, I might as well be havin' a big adventure at the time. And what could be more excitin' than being attacked by a mountain lion or gunned down by a Pod-Op?"

Celidor stared at her, nonplussed. "I really don't understand you sometimes," he admitted.

"Well, I ain't like that no more!" Viv exclaimed. "But at the time, I was miserable. So I would sneak out—"

"But what about the GPS on your bike?" Chess wondered aloud.

"It stopped workin'. But I think they got a tracker on me now," Viv said. "That's why I ain't been there in several months, ya savvy?"

"We savvy," Luciana chuckled. "But now that your friends are here, you felt you could tell us because they've already put their community in danger?"

"And because one of them is in custody. Craig Goforth. He was the youth pastor back in Adullam."

"Oh, dear God!" Rhys said suddenly. "I met him. He's at Liberation Station. He said he was from somewhere out in the Preserve. I tried to convince Dr. Moses to leave him unchipped so I could interview him further. I was just trying to buy him some time. But they never got back to me." He looked at Viv apologetically. "I'm afraid he may have already been chipped."

Viv swallowed. "It ain't ya fault, Rhys. You know how they are. If anything, I shoulda probably have done somethin'. I work outta that very buildin'. I even see Dr. Moses walkin' the hall sometimes."

Rhys's eyes opened wide and he grabbed Viv's arm. "I signed a nondisclosure form, so telling you anything about the interview could be very bad for me if they found out. But you need to know. Your friend said he knew Dr. Moses from before. He said he was from his community. He called him Yosi. He said his dad would be so happy to know he's alive!"

Viv's mouth dropped open. "Jovies! Jo-Mo is Yosi? Dr. Moses is Dawson's son!"

"Who's Dawson?" Chess asked.

"He's the pastor of Adullam. He had a son named Joseph, but his nickname was Yosi. He was *nasty* smart—like *genius*. He liked gamin' and programmin' and all that. He even built a miniature internet for the place. But when 'e was eighteen, he just up and walked away. Dawson spent months tryin' to find 'im, but 'e never could get very far. He said no matter what direction 'e took or how far 'e walked, 'e always ended back up at Adullam, an' 'e never saw any sign of Yosi in his travels."

Luciana looked thoughtfully at Viv. "I can't help but love the name of the community," she said.

"Yeah. The cave where David hid. An' I thought that was why they called it that, 'cause it was such a good hidin' place. But that ain't the only reason. Ya know how David hadda lotta people show up at his doorstep that weren't the best kinda people? From what I understand, they were broke, in debt, and depressed. But David didn't send 'em away. He became a captain to 'em. He led 'em until they became his army of mighty men.[96] That's what Dawson was like to me. He led me to Jesus. The folks there just treated me like family an' taught me how to follow Christ. Ya see, Dawson had a vision 'bout people showin' up at Adullam and gettin' taught the Word o' God. He wants their community to be a safe place fa new Christians. I wanted to stay there forever, but 'e said I might be the only chance people would have to hear about Jesus. David and his men didn't stay in the cave. They went out and fought for David's kingdom. Dawson told me I was meant to go out an' fight for the Kingdom of God."

"And it sounds like others are now venturing out of the cave," Luciana mused. She looked at Chess. "You still haven't heard anything about this? Seen anything out of the ordinary on your routes?"

"I haven't heard anything about any meetings. Of course, the only reason someone would tell me is if they could get credits for reporting it. It must be something everyone wants, because no one's talking." He shifted his weight and scratched his head. "Actually, there *is* something really unusual happening. The last time I was at the farthest end of my route, no one was waiting at the dumpster. That *never* happens. There's almost always a crowd of people waiting. So there must be a lot of people attending the revival and getting the free food."

"The Gateway Gang is capitalizin' on it," Viv said in disgust. "They worked my dad over fa talkin' to me. Thought 'e was runnin' his mouth too much about it and the State would find out. I guess they think I'm a spy. Anyway, they're chargin' entry into the outskirts now for anyone comin' to the meetin's an' makin' 'em pay whatever way they can. It's good business—fa *them.*"

---

[96] See 1 Samuel 22:1-2

"Strange. The Gateway Gang never gives us any trouble," Chess said.

Viv scowled. "Well, they wouldn't, would they? It keeps things runnin' smooth for them if there ain't any red flags. But they're takin' some serious chances these days. When I was goin' through the Dead Zone, I ran into a Discard—literally. He was wearin' one o' them hard-core respirators like they give State workers that hafta go out when the fog is bad. I tried to help 'im, but 'e ran off. I just bet 'e was a Gateway."

Chess ran his fingers through his hair and paced the floor. "I think I saw one the other day—in the State."

"What? You didn't say anything about that," Luciana said.

"Well, at first, I thought he was just a new guy. His clothes were a little better than the average Discard, but he stank like rotten milk. Of course, that's nothing unusual in my line of work, and sometimes it's worse than that," he laughed. "But this guy was trying to get from the truck yard to the subway right when that fog hit yesterday. He had a Gateway tattoo, but I thought it was a fake because he said he was going fishing in the subway before he went home from his shift." Chess rolled his eyes. "I even complimented him on his accent. Now everything makes sense, because he really looked the part. I bet he sneaked in on one of the trucks. Except for the clothes being better than normal, he looked just like a member of the Gateways."

"It's the perfect cover," Ranger agreed.

"What about the clothes?" Stasi asked. "How are they getting good clothes?"

"Sometimes some really good clothes get thrown in the trash," Chess offered.

"And maybe people are collectin' them to be able to pay the toll to the outskirts. Or maybe someone is tradin' with 'em from inside the State," Viv added.

"What could a Discard have that anyone in the State could possibly want?" Contessa asked skeptically.

"Drugs, for one thing," Viv explained. "I knew lotsa cooks back in the docks, and I always knew they had to have contacts in the State. The State folks get 'em the stuff they need ta make it, an they get a portion of the batch back. Maybe the supplier throws in a little extra somethin' sometimes, since the only thing credits is good for in the outer docks is payin' fa surgery or serious medical treatments o' some sort. So they trade other stuff."

"Well, if an odd-looking customer shows up at the café with a Gateway tattoo, you can assume I sent him, because I gave that guy one of your cards," Chess laughed.

"You *what?*" spouted Luciana.

"Well, I thought anyone who is lonely enough to douse himself in garbage and paint on a fake tattoo to get a date might need a recommendation for a nice place to eat."

"Wow, thanks," Luciana joked.

"And I thought maybe it might be a chance for him to see people who have joy and peace in their lives. It might get him curious enough to ask how they acquired that peace and joy," Chess explained.

Luciana suddenly looked thoughtful. "You know, there was an odd customer in the café the other day. A striking looking woman. Strong. I think she must work out or be a body builder. You remember her, Stasi? The blond with the mottled dog?"

Stasi smiled as she thought a moment. "I remember. You gave her a shirt."

"Yes, and I almost didn't, even though she asked for it," Luciana said. "She thought we were using a mood enhancer in the air conditioning. When I told her we weren't, I don't think she believed me. I actually think she was trying to figure out if she could get some of what she thought we were using. I just had a funny feeling about her."

"Well, since we started meeting here, the shirts aren't going to give anything away," Stasi reassured her. "They might have the right time, depending on the week, but they don't say where to meet."

"True. And that's one reason I just decided to give her a random shirt and told her to think about the quote on the table and come back to talk about it later if she felt like it." She turned to Ranger. "I really wish we could still have a practical application for the shirts, but since it isn't safe to meet at the café, I don't see how we can utilize them as a way to advertise the meetings."

"Well, at least you get some free advertising," answered Ranger, who had created the shirts in his design studio in Denver. "Even if they only brought in four souls, that's more than worth it. How can you put a price on that?"

"You can't. I guess I'm just sad that an era is over," Luciana admitted.

"Not necessarily. We may be able to meet back there someday," Chess suggested.

Luciana shook her head. "I don't know. I saw someone working on a light pole across the street. It was the same day the woman with the dog came in. When I asked Bev at the costume shop about it, she said she hadn't put in an order for it—that it had been working just fine."

"I can tell ya right now it wasn't a burned-out light," Viv said angrily. "I betcha anything they were puttin' up a camera."

"That's what I thought," Luciana agreed.

"I had a feelin' the last few times we met there that someone was watchin' me," Viv said. "I guess it's a good thing we all felt funny about it, since there's probably a camera now."

"Well, as long as my Geeves unit doesn't work, everyone is welcome here," Stasi said. "For all the neighbors know, we're just having a game night."

"Yeah, it's kind of nice to be able to have a set time," Celidor said.

Rhys cleared his throat. "Here we are, all safe and happy to be meeting in secret, when someone right now is trapped at Liberation Station, possibly paying the ultimate price for attempting to spread the gospel."

"There hasta be a reason God would allow this," Viv said bitterly. "There must be a plan."

"God always has a plan," Contessa insisted.

"I know. Some people got martyred for the gospel, and it spread even more after that," Viv said darkly.

"Horrible things happen because we live in a fallen world. But what the enemy means for evil, God can turn around for good," Luciana said.

"Yeah, I know. But when the person getting' martyred is one o' ya friends, it doesn't seem as great, somehow," Viv said, tears forming in her eyes.

"Come on, everyone. Let's pray for Craig right now," Luciana said, gesturing for the group to gather in a huddle. They prayed fervently for a time, and when they ran out of words to pray in English, those who were baptized in the Holy Spirit began interceding in other languages as the Spirit led them.

"I think I'm gonna ask my boss if I can visit with the patients," Viv said when they were finished. "I'll tell 'er I might be able to get through to 'em. Maybe then I can at least see how Craig is doin'."

"I thought your boss was scary," Stasi said worriedly.

"She is. She's like a brown recluse in a bathrobe. But sometimes she listens to my suggestions."

The group said their goodbyes and Stasi straightened the pillows on her couch in the small apartment. It wasn't a large meeting space, but it seemed expansive after meeting in a broom closet for several years. She smiled, happy she could provide a service for her brothers and sisters in Christ. It was then that she noticed her visor blinking on the end table, indicating she had a message. As she read it, her face fell.

"We have detected a short in the panel that houses your Geeves unit. A repairman will arrive tomorrow to correct this issue. We apologize for any inconvenience this may have caused. —Your fellow citizens at Unitech"

36

"*Peace I leave with you, My peace I give unto you: not as the world giveth, give I unto you. Let not your heart be troubled, neither let it be afraid.*" The words circled around and around again, like an eddy in the turbulent stream of her thoughts. Having the ability of total recall for any experience had proven a blessing and a curse for Jayka. Of course, the pesky memories that kept resurfacing could always be deleted. But in this case, the organic part of her brain just didn't seem to want to let the phrases go. It was like a puzzle that needed solving. Ever since her encounter with the quote on the table at the café, it had stuck in her mind—along with the memory of the feeling she had experienced there. When the Discard girl had shown up at her neural wall with the firewall program and had more or less repeated the quote in the jargon of the outer docks, her eagerness to solve the mystery had intensified. She had done a little research and discovered that it was, indeed, an unaltered verse from the fourteenth chapter of the book of John in the King James Bible.

The girl had openly spoken of someone called Jesus who wanted to give her peace. Was it a coincidence that this person had the same name as the Christian deity purported to have spoken the phrases thousands of years ago? Jayka couldn't accept that the girl would be talking about Jesus the Christ. If she was, then she was simply off her chip—completely loony. No sane person believed in that god anymore.

No, it was more likely the Jesus she had referred to was the inventor of this new drug. He had probably adopted the name so as to be associated with the feeling the drug gave its user, since the Messiah of the Christian religion had claimed to have the ability to give his followers peace of mind.

But then why had the girl insisted that peace wasn't a drug, but a gift you received? Perhaps she was working for her next fix, someone this Jesus person used to entice his customers. She was a Discard, after all, and any sense of peace in the world she came from would be rare, if not impossible.

Jayka had the ability to see through the avatars people would sometimes project in the neural world, and the girl was absolutely who she appeared to be, except for her hair. She could tell it was actually just beginning to grow back from having been cut short or shaved, while her virtual projection had long, wavy hair. Jayka's stomach turned. Dr. Moses had probably shaved it, just like her own hair had been shaved when she and her Podmates were being tested for compatibility with each other before implantation. The girl had been so young, perhaps Moses had attempted other methods of reconditioning or information extraction before it was determined the chip was the only option. Knowing what she had been through, it made sense the girl would want to spread the firewall program to everyone she thought might be unjustly imprisoned, reconditioned, or exploited. Looking back on her own situation, Jayka was beginning to see more clearly that even though the State had given her a sense of purpose and fulfillment, they had taken advantage of her youth and her desperation. They had given her a lifeline, but with conditions. She had escaped the horrors of the outer docks, but she wasn't truly free. *"Not as the world giveth, give I unto you."* The phrase rippled on the surface of the eddy, fascinating her with its inference: *"I'm giving you something you can keep. I'm giving you something and asking for nothing in return."* Jayka sighed. That didn't make sense for a drug dealer to give you something free, unless it was your first hit. But the implication in the quote was that this gift could last forever.

She wished she could talk with Tyrell. He still wasn't back from his assignment, and she hadn't confided in the others, but she was beginning to worry. He had been sent to the southern quadrant two weeks ago, and there had been no communication from him since. Tyrell had always been someone she could talk to easily, having come from the same rag-tag group of orphans she had joined as a toddler. He had always protected her when he could and had shown her the best places to hide from the rape gangs. Once they had stumbled upon a cache of food after taking a dare to sneak into an old warehouse rumored to be a gang headquarters. They had stolen the sack of jerky, powdered milk and ramen noodles they had found and shared it with their friends. No one ever found out who stole it, but there was a gang war that broke out soon afterward. At the time, she could only think of her empty belly and her own survival. It was only later, when she came to the State, that she had reflected on the innocent lives that were lost because of their theft. That was just the way things were in the outer docks, where you didn't know where your next meal was coming from. If you starved to death, you would most likely be somebody *else's* next meal. The State had saved her from all of that, but it had never offered her peace.

She glanced down at Macy, who had been napping at her feet and was wheezing out a soft snore. No one would guess she was the star of yesterday's performance to impress Dr. Moses when he was done with their med check. For whatever reason, Moses had postponed the thorough diagnostics until a later date, even though the fog had lifted and made it an easy trip from the barracks to Liberation Station. The fog had lasted until early afternoon, so Jayka reasoned the time frame must have conflicted with his work on the global consciousness project.

She was glad the diagnostic had been postponed. Part of her still wondered if it would be able to detect the firewall. The ability to think, unmonitored, had given her a sense of freedom she had forgotten existed, and she wasn't ready to lose it just yet. "Scrapdog, I feel like a latte," Jayka said, and immediately laughed, for she had never allowed herself to feel like doing anything so frivolous. But of course, she wasn't just going for the coffee. She changed into the shirt the woman at the coffee shop had given her, grabbed Macy's leash, and headed out the door.

As they were leaving the barracks, a girl on a hoverbike glided into a charging dock space in the parking lot. The bike had seen better days, but Jayka had never seen a hoverbike she didn't think about riding. It was the same standard gray of all privately owned vehicles, and it had a scratch on the front fender and a dent on one of the saddlebags, but it looked like fun. She had seen the cyclist before, walking the halls of Liberation Station with that arrogant new programmer and Employee Interrelations Specialist, Ainsley Abbot.

"Do you like that bike, Scrapdog?" Jayka asked, as the leash suddenly became taut in her hand. The dog's ears were pricked forward, her nose quivering as she stared in the direction of the bike. Suddenly she began barking excitedly. "What is it, girl?" Jayka said as Macy jumped and strained against the leash. She was surprisingly strong, Jayka realized. They had encountered bikes on their walks before. What was so different about this one?

As the rider dismounted and took off her helmet, she looked their direction to see what was causing all the commotion and instantly froze. Macy ripped the leash out of Jayka's hand and bounded toward the cyclist. "Scrapdog! Come back here!" Jayka commanded, but the animal ignored her completely. Jayka rushed after her, terrified that she would attack the girl, but her fears were unfounded. Upon reaching her, Macy lowered her ears and ducked her head, her whole body wagging back and forth. In an instant, she had flopped over on her side, her tail beating the ground like a drum. The cyclist dropped to her knees and began petting her enthusiastically.

"Wow, this is a really friendly dog ya have here," the girl said when Jayka reached them.

Jayka instantly accessed the girl's identity. "You're the liaison for the Outer Docks Transition Program," Jayka stated.

"Yeah. Name's Viv."

"Jayka," Jayka said simply, watching the two interact with growing concern. "Scrapdog is never this enthusiastic when she meets someone for the first time."

"Scrapdog, huh?" Viv said, scratching Macy behind the ears.

"Yes. I recently adopted her. She lives with us at the Pod-Op barracks," Jayka said, watching the girl for any reaction.

Viv stiffened slightly at the mention of the word Pod-Op. "Well, she sure is friendly," she said, standing up. Macy jumped up and put her paws on Viv's leg.

"Scrapdog, get down!" Jayka said, giving a short, instructive yank on the leash. "I apologize for her behavior. I haven't had her long enough to explore obedience training." She watched as the girl continued to scratch Macy behind the ears. "You're from the outer docks," she said matter-of-factly.

"Yeah. It's kinda hard ta hide the accent," Viv replied.

"It ain't easy, butcha kin do it if'n ya practice," Jayka said, watching Viv intently.

"Oh, I—I didn't know that Discards could become Pod-Ops. I mean—" the girl faltered.

Jayka came to her rescue. "Actually, the program is made up entirely of Unspokens. I was never elevated to the status of Discard. My parents saw to that," she said coldly. She noticed the girl kept glancing at her shirt. Jayka could tell she was trying not to stare, but her eyes seemed to be pulled toward it.

"That's a nice place," The girl said, giving up and finally gesturing to the shirt. "They make a *catapultin'* mocha."

"Yes, and I love the atmosphere," Jayka said, continuing her study of the girl. "The fact that they don't allow visors—it creates a very peaceful feeling."

"Yeah," Viv agreed, but offered nothing else.

Jayka decided to be direct. "This isn't the first time you've seen this dog. She recognized you."

"Well, she looks a lot like a dog I once knew," the girl said carefully. Jayka noticed her pulse rate had increased.

"When I found her, she was in the Preserve. But I suspect she came from the outer docks," Jayka said.

"Oh, really?"

"Yes. Her owner had escaped and had an accident. I decided to bring the dog back with me, but I have been trying to find out more information about the owner. I assume you must have known her quite well, considering the way her dog reacted to you."

"Well, I guess I probably knew her dog better than I knew *her*," Viv said slowly. "Are you talkin' 'bout that ol' pigeon trapper? Didja say she had an accident?"

"Yes. She didn't survive."

The girl was quiet for a moment, briefly glancing at Jayka out of the corner of her eye.

"I had nothing to do with her death," Jayka found herself volunteering. She knelt down and petted the dog so she could be on the same level as the girl. "I am trying to find out more about her for purely personal reasons, as my formal investigation of the incident is completed. I am amazed that as old as she was, she was she able to escape and had acquired an impressive amount of survival gear that is unavailable in the outer docks."

"Ya know how some stuff from the State works its way out there, whether or not it's legal. That ol' gal was known as a shrewd trader. Maybe she had gathered the gear all her life and was just waitin' for the right opportunity," Viv suggested.

"But how did she keep the dog safe?" Jayka asked. "When I was growing up in the outer docks, if anyone saw a raccoon or a possum or squirrel or any kind of animal, they wouldn't stop until they had trapped or cornered it somewhere and killed it for food. How is it possible this dog survived? How did she keep it hidden?"

Viv shook her head and shrugged. "I have no idea how she woulda done that."

"You knew about it, and yet you didn't try to catch it yourself?" Jayka asked suspiciously.

"Zelda was a pretty scary lady. Most people didn't cross 'er" Viv said, deciding that divulging the woman's name wouldn't matter, since she was dead.

"Zelda…" Jayka said slowly, a faraway look in her eyes. To Viv's surprise, the woman seemed to be trying to keep her emotions in check. It was very uncharacteristic for a Pod-Op. "Before I was recruited to the Pod-Op program, at a very low point in my life, the woman tried to show me some kindness," she said, making eye contact with the girl. "She offered me a piece of bread."

Jayka and Viv stared at each other silently for a while, realizing they shared a bond few people in the State would be able to understand. Viv looked back at the dog and scratched her around the ruff of her neck. "Well, I'm sure glad ya were able ta save this crazy mongrel. She was a bright spot in my past, no joke." Viv stood up and stowed her helmet in one of the saddlebags.

"It was…nice talking to you," Jayka said awkwardly. She meant it. She had been trained in many levels of social interactions, but all of them were for the purpose of undercover investigations or Pod-Op publicity events. Interacting sincerely with someone other than a Podmate was something she hadn't done since she had left the outer docks.

"It was nice ta meetcha. If ya'd like ta go to Talk-o-Lot Chocolate sometime, I'd be game," Viv said hopefully.

Jayka smiled, her severe face softening. "I'd like that," she replied. "That's where I'm headed right now, actually."

"Well, drink a latte for me," Viv said. "I hafta go ta work. And take care of Macy."

"Macy?" Jayka said, and Macy began jumping up and down excitedly.

"That was her name," Viv explained. "I'd better go now, or I'll be late!"

The two parted ways with Jayka physically dragging Macy, who was reluctant to let Viv out of her sight. "Come on, Scrapdog!" Jayka said after a few minutes of dragging the dog behind her and listening to her choke. "Macy!" she finally said. The dog stopped pulling on the leash and looked at her. "Come on, Macy, let's go!" Macy looked back toward the building where Viv had disappeared from sight and turned back to Jayka with a whine, her head lowered dejectedly. "It's okay. We can see her again," Jayka offered. She was jealous of the affection the dog obviously harbored for the girl, but she understood it. There was a bond between those who were considered the underdogs in the outer docks— apparently, even if one of those parties was an *actual* dog.

The two made their way through the subway system to the Soulard neighborhood. Jayka purposefully avoided looking at the security camera on the light pole across from the café. If her superiors knew she was knowingly walking all over someone else's investigation, they would have questions. But she had plenty of questions of her own for the State. Now that she had a firewall to protect her from being reprogrammed, she might actually be able to find a way to ask them.

When she walked into the establishment, Luciana greeted her warmly. "Hello! Welcome back. I see you brought Scrapdog with you."

"Actually, I think the name Macy may suit her better," Jayka said, deciding that perhaps the constant reminder of her past was not only unnecessary, but depressing. As her name was spoken, Macy pricked her ears forward in Jayka's direction and wagged her tail.

"Well, she certainly seems to like it," Luciana commented. "Do you have a preference on where you'd like to sit?"

"I'd like to sit at the same table I was at last time," Jayka said.

"Follow me," Luciana said.

"Interesting," Jayka said pointedly as Luciana led the way with a menu. "That's what the author of the quote on the table used to say to his recruits."

There was a sudden hesitation in Luciana's stride. "Where did you read that?" she asked.

Jayka suddenly realized that she had been caught in her own trap. The State bible had no mention of Jesus' method of recruiting His disciples. All the references to Him asking people to follow Him and His revolutionary teachings had been removed. The State placed very little importance on commitment, unless it was to its own rules and the entity called the Source, which it espoused embodied the energy of all life. The only way Jayka could have read about it was if she had seen the unaltered version of the bible. Now Luciana knew she either possessed a contraband copy or was an agent of the State with access to such files. Perhaps the woman would decide to report *her*, Jayka thought to herself in amusement.

"I didn't read it. Someone told me about it," she lied as she sat down at the table.

"I see," Luciana said.

Jayka could tell she didn't believe her. This whole thing wasn't going as she had planned. She had possibly already jeopardized someone else's investigation. She leaned toward Luciana and spoke in a voice just above a whisper. "Look. The reason I came here was because I can't get the quote on the table out of my mind. You told me to meditate on it, and I thought that was a waste of time. But I found I was unable to *stop* meditating on it. I was told to ask for someone with the same name as the author of this quote. I was told that if I trusted him, he would give me peace. So can you make in introduction for me?"

Luciana's mouth opened slightly in surprise and then spread into an amused smile. "The feeling you get here has nothing to do with the type of ...recreational substance you're thinking of. We don't use any mood enhancers in our café. We just encourage our customers to engage in good, old-fashioned conversation."

"It's more than that," Jayka insisted.

"Listen, the only Jesus I know is the one who said this quote," Luciana said. "We do not sell drugs here, and we do not refer customers to dealers. I'm sorry to disappoint you, but if that's what you came for, you're out of luck."

Jayka stared at her for a moment as she monitored the woman for the telltale physiological signs that she was lying. She was not. "You said you know the Jesus who quipped this saying. I assume you know *of* him, since he has been dead for thousands of years."

"Since you asked me, I would be glad to explain, if you're truly interested," Luciana said carefully.

Suddenly everything came together in Jayka's mind: the woman's nervousness on their first meeting, the quote on the table and the installation of the camera across the street—even the incident of the woman talking to herself on her first visit, in which she seemed to be referring to someone as "Father," all made sense now. The woman had been praying. She was a true believer in the Christian deity. Possibly the quote and other quotes Jayka had noticed on various tables were a device she used in order to entice people to ask her about their origin, which would give her a chance to legally speak about her faith to others. At some point, the woman must have slipped up and either was too open about her faith without first being approached, or had indicated that her god was the *only* god. It was a pity. Jayka enjoyed the atmosphere and was intrigued by the owner, who seemed rather intelligent and even-keeled for a Christ follower. There was no need to hammer the proverbial nail into the woman's coffin. Whoever was performing the formal investigation would make certain of that.

She smiled grimly. "I am not. But I would very much like a mocha."

Luciana nodded, collected the menu and left to put in her order. In five minutes, Jayka was thoughtfully sipping the delightfully crafted beverage. She was thinking of trying to reach out to Tyrell when she felt a knock on her neural wall. As she quickly retreated within herself, she noticed another light at her wall, very similar in brightness to the one she had seen earlier when she had encountered the girl called Piper. It was a man this time. And then she recognized him. It was the man she had apprehended in the Preserve and brought to Dr. Moses.

"How are you allowed to be here?" was all she could think to ask. She knew he had recently been implanted, but as far as she knew, he was not yet ready for a neural link and the forceful withdrawal of information.

The man smiled. "Hello. I'm extending an invitation to you to hear the Truth …an opportunity to experience peace like you've never known. I'm not asking you to link with me, but if you're interested in what I have to say, simply stand in your doorway and listen. If you aren't interested after you hear what I'm about to tell you, simply shut your door."

Jayka's knee-jerk response was to report the man immediately. But there he had said it—the word she had not only encountered, but experienced and meditated on during the past week: *peace*. She scanned the man for any evidence of malware, but could find none—only the presence of a program that seemed strangely familiar. With a start, she realized it was the same program Piper had offered her. She opened the door and was unprepared for what happened next.

She was immediately transported to an immense meadow. Other people were blinking into view, all standing very still and looking around, just as surprised as she was. In a matter of seconds, several hundred people seemed to populate the meadow, and the numbers were still growing. The meadow was not only covered in people, but it was sprinkled with all different kinds of mountain wildflowers in a variety of colors. Jayka inhaled deeply, for their scent was in the air, and as she did, she noticed the butterflies. Thousands of them were taking wing from the flowers and floating to each individual person, blinking out of sight as they crossed their neural threshold. Jayka gasped as she realized what was happening. Craig Goforth was distributing Ira's firewall program—giving people the protection they needed to keep their thoughts to themselves and continue to make their own decisions.

Her mind went back to the time she had tried to protect Dr. Moses from Craig when she had brought him to Liberation Station from the Preserve. "We were told he was dangerous, Dr. Moses," she had said.

"Not physically dangerous, Jayka…intellectually dangerous. *Spiritually* dangerous," he had replied. And yet now this man was actively giving hundreds—perhaps thousands—of people protection from the very government that had labeled him and his beliefs as a threat to modern society. She watched as the people in the meadow turned in their doorways to watch the butterflies and then suddenly realized what they had been given. A few of them blinked out of sight, apparently disturbed that they ironically had no choice in receiving a program that would guarantee they had a choice in everything in their life that followed its installation into their systems. She turned around in her doorway and noticed that although she could see no one else's neural world through their doorways (or for that matter, even the presence of their doorways), she could still see her own neural mindscape behind her, reminding her that she could leave at any time. She looked to her right at an elderly man who had a bemused expression on his face.

"Is this a mass link?" he asked as they made eye contact.

"No. That isn't possible yet," Jayka said, and then hesitated. Had they finally figured out how to perform a mass link? She checked her systems. No. She was not linked with anyone. Yet somehow, she was aware of the presence of thousands. "No, I'm sure of it. Yet somehow, we are able to communicate."

"Hah!" the man smiled broadly as he gazed about the meadow. "Did you smell the flowers? Did you see all those butterflies?" he asked.

"Yes," Jayka said. "Do you understand what happened when they entered your neural wall?"

The man turned around, appearing to look at the hundreds of people behind him, but Jayka knew he was looking into his inner world. He turned back to her, tears in his eyes, and spoke in a quavering voice. "My, my, yes! Yes, I do. And I'm so *relieved!* My therapist has been doing things to my head that I don't want. She's installing protocols so I won't think about the way the State is operating these days—filling my mind up with other things so I'll be distracted from what's really important. Now she can't get in unless I let her."

"For the first time in a long time, I feel like I can think what I want," chimed in a teenage boy to their left.

"If I understand what just happened, they won't be able to get into our heads again unless we let them. The old protocols are still there, but they can't instate any new ones," said a woman behind them. "What does this mean? Why would this guy give something like this to us for free? He obviously doesn't work for the State or he wouldn't be working against them. There has to be a catch."

As if reading their thoughts, Craig's voice could be heard throughout the meadow. "By now, you've discovered that this invitation came with a surprise gift. And you're probably wondering why. The simple answer is that the One I represent didn't intend for you to exist as mindless robots who have no choice in what you believe or what you can do. Everyone has the right to decide where they will spend eternity; and now, no one can take that away from you."

The crowd was mostly silent, listening intently, but Jayka heard someone whisper, "Do you suppose they've discovered the secret to immortality? Transferring not just our memories, but our consciousness to a digital format?"

"What I have to tell you today has nothing to do with an innovation in technology," Craig was saying, as if anticipating their questions. "In fact, the problem you have and the solution I'm going to tell you about is thousands of years old.

"You've all heard of the Source. You've been told it is the essence of all life, the origin of the creation of the universe, and the thing that connects us all to each other. You may have heard that this Source has many different names, and that all religions are an attempt to describe it. But there is only one path to the Source of all life. The Bible says, 'And there is salvation in no one else, for there is no other name under heaven given among men by which we must be saved.'[97] That name is Jesus, and that quote is just one of many that have been edited out of your State's bible, so you may not have heard it before. It doesn't fit in with the State's religious program, and it doesn't go along with their social plan. They don't want you to hear it or to even be able to think about it objectively. That's why the author of the quote wanted to make sure you had the program I gave you. He wanted to make certain you could think for yourself and make your own decisions, because your eternal destiny depends upon it.

"You've all seen the ad campaign for the chip—'Be the *you* you were always meant to be.' Well, this is the opportunity Jesus is offering you. We were created for relationship with the source of all life and knowledge and love. But at the very beginning, humankind made the wrong decision—a decision to go our own way and violate the trust we had with our Creator. It cost us the life we had in God—an eternal destiny with Him. It left us spiritually dead inside. Ever since then, humanity has been trying to bring ourselves to life with all kinds of substitutes for this severed relationship.

"The good news is, God still wants to have a relationship with us. He wants it more than *we* do! He knows everything about you. Whatever you're feeling,

---

[97] Acts 4:12, RSV

He understands, because He walked on earth as a human being. He came in the form of His Son, Jesus, and taught about God's love and healed people and showed them how to live and how to connect with their Creator. But not everyone accepted Him, since He was a threat to the status quo. The religious leaders of the day didn't realize He was actually the fulfillment of many prophecies, and they worked against Him and saw to it that He was condemned to death on a cross of Roman crucifixion. They didn't understand that even this was all part of His eternal plan. He loves us so much that He carried our sins with Him to that cross and became the perfect sacrifice, building a bridge between God and man through His death. Three days later, He rose from the dead and now lives to give us life and to be that connection between us and His heavenly Father.

"He wants to help you. But unlike the State, He won't force his agenda on you. He won't control you like a puppet. He can only help you become everything you were meant to be if you believe in Him, that *He* is the only Son of God, and ask Him to come into your life. All the feelings of guilt you have, the dissatisfaction—the feeling that something is just not quite right, or even that you have no purpose or your existence is pointless—the reason you have those feelings is that your soul is reaching for something it was created to have. You were made to be filled with all the fullness of God.[98] And since you don't know where to look to fill that empty space, you get another download on your chip or you get a new implant or you try a new drug.

"But Jesus is saying to you, 'I am the Great I Am. I am everything you need.' He doesn't want a mindless robot. He wants to be able to call you His dear child. Will you accept His offer to be your Father?" Craig waited a few moments and looked around the meadow. "If you're ready to receive Him, all you have to do is ask Him to forgive you for all the things you've done wrong and to come be the Lord of your life.[99] He will bring your spirit alive with His Spirit, and you'll become His child. You'll experience His peace. If you really want new life in Christ, you can pray this prayer with me. If you really mean it, God will come to you and fill that void you've been unsuccessfully trying to fill.[100]

---

[98] See Ephesians 3:16-19, KJV

[99] "If we confess our sins, He is faithful and just to forgive us our sins, and to cleanse us from all unrighteousness." –1 John 1:9, KJV

[100] Jesus said in John 4:13-14 that whosoever drinks of the water He would give them would never thirst, but the water He gave them would be in them a well of water springing up into everlasting life.

If that describes you, please pray with me." Craig paused briefly as he looked around the meadow. From his vantage point, he could see thousands of people —perhaps tens of thousands. Was anyone taking him seriously? Had he been clear in his message? Did they understand him? But then he remembered what Jesus had told him: "You just teach. I'll do the rest."

He took a deep breath and began to pray. "Dear Jesus, I know I've made mistakes. I know I've done wrong. Please forgive me. I believe You are the Son of God and that You died to pay for my sins—my wrongdoings. I believe You rose from the dead and are alive. Please come into my heart. Come into my life. Make me Your child. Make me brand new, and help me to live for You."

Jayka watched the crowd as Craig said the prayer. Some people were looking around, wondering if anyone else would pray. Some looked shocked and offended and immediately blinked out of view. But some were praying with him. She could see a few that had even fallen to their knees, their heads bowed. Others were looking up as they prayed. Some had tears streaming down their face. She looked at the man she had been talking to earlier, and he was staring back at her. "Did you say it?" he asked.

"I did not," Jayka replied.

"I wasn't sure, so I didn't," he continued. "But now I know I *want* to, and I missed the chance!" he cried, with a sharp intake of breath. "Do you at least remember the words?"

"You indicated earlier that you had the chip," Jayka said. "If you do, the words should be stored on your most recent memory file."

"Oh! I forgot about that! I'm still getting used to this thing," the man said. "So I guess I can just go back and listen again and pray this time—I mean, ask Jesus to come into my life?"

"Uh, I suppose you can, if you really want to," Jayka said. "If you really believe that sort of thing."

"I do, I *do!*" the man exclaimed. "All my life I felt like something was wrong with me. And now I know what it was!"

"Although I should remind you that monotheism is a dangerous belief system that can result in your imprisonment, should you proselytize. Believing that *your* way to the Source is the *only* way is not only arrogant, but intolerant, and—"

But the man had turned around and blinked out of sight before she could finish, returning to his inner world to access the file.

"How is it intolerant?" asked the woman behind her. "I happen to know some people who believe in only one god, and they don't force others to believe the way they do."

A man behind them spoke up, his voice rising in agitation. "Well, most of *my* family is from a theocracy on the other side of the world. If you don't believe in *their* god and pledge allegiance to their form of law, they'll chop off your head! That's why my family came to this country a few generations ago. And now look at our country. If you don't believe what they want, they may not chop off your head, but they'll get inside it and chop off your ability to control your own actions. And if the chip doesn't work, you end up a drooling paraplegic or choking to death on fumes in a river clean-up colony."

"But that's not the way *this* belief works—the one the man was talking about. He wasn't talking about a theocracy. He even said if we weren't interested, we could just go back about our business," the woman rebuffed. "The Jesus freaks don't force you to believe the way they do. They don't insist on it. That's what the *State* is doing, by forcing us to believe what they want us to believe. That's what they've been doing all along, and we didn't see it! They've been telling us we're entitled to be happy and that they can make us happy. But they're just doing it so they can make us conform to what they want!"

"But the man—Craig, wasn't that his name? He said our eternal destiny depended on the decision we made—on whether or not we accepted this Jesus as our God," interjected the teenage boy.

"Yeah, but it's *still* our choice," the woman said with a tone of finality.

Jayka turned her attention back to Craig, who was speaking again. "If you didn't pray this prayer today, I hope you'll think about it and change your mind," he said. "Just because you didn't do it now doesn't mean you missed your chance. It doesn't have to be those exact words. You can ask Jesus in your own words to forgive you and to give you new life in Him." Craig looked around him, as if distracted by something. When he spoke again, it was with an urgency in his voice. "I may not have much time, so I'll have to be brief, but once you've received this gift from God, it's just the beginning. You need to learn more about Him so you can grow as His child. To do that, you can read the Bible—a love letter He left to us. You'll find it if you access your most recent downloads. Everything I've told you today is true, but don't take *my* word for it. Look into the Word of God and discover it for yourself! There are scriptures about the different topics we've covered, arranged under subject headings when you open the file. It's available in all written languages, and the message you heard was broadcast in all spoken languages, in case you were wondering about all the other people throughout the world who are listening. I've recorded some messages that will help you as you begin this walk with God. All you have to do is visit this site to access them. It's protected, and since you have the firewall program, you are protected from prosecution if you visit. I—" Craig looked to his left and suddenly vanished.

Jayka looked around. Thousands of people still stood in the meadow, trying to comprehend everything that had just happened. "I hope you understand that what this man has just told you is extremely dangerous information," Jayka said to anyone who would listen. "Should you accept his invitation to make the Christian god your only belief and speak about the contraband literature you now have access to, you may be prosecuted, or at least sent to reconditioning."

"How will anyone know if we did it or not?" the vocal woman said pointedly. "They can't get in our head anymore unless we let them."

"Well, *I* will know," Jayka said.

"So, what? Are you going to report us for answering a knock at our door?" the teenage boy asked angrily.

"You don't understand. I..." Jayka faltered. Her automatic response was to identify with the State. But she suddenly realized she no longer had the same sense of allegiance she had previously held. She had sworn an oath to protect the citizens of the State. And by all appearances, the State was doing the opposite by curtailing and even forbidding and punishing certain citizens' rights. "No. No, I will not report you." Jayka said. "And I'm going to do everything in my power to protect your right to believe as you choose." She turned back to her inner world and left the meadow. Someone else needed protection now. She only hoped she wasn't too late.

37

Viv tried to appear calm as she exited the elevator and clomped purpose-fully down the hall. After visiting with Ainsley Abbot for the last forty-five minutes, she had gained permission to visit with patients from the outer docks on the pretense of being able to relate to them and make some sort of a break-through in their development as citizens. She had been instructed to go back to the front desk and receive the upgrade to her Palmscan that would allow her access. Ainsley had put in the order via her chip, and it had been ready for her when she arrived.

She didn't know if Craig would be held on the same floor as the rest of the patients or if he would be in a restricted area, but she had to try to find him and to convince her superiors that she could make a difference in his case. It wasn't much of a plan, but it was the only thing she could come up with.

Suddenly, she could hear raised voices a few rooms down the hall. "We need to end it now, Joseph! This pet project of yours is jeopardizing the push for the global link. Put aside your obsession with converting Christians who are too brainwashed to reach. They are a threat to the citizens who are easier to manipulate. Just terminate them and be done with it."

Viv quickly ducked inside the room to her left. That was Ainsley's voice.

"Or if you don't have the stomach for that, let *me* handle them. I can produce the desired outcome without the messiness of a death certificate," Ainsley said with all the warmth of a cottonmouth.

"I will do no such thing," Moses replied. "We are not trying to manipulate and control people, and we are certainly not trying to toss them out of their minds. We are trying to show them the truth! If they can just see it, no manipulation will be needed! They will gladly embrace the next evolutionary step of humanity.

It will mean an end to the threat of war ever breaking out. They will be able to understand their fellow citizens and even citizens of other nation states around the world, and they won't ever have to feel empty or isolated again."

The sound of Ainsley's laughter ricocheted through the hall. "Oh, please, Joseph. Don't be so naïve! The world will always be full of people who don't get along, whether or not they understand each other. The global link isn't about creating one big happy family. You know it isn't. How do you think you've gotten unlimited funding for this project from the beginning? It's about control. Lasting peace and global unity will only happen when there is only one ruling authority and no opposition to it. The State and the World Health Alliance couldn't care less about your idealistic philosophies about all of humanity holding hands and singing. Your global consciousness project just happened to tick all their boxes. They wanted a way to control people. You provided it."

There was silence for a few seconds, and Moses spoke. "Specialist Abbot, I am removing you from this project. You will leave immediately. Conall will escort you out of the building. We will have the personal items from your office sent to you."

Ainsley laughed again. "I would imagine Conall will have new orders soon, when the administrators discover that your soft methods of reconditioning have resulted in an attempt at global proselytizing. How he managed it is anyone's guess, but Goforth certainly pulled it off. Maybe you should become his student and he could share with you how he was able to pseudo-link with most of the chipped world?"

Viv's eyes opened wide. Her visor was pushed back on her head and muted. She had noticed a rash of notifications clicking during the last part of her visit with Ainsley, but she had been in such a rush to get to Craig that she hadn't checked them. She pulled down her visor and looked at the subject lines: "Man spreads disinformation to millions around the globe." That one was from the State, highlighted as urgently important. The rest were from global news sources, most of them sharing the same opinion. "Craig Goforth, a man of unknown origin, offends world audience with monotheistic message" "Goforth goes forth to pillage the minds of billions." The rest were from private citizens, with varying responses. She saw her former coworker, Stan, in the lineup. "Viv, I know you don't wear your visor much, but you really ought to check this out!" He had forwarded her a link called simply, "Peace with God." As she accessed it, she could see Craig standing in a flower-filled meadow, but her efforts to hear the message were curtailed by the conversation taking place down the hall.

"You know he had to have outside help," Dr. Moses said through clenched teeth. "There's no way he could have done this alone. He has no programming skills. Their community is decades behind the rest of the world."

"Which brings us to another one of your pet projects," Ainsley said.

"Ira? He wouldn't do this. I would've known about it."

"Do you have any better suspects? And then there's this report of some sort of program they received when they accessed the sight. Can you explain why we can't find it?"

"We can't find it because it doesn't exist," Moses insisted. "It's just one of those rumors people run with."

The voices stopped as the sound of heavy footsteps could be heard approaching. "Citizen Abbot, I'm here to escort you off of the premises," said an authoritative voice.

"Thank you, Conall," Dr. Moses said. "Make certain she leaves straightaway and does not access her office first."

"Of course, sir."

Viv sank deeper into the shadows of the room as Conall and Ainsley whisked by.

"This is a mistake. In a few hours, you'll be taking orders from me," Ainsley said cattily.

There was silence from down the hall. Viv accessed her Audio-boost implant and could hear Dr. Moses speaking softly. "Oh Craig, my friend. I'm so sorry it has come to this. I'm really not certain how to deal with you. I thought we were making such headway. I'm just not ready to give up on you, but I cannot allow you to poison other people's minds." He sighed, and she could hear him leave the room. She was disappointed to hear the door slide shut behind him. It was doubtful she would have access.

Suddenly, she heard a soft moan coming from the bed behind her. She turned and was surprised to see a young girl with a short fuzz of hair lying in the bed.

Viv crept closer and couldn't help but feel she looked familiar. The girl's eyes opened and struggled to focus. She moaned again and reached toward Viv. Viv came closer and held the girl's hand. She knew she needed to try to see if she could make it past the scanner into Craig's room, but the girl seemed so young and pitiful and desperate. "Do ya know 'im?" she was saying.

"Do I know who?" Viv asked.

"Did ya meetcha real Dad? Were ya able ta find 'im?" she asked earnestly, her speech slurred. "Jesus tol' me you was the same girl I met a coupla years back in the outer docks. You was lookin' for ya dad. But ya needed ta be lookin' for ya *real* Dad."

And then Viv remembered—the little girl in the dirty jacket who had witnessed to her in the outer docks. This was the same girl, two years later, her hair shaved off and a chip in her head.

Viv couldn't hold back the tears. "Yes, I did!" she said. "And it was all because ya tol' me about 'im! I tried ta find ya, but I couldn't. I heard they took ya. I'm so sorry!"

"Sorry? What for? I'm still tellin' people 'bout Jesus!" she said, and then drifted back to sleep.

Viv reluctantly left the girl and hurried to Craig's closed door. It was just as she suspected. Her Palmscan wouldn't work on this room. "Jesus, I hafta git in there! I hafta know what they're doin' to him!" she prayed desperately. Suddenly, the elevator at the end of the hall opened. Viv stepped away from the door, pretending to be looking at the number of the adjacent room. The sound of scrabbling could be heard as a mottled brown and black blur hurtled down the hall and bowled into her. "Macy!" she exclaimed. She looked up at Jayka, who was close behind the dog.

"What are you doing here? Have you seen Dr. Moses?" Jayka asked abruptly.

"I'm tryin' to see a patient. Dr. Moses was here, but he just left."

"I, too, am looking for patient. His name is Craig Goforth. I could not access his room location."

"Well, this is it," Viv said, pointing to the door.

"Although his room number was not disclosed to me, I should still have access," Jayka said simply, and waved her palm over the scanner. The door slid open and the two stepped inside. Craig was lying in bed, an IV drip in his arm. Jayka strode over to the IV bag, read its contents, and immediately turned off the pump.

"What was it?" Viv asked. "I heard Moses say he wasn't ready to give up on 'im, but Ainsley wanted to kill 'im."

Jayka turned to her angrily. "It's a sedative that affects higher brain function. It can't be administered for very long without causing permanent damage."

"I don't think Moses wanted to give Craig brain damage. I think he just wanted to stop him from tellin' people about Jesus."

"They will kill him. Since they can't program him to do what they want, they will terminate his life. He is too dangerous."

"That's kinda what Ainsley was sayin'. Although it sounded like she thought she might be able to manipulate him somehow if Moses would let 'er."

"What did they say? Hurry! Tell me everything you can remember," Jayka said as she scanned Craig's vital signs.

"She said Moses had botched it all. I think she's gunnin' for 'is job. She said he blew it with some dude named Ira, too. I think she suspicioned Ira had somethin' ta do with Craig bein' able ta preach ta millions." She paused. "Did he really reach millions?"

"He did. I was there, and I saw the whole thing. When he stopped talking and disappeared, I was afraid they had killed him. But if they continue on this drug regime, it *will* finish him." She turned to Viv again. "Where did Dr. Moses go?"

"He acted like he was tryin' ta figger out what to do next. I think maybe he was gonna go find that other fella."

"Ira?"

Viv nodded.

"Ira is a good man. I wish there were a way I could warn him," she said. Ira almost never used his visor when he was off duty, Jayka had noticed. She fixed Viv with her green eyes. "This man is as good as dead if we don't get him out of here. The State will have no patience with anything that interferes with their agenda. The only reason they might keep him alive is to see if they can duplicate what he did and develop it in their attempts at a mass link. Ira may actually be their best chance to accomplish this. I don't think they'll kill him, but they will never let him go. If he doesn't comply with their wishes, he will undoubtedly be chipped. He won't be able to keep them out if he doesn't have a way to get to his own program. But I don't know if we'll be able to locate him before *they* do."

"His own program? The one Craig handed out? So it wasn't just a rumor?" Viv asked.

"Hardly," Jayka retorted.

Suddenly Viv remembered the girl at the end of the hall. "There's this girl down the hall—I remember 'er from the outer docks. She ain't more'n fourteen, an' they got her chipped an' all drugged up."

Jayka shook her head. There were too many people to save. "I can't do anything about that. We have to concentrate on the ones we have the best chance of saving." She readied the bed for transport.

"What—are ya jus' gonna roll 'im outta here?" Viv asked.

"Prisoner transport, unless you have a better idea," Jayka said with an air of authority. "You walk ahead of me as if we just happen to be leaving at the same time."

Viv complied, but she stopped when she reached Piper's door. "Just look in here. Ya need ta see this," she insisted.

"There is no time," Jayka began, but then Piper spoke up. Apparently, her sedatives were wearing off.

"Hey! Is that the Pod-Op girl I saw the other day? Didja find peace?"

Jayka put the brake on the bed and dashed into the room. "This is unacceptable. We cannot leave Piper behind.," she said, her calculations finding no probable outcome for success.

"You know her?" Viv asked.

"I met her at my neural wall. She gave me the firewall program before Craig distributed it."

"Whaddaya mean ya can't leave me behind? Are we goin' somewhere?" Piper asked, raising up slightly in the bed.

"We're trying to get you out of here. You and Craig Goforth," Jayka explained.

"Craig Goforth! Didja hear 'im? He reached millions!" Piper said enthusiastically. She turned to Viv. "Have ya seen Janice? She's around here somewhere. She's the one who introduced Ira to Jesus. *You* know—*Janice!* Janice Druthers. You used ta work with 'er at the factory."

"We don't have time for discussion. We have to get out of here!" Jayka said with growing concern. "I cannot save all of you."

"Maybe not," said a voice from the doorway, "But you might have a better chance if I help."

The three turned simultaneously to see a scrawny man wearing glasses and an incredibly high-tech looking bodysuit, with a large suitcase in tow. Jayka's eyes widened. "Ira Owens, you must get out of here! You are a suspect in the mass pseudo-link incident."

"Add hacking and identity theft to the list of charges," Ira said. "A few moments ago, right after Dr. Moses left, an order went out from him to send the nurses on dayshift home early. I can provide digital proof of the prison transport you just spoke of, and a release of Janice Druthers." He turned to Viv. "Viv, you can take Janice out in a wheelchair. She listed you as her emergency contact when she was first implanted, so you are authorized to give her a ride home."

"She did? I am?" Viv asked.

"Well, not exactly, but it seemed plausible…" Ira's voice trailed off.

"But what about Dr. Moses? He was lookin' for you," Viv said worriedly.

"Actually, he *may* have been on his way to a meeting with the administrators. I'm fairly certain he received orders to report to them just before he left," Ira said and shrugged. "Just a hunch."

Viv's face broke into a smile. "Ira, I've only known ya two minutes, an' I like ya already."

"Surely you know they will discover what you've done," Jayka said matter-of-factly. "Not only all these infringements to which you have just alluded, but they know you must have something to do with the broadcasting of Craig's message. It's closer to a mass link than anything they've been able to produce. They will chip you and retrieve the information."

"Nope," Ira said simply.

"Don't you understand me?" Jayka began.

"Yes. But what you don't understand is that I've already been chipped. Not the standard version. I designed it myself, and was able to implant it on my own. Being a specialist in biotechnology has its benefits. It's a much less intrusive implant, miniscule by the standards of the chip you carry, and undetectable from the natural electrical impulses in my brain. The firewall program is already installed. If they attempt to chip me, they won't get anywhere with information extraction, I can assure you."

"Well, this is a surprise," Jayka said. "I had heard you were diametrically opposed to any sort of implantation other than health implants."

"I was, until it became increasingly clearer to me that my life and the lives of others may depend on it."

"Then they will find other methods of extracting the information," Jayka said gravely. "I have unfortunately been a part of these sessions. There is always a way."

"I thought you said you had to be going," Ira said, conveniently ignoring her insinuation. He turned to Viv. "Janice is in room 220. She's still pretty groggy, but I got her off whatever sedatives they were administering in her IV. She should be alright." He came to Piper's bedside and smiled. "How do you feel about tight spaces?"

"I'm purty small. I kin fit into 'em real good," Piper said, sitting up higher in the bed.

Ira grinned and rolled the giant suitcase into the room. "Viv, you'll have to take charge of both Janice's wheelchair and the suitcase for her…*personal effects*. The wheelchair has an electronic assist, so it shouldn't be too difficult. I've also arranged for a shuttle to transport you to Janice's apartment."

Viv and Jayka stood looking at Ira, momentarily in shock. "You are an extremely talented and clever man, Ira Owens," Jayka finally said. "I am honored to have known you."

"Thanks, but I'm not dead *yet*," he answered with a raised eyebrow, and then turned to Viv again. "I have disabled the Geeves unit in Janice's apartment and installed a program to convince Unitech that everything is running normally there. You should be able to converse freely in that space, and Piper will be safe there for the time being. I'm working on finding a new location for her though, since it will be too much of a coincidence that she disappeared at the same time as a false release for Janice was issued."

"Won't they just bring Janice right back here when they find out the release was bogus?" Viv asked.

"I don't think so. They really didn't have a good excuse for keeping her any longer since I installed the firewall program, unless it would be for monitoring her behavior. But they never gave her a chance to misbehave since she's been sedated most of the time. I have sent an appeal from her to the administrators to spend the rest of her recuperation at home."

"What about Ainsley?" Viv asked.

Ira's brows knit into a worried wrinkle. "Well, theoretically, she shouldn't be a problem since she was just fired, but I would be surprised if she gives up without a fight. I'll do what I can to slow her down."

"What about you? Ya can't just stay here," Viv said concernedly.

"Actually, this may be the best place for me to hide. And the suit offers me a better chance at influencing outcomes, electronically, since I'm not yet practiced at utilizing my chip. However, I do have a backup plan." He turned to Jayka. "Find Tyrell. He has the help you need." He looked at them all with a grim smile. "I'll hold them as long as I can. Godspeed," he said, and disappeared into his workroom down the hall.

38

SELAH looked out the window of Zelda's apartment. The crowd was already lining up with their cups, bowls, and jars for a helping of stew. She wondered if any of the people who were already there belonged to the group Cosmo was bringing. There were a few faces she didn't recognize, but that wasn't unusual. Attendance increased with each meeting as word of mouth continued to spread. Cosmo had instructed his men not to demand any sort of fees or pledges of allegiance as payment for passage to the area for this meeting, so perhaps the crowd would be even larger than expected.

"Did any of them think it was strange you told them to drop the toll?" Selah had asked him earlier that week.

"I tol' 'em it was all part o' gettin' as many people here as we could, on account o' da special guests we was escortin'. I tol' 'em we's gonna take 'em to da meetin's cuz dese State folk is always wantin' ta do da most dangerous ting dey can tink of. Da gang don' know da real reason we's comin' tonight, 'cept fa Creep—he knows. But all da rest o' dem is in da dark." Cosmo's expression became serious as he looked at Selah intently. "I don' how dis all gonna go down. What I hope is dat da State folk will give deir lives ta Jesus. An' I's hopin' dat mebbe, jus' *mebbe* some o' my men has already done jus' dat, an' dat tonight, mebbe *more'll* come ta Jesus. But da truth is, some of 'em ain't gonna like it—ain't gonna believe ever'ting I risked ta pull dis off. An' I may not be leader of da Gateways afta tonight. I may not be *anyting* afta tonight."

"I hope it doesn't come to that," Selah said. "We've been praying for your protection."

"I appreciate dat," Cosmo nodded.

"God doesn't always do things like we plan. Sometimes hard things happen, and we can't understand why. Then later, when we can look back on it, we understand how God was able to use those things to bring more people into His family."

"Well, don' get me wrong, Miss Selah. I don' wanna die, but I has cheated death many a time. If I die, it may be dat it's jus' my turn," Cosmo said calmly.

Selah was quiet for a moment, remembering how hard she had prayed for Miss Genevieve when she had a stroke. At the time, Selah couldn't understand why the spunky old lady had to die. It seemed like there was so much more she could offer—so much profitable time she could have left. But God had other plans. Selah knew what the Bible said about God's protection, but she also knew that Hebrews 9:27 said, *"And just as it is appointed for men to die once, and after that comes judgment, so Christ, having been offered once to bear the sins of many, will appear a second time, not to deal with sin but to save those who are eagerly waiting for him."*[101] She hadn't been given any insight on whether or not it was Cosmo's time to go be with the Lord, so there was no guarantee of his physical safety. But since he had given his heart to Jesus, the safety of his soul was secure.[102] "Do you know how many are coming?" Selah asked, changing the subject.

"Fourteen, last I heard. We's havin' ta make two trips on account o' da numbah. We didn' tink we'd have dat many, but some of 'em been talkin' 'bout some big ting dey saw on da internet. Da whole city's buzzin' 'bout it. Sump'n 'bout some dude talkin' 'bout Jesus. Some of 'em what has da chip said dis dude gave 'em a program dat protects 'em from da loon doctors what mess wit' deir heads. Dey's a few of 'em dat seem differ'nt now. Dey say dey got some new download too, but dey tight-lipped about it. I mean, dey got stuff on *us*, an we got stuff on *dem*, but dey wanna hold onto whatevah it is, ya savvy?"

"I wonder what it is?"

"I don't got no *idee*, but if I find out, I'll letcha know," Cosmo had assured her.

Selah's memory of the conversation was interrupted by a knock at her bedroom door. "Selah, it's time," Bally said, holding the pot of stew.

---

[101] Hebrews 9:27-28, RSV

[102] Romans 6:22, KJV "But now being made free from sin, and become servants to God, ye have your fruit unto holiness, and the end everlasting life.

Selah opened the door and smiled at her friend. "Well, this could be an interesting night," she said. "But I guess we'll leave the details up to God."

"We's gonna have to," Bally stated. "We cain't do nuttin' 'bout it anyway, so we mise well cast all our cares on Him."[103]

The two headed out the door and made their way to the stew station: a table crafted with skill by a grateful new convert. It was made of pallet boards, like most of the furniture in the outer docks, but it was built to be sturdy and serviceable and had been a great asset. Every time she used it, Selah was reminded of how many varied opportunities there were to serve the Lord.

She sat the pot on the table and began dishing out the stew while Bally kept people in order, a task to which she seemed born. Drey and Bester encouraged people who were waiting in line and assisted first-time attendees by making certain anyone who had arrived without a bowl or cup soon had some sort of container. The receptacles varied from soup or vegetable cans to margarine and yogurt tubs, and even Syntha-lunchmeat containers, all cleaned for use by volunteers.

"Look who's here," Bally said, nodding her head toward the end of the line.

Selah half expected to see Cosmo and his gang, but then she remembered he had sent word that something had come up at the last minute and he wouldn't be able to attend with the special visitors tonight. Instead, she spied Garrison and Lelah with their host family.

"Uh-huh," Bally said knowingly when she saw Selah's face light up. "You betta say sump'n, or I *will.*"

"You'll do nothing of the sort!" Selah said firmly.

"Hmmph." Bally raised her eyebrows and went back to crowd control.

Selah couldn't help but steal glances in Garrison's direction. She noticed that he was making conversation with some people right behind him. Lelah seemed to be enthusiastically visiting with them, as well. Suddenly she noticed one of the men was staring back at her. When their eyes met, she smiled, and he looked away, placing all his attention on the people beside him. Then she recognized him. It was one of Cosmo's men. She hadn't been able to see the arch tattoo

---

[103] 1 Peter 5:7 KJV says "Casting all your care upon Him; for He careth for you."

from this distance, but she recognized his stance. He was watchful, seeming almost to shepherd the people who were with him. Another of Cosmo's men walked alongside them, so involved with animated conversation that Selah didn't see how he could be any help at being their bodyguard. Then she spotted Creep bringing up the rear. He held his place behind them in line like a wall of defense, his eyes constantly surveying the crowd. As the group drew nearer, Selah could hear snippets of the conversation, and she remembered the talkative man from the time Cosmo had shown up at Zelda's apartment. "You is not gonna believe this," the jabber-mouthed gang member was saying, "but that stew pot jus' keep makin' the stew. It nevah runs out. Ever' night, they have these meetin's, an' folks come from all aroun' ta get a good meal an' listen to the music an' hear what the Stewmakah has ta say."

"Give it a rest, Sho-Low," said the man at the front. "You already told them the layout. Jus' let 'em see an' experience it fo themselves."

Selah smiled as Garrison's host family approached the table. "Good evenin', Miss Selah," Wallace said cheerfully.

"Hi!" Phoenix exclaimed, darting in front of his father to make his presence known.

"Well, hello there, Phoenix," Selah grinned.

"Phoenix, you can't cut in line!" Sparta said, yanking her brother back behind their parents.

"Sparta, you needs ta stop bein' so bossy, girl," Annabel scolded.

"But he cut!" Sparta protested.

"That's enough," Annabel said. Phoenix turned around and stuck his tongue out at his sister. "And that's enough outta you too, mister," Annabel said, and swatted him lightly on the behind.

"You better listen to your mama," Selah said as she bent down to grin at the children at eye level. "But I'm really glad to see you, too."

"Hi, Selah. How's it going?" said Garrison, almost shyly.

Selah raised back up and tried not to blush as she smiled at her old friend. "Fine," was all she could think of to say.

"Good," Garrison nodded. "Hey, if there's any time after it's over tonight, I wondered if we could get a chance to talk."

"Sure," she replied. "Is everything ok?"

"Oh, yeah, nothing's wrong. I just thought it would be nice to catch up."

Lelah stared back and forth between the two as a look of comprehension dawned on her face. She cleared her throat to help her friends focus on the task at hand. "Hey Selah, these are the folks we've been praying for," she said quietly as she nodded in the direction of the group from the State. "But they don't want to be treated any differently. They want to see what all the fuss is about. And some of them already know Jesus!"

Selah seemed to jolt back to the present. "Well, that's wonderful!" she exclaimed. She smiled and made eye contact with each one as she ladled out the stew.

"We've been hearing a lot about this meeting," said one of the women in the group. "I heard you were going to talk about the god they call Jesus, just like the man on the internet was talking about."

"So you heard his message?" Selah asked.

"Yeah, there aren't many that *didn't* hear it," the man beside her piped up. He turned to his companion. "And once you know Him, you'll understand why the man was willing to risk his life to tell us about Him."

"I'm not going to make a snap decision. I have to make my mind up for myself," the woman replied.

"Yes, you do," Selah agreed. "Only *you* can make the decision of whether or not to come to Christ. But I hope you decide to accept Him." Selah could feel the eyes of the tall gang member in front of the group boring into her. Suddenly, she remembered his name.

"Hey, Cade! How are things going?" she asked amiably.

Cade lifted his lips slightly in what could have passed for a cautious smile. "S'okay."

"I'm glad you all could make it," she said.

Cade nodded and continued his vigil over the crowd surrounding his charges.

"We haven't ever had any problems," Selah tried to reassure him.

"It's my job to make sure o' that, tonight," he said sharply, and beckoned his group to follow him to find a place to sit. Selah noticed he successfully booted some people who were sitting on the ground near the platform off of their claimed spots. Mild protests were made, but one look at the arch tattoos silenced all resistance. She sighed. Things were not off to a very good start, she reflected, and prayed silently under her breath.

She and her teams had been covering the situation with prayer. They had known that tonight would be different, but weren't certain exactly what to expect. Bally's words came back to her: "Mise well cast all our cares on Him." Tears came to her eyes as she realized how much Bally and the others had matured since they had come to Christ a matter of weeks ago. God was using them in a mighty way, growing them quickly for His service. To her, they shone like stars in the darkness. *"For God is at work in you, both to will and to work for His good pleasure,"*[104] she remembered the scripture from Philippians 2. *"Do all things without grumbling or questioning; that you may be blameless and innocent, children of God without blemish in the midst of a crooked and perverse generation, among whom you shine as lights in the world."*[105] While she wanted to go over and reprimand Cade for his behavior, she realized that whatever she did should be done in love, not irritation. Tonight wouldn't be perfect. But tonight, people would hear the gospel. The Holy Spirit would move, and she would not do anything to hinder that. She suddenly had an idea. "Bally, would you be willing to give up your seats near the front to those people Cade just pushed out?" she asked.

Bally hesitated a moment. "I kinda like fa us ta be up close wit' ya where we can be dere for ya if'n we need to," she said. "But I saw what happened. I'm sure we can find a place off to da side. As long as we kin still get to da front during da altar service, it'd be fine. I'll take keer of it."

Finally, the food ministry part of the gathering was over, and everyone sat down in the street to wait. Selah noticed with satisfaction that the people who had been displaced were now seated in the best location, closest to front and center, a place that was always roped off for her team. When Tunes stepped up to the platform to lead praise and worship, a feeling of expectation fell over the crowd. And while some of the secret citizens of the State were looking around, their eyes round at the strange surroundings and the unpoliced gathering, other

---

[104] Philippians 2:13, RSV
[105] Philippians 2:14-15, RSV

members of that group seemed eager to worship. As Tunes began to sing, the street and the alleyway filled with hundreds of voices giving praise to God. The Holy Spirit swept through the crowd, and people who had been weighed down by worry seemed transported to a higher plane as they worshipped.

Suddenly, a man with a voice ravaged by the acid fog began jumping up and down beside the group from the State. Selah remembered him because he had barely been able to wheeze out a "thank you" when she gave him his helping of stew. He was mouthing the words to the songs, coughing and choking in his effort. Cade watched with growing irritation, for the man was bumping into him with each jump. But suddenly, the man's voice began to grow in strength. Tunes stopped singing as he realized what was happening. "Come up here and sing with me, brother," Tunes said to the man, holding out his hand. The man scrambled forward and Tunes helped him up onto the pallet stage. The two began to sing, the man's voice growing stronger with each line of the worship chorus, until he was singing full strength, just as loudly as Tunes. The crowd cheered, for everyone around him had heard what was left of his voice before the service. *"Jesus!"* some yelled. *"Glory to God!"* and *"Hallelujah!"* could be heard. Cade looked around, his eyes wide, and then stared at the old man on the stage in disbelief. The two finished out the song, and then the crowd broke out in more spontaneous worship as the presence of God charged the atmosphere.

After praise and worship, Selah delivered a simple gospel message, as she always did, and then began teaching the people according to the scriptures which had come to her earlier. "For those of you who have accepted Jesus as your Savior, that is just the first step," she explained. "We were all created in His image, to be His lights. Once you were in darkness, but not anymore. You are no longer Discards. 1 Peter 2:9 and 10 says that *'You are a chosen race, a royal priesthood, a holy nation, God's own people, that you may declare the wonderful deeds of Him who called you out of darkness into his marvelous light. Once you were no people but now you are God's people; once you had not received mercy but now you have received mercy.'"*[106] God doesn't discard people. He gives them new life when they come to Him. And now that you know Him, your job is to share Him

---

[106] 1 Peter 1:9-10, RSV

with others. Can you imagine what would happen if the citizens of the State knew they could have peace and joy and fulfillment? I'm telling you, it would change our world! If all the people in the outer docks and the people of the State knew there is a God who cares about them, individually—if they really believed in Him and who He is, this world would be a different place. I know that if you tell others about Jesus, there's a risk you might be dragged away by the 'loon dockers.' But if enough of us shine our lights in this world and keep helping others and reaching out in love to the very people who are trying to keep us down, they won't be able to deny that we have something different! We are the lights of the world! Let's reach as many as we can!"

The altar service began, and Sho-Low and Creep kept a close eye on the group from the State. Selah could see out of the corner of her eye that Cade was watching her intently. She wondered if he was beginning to feel the convicting power of the Holy Spirit as one by one, people came forward for prayer. She noticed that Bally had been unable to push through the crowd to be with her, but was doing what she could to gradually move in closer. Drey and Bester were also on the sidelines, since they had given up their seats. As a result, this part of the service seemed a little more disorganized than normal; but Selah pushed on, determined that everyone who wanted prayer should receive it, just as normal. She noticed Creep ushering out part of the guests from the State toward one of the alleyways and remembered that Cosmo had said they would have to transport them in shifts. An hour slipped by, and still more people were coming for prayer. Suddenly, Cade was right next to her, a concerned expression on his face. "Miss Selah, there's a kid ovah here that really needs ya ta pray fo 'im —*right now!*" Selah looked around for Bally, who normally helped her negotiate the crowds in situations like this. But Bally was still on the opposite side of the street, as were Drey and Bester.

"Where is he?" she asked.

"He's ovah here next to the alley. He wanted ta come in closer, but he cain't make it ovah here cuz o' all the people. He's really hurtin'," Cade said desperately.

"Well, take me to him," Selah asked.

"Outta the way!" Cade said in a commanding voice as he took Selah by the hand. Sho-Low, who had stayed behind with the other half of the State group, herded the citizens along with her. They formed a barrier between her and the rest of the crowd. Selah felt as if she were being carried along in a river during flood stage. She looked back to see if Bally had been able to make it anywhere near them, but she couldn't see her through the people.

"Wait!" Selah said, attempting to stop.

"We're almost to 'im," Cade said, tightening his grip on her hand. Indeed, they were almost to the alley, and then she saw a State vehicle parked there, guarded by a group of Gateways.

"It's okay," said one of the citizens right behind her. "That's the car we came in. I don't know how they got it, but they brought us in it. They must be letting the kid sit inside until you can pray for him."

Selah pulled back, unaccustomed to being dragged somewhere to pray. "Selah!" she heard Bally yelling above the crowd.

Suddenly, Cade stopped. Garrison had somehow managed to worm his way through the mass of people and had stepped in front of him. "Where are you taking her?" he asked.

Cade's countenance changed in an instant, his eyes darkening, his concern morphing into anger. "Move it!" he commanded, and shoved Garrison aside. Garrison rebounded quickly, scrabbling to reach Selah and break Cade's hold on her arm. But in an instant, he was jerked off of his feet from behind, and Sho-Low's arm was wrapped around his throat.

"Don' be a hero, Romeo," Sho-Low growled in his ear. "Heroes end up in someone else's stewpot." He kept his grip on Garrison until Cade and the others made it to the car. Selah struggled, calling out for help, but the Gateways made sure she was in the middle of the State group and crammed them all into the car.

As soon as Cade was inside, the driver locked the doors and stepped on the acceleration pedal.

"Your passengers are not wearing their seatbelts," the A.I. voice said pleasantly. "This car will not operate until—"

Cade let out an expletive and began scrambling to find the belt fasteners.

"Override emergency, authorization DZ-143," the driver said suddenly. With that, the car jumped into motion and was soon speeding down the alley.

"I don't understand," said the man who had reassured Selah earlier. "What about the boy who needed prayer?"

Cade looked at him and then looked away, shaking his head as if he couldn't believe the man's naivety. "Nice work, Trajan," he called up to the driver, who was outfitted in a hazmat suit. "You have any trouble gettin' the other half to the drop point?"

"Nahh, man. Ever'ting's cool. Angel made it easy for us."

"What's going on?" the man said, alarmed. He seemed genuinely terrified, but the woman to Selah's right seemed ecstatic to be on a real adventure.

"Don't you get it? They're abducting the Stewmaker!" she said excitedly.

"I didn't sign up for this!" the man said worriedly. He turned to Selah. "I had no idea any of this was going to happen!" He turned to Cade. "Stop the car! Let her out!"

Cade turned to him with a dark expression. "What you signed up for was danger and excitement. Well, *this is it.*"

"But I want no part of this!" the man protested.

"Listen, circus freak! You is *in* this. You turn us in, we turn *you* in. Which will not work out well for you, since we have someone on the inside with connections. So keep ya mouth shut and forget what ya saw. Or I'll ask someone ta help ya forget," Cade said, his eyes glittering in the dim street lights.

"What about Cosmo?" Selah asked in the bravest voice she could muster.

"What about 'im?" Cade asked coldly.

"Isn't he your leader? Did he come up with this plan? Are you sure he would have wanted this?" Selah asked, her heart pounding.

"I don' know. You tell *me*," Cade said pointedly. "Cosmo been trustin' the wrong people, puttin' people's lives at risk—fa *what*? We don' know, cuz 'e won' tell the ones he shoulda been trustin'."

"Can you really trust this connection you have on the inside?" Selah ventured.

Cade whirled around in the seat to face her. "*No!* Of course not! But what choice do we have? Cosmo got us backed into a corner, with three of our own bein' held in a State prison, with no hope of escapin' without their brains bein' turned ta mush. That's where *you* come in. It's a trade. We bring 'er the Stewmakah, she lets our men go."

"Except that you can't trust her. How do you know she won't go back on her word?" Selah asked desperately.

"We *don't*, little girl. But we gotta do what we can. An' if'n I gotta slit her throat when she double crosses us, so be it."

Selah fell silent, her eyes darting around the cab of the vehicle. She was jammed in the middle of a group of four people. Even if she had attempted to jump into the third row of seats behind her, there were five more people crammed in that row who would impede her progress, and the doors were locked. There was nothing she could do—except pray. She tried to still her pounding heart. *"Jesus,"* she prayed silently, *"if I ever needed you, I need you now!"*

The car hurtled down the streets and passed into the Dead Zone, finally nearing a gate on the opposite side. "What's the gate doin' closed?" Cade asked the driver.

"It was open earlier," Trajan said. He slowed down. "Darken the windows," he said to the car's A.I. system. The windows automatically darkened.

Selah turned to the nervous man, who was sitting to her left, and whispered, "If the car can hear us, maybe we can ask it for help!"

"Don't try anything stupid," Cade said, having overheard her remark. "Even if ya did try ta git this car ta stop, it's only programmed to listen to the driver. An' jus' keep ya mouth shut when we git up there. I'm sure ya wouldn' want any o' ya friends in the outskirts ta have any problems with us Gateways."

Selah sank back into the seat. She didn't want anything happening to the others, and she was certain Cade wasn't bluffing, considering what they had done to Viv's father.

As the car pulled up to the gate, the guard motioned for Trajan to roll down the window. "You're really playing it safe with that suit," he said with a chuckle. "Are you worried about fog on a clear night like this?"

"Ever since the time my health implant stopped workin' right, I have sensitive lungs. They got damaged before I could get reimplanted. I can't take any chances in case the fog comes up sudden, like last time," said Trajan, in what could pass for a State accent.

"Your health implant stopped working? I've never heard of that happening!" the guard remarked.

"Yeah, those old implants are unreliable. That's why I'm gettin' the chip. It can let you know when something isn't working right," Trajan said. "Do you have it yet?" he added conversationally.

"No, I'm not really sold on it," the guard replied. "But they seem to be really pushing it these days."

"It's gonna make a huge difference for people like me," Trajan replied.

"I know they say it's a modern-day miracle, but it's hard for me to want to be first in line when they're being so aggressive with their marketing." The man leaned conspiratorially out the window of the guard station. "You know how we had so many people come down with pink eye when they first came out with 2nd Sight? Rumor is there was a conflict between it and Health 2. I don't think they always know what they're doing, you know? And they use us as guinea pigs."

Trajan tilted his head as if he was thinking about the possibility. "I don' know, man. The State has always taken good care o' me."

"Like how they took good care of you when your Health 1 failed?" the guard said skeptically, and then shook his head. "I'm sorry. We're all entitled to our own opinions, but I'm just saying you should think about it really hard before you get it."

"Sure," Trajan said. "You're probably right. I mean, you should always think things over real careful."

The guard leaned back into the station as if he was going to open the gate, and then stopped and leaned back out. "Say, you sure have been making a lot of trips back and forth tonight. Is everything ok? Do you need a bigger transport vehicle or something?"

"Nahh, this one works just fine. We just have some extra people at the clinic workin' late who needed a ride. I figured it would take too long to request a bigger transport."

"Well, when you're finished, would you mind returning this car to the guard station? I only loaned it to you the other day because the fog was so bad and you were on foot. If I don't have all my vehicles accounted for, I get written up," the man said.

"Oh, sure!" Trajan said apologetically. "Sorry if I caused you any trouble."

"No trouble yet. Just trying to avoid any in the future." The guard smiled and raised the gate. "Have a good night."

Trajan nodded and slowly drove through. After they were safely on the State side, Cade let out a *"Whew!"* and clapped Trajan on the back. "Man, you played that so cool! I didn' know you could sound like such a State baby."

"I been on the inside a few times. Ya hafta be able ta play the part, ya savvy?" Trajan replied casually, but inside the suit, he was trembling slightly.

A brief silence followed, and the man sitting to Selah's left shifted uncomfortably in his seat. "No one says 'man' anymore," divulged the nervous citizen.

"What'd ya say?" Cade asked.

"It's just…" the man began.

"Don't worry about it," the woman to Selah's right tried to reassure Cade. "Most people say 'Hume' these days instead of 'man.' He's just trying to shake you up. I still hear people use 'man'."

"When? On a fishing expedition? When they were trying to sound like someone from the outer docks?" the man said testily.

"It's nothing to worry about," the woman insisted as she placed a hand on Cade's arm in a familiar fashion. "Thank you for an incredible night! This is so much more than I paid for. But of course, tonight was free!"

"Yeah, about that," Cade said, "the show was free, but the transport is gonna cost ya."

The woman's expression soured and she withdrew her hand. "Well, that's not a very good way to do business," she snipped.

"Would you like me to hand you over to the authorities with the Stewmakah? I'm sure the State'll be interested in what business you had in the outer docks at *this* hour," Cade remarked, and silence filled the cab as the car continued its steady progress into the heart of the city.

Back at the guard station, the man on duty was making a call on his visor. "Yes, I'd like to report a possible Discard wearing a state-issued hazmat suit, impersonating clinic staff, driving a State vehicle, registered 3R587. Thank you."

39

Payton Hamby's feet made a crunching sound on the gravel road leading from his house to the Beardsley place. He had awakened early that Monday morning to the sound of someone banging on his front door. He had opened it to find Seth's son standing on the porch, his eyes frantic. "Dad needs your help," Zack said between gasps of air.

"What's wrong?" Payton asked, all his sleepiness gone in an instant.

"He said not to say anything, just to go get you." Zack bent over and put his hands on his knees, completely winded from his race to get there from the other side of the valley.

"Do we need to grab Doc Stratton?"

Zack shook his head, stood up and spit over the railing. Addy, who had been listening from inside, stepped onto the porch and offered him a tin cup of water. Zack took it gratefully and gulped it down. "I have to get back," he said with no further explanation and jumped down the porch steps, his long strides carrying him quickly through the yard and back down the road.

Addy and Payton looked at each other bewilderedly. "Well, I guess I'd better get moving," Payton said, his eyebrows raised. He went back inside to change out of his nightclothes.

"Should I go sound the alarm?" Addy asked.

"No. I think this must be a private matter," Payton said.

Addy's brow furrowed worriedly. "And…no doctor?"

"That's what he said," Payton replied. He smiled kindly at his wife as he buttoned his shirt. "Just pray."

Addy nodded, some of the worry leaving her face, and retreated into the sitting room by the chair where she always knelt to pray. As Payton left, he could hear her crying out to God. They didn't know what was wrong, but they had the attention of Someone Who did.

Much had happened in the months since Selah had left. The people of the valley were experiencing spiritual renewal. Many of them had rededicated their lives to the Lord, and some of them who had assumed they were Christians simply by being born into a Christian family realized they had never actually entered into a personal relationship with God.

An intensity was building. It had begun in the women's prayer meetings and had carried over into the regular services. As people were filled with the Holy Spirit, a hunger was growing within them. Sunday gatherings that used to last for an hour and a half, at most, went on for three or four hours, so that there was barely enough time to dismiss before the evening service. Prayer had become a priority instead of something people did as an afterthought or the fulfillment of what was expected of them. Parents spent more time praying over their children. Teachers prayed for their students. As the pastor of the little community, Payton had always faithfully lifted up each family before God in his morning prayer time. But recently, the majority of his prayers were centered on Seth Beardsley.

At first, Seth wanted nothing to do with what he called the community's ridiculous emotionalism. He had forbidden his family to attend the meetings after he had been to a service during which several people had been baptized in the Holy Spirit with the evidence of speaking in tongues. "It's nonsense!" he had sputtered, when Payton asked him what he thought.

"But, Brother Seth, it's in the Bible, right here in Acts the second chapter!" Payton had replied.

"That was for then, before people had the Bible readily available to them. It was something that happened in the early church and died with the apostles," Seth said between gritted teeth.

"Seth, do you think God would give His children a gift like that and then yank it away from them? Jesus, Himself, said that if we, being earthly fathers, know how to give good gifts to our children, how much more will He give the Holy Spirit to those who ask of Him,"[107] Payton had said gently.

---

[107] See Luke 11:11-13

"Don't twist the scriptures," Seth growled. "He was just talking about the Spirit He imparts to us when we give our lives to Him."

"Yes, yes, He is! It's the same Spirit. But why would He tell the disciples to wait in Jerusalem until they were given power from on high? The disciples already believed in Jesus and had given Him their lives. He had already breathed on them and told them to receive the Holy Spirit.[108] But He also told them that if He didn't leave them to be with His Father, the Comforter wouldn't come.[109] He said He wouldn't leave us orphans! He was going to give us another Helper to come alongside us and guide us—the Spirit of Truth.[110] If you could just experience the power and love you are given when the Holy Spirit manifests His presence in you, I think you would understand. It's better felt than tellt—er, told," Payton had said earnestly.

"You're wasting your breath on me, Pastor," Seth had said, and had stormed out of the building. It was several weeks before any of the Beardsley family were seen at church. And then one Sunday, Kiley and the children came back. Kiley confided to Addy that she had never nagged Seth about coming back to church. She had simply displayed the love of God she felt for her husband, even when he was being difficult. He had finally relented and told her she could go. Eventually, Seth had reappeared at a Sunday night service, ducking sheepishly in the back after everyone else was seated and leaving before everyone else so as to avoid any conversation. After a few such incidents, he began to come with his family again. No one ever mentioned his prior absence, but greeted him with a smile and a warm handshake. Seth seemed confused by the lack of criticism for his unexplained behavior, but kept attending. He always sat toward the back of the church, as if he was unwilling to be a participant, but too captivated to keep from coming. He seemed slightly agitated but almost wistful as he watched everyone else basking in the presence of God.

Last night, Payton had noticed him standing during the altar service, hands raised and tears streaming down his cheeks. He had felt that the man was on the point of a breakthrough in his relationship with the Lord. Perhaps this early

---

[108] See John 20:22
[109] See John 16:7
[110] See John 14:16-18

request for help had something to do with that. Perhaps Seth had been filled with the Spirit at home and was too astounded to understand exactly what had transpired.

Payton shook his head. That would explain the secrecy, but it didn't explain why he would've sent Zack over in such a rush. "Whatever it is, Lord, please help me to know what to do," Payton prayed, wishing he was in as good a shape as Zack so he could make the trip in half the time it was taking. When he arrived, everything appeared to be normal, except that Sadie was waiting outside on the porch, looking down the road. When she saw him, she went inside and then hurried back out and ran up the road to meet him. "Sadie, is everything ok?" Payton asked.

Sadie's eyes had the same unsettled look that Zack's had held earlier. "I don't know," she replied truthfully.

"Is it your dad? Your mom? Did something happen to someone?" Payton asked hurriedly.

"No. It's—" she stopped and looked at him anxiously. "There's someone here."

"What do you mean? Who is it?"

"I don't know. He's not from here," she said, her young face fraught with worry.

"Not from here? Where is he from? Is he someone from the Old Country?"

"I don't know, exactly. But he's dressed in this crazy outfit that can make him disappear," Sadie said.

"Now, Sadie," Payton began.

"No, it's true!" she insisted. "Well, maybe not disappear, but it makes it easy for him to hide. And he had some sort of weapons."

Payton's heart skipped a beat. "Did he threaten you?" he asked apprehensively.

"Oh, no!" Sadie said quickly. "He gave over his weapons as soon as he got here. He's asking for help. But Daddy wanted you to be here."

Payton began jogging toward the house, his mind flooded with questions. When he opened the door, Zack ducked his head out of the kitchen. "He's here, Mom," the young man said nervously.

Kiley stepped out of the kitchen, a platter of sausages in her hands. "Come in, Brother Hamby. We're all in here, just having a little breakfast," she said at an attempt at normalcy.

Payton removed his hat and walked into the kitchen, Sadie following at his heels. Seth was seated at the table, facing the doorway, with Denali on his lap. "Brother Seth, I understand we have a visitor?" Payton said confusedly, looking around the room. At that moment, the air around the seat beside Payton seemed to ripple, and he suddenly realized the chair was not empty, as he had previously surmised. He jumped back as a man's face appeared directly in front of him.

"Hello, sir," the floating head said politely.

"Brother Payton, this is Tyrell. He's from the Old Country," Seth said in a voice that was strangely sedate.

"I'm sorry if I startled you. It's a camo suit. Standard issue for my unit. I forgot I was still wearing the hood!" The man took down the hood, exposing the back of his head. Payton couldn't help but stare. The suit seemed to have an intelligence all its own, changing its appearance to blend in with its surroundings. "I know this must seem unbelievable to all of you. There are a lot of things where I'm from that would probably be hard for you to believe. But something just happened to me, and I need your help."

Payton stared at Tyrell, and then he stared at Seth, temporarily speechless. Finally, he found his voice. "Y-you need *our* help?" Payton stuttered. What could a community with no electricity, no communication devices, and one shotgun offer that would help a man who came from a society where clothes could think for themselves?

Seth held Denali protectively as the girl stared, wide-eyed, at the man across the table from her. "Go ahead, Tyrell. Why don't you tell him what you told me?" Seth said with an eerie calm.

"Please, sit down," Kiley said in a voice that seemed unnaturally cheerful, pulling out a chair for Payton next to Tyrell. "The pancakes are getting cold."

Payton sat down, and the family cautiously slid into their seats, all eyes on the visitor. "Brother Payton, would you return thanks?" Seth asked.

"Of course," Payton replied, although he had to admit to himself that he was reluctant to close his eyes.

"Lord, we thank you for this food and for this unexpected guest. Please bless this food and help us to have wisdom in all our…ways," Payton said awkwardly.

The family opened their eyes, but no one seemed interested in eating. No one, that is, except for Tyrell. He looked at the stack of pancakes and then picked it up with his hands, taking a bite out of it like a sandwich, resulting in an eruption of giggles from Denali.

"Not like that, silly!" Denali said, squirming on her father's knees.

"Denali, that isn't polite," Kiley said, but she couldn't hide her amused smile.

"Am I doing it wrong?" Tyrell asked. He looked to Denali for help. "How am I supposed to do it?"

Denali grinned like a possum and grabbed the butter dish. She cut off a few squares of butter and flopped them onto her pancakes, smearing them around the golden-brown surface with a fork.

"Denali, that's way too much butter," Kiley protested.

Seth looked up at his wife and grinned cautiously. "It's fine, Ki," he said reassuringly. It was the first time Payton had seen the man grin in a long time. But even Seth had to protest when Denali reached for the maple syrup. "Good heavens, Denali!" he exclaimed, as the girl drenched her stack in a river of syrup and then pushed both the syrup pitcher and the butter across the table to their guest.

Tyrell followed suit and then watched as Denali cut off a mouthful of pancakes and chewed ferociously. "Mmmmmm! Delicious!" she said enthusiastically after she had swallowed.

Tyrell took a bite of his properly prepared pancakes, his eyes widening in surprise. He nodded his head appreciatively as he chewed. "Mmmmmm! Delicious!" he mimicked Denali. Everyone around the table laughed, and the atmosphere softened. Soon they were all eating breakfast as Tyrell relayed his tale.

"As Seth was saying, I'm from the State—or the Old Country, as you call it. I was sent on a mission to find what my superiors believe is an isolationist outpost. But during my reconnaissance—my searching, that is—I began to have these strange dreams. Sometimes they would even happen when I was awake. At first, I thought my chip was malfunctioning. And maybe it was, because I was having trouble connecting to the internet. But the longer I was away from the State, the more I began to look forward to the dreams, or visions, or whatever you might call them. And although I was searching for *isolationists,*" he hesitated and looked at them apologetically.

"Tell the story," Seth said firmly, his eyes narrowing.

"Well, I began to get the feeling that I should really be looking for something else. The longer I had time to think without the State in my head, the more I felt like I was incomplete—like a puzzle with a missing piece. So I was going down this road on my hoverbike—" he paused as the expressions around the table revealed they had no idea what he was talking about. "It's like a motorcycle, except without wheels," he tried to explain.

"Huh?" Denali asked.

"Do you know what a motorcycle is?"

Denali rolled her eyes. "Of *course!* Zack has a toy one he gave to me when he stopped playing with it. It used to be Daddy's and before that it was Grampa's and—"

"Thank you, Denali," Seth interrupted. "Eat your pancakes."

Denali twisted around and gave her father a reproachful look. "How's it *go* if it ain't got no wheels?" she asked.

"Doesn't have any," Kiley corrected her. "You heard your father. Eat your pancakes." But then she turned to Tyrell and looked at him questioningly. "How *does* it go?" she echoed.

"It has powerful internal fans that push it off of the ground, almost like it's floating. And I was traveling at a high rate of speed down one of the old roads just north of here when suddenly everything turned bright—like when you look at the sun. I covered my eyes and lost control of the bike and fell off. I was thrown about a hundred yards down the road and knocked unconscious. That's when I had the most intense one of those dreams I was telling you about." Tyrell's voice quavered, and he cleared his throat, his eyes turning red.

"Are ya chokin'?" asked Denali. "Here, have a drink of my apple juice."

Tyrell smiled and shook his head. "I'm fine. It's just—what I saw," he fell silent as he was overcome with emotion.

"Take your time," Payton said encouragingly.

Tyrell regained his composure and continued. "I saw a man riding a white horse. His eyes seemed to penetrate me—like lasers cutting through flesh and bone into the center of my being. He was wearing crowns on His head—I know it sounds crazy, but He was wearing several crowns at the same time. He was wearing a robe that was drenched in—" at this point, Tyrell stopped and looked questioningly from Seth to Denali.

"Go ahead. You're not going to scare her," he said.

"It was soaked in blood."

Sadie and Zack looked at each other with raised eyebrows, but Denali seemed unphased. "That's not scary. I seen lotsa blood before, like when Daddy and Pastor butchered that mean old bull. Daddy got it all over his shirt, and –"

"Denali, let the man talk," Seth said exasperatedly.

"His robe…it had words on it. I was too afraid to look to see what they said, but all of a sudden, He was right in front of me. In the dream, I could barely move. I looked up, and I saw the words: *King of Kings and Lord of Lords*. And behind the man, I could see a huge army dressed in white uniforms. They were riding white horses. I was shaking so hard I couldn't control myself. Then the commander of the army said, *'Whom do you seek?'* And I couldn't answer Him, because I was so terrified. But I thought to myself, 'I have to warn the citizens of the State that there really *is* a threat out here in the Preserve.' And as I lay there on the ground, my hands shielding my face, I could feel His penetrating eyes. I knew then that there was no place anyone could hide from *Him*. My whole life flashed before my eyes, and it was humbling, because I could see how much of it had been centered on myself. The State says that's what you *should* do— that you are entitled to a life of happiness, and you can get it by depending on the State for everything. But as I lay there under His burning gaze, I realized it was all wrong. My life was empty, and the government had been lying to me the whole time. I was suddenly aware of all the emptiness I had been trying to fill by my service to the State. And then He said it again: *'Whom do you seek?'* And I was finally able to speak. I told Him I didn't know, but I knew I was looking for *something*. His eyes were still burning into me, revealing to me everything I had ever done. I had broken some great law I didn't understand, and there was no way I could pay for it. I couldn't stand it anymore. *'Please, have mercy!'* I begged

Him. And then He called me by name. I looked up, and the army was gone. It was just the two of us, and His eyes were full of compassion. They were the same eyes, but now I could see that even though they had such great power to see everything about me, they were also filled with great love. The commander of that great army stood before me, and He was holding out His hand. And then He said something strange: 'I have paid a great ransom for you. Your debt is paid. The charges against you have been dropped.' I couldn't believe it. I felt such relief! When I asked Him who He was, He said His name was Jesus. I swore allegiance to Him right there on the old road. He told me exactly how to find this place. He told me there were people here who could help me understand what had just happened to me. And then I woke up. When I looked around, the bike was completely wrecked. I don't know how I survived, but there wasn't even a scratch on me. In the past, I would have run a diagnostic on myself to make certain I hadn't been hallucinating. But after the incident, my chip didn't seem to be working correctly. I had no contact at all with the State and no access to the internet. I had no GPS—that means a global positioning system—it's the way we navigate. It's done through satellites, and it keeps everyone from ever being lost. I'm used to depending on all of that technology, but it was suddenly just *gone*. Basically, I was traveling blind, and I felt so helpless. I got up and started walking, following the directions given to me by the commander of the army. As I walked, I realized all the State was telling us was a sham. I began to think about what the commander had said, and I realized I didn't feel empty anymore. The State fills our heads with so much information all the time that we never have time to think. I know I have to get back and tell the other soldiers in my unit about what happened to me. But first I followed the directions the commander had given me, and I came to this house."

There was dead quiet in the room, except for Denali's smacking. Payton looked over at Seth, whose eyes were boring a hole into his plate of cold pancakes.

"It reminds me of the story of Saul on the road to Damascus," Payton remarked.

"Yes," Seth said slowly, his gaze raising to the man in the invisible suit. "Pastor Hamby, may I have a word with you in private?" he said, setting Denali down and walking out of the kitchen into the living room.

Payton remembered when Selah had fled the valley, her missionary journey undoubtedly spurred on by the threat that had been made to lock her in an abandoned cabin for observation after she had been filled with the Holy Spirit. Seth had led the charge on the witch-hunt, his suspicious nature bleeding over into the other members of the board. Surely now he would show his true colors, suggesting the man should be locked up until they decided what to do with him. But for a few moments, he simply stared out the window, as if he was so overwhelmed he couldn't find his words.

Payton looked back toward the kitchen, where he could hear Kiley attempting to make light conversation. He turned back to Seth, and when he spoke, he did so with caution and diplomacy, doing everything he could to keep from escalating the tension. "I'm glad you called me over here, Brother Seth. I assume you wanted some input on what should be done in this situation, since we've never faced it before. There's no denying the man has had an encounter with Christ. The dream he had was right out of Revelation 19. I think we need to handle this carefully, but in love. He was sent to us for help." He stopped and watched Seth, who was swallowing uncomfortably, his eyes now keeping a careful vigil on the kitchen door. "Well, brother Seth?" Payton asked in a low voice.

Seth's gaze shifted to Payton and he slicked his hair back with a trembling hand. "There's only one thing to do, Payton, and you know it."

40

THE slanting light of evening glazed the gray-bricked office buildings of Equality Avenue in warm, golden tones. Ainsley stared at the shifting colors on the deserted street, preferring to view what was actually happening in the outside world than to let her chip define reality. Not that she enjoyed the view. But one who controlled other peoples' realities could not allow themselves the luxury of a world that was tailored to her whims by the power of a chip. She had to be aware of what was transpiring in the external world, however drab or uninviting it might be. Ainsley detested the monotone colors of the State. When she was in charge, she would find a way to infuse color into the self-repairing bricks. Of course, the chip would be mandatory, and people would see things as she wanted them to be seen. She smiled smugly. Even so, the outside world would still be designed to her specifications.

She couldn't do it on her own, but she had people in place in administration —people whose minds she could overrun in an instant. Once they were programmed properly, she would have all the help she needed. Thanks to Moses and Ira, she was ever so close to being able to flex her mental muscles as the source of thought for a nation. And why stop there? She had the upper hand, so she would use it as she infiltrated global government. A rush of power sent shivers of delight through her solar plexus. Another emotion lapped at the edges of her consciousness. It was relief, she realized, although she would never admit it to anyone.

When she had absolute power, no one would ever be able to dominate her, making her feel trapped as she did when she was a small girl hiding under the covers. There had been plenty of things to hide from in the house where she grew up. Grown-ups who came to perform Satanic rites with her parents were only part of the problem. Supernatural visitors that were invited into her home had often frequented her bedroom, terrifying her with their presence. Surely when she was in control, even *they* would have to acknowledge that she was a force with which to be reckoned. She would no longer have to worry about her parents sending their emissaries of darkness to enforce their will, because *she* would be calling the shots. If anyone controlled such power, *she* would.

Soon she would meet with her friends in government and begin the takeover. Although she had complained to Moses about the recent mass pseudo-link fiasco, it actually worked to her advantage. Many leaders would work with her willingly out of concern for the possibility of future, more malevolent cyber threats. She sniffed in amusement as she thought of the incredible gift Craig Goforth had been given, and how he had wasted it by preaching ancient mythology. She would deal with Craig and Ira—and even Moses—soon. But first there was something she could no longer ignore. There was a power growing in the outer docks.

As a child, she had been very sensitive to the spiritual world. Her parents had noticed this sensitivity and had watched her for signs of the presence of demonic beings, with which they would then cultivate a relationship in hopes of harnessing their power. As the lesser demons pretended to do their bidding, Ainsley could see the higher-ranking forces in a Satanic army influencing her parents' thoughts, emotions, and motives. At times, she would see her parents turn on each other, erupting in physical violence. At other times, they would cause themselves bodily harm with self-inflicted wounds; and all the while, the demons stood by, watching in amusement. Once, she had awakened from a nightmare to see one of the smaller ones crouched in the corner of her room, ready to pounce. Suddenly, a demon with more clout had manifested and forbidden the attack. *"This one is not for you!"* it had hissed. *"This one is destined for greater things."* As the lesser demon writhed in agony from its punishment, the tormentor turned its head slightly and grinned maliciously at her. The memory was emblazoned in her mind. She determined that she would never be controlled as her parents had been. She knew that the demons always lied, and her parents had bought into it, thinking they were the masters, when they were really only puppets. Ainsley promised herself that *she* would find a way to be the master, and it wouldn't involve making deals with demons. She would find a way to grow her own power until it became absolute.

But because she could sense the presence of power, the events in the outskirts of the outer docks had not escaped her notice. The Stewmaker was given a certain level of respect, even by Cosmo. Ainsley had done a little digging, and no one knew where she had come from. She had a huge following, and although most of it was probably because of the free meals she was handing out, Ainsley sensed there was something more. And then, of course, there was the very fact that she somehow had access to an unlimited supply of food. There was no way a Discard could come up with that kind of supply without some sort of connections. She had to be working with someone in power. But to what end? And with whom?

It was time to have a chat with the woman. Whether she was a Discard or a State imposter, perhaps they could form an alliance—one that at least *appeared* to be mutually beneficial. As long as the Stewmaker's backer wasn't too high up in administration, Ainsley could always pull some strings and have her chipped, take over her programming, and then the woman's following could be hers. She laughed. If chipping became mandatory, they would *all* become her followers, like it or not. But still, there was something thrilling in the deception.

The shadows had begun to lengthen. It had only been a few minutes since Creep and Trajan had returned the first group of thrill seekers from their little jaunt into the outskirts. Ainsley had provided a shuttle for the customers at the drop point so Trajan could make a quick return to the docks for her primary target. Having Creep be involved in the first transport was Cade's idea. He was fairly certain his loyalty lay with Cosmo, and he had instructed Trajan to drop him off at the gang headquarters on the way back with the pretense of assisting Cosmo with whatever had come up. Of course, very few people knew that what had come up was a coup, and Cosmo was being held for Cade to deal with later. Cade had left his cronies with instructions on how to deal with Creep. If he saw things their way, he could stay and join ranks. If not, he might end up supplying the main course for a celebratory barbecue.

Ainsley leaned back against the building behind her. It would be another hour before they arrived with the Stewmaker. There was plenty of time to do a little research into the genius behind the mass pseudo-link. Craig's higher brain activity was minimal due to the drugs Moses was administering, so his systems might be a little sluggish, but she was certain she could discover something if she just poked around his neural net. A sneer distorted her elegant features. Moses had insisted they not attempt a link with the man until twenty-four hours after the drugs had been reduced. He planned to disrupt the pseudo-link with the drugs and then gradually taper them off so as not to impede Craig's brain function permanently. He wanted to deal with Craig once he became conscious, giving the man's brain time to heal from his recent chip implant and the onslaught of chemicals they had just introduced into the mix. "We've stopped the link. That's the important thing," Moses had said. "We can't risk leaving him permanently impaired by bombarding his mind with any new intrusions at this point." That was one of the things they had been arguing about just before Moses terminated her employment. Well, now she had some time to kill, and there was no one to stop her from doing a little exploring on her own. She folded her arms and smiled as she leaned her head back against the wall and closed her eyes. This could be an interesting ride.

She recessed into the quietude of her inner world, making a quick perusal of her systems. Everything was operating satisfactorily. Her dopamine levels were a little higher than normal, but that was due to the anticipation of what she was about to do. With a smile curving her lips, she concentrated on Craig Goforth's mind. She felt the electronic jump one always experienced during the navigation of digital networks required to complete the journey to the mind of another individual, and then she was standing in the familiar neutral ground that existed outside of every implanted person's neural boundary. But even though she knew she was in the right location, she could see no boundary.

She strained to see details in the unfamiliar panorama. An unearthly light was glowing in the distance that stretched before her. A mist was rising, partially obscuring her view, but she thought she could make out shapes of trees silhouetted against the light. Where was the neural wall? She took a step forward and was immediately struck down with such force that she blacked out. When she regained consciousness, she was once again on the sidewalk on a sleepy side street of the State, her body slumped on the ground beside the wall of the building. She blinked as the world came back into focus. *"What just happened?"* she wondered as she tried to regain her bearings. It was as if an electrical surge had occurred, jolting her out of her attempt to link. She assessed her surroundings, as one should always do when retreating into their mindscape. Nothing had changed since her first assessment before the attempt. There was no one there who could have delivered some sort of outside force to have caused such a violent disruption. With steel-willed determination, she closed her eyes and attempted once again to focus on Craig. She found herself at the same hazy location. As before, light glowed in the distance, and mist-shrouded trees blocked her view of the source of light. This time, she did not step forward, but stood still, scanning the area where the boundary should have been. Something was there. She hadn't sensed it at first because she had been so focused on her intent of penetrating Goforth's mindscape. It was hard to pinpoint, but it was definitely there; and it was immense and incredibly powerful. She trembled, in spite of her best efforts to maintain her composure, and stepped backwards. The spiritual beings she had encountered as a child had evoked different feelings when she sensed their proximity. Some instilled fear. Others, lust. Some seemed harmless or even friendly, but always ended up giving her ideas that got her into trouble. They all seemed to have their own agenda, whether veiled or blatantly displayed, and the end result of interacting with them was a sickening feeling that you had been used, duped, or violated in some manner. Whatever this creature was, it did not have the same presence. And while its power terrified her, unlike the others, it did not seem predatory in nature. She swallowed, and respectfully took another step backward. "Who's there?" she asked tentatively.

The mist dissipated slightly, and Ainsley gasped as she saw the outline of a massive wing. The light coming from the distance reflected off the surface of a drawn sword. The creature was much larger than she had assumed, and its eyes were focused on her. A voice thundered across the horizon. "I gave you warning. Keep your distance."

Ainsley flinched and took another step back. "I meant no disrespect." she said carefully. "I didn't see you earlier."

The creature unfurled its wings to their full length, and Ainsley was reminded of a whip uncoiling and snapping. The mist swirled and parted so that more of the being was revealed, and she could see it was wearing a warrior's garb. "May I ask who you are?" she said in her politest voice.

"I am Asaf, gatherer of the people."

"What people?"

"Those who have been invited to hear good news."

"Who was invited? I don't know about any good news. I didn't receive an invitation."

Asaf regarded her coldly. "You have a different agenda, one that is in direct opposition to ours."

Ainsley peered apprehensively into the fog behind the creature. "Ours? Are there more of you?"

The creature smiled slightly, and Ainsley thought she detected a faint laugh. "There are. Although I am not referring only to beings of my type."

Ainsley frowned. "What do you mean?"

"The citizens of our kingdom are as numberless as the sands of the sea," Asaf said, and Ainsley noticed a certain regalness in his bearing.

"What kingdom?" she asked tentatively. She did not like the direction this conversation was heading.

"The kingdom of the God of the Angel Armies, the Lord of all the universe …the Ancient of Days," Asaf answered, and there was a resonance in his voice that filled her with awe. She was silent for a moment as she took in the meaning of what had just been said.

"You mean, he's real?"

Asaf stared at her as if she were completely without brain function, and then his expression softened to one of pity. "Most certainly," he replied.

Ainsley was overcome with an onslaught of emotions varying from fear to sadness and even rage. "If he's real, then why have I never encountered any of you before? Why didn't you come to help me when I needed it? Isn't he purported to be the defender of the helpless? Is the reason I never got an invitation because he knew who I would become and wanted nothing to do with me? Don't you think I might have been different if he had rescued me as a child?" the words gushed out before she could think to stop them, and she was instantly irritated at herself for losing her composure.

Asaf tilted his head as if he were studying her. "Actually, you *were* sent a personal invitation nearly twenty-one years ago."

Ainsley scowled fiercely. "I have no idea what you're talking about. If it was sent, I certainly never received it."

"You *did* receive it. But your parents did not approve. They slandered the character of the person who bore the invitation. Eventually, you chose to believe your parents, even though you knew how often they had lied to you in the past."

"I don't remember anyone giving me an invitation. It didn't happen," Ainsley insisted fiercely, for a moment forgetting the magnitude of the creature before her.

"You don't remember when you were nine years old, and a classmate told you about Jesus?"

And then it all came back to her. She was in the fourth grade. It was during recess, and she was standing against the wall of the school building by herself on the playground, watching some other girls play the hand-clapping game, *Miss Gary Jack.* Suddenly she realized someone was standing beside her. She turned to see Evoka Jones, the shyest girl in the class, looking as if she wanted to say something and positively terrified at the prospect of it.

"What?" Ainsley had snapped.

"Hi, Ainsley," Evoka managed to say in a voice just above a whisper.

"Oh. Hi. What do you want?" Ainsley asked.

The girl's eyes drifted to the hand-clapping game in progress. "It looks like fun, doesn't it?" she asked.

"I don't know. I guess so. Maybe." Ainsley had never been invited to play *Miss Gary Jack.* Classmates often avoided her. There were rumors that her parents were not just Satanists in name only, but that they actually believed in a celestial power other than the Source. She stared at the girl, who seemed pale and frail in the bright sunshine. "Why are you talking to me?"

Evoka swallowed nervously. "Have you ever heard of Jesus?" she asked.

Ainsley's forehead wrinkled in confusion. "Well, yeah. If you mean that guy we learned about in history class who started some ancient religion. He was put to death, and some people said he came back to life. So some people started believing he was God, or something. Why?"

A shadow of fear passed over Evoka's face, and then she seemed to rally. "Did you know that He actually *did* rise from the grave?"

Ainsley rolled her eyes and turned back to the hand-clapping game. "That isn't possible. At least, not in that time. They didn't have all the stuff we have these days—all the technology that can make it happen."

There was a pause as Evoka tried to choose her words carefully. "He didn't need technology to make it happen, because He was the Son of God," she said softly.

Ainsley twisted her head around and gawked at her. She had just committed a federal crime, right there on the playground. And then suddenly Evoka seemed filled with some kind of power beyond herself. Ainsley could sense it, although she didn't understand where it was coming from. There weren't any demons around. She immediately did a check of the playground perimeter, and although there were some spiritual beings in the vicinity, she sensed no malicious intent.

"He came because He knew we were in trouble. He knew we needed someone to save us," Evoka was saying. "So He came and gave His life to pay for our sins. He loves all of us, and all we have to do to be saved is to ask for His forgiveness and invite Him to come live in our hearts."

"Sins? Son of God? Are you *crazy?"* Ainsley asked in a harsh whisper. "Don't you know what happens to people who talk like that?"

Evoka's gaze fell, but then she straightened herself and lifted her chin bravely. "I don't care. You're worth it."

Ainsley started to open her mouth to say something, but then stopped. What did she mean, she was worth it? So far as she knew, she wasn't even a blip on anyone's social radar.

Her thoughts were interrupted by the girls who were playing the game. "Hey, Ainsley!" one of the girls, named Jossamelle, called, "Why don't you come play with us?"

Ainsley's heart jumped. "Uh, I don't know how to—"

"Don't worry! We'll teach you," said Jossamelle's friend, Artemis.

Without a backward glance at Evoka, Ainsley scrambled through the rubber-chipped surface under the jungle gym where the girls were holding their game. Jossamelle beckoned for her to sit down. "Okay. First, you do this," she demonstrated, and guided Ainsley through the first set of moves. Within a few minutes, she had Ainsley snapping and slapping hands and knees in rhythm like an old pro. "Now, we'll add the words," the girl said with a mischievous smile. As the hand slapping began, the girls began to chant, "Miss Gary Jack-diddy-ack, diddy-ack, all dressed in black diddy-ack diddy-ack, with Satan's devils diddy-evils diddy-evils all down her back diddy-ack, diddy-ack, she went upstairs diddy-airs diddy airs to ask her mother diddy-other diddy-other for a black cat diddy-at diddy-at to sacrifice diddy-ice diddy-ice…"

Ainsley had stopped participating at the mention of Satan. She knew the rhyme well, and she knew what was happening. The girls had stopped singing and were nearly doubled over laughing. Ainsley could feel the rage boiling within her, but she gave them a bright smile. "Wow, you made new words for it!" she said sweetly. "Can I show you my version?" she looked back and forth at the two, blinking innocently as if she really didn't get their joke.

They glanced at each other in disbelief at her naivety. "Sure, Ainsley. We'd love to hear it," Jossamelle said, barely stifling a laugh.

Ainsely smiled. "Okay. But first, you have to sit close together, so I can play with both of you at the same time."

The girls scooched together, and Ainsley held up her hands. "Are you ready?" she asked.

They nodded. Ainsley looked at her right hand and drew it far to the side.

"Oh, that isn't right. You're doing it wrong," said Artemis.

With a mighty swing of her arm, Ainsley's hand sliced through the air and slapped both girls on their faces in one giant arc. "No, I wasn't," she said, as the girls gasped and grabbed their reddened cheeks. She got up and dusted herself off. They would tattle on her, of course, but it was worth it. She turned back to the wall of the school building where Evoka had been waiting, but the girl was gone. She wished Evoka could have seen what happened. The girl had said she was worth something, even if she was misguided in her spirituality; and Ainsley found herself wishing she could have shared the moment with her. Where had she gone?

The bell sounded, signaling the end of recess, and she wouldn't see Evoka until they were back in class, where the shy girl was sitting at her desk in the front row.

Ainsley wondered if maybe she could be her friend. After all, they didn't have to believe the same things to be friends; and Evoka had cared enough about her to do something truly daring. As class went on, Ainsley found she couldn't stop thinking about the verbal exchange between herself and the timid classmate. Evoka had risked much to say what she believed and to present it as absolute truth. What if there was something to it? There had been something in the air when she was speaking...something in her voice.

"Ainsley Abbot," said a voice over the intercom. "Please report to the principal's office."

The teacher stared hard at Ainsley. "Go on," she said sternly.

Ainsley slid out of her seat and headed toward the door, only to trip and nearly fall on her face. She turned around in time to see Jossamelle quickly pulling her foot back under her desk. "Ohh, be *careful,*" Jossamelle said with mock concern.

Ainsley got up slowly and gave the girl a long, steady look. "I know where you dream," she said, with narrowed eyes. It had the desired effect, as Jossamelle cringed and seemed to shrink in her seat. Half of the class was convinced she could cast spells and wouldn't hesitate to do it if she were provoked.

"Ainsley, stop procrastinating and get to the principal's office," the teacher said in her no-nonsense voice.

Ainsley gave the girl a saccharine smile and mouthed the words, *"See you later,"* as she turned to go. She looked at Evoka as she walked past her desk, but the girl's eyes were riveted to her book. Later that evening, Ainsley's parents questioned her about her visit to the principal's office. Ainsley had been told she would receive after-school detention and was at first instructed to provide both a verbal *and* a written apology to the girls who had been brutalized by her "vicious attack," as they had reported it. But Ainsley had played the State's game of equality of religion perfectly. "As a member of the church of Satan, I am expected to take part in certain acts which the general population may not understand," she had told the principal.

The principal had raised her eyebrows. "Ainsley, are you aware that the only true supernatural power in the universe is the Source? All religions are simply an expression of the divine energy created by every living thing."

"Oh, yes, of course, I understand that," Ainsley had agreed emphatically. "But I have a right to practice what I believe about the nature of the Source as long as I don't try to force other people to join my particular religion."

The principal seemed to consider what she said. "Yes, that is correct. But you must also take into account that you cannot use your religion to hurt other people. And you *did* hurt Artemis and Jossamelle when you slapped them in the face."

Ainsley looked down in mock attrition. "Oh, I didn't realize. I was just doing what I thought my religion would want me to do."

The principal stared at her strangely. "From all I've read about Satanism, it's a very benevolent faith, where diverse people groups have always been accepted with no questions asked. That doesn't seem to match your behavior on the playground today."

Ainsley thought a moment and rebounded. "Actually, it does. Those girls were making fun of my belief. They made up a rhyme to make fun of it. I didn't think it was fair." She looked at the principal with pleading in her eyes. "Oh, Principal Aziz, I have to tell you that I lied to you just now. I know my faith wouldn't want me to hit other people. But when those girls made fun of what I believe, it made me so upset! I just lost control. I didn't think it was right that they would do that to someone, just because what someone else believes is different from *their* beliefs." She completed the lie with artificial tears she was able to plumb from somewhere deep in her reserve of emotions she always held in check.

It worked. The principal straightened in her chair and glanced at the intercom button. "I knew there must be another side to this story," she said. She looked almost apologetically at Ainsley. "Now, I *must* require you to write an apology for the slapping incident. But I will *not* require you to give the verbal apology. Of course, your parents will be informed that you will receive after-school detention. I will get to the bottom of this, and all guilty parties will participate in a satisfactory resolution."

"Oh, no, Principal Aziz, that won't be necessary," Ainsley said, still sniffling slightly.

The woman smiled comfortingly at her. "Ainsley, by school policy, I *must* inform your parents you have detention so that they can arrange for transportation."

"Oh, it isn't that. It's just," she paused for dramatic effect. "I don't mind giving those girls a verbal apology. I know that they only did it because they don't understand my beliefs. I was thinking maybe I could invite them to some of our meetings so they could learn about it for themselves."

The principal looked at her, dumbfounded, and then suddenly smiled. "You know, I think that's a marvelous idea. I'm going to suggest that to their parents. Now, you run on back to class. Your detention will start tomorrow so that your parents will have time to plan for it."

"Thank you, Principal Aziz," Ainsley smiled gratefully. "And thank you for the chance to explain my family's way of believing in the Source."

Principal Aziz shook her head, amazed at the girl's apparent maturity for her age. She decided that Jossamelle and Artemis would be required to complete sensitivity training, which was held on Saturdays. She would suggest strongly to their parents that they attend one of the meetings held at Ainsley's house, but she would leave the final decision up to them.

When Ainsley explained to her parents why she had been sent to the principal's office, she was surprised by their reaction. "We *know* why you went to the office. What we don't know is why you would do something like that," her father said with a glare.

Ainsley's mouth dropped open. "I thought…" she began, but faltered. Her homelife had always been conducted by a confusing mixture of fear and praise.

"You thought we would approve of the way you handled those girls?" her father offered. He looked at her mother and shook his head. "It's like she hasn't been getting any of the stuff we're teaching her."

"She's getting some of it," her mother reassured him with a smirk. "But some things have to be taught by more than just example." She turned to Ainsley and looked at her seriously. "Baby, when you get in a situation like that, you just have to learn to stuff your feelings down so they don't explode. You have to learn to treat those people as if they were your best friends on earth."

"Well, I did, for a few seconds, before I let them have it," Ainsley protested.

"And that was good," her mother conceded, "But—"

"I thought you said Christians were stupid for doing that," Ainsley interrupted. "I thought you said they were weak for letting people walk all over them and being nice to people who treated them like trash." Ainsley was completely confused by her parents' apparent change of tactics.

"And they *are* weak and stupid. I'm not saying you should be like that. We're just trying to teach you that if you had kept up your act for a few days, or even a few weeks, you could have done so much *more*. You need to put up a good front, even if you hate someone," her mother said.

"*Especially* if you hate them," her father added. "In order to steer people in the direction you want them to go, you sometimes have to pretend you think they're wonderful, even when you think they're idiots. If you get them to want you around because you tell them what they want to hear, you'll learn more about their weaknesses and what they crave. You can use that information to make them do what you want. All you have to do is lie a little, and pretty soon you'll have them eating out of your hand," her father explained.

"Oh," Ainsley said, as her parents' cunning became clear. She wondered why she hadn't thought of that. But something was nagging at the back of her mind. "Do you really think that *all* Christians are weak and stupid?" she asked, remembering how Evoka had shown such bravery by telling her what she believed on the playground.

Ainsley's father leaned forward in his seat and fixed her with his gaze. "Of course they are, Ainsel. They serve a god who won't let them have any fun. Their religion has all these rules about what you can or can't do. If you're not good enough, you can't get into Heaven, although I'm not sure why you would want to go. Heaven is going to be boring. But Hell—" at this, he threw back his head and laughed and slapped his leg, "Hell is where the *real* party is."

Ainsley wasn't sure what to think. Most of her classmates didn't believe in a Heaven or Hell. They were taught that when you died, you became one with the Source. It was supposed to be a wonderful experience, when you would know everything and be at peace with everything that had ever happened to you and with everyone who had died and already joined the energy force. If her classmates were right, would people just float around all day? Would they have any control over where they went or what they did, or would they just be part of some huge conglomerate of souls?

"Ainsel, are you listening?" her mother was asking. "Is there a reason you asked us about Christians?"

Ainsley wondered if she should just keep quiet about Evoka. The girl seemed genuine. Even if she may not have been extremely bright, she had shown concern for her by telling her what she believed, even though it was at great risk to herself. "No reason," Ainsley said.

Her mother smiled at her with her mouth, but her eyes were dark and serious. "Now, Ainsley, you know how we feel about you lying to *other* people. But with *us*, it must always be the truth. Why were you asking about Christians? Did you find out someone at school is one of *them?*"

The last time Ainsley's parents had caught her in a lie, they had sent her to live with her Uncle Zeb for a few days. Thinking she was going on a vacation, Ainsley had looked forward to the visit. Uncle Zeb wasn't a member of the church of Satan, so there wouldn't be any of the scary satanic rites going on, and there would be cousins to play with. But once her parents dropped her off, she had realized something wasn't right. Her cousins seemed afraid of their father. Although he didn't knowingly consort with demons, they seemed to always be hanging around, influencing his decisions. At first, her cousins helped her hide whenever Zeb was drunk. But then she found they would take out their frustrations on anyone they felt was weaker than they, reenacting all the horrible things their father had done to them. She was now filling that position, and she wasn't certain which was worse, her cousins or the possibility of what her uncle might do. When Zeb threatened them if they didn't reveal her whereabouts, she could hear them coming. She scrambled out of her hiding place under the pile of dirty clothes in the corner and climbed out the window. A city bus was rumbling toward the bus stop at the corner, and she made a run for it, barely catching it before it left the stop. She had been only too glad to make it back home. "There's a girl in my class who believes that way," she found herself saying, with a bitter twinge in her heart. "She said god has a son called Jesus who paid for our sins."

At the name of Jesus, her parents seemed to recoil. "See, honey? They call people *sinners*. Everyone knows there's no such thing as sin. People are just doing what is natural," her father said. "What else did she say?"

As best as she could, Ainsley related the incident to her parents. After she was done, they told her to go play in her room, but she could hear whispers as they discussed the situation. A few minutes later, they came to her bedroom door. "Ainsel, we need you to do something for us," her father said. "We need you to report to the teacher what that little girl said."

Ainsley's face fell. She felt sick inside. She had hoped her parents would forget about it and drop the subject. Her mother came and sat down on her bed and pulled Ainsley into her lap. "You see, Christians hate us. They want to kill everyone who believes like we do," her mother said, stroking Ainsley's hair.

"But…she didn't seem like that," Ainsley said softly. She could feel tears coming to the surface and had to work hard to keep them from spilling down her cheeks. She didn't want to hurt Evoka. She was her first chance at making a real friend.

"That's because they're sneaky, and they're liars," her father said quickly.

"But I thought you said they were weak and stupid," Ainsley countered.

"Don't argue with me," he snapped. "The important thing for you to know is that they can't be trusted. We are at war with all Christians. And now, even though you are very young, you have been called into this war." He knelt beside the bed and took her face in his hands. "But this is your chance to make a striking blow against our enemy. I know you can do that. Do you understand what you need to do?"

"Yes," Ainsley muttered miserably.

"Ok then, tell me what you are going to do," said her father, who always liked to make certain she understood what was expected of her when it came to doing things that were unpleasant.

"I'm going to tell the teacher what Evoka said," Ainsley mumbled.

"Very good. And don't worry. If you have any trouble remembering what to do, our *friends* will be watching," her father said with a grin and a gleam in his eye.

Ainsley shuddered, understanding exactly what he meant. "You don't have to —they don't need to be there. I'll do it. I promise!"

Her mother smiled again. "Honey, we're just asking them to go with you so you'll have the courage to follow through with the plan."

"I don't need their help! I can do it myself!" Ainsley protested vehemently.

Her parents looked at each other, pleased with the fear they held over their daughter. "We'll see," her father said.

The next day, Ainsley carried out her parents' orders. It was the last day Evoka was seen at school. There were rumors that she was put in foster care while her parents were sent to a mental reset hospital for reconditioning. It was the era before the chip, which was still in the early, theoretical stages of development, so the State still used drugs and psychiatric methods to obtain the desired results in patients. No one knew if the family was ever reunited or transitioned back into society, because no one from Ainsley's community ever saw them again.

The betrayal seemed to scorch the ground of Ainsley's moral footing. She was afraid of her parents' punishment, but she loathed herself for giving into that fear by ratting out someone who had shown her such kindness and concern. Somehow, the news of her tattling reached her classmates and sealed her reputation as a dangerous, treacherous person. For a few weeks, Ainsley moped in guilt and depression. Finally, it was more than she could bear. She could either continue this way forever, or she could become just as dangerous and treacherous as they believed. It was all Evoka's fault for getting her into this mess in the first place. Her parents were right about *this*, at least. Evoka was stupid for telling her about Jesus, and she was also a sneaky liar. No one like Jesus could exist. Not in this world. If he did, wouldn't he stop all the evil things that happened to people? Evoka had ruined her life, and she would never allow anyone to get close enough to have power over her again.

And now, twenty-one years later, Ainsley was faced with the prospect that perhaps Evoka had been telling the truth, after all. She stared into the face of the angelic being who stood in her way. "If everything you say is true about the one you serve, perhaps he will understand why I'm here. I'm just doing this to protect myself."

"An element of that statement is true. But you are also addicted to power. And you should know that the God of all the universe cannot be manipulated," Asaf said with a tilt of his head and a knowing smile.

Ainsley swallowed nervously. The being understood her perfectly. "Listen. Maybe we can strike a deal. I really need to talk to the person beyond this boundary. Just talk, nothing more. If you let me through, maybe I can do something for you. I've heard the one you serve requires certain actions of his followers. Perhaps I can perform some function or do some service, even though I don't subscribe to his policies."

Asaf regarded her with an amused expression. "The only thing my Master requires of His servants is to do justly, and to love mercy, and to walk humbly with their God."[111]

Ainsley reflected on the statement. It sounded so vague. Surely there were specific tasks that had to be completed–some sort of pilgrimage, perhaps? In her experience, she was given little missions to carry out. Informing on Evoka had been the first of many. "So, specifically, what could I do to gain his favor? I still have some influence with people who are at war with him. I know how to affect their decisions. I even know how to make them disappear, if necessary."

"Silence!" Asaf thundered, and Ainsley trembled, in spite of herself. Asaf watched her through narrowed eyes. "You speak as if you have something to offer my Master. And you do. But the things you are offering are meaningless —even abhorrent—in His eyes. There is only one thing anyone truly possesses that He does not already own—only one thing anyone can offer to the God of the Angel Armies. And you are not ready to offer that. You are still listening to your companions. You will never be ready until you can see beyond their lies."

"What companions?" Ainsley asked, looking around her. So far as she could see, she was the sole person seeking entrance into Craig's neural world.

"The same ones which have been with you since you were an infant and your parents dedicated you to their service," Asaf said gravely.

Ainsley's blood seemed to thicken and course sluggishly through her veins. "There's no one like that with me now. I left that life. I only follow my own agenda now. I am in control of my own life."

---

[111] See Micah 6:8

"So it would seem," Asaf said. "Their deception is so complete and their presence is so woven into your thoughts that even *you* don't realize you are unknowingly carrying out their whims."

As Asaf spoke, Ainsley felt anger rising up within her. "Who are *you* to question my motives? No one controls me anymore!" she hissed.

Asaf seemed to grow in stature as he flourished the sword in his hand. "Those are not your words," he said, almost casually. "And that is not your anger."

Ainsley was filled with fury. "No one tells me what to say or how to feel or what to do. I stand alone!"

Asaf bowed his head, although his eyes continued a constant vigil. The air around him seemed electrified with power. "Master," he prayed, "open her eyes. She has been blinded by the god of this world."

As the words were spoken, Ainsley began to sense a darkness around her. Her awareness of it grew more acute with each passing second, until she felt completely engulfed in a thick, dark fog. "So much for opening my eyes. You actually made it *harder* to see. What are you doing? How are you doing this?" she demanded of the angelic being.

"I have done nothing," he replied from somewhere behind the veil of darkness. "You are merely beginning to see the reality of your situation."

Ainsley strained to see through the blackness. Suddenly, a sickening feeling jolted through her. Something was there with her in the dark. Her extremities prickled with the sense of the nearness of something powerfully evil. She stood very still, surveying the murky surroundings, and finally, her eyes settled on something. It was a vague outline, at first a darker shadow among many. She stared as it became more visible. "Who are you?" she asked.

As she directed her question toward it, the shadowy form changed and began to glow. It seemed an oasis in the dark, and she was strangely drawn to it. "Hello, Ainsley," it said warmly. "My name is not important. All you need to know is that we are on your side. We have been with you since the beginning, and we will never leave you!"

"We?" asked Ainsley.

Throughout the darkness, several other halos of light began to glow, until indeed, it seemed Ainsley was surrounded by a host of hazy lights. Trying to retain her composure, Ainsley scanned the company of beings. She had never sensed them before. "What do you mean, from the beginning?"

"Since before you were born," answered the being. "Your parents made the covenant with our master when your mother was pregnant. They knew that Asaf's master wanted to kill you, so they made a covenant with our master to ensure your safety." A murmur of affirmations rippled through the darkness.

Suddenly Asaf's voice could be heard over the mutterings. "I don't need to remind you that they speak only lies. You know this from many past experiences."

"I've never been aware of these beings before," Ainsley countered. "I would have sensed them if they were demons." Her senses must have been wrong earlier when she had felt the presence of evil, she reasoned. She must have been afraid because of their power and had simply misinterpreted the nature of their character.

"That is correct," agreed the powerful being in the darkness. "We aren't demons. We are spirit guides. We are here to guide you into all truth and to help you fulfill your destiny. We have always been here, guiding you and protecting you. We just didn't wish to reveal ourselves until now."

Several other voices added their agreement from within the darkness, a cozy chattering of support.

Once again, Asaf's voice rose above the whisperings. "You must make a choice whom you will believe. Evoka paid a high price to make that choice known to you."

"Yes. And look where it got her, stupid girl!" Ainsley snapped. She thought she could hear laughter and sniggering coming from the darkness around her.

The powerful being who wished to remain nameless hovered above her head and grew and dimmed in brightness as it spoke. "Her parents must not have loved her. They dedicated her to Asaf's master when she was born. Such a pity. If only she had known about us, we could have helped her escape that life and saved her from a meaningless sacrifice."

"Meaningless…" whispered the other beings, their voices filled with scorn.

"I can be more of a help to you now if you will listen to my advice and follow my lead," the being encouraged her. "I can protect you. You need never fear again. When you need my services, I will be there. But you will always be your own person. We never intrude on your personal freedoms and are always only interested in your well-being." The being was momentarily silent, and then added, "We can help you get past Asaf."

That was all that mattered to Ainsley at the moment. "By this I will know if you are telling the truth," she said. "Prove it to me by getting me past Asaf, and I will believe you."

"Don't listen to them, Ainsley," Asaf said urgently behind the veil of darkness. "They aren't who they say they are."

"How do I know you are who *you* say you are?" Ainsley said irritably.

"I assure you, he's not as powerful as he claims," the being of light said. "All you need to do is embrace me as your guide, and I will show you what real power feels like."

Ainsley hesitated as a familiar feeling came to the surface of her emotions. It seemed connected to some dim memory in her past. "Take all the time you need," the being said gently, interrupting her thoughts. "But you are at a crossroads. You cannot get past Asaf without help—help which I have freely offered. You must decide between Asaf's domineering master and our life of freedom. The choice is yours."

"Very well," Ainsley finally relented. After all, she could always renege on her decision later. She raised her arms toward the hazy glow. With a sudden rush the being surged toward her, enveloping her in a suffocating embrace. Ainsley cried out and fell backwards. All around her, she could hear the other beings cheering their welcomes. But the gentleness had gone out of their tone. In its place was derisive laughter.

Then she heard a familiar voice that sent a chill down her spine. *"I always said you were destined for greater things,"* said the being with a hiss. And then she remembered all those years ago—the powerful demon who had protected her from a lesser demon. She hadn't seen it since the incident in her bedroom. But it had been there all the time, lurking, possibly influencing her decisions just as she had seen others influencing her parents, waiting for the right moment; and now it had come. Could Asaf have been telling the truth, after all? "No! I don't want you!" Ainsley cried as she felt consciousness slipping away from her. "Help me!" she screamed to anyone who might hear or care. And then she fell into blackness.

41

"Janice? Janice, I have something important to tell you." Janice was just beginning to rouse from the effects of the sedation. Her body was sluggish and slow to respond. The lines between inner and outer reality had become fuzzy. She looked at her hands folded on her lap. To her surprise, she realized that she was sitting in a recliner. On the wall to her right was a picture of her parents. A cozy, multicolored afghan her great grandmother had crocheted for her was draped over her knees. "Janice, this is really important. I need you to listen." The voice would not be ignored.

"I'm listening," Janice said, looking blearily around for the source of the voice.

Viv hurried into the room, a smile spreading across her face. "Janice? Are ya awake?"

"Viv? What are you doing here? What am *I* doing here? How did I get away from that awful place? And what did you want to tell me?"

"Janice!" said a voice from around the corner, and a familiar face came into view as Piper appeared in the doorway.

"Piper!" Janice exclaimed in delight. She stared hard at the girl. "What happened to your hair?"

Piper laughed and ran her hands over her stubble, which was a little less than half an inch long. "Dr. Joe decided I needed a haircut. It only looks long when we're in our heads cuz that's how I remember it," she explained.

Janice looked around. "How did I get here? How did Piper get here? And what did you want to tell me?"

Viv and Piper looked at each other, and then Viv began to explain. "Ira faked your discharge orders and we snuck Piper out in a suitcase."

"But what about Geeves?" Janice fretted. "He can hear everything, you know."

"Don'tcha worry none about that. Ira took care o' that busybody," Piper said confidently.

"But they'll be looking for her!" Janice protested, gesturing toward Piper. "And she has a chip, so there's no place she can hide!" Janice insisted.

Piper came slowly over to Janice's recliner, leaning against it for support, and laid a small hand on her friend's shoulder. "Ira did some fancy programmin'. Somehow, he made it so even though we have a locater device, they can't find it. Somethin' about divertin' their search or splinterin' the signal."

"We don't understand how he did it, but a little while after we left the hospital, Ira told Piper about it—so we wouldn't worry," Viv explained.

Finally, Janice smiled and allowed herself a sigh of relief. "Thank you, Jesus! I'm out of that prison they called *Liberation Station!* I hope I *never* have to set foot in it again, or even *look* at it, for that matter!" She lay her head back on the recliner and surveyed her friends. "Okay, now, what was it you needed to tell me? You still haven't told me what was so important."

Viv looked at Piper again and then back at Janice. "We were in the other room. No one said anything to ya. Maybe ya thought ya heard somethin' cuz o' them drugs they had ya hopped up on," Viv suggested.

"No," Janice said, "I don't think so."

Suddenly, she could hear the voice again; and this time she realized it was in her mind. Her eyes opened wide. "I hear it again! It's Ira." She looked at Viv and Piper. "I'll go see what he wants." In an instant, Janice had retreated into her mindscape, where Ira was knocking frantically on the door to her neural wall.

"I'm coming!" Janice called as she hurried down a neural pathway that wound through barrel cacti and red rock formations. When she opened the door, Ira seemed extremely agitated. "I'm sorry it took so long," she said apologetically. "I thought it was someone calling me from the other room. I didn't realize it was someone trying to link."

Ira crossed the threshold, nervously running his fingers through his hair. "Someone is in serious trouble," he said bluntly. "Actually, two people are in serious trouble. Jesus wants us to help them."

"Well, my goodness! What can I do to help?" Janice asked.

Ira gave Janice a brief smile before a shadow of worry passed over his face. "It's very dangerous. One of the people is a girl who has been telling people about Jesus in the outer docks. She's been kidnapped."

Janice gulped. "Are we supposed to rescue her from the kidnappers? I've never done anything like that before. I'm not sure what to do!"

Ira paced back and forth nervously. "The key to rescuing the girl is in rescuing the person who ordered the kidnapping," he said, his footsteps churning the sand.

"I don't understand. Are you saying the *kidnapper* needs rescued?" Janice asked.

"Yes. She is in even graver danger than the girl she kidnapped. She was waiting for the girl to be brought to her, but then something happened."

"What happened? Where is she? How will we find her?" Janice fired the questions in rapid succession.

"She was waiting at 1507 Equality Avenue, which is where the kidnappers are supposed to bring the girl. But now she's on the move." Ira stopped pacing and faced her. "Janice, I'm afraid I'm going to have to ask you to do something very difficult."

"Well, nothing about it sounds easy so far," Janice said. "But if Jesus wants us to do it, then I'll do it. It's the least I can do after all that He's done for me."

Ira came to stand directly in front of Janice, a look of admiration and profound sadness in his eyes. "Since she has a chip, I've been tracking the woman in question. She seems to be headed to my location. I'm not certain what she'll do or what she's capable of."

Janice's eyes grew round in concern. "Ira, tell me where you are, *right now!* I may not be very steady on my feet yet, but I'll do anything to help you!"

"You haven't yet heard where I am, or who it is you need to save," Ira said grimly.

"It doesn't matter. Just tell me where to go."

"Liberation Station. Second floor."

Janice's heart dropped into her stomach, and she was silent for a moment as she looked across the desert mindscape. Clouds had gathered on the western horizon, and the blossoms of a yucca plant were jostled in a breeze that carried the promise of rain. Janice closed her eyes, and she could feel a solid foundation under the sand beneath her feet. Jesus was her rock, and she would not be shaken.

"If you just can't do it, I understand," Ira was saying. "I just helped you escape from this place, and now I'm asking you to walk right back into it."

Janice opened her eyes and smiled bravely. "I can do it. I can do all things through Christ, Who gives me strength."[112]

Ira smiled back at her. "It's because of your relationship with Him and the faith you have in Him—the paths you've been making and the scriptures you've been hiding in your heart—that He is asking you to do this. You have the power and authority needed to resolve this situation. But Jesus told me you will also have the chance to destroy a weapon the enemy would like to use against you."

Janice looked at Ira quizzically. "What do you mean?"

"You'll see. I can't explain now. There's not much time." He turned to go and suddenly stopped to face her again. "You are still very weak from the drugs and all you've been through. You may need some help from Viv. She can offer you physical assistance. She also has power and authority and has many scriptures in her arsenal. But under no circumstances is Piper to return here. I don't want Dr. Moses getting hold of her again."

Janice nodded, and Ira stepped back over the threshold and blinked out of sight. With a tremulous sigh, Janice knelt in the pathway. "Jesus, I know we don't have much time, but I can't do this without You. Please, *please* be with us!"

An inexplicable feeling of power and peace washed over her. "I am with you always, even to the end of the age,"[113] said a voice close beside her.

Janice looked up to see Jesus looking down at her, offering His hand to help her to her feet. She took it and jumped up. "If You're there to help me, I can do it."

Jesus squeezed her hand reassuringly. "I have given you authority over the power of darkness. And I will back up your authority with all of My power."[114]

---

[112] See Philippians 4:13
[113] See Matthew 28:20
[114] See Luke 10:19

Janice nodded. "Well, I sure can't do it on my *own* power. I'm not even sure I can stand up yet in the outside world!"

"Viv will be there to help you. Just remember, I came to seek and save that which is lost,"[115] Jesus said, and then He vanished from sight.

Janice squared her shoulders and returned to the external reality of her bedroom. Viv and Piper were there waiting, watching her expectantly.

"Well, what did 'e want?" Piper asked.

Janice looked up at Viv. "Someone's in trouble. Ira needs our help."

"Well then, let's go!" Piper exclaimed.

Janice smiled gently at Piper. "I'm sorry, but Ira said under no circumstances were you to come with us."

"Whaddaya mean, I can't come with ya?" Piper protested.

"Piper, y'ain't hardly fit ta walk, since they kept ya in a coma fa so long," Viv explained.

"It just isn't safe for you," Janice added.

"Where are we goin'?" Viv asked.

Janice sighed. "We have to go back to Liberation Station. Ira wouldn't have asked if he didn't really need our help. There's a girl who was kidnapped from the outer docks who's been telling people about Jesus."

Viv's eyes opened wide. "Is it Selah? If someone kidnapped Selah, there'll be an uprisin', for sure!"

"He didn't say her name, just that she was in serious trouble. But the strange thing is…in order to help *her*, we need to help the person who ordered her kidnapping."

Viv raised her eyebrows. "Who is it?"

"I don't know," Janice admitted.

Piper, who had been silent since she was told she wasn't a part of the mission, suddenly spoke up. "Ira don't hafta know I'm comin'. I can just sneak back in with that suitcase."

"*No!*" Viv and Janice said in unison.

Viv put her hand on Piper's shoulder as the small girl hung her head. "I know ya wanna help, but if Dr. Moses is there and he sees ya, not only wouldja be in

---

[115] See Luke 19:10

danger, but he would know we were all in cahoots. Right now, he just thinks I checked Janice outta the hospital 'cause there was a bogus discharge order. There's a real good chance he can't legally hold Janice an' me there with the info they have right now."

Piper was silent for a moment. "I know ya right," she said quietly.

"There is somethin' ya *can* do, though," Viv said. "You can pray for Ira and our safety and for the success of our mission."

"You can count on it," Piper said fiercely.

Janice grunted as she struggled to put down the foot of the recliner. "It's a good thing I'm not going to rely on my own strength, because there isn't much of it!" she laughed as Viv helped her out of the chair.

In a matter of moments, they were on a bus headed for Liberation Station. Janice looked down at her wheelchair that Viv had insisted she use. "Well, I'm sure I won't look like much of a threat to any kidnappers," she mused. "I've never been strong enough to fight anyone—especially not now—and we don't have any sort of weapon."

Viv squeezed her shoulder and leaned over to whisper in her ear, "Actually, we do. We have the sword of the Spirit.[116] It's not by might, nor by power, but by My Spirit, says the Lord of Hosts."[117]

Janice laughed.

"What's so funny?" Viv wondered.

"Oh, it's just what I thought about that scripture the first time I read it. When I hear the word *host,* I think about someone hosting a dinner party, or someone who seats you at a restaurant. So it didn't make much sense to me. But then I found out it means something like *armies.*"[118] She looked up at Viv, her eyes shining. "God's Spirit and a multitude of angel warriors. That's who is backing us up."

---

[116] Ephesians 6:17 (KJV) says "And take the helmet of salvation, and the sword of the Spirit, which is the word of God."

[117] Zechariah 4:6b, RSV

[118] This information is taken from Strong's Exhaustive Concordance of the Bible. The word hosts is #6635 in the Hebrew and Chaldee Dictionary portion: a mass of persons (or fig. things), espec. reg. organized for war (an army); by impl. A *campaign,* lit. or fig (spec. hardship, worship): –appointed time, (+) army, (+) battle, company, host, service, soldiers, waiting upon, war (-fare).

Viv blinked back tears. "After that time at Talk-o-Lot Chocolate when I tried ta tell ya about Jesus, and ya got so upset, I never dreamed you'd be tellin' me somethin' like that," Viv said. "I know I botched it up so bad, but somehow, someone still got to ya. I guess it was Piper who musta convinced ya. She's the reason *I* got saved. She witnessed to me years ago in the outer docks."

Janice patted Viv's hand that still rested on her shoulder, and her fingers closed over those of her friend. "No. Piper helped me learn more about Jesus by showing me how important it was to learn His Word and hide it in my heart, and she taught me how to guard my thoughts. It was your witness that saved me. Ainsley Abbot kicked me out of my neural boundary and was going to program my body to do whatever she wanted. I was sinking in chaos, out of my mind, when suddenly this memory came floating by. It was a memory of *you*, Viv. You were singing *Jesus Loves Me*. And it was because of that memory that I called out to Jesus to save me." She looked gratefully up into her friend's eyes. "You just thought you botched it, but you didn't. You loved me, and you had the courage to tell me about Someone Who loves us both. You weren't ashamed of Him, and you were willing to risk our friendship—and even your freedom, to tell me about Him. Just think…what if you hadn't?"

Viv tried to swallow the lump in her throat. "Thank Ya, Jesus," was all she could whisper.

The bus arrived at their destination and eased to a stop, lowering the wheel-chair accessible ramp for Janice to exit. "Well, here goes *something!*" Janice said enthusiastically, and the two exited the bus.

The imposing face of Liberation Station rose before them, and they fell silent as they made their way down the sidewalk. Suddenly, Viv began to sing. "Jesus loves me, this I know! For the Bible tells me so!"

Janice chimed in. "Little ones to Him belong! They are weak, but He is strong!"[119] With their courage revived, they sang their way to the entrance and stepped inside.

The foyer was strangely empty. No one was there to greet them at the front desk. "Where's the Pod-Op? There's always a Pod-Op on duty ta check ya in."

---

[119] From the hymn, "Jesus Loves Me, This I Know," by Anna Bartlett Warner

Viv wondered aloud. She approached the desk and leaned over it to glance down the hallways on either side. "Oh, Jovies!" she exclaimed.

"What is it?" Janice asked nervously.

"Someone's on the floor!" Viv rushed around the desk and gasped as she saw Conall crumpled up in a heap. "It's the Pod-Op what guards the front!"

"Is he–?" Janice couldn't bring herself to complete the question.

"I don' know," Viv said as she reached toward Conall to take his pulse.

As her hand wavered over his neck, Conall's eyes shot open. "Don't touch me!" he said hoarsely.

Viv jumped back. "I was just gonna take ya pulse, but now I see yer alive an' kickin'."

"I'm alive, but I certainly couldn't risk kicking anything," Conall said weakly. "My back is broken. If I move, it could sever my spinal cord."

"What happened? Who did this?" Janice asked as she navigated the chair to the back side of the desk.

"Ainsley Abbot. She said she needed to get something out of her office. When I told her we would send it to her and that she needed to leave, she said it couldn't wait. She just walked right past me, and when I tried to detain her, she tried to force a link with me. But she couldn't get past—she couldn't do it…" Conall tried to explain.

"She couldn't get past the firewall," Janice finished his thought.

"Do you have it, too?"

Janice nodded.

"When she wasn't successful with the link, she just picked me up and practically broke me in half. She has the strength of ten men!"

"She must have some new kinda weapon," Viv suggested.

"Not that I could see," Conall replied. "I've already called emergency services. They're on their way. I've contacted Dr. Moses, as well. The other Pod-Ops will be here as quick as they can, but most of them are on assignment. Many of them were dispatched to take care of some incidents in the city, and there's trouble in the outer docks. I don't know when they'll get here. It isn't safe for you here. Whatever business you have, it can wait."

Janice swallowed nervously and looked at Viv. "I'm afraid it can't. Our friend needs our help."

"So, Ainsley is the kidnapper? *She's* the one we need to confront—er, *help*, I mean?" Viv asked.

Janice didn't answer. Her mind was filled with the memory of Ainsley tossing her out of her own mind. "I think I know why Ira didn't tell me who we were supposed to be helping," Janice said, as she willed herself to turn the wheelchair toward the elevator.

"Where are you going?" Conall asked. "I said it's not safe!"

"We know," Janice said determinedly. "Stop reminding us!"

Viv grabbed the handles of Janice's wheelchair and began pushing it toward the elevator.

"Did Jesus really ask you to do this?" Viv asked, as the wheel chair picked up speed.

"Yes," Janice said firmly.

"Well, ok, then! Greater is He that is in you than he that is in the world!"[120] Viv said, as she pulled the chair to a stop in front of the elevator doors and jabbed at the button madly, before her brain could talk her out of it. The doors opened and Viv shoved the wheel chair into the elevator and started to punch the button for the second floor.

"Wait!" Janice said, grabbing Viv's hand. "What if she's waiting right outside the elevator door? We'll be sitting ducks!"

"Well, I can't carry ya up the stairs! Do ya have any better ideas?"

Suddenly, Janice could hear Ira calling her. She closed her eyes and listened. His voice sounded strangely calm. "Janice, I just wanted you to know that if you don't make it in time, it's ok. But you can't let anything that happens stop you from helping her. Jesus loves her. You have the power to destroy any weapon the enemy can bring against you."

"Even Ainsley?" Janice squeaked.

"I don't think that's what Jesus was talking about. You'll know it when the time comes," Ira said. "But more than just my life depends on you helping her.

---

[120] See 1 John 4:4

The freedom of thousands, maybe millions of people could depend on what you do here."

"Oh—no pressure, then," Janice laughed breathlessly. She opened her eyes. "Push the button!" she exclaimed, and the elevator began its ascent.

When the doors opened, the hallway was empty. Viv pushed Janice out into the hall, and then they could hear the sound of equipment being thrown around in an office at the other end. "I'll find you," cried a voice that was a cross between a hiss and a roar.

Fear sent prickles up Janice's spine and down her arms. Then she remembered what Ira had said. She would have the chance to destroy any weapon the enemy could bring against her. Fear could be a powerful weapon. Maybe that's what Jesus was talking about. "God has not given me the spirit of fear, but of power, and love and of a sound mind,"[121] Janice said aloud.

Suddenly the crashing sound stopped, and a figure emerged from the office. It was Ainsley, her eyes wild. "So *what?*" she growled in a voice that didn't sound quite human. "So you're not afraid of us. Do you think you can stop us?"

"Us?" Janice squeaked.

"Oh, yes. There are quite a few of us in here." A smile played at Ainsley's lips.

"Ainsley, you can't fool us. Conall said you were the only one here," Viv said in an attempt at bravery.

"Ainsley is indisposed at the moment," the voice growled.

All the color drained out of Viv's face as she realized the true nature of the situation. She straightened and faced the woman with determination in her voice. "Greater is He that is in us than he that is in the world!" Viv declared, and the demon laughed.

"God has not given us a spirit of fear, but of power, and of love—" Janice began.

"And of a *sound mind,*" the demon finished, and leered at them with Ainsley's perfect teeth. "I know what it says." There was silence for a moment as Ainsley's head tilted and the demon seemed to study Janice. "You remember what it was like, *don't* you?" it said with a smirk, and for a moment, the expression on

---

[121] See 2 Timothy 1:7

Ainsley's face very much resembled her old self. "You know, *I* didn't give her that idea. She came up with it herself—throwing you out of your own mind." Ainsley's form sauntered down the hall toward them, her lips curled into a vicious grin. "Maybe we could try that again. I quite enjoyed watching you flounder around in insanity."

Janice could hear Viv praying under her breath, pleading the blood of Jesus over them. She gripped the armrests of her wheelchair. She was supposed to help this, this *thing*? Whatever this was, it wasn't Ainsley doing the talking. But why had she risked her life—both her and Viv's lives—to save *Ainsley*? The woman had tried to steal Janice's body from her and program it to do whatever she liked and had nearly gotten away with it! Janice suddenly realized a very similar thing was happening to Ainsley right now. *"She deserves it,"* was the thought that came to her mind, and as she scowled at Ainsley, the demon threw back Ainsley's head and laughed.

And then Janice knew. The weapon wasn't only fear. It was unforgiveness. The demons were trying to give her ideas, trying to convince her not only that they couldn't be defeated, but that Ainsley deserved such a fate. Suddenly, Jesus' words came back to her: *I came to seek and save that which is lost.* Unexplainably, a feeling of compassion welled up within her. She stared hard at Ainsley's body, a mere puppet for the demonic forces that held her captive. "I forgive Ainsley!" Janice cried.

The demon seemed to draw back in contempt. "That's pathetic," it sneered. "You're wasting my time anyway. You're not the one I'm looking for. It's time to end this conversation. I've got a programmer to kill."

"Oh, no you don't! You keep away from him," Janice said fiercely.

The demon howled with laughter. "You aren't even strong enough to walk, and you think you can stop *me*?"

"No," Janice admitted. Her mind went back to the scene of her own deliverance. Jesus had commanded Ainsley to come out, and both she and some spirits of depression that had oppressed her for years had been thrown out of Janice's mind as if by a mighty wind. "Not in my *own* power. But we know Someone Who *can!* And I act under *His* authority! You horrible spirits of manipulation, come out of her in Jesus' name!" A righteous anger made Janice stand to her feet. "Get out of here, and don't come back!"

Ainsley's body suddenly lurched forward, and Janice and Viv jumped back, in spite of themselves. Ainsley writhed on the floor as she began to snarl and vomit. "Out of her! Every last one of you, in the name of Jesus!" Janice commanded. Ainsley became rigid and then suddenly grew limp.

Viv and Janice stared at the silent form. "Ainsley?" Janice finally ventured.

Ainsley stirred slightly and looked around in surprise. She stared in wonder at Viv and Janice. "They're gone!"

Viv and Janice glanced at each other and then back at Ainsley, who was hugging herself. "It's as if I can feel something warm all around me!" She stared at Janice and Viv. "Is that coming from you?" she asked.

"You must be feeling the love of God," Janice offered.

Ainsley's eyes were wide with shock. "It was as if I was on a sideline, watching these things happen as my body did them. Then you and Viv came, and Someone was with you. It was the same figure I saw with you the day I—" Ainsley stopped.

"Say on," Viv encouraged her.

Ainsley looked at Janice with newfound empathy. "I saw this person standing with you at your neural boundary after I was thrown out of your mind."

Janice smiled gently, and an overwhelming feeling of forgiveness flooded her soul. "That was Jesus. I cried out to Him, and He saved me. And He just rescued you! He was the One who asked us to come here to help you."

Ainsley was dumbfounded. "Why would He want you to help *me?* I've always thought Christians were weak and stup—" she stopped, looking apologetically at Janice. "That isn't true. I know it isn't. Especially now." She thought back to her childhood memory of the playground. "Evoka was right, after all," she said in a voice filled with wonder.

Viv and Janice looked at each other. "Who is Evoka?" Viv finally asked.

"She was a girl who told me about Jesus, but I didn't believe He could exist. Not when there were so many awful things that happen in the world. And when you two got here, all I could do was watch when just one more horrible thing was about to happen." Ainsley stared hard at Janice. "When you came into the hallway, I could tell they were worried, at first." she said. "And then one of them said it would be alright. They said they had something they could use that would keep you from being any threat."

"Unforgiveness," Janice said. "I never fully forgave you for what you did, until now." She looked into Ainsley's eyes and smiled.
"But why? After what I did to you—it's almost like what was happening to *me,*" Ainsley said.

"Maybe," Janice agreed. "But you see, both Viv and I have the Spirit of Someone living inside of us Who is more powerful than the spirit at work in the world. That Someone is Jesus. And it's His love that made us come here to save both Ira *and* you."

Ainsley looked at her, askance.

"It really is true, Ainsley," Viv added. "Jesus loves ya."

Ainsley shook her head and stared into space, as if she couldn't accept it. Then she looked back at them with an intense gaze. "When you said that you forgave me, something shifted. Something broke. You spoke as if you knew what you said would be enforced. When you commanded it in the name of Jesus, the demons started to leave. They were screaming in my head, scrambling over themselves to get away from the One who stood with you. *That* was power. But not the kind of power I'm used to. I want to know this Jesus you serve, but how can I? I've always only done things that would elevate myself, and it didn't matter who got hurt. I've—I've already killed someone," she admitted, thinking of Wayne, her undercover informant. "It didn't seem so awful then. It was quiet and clean." She shuddered. "Only now I realize there was nothing clean about it, or about anything I've done. There's no way anyone can fix me." A hardened look came into her eyes as she seemed to steel herself to her fate. "I'm a lost cause."

"Well, that's great news, Ainsley!" Janice said with a glowing smile, and Ainsley shot her a bewildered glance. "It's great because *Jesus came to seek and save that which is lost,*" Janice continued. "He told me to remember that, before we came here."

"He talks to you?" Ainsley asked skeptically.

"Well, didn't the demons talk to *you?* Is it so hard to believe that God would talk to *us?*" Janice replied.

Ainsley looked down. "I wonder if He *could* save me? I mean, I know I'll have to pay for what I've done—go to prison, or maybe even a river cleanup colony. But would He really protect me from the demons if they try to come back?"

Viv knelt beside her. "Jesus Himself said that 'For God so loved the world, that He sent His only begotten Son, that *whosoever* believes in Him will not perish, but have everlasting life,'[122] Viv said. "Whosoever means anyone and everyone."

Janice brightened. "It's all right there, in His love letter to us."

"Hah," Ainsley laughed weakly. "Could He have written a love letter to *me*, knowing how I would turn out?"

"Ya think ya so special that you're the only person God won't forgive?" Viv asked.

"Yeah," Janice agreed. "And do you think His blood isn't powerful enough to cleanse you?"

"Oh, I know His blood is powerful," Ainsley said. "It was like a covering over you both."

"Well then, why don't ya ask Him to forgive ya? Why don't ya ask Him to wash ya clean with His blood? God doesn't lie. Jesus became the sacrifice for our sins, so when ya accept that He has done this and give ya heart to Him, He honors His Word," Viv said.

"I don't know why He would want a heart like mine," Ainsley said miserably.

"Oh, Ainsley, why can't you get it through your head? It's because He *loves* you! He wants to take your life and change it into what it's *supposed* to be!" Janice exclaimed.

Ainsley gave her a sardonic smile. *"Be the you that you were always meant to be."* She laughed suddenly as she quoted the State's advertisement for the chip.

"Except when Jesus changes ya, he does it fa real," Viv said.

Ainsley hugged herself again. "I wish I could describe to you what I'm feeling right now. It's like warmth…and what I imagine love should feel like. It's—it's

---

[122] See John 3:16

…" she struggled to explain. "I didn't know how miserable I was. And having the demons take complete control was…*terrifying.*" She looked at Janice as the realization of what she'd done dawned on her. "I'm so sorry for what I did to you," she said.

"It's okay," Janice reassured her. "I forgave you. And so does Jesus."

Viv put her hand on Ainsley's shoulder. "Listen, Ainsley. Them demons are gone, but they'll be back to try again. Ya can't just fight 'em on ya own. Ya need ta have Jesus livin' in ya so they can't get back in."

Ainsley's look of joy changed to misery in an instant. "I just can't. There's no way He would want to live in someone like me."

"You're wrong!" Janice exclaimed. "He saved *me* and He lives in *my* heart. It doesn't matter what you've done. He died to save you from your sin—and from your*self!* Why would He have sent us to help you if He didn't want to save you?" Janice asked.

"I would imagine He was trying to save Ira and the Stewmaker," Ainsley countered.

"Stewmaker?" Viv and Janice said in unison.

"She's a girl I had abducted," Ainsley said, and then stopped with a look of horror. "I was supposed to meet them! I have to go!"

A sense of urgency filled Viv. "Ya shouldn't go anywhere until ya ask Jesus to be the Lord of ya life! If ya believe in Him an' ask 'im to forgive ya and come into ya heart, He'll give ya peace an' joy that no one can take away! When the demons come back, He'll be inside of ya, waitin' for 'em."

Ainsley rose to her feet. "Well, I believe in Jesus now, I can assure you of *that.* And I can't *begin* to explain how I would love to be forgiven for everything I've done." A heaviness settled over Ainsley as she realized that all of her life, she'd been trying to become invincible—incapable of being controlled or defeated by the things that had tormented her as a child. But they had been there all along, influencing her when she didn't realize it, and eventually, completely taking over. The idea that she had been powerless to stop them was horrific. "If only…" Ainsley began, and then laughed as if the thought were ludicrous.

"What?" Janice asked.

"If only Jesus *would* come in and live inside of me. If only He *would* be the Lord of my life. I would never have to be afraid again," she said, tears welling up to spill over her cheeks. She turned swiftly to them and rose to her feet. "I have to go. I have to save that girl. And maybe a couple of men I put in danger, if I can."

She turned to go down the hallway, and suddenly they heard the sound of sirens. Ainsley stopped and looked at them helplessly. "It may be too late. I don't think I can talk my way out of this one."

Janice grabbed Viv's hand. "*We'll* go. We'll go save her, won't we, Viv?"

Ainsley laughed bitterly. "These men are no one to mess with. They'll listen to me because they think I have connections and because they think I can get their friends released." She looked back at the doors at the end of the hallway. "I never did find Ira, and good thing, too. The demons wanted him dead. He made it possible for Craig to reach millions of people for your Jesus."

Suddenly, the doors to the stairs burst open. "Freeze!" a Pod-Op yelled. "Hands where we can see them!"

Ainsley sighed as the team of operatives moved down the hall, weapons trained on the three. "I'm the one you want," she said loudly as she raised her hands.

"We're well aware of that," said a voice from behind them, and Dr. Moses stepped into view, slightly out of breath from running up the stairs. "Ainsley Abbot, you are under arrest for assaulting an officer of the law and for the kidnapping of two of my patients."

"But Dr. Moses, there's someone in danger, and Ainsley may be the only one who can help her," Viv said desperately.

"Ainsley only helps herself," Dr. Moses proclaimed. "She can't be trusted. Whatever she has told you is suspect. She arranged to have the dayshift nurses sent home early and called me to a fabricated meeting with the administrators so she could kidnap my patients. She probably arranged to have Janice released early, although I'm not certain why, unless it was to create as many diversions as possible so she could do physical harm to Ira."

"I had nothing to do with any of that," Ainsley insisted.

"And why should I believe a word you say?" Dr. Moses said. "But don't worry. I'll find out the truth about everything. We'll find what you've done with Piper and Craig. Even if you plan to stop me from linking, I'll simply have Ira install Welcome 1.0 and you'll have no choice."

"I really don't think you can trust Ira," Ainsley said. "I'm not certain what that program does, but Ira is hiding something about it. I found out a few hours ago. I wouldn't have known, except some…*thing* revealed it to me."

"Your desperation to avoid the installment is just more proof of your guilt," Dr. Moses said. "Put her in the club cuffs," he instructed the Pod-Ops. "I don't know how she managed to overpower Conall, but she's obviously dangerous in more ways than just her words."

As the operatives escorted Ainsley away, Dr. Moses hurried to help Viv to her feet. "Did she hurt you, too?" he asked.

"No, we're both fine," Viv said, trying not to stare at the man she now knew to be Dawson's son.

"We came as quickly as we could. We would have been here sooner, but there was a rash of violent crimes committed throughout the city, and the Pod-Ops were busy taking care of it."

"Don't worry about us. We need to find Ira. We still don't know where he is," Janice said worriedly.

Suddenly a bumping sound could be heard coming from down the hall, followed by an "Ouch!" The three froze, and then relaxed as Ira stepped out of an office. "I'm here," he said meekly.

"Ira, my friend!" Dr. Moses exclaimed in relief and hurried to meet him. "I was afraid you had met some terrible fate!"

"No. I was hiding under the desk under the blanket we keep in the tech interface room. When Ainsley came in, she was so angry she just started tossing things around, starting with the desk. I'm a little bruised, nothing more," Ira reassured him. "I heard what you said about installing the program. You're right. I need to do it right away. Lives may depend on it."

42

Thwap thwap, thumpity thwap! Macy's tail thumped exuberantly against the floorboard of the hovercraft. Jayka looked down at the dog, whose paws were on the dashboard as she sported the closest thing to a grin that canines can manage. "Are you excited, Scrap—uh, Macy?" Jayka asked. She still wasn't used to the name. Macy answered by glancing up at Jayka and then back out the windshield. It was the first time the animal had ventured to the front of the cab, having spent every moment with Craig since they had abducted him from Liberation Station. Jayka wondered briefly about her fascination with the man, but chalked it up to the fact that he was a living human who gave little or no apparent signs of being alive. Certainly, he was warm and breathing, but that was about it. At least the mutt had stopped licking him on the nose at every opportunity. Jayka had finally scolded her severely enough that she stopped, although the Pod-Op thought she might have spied Macy licking his hand when she thought no one was looking.

As if influenced by her thoughts, Macy wandered to the back of the transport vehicle where Craig lay stretched out on a pallet. "No licking," Jayka said sternly as Macy hung her head despondently over the man's face. She looked back at Jayka and curled up beside Craig, her head resting on his arm. After a while, Jayka glanced in the rearview mirror and noticed she had nuzzled her way up under his hand so that it rested on top of her head. It seemed an inordinate amount of attention to dedicate to a stranger, but perhaps it was merely her way of showing concern, Jayka reasoned.

She turned her thoughts back to the crumbling pavement before her. Ira had said that Tyrell would have the help they needed. She knew Tyrell was in the Preserve and suspected he was on an extended mission to locate the isolationist outpost known as Adullam, believed to be the origin of both Craig and the girl who had been spotted in the ghost town of Rolla several months ago. Although Craig had not been forthcoming with information regarding its location, Dr. Moses hadn't seemed too concerned. They would learn everything they needed from the chip once the biocomponent had infiltrated Craig's neural network and they could safely link with the patient. Jayka smiled grimly. He would never get the chance.

The vehicle she had stolen was difficult for drones to detect. It was equipped with the same technology present in her uniform and had the ability to camouflage with its surroundings. Jayka had disabled the GPS unit per Ira's instructions, and they were now deep within the Preserve, following an old highway. She had learned from Piper that Ira had disabled the tracking devices associated with their chips, so they were virtually invisible until a drone used its thermal imaging capabilities. It had bought them a little time, at least. She only hoped Tyrell had the help Ira claimed he did, because otherwise, her plans would be a wasted, futile effort.

Her thoughts were interrupted by the sounds of stirring on the cot behind her and Macy's ecstatic whining. "Macy?" said a weak voice. "I thought I'd never see you again! What's going on? How did you find me?"

Jayka brought the hovercraft to a stop in the tall grass by the roadside. The fact that he had called the dog by name had not escaped her. "Craig Goforth, how are you feeling?" she asked as she made her way to the back.

Craig attempted to rise to a sitting position, and immediately a wave of nausea swept over him. "Not great," he admitted. "What's going on? Are they taking me to a different location?"

"*They* have nothing to do with you being moved. We are on our way to find another operative. We were told he would have the help we need," Jayka said.

"Help? Are we in trouble?"

"I have abducted you from the place you were being held and am transporting you through the Preserve in a State vehicle which I have stolen. To say we are in trouble is to put it mildly," Jayka said as she scanned Craig's vital signs.

"*What?* Why would you do that? You work for the State!"

"Yes, but I have also sworn to protect her citizens. It now appears that they are in danger from the present administration. People with similar backgrounds as my own are being treated as something less than human.[123] I cannot in good conscience stand by while the lives of other citizens—or future citizens—are at risk." Jayka grabbed an IV bag of fluid from a cabinet as she talked and began to reach for Craig's arm. She had left the cannula in his vein in anticipation it might be needed.

"What are you doing?" he asked apprehensively as he attempted to pull away.

"I am going to administer saline solution. You are dehydrated. To give you any liquids by mouth would most likely result in you becoming nauseated, which would be dangerous at this stage of your recovery."

Craig tried to relax and looked over at Macy, who immediately nosed her way between his arm and his body. "Where did you find Macy?" he asked.

"In the Preserve."

Craig's heart began to pound. "Was she…by herself?" he asked.

"No. She and her owner were hiding in a cave."

"Her owner?"

"Yes."

"There was only one person with her?"

"Yes." Jayka hung up the IV bag and looked Craig in the eyes. "There is obviously more to this dog than meets the eye. She was with an old Discard who had escaped from the outer docks. Later, after I returned home, I met a former Discard who had transitioned to the State, and the dog recognized *her*. That's how I discovered her name. And now I see that *you* know her name. You must have made acquaintance with the old woman who owned her. Am I to believe that more than one Discard escaped with her?"

Craig was silent for a moment. What if this whole thing—the escape, Jayka's newfound vigilantism—was all a ruse to see if he would lead them straight to

---

[123] We all have similar backgrounds in that we were all born of human parents. If you were told that your right to live was solely dependent upon whether or not your conception was planned or your parents changed their mind about having a child, would you believe that they could have called you something less than human and had the right to terminate your life? This is not where we are headed. This is where we are. Where we go from here depends on whether or not we stand up for our rights.

Adullam? "I don't mean to be rude—just in case you actually *have* rescued me and this isn't some part you're playing—but why should I trust you?"

Now it was Jayka's turn to be silent. Craig had absolutely no reason to trust her and even more reason to suspect this was a trap. "Piper," she said suddenly. "I assume you know her. She was very excited about the message you delivered. She gave me Ira's firewall program before you released it through your message. She said she was hoping I would think about trusting Jesus. At the time, I didn't realize which Jesus she was talking about. She actually said he had told her to bring me the firewall program."

"So, do you?" Craig asked.

"Do I what?"

"Do you trust Jesus?"

Jayka stared at Craig for a moment. "The only people I trust right now are Tyrell and Piper and Ira Owens…and possibly, you."

"Me? Why me?"

"Because Ira entrusted you with the release of his program which restores freedom of thought to the world. He must have had good reason. Plus, Macy seems enamored with you. She has not left your side since we helped you escape. I believe she is a good judge of character."

Craig smiled at Macy and scratched her ears with his free hand. "Who is Tyrell?" he wondered.

"He's the operative we're looking for. The one Ira said could help us. I think he was on a mission to locate the outpost of your origin, but he hasn't been back at the base for some time, and I haven't been able to link with him."

Craig sighed and stared at the ceiling. "If he's looking for where I came from, God will have to help him. It isn't easy to find."

Jayka pondered the statement. "It is true that the outpost must be cleverly concealed. Its location has eluded us although we have been looking for years. Most people thought the stories of hidden communities were just that—nothing but stories—until Dr. Moses wandered out of the Preserve as a teenager. And even *he* cannot locate it again."

"Considering his current role in changing society into an army that could be controlled like robots, I'm not surprised God hasn't helped him." He looked at the IV bag as it dripped the solution into his arm. "How do I know he hasn't programmed *you?* How do I know that isn't a bag of truth serum?"

Jayka looked at him levelly. "I can't make you trust me, just as you can't make me trust in the Christian god. If you were well enough to link, I could show you I wasn't lying, or you could link with Ira or Piper and ask them what they think of me. You may have been well enough to pull off that stunt Ira designed, but the drugs have had the desired effect on your mental processes. It would be unwise for you to attempt any neural acrobatics at this point."

Craig's eyebrows crinkled in confusion. "If you don't believe in Jesus, why are you risking your position—maybe your freedom or even your life—to save me?"

"As I said, I serve the citizens of the State."

"But I'm not a citizen."

"What you did today—you gave citizens freedom of thought. And while I do not subscribe to your belief system, I do believe that you had their best interests at heart when you spoke to them about your god. You risked your life doing so. Such a man should not be destroyed—citizen or not."

Craig was silent for a moment. It would help if he knew he could trust her. Suddenly she turned to him and raised an eyebrow. "Who is Asaf?" she asked.

Craig's heart pounded. "How do you know Asaf?"

"He just appeared at my neural wall. He claims that he knows who you are, but I am wondering if he's a covert operative trying to determine our position."

"A covert operative," Craig mused.

"Yes. He is obviously in some sort of military service. He didn't look like the sort of soldier you would want to discover was on the enemy's side. So you *do* know him? Can we trust him?"

"Yes. He's a…a friend of mine, I suppose."

Jayka frowned thoughtfully. "How have you had time to make any friends here? Especially someone from a unit in another country."

"What do you mean?"

"His uniform was unfamiliar to me. When I asked him what unit he was from, he said he was a citizen of another country. Perhaps he is someone who responded to your message? Is that how you know him?"

"We are both citizens of another country,"[124] Craig said, marveling that he actually shared citizenship with a being as powerful as Asaf. He hadn't been able to experience the inner world of his mindscape since the drugs had interrupted his message. The news that Asaf was still there protecting him gave him a feeling of overwhelming relief. The fact that the angel would have chosen to contact him through Jayka gave him an assurance that he could trust her. "What did he say?"

"He said to tell you help was on the way, and help was here."

"Oh, Jesus! Thank you, Jesus!" Craig whispered.

"What did you mean, you are *both* citizens of another country? Do you mean the same country? Do you consider the place Dr. Moses calls *Adullam* to be an autonomous country within the State? How is such an isolated community able to produce such an elite fighting force?" Jayka asked, the anxiety obvious in her green eyes.

"An elite fighting force?"

"Yes. I could see troops behind him, all in the same uniforms. They were a formidable company." When Craig was speechless for a moment, Jayka's nervousness began to grow. "Is it possible we have misjudged your outpost? Dr. Moses was convinced you were only *spiritually* dangerous, but from what I've seen, your fighting power may exceed that of the State. Does your...*country* possess a technology that has kept it hidden from us? Are you a faction of the global government that has been dispatched here to watch over us, insuring we are progressing toward the goal of global unity?"

Craig closed his eyes and shook his head. "No. That's not the kind of country I'm talking about. I've never actually been to the place Asaf is from. But I'm going there someday." He turned to Jayka. "The Discard who transitioned— the one you said knew Macy—what was her name?"

"She called herself Viv. I believe her full name is Viviana Delacruz."

"Is she all right, then? Did they put the chip in her?"

"She has not been implanted."

---

[124] See Hebrews 11:16 and Philippians 3:20

"Oh, thank God!" Craig sighed in relief. "We were afraid they had got to her—that she was chipped and maybe imprisoned. And when you mentioned that you met a Discard who knew Macy, I thought maybe she was in custody."

"No. Viv works as a liaison to the outer docks. She actually helped two other people escape from Liberation Station. Am I to believe that she has been to your community?"

"Yes. But not for quite some time. She used to come once or twice a month so she could learn more about Jesus and read Bibles that haven't been altered by the State."

"How is it possible she could have escaped detection? With all of our technology and drones we have not been able to locate the outpost. And undoubtedly, we would have seen her coming and going."

"My only explanation is that God helped her find us, and He hid her from your eyes."

"That is not possible. There are too many cameras, too many drones."

"Nothing is impossible with God," Craig said with a smile.

Jayka continued as if she hadn't heard him. "She couldn't have gone into the Preserve without anyone noticing unless she had a medical easement to traverse a road other than the causeway…" Jayka's voice trailed off as she accessed files. "Interesting. She *does* have a medical easement from when she obtained her audial implant. It has never been revoked. An oversight."

"Some might call it oversight. I call it divine intervention."

"Hmmph."

"Anyway, if we had Viv with us, maybe we could find Adullam."

Jayka frowned. "We cannot go back to retrieve Viv. If your god really did help her find the outpost, as you claimed, perhaps you should ask him to help us find it now."

Craig thought he detected a bit of sarcasm in Jayka's voice, but decided to pretend he hadn't heard it. "Absolutely, He will help us. And if you have any doubts, Asaf said as much." He looked up at the ceiling. "Jesus, You heard her. If You want us to find Tyrell, would You please lead us in the right direction? Somehow show us where to go."

Right on cue, Macy's ears pricked forward. She wagged her tail, walked to the front of the hovercraft, and put both paws on the dashboard.

"Well, Macy is ready to go," Jayka said. The dog looked back at her and barked. Then she walked back to Jayka and looked directly at her, trotted halfway to the driver's seat and looked back to see if she was following.

"She wants you to follow her," Craig said. "She did this sort of thing from the time we left my community."

"What do you mean, from the time you left your community?"

"I forgot to mention—that's where she's from. That's how Viv knows her. Macy is from Adullam," Craig explained.

Jayka stared at the dog as the pieces started coming together. "That's why you were concerned there was only one person with Macy. You were not alone when you left your home. But you were separated from your group when we found you."

"Yes," Craig replied. "The Lord asked me to let myself be found. Somehow it was part of His plan."

"I do not understand your blind trust in this god of yours. How do you know you aren't just responding to some delusion of your mind?"

Their conversation was interrupted by Macy's barking. "Instead of me trying to explain it to you, why don't you experience it for yourself?" Craig laughed. "I'm positive God used Macy to guide us to water and shelter. Besides, if anyone knows the way to Adullam, Macy probably would. She wandered there herself several years ago. Maybe she was coming from the State." It was difficult for Craig to make himself heard above the barking.

"Macy!" Jayka scolded, as she came to the front of the craft. Macy stopped barking and wagged her tail, looking from Jayka back to the road stretching in front of them. "Well, I see no harm in continuing in this direction," Jayka relented, and started up the engine. Soon the craft was humming down the old highway.

Craig drifted back to sleep, and when he awoke, the fogginess in his head had lifted. He sat up tentatively and discovered his nausea was gone. He took the IV bag from its hook on the wall and made his way to the front of the cab. "How do I take this thing off?" he asked as he sat in the seat beside Jayka.

"What are you doing up here? You should be resting," Jayka responded, but she reached over and unhooked him from the IV.

"I'm feeling a lot better. I'm actually kind of hungry. Do we have anything to eat?"

"There are some rations in the back, but I wouldn't consume a large amount right away," Jayka cautioned. As Craig rifled through the cabinet, Jayka added, "Apparently your god does not have a good sense of direction. Or perhaps your *dog* does not. We have already passed the area where you were apprehended. It was about an hour and a half ago. Macy has made no attempts to stop or change direction. Perhaps she is just enjoying the ride."

Craig came back to the front with a packet of saltine crackers. "I don't think so," he said. "Macy usually has a reason for doing things. Back in Adullam, she was always kind of a nuisance—digging in people's gardens and unlatching their gates. But ever since she left home, she's all business. It's almost like she has a directive."

They continued in silence for some time, Craig silently praying and Jayka calculating algorithms of probability that they were headed in the right direction. After another half hour, as the sun sank lower in the sky, Jayka finally broke the silence. "Macy is intelligent, but you made the trip with her on foot. If she were trying to pick up your old trail, wouldn't she need to be able to travel through the woods to stop to find it? Even if the scent trail were fresh, how could she find it anyway, traveling at this rate of speed in an enclosed cab?" She glanced at the dog, who looked back at her with her distinctive lopsided grin.

Craig stared at Macy and smiled. "I suspect she has some help."

Jayka rolled her eyes. "I can no longer entertain this foolish notion of yours that an imaginary being is somehow leading a dog to your community. We are much farther south than I had anticipated."

Craig had to admit that he had expected they would have turned off the road and into the woods by now—although he was uncertain as to how a vehicle this large could negotiate the trees. Suddenly, Macy barked and put her paw on Jayka's arm. "What?" Jayka asked the dog. Macy pawed her arm and barked again. "I don't understand you," Jayka said.

"Maybe she wants us to stop?" Craig suggested.

Jayka slowed the craft to a crawl. "There is a bridge up ahead," she noted. They proceeded with caution to the bridge, which spanned a river. Macy rushed to the door and began pawing madly at the latch. Jayka brought the craft to a stop and grabbed Macy's leash. "Maybe she needs to relieve herself," she said.

"Or maybe this is where we're supposed to turn," Craig suggested.

Jayka shot him a withering glance and snapped the leash onto Macy's collar. As soon as they set foot on the ground, Macy found a suitable area to do her business. Jayka looked back at Craig. "It is just as I suspected." She turned back toward the hovercraft, but the leash became taut in her hand as Macy refused to budge. "Come, Macy," Jayka commanded, but Macy responded by straining at the leash in the direction of the river. Although there were a few trees here and there off the shoulder of the road, the rip rap piled up under the bridge had kept the area from becoming completely overgrown, and the water was clearly in view.

"I think she wants us to follow her," Craig said.

"This rip-rap will not be easy for you to navigate," Jayka said, "And besides, she probably just wants to play in the water." Nevertheless, she started to follow the animal. As soon as she did, Macy stopped and wagged her tail and turned back toward the hovercraft. "So now she wants to ride again. I knew this was a waste of time."

Jayka and Macy returned to the hovercraft, but Craig lingered for a moment, looking out over the languid surface of the river. "Craig Goforth, we cannot stay in one spot on a roadway for very long or we may be detected. Please get in so we can keep moving."

"I just think we're missing something here," Craig responded. "I think Macy stopped here on purpose."

"Get in!" Jayka barked. She was done with the nonsensical idea that a dog could find a trail without the use of its nose.

Reluctantly, Craig climbed back inside the hovercraft, and Jayka started the engine; but when she began to move forward onto the road over the bridge, Macy barked and pawed her arm again. "Macy! Bad dog! I cannot drive with you doing that!" Jayka growled.

Macy whimpered and lunged toward the door, frantically clawing at it and barking madly. What was it going to take to make these humans understand? She was doing her best, but instead of listening to her, the female was yelling at her crossly while Craig did nothing. She looked back down at the river, where she could see the Kind Man waiting for them. He had gone ahead of them the whole time, staying to the road. But when they had come to the river, He had veered off trail. Macy knew He wanted them to follow; but apparently, they couldn't see Him. She looked at Craig. He had trusted her before. Maybe she could make him understand now. She whined as if pleading for mercy and came to him with her head down and her tail low to show him she meant no disrespect. Then she turned back toward the door and stuck her head forward and lifted her front leg, as if she had found a bird or a rabbit.

"Open the door," Craig said.

"We were just out there—"

"Open it," Craig said, grabbing Macy's leash and holding it tightly.

Jayka sighed irritably, but complied. "This is ridiculous," she added as the door hatch opened.

Immediately, Macy led Craig to the doorway, but made no move to go outside. The wind created by the hovercraft blew all around her, ruffling the fur on her neck. Once again, she stuck out her head and lifted a front paw, pointing toward the river. "She wants us to go down there. She sees something," Craig insisted.

"We don't have time for this," Jayka snapped.

"I think she wants us to take the hovercraft," Craig explained.

Jayka went to the doorway and surveyed the embankment. "Well, the initial ride might be a little rough, but once we're on the river, it should be fine," she relented. "And that would get us off of this road. Every minute we spend on it is a risk of being discovered." She closed the hatch and got back in the driver's seat. "Better strap in," she instructed. "This would be a better ride on a hoverbike." The craft turned left and plunged over the bank, clipping a few saplings on its way down. But as soon as they hit the river, everything smoothed out.

Macy returned to her post beside Jayka where she could watch out the windshield. "There. Are you happy now, Scrapdog?" Jayka had decided that when Macy was bad, she could keep the old name.

Macy responded by putting a paw on her leg and reaching up to lick her on the nose. "Ack!" Jayka complained, but she was smiling. Macy turned back to the river, where the Kind Man stood on the surface of the water. *He* was smiling at her, too; and that was all that really mattered to her.

Soon they were traveling down the river, albeit at a lower rate of speed than before. Thick-trunked sycamore trees stretched their smooth, white arms out over the water, and the occasional boulder thrust its gray head out of the river as if to challenge their passage. Macy watched intently as the Kind Man led them faithfully, slowing down for them when they had difficulties navigating the obstacles and speeding up when there was an open span of water. Shadows enveloped the hovercraft as the sun finally slipped below the surrounding trees, and their pace slowed to a crawl.

The use of headlights was out of the question, as they would be detected by any drones in the area. They were coming around a bend in the river when they spotted a large gravel bar up ahead in the growing darkness. Macy placed a paw on Jayka's arm and barked. Jayka slowed the craft and turned to the dog. "I was just thinking the same thing," she said as she pulled onto the sandy gravel bed and parked the vehicle as near to the tree line as possible. "We should probably sleep inside, but I, for one, need to stretch my legs," Jayka said.

"Same here. Watch out for cottonmouths," Craig advised as they stepped out of the craft.

"I am well aware of the flora and fauna of the area. It is programmed into my —"

"Rrarf!" Macy interrupted. She had been pulling at the leash as they disembarked and was practically hopping up and down as she strained to pull Jayka into the woods.

"Scrapdog! That is quite enough!" Jayka scolded.

Macy whimpered. Couldn't they see that the Kind Man was leading them into the forest? Were they really that oblivious?

"Quiet!" Jayka suddenly said in a hushed tone as she reached for Craig's arm. "Do you smell that?"

Craig sniffed the air. "Woodsmoke," he answered.

Jayka handed Craig the leash. "You stay here. I have a certain level of augmented vision, plus I can use my night-vision glasses."

"You're going by yourself to sneak up on whoever's out there?" Craig asked incredulously.

"Well, I'm certainly not going to march in, announcing my presence with a flashlight, a barking dog, and an invalid who probably has no experience with stealth in the woods," Jayka said in a harsh whisper.

"I don't know about this," Craig said dubiously.

"Well, *I* do," Jayka said firmly. "And you are both staying here while I check out the situation." Before he could protest, Jayka had slipped into the trees and vanished from sight.

Darkness enveloped the Pod-Op as she used all of her senses to pinpoint the location of the campfire. The smoke had a heavy smell to it that came from either using damp wood or dousing hot coals with water. Whoever was tending the fire was attempting to remain hidden. She crept along as quietly as she could, cringing when she heard a loud hiss in the underbrush. All she could do was keep moving, as she could no longer see the difference between the leaf litter of the forest floor and the well-camouflaged pattern of the different snake species of the area. The smell of the doused fire was getting closer. She stopped and waited, listening intently. A bullfrog had begun its buzzy drone near the river. A whippoorwill joined in, making it difficult to hear any clues as to what might lie ahead. Just when there was a break in the cacophonous riverside concert, Jayka heard the raspy squawk and clicking call of a starling. She froze and crouched down in the brush. This was not normal starling habitat. And so far as she knew, they did not often sing at night. It was possibly a mockingbird, she reasoned, as they were notoriously nocturnal singers. She waited, and the call repeated several times, always the same series of raspy squawks and clicks. That was no mockingbird. She stood tall in the darkness. "Tyrell?" she ventured.

"Hello, soldier," said a familiar voice. She switched on her flashlight. In front of her were Tyrell and a few other nervous looking people in a small clearing where the river had deposited gravel during flood stage. Were these people the help that Ira had mentioned?

"Where have you been?" Jayka asked breathlessly as she stepped into the clearing. "I thought you must be lost!"

Tyrell grinned. "I was. But now I'm found." He grabbed her in a bear hug and then gestured to the others. "Meet my new friends. Something amazing happened to me. I didn't understand it very well at first, but these people have helped me."

"So, these people—they're from Adullam?" she asked under her breath.

"No. But they have agreed to help me take a message to the State."

"A message to the State? They *want* to be discovered, after being in hiding for so long? What is the message—that they surrender?" Jayka asked in disbelief.

"No, nothing like that," said one of the strangers as he stepped forward. "We've been hiding out for too long. But when Tyrell, here, showed up at my doorstep, we knew the time had come to bring you the good news."

"What good news?" Jayka asked.

"The news that there is a God who loves you, and He wants to save you," the man said confidently.

Jayka was speechless. Was this man really willing to endanger his whole community with the proclamation of a myth?

"We were too stubborn and fearful, at first. Or at least, *I* was," the man continued. "But then Tyrell came and said he had to get back to his unit to tell them about what happened to him."

Jayka looked at Tyrell quizzically. "What happened?"

Tyrell smiled, and it was the happiest she had ever seen him. "Jayka, I have a new commanding officer. His name is Jesus Christ."

In the shocked silence that followed, the sound of barking and yipping could be heard, along with a crazy crashing through the underbrush. "It's okay!" Jayka said quickly. "It's just my dog. She must have broken free."

"Your dog?" Tyrell asked.

"Yes. We have much to discuss," Jayka said.

Suddenly, Macy bounded into the clearing, dragging her leash behind her. "Macy, what have you done with Craig?" Jayka asked. The group peered through the trees as the sound of snapping twigs was heard, accompanied by the appearance of the bobbing beam of a flashlight.

"I could hear you talking, and it all sounded friendly," explained Craig as he stumbled into the clearing.

"Craig Goforth?" Tyrell said in surprise. He looked at Jayka. "We really *do* have much to discuss."

"Indeed," Jayka said.

"Is this the operative we were looking for?" Craig asked. "Is this Tyrell?"

"That's me," Tyrell smiled and nodded at Craig.

"You were looking for me?" Tyrell asked Jayka.

"Ira told me to find you. He said you would have the help that I need."

"Ira Owens?" Tyrell asked. "How did he know?"

"I assumed you had linked with him."

"I haven't been able to link with anyone since an accident I had on the hoverbike," Tyrell explained.

"Then how did he know you had found help? And I still don't understand how these people could possibly help us."

"Do you remember that day when we brought Craig to Dr. Moses, and he told us that Craig was not physically dangerous, but that he was an intellectual and a *spiritual* danger?" Tyrell asked.

"Of course, I remember," Jayka said. Not only was she incapable of forgetting, but she had chosen to reflect on that incident many times.

Tyrell continued, the passion evident in his voice. "The knowledge of the reality of Jesus Christ and the gift He offers the human race is the most dangerous information that could ever confront the belief systems the State has been indoctrinating into its citizens. It goes against everything they have been working for. It introduces true freedom into a system that is built on control."

Jayka said nothing as she pondered the idea. Although she was no longer certain of Tyrell's mental stability, his claim was not without merit.

Craig finally broke the silence. "I guess we owe Macy an apology," he said, bending over to pet the mongrel.

"What do you mean?" Jayka asked.

"We asked God to help us find Tyrell. But when it seemed like we had passed Adullam, we thought Macy had led us on a wild goose chase. We forgot we didn't ask to find Adullam. We asked for help finding *Tyrell*. And here he is!"

Jayka froze, calculating the probability that a dog could find a person in a place it had never been—in an area as large as the one they had covered—without the benefit of any scent trail. "This is impossible," she said slowly.

"And yet, here we are," Craig said happily. "Good dog," he said, reaching down to scratch Macy behind the ears. "Somehow, you manage to listen to God when none of the rest of us can seem to hear Him."

Macy half-closed her eyes and leaned into his hand. At the edge of the clearing, the Kind Man winked at her and grinned.

43

RIVULETS of water trickled down Asha Merrit's cheeks and dripped onto the river rocks below. She once again cupped her hands in the cold water, bracing herself for the shock as she splashed it on her face. She could hear the sound of footsteps crunching in the gravel behind her and turned to see Jackson approaching with a tin cup. "You have *got* to try this," he said. "It might just work better to wake you up than splashing cold water on your face."

As Asha stood and took the steaming cup, a strange new aroma wafted through the air. "What *is* this?"

"This, my dear, is *coffee*," Jackson said. "And go easy on it. I've only had half a cup, and it's making my heart pound."

Asha inhaled deeply and sipped experimentally. "Yuck!" she exclaimed, spitting into the river. "It's bitter!"

"Well, *I* like it," Jackson announced and took the cup back from her.

Asha attempted to dry her face on her sleeve. "I'll just stick to a splash in the river. But I'm glad you're enjoying it." Her brown eyes sparkled as she watched her husband drain the cup. She grabbed his arm and squeezed it. "Craig said we can cover a lot of ground in that contraption. The woman said they won't be able to see us. It's just like Tyrell's uniform! Just think! In just a little while, we might be able to see Selah again."

Jackson put his hand on Asha's shoulder. "I was really hoping they would have heard something about her—but on the other hand, I'm glad they haven't. It means the government doesn't know about her yet."

"And they don't know about Garrison, either," Asha added. She looked up into Jackson's eyes. "Isn't that something? Garrison stayed at Craig's community for almost a year before their group left for the Old Country! We were praying for that boy even before he left—that he would give his life to the Lord. After he was gone, it seemed like a lost cause. And now he's on a mission trip!"

"I wish we knew where they were *now*," Jackson said. "And I know Paul and Megan have to be wondering."

"We're *all* wondering," Asha responded as she looked over her shoulder toward Garrison's parents, who were crouching by the small fire. Paul Scoffield had his arm around Megan, and for the first time in nearly a year, they seemed to look hopeful.

Jackson followed her gaze. "I don't think Tyrell's friend knows what to think of his plan to return to the State. I think I heard her use the term *suicide mission.*"

"Well, looking at it logically, I'd have to agree with her. We all knew the risks. Especially after visiting with Tyrell. But at the same time, after hearing all that's happening in the State—how the people are being deceived and forced into some sort of mental slavery… how innocent people are being exploited in experiments or even used as a source of food…." Asha shuddered. "How can we sit by when they are in spiritual darkness, and we have the Light they need?"

Jackson nodded. For months, the community had felt the call to take the message of salvation back to the Old Country, but they hadn't been certain how to proceed. Then Tyrell had appeared, and it was confirmation that the time to leave had finally arrived. Seth had actually been the first to publicly volunteer, much to everyone's surprise.

The Merrits and the Scoffields had been getting ready several weeks before Tyrell's appearance, planning to leave together if no one else was obedient to the Holy Spirit's leading. They were relieved when Seth made his announcement, as they much preferred to submit to leadership.

Zack and Sadie Beardsley had begged to go with their father, but Seth had told them they needed to stay home to help with the farm and not worry their mother any more than necessary.

Payton Hamby agreed to stay and continue ministering to his spiritual flock in the valley. Addy, very much relieved, informed him he was too old to go traipsing around the countryside anyway. The two of them would lead the church as it continued to pray for the expedition and for the hearts of the people in the Old Country to be receptive to the gospel.

The mission group had made slow progress. They were all sure of the general direction, but Tyrell still seemed a little disoriented without the use of his built-in computer system. Even if they had a current map, it was going to take a long while to make the journey on foot. And then Jayka had arrived, ironically looking for *their* help.

Asha snuggled against Jackson in the cool, damp air by the river. "Do you think they'll listen?" she asked.

Jackson pursed his lips in thought, his beard bristling. "We have covered it in prayer. We have been asking the Lord to lift the veil of deception from their eyes so that the light of the gospel of Christ can be revealed to them.[125] We have been casting down imaginations and every high thing that would exalt itself against the knowledge of God,[126] and that includes any lies the State has been feeding them. And aside from that, we've been binding the enemy in the name of Jesus, coming against any lies Satan might be whispering in their ears.[127] Jayka said that when Craig shared his message of the gospel, she saw several people make the decision to come to Christ. I am certain that part of the reason they were receptive is because we have been praying. And we aren't the only ones! Craig's community has been praying for years." He stopped suddenly and looked Asha in the eyes. "We thought we were the only place left in the country where people still believe in Jesus.[128] But now we know about Adullam. I wonder how many other hidden communities there are? Craig even said there were secret Christians in the State—remember the girl he said would come visit them? Who knows how many might be waiting in the wings, getting ready for the Director to call them on stage?"

"For such a time as this," Asha added.

The group had agreed to try to find Adullam before they headed for the State. Craig was certain they might find a few more people who were willing to go. Asha shivered, but it wasn't from the cold. The Holy Spirit had put an urgency

---

125 See 2 Corinthians 4:4

126 See 2 Corinthians 10:3-5

127 For an excellent book on how to pray for lost loved ones, see *Intercessory Prayer*, by Dutch Sheets.

128 In 1 Kings 19:14-18, when Elijah was severely depressed and said he was the only prophet left who had not been killed by his own people, God told him he would leave seven thousand in Israel who had not been unfaithful by following Baal. Sometimes, you may feel like you are the only one following the Lord, but you are not alone in the Kingdom of God!

in her heart, and her excitement was mounting. She knew that logically, she should be afraid. But she had stopped listening to humanity's logic. "With man, this is impossible; but with God all things are possible,"[129] she quoted. Jackson kissed her on the forehead and held her close to his chest.

"It's time to go," Tyrell called from the door of the hovercraft. It seemed he was calling to them from the portal of another world. The hatch was the only visible portion of the craft, floating a foot above the gravel bar.

"Shall we?" Jackson said, his blue eyes twinkling.

Asha flashed him a dazzling smile, and the two crunched across the gravel to the doorway and disappeared inside.

---

[129] Matthew 19:26, KJV

44

Ainsley looked apprehensively toward the perimeter of her mindscape, very much aware that Ira would be there soon, ready to install the program which would give Dr. Moses access to her habits and motivations. The thought was a juggernaut of dread that rolled inexorably outward from her neural core to greet the impending doom. She had just been delivered from demonic forces that had been attached to her all her life, influencing her from behind the scenes, and finally, completely taking over. The elation she felt now was indescribable, almost enough to overcome her fear of being programmed. Was it to be ended so abruptly by a mere human being who would have the power to turn her will as he pleased? She paced back and forth just inside the gateway to her mind. Of course, the others—their patients—hadn't been aware of the programming and what it did to them. They didn't know what was coming, so they didn't have to be afraid. But Ainsley knew—or at least, she thought she knew. With the program would come the end of her freedom—a freedom ironically brought to her through the help of Janice, whom Ainsley, herself, had attempted to program and create into her own image. "Poetic justice," she laughed, but the sound of her laughter had lost its musical ring.

Why had Janice risked her life for her? And Viv, whom she had attempted to manipulate into a relationship through veiled threats—she had been there, as well. They said Jesus had asked them to come. But *why?* Because He *loved* her? That's what they had said, but it sounded ridiculous. Ainsley strode furiously, kicking up clouds of the white sand near her neural wall, her thoughts punctuated by each turn. It was obvious Jesus was real. He was as real as the demons she had been hosting. It was obvious that He had power. The demons were no match for Him. But it was hard to believe that Someone with that kind of power would have a love for those who were weak and helpless to defend themselves—that He would come alongside them and protect them and fight for them.

Weakness was intolerable to Ainsley. It was what she hated in others. It was what she hated in herself. There was no way she could stop them from programming her, and she hated her own helplessness. She stopped her pacing, suddenly aware that someone was watching her. As she spun on her heel, she could see Ira just outside her boundary. She noticed absently that a soft light seemed to emanate from him. It would almost be comforting, had she not known his purpose for being there.

"Ahh, there you are," she said, attempting to hide her trepidation with a smirk. "So you've come to work your magic so that Joseph can work *his*. I've always wanted to know how you did what you're doing. I suppose I won't be aware once you install it, but I would like to know your secret, if only for a few moments. For instance, how do you get into people's minds in the first place? I don't imagine you're the sort who would force your way in." Ainsley found her nerves would no longer allow her to keep still, and she began pacing again.

Ira regarded her patiently, his hands behind his back. "Have you given any thought to what Janice and Viv said?" he asked.

She turned to face him and stepped closer to her boundary. "I suppose you overheard that part of the conversation?"

"I overheard the whole thing. If you're worried about Dr. Moses invading your mind, what about those *other* things you had inside? They may be gone for a while, but if you don't let Jesus in, they'll be back. They may even bring others with them,"[130] Ira said calmly.

Ainsley's eyes widened. "*You* believe in Jesus?" She laughed mirthlessly. "That explains it—the incurable morality, the reluctance to force yourself on others. Now I understand."

"Actually, I only recently gave my life to Jesus. But I think many people have an inborn working knowledge of right from wrong. They just choose to ignore it."

"As you are doing presently," Ainsley snapped.

---

[130] See Luke 11:21-26

"So you admit that forcing others to become unwilling participants in what you deem best for them is wrong?" Ira asked rhetorically.

Ainsley smirked again. "I was of the understanding that your God commands you *not* to do things that are in actuality just natural ways for us to behave. So what's the difference?"

"The difference is that He never *forces* you—even after you give your life to Him. You always have a choice."

Ainsley studied the man for a while. He didn't seem like much of a threat. He must possess some tactic—some skill of cunning—which he used to get inside a person's mind. She couldn't presently detect it, but she certainly wasn't going to go down without a fight. "Well, what are you waiting for?" she finally asked, planting her feet firmly on her mindscape.

Ira looked down for a moment, and then back up at her with an odd smile. "Your freedom lies in your own hands now, and it all depends on trust."

Ainsley looked at him sideways. "I'm listening."

"I couldn't install the program in you until I tweaked it a little. This version is just for you. Welcome 1.0 can only be installed on individuals without a programmer's I.P. address. Programmers can *carry* it, but they can't receive it. However, since you never listened to Craig's message, you aren't even a carrier yet."

Ainsley's eyes narrowed. "What does Craig have to do with—" she stopped, her eyes widening. "You *were* involved! I knew it! I knew you had something to do with the mass pseudo-link. And the program that was rumored to have been distributed was actually Welcome 1.0! It's just as I suspected. You were playing us all along," she said, a sense of admiration sweeping over her. "Ira Owens, you old devil, you!"

"If you trust me enough to accept the program, you can have it, and then you'll see its true purpose. But what I really hope is that you'll trust Jesus enough to let Him be the Lord of your life. His destiny for you is much better than the one you have mapped out for yourself. If it were up to me, I would have programmed you to be a nice girl who bakes cookies and knits sweaters for Discards." Ira grinned briefly as Ainsley glared at him. "But Jesus had other ideas. He wants me to give this to you." Ira brought his hands around from behind his back, and Ainsley could see that he was holding a bouquet.

She gawked at him, and then burst into a fit of laughter. "How quaint. Jesus wants you to give me flowers for Him. Tell me, if I accept them, does this mean we have to go out on a date?"

"I think He's thinking of something more permanent. Just consider the flowers as an expression of His love for all of us."

As she studied the bouquet, Ainsley could see that the flowers were more than met the eye. "So this is it? This is Welcome 1.0?"

"This is the updated version, with a special allowance for your I.P. address. You can trust me and take it and secure your freedom—at least from Dr. Moses. Or you can refuse it and Moses will just force his way in and program you however he likes."

Ainsley looked up from the flowers into Ira's eyes. Even now, he could be lying, but she didn't think so. It wasn't his M.O. She walked to her gateway and cracked it open. Ira handed her the flowers, and as he did so, she could smell their fragrance. Before she knew what she was doing, she had inhaled deeply, and was surprised when some butterflies escaped the blossoms and fluttered toward her neural core. Her eyes grew round with comprehension, and she stared in amazement at Ira. "You clever dog!" she exclaimed, and Ira blinked out of sight.

In a few moments, she could see Dr. Moses as he typed code into a false neural core just outside of the firewall she had been given. Ira had given her the incredible gift of neural freedom. By all accounts, almost everyone on the planet who wasn't a programmer had it—an ingeniously designed virus that protected the host's freedom of thought. He had given it to her, she realized, so she would still have the opportunity to make a decision about Jesus Christ. He must think he could trust her. How could such a genius be such a fool?

She watched as Dr. Moses finished his work and left. A quick trip to her neural core confirmed that everything was as she had left it, except for the addition of the firewall program. Gratitude washed over her. She might just have to have to find a way to thank Ira, as detestable as the prospect was to her. Her thoughts were interrupted by the sound of a knocking at her neural gate. Could Ira be back so soon? What could he want? Ainsley hurried to her wall and stopped.

There was a figure standing at the door, unearthly light shining from Him like a beacon. A lump formed in her throat as she cautiously approached the gate. "I know Who You are," she said, shielding her eyes from the blinding light. "I believe You are Who Janice and Viv say You are."

The intense glow emanating from Jesus dimmed to a level that was tolerable to her eyes, and He smiled wistfully at her. "Yes. But the devils also believe, and tremble.[131] You believe in Me. But would you like to *know* Me? Will you open the gate and let Me in?"

"Part of me thinks You'll just leave after You realize I only want You for protection. There. I've said it. So You can go ahead and leave, if that's how You feel after knowing," Ainsley said with a caustic glare.

Jesus regarded her quietly. "You say that you only want Me for protection. But in truth, there are things you've done that you know are unequivocally wrong. They have stained your conscience, no matter how deeply you have buried them, and only I can take them away."

Ainsley rolled her eyes, but at the same time, memories were surfacing. As she looked around at the white expanse, she could see incidents of her past rising up, unbidden, from beneath the sand. They were dark, treacherous things she had done that she thought she had buried deep enough to forget.

"You don't have to carry those things anymore," Jesus was saying. "You don't have to keep burying them. There is no hole deep enough, Ainsley. This is not something you can fix on your own. But there is forgiveness. There is forgiveness for *you*, too."

Ainsley looked out over her mindscape, her gaze dancing over the ugly memories. "You don't know what I've done."

"I know everything about you. I know about what you did to Wayne. I know about how you plan to use My servant, Selah—known to you as the Stewmaker. I know the things you did to place yourself in the position of power you have right now. Even now, you think you could discredit Dr. Moses and be on track to running the world the way you see fit. I know you want to keep pushing forward because you think no one has ever truly had your best interests at heart.

---

[131] See James 2:19

Your parents had plans for you since before you were born. Even though you did everything you could to protect yourself from their designs, you have been walking the path they created for you—with the help of the Father of Lies. But I know the plans *I* have for you. They are plans for your good, and not for evil, to give you a future and a hope.[132] You may think you only want Me for protection. But once you get to know Me, you won't ever want Me to leave." Jesus paused and looked toward an especially prominent memory that dominated the horizon. "You were so close on the day Evoka told you about Me."

Ainsley swallowed and blinked, her view of the monument to that incident distorted by tears held in check. "You were there that day?"

Jesus smiled in reply.

"That's the thing I regret the most. Turning her in made me feel like there was no turning back."

"Your parents placed you in a terrible position. They used fear to control you."

"But I still had the choice. I could have refused." Ainsley stopped and looked up at Jesus. She almost hated to ask, but she felt she had to know. "Whatever happened to Evoka? Did she get to stay with her parents?"

"Sadly, no. She was raised in foster care. Her parents did not survive the reconditioning process."

There was a sharp intake of breath as Ainsley felt the magnitude of her betrayal. Quickly, she attempted to divert the blame. "How could You expect anyone to want to follow You when You don't even protect those who *do?*"

"Evoka's parents are alive and well with My Father. Their time on earth is just a passing blur of a memory, and they are still celebrating that they did not deny Me."

"I thought *Hell* was the place where people partied," Ainsley quipped.

"From what you know of demons, do you really believe that?"

Ainsley shuddered involuntarily, and then looked into Jesus' eyes. "I don't understand You. I can tell that You care about me. I know You realize I might

---

132 See Jeremiah 29:11

just want to accept Your offer in order to keep the demons away and to keep from going to Hell. Why would You want to help someone like that who just wants to use You?"

"I'll take you any way you want to come, and for any reason you may think you may have. You say you just want to come to Me to keep from going to Hell. But your anguish concerning what happened with Evoka says otherwise."

Ainsley's heart felt as if it were made of lead. "Why did she ever tell me about You? I didn't want to report her. I should never have asked my parents if they thought all Christians were weak and stupid. Then, they would never have found out one of my classmates had witnessed to me. Why did she have to be so brave?" Ainsley clenched her fists and screwed her eyes shut as tightly as she could, but she could no longer keep her tears inside.

"She did it exactly for the reason she gave to you. You are worth it," Jesus said solemnly.

"How can You say that? Because of me, a family was torn apart. Because of me, her parents died."

"None of this would have happened if society had not chosen to turn its back on Me. But it did. And you had a choice of saving your friend or saving yourself. You chose yourself. Very few people—even adults—would have chosen otherwise."

"But that doesn't make it right. I wish I could take it back. I wish I could go back and change what I did."

"But you can't. It's done."

"But it's not done in my heart," Ainsley cried. "That decision has affected every other decision I made. It's *still* affecting me. And even though I tried to be angry at Evoka, what I really wish was that I could tell her how sorry I am."

"You may not be able to tell Evoka. But you can tell Me."

Ainsley stared at Him. "How does that change anything?"

Jesus looked at her with great compassion. "It changes *everything*. The state you're in is the result of a sin committed long ago—not the sin of reporting your classmate. I'm talking about a sin you would consider ancient, or perhaps even mythical. But its results are still felt today, because it brought spiritual death to the world. Ira was right when he said most people have an inborn knowledge of what is right and wrong. Yet even those who choose to do right aren't exempt from sin and its punishment.[133] The result of that first sin was death. But the gift of My Father is eternal life through Me.[134] I know you've never heard this before, but if you accept this gift and admit to Me that you have sinned, I am faithful and just to forgive you of your sins and to cleanse you of all unrighteousness."[135]

"If all that is really true, I want it," Ainsley whispered. She waited to hear the voices that had always been there to tell her otherwise—that there was no redemption for her, and that there was no such thing as forgiveness.

"I know what you're thinking. I have stopped the lies of the enemy so that you can make this decision for yourself. You've already confessed to several sins. Why don't you take that next step? Do you realize I've already paid for your sins? Everything you've ever done wrong—I carried it to the cross long ago. All you need to do is acknowledge them and take My gift of salvation. What I'm offering you is more than just freedom of thought. It's freedom from sin and the guilt it brings... freedom from fear. And eternal life with Me."

Ainsley's stomach fluttered like the butterflies from Ira's program. She quickly stepped forward and opened the gate.

She was unprepared for what happened next. As Jesus stepped over her threshold, something on the inside of her came alive. She looked around wildly to see what had just taken place, but the only noticeable difference to her was a soft glow that was beginning to shine from her neural core. "What just happened? What did You do to me?" she asked.

"I gave My peace to you. That's the light you see. But first, I brought life into your spirit. Because I died for you and conquered death to rise from the grave, I can give you the same resurrection life that I have. What you felt was your spirit coming to life, and that isn't something that can be seen with the natural eye."

"Why would You do this for me?" Ainsley asked incredulously.

"Because I have loved you from the foundations of the world. I knew about you before the creation of the earth, when I decided I would create you in the future. I have been waiting for this moment since before the beginning of time."

---

[133] See Romans 3:23
[134] See Romans 6:23
[135] See 1 John 1:9

Ainsley stood in awe as waves of love swept over her. No incident of past abuse, emotional or otherwise, could escape the overwhelming tide of His healing love. Even the ones she kept hidden deep within the innermost vault of her being would eventually be exposed to its power. Behind her, she could hear explosions and the sound of crumbling walls, but her boundary remained intact. As if reading her thoughts, Jesus suddenly spoke. "That is the sound of strongholds coming down. You have many, and some may take time to dismantle—in fact, they may take years, depending on how tightly you hold onto them. The work I accomplished through Janice and Viv was just the beginning of your deliverance. I have begun a good work in you, and I will continue to perform it until the day I return for My children."[136]

"Return?"

"I will not leave you like an orphan with no one to comfort you.[137] My Holy Spirit will be with you to guide you. And someday I will come again to bring you home with Me, so you can live with Me forever."[138]

Ainsley looked around for the memories of her past that she had buried. They were still visible just above the sand, like tombstones protruding out of the ground. "These things that I've done…they're still here."

"You still possess the memory of them. But as far as I'm concerned, they don't exist. Someday, you will learn to forgive yourself, and when you see them, they won't have the crippling power over you that they used to have. Instead, they will be reminders of the power of forgiveness and My love."

Ainsley wasn't certain what to say. She felt lighter, as if a weight had been lifted off of her. "What can I do to repay You?" she asked suddenly. "There has to be something I can do—something You might want."

Jesus shook His head. "My salvation is free. But I would love it if you would spend time with Me every day. You know so little about Me, and much of what you've been told is lies."

"That's it? You want me to spend time with You? To get to know You?"

"Yes. I wrote you a letter. If you would read it, you'll understand Me better. You'll know My heart."

---

136 See Philippians 1:6
137 See John 14:18
138 See John 14:1-3

"You're referring to the Bible, of course…the love letter Janice was talking about. I'm not certain I have access to the unedited version anymore."

"Don't worry. My daughter, Piper, will give you a copy. I'll send her over."

Ainsley looked up at Jesus, in awe of what had just happened. "I still can't believe it! I feel…clean!" Suddenly her eyes widened as her mind was brought back to the present. "The Stewmaker! I need to help her! They were bringing her to me. I have to meet them at the drop point, and Joseph will never let me leave!"

Jesus put His hand on her shoulder. "You may not be able to meet them, but you can pray."

Ainsley looked at Him hopelessly. "I've never prayed before. I couldn't begin to know how."

Jesus smiled. "You say you don't know how, but you've been engaged in prayer for the past fifteen minutes."

"Do You mean to tell me that prayer is as simple as a conversation?" Ainsley asked.

"It can be as simple as a conversation, or as intense as an exchange on a battlefield. My Word explains that the effectual fervent prayer of a righteous man avails much."[139]

Ainsley looked down. "No one could call *me* righteous."

Jesus put His hands on her shoulders and waited for her gaze to lift to His. "*My Father and I do.* You just traded your sins for My righteousness." He waited for the meaning of His words to sink in and then continued. "Now, Selah could certainly use your prayers—although even if her life on earth would end today, she would be with Me in eternity. But the men she is with—the ones who don't know Me—they are the ones in real danger. Pray that their eyes will be opened and they will change their minds."

"Can't You just *make* them change their minds?" Ainsley asked.

"If I forced them to follow Me, do you think they would truly be free?" Jesus asked.

Ainsley shook her head. She, of all people, understood this. "Very well. I will pray."

---

[139] See James 5:16

45

"WHERE is she?" Cade muttered under his breath. They had arrived at the drop point where the second transport waited to shuttle thrill-seekers back to their places of residence. Before releasing their customers, they threatened to expose them if they leaked any news of the kidnapping. The shuttle rumbled away, and the street had remained quiet.

Trajan, noticing Cade's nervousness, peered through the windows into the shadowed alleyways. "Sometimes I hafta wait a little while fa Angel. Important folk stay busy, an' sometimes they cain't be places on time," he suggested.

"Well, if she takes too much mo' time, we gonna hafta leave," Cade said, his eyes straining to see into the darkened windows of the empty buildings.

"What about our men she holdin'? What she gonna do to 'em?" Trajan asked.

"Hey, the deal was we meet her here at a certain time. We give her the Stewmakah, she give us the twits. We already waited five minutes past." Cade's nerves were on edge. Something was off. Everything in him was telling him to leave. He pushed the feeling down and shook his head. "They may be twit-headed, but they's still ours. We's waitin' five mo' minutes. Then, we's leavin' fa the docks. We kept up our part o' the bargain. If she knows what's good fo'er, she will remembah that an' honor it." Angel didn't seem like the type that would think twice about double-crossing someone. But they did have a little leverage. They were holding the leader of the Gateways, who had been the main thrust in the illegal "excursion" trade and could implicate Angel for her involvement. They also had the Stewmaker, whom Cade was convinced was another State spy. He turned to her suddenly. "Where you from, little girl?"

Selah blinked, her eyebrows scrunching up as if confused. "You know where I live," she said. "Zelda's old place. You were there that day with Cosmo and

Creep and Sho-Low."

"Don' get smart with me, girl. You know what I mean. Where you is *really* from, that's what I wanna know. Cuz ya ain't from the outskirts. Y'ain't from *anywhere* in the outer docks. Angel, she may be puttin' up a front fo' ya by astin' ta see ya like she don' know who ya is, or mebbe you two is jus' workin' a differ'nt side o' the same coin. But I know a Discard an' a Unspoken when I sees one, an' you ain't it." Even as he said it, Cade wondered if Angel and the Stewmaker had conspired to lure them into a trap. If so, it would to be their demise. He would make sure one of them didn't get out of it alive.

"Man!" Trajan exclaimed suddenly. "I wished I had thought o' this earlier." He looked back at Cade from the driver's seat. "We shoulda had one o' them circus freaks flash 'er hand. It gives 'em a readin' on the other person, an' they can look it up on their Viser or their chip, if'n they has one. They coulda told us where she was from."

Cade slammed his palm down on the back of the seat and cursed. "That woulda been a good *i*dee. But they's long gone."

The vehicle's A.I. system suddenly spoke, making the two men jump. "If you need to inquire about a citizen's origin, I have a built-in Palmscan in the dashboard on the middle console."

After recovering from the initial shock of the computer joining the conversation, Cade turned to Selah with a no-nonsense expression. "Gimme ya hand, little girl." When Selah remained motionless, he grabbed her right arm and dragged her over the back of the front seat, where Trajan quickly slapped her hand against the scanning device.

They waited in silence as the scanner lit up and attempted to find an implant. "No Palmscan detected," the A.I. voice said.

"Try again," Cade said, and when the car did not comply, he swore and ordered Trajan, "Tell it to try again!"

"Check it again," Trajan said.

Again, the scanner screen lit up, but the characteristic beep normally heard when citizens flashed each other their palms or ran their hands across a Palmscan device was absent. "No Palmscan detected," the A.I. repeated.

Cade let go of Selah's hand, and she slid back into her corner of the vehicle, rubbing her wrist. Cade's eyes seemed to bore a hole through her. "I don't care what this car brain says. You ain't from the outer docks," he insisted. And then his eyes lit up. "Ya gotta be kiddin' me," he said, as he stared at Selah.

"What?" Trajan asked. "Ya think the State somehow covered her implant ta keep it from readin', in case somethin' like this happen?"

"Nahh, man," Cade said, continuing his study of Selah. "You ain't from the outer docks, but y'ain't from the State, neither. Y'ain't from nowhere around here!" He turned to Trajan, a smile spreading across his face. "Trajan, we done hit the jackpot. There ain't no way we's handin' this lil bit ovah ta Angel."

"But what about the twits?"

"I think once the State finds out what we got, we kin have whatevah we want."

Suddenly, headlights sliced through the shadows of the empty street in front of them. "Take us home, Trajan. We gotta keep this offer off the table fa now."

Trajan wheeled the car around and sped off in the opposite direction. The car behind them followed closely. "Cain't you go any faster?" Cade barked.

"It's not lettin' me. I got ma foot down to the floor," Trajan said. "Go faster!" Trajan said desperately, pounding his fist on the dashboard. "Override emergency, authorization DZ-143!"

"I no longer respond to that authorization code," the car said pleasantly, and began decelerating.

"What're ya doin'?" Cade yelled.

"It ain't me! I don't got control no more!" Trajan yelled back at him.

Headlights appeared in front of them as the car slowed to a crawl and finally stopped. Cade and Trajan grabbed at the door handles frantically, but they were locked in. "We ain't goin' down like this," Cade said as he suddenly grabbed Selah, holding a shank to her throat.

"Jesus, please help me!" Selah prayed silently, eyeing the sharp point that hovered inches from her neck.

"You are under arrest for impersonating a state employee and for the unlawful use of a state vehicle," the A.I. said. "This vehicle is now under control of the State and will be driven to the nearest detaining facility, where you will be questioned and await sentencing."

"Tell them we have a hostage," Cade said to the car. "You tell them if they don' send this car back to the outer docks, we'll kill 'er."

"Her death is acceptable," the car said in its warm tone. "I have scanned her and found her to be either a Discard or an Unspoken. Under new legislation, even Discards who refuse to obtain citizenship are no longer considered human and may be used for a variety of purposes."

"You don' get it! She ain't a Discard or a Unspoken. She from the Preserve! She got intel to the secret hideouts ya been lookin' for. Mebbe we should jus' kill 'er right now!" Cade yelled, tightening his grip around Selah's shoulders.

There was a slight pause. "That will not be necessary. Release the hostage."

"How stupid do you think we is?" Cade squawked.

"Probability of your I.Q. exceeding 95 is less than—"

"Shut it!" Cade yelled. "We're not lettin' 'er go until we see our men safe to the docks. You let go the three ya got, an' let us back across the border. Then we turn 'er ovah to ya."

The car was silent for a moment. "Very well. We will arrange for your men to be released. This vehicle will transport you through the Dead Zone and release you at the gate, where you will relinquish the prisoner to us."

"I wanna see our men. I want them to come with us, *in this car,*" Cade insisted.

"Very well," the A.I. complied after a short silence.

"This is too easy," Trajan whispered to Cade, but Cade silenced him with a look and shook his head slightly.

Selah closed her eyes. The State didn't care about Discards or Unspokens, this much she knew. As soon as she was released, they would undoubtedly shoot the Gateways and take her into custody. Cade had to know this, she reflected. So he was probably planning to kill her before *they* were killed so the State wouldn't get what they wanted. She took some slow, deep breaths to attempt to calm herself, but it wasn't working. *Jesus, I'm scared! I would really like to live! But I know You know all things, and You have a plan,* she prayed. Inexplicably, a feeling of peace came over her. Her pounding heartbeat slowed to an acceptable rhythm. Her immediate future was uncertain. But she knew that her eternal future had been secured long ago.

The three waited in the car for what seemed like an hour, but was in reality only twenty-five minutes. Another State vehicle came into view. The doors opened and three men stumbled out, still dressed in hospital gowns. They squinted into the headlights of the transport vehicle and shuffled slowly toward it. As they approached, the back door opened and the three climbed inside. "You idiots! You sho is a lotta trouble," Cade said, finally relaxing his grip on Selah and clasping each of them by the hand as they slipped into the back seat. The door locked again behind them.

"What's goin' on? Where's Cosmo?" Dune asked.

"Cosmo ain't runnin' things no more," Trajan explained. "Cade, *he* the one what gotcha out. He the new boss man."

There was a brief silence as this new bit of information sank in. "Thanks, man," Dune said and nodded to Cade.

Tank leaned forward into the middle row to study Selah. "Hey, ain't that the Stewmakah?" he asked. He leaned closer. "Hey, Selah. Don' you worry none. It's all gonna be ok."

Cade stared at Tank. "Selah?" He looked down at his captive and back at the bulky henchman. "You on a first name basis?"

"Ever'one in the outskirts knows Miss Selah," he explained.

"So dey jus' lettin' us go?" Ox asked. "Dey didn' tell us nuttin'. Dey jus' said ta git movin', cuz dere was gonna be a prisoner change."

Trajan shook his head. "Dang, Ox. You is as smart as ya name. They ain't jus' lettin' ya go. It's a prisoner *ex*change, like they said."

When Ox gave him a blank look, Cade spoke up. "It's a trade, man. *You* three fa the Stewmakah."

"Oh, yeah!" Ox said, chuckling. "Ya know, dem State folks is ate up. Dey talk 'bout how da chip make 'em smarter. It ain't done nuttin' fa me."

Cade whirled around to face Ox. "You got the chip?"

"They chipped us, an' they was waitin' til we healed up to grill us," Dune explained. "An' that Angel girl that Cosmo took up with—that ain't her *real* name. She work fa the State, right unda the Moses fella what came up with the chip. She was gonna ast the questions, but she nevah got 'round to it afore they decided ta let us go."

Cade and Trajan exchanged glances. "Well, at least they might not kill us, jus' yet," Cade said.

"Kill us? I thought dis was a *trade!*" Ox said worriedly.

"What do *you* think?" Cade asked pointedly. "I don' trust 'em. But even if'n they let us live an' let us go, you'ns cain't nevah come hang with us, knowin' what we know now. If you'ns got the chip, they's jus' gonna use ya ta keep an' eye on us. You know they can track ya with it, right? An' they might even be able to listen to what you is listenin' to, somehow."

"Like they's listenin' to us with the car now," Trajan interjected. Cade glanced at him briefly, a hollow look in his eyes.

Ox's eyebrows squinched into a wrinkle. "We cain't go home? Da gang's da only fambly I got!"

Cade placed his hand on the man's arm and gripped it tightly. "Sometimes family hasta sacrifice fa family. You is still in the gang. Ya just cain't be with us, is all."

Ox looked down, and then out the window, attempting to hide the trembling of his lower lip. Tank put his hand on Ox's shoulder and squeezed. "Hey, man. You ain't nevah alone. Remembah?"

Ox looked back at his friend and suddenly smiled. "Yeah! I remembah. We gotta friend who stick closah dan a bruddah."

Trajan looked at Ox curiously. "Whatchu talkin' 'bout, bruh? *We* is ya bruddahs. Ain't no one closah than a bruddah."

"Yeah, dey is," Ox insisted. "His name is Jesus. Ain't dat right, Selah?"

Selah swallowed and attempted a brave smile. "You got it, Ox."

Dune rolled his eyes. "Don't pay no mind to 'em," he said, directing his comment to Cade. "Ya see, we had this dude show up at our wall—that's what they call it in ya mind, when someone wants ta talk to ya—they can talk to ya in ya head, but they cain't come past this wall ya got. Anyway, this dude shows up an' tells us about Jesus."

"*Jesus?* The one they swear by?" Trajan asked incredulously.

"We was in dis big beautiful place wit' grass an' flowers such like I nevah seen afore!" Ox exclaimed, making a sweeping gesture with his arms.

"Like I said," Dune continued, "don't pay them no mind. They bought into the dude's story. But I didn'. I know who ma real bruddahs is. I won't be spyin' on ya none with the chip."

Trajan looked at Dune with a pained expression. "Don'tcha see, man? There ain't no gettin' outta it. Ya cain't hang with us no more, cuz you is *livin' spyware.*"

"Wha—? No! No, no, *no!* We kin take it out! I betcha at the clinic they kin take it out," Dune insisted.

Cade cleared his throat. "From what I understan', that don't work out so good."

The vehicle was silent for a while as it wound through a brightly lit business district. Acid fog was low tonight. Even though there had been outbreaks of violence earlier that evening, they had been immediately quelled by the Pod-Ops teams, and a temporary curfew had already been lifted. Citizens had begun to emerge on the streets again to engage in the city's nightlife. None of those who frequented the sidewalks in front of restaurants and bars would guess the caravan rolling past contained anything but government administrators or Pod-Ops enroute to their next assignment, and the dismal drama unfolding inside the lead car would disappear, unreported, into oblivion.

Cade stared out the window, and as he watched the carefree citizens of the State laughing and chattering on the street, his heart felt like it was caving in upon itself. He looked down at his hands. The ring Cosmo had given him reflected the glow of the streetlights, flashing and dimming as they passed. Cosmo had given it to him to cement his position as second in command. At the time, Cade had swelled with pride. He was going to be somebody—someone his brothers could respect. He would earn their loyalty, just as Cosmo had done when he became the leader. But a fistful of bad decisions and murky communications had eroded his trust in the man. Cade had thought if given the chance, he could do better; but he was wrong. In trying to prove his sincerity and put the lives of his crew as paramount, he had led them all into an ambush. "The best laid schemes o' mice an' men gang oft a-gley,"[140] he mumbled.

---

[140] From the poem, "To a Mouse," by Robert Burns

Dune leaned over the back of the second row of seats. "Mice and Men Gang? I don' know them. Is they movin' in on us? Is that some gang in the State behind all o' this mess?"

Cade shook his head and half-smiled. "Nahhh, man. That's just somethin' my grandaddy used ta say when things didn' go his way."

The wall to the Dead Zone rose in the distance, its security lights shining like welcoming beacons to the five men. Cade tried to swallow the lump in his throat. Power had been the game with the Gateways. Power and provision. He would have given anything to hand that power back over to Cosmo, but that wasn't possible. Insurgence was unforgiveable in the gang. If he no longer wanted the responsibility of leadership, there was no way he could ever go back home. He stared at Selah, who sat quietly with her hands folded in her lap. Her lips were moving as she silently mouthed words to herself—or maybe she was praying to the God she served. A question burned in his chest, and he could no longer keep silent. "Hey, Stewmakah. Whyd'ja do it? Whyd'ja throw away ya freedom ya had outside ta come live in this piece o' trash place? Ya had ta know they'd find out aboutcha. Ya had ta know they'd come gitcha an' lock ya up."

Selah regarded him calmly as they passed through the gate into the Dead Zone. "The message I bring is for the people of the State, too. Maybe it's time to tell *them*, now."

"Tell them what?" Trajan asked.

Cade shook his head and smiled slightly. "You *believe* it," he said. "You *believe* everythin' ya tellin' them folks at the meetin's. Believe it enough ya left a life most of us only dream about."

Selah stared evenly back at him. "You are all worth it. Jesus died for you. That proves how much you mean to Him and to God, His Father." She looked at all of them one by one, meeting their gaze. "I didn't want to leave, at first. Most people where I'm from don't want *anyone* to leave because they're afraid of being discovered. But God had asked me to come. And when I thought about all the people who may never have heard about Jesus, all my arguments for staying seemed empty. The message was too important. How could I keep it to myself, when people were dying without ever hearing the name of the One who died for them? How could I stay where I was, when I knew He had asked me to go?"

Cade stared at her in wonder, and then looked out the window. The girl answered to a higher Boss than he did, one that asked her to take risks even more dangerous than Cosmo had asked of his men. He turned back to her. "Seems like a fool's errand, ta me. Whaddaya git fa riskin' ya life?" he asked. "Ya gotta git somethin' outta it."

Selah looked at him, her eyes shining. "Brothers and sisters. Souls pulled out of darkness and into light. Every person who gives their heart to Jesus is a new birth in the Kingdom of God. I obey God because I love Him. But the more I serve Him, the more I feel His love for people and begin to understand what He really wants. And He wants *all* to come to know Him! Being able to help Him reach other people is an honor I will not lay aside." She marveled as she heard herself speak. Her boldness was not her own, she realized. The Holy Spirit was giving her strength.

The vehicle slowed as the gate to the outer docks came into view, finally coming to a stop with its fender at the border. "You will now exit the vehicle and pass through the gate," said the A.I. system.

Cade looked at his men. "I think y'all know how this is gonna go down. They's gonna shoot us an' take the Stewmakah fa intel. But we ain't gonna let 'em git what they want." He turned to Selah. "It ain't fair, but we can't let 'em git the upper hand. An' you gotta know, if they git ya, they gonna chip ya an' make ya tell 'em where ya people is out in the Preserve. This may not make sense to ya, but it ain't in ya best interest ta leave here alive."

Selah stared back at him. "To live is Christ, and to die is gain,"[141] she said softly, her heartbeat in her throat.

Cade reached for the door handle, but suddenly, Tank put his hand on Cade's arm. "Man, wait a minute." He looked at Dune and Ox. "Did y'all hear that?"

"What?" Cade and Trajan asked in unison.

Dune nodded. Ox's eyes grew wide. "It ain't right. Can ya believe dey'd do dat?" Ox asked in disbelief.

"What is it?" Cade asked.

---

[141] Philippians 1:21

Dune looked at Ox and Tank and shook his head, pointing to his ear and then to the vehicle's dashboard. "Let's step outside," he said to Cade. "We need ta tell ya somethin'. An' we can't tell it in here."

Cade looked at Trajan and nodded, and the group filed out of the vehicle, Cade's arm locked around Selah's neck. As soon as Dune, Ox and Tank were outside, they huddled around Cade, Trajan and Selah, using the bulk of their larger bodies as a human shield. "They expect us ta kill ya," Dune explained. "They done ast us all ta kill the two o' you'ns and bring 'em the girl."

"They gave the order with that chip, an' they thinks they kin force us ta do it. But they cain't! They cain't make us do nuttin' we don' wanna," Tank said in an excited whisper.

"Dey tink dey kin order us aroun', but dey don' know we got sump'n what keeps 'em from makin' us do stuff we don' wanna," Ox said with a broken-toothed grin.

Cade's eyes flashed in anger. "But they's still *expectin'* ya ta do it. An' if ya *don't*, they is prob'ly just gonna kill us all an' take 'er anyway," Cade said. "We ain't gonna give 'em what they want," he said, and reached for his shank. Selah struggled to slip out of his grasp, flailing and kicking, but his grip around her neck was blocking her airflow.

Suddenly, Tank gripped Cade around the wrist. "We ain't doin' that," he said.

"Whaddaya doin'?" Trajan squawked.

"We ain't killin' you'ns, an' we ain't killin' Selah, neither," Tank announced.

"Don'tcha see?" Cade said exasperatedly, as Ox grabbed him from behind. "They's gonna kill ya when they find out y'ain't their robots like they thought ya was. We's all as good as dead!"

"Killin' someone like that—it ain't right," Tank said.

"He's right, Cade," Dune said. "Give us the shank."

Cade looked at Dune in disbelief. "I woulda thought that *you*, at least, was smart enough ta understan' what's goin' on here," he said, but relinquished his hold as Dune grabbed it out of his hand. What happened next transpired so quickly that Selah was unsure of the order of events until it was all over. Dune made a quick movement with his arm, and Cade's grip on her suddenly loosened.

She felt something warm and wet running down the back of her neck, and then was pulled to the ground as Cade collapsed behind her.

"Dune? Wha—" Tank began, but his cry ended in a gurgled shriek as Dune slashed through his jugular.

Ox, his eyes wide, lunged at the man in a wild tackle, but as he landed on top of Dune, the shank found its mark, sinking deep into Ox's chest, into his heart. "Sorry, brother," Dune said as he crawled out from underneath the man. "But if we don't kill them, they is gonna kill us. An' if we can't go home, we gotta do what we can to survive." Ox gripped his chest and stared at Dune in disbelief as his heart beat raggedly out of rhythm. His eyes turned to find help from Trajan, but the nimble runner was already speeding away from the well-lit road toward the darkness of the nearest alley. A shot rang out, and Trajan dropped to the ground, his body crumpled and his legs sprawled in their last stride.

Dune looked around for the sniper as he held his hand out to Selah, who was covered in Cade's blood. She scrambled to her feet, her eyes searching the rooftops. "Don't worry, princess. They ain't gonna kill us. You is too valuable, and I done what they wanted."

Selah looked around them at the fallen men. "H-how—how could you do that?" she stuttered.

"Like I said, I gotta do what I can to survive," Dune said. "It's the law of the docks."

Selah backed away from him, nearly tripping over Cade's prone form. Dune shook his head, looked down and then back up at her again. "There ain't no gettin' outta it," he told her. "You cain't outrun 'em. Ya might as well come peaceable-like."

"You didn't have to kill them!" she exclaimed. "You still had a choice!"

Dune's expression darkened. "That's right. An' I chose ta survive. Now, come on! I'm bringin' ya in, like they tol' me to," he said firmly, reaching toward her. When Selah made no move to comply, Dune made a quick lunge at her.

Selah heard a loud *pop,* and the man fell to his hands and knees. She looked around at the rooflines, barely visible in the darkness. *"Stop!"* she yelled, waving her arms. *"Stop shooting!"* She rushed to Dune, who was now lying on his back. It was obvious the man was mortally wounded, a growing crimson stain spreading across the white hospital gown. "It's not too late!" Selah said hurriedly. "You can still ask Jesus to be the Lord of your life!"

"Whaddaya mean?" Dune asked through ragged breaths. "O' course it's too late. I's dyin'." He looked over at the fallen figures around him. "I killt ma own bruddahs. God, forgive me!" he gasped, and then the light faded from his eyes.

Selah stared at him in horror. Was it enough? Did he really believe in Jesus and His power to forgive, or was it just a dying man's regret? "You did all you could," said a voice behind her. "As the man said, he made his choice." Selah turned to see a man of small stature, flanked on both sides by a team of Pod-Ops. She turned to Dune and began sobbing uncontrollably. "She's going into shock," the man said as he slowly approached Selah and knelt in front of her, offering her his hand. "My name is Dr. Moses. You're safe now. We're going to help you."

Selah stared at him through tears, recognizing his name as the one feared by Discards, Unspokens, and—it had been rumored—even citizens of the State. Without thinking, she leapt to her feet and ran. The darkness of the alley was too far away, and she hadn't even reached Trajan's body before she was intercepted by a Pod-Op. She struggled, but the soldier had been trained in ways of holding prisoners. "You should stop struggling," the soldier said, and Selah was surprised to find it was the voice of a woman. She had never met a woman of such physical strength. "You can't get away from me, and if you persist on trying, I will have to restrain you in club cuffs, which can result in a very unpleasant experience."

Selah grew rigid in fear. *What am I supposed to do now?* she prayed silently. *What if they put a chip in my head? What if they never let me go?* The idea of being locked in a cell—away from any form of sunlight, with some sort of digital components taking over her mind—was terrifying. "Jesus, help me!" she whispered audibly.

Suddenly, she felt the woman's grip soften. "Take heart, soldier," the woman whispered. "You are not alone." Selah turned and looked into the woman's eyes. "My name is Sloane," the Pod-Op was saying. "I will do everything I can to help you. But for now, you must come with me."

46

Morning painted the crumbling tenements of the outskirts, brushing the tops of the buildings with an orange hue. Sunlight tiptoed far above the dense, fog-filled streets, leaving them cloaked in toxic, atomized acid. After news of last night's kidnapping filtered through the crowd, revival attendees had refused to leave, interceding in prayer for Selah well after midnight. But then the fog had begun to roll in, and everyone was sent rushing to their homes to escape the fumes. Those who had traveled far sought temporary shelter in the neighborhood, and prayer had continued behind closed doors. Many had spent a sleepless night. Garrison was one of them. He peered out the window into the impenetrable fog, his fingernails digging into the windowsill. Bally exited Selah's room, where Drey, Lelah, Chandra and Dania had spent the night. "Did ya even go ta bed?" she whispered, trying not to awaken Garrison's host family and Thom, who were sleeping on blankets on the other side of the room.

Garrison shook his head. Bally came to stand beside him, and the two stared at the muddy green fog swirling outside the window. "It hasn't done dis in weeks," Bally said. "Why now?"

Garrison shook his head and rubbed his eyes. "I dunno. Maybe God's trying to keep us here, because if it was a clear day, I would be on my way to the Gateways, demanding to see Selah."

Bally snorted softly. "Lotta good dat would do ya. You'd just end up dead in some alley."

Garrison was silent for a moment. "I don't know. Would I? A lot of people are upset about this. If enough people came together, would they be able to fight us all?"

Bally snorted again. "Da Gateways is good at keepin' ever'one too skeered ta stand up to 'em."

"But this is different," Garrison said. "I can't even understand how it happened, because Cosmo not only wanted to see his gang members get saved, he wanted to bring people from the State to hear the gospel. How is that going to work if he kidnaps the speaker?"

"I'm with Garrison," said a voice behind them. Wallace was sitting up, his back against the wall. "It jus' don' make sense. Selah was good fa business. Even if Cosmo was lyin' 'bout wantin' ta spread the good news, why would he steal the main event?" Annabel moaned slightly, and Wallace gingerly extricated himself from the blanket and picked his way carefully through his sleeping children. "Ya know what *I* think? I don' think it was Cosmo's *idee*."

The three jumped when a loud banging was heard at the front door. Bally rushed to answer it, concerned for anyone who might be stranded in the fog. When she opened the door, two figures wearing respirators and homemade hazmat suits constructed of trash bags and duct tape burst into the apartment, nearly bowling her off of her feet. One of them quickly closed the door behind them. Bally and Garrison backed up as fumes hung close to the entrance, and the shorter figure ripped off his mask.

"Cosmo!" Bally exclaimed. "Where's Selah! What have you done wit' 'er?"

By this time, everyone in the house was stirring. Wallace's family huddled together on the other side of the room. Selah's bedroom door opened, and Dania and Lelah filed outside, with Drey and Chandra close behind.

"I didn' have nuttin' ta do wit' dat," Cosmo declared. "Cade an' Trajan cooked up a coup. Dey took Selah ta trade fa our three men what got caught out in da Preserve. But it all went haywire."

"Jus' supposin' I kin actually trust anyting what come outta ya mouth," Bally began.

"I'm tellin' it true," Cosmo said.

The taller visitor, a hulk of a man, had been fumbling with his mask and finally managed to remove it. "He ain't storyin', Bally. We done been held at the headquarters, Cade's orders. But then when his big plan went south, the gang decided Cosmo wasn't sich a bad leader, afta all," he said in his deep voice.

"Creep!" Bally exclaimed. "At last, a face I kin trust," she added, glaring at Cosmo, but when she saw the man's pained expression, she instantly regretted the remark. "I should'na said dat," she admitted. "I know ya done got saved. It's jus' dat, when Selah got kidnapped, what was I ta tink?"

"He wasn't in on this, Miss Bally," Creep reassured her.

"No, I wadn't. Cade didn' like da way I was runnin' tings. He thought I was takin' too many chances wit' da bruddahs' lives. An' 'e wadn't wrong. But in da end, I was tryin' ta *save* deir lives. I wanted 'em ta meet Jesus, an' I wanted ta save da lives o' da men I had ordered a hit on." When Bally raised her eyebrows at his last comment, he added, "That was *afore* I met Jesus." He shook his head and turned away as tears filled his eyes. "I lost 'em," he said.

Creep laid a hand on the man's shoulder comfortingly. "Ya did ever'thing ya coulda, bro."

"What happened?" Bally asked gently.

Garrison stepped forward. "What about Selah? Is she okay?"

"As far as I know, she is," Cosmo said, "But da State done took 'er—afta dey killed da three boys I was tryin' ta save, plus Trajan an' Cade. Dey mighta got Sho-Low, too, cuz nobody knows where he at."

Creep's lip turned down at the corner. "Sho-Low layin' low, that's what he doin'. He wasn't in that sled. I think we'll see him again, whether we like it 'er not," he said, patting Cosmo on the shoulder.

"Reggie saw da whole ting," Cosmo explained. "He wadn't completely sold on da *idee* o' Cade bein' boss man, an' 'e decided ta sit an' wait in a alley near da gate ta watch what was goin' down. 'E said Dune turned on all of 'em. But den, dey was all in hospital garb, like dey's been worked on, ya savvy? We can't hold Dune accountable fa what 'e did, if'n 'e was all wired up. Dune killed 'em all, 'cept Trajan. Sniper took Trajan out. Den dey shot Dune an' grabbed Selah."

"We have to get her out of there!" Garrison said desperately.

"An' how's you s'pose we do dat?" asked Cosmo.

"We could get all of the people who were praying for her last night at the meeting, and anyone else who might listen. We could march across the Dead Zone as a group and demand to be heard!"

Bally looked at him as if he had been smoking something he just scraped off the bottom of his shoe and rolled into a scrap of newspaper. "Whatchu tink dis is, *America da Beautiful?* It won't do no good. Ain't no one evah done nuttin' like dat," she sputtered.

Garrison stared back at her. "Then how do you know it wouldn't do any good?"

Bally shook her head and put her hands on her hips. "It jus' don' work like dat aroun' here. People jus' don' come togedder like dat. It ain't nevah been done, cuz folks is too busy tryin' ta find 'nuff food ta eat. It's ever' man fer 'imself."

"But that was *before* they met Jesus. They might feel differently now. They certainly have more food in their bellies now. They might be willing to come together for the right reason, or even if it was just so they could keep getting a free meal," Garrison suggested.

Wallace looked from Cosmo to Bally. "Selah has given these folks the message of Jesus. She's given 'em food, and she's loved on 'em, prayed for 'em, taken the time ta git ta know 'em. No one has ever done anything like that aroun' here. An' when this fog lifts, the word is gonna spread past the outskirts that she's been kidnapped," he said. "Someone offered 'em hope, an' then the State jerked it away. I think ya might be surprised how much they care. I think ya might be surprised how folks might be willin' ta do whatevah they can ta help."

Cosmo looked down. "I cain't order ma crew ta do nuttin' dat would put 'em in danger. I'm done wit' givin' orders like dat. But I can tell 'em what *I'm* gonna do, an' I can invite 'em ta join me, if'n dey want."

"I'll go witya," Creep said, squaring his broad shoulders.

"I'll go, too!" Phoenix announced, jumping out from under his blanket.

"This ain't fa kids, Phoenix," Wallace said. "This is dangerous."

"*I'm* dangerous," Phoenix growled, brandishing his tiny fist.

Sparta grabbed his hand and wrestled his arm to the ground. "Phoenix, quit showin' out."

"Settle down," Annabel said as she laid a calming hand atop her children's heads. She looked at Wallace. "I imagine there'll be a lotta kids what wanta go ta somethin' like that. Little kids love Selah. I'm not sure we kin keep 'em away

—not all of 'em. Whaddaya think'll happen if the State decides ta open fire on us?"

Lelah's eyes grew round. "They wouldn't shoot little children!" she exclaimed, and when no one said anything, she turned to Bally. "They wouldn't do that, would they?"

Cosmo stared at the floor with a somber expression. "Reggie—he work at da clinic. An' he say dey jus' come out wit' some new law what say Discards an' Unspokens ain't real people. Dey kin do wit' 'em whatevah dey want."

Bally whirled around to face him. "What? When did *dat* happen? You sayin' none of us *mean nuttin'*? Even da ones what has a *D.I.N.?*"

"De way I understan' it, if'n ya ain't a citizen, ya ain't human an' ya ain't alive. An' if'n y'aint alive, ya don' got no rights," Cosmo said darkly.

"But we *is* human, plain an' simple!" Bally exclaimed. "We is livin', breathin' human bein's, no mattah whether we got a piece a paper dat say so. What dey tink we is, *pigeons? Trash pandas?*"

"Nahh," Drey drawled. "Dem is got more rights'n us. You try an' kill a trash panda or a pigeon in da State, ya git jail time. An' even dey dogs got adoption papers. Cain't even have a dog unless ya prove ya kin take keer of it." She scowled. "My granny could show 'em how ta take keer of a dog. She say dey was stringy, but dey fat made a good broth."

Garrison shook his head as if trying to rid himself of the mental picture that Drey had just dredged up. He studied his new friends from the outer docks. "How many people know about this new law? If they don't know yet and we tell them, that'll be even more incentive for people to come—even people who never bothered to come to the revival meetings."

"Or will it be more reason for 'em to stay home?" Cosmo asked. "Before, most of 'em had a D.I.N. ta protect 'em. Now, dey got nuttin'. Nuttin' but a hope dat some human decency still exist in da world an' da gov'ment won' jus' mow 'em down."

"There must be some people in the State who are against this new ruling. If we march peacefully to the city, do you really think the State would open fire? I would think there would be an outcry from citizens who felt it was an outrageous act of tyranny," Thom said from his seat on the pallet table.

"Dat's jus' da ting. We may be peaceable, but dey news feed tell it howevah dey want. Dey could make us out ta be lootin' an' riotin' an' goin' on a killin' spree. Dey kin doctor it up, an' da only ones what know da truth is da citizens what might be dere ta see it in person," Cosmo explained. "On da udder hand, dey really *is* some people in da State what keers 'bout Discards. Dey had a vote ta pass dat law. An' from what Reggie heard from da State folk at da clinic, it shouldn'a nevah passed, accordin' ta how people voted. Da people at da clinic was real upset 'bout it. Dey is folks in da State what is good people. Dey's even people left in da *gov'ment* what's good people. Dey's jus' skeered. Da State say dey know what's good for us. So dey make all da decisions. An' when dey vote on sump'n, if'n it don't turn out like dey want, da people in power jus' make da votes go whatevah way dey want."

"But aren't the people in power voted for by the citizens?" Dania asked. "Aren't they supposed to cast their vote according to the people they represent?"

Bally and Cosmo laughed. "Dat's a good one," Drey chimed in. "Dey ain't had a real election since my great, great grandaddy was alive. An' even den, it was rigged."

"Who knows who is *really* holdin' da reins," Cosmo said. "Like Bally said, dis ain't America da Beautiful no more. Da world is jus' one big crappy family, wit' da real power in some place overseas."

Garrison sighed. "Well, I know this isn't a perfect plan, but it came to me when we were praying last night, and I couldn't get it out of my head. It's what kept me awake. I've been praying about it all night. But I know we shouldn't do anything like this without the Lord's direction. Did anyone else have the same thought? Does anyone else feel led to do this?" In the silence that followed, anguish seemed to burrow its way into Garrison's soul.

"I did," Bally finally relented. "But I thought it was jus' cuz I felt guilty. I'm s'posed ta be watchin' out fa her. An' I let 'er down!" She turned to the wall, and Chandra rushed over to comfort her, followed by the other girls.

"I thought maybe we could sneak in and rescue her, but I realize that sounds ridiculous. It's impossible." Thom said.

Cosmo shifted his weight, and the trash bags crinkled and squeaked. "Not *impossible*. Jus' not *likely*," he said. "I sneak people in an' out all da time. But none o' dem was ever bein' held by da gov'ment. An' we had inside help. But from what I know, our only good contact was da one what *ast* fa da Stewmakah —*Selah*, I mean—in exchange fa our three men. So dat is out."

Garrison suddenly stood taller and looked at Cosmo. "You say Reggie said the people at the clinic didn't agree with the ruling. Chances are, they may know some other people who don't agree." He turned and looked at the group from Adullam. "We all have a contact in the State who wouldn't stand for something like that."

"Viv," the girls from Adullum said in unison.

"And *she* has friends who wouldn't agree with the new law," Garrison added. He turned to Cosmo again. "If there were enough citizens scattered throughout the crowd, would the State be as likely to fire upon us?"

Cosmo raised his eyebrows and looked at Creep. "Dey would hafta be a lot of 'em, scattered here an' dere."

Drey ambled over to lean against the pallet table with Thom. "Hey, how many people you reckon got dogs 'er some sorta animal dey take keer of in da State?" She looked around the room. "An' how many pigeon trappers we know?"
All eyes turned to Drey, and Cosmo's face broke out into a wide smile. "Drey, you is jus' about da smartest ting in dis room!" he exclaimed.

Drey smiled and her face flushed pink through her orange freckles. "Even a blind squirrel finds a nut once in a while."

47

SELAH pressed her forehead into Maggie's warm flank. The milk made a rhythmic *swish, swish* sound in the bucket as she worked to empty the Jersey's swollen udder. Selah could smell the sweet oats in the feed box as Maggie crunched contentedly on her feed. She sighed. Even though it was hard work, there was something peaceful and meditative about milking a cow. The level of milk in the bucket rose slowly as she worked. Outside, the resident rooster crowed his welcome to the rising sun.

"Aren't you finished yet?"

Selah sat up on the milking stool and leaned back to see her father coming through the barn door. "Dad!" she said, and in that instant, she felt like a much younger version of herself. She jumped up from the stool and ran to embrace him. "It's so good to see you!" she cried.

Jackson Merrit laughed. "Yeah, I haven't seen you since breakfast!"

Selah smiled up at his twinkly blue eyes. "It seems like so much longer than that, for some reason," she said.

"Hey, where's *my* hug?" asked Asha as she came through the corral gate.

"Mom!" Selah ran to meet her mother and grabbed her in a bear hug.

"Easy!" Asha joked. "You're going to squeeze me in half!"

"Whoops," Jackson said. "Selah, you left the bucket where Maggie could—ahh, rats!"

Selah turned as she suddenly realized she had haphazardly left the milk pail where Maggie could kick it over. All her hard work was sinking into the straw-strewn floor. She rushed over to see if any was left in the pail. A mere quarter cup remained of the gallon she had collected. "Oh, you stupid cow!" Selah said crossly.

"I think your insult might be misdirected," Jackson said, and winked at her when she flashed him a look.

"I don't even care," she said, although it seemed like ages since she had had any milk. She must have had some at breakfast, but she couldn't recall. "I'm just so glad to see you again. I'm so glad to be here, in our own barn, with my own cow. I can't even remember why I left in the first place. Why would I leave all this? The troubles of the Old Country don't have anything to do with us. What was I thinking?"

Suddenly, Asha and Jackson looked as if they had seen a ghost. They were looking at something behind her. Selah spun around. "We'll take that," said a small man in a lab coat as some soldiers untied Maggie and led her away. "This barn is ours, as well, and everything in it. All of this land and property belongs to everyone, *and* to no one," he announced. Selah recognized the man as someone she had seen recently, but she couldn't remember where.

"That is *my* cow, and this is *our* barn. We've taken care of them for years. My father helped plant and harvest the oats stored in that grain barrel. You can't just come in and take away everything we've worked so hard for!"

"It isn't fair that some people have nothing, while you have so much, so we are distributing everything equally," the man explained.

"But they didn't work for it! They don't know anything about taking care of a cow!" Selah protested.

"What difference does it make? This is the way to do things fairly. Equality. No one has an advantage over anyone else. It says as much in the Declaration of Dependence. Everyone has the right to Healthcare as deemed necessary for the good of the majority, Liberty within the boundaries of the law, and the pursuit of Happiness as deemed appropriate. Governments are instituted among humans, deriving their just powers from the consent of the State—that whenever any group of people becomes destructive of these ends, it is the Right of the State to alter or abolish them, laying its foundation on such principles and organizing its powers in such form, as to the State shall seem most likely to effect their Safety and Happiness. Your family and the other families in this valley are destructive of the rights of others. *You* do not own that cow. We *all* own that cow. We will all share her, as the State sees fit."

"But what if they let her out in the Johnson grass when it's stressed? She'll die!" Selah wailed.

"That is ridiculous. Cows don't eat grass. That is barbaric. No wonder it's stressed. Can you imagine, if you had to worry about someone eating *you?* It's cruel, the way you've been destroying vegetative life and using this cow for her milk. That milk should go to her offspring. And I've heard that some of you even eat the individuals to whom she gave birth! It is *you* who have no right to own an animal. As if an animal could be *owned!* Animals should be cared for as equal citizens."

"You don't understand," Selah insisted. "Maggie has so much milk that her calf can't possibly drink it all. She might get mastitis if I don't keep milking her."

"You obviously have no idea what you're talking about," the man said sharply, and shoved Selah into an empty stall, slamming the gate behind her. "You can stay here until you recant your barbaric beliefs about animals and plants and personal property. In fact, we will put you to work so that you can pay for your infringements and provide sustenance for those who find manual labor to be offensive."

Selah reached for the latch on the stall door and immediately received an electric shock. "I wouldn't try that again, if I were you," the man said with a smile.

Selah looked wildly around for her parents. "Mom! Dad! Where are you?" she cried. She looked around the barn, which was strangely no longer made of wood. In place of the weathered boards were gray bricks that seemed to swallow any light that hit them. As she strained to see out the barn door, she could barely make out the forms of her parents as they were loaded into a cattle car of a train, much like the ones she had seen in Miss Genevieve's history books. "Where are you taking them?" she demanded.

The man pursed his lips and looked toward the train car, which bristled with the arms of people reaching through the slats in the boards, begging for their freedom. "Ahh, yes. Well, it seems their parents never came forward with a Declaration of Intent to Nurture, and they never filed for citizenship. But no worries, they will make good dog food."

"Nooooo!" Selah screamed and sat bolt upright in bed. Her breath came in uneven gasps, and sweat matted the hair on her forehead. She looked around the dimly lit room. How long had she been here? Time had a strange way of passing when she couldn't see the sun. All around her, the walls of the room were the same monotonous gray she had seen in the walls around the outer docks and the Dead Zone.

She swung her legs over the bed and reached behind her head. A feeling of relief swept over her. She had not been implanted. Unless, of course, this was a dream within a dream. She dropped to her knees and cradled her head in her hands. "Jesus!" she whispered. "Is this real? Am I awake?"

Suddenly, the door slid open. Selah looked up to see the small man from her dream enter the room. He was accompanied by the female soldier who had called herself Sloane. The events of the previous night came back to her in a rush, leaving her feeling dazed. "Good morning, Selah. How are you feeling?" he asked.

Selah stood up cautiously. "Dr. Moses, right?" Selah asked. The man nodded and smiled. "Why am I here?" she asked, not knowing what else to say.

"I was hoping you would tell *me,*" Moses said. "I think we both can agree you're not from the outer docks. I've heard you have been filling people's minds with false hope, directing their allegiance to a mythical god instead of the resources of the State."

"It isn't false hope," Selah said quietly, her gaze riveted to the floor.

"Isn't it?" The man's smile never reached his eyes. "Since you've been here, have you prayed for your god to save you?"

Selah's gaze rose to meet his. "He already saved me."

Dr. Moses' expression turned sour. "We'll have pie in the sky by and by. Yes, yes, I know all about that. But has your god ever done anything for you in the here and now? Something that you can prove?"

"Give me a piece of paper and a pencil, and I can start writing, if you want," Selah said casually.

"I'd be careful what I admitted to," Moses replied. "And I'll ignore the reference you've just made to the wasteful use of trees for antiquated writing methods —although we already have footage of you killing a rabbit and a snake in the

Preserve. That's more than enough to put you away for quite a long time. Instead, why don't you tell us where you came from and how to get there? You can have a reduced sentence, since you probably had no idea you were breaking any laws, and you obviously had no choice in where you were born. Perhaps your parents didn't, either. Exactly how long has your community survived on forbidden land?"

Selah stared silently back at him.

"Very well," he continued. "But it is only fair to warn you that I can eventually retrieve any information I need. It is your choice as to whether it is with or without your consent."

As he stood to go, an image suddenly flashed through Selah's mind. A young boy was traveling with his parents on vacation. They kept attempting to show him the majesty of the surrounding meadows and the large herds of something that resembled very large deer. But the boy was so absorbed in a little hand-held computer that he wouldn't even look up. He held on tightly to the tablet, his eyes glued to the screen. *"Look, Yosi!"* his parents pleaded.

"No! I'm talking to my friends now," he grouched. As he said it, a barrier slid down from out of nowhere, separating him from his parents and everyone else around him. His parents pounded frantically on the glass-like prison, but the boy ignored them, busily seeking acceptance from people he had only known in a virtual world. The room came back into focus as the image faded, and she knew she was looking at the boy in the vision, some twenty years later.

"Why did you do it, Yosi? Why did you shut out the very people who loved you? You not only shut *them* out, you shut out everyone else, as well. You thought they were holding you back, but your prison is one of your own making." Selah stopped speaking, and the man's look of surprise was mirrored in her own. She had never before received a word from the Lord concerning someone's personal history and the condition of their soul. "Even now, the Father is waiting for you to change your mind about Him. Even now, He can free you from the prison you have created."

"You *are* from Adullam!" Dr. Moses exclaimed. "I had thought perhaps you came from another community farther to the south. Tell us how to find it, and life will be much easier for you."

"I've never been to any place called Adullam," Selah replied evenly.

"Stop lying! Don't you realize I have the authority to take from you any information you insist on withholding?" Dr. Moses said angrily.

"Her physical responses would suggest that she is not lying, Dr. Moses," Sloane remarked judiciously.

"Quiet!" Moses barked, but he had noticed it as well. His chip had recorded and played back her breathing and pulse rate and the dilation of her pupils. All pointed to the fact that she was indeed telling the truth. Without another word, he turned and exited the room.

Sloane gave her a reassuring glance and then followed him. Her pace slowed as she processed a visual recording from a drone. The image was being sent from a wall camera on the border of the Dead Zone. "Dr. Moses, it appears there may be trouble in the outer docks," Sloane reported.

"I see it," Dr. Moses said as the footage showed up on his feed. "You may assist your Podmates."

Sloane glanced back at the room where Selah was being held. "Respectfully, Sir, I believe I may be of more use here. I believe the girl may trust me to a certain degree, as I was first on the scene to successfully make physical contact."

Dr. Moses looked at her strangely. "You ran her down and captured her. I fail to see how that elicits trust."

"Considering what she had just experienced at the time, I believe my…*interception* of the girl may have offered a comparative state of comfort and security to the preceding chaos," Sloane offered.

"Very well. Jayka and Tyrell are already missing in action. We don't want another one of your team disappearing," he said with a distracted frown as they headed to the elevators.

The doors slipped open as if on cue, and Ira stepped out. "Dr. Moses, I've been looking for you. There's a demonstration in the outer docks. The administrators are calling for it to be put down immediately, but it seems very peaceful."

Moses did not slow his pace, striding purposefully into the lift with Sloane in tow. Ira turned on his heel and joined them. "What could have gotten into them?" Moses muttered. "They've never revolted before."

"I don't think they're revolting," Ira said. "I think they're just marching."

"Of course. It must have something to do with the recent ruling on Discards not being human," Moses muttered.

"A ruling which you know is preposterous!" Ira hissed under his breath.

"Careful, my friend. The walls have ears," Moses cautioned him. "I had nothing to do with it. And I don't agree with it. But if Discards refuse to become citizens, what can we do? If they agreed to be chipped, then the world would see they're still living human beings, just like the rest of us."

"They don't need a chip for the world to see that. You only have to open your eyes to the facts of human physiology," Ira glowered.

"Humanity is evolving," Dr. Moses began.

"And I would argue that it is *de*volving. Anyone with the ability to reason can see that there is no difference between a Discard, an Unspoken, and a citizen of the State," Ira said, spitting out the words like bullets.

Moses opened his mouth as if to reply, and then stopped. "I am being asked to come to the drone readout room responsible for outer docks surveillance. Would you care to join me? Perhaps it will refresh your appreciation for your current position," Moses said pointedly.

Ira clamped his mouth shut. When they arrived at the drone readout room, Moses looked around and frowned. "Where is Ainsley? I sent an order for her to be escorted here to provide input, since she has been heavily involved in the social networking of the outer docks. Whether her activities were nefarious or not, she could still provide useful intel."

The group studied the screens, which recorded a large group of people advancing toward the Dead Zone. Suddenly, Sloane stiffened and looked at Dr. Moses. "The administrators are ordering Pod-Ops to open fire if the group passes through the gate."

A momentary look of discomfort passed over Moses' face, quickly replaced by studied reticence. "Well, they know the rules. If they want to live in the State, they have to become citizens and get all the implants along with the rest of us."

"I don't think they want to live in the State," Ira said, pointing to one of the screens. "Look at that sign."

"Discards are human," the sign read. It was being held by a man who was obviously a member of the Gateway Gang, his left eyebrow replaced by an arch tattoo. "That's the leader of the Gateways," Sloane announced.

One of the monitors leaned back in her chair and gave Dr. Moses a peculiar smile. "Perhaps this could clear up any confusion as to why Ainsley isn't here," the woman said, pointing to one of the screens. She accessed the nearest camera with her chip and zoomed in on the crowd of people quietly marching down the road. Ainsley was on the front row, holding a sign that read *"Free Selah!"* Right on cue, she looked directly into the camera, smiling and waving as if she were a homecoming queen in a parade.

"What is she doing? How did she get out?" Dr. Moses fumed. "She must have somehow circumvented my programming and compromised someone on staff!"

"Wait, isn't that someone who works here?" said another monitor, pointing at a screen with another view of the crowd. A shock of white and red hair bobbed in the mass of people, and Ira could see Viv's face as she chanted and held a sign that read, *"One nation under God, with liberty and justice for all."* Beside her, Janice rolled along in a wheel chair, with Piper sitting on her lap.

Moses' eyes bugged out as he pointed excitedly at Piper. "That girl! We must arrest her at once!" he said to Sloane. "Inform your team! She escaped this facility, and now I'm beginning to think our liaison to the outer docks was behind all of it!"

Sloane stared off into space and appeared to be contacting her Podmates, while Moses continued to fume. "She must not be shot. I've put too much work into her. I'm on the verge of a breakthrough. She was making such progress, with the help of Ira's program. *She cannot be shot!*" He looked frantically from screen to screen as the crowd neared the wall. He turned furiously to Sloane. "Why hasn't your team apprehended her? She could be killed once they cross into the Dead Zone!"

Sloane turned to him stoically. "No one will open fire on that crowd, even though the administrators have ordered it. I have identified no less than fifty other citizens besides Janice Druthers and Ainsley Abbot scattered throughout the group. There are undoubtedly more. And they have brought animals, which as you know, are now considered citizens of the State."

As she said it, one of the monitors zoomed in on a citizen carrying a Pomeranian. As Moses and Ira leaned closer, they began to see a menagerie of dogs, cats, and rabbits on leashes or wearing harnesses, led or held by citizens. Even many of the Discards carried pigeons, either in cages or held securely by jesses.

"To fire upon that crowd would violate several laws of the State," the monitor remarked as the people stepped through the gate into the Dead Zone.

"Dr. Moses, I am receiving footage from another drone," Sloane announced.

"Haven't we seen enough?" Dr. Moses asked. "We must act! We can't be paralyzed by indecision. We may not be able to disperse the crowd by shooting at them, but we could certainly use teargas."

"We cannot, actually," Sloane said. "Teargas can be fatal to birds."

Moses stared at her in disbelief. "So what is this new development? Could it get any worse?"

"That usually isn't a wise thing to ask," Ira said wryly.

"This footage isn't from the Dead Zone," Sloane explained. "It's from a drone within the Preserve. I've been accessing its feed for the past ten minutes." Sloane redirected the drone feed to one of the screens, and a view of the woods near the causeway just outside of the city came into view.

"I don't see anything," Dr. Moses said impatiently.

"Just wait," Sloane instructed.

The room was silent for a few moments, and then one of the monitors pointed at the lower right corner of the screen. "There. I thought I saw something." The group strained to see any movement or a hint of a pattern in the vegetation. "I could've sworn I saw something," the monitor insisted.

Suddenly a strange line appeared at the edge of the woods and began growing in size. "It's a camo-shuttle," Sloane said and smiled quietly, for with the door now opened, she was able to detect Jayka's digital signature. People began piling out of the craft. It had been filled to capacity. Last of all, Jayka and Tyrell stepped outside.

"Jayka, I'm watching you onscreen," Sloane messaged to her Podmate. "I can't hear Tyrell. I see him, but his signature is silent. What is going on?"

There was a slight pause, and then she could hear Jayka's voice in her mind. "I cannot explain Tyrell's condition. But these people—*and Tyrell*—feel they have something very important to say. We have been shuttling them here for the past few hours. I am hoping they will be given the chance to speak. If not, I will die trying to defend their right to do so. Jayka out."

At that, Jayka and Tyrell turned around to face the edge of the forest and held up their right hands in the Pod-Ops signal for *advance.* Suddenly the woods seemed to come alive. People began piling out of the edge of the forest and climbing up the embankment to the edge of the causeway. The crowd, which numbered well over a hundred, began walking up the old road beneath the causeway toward the city, which was a mere half-mile away. Dr. Moses turned to Sloane. "Report to your team. The administrators are requesting all Pod-Ops report for duty."

"Understood," Sloane replied. She exited the room without another word.

Moses moved closer to the screens, searching each one and requesting views from other surveillance cameras. "There!" he said suddenly, pointing to a face in the crowd. The monitors zoomed in, and Moses seemed to take a step backwards.

"What is it?" one of them asked.

"That man…that man is my father," Moses replied. There was a sharp intake of his breath as he saw Sophia's face appear next to Dawson. "And that is my mother." His face grew ashen as he heard an order go out from the administrative line. "No! You mustn't!" he cried. "We need them alive. We need them *all* alive!"

The monitors looked at each other apprehensively. "I was just able to pick up the feed from the administrators' office," one of them announced. "They've ordered the Pod-Ops to prepare to open fire." He turned to the screen. "It would have been interesting to know what in the world they were thinking, coming here—and where they were from, for that matter."

"You cannot do this!" Moses was saying desperately. "We need them for— for experimentation for my program," he said to the administrators, grasping for some excuse to avoid the bloodshed.

"There are too many to process," came the reply. *"Besides, you have all the experimental fodder you need in the Discards, since we have ruled them expendable."*

Moses closed his eyes and focused his attention on all the Pod-Op teams in his immediate command. "I order you to stand down," he said with a firm voice of authority. "Acknowledge that you have received this order," he said after a slight pause, and then cringed as he received word from one of the administrators.

"We have severed your link with the Pod-Op teams. They are now under our direct command. Return to your duties and make no further attempts to interfere with the defense of this city."

"But they are unarmed," Dr. Moses sputtered.

"On the contrary, they are armed with the knowledge of how to survive without the aid of the government. They cannot be allowed to continue. They are a threat to our agenda."

"But I can change them! Soon you won't have to worry about control. The mass link will take care of all that!"

"This conversation is over," the administrator replied, and Dr. Moses put his hands over his face as he heard the order go out to open fire. The monitors watching the screens hunched slightly, as if preparing for impact; and the ones accessing the footage via their chip sat up in their chairs, their hands gripping the armrests. Seconds ticked by, and the crowd of people on historic I-44 marched steadily forward.

"Nothing's happening," one of the monitors said, barely above a whisper.

"The order just went out again," said another.

Moses opened his eyes and looked at the screens. "What's happening?" he asked.

The monitor with direct access to the administrator's office turned to him, her eyes registering shock. "The Pod-Ops are refusing to open fire. They have sent in secondary troops, but they have given the same response."

Suddenly the door to the room slid open, and Ira recognized Vicey, his old coworker. "We just picked up something from a wall cam in Denver!" she said excitedly. "Switch a screen over to that feed. You've got to see this!"

As the screen flashed and the feed from Denver appeared, the room was filled with a collective gasp and expressions of "What the—?" "Zoom in!" and "What in God's name is going on?"

Ira's face spread into a wide smile. "In *God's* name, the *right* thing is going on!" No one seemed to hear him, for their eyes were all glued to the screen. Surrounding Denver was a crowd of people numbering in the hundreds.

"What do they want? Where did they come from?" Vicey asked.

"There are reports coming from all over the State," one of the other monitors interrupted. "Almost every consolidated city, nationwide, has been approached by crowds of people coming from the Preserve. All of their outer docks are crawling with Discards marching through the Dead Zones to protest the recent ruling, and citizens have come out to join them!"

"Look at that sign. What does it say? Zoom in," Vicey demanded.

As the monitor complied, the sign came into focus. *"We have come to the Kingdom for such a time as this,"* the sign read.

"I don't get it," Vicey admitted.

"It's a reference from the book of Esther," Dr. Moses said.

"I've never read that book. I've never even heard of it," Vicey said.

"Well, you wouldn't have. None of you could have recognized that quote. The only reason I did is because I came from a theocratic isolationist society, apparently much like the one these people hail from, where the Christian Bible is given credibility."

"They don't look like isolationists now," one monitor remarked.

"What is it supposed to mean?" Vicey asked, her face screwed into a quizzical frown.

"In the book of Esther, an entire race of people was destined for slaughter. The queen was secretly a member of this race, and her uncle asked that she speak to the king on their behalf. When Esther reminded him that she would be risking her life to do so, he replied that if she kept silent, she would perish, but that she may indeed have come to the kingdom for such a time as this, to bring salvation for her people."

"But the State isn't a kingdom, per se," Vicey argued. "That form of government is extinct."

"I don't think that's the government they're referring to," Ira interjected. "I don't think they're talking about an earthly kingdom at all."

Moses turned to Ira with an appreciative smirk. "They think they were born to participate in this uprising for the furtherance of what they would call *the Kingdom of God* and *its* agenda. Very astute, Ira."

The monitor with the administrator feed held up his hand to silence the room. "All of the Pod-Ops have refused to fire upon the Discards and the people from the Preserve. The other troops are following suit…Wait a minute," he paused. "I lost my feed." He looked at the others. "The signal from the administrative line has been interrupted."

The screens in the monitor room flickered and went black. "What's wrong?" Dr. Moses asked. "Did we lose connection somehow?" A few seconds later, the screens lit up again, but instead of the feed from surveillance cameras, they all presented a scene from a flower-filled meadow. Moses scowled as the screens zoomed in on a lone figure who was beginning to speak. "It's Craig Goforth! This is the content of the mass pseudo-link that was somehow perpetrated. They've been trying to remove it from the internet, but have been unsuccessful. What's it doing on our surveillance feed?"

"Maybe we should listen and find out?" Ira suggested as casually as possible.

Moses looked at him and glared. "I've reviewed this footage before."

"But did you really listen to the content?" Ira asked.

"What is the point? You know it's full of Christian propaganda and antiquated belief systems!" Moses sneered.

"Shhhh! I want to hear this," a monitor said, and then realized who she had just shushed. "I'm sorry, sir. It's just—I wasn't a part of the link because I haven't been chipped yet, and I haven't had the chance to see it online."

Moses folded his arms and wrinkled his lips in disgust. "Very well, but I'm going to meet with the administrators and figure out what's going on." He stormed out of the monitor room, and all eyes were glued to the screens. Craig's message was allowed to air in its entirety, to the point where it had been interrupted through the intervention of Dr. Moses and Ainsley. The screen went dark for a moment, and afterwards, one of the wall cameras was again accessed.

"What's this?" one of the monitors queried. "It's almost as if they have control of the wall cam."

The camera was from the boundary wall of the Preserve outside of the city of St. Louis. It zoomed in on Tyrell, who was surrounded by the people who had travelled there from their hidden communities. "My name is Tyrell. I was a

Pod-Op in service to the State. But now, I serve a higher form of government," he began.

One of the monitors turned to Ira. "I'm receiving reports from monitors in other cities. This is being broadcast Statewide."

"I have learned that even though I was labeled as an Unspoken, that I am fearfully and wonderfully made.[142] There was Someone who designed me with a purpose in mind, and He designed each one of you, as well. Craig just told you about Jesus, and I want you to know that I am living proof that someone who has done horrible things in the name of the State can be forgiven and accepted into His Kingdom," Tyrell said.

Jayka, visible in the view behind him, looked away from the camera, but not before Ira noticed there were tears in her eyes.

Tyrell continued. "Even though I've done things I wish I could forget, Jesus forgave me. He gave me peace inside that I can't explain. I know that many of you struggle with anxiety and fear of the future. But I want you to know that with Jesus, no matter what happens, you are His. He loves you and is reaching out to you through all of these people with me here today." Tyrell stepped aside, and one by one, people began sharing their testimonies. After a while, the feed switched to the camera in the outer docks of Los Angeles. Discards and Unspokens began telling their stories of people who had come from the Preserve to tell them about a man called Jesus. The disenfranchised from the outer docks of Chicago told of how Christians from underground churches had ministered to them and told them of the hope they could have in Jesus Christ. The footage continued, moving from city to city, where similar stories had played out.

"Who is coordinating all of this footage?" a monitor asked aloud. The room was silent except for the news of the gospel that was spreading around the globe.

Vicey turned to find Ira. "Can you believe this?" she whispered, but Ira's eyes were shut as he concentrated on using his chip for the orchestration of the largest evangelistic broadcast in history.

---

142 See Psalm 139:14

48

"ON your feet, soldier!" Selah jumped and looked in the direction of her doorway, which had just slid open. No one was there. Or at least, no one *seemed* to be there. A face suddenly appeared as Sloane opened the visor of her helmet. "Put this on," she said, tossing a bundle in Selah's direction. Selah opened the sack and found a bodysuit, complete with boots and gloves and a hood. "Hurry, we don't have much time," Sloane urged. Selah slipped on the suit and stared wonderingly at her hand, or the space where her hand should have appeared. The chameleon-like clothing given her by Sloane rendered her nearly invisible. "Keep hold of my hand. If anyone passes us in the hall, stand against the wall and be still," Sloane instructed.

Selah nodded and grabbed Sloane's outstretched hand. The two stepped into the hall, which seemed strangely empty. Liberation Station nursing staff were all at the nursing stations, watching the unexplained commandeering of the State's surveillance feed and its redirection to a State-run media channel, while programmers frantically attempted to locate the source of the redirection. Selah and Sloane proceeded, undetected, into a restroom, where Sloane took off her helmet and deactivated the camouflage technology of her uniform. "I entered this restroom before I came to see you, but left undetected. Now I will leave without camo tech activated, so as not to arouse suspicion. Put on my helmet. It is more effective than the hood. Stay close, and keep quiet."

Selah nodded and followed Sloane out the door, half-jogging to keep up. As they exited the building, Sloane nodded to the officer at the door, who was taking the place of the Pod-Op who had left earlier to confront what the State was calling a "highly coordinated attack." "Leaving a little late for the party, aren't you?" asked the officer.

"I was unavoidably delayed," Sloane said, resting her hand on her stomach.

"You must've had the Syntha-Meatloaf in the cafeteria. That stuff ought to be illegal," the officer joked. "Hey, maybe they could use it as a weapon against the rioters!"

"You don't seem very concerned about the safety of our city," Sloane reprimanded him.

"No, I'm not. You Pod-Ops always have everything under control," he replied.

Sloane nodded and smiled at him, and she and her invisible shadow exited the front door. In the parking lot was a row of hoverbikes. Sloane headed for the third bike in the row. "Get on behind me and hang on tight," she told Selah, facing away from the building cams so anyone reviewing the footage wouldn't be able to read her lips.

The bike shuddered to life, and Selah found herself weaving in and out of the busy streets of the city, her arms wrapped tightly about her rescuer. "What did he mean, *rioters?*" Selah asked.

"I forgot—there's no way you could have heard about what was happening. There are demonstrations in the Dead Zone and just outside the city walls in the Preserve. It isn't just happening here, either. There are people arriving at the borders of almost every city across the State."

"What are they rioting about?" Selah asked.

"None of them are rioting. It's just a spin the State was attempting to put on the story so they could have the excuse to eradicate the crowds without any question from concerned citizens. All of the demonstrators have appeared peaceful, but many are holding signs protesting a recent ruling that Discards are not human beings and should not even be considered to be alive." Sloane paused and gave Selah a backward glance. "And there are others who are proclaiming a message of love and salvation through Jesus Christ. But I have a feeling you know a little about that message."

Sloane increased in speed as she neared the entrance to the Dead Zone. "We may have trouble getting through the crowd," she said.

"Where are you taking me?" Selah finally asked. She hadn't cared before, as long as Sloane was helping her escape. Suddenly her grip on the Pod-Op tightened as she saw Garrison's face in the crowd. "Stop! That's my friend! Can you let me off here?"

The bike slowed a little as Sloane hesitated, and then she circumnavigated the crowd, turning the bike north in a route parallel to the wall. "Hey, did you hear me?" Selah cried. "Those are my friends back there! You can let me off now!"

"I'm afraid I can't do that," Sloane said in an emotionless tone as the bike rocketed forward. Selah held on tightly. She momentarily had the idea of jumping off, but that was before the wall to their right had become a gray blur. The wind tore at the legs of the Selah's camo suit, which was slightly too big for her. She had thought Sloane was rescuing her, but now she wasn't so sure. Had she escaped from kidnapping and prison, only to be kidnapped again?

Ten minutes later, the bike slowed as the East Gate of the outer docks came into view. Selah's body tensed as she prepared for what she thought might be her only chance to escape. As if reading her mind, Sloane gripped Selah's arm and sent the bike hurtling through the entrance, returning to full speed again once they were through the opening. "I wouldn't do that at this speed," Sloane advised.

"Where are you taking me?" Selah repeated the question drearily.

"You will see soon enough," Sloane said mysteriously as they wound through deserted alleyways and nearly-abandoned sideroads. It seemed to Selah that they had turned toward the south again. They whizzed by the dilapidated buildings, and Sloane seemed to have an uncanny sense of which streets would be empty to afford them the easiest passage. Eventually, the sideroads dwindled into the most rundown apartments of the outskirts. Still, Sloane kept the bike at blinding speed. They were past the outermost roads, and Selah could see the outer wall coming into view. Sloane sent the bike into a wide turn to the west, skirting the perimeter of the boundary to the Preserve. Watching the wall as it sped by, Selah thought she spied a vine crawling up the brickwork, covered with clusters of purple blossoms. It was Zelda's wisteria vine! Sloane slowed the bike for a moment, nodding toward the wall. "This vine has somehow caused the wall considerable damage," she commented. "We were ordered to leave it undisturbed so as to observe any illegal traffic. The blooms are quite beautiful, for such a destructive plant."

Selah said nothing, but smiled as she thought of Zelda. She wondered where the old woman was now. Was she still living free? Had she made it to shelter? Did she have enough to eat? Her thoughts were interrupted by the scene unfolding before her. Military troops were stationed at what appeared to be a gate into the Preserve. The bike slowed slightly as Sloane signaled to the soldiers nearest the wall. They moved aside to allow her passage, and the bike proceeded, unhindered, to the gate. Selah sucked in her breath as the trees and grasses of the Preserve came into view. She hadn't seen anything but gray walls and crumbling buildings for months. But it was the sight beneath the shadow of the causeway that commanded her full attention. A crowd of people were gathered there, quietly listening as individuals stepped forward to face one of the wall cams. "What are they doing?" Selah asked.

"They are telling the world about the difference Jesus has made in their life," Sloane said. "And the world is listening. We aren't certain who is responsible, or how they've managed to do it, but the messages of these people are being broadcast through the State media channels. It is such an unprecedented event that it is even being broadcast overseas."

Suddenly, a golden-haired Pod-Op standing at the edge of the crowd waved at them. "I've seen that woman before," Selah said.

"Jayka!" Sloane called out, and brought the bike to a stop beside her Podmate. "I was worried about you. And Tyrell?"

"He's fine," Jayka answered, grasping Sloane's hand firmly. "I can see you brought a friend," she added, nodding in Selah's direction.

Selah took off the helmet. "That's funny. You were able to see me now, but you couldn't see me several months back, when you captured that man under the causeway!" she laughed. "I wasn't even wearing an invisible suit then."

Jayka frowned in confusion, and then as she accessed her chip for the memory, a smile lit up her face. "You were there that day? Were you hiding nearby?"

"Not really. I was actually trying to get your attention. But God kept me hidden."

Jayka looked at her intently. "That does not sound very probable. But there are many things that have happened lately that do not seem...*probable.*" She turned to Sloane. "I understand that you are under new orders."

Sloane nodded. Jayka's eyes narrowed. "Then you may proceed."

Sloane tilted her head in farewell, and the bike crept along the crowd. "Where are all these people from?" Selah asked.

"Apparently, there are hidden pockets of Christian communities located throughout the Preserve. We have never detected any of them, but they were there, nonetheless. None of them seem to have been aware of each other, and yet they all decided to advance on the State at the same point in time, at the same time as the outer docks demonstrations."

Selah looked hopefully through the crowd, and then forced herself to be realistic. No one from her community would be there, she was certain of that.

"Selah?" said a voice suddenly to her left.

Sloane brought the bike to an immediate stop and Selah jumped off. "Dad?"

"Asha! Asha, she's here!" Jackson bellowed over the crowd behind him, and then Selah was swallowed in the arms of her father.

49

In the months that followed, the government wobbled on the unsteady legs of its rebirth. The exposed plans of the World Health Alliance to use Dr. Moses' research for absolute mind control eroded any trust in that particular institution. Many were horrified that they had willingly complied to receive the implant needed to turn themselves into organic, programmable robots. News of the State's complicity with and advancement of the Global Alliance's attempts of absolute control through a mass neurological link gave the people incentive to withdraw from the organization and become an independent nation once again.

Proof of the plot had been provided by an unlikely source. In one of the most surprising developments of the investigation, Ainsley Abbot, who had somehow managed to escape Liberation Station in order to join the protesters but had not been seen since the demonstrations, appeared two days later on the Pod-Op base to surrender herself to authorities. Many of the crimes to which she confessed could not be verified due to her skills at destroying evidence at an earlier date. Janice, the one person who could have corroborated one of the most serious crimes, refused to press charges against her and continued to visit her in prison. Ainsley's cooperation with authorities helped bring several high-end government officials who were involved into custody, and she was spared the death penalty. Joseph Moses, who came peacefully with authorities, insisted he was a visionary who had humanity's best interests at heart. Although vilified by many, it was the consensus of the intermediary government that Moses was an idealistic scientist with dreams of making the world a better place and had been merely a pawn in the hands of the State. Through a modification of his chip, his ability to neurally link was severed, his access to the internet, terminated. After serving time in prison for his mistreatment of the individuals formerly known as Unspokens, he was placed under house arrest. As time passed, he looked forward to seeing his parents, who visited him faithfully.

Along with the nation's decision to become autonomous came the weight of this monumental responsibility. Many were terrified of governmental collapse. They had come to depend on the State for their every need, and the State had come to depend on the global government. The uncertainty of the times seemed overwhelming. One thing was unequivocally clear: the status quo could no longer be tolerated. With the nation's military no longer obeying orders issued to them by a godless administration, there was fear that martial law might be the new norm. But it was the Pod-Op team leaders, who had come from humble backgrounds and proven their commitment to the protection of the people, who stepped up to serve as peacekeepers until new elections could be held. The Pod-Ops' insistence that the government provide national elections without the ability of tampering with ballot boxes alleviated the public's fear that the military jurisdiction would be permanent.

So much history had been rewritten that the nation was unsure of its past and how best to proceed. However, there was one government worker that all of the military seemed to respect, and he was busily researching the history of the United States of America before its spiral into socialism. He spent weeks familiarizing himself with records of its foundation that had been housed within the hidden communities of the Preserve, where they could not be corrupted by the State government.

"Here is a copy of the document you requested," Rhys said as he came into Ira's office. Ira looked up at the man who had done so much to protect and disperse an accurate version of the Bible during his employment as a curator at the Museum of Religious Convergence. "Thank you, Rhys. Where did you get it, may I ask?"

"This came from a valley in the region of the Ozarks plateau."

Ira smiled. "Oh, yes! Selah's community." By now, everyone in the city of St. Louis knew Selah's name, although some thought her last name was Stewmaker. Her story was just one of many people who had stepped out in faith and answered the call to be a missionary within their own country.

"This particular book is from a beloved teacher of that valley."

"I would like to meet her."

"So would I. But she passed away over a year ago. Her name is inscribed within the cover. The leaders of the community have asked if we could display the book opened to this document in a prominent place, such as a museum, where the public could have free access to it. They said the owner would have liked that."

Ira carefully took the book with gloved hands to protect its pages from the oils in his fingers. On the inside cover was written the name *Genevieve Gutierrez.* "Thank you, Rhys." He said, and opened the book to the place marker.

In Congress, July 4, 1776

The unanimous Declaration of the thirteen united States of America

When in the Course of human events, it becomes necessary for one people to dissolve the political bands which have connected them with another, and to assume among the powers of the earth, the separate and equal station to which the Laws of Nature and of Nature's God entitle them, a decent respect to the opinions of mankind requires that they should declare the causes which impel them to the separation.

We hold these truths to be self-evident, that all men are created equal, that they are endowed by their Creator with certain unalienable Rights, that among these are Life, Liberty and the pursuit of Happiness.–That to secure these rights, Governments are instituted among Men, deriving their just powers from the consent of the governed, –That whenever any Form of Government becomes destructive of these ends, it is the Right of the People to alter or to abolish it, and to institute new Government, laying its foundation on such principles and organizing its powers in such form, as to them shall seem most likely to effect their Safety and Happiness. Prudence, indeed, will dictate that Governments long established should not be changed for light and transient causes; and accordingly all experience hath shewn, that mankind are more disposed to suffer, while evils are sufferable, than to right themselves by abolishing the forms to which they are accustomed. But when a long train of abuses and usurpations, pursuing invariably the same Object evinces a design to reduce them under absolute Despotism, it is their right, it is their duty, to throw off such Government, and to provide new Guards for their future security.–Such has been the patient sufferance of these Colonies; and such is now the necessity which constrains them to alter their former Systems of Government. The history of the present King of Great Britain is a history of repeated injuries and usurpations, all having in direct object the establishment of an absolute Tyranny over these States. To prove this, let Facts be submitted to a candid world.[143]

The document went on to describe the unfair practices of the King of Great Britain. Ira rested his chin on his hands and drummed his fingers on his upper lip. "To think we had escaped tyranny, only to embrace it several centuries later," he said in wonderment.

"Incredible, isn't it?" Rhys mused. "And the same can be said of us, spiritually. Some of the first European settlers came here to escape religious persecution and to pursue freedom to worship God as they chose. And our government was to the point of institutionalizing people for sharing their faith!"

Ira shook his head. "There are many ugly things in America's past." He thought of the hidden tribes of indigenous people in the Preserve who had come forward to add their voices to the formation of the new government. It was a fresh start for everyone—painful, like any new birth, but a chance for the voice of every people group to be heard and weighed equally. "But there are many beautiful things, as well," Ira added. One such discovery he had made was an unaltered copy of the Constitution of the United States in a vault of the National Archives. Corrupted internet versions were immediately taken down, and the original was disseminated through government websites and social media.

---

[143] Taken from the Declaration of Independence (US, 1776)

A more recent example of America's beauty was the all the souls who had come to Christ through what was becoming known as the National Rebirth Revival, named for the state of the nation as well as that of the new converts. Now that open proselytizing was no longer outlawed, meetings were being held in huge sports arenas and stadiums across the nation. Formerly underground churches were seeking new places to meet as the numbers of those they discipled grew steadily. Luciana and Chess's church had quickly outgrown their café, and they were now renting a convention center. The conversion of a nation was transforming what could have been a time of social unrest or even chaos into a time of peace and reconciliation between the peoples of the Preserve, the State, and the outer docks.

Ira's ruminations were interrupted by the sound of a hopeful voice from the hallway. "Ira, do ya guys think ya could come eat with us?" Ira smiled as he looked up to see Piper, and his smile deepened when he spied Janice close behind her.

"Of course! We need a break, don't we?" he said to Rhys.

Ira had already decided to propose to Janice. He just couldn't decide when, or how. Something about it made him more nervous than the formation of the nation's government. He offered her his arm as they walked down the stairs and grinned as he watched Piper hopping from one step to another. She would need to be cared for. He wondered how Janice might feel about adoption.

The group exited the stairs into the courtyard, where Jayka and Tyrell had invited some friends over to see the "re-birthplace" of the new nation. A few tables had been pushed together for the impromptu picnic. Craig Goforth and Viviana Delacruz were sitting rather close together, Ira noticed. Selah and her friend Garrison were there, as well as the rest of the missionary team from Adullam. Bally was heading a lively discussion, as usual, while Cosmo listened with a skeptical look.

Ira and Janice found a seat across from Selah and Garrison. "I hear you don't plan to stay much longer," Ira said to Garrison as he passed the sandwiches.

Garrison smiled and looked at Selah. "Well, we won't stay gone, and I wouldn't mind staying forever, but not everyone feels the same way about modern conveniences."

Selah elbowed him in the ribs. "I like modern conveniences just fine, but I've got a cow to milk."

Bally's bombastic antics from the other end of the table interrupted the discussion. "Don' you look at me like dat!" Bally was saying to Cosmo. "You know I ain't wrong." She turned to Piper as the girl sidled up to her on the bench. "Ain't it right dat you was da best bird trapper in da outer docks?"

Piper grinned. "Nope. That title belongs to ma old friend, Zelda." Her face fell for a moment. "I miss 'er like crazy, but I know I'm gonna see her again." She looked at Jayka, who was fending off Macy from the plate of sandwiches. "From what you said, I know she made the ultimate trade."

Jayka smiled back at her. "She did, indeed."

About the Author

Annika Goodwin grew up in the Ozark hills. She loves being in the presence of God and hearing His voice expressed through the wonders of His creation. She enjoys growing tomatoes, irises and daffodils and loves going on adventures with her husband and spending time with family and the extended family of her brothers and sisters in Christ.

Annika believes in the restoration of broken lives and has seen it first-hand in those who have participated in the New Life Restoration Center program in Hollister, Missouri.